CW00701772

CONRAD'S LADY

Conrad's Lady

Leo Frankowski

CONRAD'S LADY

This is a work of fiction. All the characters and events portrayed in this book are fictional, and any resemblance to real people or incidents is purely coincidental.

A Baen Book

Baen Publishing Enterprises
P.O. Box 1403
Riverdale, NY 10471
www.baen.com

ISBN-13: 978-1-4165-0919-6
ISBN-10: 1-4165-0919-4

Cover art by Gary Ruddell

First printing in this format, December 2005

Library of Congress Cataloging-in-Publication Data

Frankowski, Leo, 1943-
  Conrad's lady / Leo Frankowski.
      p. cm.
  ISBN 1-4165-0919-4
  1. Time travel--Fiction. 2. Mongols--Fiction. 3. Poland--Fiction. I. Title.

  PS3556.R347C658 2005
  813'.54--dc22

                                                    2005026425

Distributed by Simon & Schuster
1230 Avenue of the Americas
New York, NY 10020

Production & book design by Windhaven Press, Auburn, NH (www.windhaven.com)
Printed in the United States of America

10 9 8 7 6 5 4 3 2 1

contents

Conrad's Lady

THE FLYING WARLORD

volume four

of the

ADVENTURES OF CONRAD STARGARD

DEDICATION

I'd like to thank Phillip C. Jennings for his kind help in proofreading this series, and for his many valuable suggestions on improving it.

We're coming, you Mongols,
We're coming to kill you.
We're coming, you Mongols,
We're coming to die!
And your blood and our blood
Will fertilize meadows,
And our sons will plough them
And grain will grow high!

—Krystyana's hymn

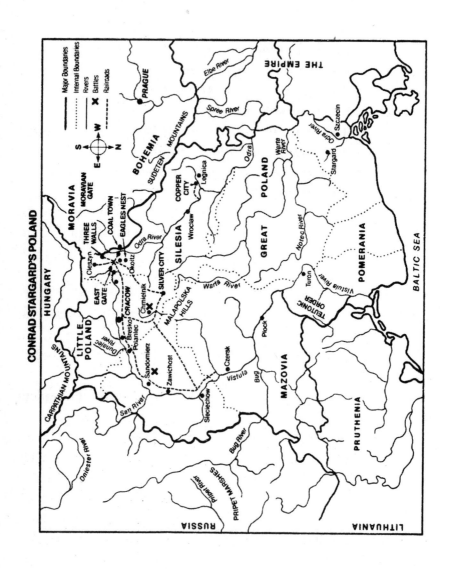

CONRAD STARGARD'S POLAND

Legend:
- Major Boundaries
- Internal Boundaries
- Rivers
- Battles
- Railroads

THE EMPIRE

BOHEMIA

PRAGUE

Elbe River

Spree River

SUDETEN MOUNTAINS

MORAVIA

MORAVIAN GATE

THREE WALLS

COAL TOWN

EAGLES NEST

Cieszyn

Okoitz

Odra River

SILESIA

COPPER CITY

Legnica

Wrocław

Odra

GREAT POLAND

POMERANIA

Szczecin

Odra River

Stargard

Warta River

Notec River

BALTIC SEA

HUNGARY

LITTLE POLAND

EAST GATE

CRACOW

Breslau

Polaniec

Chmielnik

SILVER CITY

MALAPOLSKA HILLS

Warta River

Dunajec River

Sandomierz

Zawichost

Sieciechow

San River

CARPATHIAN MOUNTAINS

Dniester River

Pripet River

PRIPET MARSHES

Bug River

Bug

Vistula

Czersk

Płock

MAZOVIA

Vistula River

Turon

TEUTONIC ORDER

PRUTHENIA

LITHUANIA

RUSSIA

Prologue

"Whoopee shit!... It's finally happening," she said. "A hundred years of tracking protohuman migration patterns on the African plain and it's finally over! It feels so good that I almost don't hate your guts anymore!"

"Well, don't get too carried away. You deserved every minute of it for dumping the owner's cousin into the thirteenth century when the guy didn't even know that time travel existed. And you deserve twice that for getting *me* messed up in it. Now get your scrawny body in the box. Time's running short!"

"Eat your heart out! I'll have my old sexy body back, and I'll take bubble baths and while you're eating carrion, I'll gorge for weeks on lobster thermidor and New York cheese-cake and—"

He sealed her into the stasis chamber, then watched the readout over the temporal transport canister count down to zero.

The tone sounded and he opened the canister, pulled out his new subordinate without glancing at him, and started to slide his previous superior in. It was *expensive* to hold the canister in 2,548,850 BC, so doctrine was to make the transfer as quickly as possible.

She was almost in when something struck him as being very, very wrong. He took a closer look at the body he had just extracted. He gagged, retched, and vomited on the floor. Then he switched off his boss's stasis field.

"—Cherries Jubilee! Hey! What the hell is this? What am I still doing here? You're holding up the canister, you ass! Do you realize what that costs?"

"So the owner has lots of money but you only have the one life. I figured I didn't hate you that goddamn much."

"You're not making any sense; get me out of this time period! I've waited long enough!"

"Anything you say, lady, but take a look at what just came out of the canister and then ask yourself if you really want to get into it."

She stared at him and then at the other stasis chamber.

The body within was shriveled and dried. It was laying on its side, a look of horror on its face. Its fingernails were all ripped off as if the man had tried to claw his way out before his air was exhausted.

"His stasis field must have failed," he said.

"But that's impossible! You know that's impossible! The circuitry for the stasis field is always built *inside* the field itself. Time doesn't exist inside the field, so how could the circuitry possibly have had *time* to fail?"

"Yeah, I know. But I still say that something is screwed up somewhere. The trip here takes six years subjective, and he had maybe two hours of air in the can. But that's not the big question. The biggie is whether or not you want to take the trip back. Me, I wouldn't risk it."

"Well, this chamber that I'm in hasn't failed. Why should it fail just because the other one did?"

"You know better than that, bitch. You're in the same damn chamber he's in. Right after sending you back, I got to send the empty chamber back to yesterday. It makes for a quicker turn-around that way. But I ran a self-check on it last night and it checked out perfect. So make up your mind. You're costing the owner a million bucks a second."

"Screw the owner," she said, squirming out of the chamber. "I'm not going anywhere till I see a live body crawl out of this thing!"

"Then help me get this dead one into your chamber. We gotta let the people uptime know what the problem is and we don't have much time to do it. Getting the body should be explanation enough!"

"Why not just ship him in the one he came in?"

He got the surprisingly light corpse into the other canister. "Lady, your big problem is that you're dumb."

He sent the canister back uptime and waited for a reply.

He waited for a long, long time.

Chapter One

FROM THE DIARY OF TADAOS KOLPINSKI

My people was always boatmen on the Vistula. My father was a boatman and his father before him, and my great-grandfather was one, too. I still would be, except I lost my boat a few years back. I would have lost my life with it, if it hadn't been for Baron Conrad Stargard.

I was maybe the first man to meet him in Poland, next to the priest, Abbot Ignacy at the Franciscan Monastery in Cracow. I was stuck on the rocks on the upper Dunajec with no one but a worthless little Goliard poet to help get me off. It was the poet's fault that we were hung up in the first place, since the twit rowed to port when I yelled starboard, but that's all water down the river. It was late in the season, and the weather was cold. Another day, and the river would be froze over and I'd lose my boat and cargo, all I owned, and maybe my life, too.

Then along comes this priest and with him was Sir Conrad. He was a giant of a man, a head and a half taller than I am, and I'm no shorty. He was pretty smart, and after I'd hired them two, we got the boat free in jig time with a line bent around a rock upriver, following Sir Conrad's directions. Never saw the like of it.

He told me he was an Englishman, but I never believed it. He didn't talk like no Englishman and he'd never seen an English longbow!

Now me, I'm a master of the English longbow. There's no one no where who can shoot farther or straighter or better than me, and that's no drunkard's boast. It's a gift, I tell you, and many's the time I've hit a buck square in the head at two hundred yards from a moving boat. I did it in front of Sir Conrad, and he helped me eat the venison.

And if you don't believe me, you meet me down at the practice butts some time, and I'll show you what shooting is all about. Only you better be ready to bet money.

We got that load to Cracow and I paid off my crew, me spending the night aboard to ward off thieves. Good thing, too, because three of them tried to rob me that night and kill me, besides. I was asleep, but at just the right time Sir Conrad shouts me awake, while he was holding a candle to me.

I tell you there was three of the bastards on my boat, coming at me with their knives drawn! I killed the first one with a steering oar, broke it clean over his head and his head broke with it. I threw the broken end at the second one and when he raised his arms to ward the blow, I caught him in the gut with my own knife, just as slick as you please.

The third one, he tried to get away, but in that kind of business, where you're a stranger in town, you best not leave no witnesses! Any thief would have a dozen friends swear that he was an honest man and *I* was the murderer.

So I bent my longbow and caught the bastard in the throat as he ran along the shore. Nailed him square to a tree, I did, and he stuck there, wiggling some.

Sir Conrad, he had his own funny knife out, that one that bends in the middle, but I wouldn't let him finish the thief. After all, it was *me* they was trying to rob and kill, so the honors was mine. Anyway, that was a good arrow, and I didn't want the fletching messed up. I cut the thief's throat and saved my arrow, and I guess Sir Conrad, he was a little mad because he wouldn't help me slide the three bodies into the river current to get rid of them. He even threatened to call out the guard!

But I got him calmed down just fine and he went back to the inn where he was staying at. That was the second time he saved me, because if them thieves had of caught me asleep, I'd be a dead man, and my cargo gone besides.

Well, I got me a good price for my cargo of grain and spent the winter in Cracow with a widow of my acquaintance.

The next summer a friar brought me this letter. He was the same kid what used to be a Goliard poet and worked for me the last fall. He read it to me, and it was from Sir Conrad and it had Count Lambert's seal on it. They wanted me to come to Okoitz and teach the peasants there how to shoot the longbow. I was sort of tempted because I'd heard of beautiful things about Okoitz. They said that Count Lambert had all the peasant girls trained to jump into the bed of any knight that wanted them, and if Sir Conrad could qualify for them privileges, then why not me as well? At least I could dicker for it, if they really wanted me that bad, and they must have, since they wrote that letter on real calfskin vellum. Not that I was about to give up my boat and the Vistula, you know, but it might make a fine way to spend a winter.

But just then I had a contract to deliver a load of iron bars to Turon, and two other ones to buy grain on the upper Dunajec and sell it in Cracow. I didn't have the time to find someone who could write me a letter to Sir Conrad, so I told the friar, him what brought me the letter, that I'd reply to Sir Conrad when I got back, in a few weeks, like.

That trip went just fine until I was heading down the Dunajec again. The water was high, so I was working the boat alone, and I saw a buck at the water's edge in the same place where I'd bagged two other ones before, where a game trail comes down to the water. I was out of meat, so I shot that buck square in the head and pulled for shore to get it aboard before I got caught poaching.

Only it wasn't a buck I shot! It was a stuffed dummy with a deer skin on it, and the baron's men, they had me surrounded before I knew what was happening. They stole my boat and cargo, "confiscated" it, they called it, and I never did see it again. They would have hung me except I had that letter, written on good calfskin vellum it was, with Count Lambert's seal on it.

The baron said he wasn't about to offend a lord as high as Count Lambert, not without finding out what that man would pay for my life. They was all eating and drinking while I was tied up in front of them, and every round of wine they drank, they'd decide on a higher price for my ransom. By the time they was near dead drunk, they had this priest write up a letter to Count Lambert saying that if he didn't come up with four thousand pence in six weeks, they'd hang me for poaching, and I knew I was a dead man. I'd never seen that much money in one spot in my whole life, and the count didn't even know me. Who'd spend a fortune to save a man they'd never even met?

So they chained me with shackles riveted around my wrists and ankles and threw me into this tiny cell in the basement, with barely room to lay down. The only food I got was some table scraps every third day or so and they was stingy with the water. They wouldn't even give me a pot to piss in, and I had to piss and shit on the floor of my cell. But that whole castle stank so bad that they didn't even notice the stench I added. In a month's time, I was covered with my own shit, and being hung didn't seem like such a bad thing after all. At least then I could stop smelling myself!

Then along comes Sir Conrad, all decked out in red velvet and gold trim, with good armor under it. There was another knight with him, Sir Vladimir, and two of the prettiest girls you've ever seen, Annastashia and Krystyana. He paid out four thousand pence in silver coin and got my bow and arrows back, too, but I had no such luck with my boat and cargo.

A blacksmith knocked the shackles off me and it was strange to stand there in the bright sun with clean air to breathe, trying to make myself understand that I was going to get to live again.

Sir Conrad said I owed him four thousand pence, and I'd pay it off by working for him at three pence a day, the same pay that I'd given him the last fall. That was five years pay, even if I saved every penny of it, and many's the time I wished I'd paid him the six pence a day he'd asked for in the first place, instead of dickering him and the priest down to something reasonable.

They all stayed upwind of me until we got to an inn, and the innkeeper wouldn't let me inside until they'd given me a bath in the courtyard. They burned my clothes and I had to make do with a set of Sir Conrad's with the cuffs rolled up.

So we headed north and west, and when we got to Cracow, the ferryboat there had been changed at Sir Conrad's suggestion. It had a long rope running upstream to a big tree on the bank, and by adjusting that rope, the ferry master could take the ferry back and forth without needing any oarsmen!

I'd known Sir Conrad was smart, but this amazed me. I was still staring at it when we was attacked by a band of unemployed oarsmen. They blamed Sir Conrad for robbing their jobs, and maybe they was right. Sir Conrad, he got knocked off his horse by a rock that hit him square in the head, but Sir Vladimir, he went out and started smashing them oarsmen, and darned if Sir Conrad's mare didn't go out there and help him with the job. That horse is spooky, smarter than a lot of men I've hired. Sir Conrad says she's people, and he even pays her a wage for her work, swearing her in just like she was a vassal, but she scares me sometimes. It just ain't natural.

I got my bow bent, but I noticed that Sir Vladimir was using the flat of his sword on the oarsmen, so I didn't kill nobody either. I just nailed a few of their arms to some trees and buildings, me being that good a shot.

Once Sir Conrad got his wits back, he talked to the oarsmen and said that if any of them couldn't find work in Cracow, well, they could come to his lands at Three Walls and get work there. Most of them took him up on it, too. So did a lot of others that never was oarsmen, but it wasn't my place to say nothing. Why should I cost a man his job?

Sir Vladimir, he led the party right up to Wawel Castle, and all the pages and grooms scurried around like our party was real important. I got put up in the servants' quarters, of course, not being quality folk, but it wasn't bad. Them castle servants eat good, and I was still a month behind on my eating.

Besides filling me up on food, them servants filled me in on what was happening. They said that Sir Conrad got on the right side of Count Lambert by building all sorts of machines for him, and the count gave Sir Conrad a huge tract of land in the mountains near Cieszyn. Sir Conrad was building a city there when he heard I was in trouble and he got into a cesspool of trouble hisself on the way to get me.

They said he met a band of Teutonic Knights what were taking a gross of young heathen slaves to the markets in Constantinople, and Sir Conrad wouldn't allow them to do it. He said they was molesting children, so him and Sir Vladimir chopped up them seven guards and took the children back to Three Walls.

The trouble was that them Teutonic Knights, or Crossmen they're called, are the biggest and orneriest band of fighting men within a thousand miles, and they wasn't about to let Sir Conrad get away with robbing them. There was going to be a trial by combat, and Sir Conrad was going to get hisself killed, sure as sin. Nobody beats a Crossman champion in a fair fight, and mostly they don't fight fair.

I tell you that if you ever want to know something, you just ask a palace servant. They know everything that's happening, which is probably the reason that Sir Conrad won't have any. Lots of people works for him, you understand, but he gets up and gets his own meals just like everybody else.

We went to Okoitz, and I could see why Count Lambert was so impressed with Sir Conrad. There was a huge windmill, taller than a church steeple, and it sawed wood, worked hammers, and did all sorts of things, and there was this big cloth factory chock-filled with the damndest machines you ever saw, making cloth by the mile.

It was also filled with the finest collection of pretty girls in the world, and didn't none of them wear much. They was all crowding around Count Lambert and Sir Conrad, hoping to get their butts patted or their tits pinched. Not that any of them would pay any attention to the likes of me. I wasn't a knight and they didn't have time for us common trash.

Then, like there wasn't a gross of pretty girls after his body, and the Crossmen wasn't going to kill him, Sir Conrad invents a flying toy called a kite, and spends a week building them. He's a very strange man, that one.

Then we went to Three Walls and I got put to work, mostly doing guard duty at night. It wasn't so bad, since Sir Conrad let me hunt all I wanted, just so that everything I shot went into the pot, which was fine by me. I ate my share of it, and so did Sir Conrad. One of his rules was everybody ate the same, and there was always plenty of it. I respected him for that, even though a lot of the others just thought he was crazy.

At first, there wasn't much at Three Walls but a big sawmill and some temporary shacks, but they got some fine buildings up real quick before the snow flew, and since Sir Conrad planned it all, you just know they was full of odd things.

The strangest were the bathrooms, where they had flush toilets and hot showers and more copper pipes than you ever seen in your life. And some damn fine scenery, since the girls used the same showers we did. Not that any of the young ones would have much to do with me, no, they was all wanting a real knight and maybe even Sir Conrad.

But I found me another sensible widow and just sort of moved in with her. Nobody said anything about it and in a few weeks somebody else was using my bunk in the bachelors' quarters, and that was fine, too.

Come time for Sir Conrad's trial by combat, everybody in Three Walls went to Okoitz to watch it. I got to talking with Sir Vladimir and Friar Roman—him what used to be the Goliard poet—along with Ilya, the blacksmith. We all allowed as how it was a rotten shame that a fine man like Sir Conrad was going to get hisself killed, and especially by them filthy German Crossmen.

And we came up with a plan to do something about it. The friar had a painting kit with some gold leaf in it. He was going to cover some of my arrows with gold, and the blacksmith, he had some steel arrowheads that could cut any armor. I was going to be up on top of the windmill, and if Sir Conrad got into trouble, I planned to shoot me the Crossman champion. Once I did that, and golden arrows came down out of the sky to punish the evildoers, the others would be in the crowd shouting "An Act of God!", "A miracle!", and such like nonsense, since who'd look for the perpetrator of a miracle? How could they punish me or Sir Conrad for an Act of God?

When the time came, we was all ready. Sir Conrad got hisself bashed out of the saddle on the first pass, and the Crossman, he came around to finish him off. I let fly and then hid myself, but somehow I must have missed him clean because when I looked up, him and Sir Conrad was locked in a close fight. Since I missed once, I was afraid that the weight of the gold leaf was throwing off my aim, and I didn't shoot for fear of hitting Sir Conrad. Just as well, because Sir Conrad kicked the Crossman's smelly arse! He played with the bastard, first throwing away his shield and then killing him with his bare hands!

Then when the fight was over and I was getting ready to climb down, four more Crossmen charged onto the tourney field at Sir Conrad. I had my bow bent real quick and let four arrows fly as fast as you can blink! This time, I watched them fly through the low clouds and come out again to hit every one of them Crossmen square in the heart! I tell you I got four out of four, and every one of them straight in at three hundred yards! I killed every one of them fouling bastards and their empty horses ran past Sir Conrad on either side.

Then, right according to plan, everybody was shouting "*A miracle!*" and "*An Act of God!*" The blacksmith ran out on the field, to be the first one there to recover my arrows, since we figured that nobody would believe God using gold-*covered* arrows. God would use real solid gold if He used anything. It was best to get rid of the evidence.

But when Ilya tried to pull out the first arrow, it bent in his hand! It really was *real solid pure gold*!

I got religion about then, saying my prayers every night like the priest taught me and going to mass every morning. I did that for about a month and then was my old self again, or pretty near. Only I don't make jokes about the stupid priests anymore and I try to watch my language, except when the shitheads push me too hard.

So Sir Conrad lived and them kids all grew up proper at Three Walls instead of being slaves to the Mussulmen. And nobody thought to catch me for killing them Crossmen, if it was me that shot them and not God. It was some damn fine shooting, Whoever did it.

So we all went back to Three Walls, right after Sir Vladimir married Annastashia. I went back to the Widow Bromski and spent most of the next four or five years hunting and standing guard, except for a few side trips with Sir Conrad. Well, besides that I got me a fine education at the school Sir Conrad set up, but I guess that shows up in my writing.

They was always building something new at Three Walls, and some of it was pretty exciting, especially the steam engines. In my off-hours I got to looking at them and talking to anybody what knew much about it. I tried to get Sir Conrad to transfer me to one of the machining sections, but he wouldn't do it. He said he had plenty of good men who could run a lathe, but only one man who could shoot like me.

After that, about the only thing that happened that was worth talking about was once when we was all going to a new site that Sir Conrad got from Duke Henryk to open up a copper mine. We got word that there was a bunch of foreigners in Toszek, just a mile up the road, that was murdering people and burning women at the stake! Naturally, we went right there, and Sir Conrad and another knight went in to arrest the bastards—there must have been five dozen of them—while I got up on a shed to back them up with my longbow.

Well, these foreigners, some kind of Spaniards they was, they didn't want to be arrested so naturally a fight got started. All our workers got into it and I let fly with all the arrows I had, a dozen and a half of them. I only missed but once, when the fletching let loose on an old arrow, but that one time was when a soldier was coming at Sir Conrad and all I shot was some priest standing behind him. Sir Conrad's horse killed the bastard, kicked him square in the face and killed him dead, but like I said, that's a spooky horse!

I felt bad about missing, since Sir Conrad had saved my life three times, and up till then I'd only saved his once, but he wasn't mad about it. Like I said, he was a fine man.

We took prisoner such of them as we didn't kill and we divvied up the booty and I got three months pay out of it, besides a fine sword and a knife. Ask me and I'll show them to you sometimes.

Then they had a trial where everybody could speak their piece, and the foreigners, they said that they was only killing witches, and after that we hung the bastards. I never heard of nobody hunting witches from that time on.

So it wasn't so bad, working for Sir Conrad, but I got to yearning for the river. Being a boatman gets into your liver after a while, and when you been doing it for four or six generations, it sticks heavy in your blood. When I was close to working off my debt, I went to Sir Conrad to talk about it, or rather I made an appointment to see him with Natalia, his secretary. He was a busy man. And he wasn't "Sir" Conrad any more. Count Lambert had bumped him up to "Baron" now.

I was hoping that he'd stake me to a boat and cargo, or maybe let me work a few more years at the same rate so I could buy my own, but he had other ideas.

He said that he was going to build a fleet of the finest riverboats ever seen, and every one of them powered by one of his steam engines. They'd each carry a dozen times the cargo of any boat now on the rivers, and they'd go six times faster, upstream or down!

I asked what would happen to the other boatmen on the river and he said that we'd have to hire them, but he needed a good man to be boss, a man he trusted and a man who could speak the language of the other boatmen. Then he asked me if I was interested in the job.

I near fell off my chair! Hell yes, I was interested! Me running all the boats on the Vistula! Damn right I was interested!

He said good, he wanted me. And it wasn't only the Vistula. There was more cargo to be hauled on the Odra than on the Vistula, what with his installations at Copper City near Legnica and Coaltown north of Kolzie. On top of that, these boats wouldn't only be just for cargo. They'd be armored to stop any arrow and armed with weapons he didn't want to talk about just yet. He said the Mongols were coming in a few years and they would try to kill everybody, but we would stop them, and we would do it with the riverboats if that was possible. If that failed, he had an army building at the Warrior's School, and that would be the second line of defense. But the men on the boats would have to be warriors too, so I would be in the first class through, now that they was almost finished training the instructors.

Now that took me back a peg or five. I'd heard a lot of stories about that school and wasn't none of them good. It was supposed to be a secret, but everybody knew that three-quarters of the men who started didn't live through it and I told Baron Conrad so.

He said that I'd been listening to a lot of old wives' tales. That while only a quarter of the first class graduated, only one in six had actually died. Most of the rest had been washed out for injuries, or physical or mental problems, and anyway the next class would not have it so hard. They were projecting a fifty percent graduation rate. On top of that, everybody who worked for Baron Conrad would soon have to go through the school, so I might as well get it over with, before I got any older. Younger men had a better survival rate.

I said I didn't like them words "survival rate," but Baron Conrad said he only meant the ratio of men graduating, and nobody wants to live forever, anyhow.

I said it was my Christian duty to try, but Baron Conrad, he told me that it was still a secret, but that all of that first class was going to be knighted, and the next one was, too. He told me to think about all them pretty young girls I saw in the shower room every day and to think about the old widow I was living with. Yeah, I guess he knew about it.

So I thought about them eager young smiles and the Widow Bromski's scowling face, and about them bouncing young tits and her sagging dugs and that's what done me in.

Chapter Two

FROM THE DIARY OF CONRAD STARGARD

The weather was so beautiful that Krystyana and Sir Piotr had elected to have their wedding ceremony, complete with church service and reception, held outside. Since Sir Piotr was the local boy who had made good, the priest and everyone else went along with it.

And of course, since everything had to be done as ceremoniously as possible, the mass went on for over an hour and I had some time to get some thinking done. I was working on my next four-year plan.

Yes, I know that socialists are supposed to write five-year plans, but in less than four years the Mongols were going to invade, and there didn't seem to be any sane reason to plan much beyond that. If we could lick the Mongols, we'd have a whole lifetime to plan things. If not, well what was the point? We'd all be dead.

For the last five years, I had been working mostly at getting our industrial base going. We now had a productive cloth factory and a sugar refinery here at Okoitz, and a copper-mining, smelting, and machining installation at Copper City, that Duke Henryk owned. More than a dozen of Count Lambert's other barons and knights had various light industries going at their manors, mostly to keep their peasants busy during the winters. Some of them were my vendors, making boots and uniforms for my future army.

At the Franciscan monastery in Cracow, we had a paper-making plant, a printshop, and a book bindery. And besides books, they were also producing a monthly magazine.

I had three new towns of my own running. There was Three Walls, where we were making iron, steel, coke, cement, bricks, and other ceramics, and machinery, plus several hundred different consumer products. It also had a major carpentry shop, set up for mass production, and a valley filled with Moslem refugees that functioned as an R&D center and a gunpowder works. There was Coaltown, where we were making coke, bricks, glass, and chemicals. And there was Silver City, in the Malopolska Hills, where we mined and refined lead and zinc.

Silver City got its name when my sales manager, Boris Novacek, refused to let me call zinc by its rightful name. He said that a zinc was a musical instrument, and that it was stupid to use the same word on a metal. He wanted to call it "silver" and pass it off as the real thing, but I wouldn't let him do it. We compromised on "Polish Silver," and the name stuck.

In addition to the factories and mines, a major agricultural revolution was taking place, mostly because of the seeds I'd brought back with me, but also because of the farm machinery I'd introduced.

Understand that none of these installations was really up to twentieth-century standards. At best, some of it was up to nineteenth-century standards. Everything was primitive and on a small scale. Most of the work was still being done by hand, and the most useful and cost-effective piece of farm machinery I'd introduced was the wheelbarrow. Well, the new steel plows worked well, and the McCormick-style reapers sold well even if they were too expensive. A whole village had to club up to buy one.

Nonetheless, worker productivity was four times what it had been when I'd arrived, and things were constantly getting better. The infant mortality rate was way down, too, because of the sanitation measures I'd introduced. Of course, the birth rate hadn't changed to any noticeable degree, so the place was crawling with rug rats, but what the heck. There was plenty of room for them. There was an underpopulated world out there.

Eagle Nest was nominally an aircraft development center, but I completely doubted if a bunch of twelve-year-old boys could really develop practical aviation. I'd helped build it to keep my liege lord happy and because in the long run, it was actually an engineering school, which we needed.

Lastly, I had the new Warrior's School ready to go, and my corps of instructors trained. My army was to have three branches.

The first branch would be made up of my existing factory workers. They would all have to go through an abbreviated basic-training period of six months and then train one day a week after that. The problem was that I would have to send the managers through first, since we couldn't have a situation where the subordinates were knighted and the managers were commoners. Discipline would vanish! There wasn't time to send the managers out in small bunches, so there was nothing for it but to send them all at once, which involved running the factories with untrained, temporary managers. It was scary, but I didn't see any way around it. Everybody in the top two layers was told to pick a man from below and teach him how to do his job in ten weeks. Only thirty-five men were leaving, but they were my *best* thirty-five men. There were screams and moans from all quarters, but I got my way.

Furthermore, all new hires, women as well as men, had to go through the six-month training period before they could start work. I required the women to be trained because when we went off to war, I planned to take every able-bodied man with me. The women would have to "man" the wall guns and other defenses without us. And this meant setting up a training program for the wives of my managers as well.

Then there were the river defenses. If the weather was right, and the rivers weren't frozen, we just might be able to stop the Mongols at the Vistula, or even at the Bug. We already had good steam engines and a carpentry shop set up for mass production. Steamboats should be a fairly straightforward proposition. The troops manning them would be hired from among existing riverboat men and then put through the full-year basic-training program. Then, after that, they'd have to learn about fighting from a steamboat on the job.

The regular army would be a full-time group based on the training instructors I already had. Besides training everybody else, they had to multiply their own numbers by at least six each year for the next three years, and then twice more in the last year to get us an army big enough to do the job. And those were absolute minimums. Anything less than fifty thousand men would just get us all killed. The production quotas for the factories were set up for a hundred fifty thousand.

From an economic standpoint, land transport was even more important than river transport. All of the roads were so bad that it was almost impossible to get a cart over them. Almost all goods were transported by caravan mule, and the best of them could only carry a quarter ton. They could only do thirty miles a day and had to be loaded and unloaded twice a day at that. But on level ground, on a steel track and steel wheels with good bearings, a mule should be able to tow two dozen times what it could carry on its back.

But more important than economics was the fact that my army was being trained to fight with war carts. Swivel guns mounted in big carts would fire over the heads of the pikemen towing the cart. I had to get the troops to the battlefields quickly and in reasonably good shape. It was time to build railroads.

And if I was going to build a transport system, I was going to build it right from the beginning. All the railroad tracks would be wide gauge and that gauge would be absolutely standardized. And we would containerize right from the start. Our war carts were six yards long, two yards wide and a yard and a half high. That would be our standard container size. All chests and barrels would be sized to fit neatly within the container, and anything nonstandard would get charged double rates, at least. The four wheels on a war cart were two yards high and mounted on casters, and each could be locked either fore and aft or to the side. Fore and aft, the center of the wheels were two yards apart, so that was the standard track gauge, and future carts would have flanged wheels to keep them on the track. If they tore up the ground when going cross country, tough.

Then we needed maps, and there weren't any. How a medieval general ever commanded troops without adequate maps was beyond me, and I didn't intend to learn. I'd had the machine shop make up some crude but usable theodolites (they didn't have a telescope on them, just iron sights like on a gun) and I had a good mathematician, Sir Piotr, to put in charge of the project. He could train others.

And we needed radios. Integrated circuits, transistors, and even *tubes* were well beyond us, and would be for years. I'd been able to muddle my way through a lot of things because I was too ignorant to know what I was getting into. With electronics, I knew what the problems would be, and they frightened me! Where would I get the rare-earth oxides needed to make a decent cathode? How would I develop alloys with the same temperature coefficients as our glass to take wires into the tube without shattering it? How could I possibly get a good enough vacuum?

But working radios were invented long before there were tubes. They used spark-gap transmitters and coherers to pick up the signals, and with enough work, I thought I could get one going. With radios, I could effectively double our speed, since I wouldn't have to send a runner to convey every order. Speed was the one area where the Mongols would be our undoubted superiors. Those shaggy ponies could move!

Radios were an absolute first priority.

The mass ended and we all walked over to the reception area. I stood in line to kiss the bride, even though I had done it all-too-many times before. Cilicia kissed the groom full on the mouth and warmly, probably because she too was glad to see Krystyana married off. As we went to the sideboard to get a couple of glasses of mead, my liege lord came up.

"Ah, Baron Conrad! You seem to be enjoying yourself!" Count Lambert said. Cilicia remained silent around my lord. They didn't get along.

"I might as well, my lord, seeing as how I'm footing the bill for the wedding feast," I said.

"And the dowry as well, I suppose?"

"Of course, my lord. After all, I've had three children by Krystyana and it seems the least I could do. I'm just glad that the kids will have a proper father."

"Indeed. I'm surprised that the Church hasn't come down on you for it."

"I'm sure that they are keeping careful notes, my lord. The inquisition concerning me is still up in the air."

"That's not all that's up there! I trust you've looked up some-time in the last hour?"

I hadn't, but I did so now. There was this thirteenth-century sailplane circling overhead.

"I guess I must have been thinking about something else, my lord. There must be quite a thermal above the town."

"Quite. It's doubtless helped by the way every fire in the town is burning bright on a warm, calm day. You don't think that's cheating, do you?"

"I guess not, my lord. We never qualified what it had to do to stay up, only that it had to fly for two hours. It looks like it's climbing. The wager is yours."

"Good! Then where is my aircraft engine?"

"Still in my head, my lord, but I'll get working on it as soon as I get back to Three Walls. Perhaps I can deliver something to you in a few months."

"It will take that long? The boys were hoping to get started immediately!"

"It will take at least that long, my lord. Do you realize what you're asking? It's not just designing and building the mechanical parts, though that's going to be hard enough! I have no idea how we'll go about machining a crankshaft on one of our lathes! There's a lubrication system to worry about and a carburetion system. And how am I to make a spark coil with nothing but beeswax and paper for insulators? And spark plugs! Thermal expansion problems alone could kill us right there! And—"

"You will solve it, Baron Conrad. You always have before. Shall we say by the Harvest Festival, then?"

"My lord, I will work on it diligently, but I cannot promise results by any fixed date. There's the problem with fuel. I *think* we can use wood alcohol, but—"

"We'll discuss it again on the Feast of Our Lady of the Harvest. Oh, yes. There was another thing I wanted to talk over with you. When first you came here, you showed us the *zipper* things that fastened your clothes and equipage together. You distinctly said that you could show my workmen the way of making them. Well, almost six years have gone by and you still haven't done it. I want you to start on that as well."

"My lord, don't we have more important things to worry about than zippers? In less than four years, the Mongols will be arriving. There are all sorts of things that need doing if we are to survive that."

"Indeed? Like what? You are training some very good infantry, and you should have plenty of them in time. As to the cavalry, well, our Polish knights are always ready. All the more so once you have them in plate armor. But I've seen your stamping presses work, and they'll have no difficulty getting the job done. As to the air force, if you can build the engines you promised, the boys and I can do the rest. What more remains to be done?"

"Plenty, my lord. Remember the binoculars I gave you on the first day we met?"

"Of course! Marvelous things! I keep them in my chambers."

"Well, I think we may be able to produce something similar called a telescope. It will be bulkier and will be used over only one eye, but it should do the job. What if I could have enough of them made so that you could give one to every Polish baron, count, and duke before the battle? What would that do for your fame?"

"I like it, Baron Conrad, and I would even pay the cost of it all, in cloth of course."

"Then I'll put a team to working at it, my lord. It would help if I could borrow those binoculars back for a week or two."

"Take them for as long as you need them. But what does that have to do with zippers and Mongols?"

"I'm just trying to say that we have a lot more to do. Now let me tell you about railroads. . . ."

The conversation went on for hours while the party went on around us. The upshot of it was that Lambert would provide the land to run a line from Coaltown to the Vistula, and from Three Walls north to the line, along with two square miles of land along the Vistula where I would build a fort and a riverboat assembly factory. The fort would be at Count Lambert's expense, in cloth, and he would be in nominal command, but I would see to the manning of it, since the people there would be working at the riverboat factory and the railyard. I would build the track at my expense, and all my goods, and the duke's, would travel on the line free. Others could use it by paying a toll to Lambert, but they'd have to rent railroad cars from me. After that, we'd run a line from the east end of the line to Silver City, and that part of it on Count Lambert's land would be managed on the same basis as the rest.

Medieval business deals were always complicated, especially when Count Lambert was in something like his current mood. Actually, I didn't care who owned what, so long as the job got done. As to the division of the profits, well, I'd have to keep my liege lord happy in any event. After that, the accountants all worked for me so he would be rewarded as I saw fit!

"Done, Baron Conrad! This has been a good day's work! I feel right about it. But I still think that when the Mongols arrive, we should be dressed in our best, so do get to work on that zipper machine, won't you? At your own expense, of course."

With that, he got up and walked away and I started thinking about how one would go about building a zipper-making machine.

Interlude One

I hit the STOP button.

"Tom, something's been bothering me since you mentioned it a few days ago."

"And what is troubling you, my son?"

"Well, you said that you found out about Conrad's trip to the

Middle Ages when you went to the Battle of Chmielnick during the Mongol invasion. You said that the battle you saw had a different outcome than what's written up in the history books. And you said that the investigation teams you sent out came back duplicated. Why weren't *you* duplicated as well?"

"Well, *I was!* It was strange, meeting myself. Not because running into yourself is all that odd. With time travel, we do that all the time. But protocol is that the senior self always talks first, and the two of us just stood there, each waiting for the other to speak first, since neither of us remembered being there before. It was quite a while before I asked him why he didn't say something. Eventually, we figured out what happened. Being a sensible person, both of me, I decided to timeshare the management of the place with my other half. We flipped a coin and I got it for this century and he gets it for the next."

"Good Lord!"

"Well, what else could I do? Fight myself? I suppose it would have been more complicated had I been married, but after a bit of youthful insanity, like Conrad, I'm not the marrying kind."

He hit the START button.

Chapter Three

FROM THE DIARY OF CONRAD STARGARD

Part of my deal with Count Lambert was that I would spend two days a month looking over the projects we had going at Okoitz, so I couldn't go back to Three Walls immediately. I checked the windmills and went down the coal mine. I looked over the progress made on Count Lambert's new castle, which was now more than half built, and spent more time than was necessary in the cloth factory, mostly because all the girls working there wanted to talk to me about something or another. Mostly, they were just trying to get me interested in themselves, and since I was still pretty seriously involved with Cilicia, they were out of luck. None the less, it's fun being pursued by scantily clad young ladies, even when you don't intend being caught, so I ended up spending half of both days there. Cilicia spent her time teaching dancing to the ladies of the town, charging all the traffic could bear.

Then it was back to Three Walls, where I got a half dozen research teams going on the new projects. My usual approach to research was to set up a team of two young men, apprentices, generally, along with one older craftsman. The rule was that they had to try out everybody's ideas, and the older man was not allowed to squelch the dumb ideas that the kids came up with. I reviewed the progress with each team every week or two and threw in my own thoughts, and usually something workable resulted. On really important things, I'd set up two competing teams and let them work independently. The reward for all this, besides their pay, was in the form of cash bonuses if they were successful and the fact that if the new product went into production, the men on the research team were the obvious people to manage the new factory, so promotions were in order.

The railroads and the steamboats were just a matter of design and build, with little real research required at first. Sir Piotr's first survey job was for the railroad track.

Yashoo was sent with a crew to the new lands, which we called East Gate, to build a boat-assembly building and the foundry got busy making cast-iron railroad track. The construction crews were scheduled to go through the Warrior's School in the winter, when there wasn't much else for them to do anyhow.

We didn't have the machinery necessary to roll steel track, and with the comparatively light loads that our track would be handling, malleable cast iron was good enough. Cast iron also had the advantage of being not worth stealing. A blacksmith couldn't make anything out of it. If he tried heating it and beating on it with a hammer, it just crumbled. This fact, coupled with Anna's outstanding ability to sniff out thieves, reduced our theft problem to almost zero.

I was almost tempted to try to build a telegraph again, but not quite. There was no way that I could make copper not worth stealing, and the Mongols would probably be smart enough to cut our lines once the invasion started, so its military advantage would be nil.

Our rolling stock consisted of small flatcars big enough to carry a single container, with a load limit of ten tons. A tenth the size of modern cars, they were huge by the standards of the thirteenth century. They would all be horse or mule drawn, since our line would be only thirty miles long. There wasn't any need for greater speed and the mules already existed. Locomotives were for the future.

Sketching up the boats and the railroad took less than a week, since I had a staff of draftsmen (and draftswomen) now. The aircraft engine was something else.

My first thought had been to make an air-cooled single cylinder two-cycle engine, the sort that is used on lawnmowers, but I got to worrying about balancing it. Static balancing would be no great problem, but dynamic balancing without any sort of test equipment seemed impossible. The thought of vibrations tearing one of our frail wood-and-canvas planes to shreds in midair bothered me.

I went to a two-opposed cylinder design, where both pistons went out at the same time. If every part was identical to its opposite part, it all should balance perfectly. I hoped.

Lubrication? All we had was various animal fats and imported olive oil. I designed a pressurized lube system, knowing that it would be contaminated with the wood alcohol I hoped to use. After that, we would just have to try different mixtures and burn out engines until we found something that worked reasonably well.

Carburetion? All I could do was to sketch up what I think I saw in a textbook fifteen years ago and hope.

Ignition? I put one research team to work on a magneto system and another on the battery-and-coil type and again I hoped.

Then there were the mechanical parts. The engine had to be as light as possible, which meant that I needed the best possible strength-to-weight ratio. Sad to say, our best cast steel was weaker than ordinary cast bronze. Bronze was expensive, since it was made, in part, of tin that had to be imported from England, but hang the expense. I'd get it out of Count Lambert somehow. Everything on that engine was bronze except for the bearings (another research group), the cylinder liners, and the piston rings. These last two were cast iron, just like on many modern engines.

As more and more problems were encountered, more research teams were set up. Did we have a ceramic that had a coefficient of expansion similar to some metal we already had, so we could make a spark plug that didn't shatter when the engine heated up? Get the machinists to make spark plug jackets out of as many metals as they had, and for each type, have the potters mold in all their different types of clays and try to fire them. Could we insulate wires with some sort of varnish? Put a team of alchemists on it!

But many of the problems had to be solved sequentially, rather than in parallel. We couldn't test bearing materials without a working engine, nor could we work on lubricants or carburetion or propellers. The first big snag was ignition, and the problem there was the lack of a decent electrical insulator for the spark coil. The damn things kept shorting out.

While this was going on, there were innumerable problems with the factories, since the entire upper management, everybody above the foreman level, was out playing soldier. And besides Three Walls, I still had to keep tabs on all the other installations, which were also running without their best men and women.

Then there was the problem of the barony that I had just been given. It was previously owned by my enemies, the Jaraslavs. These men had hated everything about me and as a result, they had refused to allow any of my innovations on their lands. Because of this, the barony was the most backward in the duchy. The spring crops were already planted when I got the place, so not much could be done in that direction until next year, but there were a lot of other things that needed doing.

The school system had to be extended into it. That meant more work for Father Thomas, who ran the schools, but not much for me. Along with the schools went our distribution system and the mails. Boris's job. Teaching the farmers about the new crops and machines? I managed to "borrow" two dozen of Count Lambert's more mature peasants, men with grown sons who would just as soon take over the family farm. I made these men my bailiffs and assigned farmland to them scattered over the barony, along with a complete set of the newest farm equipment, with the understanding that they had to teach their new neighbors about the new stuff.

Understand that none of these were trivial jobs. That barony was *big*! There were four thousand three hundred peasant families living on it. No wonder Baron Stefan had been able to ride around with solid gold trim on his armor!

As to the fifty-odd knights and their squires that were sworn to Baron Stefan, I pointed out to them that their previous liege lord had been killed in a fair fight when he was fully armed and on horseback. And that this deed had been done by scrawny and naked little Piotr, one of my students at the Warrior's School. If they wanted to swear to *me*, they had to go to the school, too. And there was a school for their wives as well.

Those who had manors still kept them, but it was many years before they could do more than occasionally visit. They were in the army now!

All told, it was a rough summer and fall.

In the middle of this, my alchemist, a heretical Moslem named Zoltan Varanian, came to me with a vast grin on his face. He wanted to show me something in the valley I had set aside for the use of his people. He took me to a cave in the hills, which had centuries of bat droppings on the floor.

"You see?" he said. "We will no longer have to haul shit up here to make into your gunpowder, my lord! On this very floor is sufficient to make nine hundred tons of gunpowder! I have calculated it!"

This was extremely good news. Getting enough manure to meet the gunpowder quotas was a problem, and the peasants complained that we were taking the only thing they had to fertilize their fields. Furthermore, the manufacturing process for gunpowder was one of our major secrets, as were the ingredients that went into it. Having an internal supply of saltpeter eliminated one possible security leak. On top of that, why couldn't bat droppings be used as fertilizer? There were a lot of bat caves around.

We still had a problem with the sulfur needed, and were importing it from Hungary in the form of cinnabar, mercuric sulfide. We were just storing the mercury, except for a little that was used in thermometers, but it would find a use someday.

The annoying thing was that Poland has vast deposits of sulfur, but they are so far down that we couldn't get to them without some sophisticated drilling equipment that we hadn't had time to develop. Many of the ores we were mining were sulfides, and in roasting them, we were able to recover the sulfur dioxide and convert it to usable sulfuric acid. But taking sulfuric acid back to sulfur is harder than getting toothpaste back into the tube! As Zoltan put it, "Can the child be put back into the mother?" For the foreseeable future, we were stuck with imported sulfur.

I gave Zoltan my hearty congratulations, and two dozen huge bolts of Count Lambert's cloth as a bonus.

By fall, the team working on the zipper was successful, since all they had to do was duplicate the zipper on my sleeping bag, and this mollified Count Lambert somewhat, but the boys at Eagle Nest were disappointed with me. They had done their part and I had failed to do mine. I finally invited the entire senior class to Three Walls so that they could see the problems we were having with the aircraft engine and try their hands at solving some of them.

And the little bastards did!

A fourteen-year-old kid came up with an incredibly simple and efficient ignition system. Our cigarette lighters made a spark, didn't they? They worked on the principle of hitting a quartz crystal, didn't they?

So he made a spark plug with a hefty quartz crystal inside of it, which was struck by a little hammer connected by a linkage to the crankshaft. It didn't need insulation for the wires because there weren't any wires!

So we named the system after him, calling it the Skrzynecki ignition, and threw a party in his honor. What troubled me about it was the fact that I should have thought of that one myself. After all, I was the one who had designed our lighters in the first place. I just had to put it down to a mental blind spot.

It took a few months to beat down the other problems, but by Christmas we had an engine that could run for six hours without an overhaul and that was good enough for starters.

By spring they had six powered aircraft flying. It is astounding what a bunch of motivated kids can come up with!

Of course, the same electrical problems that plagued the engine also troubled the radio. To make a spark-gap transmitter, you have to have a spark. So I used a variation on the Skrzynecki ignition to power the transmitter. To transmit, somebody had to turn the crank so that a dozen little wooden hammers beat on a big quartz crystal, but that was no big problem.

Waxed paper and gold foil (the only really thin metal available) made a usable capacitor, a large, carefully made air core coil of bare wire served for a choke, and a long bare copper wire served as an antenna.

The receiver had a similar antenna connected with an identical coil and capacitor. This in turn went to a coherer, which was little more than a glass tube with iron filings in it. If a signal was picked up, the iron filings slightly welded themselves together and the resistance through them went way down. This let a low voltage current go through a relay which went "click" and tapped the coherer, shaking loose the iron filings to wait for another signal. It was a year and a half getting a pair of transceivers working that could send and receive over two dozen miles, and they weren't very dependable, requiring constant fiddling on the part of the operators, but they were good enough. We went into production with them.

About then, I somehow found time to polish up the books

I had been writing. Over the years, I had tried to write down everything I could remember about science and modern technology, and over time these scattered notes had turned themselves into about two dozen books. Or perhaps I should say pamphlets, since none of them was more than three dozen pages long, and in fact the longest of them was the poetry I had remembered.

One was called *Concerning Optics*. Everything I knew in twenty-nine pages. Another was *Power Transmission*, eighteen pages. It was frustrating! Here was everything I remembered from seventeen years of formal education, and a lot of reading besides, all in one short stack of papers! Even then, some of them wouldn't be useful here for many years, and books like *Computer Design, Programming and Semiconductors* were filed for future publication. But *Bridges*, and *Canals, Locks, and Dams* could aid contemporary builders, and there was no reason to withhold the information. I got the stack over to Father Ignacy and ordered six thousand copies of each, with woodcut illustrations. He was awestruck, but said he'd start having it done.

Around Christmas, Sir Piotr brought me copies of his first maps, the first accurate maps ever done of my own lands. He was an amazingly good mathematician, and after some years of tutoring on my part, he was starting to pull ahead of me. Certainly, his books on arithmetic, algebra, and trigonometry were better than mine, and we published his instead of what I'd done. He himself, with the help of the accountants that used to work with him, had written a book of trig tables, and had worked out the techniques necessary for accurate mapmaking. Those got into print as well, and we paid decent royalties.

There was a compass rose on the map, so naturally I turned it so that the arrow pointed up and I could read the words. I stared at the representation of the land that I had been riding over for years and I couldn't make heads or tails of it.

"Sir Piotr, there's something very wrong here. This isn't my land."

"But of course it is, my lord. I could hardly make a mistake like surveying the wrong property."

"But . . . you've got Sir Miesko's manor south of Three Walls. It's north of us!"

"Right, my lord. It's north of us."

"Then why do you have it at the bottom of the map?"

"Because I put south at the top of the map, my lord."

"You put *south* at the top of a map?"

"Yes, my lord. I worried a bit about that, since of course it's traditional to put east at the top—"

"*East,* for God's sake?"

"Of course, my lord. But I knew you'd want things done in a sensible and rational manner, so naturally south goes at the top."

"Naturally. Would you please go over your reasons for that conclusion?" I'm not sure whether it was caused by graduating from the Warrior's School, being knighted, or marrying Krystyana, but Piotr just didn't get intimidated anymore.

"Happy to, my lord. Your prime referent has always been your clock. All of our angles are measured as though they were the time of day it is when the fat hand is at that angle. At least that was the system you taught me. The fat hand corresponds to the position of the sun when the clock is south of the viewer, and all of your clocks are always mounted on a south wall for that reason. Therefore, all of the angles shown on the map correspond to the normal clock if the map is placed up next to the clock. Since the map corresponds to the land, and the land, looking south, has the more southerly portions appearing to be higher, this just naturally puts south at the top of the map. In addition, everybody knows that the mountains are to the south of us, and the plains and the sea are to the north. The mountains are higher, so naturally they go at the top."

I had to stare at it for a while and think about it, but in the end I had to admit that his way was more consistent.

It was more consistent to read our angles clockwise rather than counterclockwise, as it is done in the modern world, so we did it that way.

In the modern world, electricity flows from negative to positive. It happened that way because Ben Franklin knew that something was flowing, but he guessed wrong about the direction. Since I was starting out fresh, I corrected Ben's error. Our electrons were positive.

The controls on the aircraft worked the opposite of those on twentieth-century planes, because the boys started out flying hang gliders. With the usual control stick, if you want to go down, you push the lever away from you, but on a hang glider, which steers by the shift in body weight, to go down you must pull on the stick to pull your body forward. So when they started making gliders with control surfaces, it was natural for them to make it so that you pulled the stick to go down. Exactly the same thing happened with turning left and right. Sensible, but the opposite of what I was used to.

And on the riverboats, the same damn thing happened. I'd installed a conventional ship's wheel, but Tadaos had insisted on reworking the steering apparatus so it would be more "natural" for him. He was used to steering with a tiller bar, where to go to the right, you push the bar to the left. "Natural" for him was to move the top of the wheel to the left to make the boat go to the right. I had to do it his way or fire him, and just then I didn't have a replacement.

Yes, I know we were all Polish, but is that any reason why everything has to come out backward?

Chapter Four

FROM THE DIARY OF TADAOS KOLPINSKI

Well, they dang nearly killed me, but they didn't.

They shaved me naked and yelled and screamed and ran me up and down mountains and cliffs, and ropes, and all the while singing damn fool songs and blowing on horns and beating stupid drums. They got me up every day before dawn to swear the same dang oath, like I didn't remember it from the last two hundred mornings we'd said it, and then came at me with pikes and swords and axes, and they made me do the same to the others. They made me walk funny and talk funny and smile when they was shouting at me.

You see, one of the twelve things we was always to be was cheerful, and I think that was the hardest of the bunch. I finally figured out that if I squinted my eyes and gritted my teeth at them, I could usually make them think I was smiling.

Worst yet, they made me go the first six months of it without getting drunk or laid.

Sometimes, I think it was that last that kept me going, knowing that once 1 got out of this hell, all those pretty little girls would be waiting for Sir Tadaos to service them. I lived for that, and like I said, I nearly died for it.

A lot of men did die in that training, but not in my platoon. I guess I was lucky in that I was put in with the baron's managers for the first six months, and not many of them men washed out. I mean that they could all read and write already, and they was mostly pretty sensible. A few got hurt pretty bad on the cliffs, but even they graduated. I thought that I was going to graduate with them, but no, the day before the rest went through the firewalking ordeal and the vigil, they told me that I was scheduled for the whole year-long program. I went and talked to Sir Vladimir about that, since he ran the school and I knew him pretty well. Hell, once he let me use him for target practice, but that's another story.

Anyhow, he said that there was nothing he could do about it since the baron, he had put it in writing and that was that. But he did give me a pass to go to Three Walls for three days, so I could get proper drunk and visit the Widow Bromski. Seeing her again after spending six months dreaming about those sweet young things, well, it helped to get drunk first. I'd worn my armor coming in, but I guess I didn't fool anybody. Certainly not any of the girls. They must have some kind of secret code about that sort of thing. But at least I got good and blasted with the girls at the Pink Dragon Inn. Course, that's a look-but-don't touch sort of place, but I tell you it's well worth the looking.

So I went back to Hell, and this time they put me in with the baron's new knights, them what he got after little Piotr killed Baron Stefan and Conrad stepped into the old baron's shoes. They was pretty standoffish at first, but then one day Sir Vladimir called me "Squire Tadaos" in public, and those knights and squires loosened up some.

I guess I did learn something there. I got to be real good with a sword, one of those long skinny ones you wear over your left shoulder. I could hold my own with an axe or a pike, though I don't much like a pike, and I found out I was near as good a shot with one of them swivel guns as I was with my bow. I could outshoot anybody, the instructors included.

So at last came the day when we was to graduate. They made a big to-do about it, but me, I was just glad it was over. The others was worried about walking on fire, but not me. If Piotr and all them managers could do it, I knew I wouldn't have no trouble, and I didn't.

Look here. Every man in the world has snuffed a candle with his fingers without burning hisself, and walking on coals is just the same thing in a bigger way. Anyhow, I did burn myself a little, though I didn't feel nothing at the time.

Naturally, I had brains enough to go through it all with a straight face, not wanting to be dropped this late in the thing. I know when to keep my mouth shut.

After that, there was some hocus-pocus about sitting up all night and seeing if we had halos in the morning. I guess I never been much of a religious man, except once there, and that didn't last long. But I learned long ago that if you play the game and look nice, there's a whole lot less trouble. So we waited up all night and the sun come up and didn't none of us have a halo showing on the fog. There wasn't even no fog!

So this priest, he says that one of us must not be in a state of grace, and that we'd have to pray all day and try it again tomorrow. We was all pretty disappointed.

Them knights, they all took it real serious and did some real soul-searching, so naturally I had to look like I was doing the same. But any man with half the brains of a cow should be able to figure out that you can't see your shadow on the fog, halo or no halo, when there wasn't no fog in the first place!

So we stayed up the whole day in prayer, and the next night in vigil and again there wasn't no fog. I thought some of them knights was going to die right there from the humiliation of it. They figured God was rejecting them for their sins, and of course, I couldn't tell them no different.

So a third day and night went by without no sleep and in the middle of the night, Baron Conrad came by. He hadn't been there the other two nights, and I figured he knew when it'd be foggy. I always knew that man was smart.

So we finally got fog and saw our shadows in it. What they got so excited about was something I'd seen a hundred times before, only looking into green water instead of fog. Sort of these rays of light seem to come out of the head of your shadow. Every man on the river has seen it, them with brains enough to look down, and fog is just another kind of water, isn't it?

But it wasn't my place to say nothing, so I got in line with the others and was knighted and sworn in and became Sir Tadaos Kolpinski.

We slept in that day and threw a party that night with the help of some beautiful young girls from the cloth factory at Okoitz. The next day, they gave me a full purse of silver and lent me a horse, so I gave one of them girls a lift back, because Okoitz was the place I intended to spend my month's leave.

I had a month off, and after the first day, I just sent the horse back to the baron, cause I wasn't going nowheres else. That place is even better than the stories they tell about it! They not only had the prettiest and the eagerest girls in the world, they had two shifts of them! You could stand there smiling in your red-and-white dress uniform, with all your brass and boots polished, watching them as they paraded out after the end of their work day, and none of them wearing much of anything. Then when you saw one that suited you, you just smiled and asked her if she wanted to have a beer with you, and never one of them turned me down.

Then in the morning, when you'd eaten and drunk and fornicated all night, you walked her back to the factory and there'd be the night shift coming off work, rubbing the limelights out of their pretty eyes and wondering what they'd do with themselves all the lonely day.

I'd just spent a year in Hell, but now I was in Heaven!

This went on for three weeks, when one night I was sitting in the inn with two of the prettiest girls in Okoitz. Good friends and roommates they was, and I'd had the both of them before, one at a time, and that night I couldn't decide between them so I took them both, and they said that sounded like fun.

They was both wearing about what the waitresses at the inn wear and, that's to say, nearly nothing. They said it was the new style at Wroclaw, and I sure didn't make no argument about their tits hanging out. Not that theirs really hung, you understand, being of the young, conical variety.

We was all laughing and talking when Baron Conrad comes up. I asked him if I could buy him a beer, or maybe a mead would be more fitting for one of his exalted rank. He said it had been a hot day, and if I was buying beer, he was drinking it. Course, he never had to pay for his drinks anyway, seeing as how he owned this Pink Dragon Inn and fifty others besides, but it felt good playing host to my liege lord. He downed it quick and bought the next round for the table, just like he was a normal man and all.

Then he got down to business. He said that I was going to have to cut my leave short. It seems that the first steamboat was all built ahead of schedule, and if I figured to be its captain, I'd better be in East Gate tomorrow by noon.

Course, I wouldn't of missed that boat for all the girls in Okoitz, now that I'd had three weeks of them. But I figured that it was worthwhile complaining about it, since the baron might sweeten the pot a bit to get me there. It's the squeaky oarlock that gets the oil.

So I said that it would be hard, tearing myself away from these poor girls, leaving them to God knew what sad fate.

So the baron, he says that if I was worried about their futures, why, I could marry them if I wanted to.

I said I couldn't marry them both and he said I could if I was of a mind to. Hadn't I read the manual and rules of the Radiant Warriors?

Well, they'd given me this little printed book just as I left, but I hadn't read nothing and I had to admit it. So the baron says that any knight in our order had the right to have a servant, with his wife's permission. And a servant of ours had all the rights of a wife, so it was the same thing, except for the church ceremony, of course.

Well, that sort of flabbergasted me, and I said I didn't know which one I should marry. I don't rightly know if he was serious or not, but he says that if I couldn't decide, I should let the girls do it. Let them flip a coin, he says.

Before I can blink twice, the girls are grinning and nodding at each other. One of them digs a silver penny out of my purse and flips it in the air. The other calls "crowns," and that was the way that I proposed to Alona. I never had a word to say about it.

Course, the girls were both jabbering now, working out the details. If I had to go to East Gate tomorrow, why, Alona's village was only a half mile off the new railroad. She could come with me and I could speak to her father and post banns at the village church, because that's where she wanted to be married. Then Petrushka would be her bridesmaid and right after the ceremony, she'd become the servant.

All this was fine by Petrushka, so the girls had it all settled while me and Baron Conrad never said a word.

Then the girls left in a hurry to tell all their friends and I was left staring at the baron. I think that if I hadn't been drinking and fornicating for three weeks, I might have had enough sense to shout "NO!", but I had been and I didn't. The baron, he just seemed amused and said that under the circumstances I didn't have to get to East Gate until tomorrow *night*.

But looking back on it all, I tell you that if I had been sensible that night, I would have made the biggest mistake of my life.

Them girls was everything a reasonable man could want, and we've been mostly happy together.

So the next morning, I rented us two horses, one with a side-saddle since Alona didn't figure it was smart wearing the Wroclaw styles home, but had on a nice wool dress she'd made. We got there before noon and I talked to her old man and the priest and we settled everything real quick, since I didn't much care about the dowry and all, what with me making eight pennies a day now. Then I left her with her folks to visit for a day or two and got to East Gate before dark.

They had limelights up around the dock area, so I went out to look at my new boat right after supper, and she was a beauty! She was painted red and white, with gold and black trim, and a big white Piast eagle was painted on her side, just like the one on the back of the dress uniform. She looked more like a castle than a boat, what with her tall, flat armored sides, and there was crenellations all around the top and turrets at all four corners.

I swear I loved that boat more than the girls I was going to marry.

She was huge, fully three dozen yards long and ten wide. She was two and a half stories tall and armored with steel thick enough to stop any arrow but one of mine! She could carry sixty tons of cargo in six containers, and had fourteen cabins for passengers as well, plus five more for the crew. Yet the night guard told me that she only drew a half a yard of water with a full load!

I went down to the engine room and who do I find there but Baron Conrad hisself. I told him this boat of his was the finest looking thing I'd ever seen, both my girls included, and he said he was glad I thought so, but I better not let them hear that. Then he showed me all over that engine. It had a tubular boiler that ran at two dozen atmospheres, and a sealed condenser below the waterline so we got full power from it. It had a separate distillery run off waste heat, with its own condenser to make distilled water for the main boiler, so he didn't figure we'd ever have a fouling problem. It had two big double expansion cylinders that turned a paddle wheel that was two stories tall. There was a kitchen that could feed a whole company of men. There was even a bathroom with hot showers!

Then he got into the armament. We carried twelve swivel guns aboard, plus four steam-powered guns in the corner turrets he called peashooters. These fired ball bearings at the rate of three gross rounds a minute, one after another. And there was two steam projectors, Halmans, he called them, that could throw three pounds of death at the enemy. And during wartime, the boat was set up to carry a full company of men with all their equipment, including their war carts!

Then he told me I better get some sleep, because we was going to take her out in the morning.

Chapter Five

FROM THE DIARY OF CONRAD STARGARD

We took the steamboat out with a skeleton crew: an engine operator, a fireman, Tadaos and myself, plus a dozen of the carpenters and machinists who had helped build her. And of course I brought Anna along, since she didn't like being far from me, and her senses were better than a human's. There was always the chance that she would spot something wrong before the rest of us did.

One of the watertight compartments below deck leaked a bit, but that was not serious. There were two dozen of them, and it could have been holed without endangering the boat. There were no other hitches, except for Tadaos' problems with the steering wheel. Once, when he wasn't sure if the water ahead was deep enough, we sent a man out ahead of the boat, walking. As long as the water stayed above the guy's knees, we were safe!

I'd planned to just take her a few miles downriver and return, but with things going so well, we went all the way to Cracow. We took up half the dock and drew quite a crowd, so I told Tadaos to speak with the riverboat men and try to talk them into joining the army. We were advertising in the magazine, but most of these men couldn't read.

I rode Anna up to Wawel Castle to pay my respects to the duke and see if he wanted a ride. Duke Henryk the Bearded was even more important to me than Count Lambert, and without the duke's support, I couldn't have accomplished a tenth of what I had. On the way there, Anna gestured that something was wrong, but she didn't know what it was.

The guard at the castle gate looked glum, but he recognized us and let us in. I didn't find out what was the trouble until I asked the marshal, the man in charge of the stables, where I could find the duke.

"Young Duke Henryk is in his chambers, my lord, but I wouldn't bother him just now."

"*Young Duke Henryk?* What are you talking about? The duke is over seventy!" I said.

"You hadn't heard, my lord? Duke Henryk the Bearded was killed last night. Duke Henryk the Pious now rules."

"Good God in Heaven! How did it happen?"

"It was one of his own guards that killed him, my lord, a Sir Frederick. Shot him with a filthy crossbow while he was asleep. The other guards chopped up Sir Frederick, killed him on the spot, so I don't guess we'll ever find out why he did it."

I left Anna with the marshal and went to young Henryk's chambers. Actually, he was ten years older than I was, but he still might want someone to talk to, and I knew the man fairly well. In any event, I could hardly leave the castle at a time like this without his permission. There was a crowd around his closed door, but just as I got there, the door opened and the new duke came out. He was wearing an army uniform.

"Ah, Baron Conrad. You got here quickly."

"In truth, your grace, I didn't hear the news until I arrived."

"Your grace?" he mused. "Yes, I guess I am that now. I've been going over my late father's private papers. I want to talk to you alone. The rest of you, please tell everyone that I will want to see every noble in the throne room in two hours, but for now, disperse. Come in, Baron Conrad."

"Thank you, your grace. May I say how sorry I am about your father's death?"

"No sorrier than I am, I assure you. But things must go on if I am not to waste the work he spent his life on."

"Have you any idea why Sir Frederick would do such a thing, your grace?"

He thought a moment. "My father was often rude to the man, but there must have been more to it than that. My father made many enemies. He had to knock a lot of heads together to get the lords of both Little and Great Poland to swear allegiance to him. There are a lot of young hotheads out there who thought that they would inherit petty dukedoms and who now find themselves only becoming counts or even barons. Doubtless one of them got to Sir Frederick somehow. But which one? I doubt that we'll ever know. But I tell you this—every noble on my lands is going to swear allegiance to me, and those who don't are going to *wish they had!*"

"Whoever did it might come after you next, your grace. Perhaps you could use a special sort of bodyguard. I'm sure you've heard many stories about my horse, Anna. The truth is that she's not really a horse. She's almost as intelligent as a man. She's absolutely loyal and she's saved my life many times. The first of her children are of age now, and I'd like you to have one of them, sort of a permanent loan. The young ones are identical to their mother, and might save your life."

"Can they run like she does?"

"Yes, your grace."

"Then I'll take one. But that's not what I wanted to talk to you about. My father's secret letters to me say some astounding things about you. Are you really from the future?"

"Yes, your grace. I was born in the twentieth century."

"And you don't know how you got here?"

"Not really, your grace. I think it had something to do with an inn I slept in, but that inn is gone now. Certainly my own people never had a time machine."

"But you were Polish, and a sworn officer in the military."

"I *am* Polish, your grace, and once an officer, always an officer."

"Yes, yes. Then your knowledge of the Tartar invasion is one of simple historical fact?"

"Yes, your grace. But in truth, I am no longer sure just what a historical fact is. In my history, at this time there was nothing like the factories or railroads or aircraft or steamboats that I have built here. My being here has changed things, and I have no idea whether or how these changes will affect other things. In my time, the Mongols invaded Poland in late February and early March of 1241. Two major battles were fought, one at Chmielnick on March seventh, and another at Legnica two weeks later. We lost both battles."

"But you don't know if these things are fixed by fate?"

"No, your grace, I don't. I'm praying that they are not. It is my intent to defeat the Mongols and kill them all."

"I see. Well, you may rest assured that the 'Mongols,' as you persist in calling them, are indeed coming. They are already invading southeastern Russia. We just got word that the city of Vladimir has fallen. They said it had been larger than Cracow. But it's gone now, with almost every man, woman, and child slaughtered. The Mongols even killed every animal—why, I do not know."

"Perhaps they simply enjoy killing, your grace."

"I see. You were definitely not sent here by anyone?"

"Not to my knowledge, your grace, but I got here somehow. Someone must have done it."

"Well. I'll expect you and any of your knights that you have with you to swear fealty to me this afternoon. Tell me, if you hadn't heard of my father's death, why did you come here today?"

"It seems trivial now, your grace, but we just got the first riverboat working. It's tied up at the docks here in Cracow. I came to see if your father wanted to ride it."

"Perhaps tomorrow I might have time to inspect it. For now, good day, Baron Conrad."

I scrounged up some writing materials, wrote some quick letters, and then went down to see Anna.

I met Lady Francine in the courtyard. She had been the old duke's companion (Paramour? Assistant? Toy?) for some years, and we had been friends for even longer. Perhaps next to Cilicia, she was the most beautiful woman in Poland. I gave her my condolences and invited her to join me on my errand.

"I would love to, Baron Conrad. But do not be so downhearted," she said with her thick French accent as we walked to the stables. "The old duke had a long full life, and he died without pain, yes? How many others have done the same?" She was wearing a most modest dress that covered her from wrists to chin to ankles, a far cry from the miniskirt and topless styles the old duke preferred.

"I suppose you're right. That's a most attractive dress, my lady."

"It is the style that will be worn at court from now on, I am afraid. Everyone knows the young duke's displeasure with the styles preferred by his father."

"Perhaps it's just as well, my lady. The bare-breasted style was lovely on you and on a few other young women, but on the battle-scarred spinsters who were wearing them, well, perhaps it's all for the best."

"My only regret is that the bare styles had to arrive in the wintertime, and these cover-it-all things must needs be worn now that summer is finally here. If only the old duke could have lived five months longer!" She smiled at her own audacity.

"Still, he'll be missed."

"All too true."

"But what about you, my lady. What is to happen to you?"

"Indeed, I do not know. I am not in want. Much to the contrary, for I had little chance to spend my excellent income. Also, the duke saw fit to elevate me to the peerage. I am a countess now, with a large estate near Wroclaw. But as to what I will do, I do not know."

"Don't worry, my lady. The most beautiful woman in Poland will not be left alone for long."

"Oh, the boys are already flocking around, but only boys. Not men like you."

I was saved by our arrival at Anna's stall.

"Anna, I have some errands for you to run." I threw on her saddle and cinched it down. "This letter is for Tadaos down at the boat. He is to come here right away, so give him a lift up here, drop him off at the gate, and then be on your way. This one is for the people at East Gate, since they have to be worrying about us. And this one is for your servant, Kotcha. If you haven't heard yet, the old duke was killed. I think that the young duke would be a lot safer if one of your daughters was with him. Do you think one of them would like that?"

Anna nodded YES.

I put the letters under her saddle where she could get at each of them individually. "Oh, yes. This last letter is for anyone silly enough to try to stop you. On your way, girl."

Anna sped out of the stables and past a startled guard. I waved to the man so he would know that nothing was wrong.

"Such an amazing beast!" Lady Francine said.

"Not a beast at all, my lady. Anna's people."

"Still, would that I had such a mount."

"Well, Anna's not exactly for sale."

"But you said that she had children."

"She does. But I also said she was people and you didn't believe me. One doesn't sell children, my lady."

"Well, I never offered any money, my lord."

"Sorry. It's just that I feel protective toward her. Everybody tries to treat her like a dumb animal and I don't like to see her feelings hurt."

"You always take so much upon yourself, Conrad. You cannot change the whole world."

"It's strange, my lady, but you know?—I really think I can. But while I can't give you Anna, I can give you a lift. After the funeral, if you want transportation back to your estate, I can provide a steamboat to East Gate and a railroad to Coaltown. Or you could stay a while at Three Walls if you like."

"Much of my last stay there was enjoyable, my lord. Perhaps

I shall get a job again as a waitress at your inn, yes? I still qualify."

That was her way of telling me that she was still a virgin. Well, the duke was a very old man. But while I enjoyed the tentative way she was offering herself to me, I had the feeling that she wanted much more than a casual affair. And the whole idea of marriage *scares me shitless*!

I was saved again when a page called us to the throne room. We got there just as Sir Tadaos came puffing in.

"Your uniform's a mess, Sir Tadaos. It's filthy! Don't you know that you are about to swear fealty to the new duke?"

"It's not like I had a spare to change into, my lord. I didn't even know we was coming to Cracow! And I was fixing the cabling on the steering wheel, and—"

"Well, there's nothing for it now. We'll have to bluff it through. Come and sit by me and do what I do. My lady?" I said, offering Lady Francine my arm.

And thus it was that I swore fealty to Duke Henryk the Pious of Silesia, Little and Great Poland, and my future king if I had anything to say about it, standing between a filthy subordinate and a woman I was afraid of.

Chapter Six

Anna came back as soon as the city gates were opened the next morning, and with her were all four of her oldest daughters. They said that they all wanted to work for the duke, and figured that he should make the decision between them. Of course they said this in a combination of the sign language we'd worked out and by my playing a game of twenty questions with them.

The funeral was held the next day. Embalming techniques were unknown, and in the summertime, well, these things couldn't be delayed. The old duke was placed in the crypt below Wawel Cathedral.

The morning after, I was trying to talk the kitchen help into scrambling me up some eggs, since nobody else in this century ever ate before late morning and I was partial to a decent breakfast. But word came that the duke would speak to me, so I missed another breakfast.

When I arrived before him, the duke looked up from a stack of parchment. We were producing some decent paper now, but everything official was still being handwritten on real sheepskin parchment, when it wasn't on the even more expensive calfskin vellum.

"Ah, Baron Conrad. Riders have been sent out to every noble in Little Poland, telling of my father's death and my requirement that they all swear allegiance to me. It will be a few days before they start getting here, so I have time to inspect that boat of yours. Also, the marshal tells me that there are now five 'Annas' in the stables, but I suppose you know about that."

"I do, your grace. The children felt that you should choose among them."

"Then let's do it."

At the stables, the duke said, "By God, they *are* identical. How do you tell them apart?"

"I have to ask them who is who, your grace. Anna, please come here by me, and the rest of you get into alphabetical order, so I can introduce you properly."

There was always a crowd around the duke, but this drew a bigger crowd than usual. I noticed Count Lambert's sister-in-law, who was trying to flirt with me as always. Both she and her husband, Count Herman, were of the opinion that people should be respected on the basis of their rank, and only on that basis. To her mind, this made her infinitely desirable, despite the fact that she was ignorant, supercilious, intolerant, married, and shaped like a pear. I ignored her, as was my custom.

I introduced Anna's children, and each bowed properly to Henryk. Everyone was familiar enough with Anna not to be too astounded.

"They're all perfect, and I don't see how one could possibly choose between them. I'd be forced to choose a horse by its saddle. But they're not really horses, are they?"

"No, your grace."

"Well, we must call them something. You keep calling them 'people,' but they're not really like ordinary people either, are they? What say we call them 'Big People'?"

"Well girls, what do you say?"

They all nodded YES, that was fine by them.

"We all seem to think it an excellent term, your grace."

"It's all settled, then. Well, Big People, am I correct in assuming that you all would like to serve me?"

The four sisters nodded YES.

"I see, and I thank you. Baron Conrad, you have offered me the loan of one of these lovely ladies. But what if I was attacked on the road by a superior force? I might then have to run for it, wouldn't I? But I would hate to run if I had to leave my wife or sons behind. In fact, I likely wouldn't do it. Could I prevail upon you? I know you have others like these growing up. Could I have all four?"

"You are a hard man to refuse, your grace. Of course. Since the Big People are willing, you may have the loan of all four."

"And that's another point. Why do you keep saying 'loan'? Many would simply make it a gift."

"Three reasons, your grace. One is the fact that they really are people, which you are already forgetting. I can't give them away because I don't own them. They are sworn to me and I pay them a regular salary, so I can loan out their services. The second is that I want to keep very careful control over who has them. I don't want them abused, and I wouldn't want an enemy to have them. The third is that I want all their fillies returned to me, again so that I can take proper care of them, and keep control over who has them."

"You seem adamant on these points, Baron Conrad."

"I am, your grace. Surely you can see my reasoning."

"I suppose I can. Perhaps I was being greedy. But what if there were enough for all my retainers? For all my knights! Such an army would be unbeatable!"

"Perhaps in time that will be possible, your grace. They reproduce rapidly. Indeed, all five that you see here are expecting, and each will have four fillies. In twenty or thirty years, they could outnumber people, if they wanted to. I assure you, we'll discuss such a mounted force when the time comes. For now, I suggest that we go for a ride. You notice that none of them has a bridle. They don't need them. Also, I'd thank you if you took off your spurs."

"What? Oh, yes. I'd forgotten that."

Two of his knights bent down to remove the duke's spurs, and I noticed Lady Francine join the crowd.

"Baron Conrad, may I join your group?" she asked.

"I'm sorry, my lady, but I believe the duke already has his party chosen."

"But there would be room for me if you put that thing behind your saddle on Anna."

"That thing" was the sidesaddle I'd had made to fit behind a regular saddle so a passenger, Cilicia for the last few years, could sit comfortably. It was sort of a pillion with a foot rest. Kotcha had given each of Anna's children one of my saddles, every single spare one that I kept for my own personal use, and I had the feeling that it would be awkward getting them back. This way, I could at least save the sidesaddle. I gestured to a groom to switch the thing.

"Then I would be delighted to have you riding apillion, my lady."

The duke mounted up along with three of his armed guards. They each carried an oversized shield and they'd had brains enough to remove their spurs.

"We'll go out by way of the Carpenter's Gate, then take the outer road to the docks," the duke announced. "That should let us give the Big People a good run."

I gave Lady Francine a lift into the rear saddle. She was a lot fleshier than Cilicia, but in fact she was lighter, not having the dense, muscular dancer's body that Cilicia has.

Once we were out of the city, I told Anna to go at her best speed, to show the duke what running was. We were soon going at a solid run, doing about the speed that a modern thoroughbred can run, but where an ordinary horse might match our speed with a tiny jockey aboard and for a mile, Anna and her kin could do it with two full-sized people on their backs, and keep it up all day!

Nonetheless, Anna was carrying double and her daughters pulled ahead of her. They were two-gross yards ahead of us when the attack occurred.

Suddenly, an armored man stood up in the bushes a gross yards from the road. He leveled a crossbow at the duke and let fly. The guard to the duke's right, a lefthander who carried his shield on his right arm, had remarkably good reflexes. He raised his shield in time to deflect the bolt high into the air.

But at the same time, two other crossbowmen were raising on the left, hoping to catch the duke's party off guard. They didn't. Those guards were on the ball, and Anna's daughters weren't being slouches, either. They had the duke surrounded, and the guards were holding their shields, not to cover themselves, but to cover the duke! It was as though they considered their own bodies as extensions of their shields. The next two bolts were stopped, one by a shield and one by a guard's arm.

The duke's party continued down the road, not knowing how many assassins they faced. But from my vantage point, I was sure that there were only the three of them. Sad experience had taught me that speed was more important than planning. When in doubt, charge straight in! I signaled Anna to attack the two on the left.

They were franticly trying to rewind their crossbows, hoping to get off a second shot. I don't think they saw us coming. Anna can run very quietly when she wants to, although she says that it's a lot more work. We were only a few dozen yards away when they noticed us. I had my sword out, but I wasn't wearing armor or carrying a shield. Heck, I'd started out dressed for a boatride. A knight is always supposed to be ready for emergencies, but that's often hard to do!

Anna passed to the left of the first man, and I found that he had stuck his sword in the dirt so as to have it near if he needed it in a hurry. He dropped his crossbow and swung his sword at me. I wanted to take prisoners, since these men probably had something to do with the old duke's assassination, but all I could do under the circumstances was to chop down at his sword as hard as I could. My sword went right through the crossbowman's blade, and through his helmet and head as well.

Before I could recover from the blow, Anna was already onto the second man. She just went right over him, trampling him flat. She turned and I saw that there were four hoofprints in the assassin's chest. He had squirted out of his armor like toothpaste from a tube hit by a sledgehammer.

We turned to see the last assassin mounting his horse and leaving.

"Catch him, Anna!" I shouted, but she was already on the way.

"This is so exciting!" Lady Francine shouted.

This shocked me. Would you believe that I had actually forgotten that I had a beautiful woman riding at my back? Worse yet, that I had gone into combat without even considering that I was risking her life!

"My lady!" I yelled, and Anna picked up from my body language that I wanted to stop.

"NO, NO!" Lady Francine shouted. "We must catch him! He must know who had the duke murdered!"

She was right, of course. Her safety and mine were unimportant compared to insuring the young duke's safety. The mystery had to be solved.

Anna picked up speed as she felt my new resolve. The assassin had quite a lead on us, but we caught up with him within half a mile. He ducked into a woods, trying to shake us, but it did him no good.

"We need a prisoner, Anna!" I shouted, as we approached him from the rear. She nodded okay. My thought was to hack off one of the horse's hind legs and then deal with the rider at our leisure. I never had a chance to, since Anna had similar ideas. She broke both of that animal's rear legs with her forehoofs. The horse went down in a heap. The rider flew over its head and stopped abruptly against a big tree trunk.

We dismounted in a hurry. The horse was still alive but the rider was not. He had both a caved-in forehead and a broken neck. One hundred percent overkill.

"Damn! Not a single prisoner."

"Your sword, Conrad! It went right through that knight's sword, and his helm and head as well!"

"Yes, it's quite a blade. I wish I knew how it was made." I bent to search the dead knight, hoping to find some clue to who he was.

Interlude Two

I hit the STOP button.

"Hey, Tom, how was that sword made?"

"It happens that I am well informed on that subject, seeing as how I invented the process and made that particular sword myself," he said smugly. "First you get a good quality Damascus steel blade, which, by the way, were mostly made in India. Damascus was nothing more than a distribution point. You split the blade in half the hard way, right down the middle, through the edge."

"How do you do that?"

"Simple. You line up a nonlinear temporal field just right, then send one half of the blade a few minutes farther forward in time than the other. This gives you perfectly smooth surfaces, and since you're working in a vacuum, those surfaces are pretty reactive, chemically. Then you put a thin slice of diamond between them, about a hundred angstroms thick. You get that by slicing it off a larger block, using the same temporal cutting technique as you used on the blade. Then you clamp this sandwich together at four thousand PSI for two hundred years in a hard vacuum at room temperature. This welds the pieces together without harming the crystalline structure of the steel. You end up with as perfect a sword as is possible, with a pure diamond edge."

"Uh-huh. Where did you get a block of diamond that big?"

"Simple. You just put a block of graphite somewhere at thirty million PSI and two thousand degrees for twenty thousand years. It's not as though you need a flawless, single crystal."

"Oh. Is that all. I should have known." I hit the START button.

Chapter Seven

FROM THE DIARY OF CONRAD STARGARD

Lady Francine was flushed. "That was very . . . exciting, my lord."

"The first time you've seen combat? Well, try not to let it upset you." I was checking the dead man's pouch. Of course, nobody carried any ID in this age, but there might be something identifiable.

"I am not upset, I am . . . excited. Take me, my lord. Please."

"What? My lady, you don't know what you're saying. Look. Violence excites a lot of people sexually. It doesn't get me that way, but it's not uncommon. It's nothing to be ashamed of, but don't lose your head." I went over to dispatch the wounded horse, not looking at her.

"I know exactly what I am saying. Take me. Now."

"Here? Lady, besides the violence, you were just bouncing your butt on Anna's hindquarters. That can get you horny, too, but for physical rather than psychological reasons. Anyway, you're a virgin and—" I was still avoiding looking at her. I took out the wounded horse by cutting its head off. Then I checked its saddlebags. Nothing.

"I am a twenty-six-year old virgin and I know exactly what I am doing. Look at me. Please?"

I looked at her. She had stripped down to her slip, and was naked to the waist. Lord, what a magnificent body. I went over to her.

"You know I'm not the marrying kind. I can't promise—"

She put her arms around me. "Do not promise anything, do not say anything, just take me. Do it now."

Well, the woods were fairly secluded and there is a limit as to how many times a normal man can say "no" to a beautiful woman. And if the violence and bouncing had turned her on, well, I have my hot buttons, too. One of my major ones involves holding a beautiful, passionate and nearly naked woman in my arms.

If she wasn't totally rational, well, neither was I. I pushed my own future regrets aside and took her, with a dead horse on one side of us and a dead man on the other. But the taking of a virgin is a time-consuming affair, if one is not to be a total klutz about it, and it was over an hour before we sat up on the woodland moss.

I noticed a knight in the duke's colors sitting a hundred yards from us with his back turned.

Embarrassing as hell. Once we were dressed, I shouted, "Okay! You can turn around now! What are you doing here?"

"My lord, I was sent with others by the duke to see to your safety and come to your aid, though when we found you we thought our assistance might not be welcome. We have reported your safety to the duke, and have your other rewards of combat, that is to say, your booty, packed and ready for transport." His left arm was bandaged, but it didn't seem to bother him.

"Thank you, I suppose. Did you report what we were doing to the duke?"

"It was needful, my lord, since he asked about the delay."

Great. The rumormongers would be going for months over this one. Yet Lady Francine didn't look the least bit embarrassed. She looked as if there were canary feathers on her mouth.

"I take it that the duke is at my boat?"

"Yes, my lord."

"Then we'll be going there now. Clean up the rest of this mess," I said, gesturing to the dead knight and horse. "And then bring it all to the boat. The duke will want to examine it."

"And after that, my lord?"

"After that, you can keep it. Divide the booty up among your fellow guards."

"Thank you, my lord, you are most generous! But then, you have taken a far greater reward for yourself."

"Shut your damn mouth!"

At the boat, the duke was smiling. "Well, Baron Conrad, they tell me that you killed all three would-be assassins, and with a lovely lady at your back, besides!"

"I killed one, your grace. Anna got two, and one of those was an accident. We were trying for a prisoner, but he was killed when his horse went down."

"A prisoner? But who would ransom an assassin? To do so would be to admit one's guilt!"

"I wasn't worried about a ransom, your grace. But the men who were trying to kill you were probably connected to whoever was behind the death of your father."

"Yes, of course. Stupid of me. I think my father's death must have affected me more than I had thought. Well, I shall instruct my guards to try to capture assassins in the future, and if we can't identify the men you killed, I'll have their heads set on poles in the marketplace, across from St. Mary's Church, with a reward posted for any information about them. For now, your excellent Sir Tadaos has shown me around the boat during your absence, and I suggest that we take it out for a ride."

They had the booty on board before Tadaos could get a head of steam up. We went downstream to the limits of the duke's lands, halfway to Sandomierz, and then back past Cracow to East Gate. Lady Francine stayed close to me the whole while, but I stayed close to the duke, so she couldn't speak what was on her mind.

The duke tested all our weaponry himself, and was both

impressed and troubled by it. He'd seen the swivel guns before, though this was the first time he'd fired one. The Halman Projectors were essentially steam-powered mortars, of a type that was used on merchant ships during WWII. We fired off a number of dummy rounds and one grenade. The peashooters were turret-mounted steam-powered machine guns. They worked as well on the boat as they had in the shop, with one problem. They drew so much steam that firing a single one of them noticeably slowed the boat. Something would have to be done, but I wasn't sure what.

What troubled the duke was that these weapons could rip up any group of mounted knights, and there wasn't much that conventional forces could do about it. And the duke's power was ultimately based on his knights.

"Good, Baron Conrad. We will need dozens, many dozens of these boats. With them, if the rivers be free of ice, you might stop the Tartars from killing my people. But in so saying, I am chanting the doom of my own kind."

"Not so, your grace. Poland will always need leaders and the land must have a king."

He looked at me strangely. "Yes. But who?"

I got off at East Gate and offered to have Tadaos run the duke back to Cracow. He said he preferred to ride back on his new mounts, and left. One of the guards made quick arrangements with Tadaos with regards to the bodies and booty, and Francine sent a note back with the guard concerning her servants and luggage.

Lady Francine stayed with me and seemed to take it for granted that she would continue to do so.

As soon as we were alone, I said, "I once asked you if you wanted to join my household. You know that offer still stands."

"To join your household? To be one among many?"

"Not so many. Actually, you'd be one among two."

"Two. Do you mean that foreign woman?"

"Cilicia, yes. And you yourself are something of a foreigner here, my lady."

"I had hoped for something better."

"It's all that I have to offer, my lady. I couldn't dump Cilicia. She's heavy with my child. And I've told you that I'm not the marrying kind."

"I must think on it."

Well, she didn't seem to think much, but continued acting as if she owned me. We got back to Three Walls the next day and I introduced her around.

She'd met Cilicia a few dozen times when she was with the old duke, and always they had been cordial, even friendly with each other. Now all that was changed. You could see little lightning bolts flash between the two women, with plenty of fireworks and the occasional atomic blast!

It was an awkward, unpleasant situation, and I did my best to ignore it. I found myself working late in the shops and hoping that the ladies would come to some sort of an accommodation. I tried to be fair, and took them to bed on alternate nights, but their concept of fairness was different from mine. At last, I tried to sit them down together and get them to talk it out, but they both just sat there radiating hate.

After a month, Lady Francine rather stiffly thanked me for a pleasant visit and said that she was leaving for her estate. She stressed that I would always be welcome there, but that she would not be returning to Three Walls.

We gave her a nice sendoff, and I breathed a vast sigh of relief. Having the two most beautiful women in the country was nice, but it was not worth the total absence of domestic tranquility.

I think I must be growing old.

Yet ever after, I could not help but visit the countess at her manor, once or twice a month. And always I stayed the night.

FROM THE DIARY OF TADAOS KOLPINSKI

In the summer of 1238, I married Alona and took Petrushka on as a "servant" as we'd agreed, and we was as happy as three people could be. The captain's cabin on my boat was bigger than a lot of the houses we'd all lived in, so that was no problem, and the girls just naturally took over the kitchens and all, just like the boat was a house.

I even got them both on the payroll, at two pence a day, each.

Most of that summer, while the people at East Gate was building a dozen new boats, we went up and down the Vistula and its tributaries, setting up small depots with the help of Boris Novacek, him with no hands, and his wife, Natasha.

The idea was to have a depot every twelve miles or so along all the rivers, where they'd buy and sell goods, or contract goods for shipment. Every one of these was to have a radio, once we got them, so we'd know when to stop, but for now they just ran up a flag.

'Course, once it started working, every boatman on the river started howling about how we was ruining them, since we was charging half what was usual. I kept telling people that if they could get through the Warrior's School, they could work on the steamboats, and maybe get one for their own. Well, a lot of them went to that school, and more than half of them got through it alive, but we was always pressed for enough good boatmasters.

Yet I don't think we put anybody out of business. We collared the long-run trade, sure, but once we got going, there was just a whole lot more trade going on! The short-run stuff and running up small rivers kept all the boatmen busy enough.

But for me, the best part was the baron's strict orders that we wasn't to pay no tolls! He said that despite the fact that we was engaging in trade, this was a military craft engaged in defending the country. It was owned by a baron and commanded by a knight, and if anybody didn't like it, they could challenge me if they wanted to. Their boat against mine! Didn't nobody take me up on it, though, except maybe once.

There'd be their toll boat out there and I'd come steaming past them just as smooth as you please, and I'd wave at them bastards as I went by.

Even that jackass Baron Przemysl had a toll boat out when we went up the Dunajec. Just like I was ordered, I explained why we wasn't to pay no tolls. 'Course, I had to explain to them that I was the man they jailed for poaching some years back, and suggest to them what I felt about their morals and standards of cleanliness. They got abusive in return, and I decided that this was a sufficient affront to my knightly honor as to constitute a challenge. Anyhow, they wouldn't get out of my way, so I just ran the buggers down and dunked them. 'Course, they was wearing chain mail, and they didn't come back up again, but that was their problem and not mine.

I tell you that it was worth more to do that than all the money I got paid for doing it. No man ever said wrong about Baron Conrad when I was around, or at least not twice!

But there was a lot of petty nobles that wouldn't let us set up depots because of the way we didn't pay no tolls. They didn't bother Boris none. He just spread the word that we was paying to set up our depots this year, but next year we wouldn't. And the year after that, if anybody wanted a depot, they'd have to pay *us*.

And you know, some of them that wouldn't have us at first later on paid us to come. There was profit in having a depot on your land, and in time, a lot of them depots got a Pink Dragon Inn by them, and there was profit in that, too.

Well, come fall, both of my ladies was bulging, and they both had their kids within a week of Christmas. Now, I knew that that was only seven months from the time I met them, but the saying is that a kid takes nine months, except for the first one, which can take any time it wants to. I never said a thing about it to them, since a grown man knows when to keep his mouth shut. I knew when I had a good thing going, and I wasn't going to let a few little months upset it.

But after that, we tried to work it so only one of them got pregnant at a time.

Chapter Eight

FROM THE DIARY OF CONRAD STARGARD

By the fall of 1239, all the people who worked for me at any level above the bottom had gone through the Warrior's School, with the exception of a few like Boris Novacek, who had no hands. There was even a four-month winter school for the peasants on my new barony. Three years of it and they could be knighted. But a lot of men didn't make it through, and I had to be fairly brutal about weeding them out. Since they were sworn to me, I couldn't fire them for not passing, but I wouldn't let them stay on in any kind of a managerial capacity, either. Mostly, I just demoted them down to apprentice, no matter what their skill level, and I gave some of them plots of land and let them be peasants. Many took this pretty hard. Some people quit and there were even a few suicides, but I was adamant.

To keep in practice, everybody spent one day a week in military training. Not the same day, of course, since the factories had to keep running full blast if we were going to meet our production quotas.

I would have preferred a system where the men who worked together fought together, but there was just no way we could do that. In the factories, each section had people with specialized skills. If they were all off and in training on the same day, their machines would be idle.

As it was, most work teams had seven men, counting the leader, who was always knighted. The bottom rank was made up mostly of pages and squires. On any one day, five of them would be working, one would be at military exercises and one would be enjoying his day off.

This meant working Sundays, and I got a lot of flak about it, both from the men and from the Church. I tried to prove to them that what God meant was that they should spend one day a week in prayer and rest, and the original Sabbath was on Saturday, anyhow, but they were still mad at me. We tried juggling schedules, hoping to keep everybody happy, but that didn't work either.

On top of this, virtually every industrial job was worked in two shifts, one days and one nights, and that was another set of headaches.

Finally, I just threw a temper tantrum and said they could do it my way or they could leave. Very few quit.

We tried to keep the training as amusing as possible, with contests, races, and that sort of thing. To a certain extent, we were successful and military sports became the big game on campus. At Three Walls, these drills and games were generally held on the "killing ground" in front of the walls. This was where we held our portion of the yearly Great Hunt, the harvesting of the wild animals on our lands. It was a great alluvial, fan shaped area, almost a mile to the side, and was surrounded by a vast tangle of Japanese roses, fully five yards high and twice that thick. Barbed wire would have been inferior as a military defense!

It wasn't only the men who did military training. The women had their duties as well, concentrating on defending the walls. They got proficient with the swivel guns on the outer wall, as well as with grenades. They didn't work out with the pike or halberd, the usual woman's arms being a little weak to handle these big weapons, but most of them were decent with a rapier.

Lady Krystyana became a master swordswoman, always winning the women's championship and outfencing me most of the time. She seemed to get a special thrill out of scoring on me, I suppose in revenge for all the years I'd spent sticking it to her.

But these exercises were a problem for the night shift, since despite fudging things by an hour or two, most of their training day happened in the dark.

Sir Ilya was my night shift manager at Three Walls. He had wanted this job because his wife was incapable of sleeping in the day, and the arrangement suited him. He just got a bunk in night shift bachelors' quarters and mostly ignored her, despite my orders to the contrary. After a year of being ignored, she ran away with Count Lambert's blacksmith to places unknown. It was two weeks before Ilya noticed it, and then only when he checked his account at the bank. Not that he tried to find her, or replace her, or even take on a "servant." A bachelor's life suited him.

But despite his marital problems, Ilya took his work seriously, and if military duties were part of his job, he did it. But he did it in his own way.

He figured that what we needed was a special group of men trained to fight at night. He even named them "The Night Fighters." As a group, they worked out the techniques for silent fighting in the dark. I helped them where I could, mostly telling them about commando stuff I'd seen in the movies, but they got good at it. They learned to walk quietly in total darkness, the leader signaling the men behind him with a string they all held in their left hands. They practiced with the knife and with the garrote, their version of which was a steel wire with a couple of wooden spools and a strange, one way slipknot. I think it might have been the world's first disposable weapons system. It only worked once. But since you weren't likely to miss with one, once was enough.

And they played games, just like the day shift, only different. One of theirs was "steal the pig." This was played with a live pig, one scheduled for tomorrow's supper, since the pig often did not survive the game. It was played in pitch darkness, and if there was a moon out, they'd play it in a basement. The pig wore a harness around its body which was tied to a pole with a three-yard rope. A lance of seven men was assigned to guard it and another lance was given the task of stealing it. It was played in full armor, and no weapons were allowed except on the pig. After that, anything went! Real class was to steal the pig without the guards knowing it was gone, but decking them all out cold was fair.

Games of this type put a premium on quiet motion, which wasn't easy in regulation plate armor. They naturally got to working on the armor. I told them that we could not possibly make new stamping dies, not this late in the game, so they worked within those limitations. What they came up with was a set of armored coveralls. It used the same pieces as our standard armor, but each piece fit into a sort of pocket sewn in the garment. Baggy when you first put them on, they had zippers up the sides and on all four limbs which snugged them up properly. Where the plate armor couldn't cover, as on the armpits and on the inside of the knees and elbows, pieces of chain mail were sewn in.

One of the beauties of this design was that you could get into it in a hurry. It took a quarter-hour for a man to arm himself with our standard armor. With Night-Fighter armor, it was a matter of a minute.

Another problem with any plate armor was that it didn't breathe. Steel is impervious to air. This was no problem in the winter, when we normally wore quilted goose-down long underwear, but in the summer, you could suffocate in there, and cases of heat exhaustion and even heatstroke were all too common.

They worked out a system of forced ventilation. In the summer, you wore a set of thin linen long johns that had zippers all over the place. These zippers matched up with zippers on the inside of the armored coveralls. Since the armor was about a finger's width bigger than you were, all around, the result was a number of separate compartments all over you. The front of your shin was one compartment and the back of it was another. There were valves, simple flaps covering holes, at the knees and ankles, such that cool air could come in at the ankles and go out at the knees. As you walked, you naturally moved around inside this oversized armor, and this motion pumped cool air in the bottom and hot air out the top. Since there were eighteen of these compartments around your body, you stayed reasonably cool. Not like you'd be in a pair of shorts and a T-shirt, but cases of heat exhaustion became rare.

They did talk me into a summer helmet, which resembled a Chinese coolie hat, and we tooled up for that.

Their system was so superior to what we had that I made it the army standard, for the men anyway.

There wasn't much to setting up for the new armor. A number of conventional knights were looking for something for their peasants to do as a winter money-maker, so we set them up sewing armor coveralls.

I'd originally issued the same armor to the women that I had to the men, but the girls didn't like it. It had to be of the same thickness as the men's or it wouldn't be able to stop an arrow, and they said it was too heavy.

Since they would be fighting only from the walls, where the parapet protected them from the waist down, they soon discarded the leg armor. They said that the gauntlets made it hard to operate a gun, so they got rid of them, too. But the man's sword had only a small hand guard, about what you'd find on a Japanese sword, since the men wore steel gloves. Without authorization, the girls got the shop to tool up a special big hand guard, like they put on a modern épée.

And the standard breastplates. No style at all! Completely without my permission, special tooling was made, *thirty-two expensive dies in all,* just to satisfy them.

Now their breastplates had breasts on them.

And having done that, they thought that it was prettier polished and shiny, so they didn't go the practical coverall route. They'd even come up with a zowie-looking helmet with a Greek-style crest on it when I put my foot down. There was no face guard, and it didn't protect the neck at all, since the girls wanted their hair to show! I ranted and swore that this was a stupid design and a stupider waste of resources. They said, yes, sir. You're right, sir. We'll do it your way, sir.

Then two months later they were all wearing these new helmets!

I never could find out who made the dies, since they knew I would have fired the bastard, and the production schedules on the stamping presses showed no time allotted to the silly things. How they got them made, I don't know, but soon the ladies at all the other installations were in the new outfits, too.

But *you* try holding back a bunch of women when they get a bright idea.

Then to top it all off, the duke saw the ladies' helmets and thought that, gold-plated, they'd be just the thing for a ceremonial guard! I managed to talk him out of it. They wouldn't have fit a man, anyway, a female's head being much smaller than a male's. Darned if I was going to let any more draw dies be made.

Strange to say, despite its obvious advantages, the new coverall armor didn't catch on with the conventional knights.

Of course, during all this time, we'd been selling plate armor at decent prices to anyone who wanted to buy from us. Well, we wouldn't have sold to a Mongol, but none of them applied. But after three years of selling polished plate armor, it was all the rage among the hawking and hunting set. While our troops were discovering camouflage paint, they wanted to shine. There was nothing we could do about it, so we let them have their own way.

Another thing the Night Fighters did was with the swivel guns. They put a big pie plate of a flash suppressor at the muzzle of the gun. This did two things for them. For one thing, it stopped the muzzle flash from blinding the gunner at night. For another, it reflected all of the light forward, and they worked out a system where each gunner fired just after the man to his left. This let him aim by the flash of light caused by the last gun going off. From a distance, it looked like a string of chase lights on a theater marquis, but they got reasonably accurate with the system. Flash suppressors soon became standard for all our swivel guns.

Innovation was the name of the game at Eagle Nest, where a sturdy band of very young men were busily conquering the skies. Actually, they were getting too innovative, and I had to work at converting their efforts from research to production.

They had started out with motorless sailplanes, and their aircraft showed that heritage. The wings were long and thin, the bodies long and sleek. They were all high-winged, since I'd always been aiming at observation craft, and even with motors, they still had to be catapult launched.

This catapult was built on top of an ancient, man-made hill about six dozen yards high, probably some sort of prehistoric defensive structure. The hill was conical, with a flat spot on top about two dozen yards across. We built a low, circular concrete wall, and the catapult rode on this wall, so as to point into the wind. The catapult itself was a wooden ramp, six dozen yards long and angling upward at a half-hour angle. A rope ran from the back of the catapult to a pulley at the front, then back halfway to the center where it went over another pulley and then was attached to a massive concrete weight that was hung over a well we'd dug in the hill.

To launch, a plane was hauled up the hill and loaded onto the catapult. Then four dozen boys walked up to the front of the catapult, grabbed the rope, and hauled it back to the plane. With practice, they got so they could launch a dozen planes an hour this way.

But instead of building a few dozen planes of the best design we had and "fine tuning" them, they wanted to continue designing whole new ones. Part of the problem was that I'd once mentioned that a canard-type plane, with the propeller in back and the elevator forward of the wing was more efficient than the conventional design, but that these planes were too difficult for us to design and fly. The boys took that as a challenge, and Count Lambert was on their side. It took me three temper tantrums, and them four deadly wrecks, before they went into production on a standard, conventional aircraft.

Even with that, crack-ups were so frequent that they rarely had three planes ready to fly at any one time, and the price they willingly paid in lives still gives me nightmares.

Chapter Nine

About this time, we began to notice that there wasn't enough money to go around. I don't mean that we were spending more than we made. Far to the contrary! Our products were being sold all over Europe, and the local currency had become a hodge-podge of pennies, deniers, pfennigs, and what have you, minted in dozens of different places. In theory, all these coins were of the same value, but in fact, their weight and silver content varied all over the map.

But despite this influx of foreign coins, there still wasn't enough to go around. I was converting Poland from a barter economy to a money economy. Peasants who had rarely needed or even seen money in their lives suddenly found that they wanted money to buy the things we sold, and that they could get money by selling their crops, now that the railroads and steamboats were operating and they could get those crops to market. The lack of silver coin was causing a serious deflation, and the prices of things were dropping precipitously.

I, of course, had all kinds of money, and at first I tried to counter-act the deflation by raising the pay scales of the people who worked for me. I kept the bottom rate the same, a penny a day, since we always had a waiting list to get in, even with the military-training requirement. But after that, pay doubled with each promotion. There were three grades of nonmanagerial workers, warriors, pages, and squires, earning one, two, and four pence respectively, and from then on, well, a man could get rich working for me.

But it didn't help the deflation a bit. Most of the extra pay was spent in my stores and my inns, or left in my bank. Very little of it got out to the general public.

Then I tried buying things I didn't really need, mostly land. I started buying up land along the rivers because I had some vague ideas of one day building a series of forts along them. But not that much land was for sale, and buying land was not as easy as it would be in the twentieth century. There were all sorts of incumbrances involved, oaths of fealty, requirements of military service, the rights of the peasants living there, strange taxes, and what not. I managed to get out of most of these—but not peas-ants' rights—with one-time cash payments, yet it did not cure the major problem that I was trying to solve. When I bought land from some nobleman, he usually spent the money to buy the things that my factories were making! He wanted arms and armor, glass windows, and indoor plumbing. The money came right back to me and the deflation continued!

Furthermore, I couldn't resist making the land I'd bought productive and profitable.

Surely, this was a problem that no capitalist ever had to cope with!

Charity work was another matter. With the assistance of Abbot Ignacy and his monks, I worked hard at helping the poor. We set up soup kitchens in the major cities and a large leper colony on an isolated estate that I'd bought. But the engineer in me hates waste, and the waste of human potential is the worst sort.

Many of the poor were that way simply because they could not find honest work, so I gave it to them. I set up nonarmy construction groups to build railroads and bridges. They were supervised by army personnel, of course, since there weren't many trained, technically competent people outside it. We were running tracks as fast as the blast furnaces could cast them, and most of our lines were double-tracked, so we didn't have to worry much about scheduling. With a single-tracked line, you have to make sure that a train isn't coming north before you take yours south. Double tracks can be treated just like a highway.

Some of the poor were children, orphans. We set up an adoption service, and many of these kids were adopted by army families. Some of the poor were old or feeble. In the cities we set up factories that turned out knitted goods, much of which were bought by the army. We always needed socks and underwear.

Undoubtedly, all of this did a great deal of good for the people. I think it made me something of a people's hero. At least they insisted on cheering whenever I was around, though in fact I would have preferred some peace and quiet. And what do you do when children and old women insist on kissing your boot, for God's sake! It was embarrassing. I got to giving a standard speech, thanking them, but saying that I didn't like people yelling at me, and if they wanted to do anything for me, they could pray in church for my soul, which needed it. It didn't help much. Most people would rather yell than pray.

Yet the prices kept on dropping and my coffers stayed full. Even feeding the indigent, we had to buy from the farmers, and the farmers made enough money to buy our plumbing supplies and glass windows. Raising my prices didn't help either. They just bought less, but spent the same amount of money, so I put prices back where they had been.

In the middle of this charity work, Abbot Ignacy became His Excellency Ignacy, Bishop of Cracow, and he stepped lightly from the regular clergy to the secular branch of the Church. How much I had to do with this promotion, I don't know.

Despite his elevation, Bishop Ignacy remained my confessor, and I made a point of seeing him at least once a month. He had traded in his humble monk's robe for the glorious raiment of his new office, but he wore his embroidered silks and velvets with the casualness with which he had treated his old brown smock when we had camped along the river, so many years ago. His new office, in his palace near Wawel Cathedral, was as ornate as a church altar, with brightly painted carved wood encrusting the walls and ceiling, but he had moved one of our standard wooden desks into it, the sort that our cabinet shop turned out by the gross.

"Ah, Conrad! Have you come to confess again? Have I told you how much I like these desks you've designed? What with all the drawers, I can keep everything at hand. I've recommended them to all my priests."

"Uh, yes, no, and thank you, your excellency." I made a mental note to have a special desk made that would match his office, rather than looking like a computer in a church.

"Oh, 'Father' is sufficient when we are alone, Conrad. Did I tell you that there is word on the inquisition the Church is conducting in your regard?"

Ever since arriving in this century, an inquisition had been hanging over my head. The Church was trying to decide if I was an instrument of God, perhaps to be canonized, or an instrument of the devil, to be burned at the stake. I couldn't help being a little anxious about it.

"What has happened, Father?"

"Well, you recall that when first you came to this century, I wrote up all the particulars quite diligently and presented them to my abbot. He, in turn, quickly annotated my report and within the month sent it to this very office. The bishop of that time felt that the matter would best go through the regular branch of the Church, rather than the secular, so he sent it back to my abbot with that recommendation. My abbot then sent it to the home monastery as soon as someone could be found who was going in that direction, and the speed and diligence of all concerned was such that the home monastery in Italy was able to reply back to us within the year."

"Yes, Father, but—"

"But the home monastery was sure that this was a matter for the secular branch, so my abbot sent the report, with notations, back to the Bishop of Cracow. But by this time, you had established yourself in Silesia, which of course is in the Diocese of Wroclaw. The Bishop of Cracow therefore sent the report to the Bishop of Wroclaw, who forwarded it to the Archbishop at Gniezno. From there, it was sent to Rome, with further notations. Rome then replied with a request that the Abbot of the Franciscan monastery here confirm the report. By this time, however, I was that very personage, and having all the facts at my fingertips, as it were, I was quickly able to comply, and provided an update on all your doings."

How could I forget that? After three years, all that had happened was that Father Ignacy had written a letter to himself, and then he had replied to it!

"Yes, Father, but—"

"Now, since all this had transpired within a few years, you can see that the matter was being pushed forward as quickly as possible. But then several years went by in which I heard nothing, so I took it on myself to write a letter of inquiry to Rome. As it turned out, my reply to the report had somehow gone astray somewhere between Gniezno and Rome, no one has any idea what happened to it, and the merchant who carried it was never seen again. Fortunately, the Archbishop of Gniezno had caused to be made a true copy of the entire annotated report for his files.

A copy of this was made and again it was sent to Rome. Rome's reply returned through proper channels only a week ago, and it orders that a full inquiry be made by the Bishop of Cracow, who at this time again happens to be me. Of course, I complied immediately, and a full report is again on the way to Rome, through channels, of course."

So Father Ignacy had for a second time answered his own report! And nothing of significance had transpired in seven years! It made me want to scream and pull out my hair! But, with work, I kept my cool.

"So Rome still doesn't know much about me, Father?"

"How can you say that, Conrad? They've seen my reports, haven't they? They also subscribe to the magazine you started and get a copy of it every month! People are learning Polish just to be able to read it! Your books and plumbing supplies are all the rage in Rome, and everyone there has one of your lighters! Of course they know about you!"

I sighed. After Confession, I mentioned that I was going over to the monastery to talk to the artist, Friar Roman.

"Then I've saved you a trip, Conrad. I brought Roman over with me, I think mostly to keep an eye on him. He had been using the wealth he gained from designing church windows to hire young ladies as models, and was posing them most immodestly!"

"In most cultures, your excellency, that would be considered an artist's prerogative."

"Not in *my* church, it isn't! What did you want to see him about?"

"Lithography. It's another printing process, well suited to art work. We have accurate maps of much of Poland now, and I need many copies made of each. I have a new machine almost ready at Three Walls, and I want to teach him how to use it, since it takes an artist."

"Three Walls would be just fine, Conrad. Take him for as long as you need him. But you keep that boy away from Okoitz! If it was in *my* diocese, there'd be some changes made there, I assure you!"

"Yes, Father."

Friar Roman was delighted to get out from under Bishop Ignacy's thumb, and caught the next boat to Three Walls.

The deflation was still troubling me, and I finally realized that to inflate the economy back to its previous levels, I was going to have to add new money to the system. With the duke's permission, I started making my own coins, with his likeness on one side and a Polish eagle on the other. For some years, we had been refining zinc and calling it "Polish Silver." No one had paid much mind, but the fact was that we were the only people in the world that had this technology. I made it a *secret* technology.

The only problem was that to use zinc for coinage, I had to drastically raise its price. I could sneak it into the brass, since very few people realized that brass was an alloy of copper and zinc. They acted like it was a separate metal. But the price of pure zinc items had to go up and the price of galvanized iron skyrocketed to the point that sales went way down.

I wrote a series of articles for our magazine, explaining the cause of the deflation and what I intended to do about it. My alchemist, Zoltan Varanian, made an analysis of the silver content of each of the six dozen supposedly identical coins that were in circulation, and I published it. The silver content of those coins varied from forty percent down to as little as three percent!

The result was economic chaos for a half year. But at the same time, I came out with a series of zinc coins in various denominations. I rated zinc at one-sixth the value of pure silver, but the whole concept for different denominations was new, and it took some people a while to get used to it. But in our money system, with a few large coins you could buy a horse, and with the smallest, a kid could buy a piece of candy, something that was not possible before.

In one of my magazine articles, I made a serious oath that the content and weight of my coins would be absolutely constant, that we would trade any worn (but not clipped!) coin for a new one, and that we would trade our coins for standard silver coins on demand. "Polish Silver" caught on.

Then we started buying everything in sight! We bought land,

we bought furs, we bought amber. We bought land in the Bledowska Desert, built huge granaries there, and set up a constant
pricing system for purchases and sales, buying grain by the hundreds of tons! We even bought silver and gold. But mostly we
bought land. In a few years, we owned most of the land within
five miles of the Vistula, the Odra, and many of their tributaries.
Once we had the time, I was going to ring Poland with a line
of concrete forts!

But all this land aggravated some of my other problems. Besides
being the owner, I had to be the police force and the judge as
well. The police force wasn't a big problem, since I had set one
up years ago. Whenever one of my bailiffs had a problem he
couldn't handle, he called in a detective. And now that these men
were partnered with Anna's progeny, their arrest rate was near
perfect. The Big People could smell out a thief or a murderer
every time.

Most of the other Big People were working carrying the mails,
and the speed of mail transport was doubled. After the first few
months, we started using them without riders, and except for
some astounded travelers, there wasn't a hitch.

But what I needed now was some judges and lawyers, and
the man I knew who was most knowledgeable of the law was
Sir Miesko. He had been my next door neighbor for years. Well,
his manor was six miles away from mine, but that's the way
these things went. He was my assistant Master of the Hunt, and
in fact ran the thing on all the duke's lands. He got all the furs
taken each fall, and this had made him rich. He had once been
my biggest vendor, providing food for Three Walls, but now was
one of my best customers. He'd built a truly fine castle using my
building supplies, and many of the features of my own defensive works, like the combination granary and watchtower, were
invented by him.

He'd been a legal clerk, the closest local equivalent to a lawyer,
before he was knighted for valor, so I asked him to head up my
legal department.

"I'd like to, Baron Conrad, but I just can't. The Great Hunt
takes up a lot of my time, and running my manor takes up more.

You know that all of my boys have joined your army instead of helping me out around here, and, well, I'm just not as young as I used to be."

"Damn. I can see your point, though. Okay, if not you, then who? Do you know a truly honest man who knows the law?" I said.

"That's a hard one, Baron. Somehow, the more a man knows about the law, the less he seems inclined to obey it! But yes, one man comes to mind. He's only a few years younger than I am, but he doesn't have my responsibilities. We worked together in my youth, and we've kept in touch. Adam Pulaski, he's your man."

So I got in touch with this Pulaski. I set him up with three younger men, one to act as prosecutor, one to be defender, and one to be court recorder. I sent them out to take over my case load. I had to approve all their actions, of course, and any capital offenses had to be taken to my liege lord, Count Lambert, but they were the start of the army court system.

Before the Mongol invasion, prices were back up to where they had been before I had arrived. After that, we just watched the prices of a dozen common commodities, and if the average price got too low, we brought it back up by making more coins and buying things we didn't need.

Chapter Ten

By the spring of 1240, I knew we'd be ready. The Warrior's School was completed, even though everybody was calling it "Hell" now. The main building was a mile square and six stories tall, surrounding a collection of mess halls, parade grounds, churches, huge warehouses filled to the rafters with military goods, an induction center, and even a synagogue.

I was surprised to find how many Jews I had working for me. The Jews were a new element in thirteenth-century Poland, most of them coming in with the Germans in their peaceful "invasion." There were no racial tensions at the time, mostly because the Christians were rarely aware of the Jews. In fact, most people didn't even know of their existence as a separate religious group, lumping them in with other foreigners.

But most work crews were eager to get them when they could. Jews were perfectly willing to work on Sunday, providing they could get Saturday off, or Friday night in the case of night-shift workers. The vast majority of my people were Catholics, and the more Jews in your crew, the better your chances were of getting Sunday off.

A delegation of rabbis had once come to me, asking if they could set up a ghetto at Three Walls, the way they were being set up in the increasingly German-dominated cities. I wouldn't do it.

I would like to make it clear that these ghettos were not slums where the unfortunate were stuffed to get them out of the way. The ghetto was a portion of the city where Jewish Law, rather than Christian Law, was practiced. In the ghetto, the Jews had their own council, their own schools, their own courts, and what amounted to their own police force. Furthermore, there were special courts to handle problems between Jews and Catholics, and an attempt was made to keep these fair. The ghetto was a privilege that the Jews sought and paid cash for.

In the world I grew up in, and I am becoming convinced that it was a different world than that which I am now living in, the Jews came to Poland at about the same time, and settled in the cities.

There is a natural animosity between city dwellers and rural people. Before the days of movies and television, they lived in such totally different environments that neither comprehended the lifestyle of the other.

Yet each needed the products of the other. The cities needed food and the countrymen needed the manufactured goods of the cities. They traded, but each soon felt that the other was out to cheat him, and so retaliation seemed the sensible thing to do. Once this started to happen, the myth had become truth, a self-fulfilling prophecy.

When this difference in lifestyles was added to differences in language, differences in customs, and differences in religion, these animosities naturally were accentuated. There were even differences in political allegiances, for many cities within the political boundaries of Poland became members of the Hanseatic League, and no longer swore allegiance to the Polish Crown.

And in Silesia, the countrymen were Polish, the nobles were sworn to the German Holy Roman Empire and mostly spoke German, and the cities were allied with the Nordic Hans! And part of each city was yet another separate political entity, the Jewish ghetto! A crazy system, yet it survived for centuries!

The truth is that the Jews in Poland maintained their separate culture for *seven hundred years*! They did not learn Polish, the language of the people around them, but continued speaking German, although in time their language drifted so far from standard German as to become a separate dialect, Yiddish.

The Jews called the people surrounding them *goyim*, cattle, and were sure that these farmers were out to poison them. And indeed, there were unscrupulous farmers who tried to make a quick profit. Not many, but some. The Jews overreacted with a ridiculously strict adherence to the biblical dietary codes, having a religious leader inspect all food eaten, and cheated a dumb farmer whenever possible.

In the early thirteenth-century Poland, Jewish dietary rules were not nearly as evolved as they became later.

The countrymen became convinced that the Jews stole Christian babies for sacrifice at their religious services. This was of course not true, but a few Jews did engage in kidnapping Christians and selling them as slaves to the Moslems, a thing that Christians generally could not do since the Moslems usually refused to trade with Christians.

Without a basis of mutual understanding, the actions of a few criminals became "what everybody knows."

Having said all this, I must point out that Poland was the best place in Europe for a Jew to be, at least up until World War Two. Everywhere else, it was worse. The Jews were thrown out of England, France, Spain, and many other countries. All their property was confiscated, and many of their people were killed. This never happened in Poland, at least not until Poland itself was conquered by foreign powers. There has always been an official policy of toleration, no matter what most people actually felt.

Separate peoples, hating each other and misunderstanding each other, they lived together because they needed each other.

I wasn't going to let this happen again, at least not on my lands. The Jews were welcome as individuals, as was anybody else. Well, I wouldn't want an Atheist around, but in fact I never ran into anyone who would admit to being one. But if I let the Jews segregate themselves, they would keep to their own German language and their own customs. They never would become part of *us*, and racial tensions would inevitably develop. I let them have the use of some of the common rooms for their own religious services and religious instruction. Where the rabbis were sufficiently educated, we hired them into the school system, and the Jews could always wrangle it so they got Saturday off. But separate housing, separate schools, separate laws, and separate dining facilities were out!

Well, I did have the kitchen staff put up a little sign when something was grossly nonkosher, since many traditional Polish foods were based on blood and others on pork. A Jew would sometimes get violently ill if he found out that he had just eaten *kishka*. Anyway, you only get a little bowl of blood from a duck, and there is no point in wasting *tchanina* on somebody who doesn't appreciate it!

Now, I know that I was at the very same time keeping the Moslems sworn to me segregated from the rest of the country. But it was not my intent that this should be a permanent situation. One day, we would defeat the Mongols and drive them back to where they came from, at which time I meant to help Zoltan Varanian's people resettle their original homeland. And if we didn't beat the Mongols, we'd all be dead anyway, so the problem would solve itself.

Count Lambert's new castle was completed, and he was vastly

proud of it. It really was a functional military defensive structure, with thick masonry walls six stories tall, crenellations, machinations, turret towers, and all the rest. It was completely fireproof, with even the floors being made of masonry, rather than the usual wood. It had room for all of his peasants as well as the four-gross young ladies that worked at his cloth factory. Further, he could play host to half the nobility in the duchy and have beds for everybody.

And it had glass windows, indoor plumbing, and steam heat. There were even gaslights in the public areas. There was a church, a granary, huge storerooms, a sauna, and an indoor swimming pool. There was even a system of conduits going to every room, so that when we got electric lights and telephones, these things could be easily installed. The kitchens and dining rooms were such that everybody ate there, and private cooking was frowned on.

I think I was as proud of that building as the count was.

The fort at East Gate was up as well, and it had gone up much quicker, since at Okoitz I had used vaulted construction throughout, but at East Gate I used prefabricated reinforced concrete for the floors and ceilings. Not as pretty, but it sure was cheaper.

I was sure that this fort was impregnable. The outer walls were seven stories tall and made of thick, reinforced concrete. It was surrounded by six tall towers, which were really storage silos for hay, grain, and coal, but each had a fighting platform on top, and a dunce-cap roof to protect the fighters. These towers were connected to the main fort by underground tunnels. An enemy attacking any point would be in a crossfire from at least two and usually four directions. A two-story wall (that doubled as a long barn for the mules that pulled the railroad carts) surrounded the entire complex, connecting the towers. It wasn't high enough to stop men with ladders, but it would stop horses and siege equipment.

The ground plan was a symmetrical hexagon, and what with the six surrounding towers and walls, it resembled a snowflake. We ended up calling the design just that, and I got to toying with the idea of someday building hundreds of them.

Let the Mongols try and take this one!

I think that we bragged about it too much, and that this contributed to a major tragedy. But I get ahead of myself.

➤   ➤   ➤

Three Walls really had three walls now, and the outer one was of sturdy concrete. There were towers above the surrounding cliffs, and all sorts of dirty tricks were built in as defensive measures.

And all my other installations at Coaltown, Silver City, and Copper City were similarly fortified. This was necessary because when we men went off to war, we needed someplace safe for the women, children, and old folks. And it was not only our own dependents that we had to protect, but those of everyone else in Silesia and Little Poland. I calculated that by stacking people in like cordwood, we'd have enough room to save them all. And while they might eat a lot of *kasha*, there would be food enough to feed them all as well.

Except for adding wall guns, I'd left the castle I'd inherited from Baron Stefan alone, and in fact rarely used it. It was well enough designed as a defensive structure, but the moat made it difficult to add a sewage system. The peasants in the immediate area used the castle for weddings and what not and, come the invasion, would retreat to it for safety, but aside from that, I really didn't see much use for it. Maybe someday I'd fill in the moat and put in a septic system.

Eagle Nest, on the other hand, got only a single, separate concrete tower, which doubled as a control tower for the airport. If attacked, the boys could go there and be safe enough, since the thing was nine stories tall. There simply weren't enough people there to defend a wall long enough to surround the entire airport, and there weren't enough peasants nearby to help them. I was sorry to do it, but we had to treat the whole wooden complex as expendable.

The old cities weren't in very good shape either. The walls around Cracow were only three stories tall, and a wall that low can be scaled. Wawel Hill was well enough fortified, but the city below it looked likely to fall if it was seriously attacked. But try to get those damn merchants to spend a penny they didn't have to! I offered to sell them guns and to train their people as gunners, all at cost. They bought only a dozen swivel guns for the whole city and considered this to be sufficient!

Wroclaw was in similar shape, and Legnica! Legnica still had *wooden walls!*

We didn't have room enough inside our fortifications for the farm animals, so doctrine was for the animals to be released to try their luck in the woods. At least the wolves were pretty much eradicated now, what with the Great Hunts and all. A program of branding was underway, so that the animals could be returned to their owners after the invasion.

We had a similar program going to identify people. My own troops had dog tags, of course, but we enlarged the program to include the conventional knights as well. The service was free, and most of them took us up on it. If they fell in battle, we could at least mark their graves.

The radios were working, although they weren't all that dependable. They weighed two-gross pounds each and had a range of only thirty miles and that only in good weather. A lightning storm within fifty miles could drown them out, and they required endless fiddling by the operator. Nonetheless, we'd gone into production, and produced them by the thousands. There was one on every steamboat and one at each depot. Every Pink Dragon Inn had its radio, and there were four at each of our major installations. In addition, one war cart in six had a radio, so each company could keep in touch. Getting enough trained operators was a huge problem, but people were being trained as fast as sets were being built. Most of them were still pretty slow, but we kept them in practice.

With only nine months to go before the Mongol invasion, Zoltan came to me with a new device. Our swivel guns used brass cartridges. They were breech-loading and clip-fed. But after years of fruitless effort, the alchemists had been unable to come up with a dependable primer to detonate the black powder in the shell. What we were using was a firecracker wick on the back of each shell that was lit by an alcohol burner near the breech. It was a clumsy alternative, but it was the best we could do.

Zoltan presented me with a new cartridge and a new gun to

fire it. Each cartridge had what amounted to a spark plug in the base, and the bolt of the gun contained a piezoelectric crystal to provide the spark.

This was the same system that we had been using for years on our lighters, and the same system that the boys at Eagle Nest used on their aircraft engines, and the same system we used on the spark-gap radios. And for years, it hadn't occurred to me or anyone else until now to use it to ignite gunpowder!

In truth, I had to take the blame for this one myself. I had made gunpowder a secret thing, something you weren't supposed to think about. I had kept Zoltan working on chemical projects and generally away from the Christians working on almost everything else. Secrecy is hell on innovations, and it was all my fault.

To make things worse, there was no time to convert the tens of thousands of swivel guns we had already made. We would have to meet the Mongols with obsolete equipment.

I designed a simple, single-shot pistol to use the new cartridges, and a few hundred of them were made in time, for use by officers. It had a breaking action like a shotgun, and had the general appearance of an old-style dueling pistol. I also designed a submachine gun along the lines of the Sten gun, but only prototypes were made. There just wasn't time!

Then we got word that Kiev had fallen, the walls had been stormed, and the armies slaughtered. The tales we heard from the few survivors were ghastly. They told of old people tortured, young women raped, and children hunted down in the streets for sport.

No one doubted that we were next on the list.

FROM THE DIARY OF TADAOS KOLPINSKI

I was Komander Tadaos now, and making sixty-four pence a day! It makes me wish my father could have lived long enough to see it! I had eighteen boats on the Vistula, and twenty-two on the Odra.

'Course, only three of those Odra boats was real fighting boats, two operating above Wroclaw and one below it. The rest were low, skinny things that could make it under the bridges at Wroclaw. There weren't any bridges on the Vistula, nor were there any on any of the tributaries that you could get a fighting boat up, but those Wroclaw bridges was a pain!

We could build new bridges wide and tall enough. Baron Conrad's book on them showed just how. But the damn city father (mothers, the lot of them) wouldn't hear of tearing their old ones down.

I figured that with twelve barrels of gunpowder, we could do in one of the bridges some dark and stormy night and claim it was lightning, an Act of God, but the baron wouldn't let me do it. He said it would take thirty barrels, easy, and the rubble would likely block the channel. And he said that the duke wouldn't like it, so that ended it.

But someday, I was going to find a way of getting me them thirty barrels and trying it!

All the boats was way overmanned, since we had to train crews for the new boats being built. Come spring, I was to have three dozen on the Vistula alone. What's more, we had a gas generator on all our fighting boats now, and limelights on top of the turrets. These lights had big reflectors that turned with the gun below them, and we could run and fight in the dark, so we needed night crews as well as those for the day.

We had flamethrowers now, too. These was a big barrel of pitch and wood alcohol in the bow with sort of a fire hose on the end. There was a lighter built in it, and when we put steam pressure to the barrel, we could squirt fire for six dozen yards! 'Course, it only worked for about a minute, but that was a lot.

We was always doing target practice, mostly with the Halmans and the peashooters, since they didn't use no gunpowder and was cheap to shoot. The peashooters didn't draw nearly the steam now that they used to, and I was pretty proud of that, since it was my doing. I came up with a valve that shut off the steam, just for an instant, while a new ball was dropping into the chamber. It was a little like the valve the baron designed for the bottom of the Halmans, which let loose a blast of steam when the round hit the bottom, only sort of backward. Anyway, the baron, he was tickled red over it cause now we could fire all four peashooters at once and still power the boat. I got two thousand pence as a bonus and they named that valve after me.

But like I was saying, there was a target range set up about every two miles on the rivers, and we used them. These targets was set up by young boys after the baron wrote a magazine article asking them to do it. They was pretty good at coming up with interesting things to shoot at, since they wanted us to do all the shooting we could. See, the ball bearings used by the peashooters and the dummy rounds from the Halmans was all reusable. After we'd go by, the kids would be out there digging them up so they could turn them in for the reward on them. Since we gave them about a quarter of what it would cost to make new ones, everybody came out pretty good.

Then somebody found out that the Halmans could shoot a potato about as well as a dummy round, and we got to shelling the other steamboats as they went by. The baron told us to stop before somebody got hurt, but everybody on deck was required to wear armor, and no potato ever hurt an armored man. Why, after coming out of a Halman, they was half cooked, anyway. And moving targets was more interesting, so that order sort of got misplaced.

I was having a row with my wives. They both got pregnant at the same time again, which they'd agreed not to do, and I was finding myself having to do without. Can you believe that? Two wives and still going horny?

Well, they said it was as much my fault as theirs, it taking two to accomplish anything, but you know how women like to come up with excuses. Then they said that at least this time, they'd both be mine, and I hit the ceiling! I said that the first two was mine, and I'd wallop anybody who said different!

Then I said that what with my rank and all, I was allowed a wife and four servants, and I was going to Okoitz to find me another one. They said that it took their permission, too, and they had to pass on any girl I picked. So we left two of the kids with a family at East Gate and we took one of the passenger carts to Okoitz the next time we had a few days off.

Well, you know I found me a pretty and willing girl in just no time at all, and so did they. The trouble was that they wasn't the same girl, and we had us another row about it. Finally we compromised and I took the both of the new girls on. But that's going to be the end of it, unless all four of them get pregnant simultaneous. If they do that on me, well, I'm still allowed one more, and after that I'll just have to get me some more rank.

Chapter Eleven

FROM THE DIARY OF CONRAD STARGARD

There were Mongols in Cracow, but they weren't invading just yet. This was a diplomatic party, and the duke wanted me and some of my people there to advise him.

We'd had plenty of warning about their coming, since they were spotted at one of our depots on the River Bug. The operator there got out a radio message fast, and she was bright enough to warn away the steamboats in the area. I don't think they saw any of the planes, either.

I knew that it was important to make as brave a show as possible, but at the same time I didn't want them to see everything we had. Word went out on the radio that the steamboats and airplanes were to avoid the Mongols, the guns were to be taken down and hidden, and that the radios themselves were not to be talked about.

I'd never publicized the radios, but I knew that scattered around as they had to be, there was no way of keeping their existence a secret. Operating principles were something else, but since few people knew them anyway, I wasn't worried.

In fact, I needn't have worried at all, since people who did hear about them didn't believe it. They'd believe in a steamboat because they saw it, and the same was true with the airplanes, which still had people running outdoors and pointing upward whenever one went over, but a machine that made sparks and talked to people miles away? . . . Nawww. . . .

I wanted the Mongols to be afraid of us, but for the wrong reasons. There wouldn't be enough of Anna's mature children to make a difference in the invasion. Oh, they'd stand night guard duty and run messages, but there would only be thirty-three adult Big People by the time of the battle, and that wasn't enough to tip the scales.

Still, if I could make the Mongols worry about fighting a highly mobile cavalry force, they might conduct their strategy accordingly, and that couldn't do us any harm. Mobility was where we were weakest.

I collected all the Big People I could, twenty of them counting Anna, along with some of my main people, and rode to Cracow. I brought Sir Vladimir, Sir Piotr, and the Banki brothers, among others.

I brought Cilicia along, and I had the others bring their wives. We came in civilian clothes and without armor, my idea being to lend the occasion as little dignity as possible.

We arrived in the early morning, just hours ahead of the Mongol delegation. Duke Henryk met with me and asked me to do the bulk of the talking at the preliminary meeting, since I apparently knew more about the Mongols than anybody else.

"Just stand on the dais by my left hand, Baron Conrad. Should I want to talk to them directly, I shall signal you. But talk as you see fit."

A number of counts were up there as well, sort of an honor guard. The throne room was filled with gawkers, but all of my own people were there as well. This was supposed to be just a formal meeting, with further negotiations to be held in private. At least that was what the duke thought. I had somewhat different ideas, and the Mongols were way out in left field!

The Mongol ambassador entered with twenty warriors at his back. Surprisingly, he spoke very good Polish.

"I have come—"

"A moment," Duke Henryk said. "First off, who are you? Are you a Mongol?"

"No. I am a Tartar."

The duke gave me a smug look, but the ambassador continued.

"I am a Tartar but the great Ogotai Kakhan is a Mongol. They are slightly different tribes, like your Silesians and Mazovians."

"Thank you for clearing that up. Now, you were saying?"

"I have come to accept your submission to my lord, Batu Khan, and to the great Ogotai Kakhan, Lord of All the World!" He was bowlegged and he stank, but you couldn't accuse him of not coming to the point. His head was shaved, leaving ridiculous tufts of hair on his forehead and behind his ears, but then military organizations generally adopt funny haircuts. He wore gaudy silk brocades that might once have been attractive, but now were grease-stained and filthy.

Yet he wasn't at all what I had expected. He didn't look like a Mongol! He did not have slanty, black eyes. They were green and Caucasoid. His skin, under the dirt, looked to be white, rather than yellow, and his hair was not black. It was red! And none of his men were "Mongoloid" either.

Rather than answer the man, the duke glanced at me, so I said, "That's quite a statement. Why should we want to do such a thing?"

"Why? You will do it because you want to live!"

"We've been doing a pretty good job of living without the khan. Why should we want that to change?" He wasn't using any honorifics on me, so I didn't see why I should use them on him.

"You talk like a fool or a crazy man! All men must submit to the kakhan!"

"*I'm* a crazy man? I hope you realize that your last few statements sound like those of a rampant megalomaniac. But I repeat my question. Why should we want to do something as silly as bowing down to your kaka?"

"That's *kakhan*, you fool, and you will submit or our swords will take all your heads!" He drew his sword for emphasis. Apparently, he felt that I wasn't playing my role properly.

"Oh. With swords like that? May I see it?" He handed it to me. It was good Damascus steel, better than what most of the conventional knights carried. But I couldn't let him get one up on us.

"A pretty handle," I said. "Where did you steal it?"

"I won that blade at the Battle of Samarkand, when the fools there refused submission."

"Well, that's a bit far to go. Mine only has an iron hilt. May I test them?"

"Destroy your blade if you want!"

I drew my own sword. Setting the tip of his blade to the marble floor, I shaved a thin wire of steel off the edge of his sword.

"The edge is soft," I said, throwing the wire to him. Then I put my blade tip to the floor, edge up, and swung at it with his. His blade was cut in two. "The shank was weak. Next time, don't steal a sword because of its flashy mountings." I tossed the pieces back to him.

The emissary was livid. This was not going as planned. "It is not weapons that win, it is the men behind the weapons!"

"You know, I've been saying that for years. That's why I know that we have nothing to fear from you people."

"The kakhan has the finest army in the world!"

"He has a bunch of undisciplined goat herders, suitable only for murdering helpless women and children. True warriors need not fear them."

"Undisciplined? You lie! Choose three of my men."

"If you wish. That one, that one, and that one." I'd picked the three most gaudily dressed of his entourage, and I think I picked right. I must have singled out someone pretty important, since a trickle of sweat went down the ambassador's cheek. I could see him weighing the loss of face against the loss of someone special. Face lost out.

"The first man you picked is Subotai Bahadur. He, like me, is sworn to report to Batu Khan. You must pick another."

"As you like. How about that pretty little guy on the end?" I later found out that this man was the ambassador's son, but the father didn't bat an eye.

He spoke briefly to the three men in what must have been Mongolian. Then he said, "I have just ordered these men to cut their own throats, as a demonstration of their loyalty and obedience to the kakhan!"

And those three men did it! One after another, they stepped forward, said some sort of prayer, drew their belt knives, and cut their own throats! There were gasps of horror and disbelief from the audience. I glanced at the duke and he looked a little pale.

If word of this got around, Polish morale would suffer. I couldn't let them outdo us, but I wasn't going to see if any of *my* men felt suicidal! So I laughed at him.

"Well, don't feel too bad about it," I said. "We have crazy people in this country, too. Of course, we try not to show them off in public when company is calling, but I suppose that customs differ. How about that one? Would he cut his throat, too?"

"Any true Mongol would obey orders!"

"Then let's see it!"

And damned if he didn't order it and the poor bastard ended up bleeding on the floor along with the others.

"And how about that one?" I said.

"What are you trying to do?" screamed the ambassador.

"Well, I figured that if we could get every Mongol to cut his fool throat, we wouldn't have to fight a war next spring." The room exploded in laughter.

"Were I not forbidden by my lord Batu to fight, I would kill you here and now!"

"It wouldn't be much of a fight, especially since you don't have a sword anymore. Why, any of our women could beat any of your fools with a sword. Even little Krystyana over there could take on any one of you, and she's had six children."

"Could I, my lord? Could I really fight him?" Krystyana said as she eagerly stepped out from the crowd. She was in court dress and so of course was unarmed, but she had borrowed her husband's sword with such vigor that Sir Piotr had a thin trickle of blood running down from his left ear.

"Well, I was just talking, Lady Krystyana. This is a diplomatic meeting, and not the place for a fight."

"Ah! You make a foolish boast and then you try to wiggle out of it! I say that you must back up your boast!"

"I suppose, if you insist. Sir Piotr, what do you say about this? She's your wife, after all."

"My lord, when she's in this mood, I've found it's best to let her have her own way."

"Very well then, pick your best swordsman," I said to the ambassador.

"Let the lady choose her own executioner," he said with a greasy smile.

"I want *that* one," Krystyana said. "He's wearing the most gold, and I get it when I win, don't I?"

"To the victor goes the spoils, my lady," I said.

"Good! Of course, I can't fight in *this* silly outfit!" She said, as she stripped her clothes off. The Mongols were all wearing armor and she was proposing to fight naked!

At this time, Poland didn't have a nudity taboo, so a naked lady wasn't all that unheard of, but the duke had let it be known that he wanted a complete coverup in his own court, and thus far, no one had ever dared defy him. I glanced at the duke again, but he just looked up at the coffered ceiling.

The Mongol acted as if he was just going to walk up and murder her. Krystyana parried his blow easily and gave him a horizontal cut on the forehead.

This startled the man, and he started hacking in earnest. It got him nowhere. He might have been good at saber fighting on horseback, but his footwork was almost nonexistent. The parries used on horseback are different from those used on foot, and are slower, since on a horse you have the animal's neck between your legs and it gets in the way.

But mostly, he'd never seen a rapier before, whereas Krystyana had often fought rapier against saber. She'd beaten me that way quite a few times.

So she played with him. She added a vertical cut to the one horizontal one on his forehead, making a perfect Christian cross. Then she put a cross on each cheek, and during all this had not taken a cut herself.

She was making the Mongol look like a buffoon, which was wonderful. She was savvy enough to realize that we had to take people's minds off the dead bodies on the floor.

The crowd was going wild, and the ambassador was turning livid purple.

"She's making a Christian out of him!" Piotr yelled.

"Does that count as a Baptism?" somebody shouted.

"No! That's Extreme Unction!" another wit called back.

"Krystyana, didn't your mother tell you not to play with your food?" yelled someone else.

She was working at cutting the Mongol's armor off when I said, "I think you've made your point, Lady Krystyana. Kill him and be done with it."

"Yes, my lord. On the count of four! One! . . . Two! . . . Three! . . ."

And she skewered him, straight through the heart, on the count of four. Then she bowed to the duke and to the crowd, picked up her clothes, and retired. The applause rocked the castle!

I turned to the ambassador. "With regards to your request for submission, the answer is no."

"And who are you, to say this thing? What is your name and station?"

"I am Baron Conrad Stargard."

"What! I have been talking to a mere baron?"

"Surely you didn't expect our duke to dirty his lips by talking to such as you? I'm the lowest ranking man up here!"

The Mongols turned and left, leaving their dead on the floor.

The duke stood and motioned for me to follow. Once we were alone in his privy chamber, he turned and glared at me.

"Damn you, Conrad! I asked you to conduct a preliminary interview, not to set policy for me!"

"Yes, your grace. I guess I sort of got carried away."

"You 'sort of got carried away'? Were my father still on the throne, you would be carried away in a *coffin*!"

"Yes, your grace."

"'Yes, your grace!' Is that all you can say?"

"Well, your grace, what other outcome could there have been? Surely you never considered submitting to them! You know what has happened to every other people that has done that. They make insatiable demands, require hostages, and ruinous tribute! Poland under the Mongols would be a living hell until they killed us all! Then it would be a dead one!"

"I know, I know. But there was no need to make them mad! You've told me that their plan is to simultaneously attack both Poland and Hungary. After what you've done, they just might come at us alone with all their forces! King Bela can put two knights in the field for every one that Poland can, and I include Sandomierz, Mazovia, and the Teutonic Knights as being with us!"

"Then maybe I've done some good, your grace. If I've made them mad enough, they'll go straight back to Batu Khan without talking to the other Polish powers. There was always the chance that they could have split us up, or talked some of the others into being neutral."

"That would never have happened, Baron. We may not be united, but we Poles would always stand together against a foreign aggressor."

"I hope you're right, your grace. But the Crossmen aren't Poles, they're Germans who have no great love for us. The Duke of Mazovia is a fourteen-year-old boy! Who can tell about a child?"

"Perhaps the Teutonic Knights are a cipher, but if the Duke of Mazovia's youth causes problems, they will be in the other direction, entirely. He might rashly charge into certain slaughter, but he won't prove a coward."

"Yes, your grace."

"As to the Mongols, well, we'll talk to them again tomorrow."

At this point, a page knocked, entered and announced that the Mongol party had left Wawel Hill.

"Damn!" the duke said. "Baron Conrad, go after them and see what you can do about extending the negotiations."

"Yes, your grace," I said, fully intending to do just the opposite.

I had had my people dress, not in armor or even dress uniforms, but in civilian court garb, and our embroidered velvets shone in all the colors of the rainbow and then some. Some of the colors that Piotr wore had to be unique!

Since we were all riding Big People, we caught up with the Mongols within the hour.

"Hello, ambassador. You left without your honor guard!" I said.

"More of your insolence, Baron Conrad? You call this bunch of fops an honor guard? Why, none of you are in armor and half of you are women!"

"What's more, they're our better half. Why should we need armor in our own country? None of our people would harm us and these woods were cleansed of wolves years ago. Haven't you ever been in a civilized country before?"

"I've seen silly fools before, riding sleek horses."

"Speaking of which, can those little ponies of yours run? What say we race, say from here to the River Bug."

His men had four spare mounts each and he could see that we didn't have any. He said, "Are you suggesting a wager, Baron?"

"Why not? Shall we say a bag of gold to the winner?"

He insisted on seeing my gold, but we made the bet. We soon left them in our dust. When we were about six miles ahead of them, we stopped by a brook and broke out a picnic supper. We were well into it before the Mongols caught up with us, their horses lathered with sweat.

"Care to join us, ambassador?" Krystyana shouted and waved. "There are plenty of leftovers!"

"A Mongol eats in the saddle!" The ambassador was not amused. They rode on.

We passed them again a while later, and I slowed down to chat. "I notice that you have changed horses already. Surely those little things can't be tired yet!"

"Changing horses is the custom of my people," he said stiffly.

"As you like," I said, "but it's obvious that this is not a fair contest. We'll try to make it more even."

With that, Anna and I went to the front of his column, circled ahead of it, ran back to the end, then back to the front again, literally running circles around them. The others in my party joined in the fun, laughing and shouting while the Mongols galloped stoically forward.

Toward dusk, we again left them behind, and when they caught up with us, we had a big campfire going, and Cilicia was dancing for us around it. Piotr and two of the Bankis were playing recorders and the rest of us were keeping time by beating on saddles and swords. A glass bottle of wine was being passed around. I was stretched out with my back to a tree.

Cilicia timed it such that they got a good eyeful of her magnificent nude body, then ended the dance by falling naked into my arms.

"Again you work to humiliate me," the ambassador said. "What manner of devil's spawn are you riding?"

"These? Why, they're just ordinary Christian horses. In fact, these are all just mares. We keep the stallions for battle, when you really need something big and fast. Haven't you seen good horses before?" I asked.

"We have fought Christians before. All the Russias do homage to us! But they did not have such animals as these!"

"Oh. Well, those were Orthodox Christians. We're Catholics. There's a difference."

"Your false gods have nothing to do with your horses!"

"Don't tell them that! They might get mad. They're all very religious," I said.

"Bah! They might be fast, but they would never last through a campaign. Sleek horses like those must eat grain! They'd starve if they had to travel across the steppes!"

"Well, we have a lot of grain for them to eat, but in fact they prefer fresh grass when they can get it. And in a pinch, they can eat darned nearly anything. Anna! Come here, girl!"

The ambassador looked astounded as Anna came up.

"Anna, this man doesn't think that you can get along without grain. Would you please eat that tree for him?"

Anna looked at the pine tree I'd pointed to, winced, and made an expression of a bad taste in her mouth. Then she looked wistfully at a young apple tree near by.

"Oh, okay. Eat the apple tree instead."

Before the dumbfounded Mongols, Anna and a few of her daughters ate that tree right down to the ground, biting off chunks of wood and chewing them up.

"Well," I said, "this has been a pleasant diversion, but we didn't bring our camping gear with us. There's an inn a dozen or so miles up the road, right on the River Bug. We'll wait for you there and collect on the bet."

"Mongols prefer to sleep under the stars!"

"Suit yourselves. You're welcome to the fire, but be sure to put it out when you leave. Forest fires, you know."

The Big People came when we called them. We saddled up while Cilicia put her clothes back on and galloped off into the pitch-dark night. Big People have the most amazing eyesight. They really can see in the dark.

It was another of my Pink Dragon Inns, one I hadn't visited before. The innkeeper promised to wake me when the Mongols arrived, but they never came. Later the next day we got word that they crossed over into Russia a few miles upstream.

"They cheated on their bet!" Sir Vladimir said.

"Don't worry," Sir Piotr said. "We'll collect in the spring."

Chapter Twelve

All the factories were idle and no one manned the machines. The mines were no longer functioning and the furnaces were cold.

The farms no longer had farmers and the countryside looked abandoned.

Right on schedule. The winter of the war was coming and almost every able-bodied young man in southern Poland was training for combat. Our propaganda, appeals, and sometimes outright orders had borne fruit, and from all the lands controlled by the duke came a hundred thirty thousand new men to Hell. In a few weeks, a square mile of nearly empty buildings became the most populous city in Europe. Every skilled man I had was needed to train the new troops, and if we lacked some piece of military equipment, we would just have to do without it. There was no time to build more.

Squires and pages found themselves knighted and training their own lances of six men each. Knights were now knight banners and even captains, and above that we were hard-pressed to keep the command situation from becoming chaos.

Hell itself was chaotic, or at least it must have seemed so to the new men that arrived. There were big signs everywhere, but half of the new people couldn't read, and there was no time to teach them. We even got to painting some men's barracks number on their sleeve so that they could compare it with the numbers over the doors to find their bunks.

But somehow, arms and armor were issued and fitted, men were fed, and training went ahead full blast. There was very little skull work in the training schedule now; the men were not taught to read and write, and there was little mention made of strategy and tactics. We already had all the leaders that we were going to get, and we had only four months to train the men who would do most of the actual fighting.

It was drill and drill and drill, with pike and axe and gun. Even the sword was deemphasized, since it takes years to make a swordsman. The new troops were issued axes as a secondary weapon. Most of these farmboys already knew how to use an axe.

And amid all this work, doing something that none of us had ever done before, dealing with six times as many people as we had ever handled before, trying to keep track of millions of details without the aid of a computer or even a decent bureaucracy, my liege lord, Count Lambert came visiting.

"Baron Conrad, there is a very serious matter that I wish to speak to you about."

"Yes, my lord?" Shit. A brand new steamboat had just sunk the first time it slid down the ways, six tons of battle-axes had been found to be improperly heat-treated, and we seemed to be out of size-five shin guards. What did *he* want?

"Can we speak privately?"

"Of course, my lord." I led the way back to my private office, leaving Piotr to track down the fifty-five cases of missing maps.

"It's my daughter, Baron Conrad. She's come to Poland, and I'm worried about her."

"Your daughter, my lord? I'd forgotten that you had one. Well, except for the children that you've gotten off your peasant girls—but I gather you aren't talking about one of them."

"No, no, of course not. I mean my real daughter, the child of my deceased wife."

"I'm sorry, my lord, but I hadn't even heard that your wife had died."

"I suppose that we can allow for the fact that you've been inordinately busy lately, and of course you never met the woman. She lived with her relatives in Hungary for her last eleven years, and of course our daughter was with her. But now that she is dead, my child has returned to me."

This sudden outbreak of parental love surprised me. I'd never known the count to get sentimental about anything before, and his habits with the girls at Okoitz were such that he must have fathered *hundreds* of children. Oh, he always made sure that the girl was married off properly, and with a decent dowry, but his interest always stopped at that point. Why bring the problem to me?

"I suppose that will make for some changes in your household, my lord, but I can assure you that children add a lot to a home. She'll doubtless be a great comfort to you as you grow older." Just smooth it all over with honeyed oatmeal, I thought. Sometimes that works.

"Well, there is that, but don't you see? She's not exactly a child anymore. She's a young woman! She's fourteen years old and it's my duty to find her a proper husband."

"That's certainly fine, Christian thinking, my lord, but why discuss it with an old, confirmed bachelor like me? Better you should go talk to all of your female relatives and have them be on the lookout for a suitable young man."

"You know that most of those old bitches don't like me, Conrad, and anyway, I know the man I'd want for my heir."

That was the first time in nine years that he had called me just "Conrad." I was beginning to get a very bad feeling about this conversation.

"What's this talk about an heir, my lord? You're barely over forty and you come from a long-lived family. Why, you'll probably live longer than your uncle the old duke did!"

"Lately, I have had a premonition of death. I feel it strongly, and I am worried." He shook his head.

"We're all concerned about the invasion, my lord. Any of us could fall in battle, but a knight doesn't worry about that sort of thing, does he? Anyway, if you've come for my advice about your daughter, it's to let the girl pick her own future husband. She'll be a lot happier that way, and it will vastly increase your domestic tranquility."

"But I didn't come for your advice, Conrad. I came for your consent!"

"My consent, my lord?"

"To marriage, of course!"

"To marriage!" I stood. For the first time in twenty years, my voice broke and it came out like a squeak.

"Of course! What do you think I'm talking about? I want you to be my son-in-law! I want you to marry my only child and be my heir."

"But, but I'm just not the marrying kind! The whole institution frightens me! No, no, my lord. I would never make a decent son-in-law! You'd learn to hate me. So would she!"

"Nonsense, my boy. Why, you and I have gotten along for years with never a cross word. All the women around seem to love you. Why should my daughter be any different?"

"What's this 'my boy' business? I'm only two years younger than you! I'm an old man! You shouldn't saddle your daughter with an old man! She'll end up being a young widow, and you know all the trouble they get into!"

"Again, nonsense! You're as healthy a man as I've ever met, and any woman with any brains about her prefers a mature man to a young stripling."

"They didn't when *I* was a stripling!"

"Well, that simply proves your prowess! None of your ladies are complaining, are they?"

"It's not a matter of my ladies, my lord. For years now, I've been satisfied with just one, Cilicia. She's heavy with our second child now. I couldn't possibly leave her."

"Well, you wouldn't have to leave her, just sort of get her out of the way for a while. Anyway, I know full well that you haven't been absolutely faithful to her. You manage to get to Countess Francine's manor at least once a month."

"She's an old friend."

"And a close one, no doubt. But that's all one to me. Just keep up appearances, and you'll hear no complaints from your father-in-law."

"My lord, I've never even met your daughter."

"So? She's a normal, healthy girl. She has all the standard features. What more can be said? And she'll learn Polish soon enough, so that's no problem."

"She doesn't even speak Polish! Well, I don't speak any Hungarian! What do we do? Invite an interpreter to bed with us?"

"Mind your manners, Conrad. This is my own flesh and blood we're talking about."

"There are hundreds of girls that are your own flesh and blood! And all the rest of them can at least speak the language! Why don't you make me marry one of them?"

"Conrad! Control yourself! If this goes on, you shall anger me."

"See what a lousy son-in-law I'd make? We had an excellent relationship until it was torn asunder by the mere mention of marriage! Find another man, my lord. I don't want to get married!"

"That's your final word, then?"

"Yes, my lord, it is."

"Well then. It has certainly been a pleasure having you for a vassal, and the experience has been vastly profitable. Tell me, where were you planning to go next?"

"My lord, what are you talking about? You can't fire me like a bricklayer who's finished his job! We made an oath together, and that oath gives you no right to force me into marriage."

"True. We made an oath. Do you remember it? It was Christmas time, almost nine years ago. True, I don't have the right to force marriage on you, but you made one strange addition to the standard oath, which at the time I thought inconsequential, but now it comes into the fore. You swore fealty to me for only nine years! Those nine years will be up in three weeks, at which time our agreement is off! So I wish you well. Be sure and fill your saddlebags before you leave. Take a few carts of gold with you if you wish. But I am not minded to renew my oath with one who would so crassly insult my own daughter as to refuse her hand in marriage."

I was dumbstruck. I *had* put that in my oath! At the time, I wasn't sure whether I could get technology going in this century or not, and if I couldn't I wanted to have the right to be somewhere else than in the middle of a Mongol massacre, where one more dead body wouldn't have done Poland much good. I had left myself a coward's way out and now I was paying for it!

"But—but the army, the boats, the aircraft! I'm needed here now more than ever! You can't do this! Not to me nor to Poland."

"Wrong, Baron. Or at least 'baron' for the next three weeks. I can do it and I intend to do it. Sir Vladimir can handle the army properly, I'm sure, and Sir Tadaos can do what's right with the steamboats. And the aircraft? Well, I'm already in charge there!"

"Well, I won't stand for it! I'll go talk to the duke about this!"

"Feel free, but I've already discussed the matter with him. You know that he has long been displeased with you concerning the way that you have consistently lived in sin since coming here.

He thinks that you should get married and that my daughter would be an excellent match. He has already given his blessings on the union!"

"But my lifestyle is a good deal more moral than yours!"

"True, at least by any sensible standard. But I am a mere back-woods count, whereas you have made yourself into a hero. Heroes have to live upright lives! After all, the youth of Poland looks to you for guidance! Myself, I think where you went wrong was all the charity work. You should have left those wretches alone."

"But this is filthy, rotten blackmail!"

"Yes, it is, isn't it. Shall we say the day after Christmas for the wedding? The Bishop of Wroclaw has already given dispensation for the posting of the banns."

"Damn you, Lambert! God damn you straight to hell and the devil!"

I stormed out of my office, pushing aside a startled secretary who was standing in the doorway. I went down to the stables, threw a saddle on Anna and charged back to Three Walls. I told the stable girl, Kotcha, to put Anna's best saddle and barding on her and went up to my room.

I put on my best armor, not my efficient Night-Fighter suit, but the fancy, engraved, gold-plated stuff they'd given me for Christmas a few years back. I threw my wolfskin cloak over my shoulders and went down to the strong room. I came back up with my saddlebags filled with gold. To hell with the silver, the gold would do. It was all that I could carry, anyhow.

Then I headed down the trail, or railroad track now, and at the first intersection I headed not east, toward the Mongols, but west, toward France! I'd heard a lot of nice things about France. Maybe I could even learn the language.

Nine years in a country that punishes a man for helping the poor! Well, to hell with them! To hell with them all.

We rode like thunder for hours and Anna never let up. She didn't know where we were going or why, but I wanted to go and that was enough for her. The one good friend I had.

Darkness was closing in as we rode by the trail to Countess Francine's manor. Well, it was a bit cold for camping out, and

I hadn't brought my old camping gear along, anyway. Maybe Francine would like a lift back to France.

She was a countess while I was only a baron, despite the fact that her county was much smaller than my barony. She only had six knights subordinate to her, yet she was my superior in status. Because of this, she absolutely refused to use my title or her own when we were together, and got unhappy when I used them myself. I think she thought I really gave a damn about that sort of thing.

Her watchman must have called her, because the drawbridge was lowering as we approached, and she stood just behind it, waiting.

"You come gaily clad, my friend!" she said as she warmly embraced my cold armor.

"It seemed like a good idea, if I was going to France."

"France! But you must come inside and tell me all about it!"

A marshal came up to take care of Anna, but I slung the heavy saddlebags over my own shoulder. I just wasn't very trusting anymore.

At supper, Francine got the whole story out of me.

"So you charged away like a hero in a fireside tale, without even a change of underwear." She giggled. "Oh, you poor little dumpling."

"Well, I don't think it's the least bit funny."

"Of course it is not, darling. It is horrible. You have been rudely treated by a man that you have done everything for. You have a perfect right to be angry, but if Lambert has made himself your enemy, then you must fight him! You have done great things here and you must not let them be stolen from you!"

"The truth is that I really don't give a damn anymore."

"You have just worked too hard for too long and have treated it all too seriously," she said.

"Call it a long vacation, then. Say, fifty years or so. France still seems like a great idea. Would you like me to give you a lift there?"

"To ride with my knight and hero back to my homeland? Oh, Conrad, what a romantic thought! But France is not Poland and if you did not marry me, people would call me a strumpet! Would you let them do that to your poor damsel?"

"And so I would have to do the very thing I was running away from. You're pretty good at popping balloons."

"And someday you must tell me what a balloon is, but not right now. Think! If you do not care about your wealth or position, what of the people who are depending on you? What of the noble Sir Vladimir? What of earnest little Sir Piotr? And Lady Krystyana. I know you loved her once. Has that love turned to such hate that you would abandon her to the Tartars?"

"No. I guess not."

"Then you must stay in Poland and find a way to resolve your problem with Lambert. We must plan our strategy! We must confound your liege lord and defeat him!"

"Well, I can hardly go out and fight the man."

"Of course not. You have a hundred fifty thousand fighting men and he does not have a hundred fifty, yes? How could there be a fight? You could massacre him if you wished, but that would be immoral. No. You must use a woman's arts of persuasion and intrigue, and I am the woman to help you with this. First, you must realize that you have many friends in the very highest places. The Bishop of Cracow is your friend and confessor, yes? And the duke himself is a member of your order of Radiant Warriors. And you have me. I spent many years by the side of the old duke. I know where all the bodies were buried and was privy to all of the old duke's secrets."

"All? You mean . . ."

"Yes, all. Even about you. An old man will always tell everything to an adoring young woman."

"Then . . . tell me what you know about me."

She glanced around to see that the servants were out of the room, then said quietly, "I know that you have come to us from the far future in some way that even you do not understand. Is that enough?"

"It's way too much. You shouldn't have been told."

"But I was. Don't worry, darling, your secret is safe with me.

I swear that you are the only person I have ever told it to, and ever will."

"And it doesn't bother you?"

"It is passing strange, but I love you still."

"Well. You mentioned strategy. What do you think we should do?" I asked.

"First we must speak to the duke. We must do this right away, before Count Lambert has a chance to see him again. We must find out where he stands on your marriage to Jadwiga, and—"

"Who?"

"Jadwiga. Oh, you dumpling! You do not even know the name of the girl they are trying to marry you to?"

"The count never mentioned it."

"Well, now you know. Knowing the young duke as I do, it is quite possible that he really does want you to get married. He is such a prude about some things! Has he ever mentioned it to you?"

"I'm afraid so. Quite a number of times, as a matter of fact."

"Then you just might have to get married."

"What!"

"Hush, dear. It is not the end of the world. You have been living with Cilicia for many years now, yes? Nothing need change if you were married to her. It could be done quietly, a few minutes with a priest. Is that so bad?"

"I can't marry Cilicia. We couldn't have a Christian wedding because she refuses to become a Christian! Believe me, I've been trying to convert her since we first met. And even if I was willing to become her brand of Moslem, which I'm not, her father has some sort of complicated theological reason why I couldn't join their church, or whatever they call it. The whole thing is simply impossible!"

"Then marry me. You have been coming here every few weeks for years. That would satisfy me, if I could get no better. Nothing need change, darling."

"But . . ."

"Then think on it. Come love, we must be up before gray dawn to ride to Cracow and see the duke. Let us go to bed."

Even after a vigorous bout of lovemaking, I had a hard time getting to sleep that night. Francine was asleep with her head on my arm, her back to my stomach, spoon fashion. I was careful not to wake her, but I needed a good think.

Okay, I told myself. You've got this phobia. Nothing to be ashamed of. Lots of people have phobias.

You've got to stay in Poland and fight this invasion. That's a given. A lot of good people are counting on you. You can't let them down. You've made promises and you have to live with them.

Is that what really scares you about marriage? The fact that it's a lifetime promise, without any way out if you were wrong? But you've made so many other promises, and you can't get out of them, either. You didn't go into a cold funk when you swore to Lambert, did you? Oh, you let yourself have a coward's way out, but that's one of the things you're regretting now, isn't it?

But if you're going to stay, you've somehow got to placate Lambert *and* the duke. Lambert isn't going to let up, you know. Once he gets an idea into his head, he's like a bulldog clamped down on a bull's snout. As long as there is any chance that you will marry his daughter, he'll be in there conniving a way to force you to do it.

And the duke. He wants everybody to live a fine, conventional and Christian life, just like in all the stories the priests like to tell. He would have had Lambert back with his wife years ago if she hadn't been out of the country and the duke's jurisdiction, that's sure. If you were married, you'd have the duke solidly on your side against Lambert. What's more, once you were married, Lambert would give up on his plans for you and his daughter. He's a bulldog, but he's not stupid.

So getting married is the rational thing to do at this point. It solves all the conflicting problems of duty, morality, your boss, and your boss's boss.

So why aren't you rational about it? Because you're scared shitless, that's why! All this business you keep telling yourself and everybody else about rationality and the scientific method is just a hypocritical ball of lies! Underneath, you're just a wad of primeval fears, a caveman huddled around his campfire, afraid of the dark, a whining neurotic desperately in need of professional help!

Well, maybe not that last, but you sure need help. Look, would it really be so bad? This woman in your arms, is she so bad? She's beautiful. She's easily the best looking Christian you've seen since you got here. She's mature, well educated, and damned intelligent. What's more, she wants to marry you, and you damn well know you'll never get a better offer. You're almost living with her now. Is she really asking so much? One little church ceremony? It could be over in minutes, in some obscure little village church.

Five minutes. It could be over in five minutes. You're man enough to stand up to that, aren't you? It would solve your problems with both Lambert and the duke, and would make a very nice lady very happy. Like she said, it would make no difference in your lifestyle. Nothing need change at all. You could do that, couldn't you?

Yeah, I thought, I suppose I could. But just a little ceremony.

Francine snuggled even closer in my arms.

In her sleep, she murmured, "I am so glad that it is settled." Then she was quiet once more.

I don't like it when things like that happen.

In the morning we both sort of half awoke and calmly, warmly I was inside of her again.

"Francine, do you really want to marry me?"

"Of course, darling, with all my heart!"

"Then let's do it."

This brought on a smile and a squeal and a hug and a kiss that quite literally took my breath away, followed, naturally, by far more enthusiastic lovemaking.

Later, she said. "You really want this? I have not done anything unfair to get you?"

"Yes, I want you, and your magnificent body is a most unfair enticement."

"Good. I did not want you to think you were forced. But

if you are going ahead freely, there is something that I must tell you."

"What?"

"That you are going to be a papa again, and this time, I am going to be the mama!"

I should be getting used to this sort of thing, but I'm not.

Interlude Three

Tom hit the STOP button.

"What the hell goes on here!" he shouted.

"What are you talking about?" I asked.

"I'll show you!" He pushed the intercom button. "I want the asshole who edited this tape front and center, here and now!"

A man dressed in a conservative brown T-shirt and shorts stepped in immediately. Another advantage of time travel is that you always have time to get to meetings promptly.

"Sir?" the man said.

"Just what are you trying to pull?"

"Sir? What are you talking about?"

"This tape! It has Conrad getting ready to marry Lady Francine! When I viewed it last week, she talked him into marrying Lambert's daughter. If this is some kind of joke, mister, I don't like your sense of humor!"

"But sir! I edited that tape, and he didn't do either one of those things! He went on toward France until an emissary of the duke caught up with him in Worms and talked him into returning to Poland!"

"What?" Tom thought a minute. "If this is a joke, the prankster will spend the next century doing anthropological work on Eskimos! But right now, I want you to get your staff together and find out who the joker is. I want to see how this version comes out, but I'll see you and your people in two hours. Now get out!"

The man bolted out the door.

"Tom, I don't think he fudged it," I said. "I mean, he would have to have found actors who were exact doubles for Francine and Conrad. He would have to build perfect sets and backgrounds. It's not the sort of thing that would be done as a joke!"

"I know. But the alternative is frightening. It means that we are seeing a temporal split right here. Two temporal splits!"

"But how could something that happened in the thirteenth century affect us? We're seventy thousand years in their past!"

"I don't know, but it scares the shit out of me!"

He hit the START button.

Chapter Thirteen

FROM THE DIARY OF CONRAD STARGARD

Anna carried us both through the day, and that night in Cracow, the duke granted us an immediate private audience.

"Baron Conrad. I'm glad you're here. I was about to send men out in search of you. But the matter which we must discuss, well, are you sure that you want the Countess Francine present?"

"Quite sure, your Grace."

"Very well, then. What is this business between you and Count Lambert's daughter? Dalliance with peasant girls and heathens is bad enough. Trifling with the peerage is something else!"

"Your Grace, I have never met the count's daughter! I have never seen her, let alone touched her. I had forgotten that she even existed until Count Lambert told me yesterday that she is in Poland!"

"Then what's this business of his insisting that you marry her?"

"I don't know, your Grace. I was shocked by his demands. He said that you had approved the marriage."

"Well, he asked me if I would approve such a marriage, and of course I said I would do so. You know that I would be delighted to see you married. This business of your cohabitating with an infidel Moslem is shameful, and your fornications with my ward are even worse!"

"Your ward?"

"Countess Francine here, of course! She's not married and she has no family in the country, so she must have a guardian, and who else but a duke could be guardian to a countess? Use your head, man. It's complicated by the fact that she was my father's friend and is quite capable of taking care of herself, but nonetheless I am personally responsible for her before God, and you have been bedding her!"

"That is the other matter that I would like to discuss with you, your Grace. The Countess Francine and I would like to be married."

For the first time, the duke relaxed and smiled. "And is this your wish as well, Countess?"

"With all my heart, your Grace."

"Then with all mine, you have my approval. But back to the matter at hand. My impression was that you, Conrad, had been the instigator of the marriage proceedings between yourself and Jadwiga. I mean, that's the usual thing! If two people wish to get married, they talk to the girl's father, and if there is a major inheritance involved, the father talks to his liege. I thought that in approving Lambert's request, I was granting *your* wishes!"

"I swear I knew nothing of it, your Grace."

"Well. For now, I'll take your word for it, but if you're lying to me, I'll see you hung! All I know of this is that your secretary, Lady Natalia, came to me this morning and reported your conversation with Count Lambert *verbatim*. She even had it in writing, though I could scarcely believe it! Does she always do things like this?"

He tossed a sheaf of papers at me. I quickly scanned it.

"She has a remarkable memory, your Grace. The door was open and I guess we were pretty loud. But this is what was said, word for word."

"She also told me that you had taken all your ready gold and had headed west without explaining to anyone. She was deathly worried about you."

"I'm sorry I upset her, your Grace. I was pretty upset myself."

"As I suppose I would have been in your position. This business of only swearing for nine years. I suppose that's true?"

"Yes, your Grace. At the time, I didn't know how long I would want to stay."

"I see. But later, when you were enlarged to a barony, you must have sworn again to Lambert. Was there any time limit made in that oath?"

"No, your Grace."

"Then the second oath supersedes the first. Count Lambert had no right to threaten you with escheating your lands. Also, if you are to marry Countess Francine, you must be enlarged to her county. That is to say, you must swear fealty to me as my count, though you will also remain Count Lambert's baron. You will be his subordinate, yet his equal in status. As to Lambert, you will have no further problems with him, I assure you. He and I will have a serious talk! For the rest, see a priest, or perhaps the Bishop of Cracow, since he's a friend of yours, and post proper banns. Your oath of fealty can be taken at the wedding."

"Yes, your Grace, although we had thought that just a simple ceremony—"

"What! My ward being married in a back chapel like an eloping peasant? I wouldn't hear of it! You shall be married in Wawel Cathedral before all the nobility of the land and I shall give the bride away! Now be off with you both and, uh, separate bedrooms until the wedding, right?"

The next morning, Bishop Ignacy was as pleased about the wedding as the duke, and the date was set for three days after Twelfth Night. Francine stayed on in Cracow to help with the arrangements, but I still had a war to get ready for.

Word of my engagement had gotten to Hell before me, and I had to put up with a lot of stupid cheering, but I soon got things back to business.

"The steamboat that sank has been brought back up," Natalia reported. "And the boatyard says they'll have it fixed in a month. Sir Ilya has taken over the problem of those axeheads. He says that he was tempering axeheads over wood fires nine years ago and he can still do it. They found three containers of size-five shin guards labeled size one, so that's all right, and one of the cooks from mess hall eleventeen brought over the fifty-five cases of maps and wanted to know how he was supposed to cook them so that even a grunt could eat it. They got delivered to him in the same container as the seven cases of applesauce he'd ordered."

"So problems are being solved," I said.

"Yes sir. But there are eighty thousand rounds of swivel gun ammunition that were cast oversize and won't fit in the chambers. Coherers—is that how you pronounce it?—coherers for the radios have been breaking faster than expected and we're almost out of spares, and six thousand sets of goose-down underwear were found to be stuffed with chicken feathers. They say they're too scratchy to wear."

"So things are back to normal," I said. "And Natalia—thank you. Thank you for everything."

That night I went back to Three Walls. Cilicia had already left, gone back to her father in the valley I had given his people. Well, all right, I'd miss her, but she had to do what she had to do. She'd taken our boy with her and that was not all right. He was my son and by God he'd be raised a Christian, and that went double for the one in the cooker.

But then I cooled down and decided that this was not the time to push it. Maybe Cilicia would come back. Maybe we'd all be killed in the invasion. And maybe the horse would sing.

Later. We'd see about it later.

For now, there were mass maneuvers with the war carts.

I think I was dreading my wedding more than the Mongol invasion. It was not a pleasant Christmas, in part because of my worries, but mostly because we really didn't celebrate it. We held a High Mass in the morning and served a better than average dinner, then spent the afternoon in training. There were complaints from all quarters, but we couldn't waste the time. Furthermore, the men couldn't have their families with them, and I would rather have them mad than maudlin.

My wedding preparations went on without me. Countess Francine wrote me constantly and visited me twice at Hell to keep me updated, although she insisted on sleeping alone. These wedding customs are ridiculous! With both Cilicia and Francine unavailable, sexual frustration was added to all my other problems. After a week, Natalia got together with Krystyana, who had taken over food preparation at Hell. They started sending me young peasant girls on the theory that I shouldn't go to waste. Bless them.

Despite the war preparations, the duke was planning to make my wedding the major social event of the year! Every count and baron under the duke was expected to attend, and the dukes of Sandomierz and Mazovia were coming along with their peerages. This when we should have been sharpening our swords!

But there was nothing I could do about it.

Years ago, I had mentioned cutting gemstones to my Moslem jeweler, and now he gave me a faceted stone that I think was diamond. It wasn't as sparkling as a modern gem, but maybe that was because the jeweler didn't have all the angles exactly right. At least it cut glass. I had it set in a gold ring and Countess Francine was pleased with it, but nobody had ever heard of an engagement ring before. It started a new fad.

The day approached and I left for Cracow with my best three-dozen men and their ladies. We got there to find out that the heralds had taken over the seating arrangements in the cathedral and there was room for only barons and better. My own party wouldn't be able to attend!

I went to the duke with the problem and he swore me in as count a day early. Then I swore in my whole party as barons! I even swore in Novacek, who had never been knighted! Damn all heralds, anyway.

Word was that this was to be a military wedding, and all were to be dressed in their best armor. Well, I had my gold stuff and my best man, Baron Vladimir, had managed to scrounge up a similar set, as it turned out, from Count Lambert. But most of my people had only Night-Fighter armor, efficient but not decorative. They did what they could, bleaching it white and adding bright red baldrics. They certainly stood out among the polished plate.

For me, well, it was like I had agreed to have my leg amputated with an axe, and then the doctors decided to do it with a grinding wheel instead.

Somehow, I survived the ceremony.

Why is it that men smile at a wedding and women cry?

Afterward, there was a reception that filled most of the rooms in Wawel Castle. I was trying to be agreeable to a crowd of people that I hardly knew when Count Lambert came up.

"May I offer you my congratulations, Count Conrad, as well as my apologies? I realize now how crass and crude I was to handle that matter in the way I did. Can you forgive me?"

"Of course, my lord. At least I think I still address you that way. There is nothing to forgive. We were both overwrought and the less said now the better."

"I quite agree. And as to your form of address, my friend, well, you can call me anything you like but a coward. I think that equals speech would be most appropriate, don't you think so, Conrad?"

"That sounds good to me, Lambert." I smiled, though I knew our relationship would never again be the same.

Finally, things settled down enough so that Francine and I could sneak off and enjoy our first night together in a month and a half.

Early the next morning, Duke Henryk called the visiting dukes and all counts present to a council of war, and I finally saw why attendance at this event had been mandatory. The wedding had been a cover for the council.

Besides the Polish nobility, the Grand Master of the Teutonic Order was there with a dozen of his masters. There was bad blood between the Crossmen and me, so they had not attended the wedding. There was also a representative from the Knights Hospitalers, as well as nobles from both King Louis IX of France and Emperor Frederic II of Germany. Duke Henryk had been doing his homework.

After an opening prayer, Duke Henryk introduced the envoy from the King of France. Speaking through an interpreter, this marquis pledged the support of France to our cause, and said that already, three thousand lances of French knights were coming to our aid, a total of about nine thousand men, a third of them nobles, a third squires, and a third crossbow men.

The emperor's envoy made a similar statement, promising half again as many men as the French, as well as supplies for the French forces as they crossed the Holy Roman Empire.

You could see the mood of the room lightening. The Polish knights wouldn't have to fight alone! We had powerful friends coming to our aid!

Duke Henryk spoke of strong contingents of Spanish, English, and Italian knights coming to Poland as well. He had been in communication with King Bela of Hungary and Tzar Ivan Asen II of the Bulgarian Empire. Since these two empires were threatened with invasion at the same time as Poland, he could not in good conscience ask them for aid. But they had agreed that should any of the three powers defeat the Mongols in its own country, that power would then go to the aid of the others.

With emperors and kings accounted for, the Knights Hospitalers stood and promised six hundred knights to our aid, which was almost all that they had.

The Teutonic Knights promised only five hundred, saying that their men were on the frontiers as well, and they could not leave those borders undefended. All present knew that was bullshit. The Crossmen had over three thousand men and the Pruthenians against whom 2500 were supposed to be guarding were no serious danger. At worst, they might do a little cattle-raiding and, what with all the animals running free, they could take their pick without hurting anybody. I got madder when I found out that to get even this little help out of the Crossmen, the duke had had to promise to rescind his father's ban on their order in

Silesia. I'd nearly gotten killed getting them thrown out! There was nothing I could do about it now, but someday I was going to get those bastards.

Duke Boleslaw V of Mazovia stood and pledged every man he had, about sixteen thousand of them. In the history books, he's called "the chaste" or "the bashful," depending on whether the particular historian liked him or not. The nickname had to do with his love life, not his fighting. At fifteen, he looked to be a hell-raiser.

The Duke of Sandomierz followed suit, pledging twelve thousand men. Knighthood was not really well established in Sandomierz and Mazovia. The men fought in family groups rather than in feudal levies, and the concept of nobility was somewhat different. Not that it mattered much right now.

Duke Henryk announced that from Silesia, Great and Little Poland, he would lead twenty-nine thousand men into battle, over half of whom were knighted, and that he did not include in this total the infantry that I was training.

I was the only mere count who spoke at that council. I said that they all knew about the arms and armor that my men had made. Indeed, most of those present were wearing our products. They knew about the steamboats, but were surprised to learn that there would be three dozen of them on the Vistula alone. The aircraft were well known, and I spoke a bit on the advantages of aerial reconnaissance, until the duke motioned for me to hurry it up.

Then I announced the radios and told what they could do. I don't think anybody believed me! They'd all heard tales about my Warrior's School, but when I said that we would march out with a hundred fifty thousand fighting men, there were looks of stupid disbelief and a few people laughed. They simply didn't think in terms that large.

I was red-faced when I stepped down.

Nonetheless, there was a feeling of buoyancy and confidence in the room. We had the men, we had the power, we had allies coming in from all of Christendom!

Then Duke Henryk announced his battle plan and things started to fall apart. He said that all the foreign contingents, most of which were already on the way, would be gathering at Legnica, and that the rest of us should meet them there. We could then have a single, strong, unified army with which to advance eastward toward the Mongols.

The knights of Little Poland, Sandomierz, and Mazovia were not the least bit pleased by this plan! It meant that they would have to march hundreds of miles west, wait for the foreigners to arrive, and then march back again! And while this was going on, their own lands would be completely at the mercy of the Mongol invaders with no one to defend them!

Young Duke Boleslaw was the first on his feet, shouting. "Henryk, do you expect me to abandon my own duchy, my own people, to go off to your estates to defend your lands? Because if you do, you're crazy! My lands, and those of Sandomierz and Little Poland are in front of yours! The Tartars must go through us before they can touch your precious lands! It is *you* who should come and support *us*!"

Duke Henryk was on his feet. "We *will* come in your support! But don't you see that we must come *together*? If every man stands and defends his own manor, the Tartars will chew us up one by one in little bites! If we join together in a single army, we will be invincible! The choice of Legnica as a rallying point is the result of simple geography. It is the center point of all the knights who will be fighting on our side, the center of gravity, as Count Conrad would call it. Yes, it is on my lands, but it has to be on somebody's lands! Further, arrangements have already been made to feed and house the vast number of fighting men who will be gathering. Can any of you provide such a thing? Can Sandomierz or Plock feed so many men?"

"Merchants will come," Duke Boleslaw said. "They always do! I say that I will defend eastern Poland with my life! I will not run back for three hundred miles while my people are murdered! I will defend, and if you and your foreigners can come up in time to help me, I will be forever grateful to you. But if you are late, may God have mercy on you, because no one else will!"

And with that bit of bombast, the kid stomped out of the room, followed by all the men of Mazovia. After a few awkward moments, the Duke of Sandomierz stood and followed him, and in a few minutes, the hall was half empty. Even those men from Little Poland, men from the Cracow area who were personally sworn to Duke Henryk, had left. To them, the decision to be made was between abandoning their lands and peoples, or abandoning their oath to their duke. And they had made it. Even many still in the room seemed uncertain.

"Well," the duke said. "It seems that we must fight without them. But at least you men are with me, and Count Conrad's men outnumber by far all those that have left."

I had to stand. "Your grace, don't you see that I can't bring all my men to Legnica, either? I have a major force in my boats on the Vistula. I cannot bring those boats overland to the Odra. They must be used in eastern Poland or not be used at all! The aircraft will be far more useful than you now realize, but we only have one airport! That airport is near Okoitz, which is east of Legnica, and if it is overrun, the planes are useless! My infantry needs the railroads to travel quickly. We have built extensive tracks along the Vistula and through the Malapolska Hills, the area that we will need to defend first. If we can win there, western Poland is safe. But the railroad net is thin in western Poland and nonexistent in many areas. We haven't had time to expand it yet. My men can not effectively fight in western Poland!"

"So. You, too, Conrad?"

"Your grace, I am not abandoning you, but don't you realize what the radios and the rails mean? It is not necessary for all of us to be in the same spot for us to be together! With good communications, we can work in concert even though we are hundreds of miles apart."

"Count Conrad, I don't understand what you're saying. But what I do know is that every man true to me will join me at Legnica before the first of March!"

With that he got up and left, and the council of war was never called again. Instead of one Polish Army, there were now three of them. Those in the east under Duke Boleslaw, those in the west under Duke Henryk, and those men sworn to me. We were in pieces before the Mongols had even arrived.

Chapter Fourteen

There wasn't much time for marital bliss. Not with the war just weeks away. Francine moved into Hell with me, but that was only temporary. The place for her when it started was Three Walls, only she didn't see it that way. She had visions of herself being a female power behind the throne.

We were arguing about that one night in bed. "Look, love. Three Walls is my home. It's where I normally live and work. It's also my biggest installation, and my best defended. On top of all that, it's the one farthest back. Before the Mongols dare attack it, they must first destroy East Gate. Then they must take out Sir Miesko's formidable manor, as well as Hell, or they have an enemy at their rear. They'd even be well advised to destroy Okoitz before they tried to take Three Walls. It's a matter of simple geography."

"Geography, yes. But not politics. It would be best if I were in Cracow. There I can do you some good."

"I don't need you to do me any good. I need you to be alive. You will have a much better chance of staying that way at Three Walls."

"You have no feeling for the politics of the situation."

"I don't give a damn about the politics of the situation! The city walls at Cracow are made of old crumbly bricks. They are only three stories high, and they are defended by only two dozen guns. Do you know what came into the office today? An order from the city fathers of Cracow for two thousand swivel guns, to be shipped immediately! They should have placed that order two years ago!

Then it could have been filled! Now, I could fill it only by stripping the guns from the walls of other cities, and I won't do it!"

"You see? If you had understood the politics there, you could have sold them those guns at the time, yes?"

"It's not that I *wanted* to sell them the guns! I've never made a penny selling arms and armor! It's just that the city is weak and the people there don't have much chance if they're attacked. You are going to Three Walls. I am your husband and you will obey me in this!"

"What happened to letting each other live our own lives?"

"I'm still for it! But you have to be alive before you can live! Now shut up and go to sleep. I have other things to worry about."

"What other things, my darling?"

"Treason, for one. There is no way that I can obey the duke and retreat to Legnica. That move would destroy the usefulness of everything that I've done here. I must disobey him."

"So. This must be?"

"Absolutely. There is no way around it. I wish I could obey him, and after the war I hope he still wants me for a vassal, but his battle plan is Just Plain Awful."

"Then perhaps I should be going to Legnica, yes?"

"No! You are not going anywhere but Three Walls. And I, well, I'm going to Okoitz in the morning."

"And why do you go to Lambert, whom you do not like anymore?"

"I go there to add conspiracy to my treason, and compound it with sowing disaffection among the duke's loyal men. If I'm going to send out the riverboats to hold the Vistula, and maybe even the Bug, I'm going to need the aircraft to help patrol the area and watch for the enemy. Lambert is in solid control of the boys at Eagle Nest, so I have to talk him into joining me."

"And you say that you do not care for politics."

"I don't. And I'm sure not looking forward to tomorrow's meeting."

At Okoitz, Lambert was effusive.

"Ah, my dear Conrad! It's so good to see you again! I trust

you've come for your usual monthly visit. I want you to look over our defenses here one more time. Those old women you sent to teach my girls how to defend the place seem to know what they're about, but defense is really a man's business, what?"

"I'd be happy to go over the defenses, my lord, but there's another matter to be discussed."

"Now, what's this 'my lord' nonsense? I thought we agreed to treat each other as equals, as brothers, even!"

"Sorry, Lambert. Just habit, I suppose."

"Good! Now, what was this other matter?"

"Treason."

"Dog's blood! Whose?"

"Mine. Maybe yours as well."

"What the devil are you talking about?"

"I'm talking about the duke's battle plan. You were at the council of war. You saw what happened, and you heard what I had to say. It still goes. If I follow the duke's plan, everything I've done here is wasted. Poland will fall and most of us, the duke included, will likely be killed. I'm going to have to disobey him."

"I see. But you've always had an obligation to a Higher Power."

"What do you mean?" I said.

"Prester John, of course! I figured out who sent you here long ago. The greatest Christian king of all, Prester John."

Good lord! Lambert told me about this fantasy of his nine years ago, but he hadn't mentioned it since, so I'd hoped he'd forgotten about it. Yet my oath to Father Ignacy still stood, and I couldn't tell him the truth of the matter.

"You are silent," Lambert continued. "Well, I understand your problem and your oath of silence. But to answer your implied question, I'd say that your duty to your king takes precedence over your later oath to the duke, so you are safe on moral grounds. As to the practical considerations, well, if your strategy is right and the duke's is wrong, then you will be a hero and there won't be much he can do to you. If the duke's strategy is right and yours is wrong, then you are likely to die on the battlefield, and again there won't be anything he can do to you. Offhand, I'd say that your treason is a safe one."

As safe as a tomb, I thought.

"Thank you, but I didn't come here for your moral support. I came here for your physical support. My boats are going to need your aircraft to show them where the enemy is concentrating. Can I count on your help here, though it be treason on your part?"

"You can count on my help and that of the boys from Eagle Nest. We'll be up there, you may be sure! But how would that be treason to the duke? My oath to him requires that I send him so many knights in the time of his need. I shall do so, and then some, for I now have more men than my oath requires, despite the loss of those knights that once served Baron Jaraslav and now serve you. In truth, since you are arming all of my knights and squires and my barons, and I need only provide training and a horse, in the last six years we have been able to more than double the number of knights that serve me. I was wise to accept your offer, you see.

"And while my oath does not require it, I have told him that we shall be watching the enemy from above, and reporting their movements to him, and this, too, I shall do. If we also tell your boats what we tell the duke, how is that treason? It's just the sensible thing to do. We're all fighting the same enemy, after all!"

"You have relieved my mind, Lambert."

"If you say so. Myself, I can't imagine how you thought I could have done otherwise! Now then, shall we see to my defenses? And afterward, you shall have supper here with me and my daughter, and you shall see what you missed out on!"

FROM THE DIARY OF TADAOS KOLPINKSI

In the last week of February, the ice on the Vistula was breaking up some, but it wasn't gone. Like usual, it'd drift downstream and jam up at some turn, then more ice would pile on top, then that night, sure as Hell for a Heathen, it would turn cold again and the whole damn thing would freeze solid.

I had three boats on the river and we was loaded with bombs, something new we wasn't sure would work. They was big iron barrels filled with gunpowder and weighted so's they'd just barely sink. There was a slow fuse in a bottle in one side, and the idea was when you came to a jam, you lit one, screwed down the cap, and got it over the side before it blew up in your face. It was supposed to drift with the current under the jam while you was paddling backward under full steam.

Sometimes it worked. Sometimes it drifted too far or not far enough. Once it blew and took the whole damn boat with it!

At least I think that was what happened. Nobody from *The Pride of Bytom* lived to tell about it. We just heard the blast around the bend, and when my own *Muddling Through* got there, well, there wasn't much left. Every barrel in her must have blown with the first one.

But we was pushing the ice downriver, and not that much was coming from upstream behind us. Once we got past Cracow, I ordered the other boats out, so's we could at least patrol what was clear. They went down their ways without a hitch and each loaded up with six war carts and a full company of warriors.

We continued north with the *Hotspur*, blowing ice and sometimes getting a shot at a Mongol patrol, until we got to the River Bug. It was froze solid and there was nothing we could do about it. We was out of bombs then, and there wasn't no way we could work upstream, anyhow. I'd hoped to save maybe three dozen of them bombs for another project I had in mind, but there was no way to do it, what with the loss of *The Pride of Bytom* and all. We couldn't get up the Dunajec either, so all of Poland east of the Vistula was left open to the enemy.

But we did what we could, damn it! What else *can* a man do?

The other boats was running into bigger patrols and we turned back to pick up our troops at East Gate. It took a while. Doctrine was to give refugees a lift across the river when we weren't actually in a fight, and we had to stop and ferry God knows how many thousands of people across.

The planes was up and flying whenever the weather was decent, and they'd tell us about refugees and Mongol patrols. They had these big arrows with a long red ribbon on them that they'd drop right on your deck. They'd stick right in the wood and it was amazing they never killed nobody. But there'd be a message in the arrowhead that wasn't hardly ever wrong. Them flyboys was okay.

In two places we found river ferries that we put into service and to hell with their owners. They was both of the long rope kind that Count Conrad invented years ago. In both places I put two of my men ashore to work them, since a civilian couldn't be trusted not to run. Not one of those four men lived. They stuck to their jobs till they was all killed. Let me tell you their names. They were Ivan Torunski and his brother Wladyclaw, and John Sobinski and Vlad Tchernic. Good men, every one of them.

That was all we could do for them refugees, though. Lift them across and give them a map showing where they was and where the safe forts was. Maybe some of them made it alive.

We'd been telling people for years that noncombatants should evacuate by the first of February, handed out leaflets and wrote magazine articles, but the fools wouldn't move until they was burned out and half of them was dead. But you can't let a kid die just 'cause his folks are dumb!

Then half the idiots would want to ferry their cow across, too, when there wasn't hardly room for the people! But doctrine was to leave the animals for the Mongols to eat, cause if they couldn't get animals, them bastards would eat humans!

Our own people was out of there long before that. The inns and depots was long closed down except for the radios. The baron had called for volunteers to man the forward radios so we would know where the enemy was. Almost all of those people, half of them women, stayed at their posts. Sometimes there was some last words, sometimes not. Usually we found out that a site had been taken when the radio went off the air.

When we got to East Gate, Count Conrad was waiting for us.

FROM THE DIARY OF CONRAD STARGARD

On the last day of February, we seemed to be ready. We had to be, for we were moving out at dawn. The new troops hadn't been given the graduation ceremony that all the other classes had gotten. There was simply no way that we could have scheduled that many men to do the hillside vigil. The halo effect didn't happen that often in the wintertime, and anyway, these men weren't being knighted. With only four months of training, and all of it physical training, they just weren't ready for it.

But every one of them was armored and armed, and they knew how to use those arms. Their equipment had been inspected hundreds of times, as had the contents of their war carts. They had spares, bedding, food for a month, and a ton of ammunition in each cart.

That afternoon, people were running to me with scores of last minute problems, things that should have been done earlier, or things that should have been done without my knowledge. I think that everyone else's nerves were about as shot as mine, and they all wanted stroking. Well, I wanted it too, and I wasn't getting it either. I was growling at people.

At this point I got a surprise visit by two priests. They spoke Italian and Latin. I spoke Polish and Modern English. I don't even understand how they got in to see me, but I had them sit in the outer office and had a runner find Father Thomas Aquinas. Maybe he could figure out what they wanted.

Fifteen trivial problems later I was getting ready to start chewing holes in my desk. At this point Father Thomas came in.

"It's the Inquisition," he said. "Was there an inquisition being held concerning you?"

Good God in Heaven! Nine and a half years had gone by since the thing had started, and they had to pick today of all days to show up.

"Yes," I said, "but it concerns something that happened long ago. Ask them what I can do for them."

They talked a while in hesitant Latin, their arms stiffly at their sides. Then they seemed to discover that they all spoke Italian and the conversation speeded up considerably, and their arms started waving. They brought out a thick sheaf of parchment, but wouldn't let Father Thomas see it. They handed it to me. I looked it over. It was all in Latin.

"They want you to read this and say if it is the truth," the Father said.

"Tell them that I'm sorry, but I don't speak Latin. I don't read it or write it, either."

They looked sheepishly at each other as Father Thomas translated what I had said. There was more conversation, and I finally got the idea that they weren't allowed to tell Father Thomas what the case was about. They couldn't tell it to the interpreter and they couldn't speak my language. And it hadn't occurred to the silly twits until now that they might have a problem!

They argued between themselves for quite a while, mostly in what had to be unfinished questions, for there were a lot of pregnant silences and glaring eyes. I didn't know whether to laugh or to cry, but I figured that either one could get me into trouble, so I just hung in there. Finally, they came up with what they thought was a suitable question, but maybe it didn't translate well.

"What do you think is the truth of the matter in which you might think we are talking of?"

I had to puzzle that out a bit. Then I said, "If this is concerning the matter that I think it might be about, I regret to inform you that I made a solemn oath to Father Ignacy, who is now the Bishop of Cracow, in which I vowed to discuss the matter with absolutely no one. I therefore can't answer what I think might be your question."

I had to repeat that three times before Father Thomas dared make a stab at translating it. Even then, they talked a long time in Italian before they got back to me.

Father Thomas looked at me and said, "I think what they want to ask you is 'What should we do now?'"

"Tell them that they should talk the matter over with his

excellency, the Bishop of Cracow. Draw them a nice map. Use small words and big letters. Point them on the road and wish them well."

"Yes, sir."

The clergy left and I got back to work. With any luck, the twits would run into a Mongol patrol and the next bunch the Church sent, in another ten years, might have some of the brains that God surely had intended to give them!

We formed up at dawn on the morning of March first, the training completed. A hundred fifty thousand men stood at attention on the great concrete parade ground.

I nodded to a priest, who said a quick mass without a sermon. Few of the men could have heard him, anyway. Then I nodded to Baron Vladimir, Hetman of the Army, and he led the troops in the oath that I had cribbed years ago from that of the Boy Scouts. It was fitting. Many of these troops weren't much older than Boy Scouts.

We raised our right arms to the rising sun, and a sixth of a million men chanted with me:

"On my honor, I will do my best to do my duty to God and to the Army. I will obey the Warrior's Code, and I will keep myself physically fit, mentally alert, and morally straight.

"The Warrior's Code:

"A warrior is: Trustworthy, Loyal, and Reverent. Courteous, Kind, and Fatherly. Obedient, Cheerful, and Efficient. Brave, Clean, and Deadly."

Hearing that many men chant it, well, there was quite a difference from that first class of thirty-six men we graduated four years ago.

"Hetman," I said, "advance the army!"

Vladimir raised his voice and shouted to his three kolomels, "Kolumns, advance!"

And the three kolomels, the Banki brothers, turned to their eighteen barons and shouted, "Battalions, advance!"

And eighteen barons turned to a hundred komanders and shouted, "Komands, advance!"

And a hundred komanders turned to six hundred captains and shouted, "Companies, advance!"

And six hundred captains turned to thirty-six hundred banners and shouted, "Platoons, advance!"

And thirty-six hundred banners turned to twenty-one thousand knights and shouted, "Lances, advance!"

And twenty-one thousand knights turned to a hundred twenty-six thousand warriors and shouted, "Warriors, advance!"

And a hundred twenty-six thousand warriors shouted, "Yes, sir!"

It made a nice ceremony with a good crescendo effect. It would have been nicer if we could all have swung out right then and there, but of course there were the war carts. The men marched out to them, and the first few hundred were already on the tracks, but it was almost noon before the last cart went out the gate. Not that the departure was disorganized, far from it. We were double-tracked and the men moved out at a quick march, but it takes time for thirty-six hundred big carts to move down a pair of tracks. The column was sixteen miles long.

Yet once moving, they didn't stop. Early on, we had found that eighteen armored men could easily tow a war cart filled with their arms and supplies, and with the rest of the platoon riding on it, so long as it was a railroad track. A cook stove was slung from the back of the cart, and three cooks could keep the men fed. There was room for the other half of the platoon to sack out on top of the cart or to be slung from hammocks below it. Working three hours marching and three hours resting, they could go on indefinitely, making six dozen miles a day without ever breaking into double-time. Most caravans were happy to do two dozen miles, and few conventional military columns could do that! Actually, providing we could stay on the rails, we could probably outrun the Mongols. Providing.

I sat on Anna, watching them go out the gate. There was a big crowd outside cheering them on, dependents and refugees who were waiting to move into Hell as we left. Odds were that they were cheering more because we had vacated the premises than because we were going out against the enemy. Some of those people had been out there in the snow for days.

But there were others whose job it was to worry about those left behind. My job was with the riverboats. I was about to leave for it when a strange company of troops came up. I say strange because they were out of uniform. They had turbans wrapped around their helmets. Then I spotted Zoltan sitting on one of the carts. I went up to him and rode by his side.

"Zoltan, what the hell are you doing here?"

"Doing, sir? Why, I am riding off to war against my ancient enemies, the Mongols! We have many old scores to settle with them as you would say. And you must not call me Zoltan, sir. Not here. Now I am Captain Varanian of the two-tendy-eighth."

"But I never said that you could join the army! This is a Christian army!"

"True, my lord, but you never said that we couldn't, either. As to the Christians, we are not prejudiced, and we keep to our own company in any event."

"There's a whole company of you? How is that possible? Eight years ago there were only fifty men in your band, and no children. How can there be two hundred fifty of you now?"

"Oh, the word spread of your generosity and our security under your protection, my lord. Others of my people who were scattered over the world came to us in ones and twos and what could we do? Could we send them back to the cold and cruel world? So we took them in, even as you took us in. And now they repay you, with their lives, perhaps."

"I thought that there were only a hundred families of you."

"From Urgench yes, my lord. But there were many other cities in Khareshmia that is no more. Is it not enough that we join you in this Holy War?"

"Yes, I suppose it is, Captain. Carry on." I just hoped the Church never got wind of it.

The last company in line were specialists in cart repair, set up to get stragglers back on the road. Once they went by, Anna and I rode the trail beside the track and the men cheered us the whole way. I smiled and waved at them until my arm got sore, then switched arms. Good. Morale couldn't be better.

Halfway to East Gate, we passed the first of them, and Anna went over to the track. She said it was easier to run on the wood than on the ground. Springier.

I got there to find the RB1 *Muddling Through* just rounding the bend with the RB14 *Hotspur* right beyond her. There were also three companies of troops waiting to board them. They hadn't heard about the loss of the RB23 *The Pride of Bytom*, so I told the captain of the company that had been assigned to it that he would have to join up with the regular army. His boat ride was gone.

I turned to Anna.

"Well, girl, this is where we part company for a while."

She gave me an "I don't like this" posture.

"Now don't start that again! We talked this over weeks ago. There wouldn't be anything you could do on a boat but take up space. Baron Vladimir needs your help. You like Vladimir, don't you?"

She nodded YES, but sulkily.

"I know you don't want to leave me. I don't want to leave you either, but this is the sensible thing to do. Look, give me a hug."

I hugged her neck, her chin pressed firmly to my back.

"Anna, you know I've loved you since we first met. You've always been my best friend, and no matter what happens, you always will be."

She signaled "ME TOO." I felt a tear forming.

"Good. Now be off with you, love, and take good care of Vladimir! I love you!"

She galloped back west.

Captainette Lubinski, the woman commanding East Gate, came out to report to me.

"We have over twenty thousand people in there, sir. I tell you that they're stacked up to the stone rafters! We can't possibly take any more!"

"Then don't," I said. "There's plenty of room in Hell. Send all the newcomers there."

"But everybody wants to be in here!" she said. "They've all heard that this fort is invincible."

"It just might be. But there is a limit as to how many people it can hold. You'll just have to shut your gates and tell them to walk another day to Hell. It's the only thing you can do! Oh, give them some food and water, of course, but send them on their way!"

"Yes, sir, but some of them—"

"But nothing, Captainette! It's not what *they* want that counts! It's what *we* can possibly do! You have your orders. Dismissed."

She was crumbling already, and the battle hadn't even started. I wondered if I should replace her, but I didn't know any of the other women here well enough to pick her replacement. Maybe she'd be all right.

The boats pulled up to the dock and their front drawbridges went down. They must have been carrying a thousand refugees each.

"Send those people on their way to the Warrior's School!" I shouted to the troops standing around. "There's no room for them here!"

Baron Piotr had gotten there before me, and he had his crew organized. He was to run Tartar Control, our command and control center, acting as my chief of staff. He only had two dozen radio operators and clerks under him, but in fact he would be running the Battle for the Vistula—under my occasional direction, of course.

The RB1 *Muddling Through* was a command boat, the only one we had. It had six radios instead of the usual one, so we could cover all the frequencies that we used without retuning. It had an operations center with a big situation map, plus bedroom space for all the extra people. Aside from that, it was just another steamboat.

It was late afternoon by the time the boats had taken on more coal and supplies, loaded the troops, and headed downstream. As we left, two other boats were coming up to replenish their coal. I gave their masters a chewing out over the radio for being so bunched up.

RB1 EG TO RB18 EG AND RB26 EG. WHAT ARE YOU?
TWO WOMEN WHO MUST HOLD HANDS ON THE WAY
TO THE POTTY? THE NEXT TIME I SEE YOU SO CLOSE
TOGETHER, I WILL PERSONALLY DRESS BOTH OF YOUR
BOAT'S MASTERS IN BUNNY SUITS! CONRAD. OUT.

Our range being as short as it was, the rules were that any boat between the sender and the receiver should relay the message onward. In this case, where all units concerned were at the same location, it shouldn't have been relayed at all, but the substance of the message was such that I knew the radio operators would send it the full length of the line, which is what I wanted.

Doctrine was that the boats should be evenly spaced. We had three-gross miles of river to patrol, upstream and down, with three dozen boats. They should have been two dozen miles apart!

We got on the radios and had all boats report their positions and headings. If they bunched up, that meant long stretches of the river weren't being patrolled. It also meant that boats might be so far apart that radio messages between them might not be received, and that could cut our communication lines in half. We put markers on a map and started getting things organized. By midnight, we had schedules for all of them, where they should be at what time, assuming they weren't involved with refugees or Mongols. Even then, they were supposed to try to make up the time, since the schedule had them moving at only half speed.

At dawn, the RB9 *Lady of Cracow* reported a heavy enemy concentration across the river from Sandomierz. I told them to make a three-mile switchback, letting them hit the concentration three times. They complained vigorously when I ordered them to continue the patrol, but the RB20 *Wastrel* would be on station in minutes to take over the load.

The next four boats by there did the same, while we saw only scattered patrols. I wasn't going to let a bunch of boatmasters, excited at their first contact with the enemy, upset our schedules! As long as we could keep the bastards on the east side of the river, we'd get them all eventually.

But when we got near Sandomierz, I saw that they hadn't been exaggerating a bit. Through my telescope, I could see the Mongols had troops thirty deep along the shoreline. More importantly, at the shoreline men and horses were piled five and six high, and dead! There must have been twenty thousand dead along that sector of river, but they kept on coming. The riverboats were earning their pay!

Chapter Fifteen

I ran below decks and told Piotr to order the closest dozen boats to join the fun. We could just cruise up and down, raking them with everything we had except the flamethrowers, which had to be reserved for bridges.

That done, I opened the hatch to go back up on deck. A dozen Mongol arrows flew in at me! Four stuck in my armor and by the time I had them pulled out, I had been hit two more times. But I wasn't hurt. That armor really worked! So I ignored the arrows and pressed on.

On deck, the men looked like pincushions and were laughing about it. The deck itself was so filled with arrows that you couldn't take a single step without breaking some. Tadaos had the boat running a few dozen yards from shore, letting them hit us but making sure that we couldn't miss!

I saw a warrior go down with an arrow in his eyeslit; and another man take his place at the gun before the first had hit the floor. But the medics were right there and there wasn't anything I could do. Men running up ammunition moved with a skating motion that broke off the arrows so they wouldn't have to step on them.

The noise was deafening. Both starboard peashooters were firing without letup, throwing six hundred rounds a minute into an almost solid mass of Mongol troops. Those iron balls had about the ballistics of a carbine bullet. When they hit a man, he was wounded or dead, armor or no armor. Shooting into that tangled mass, I don't see how any of them could possibly have missed.

The sides of the boat were two and a half stories high, with smooth surfaces so they couldn't be climbed. But I saw a Mongol try to get in by grabbing on to the paddle wheel. I got my sword out, but before I could swing, the man was killed by one of the arrows flying at us. His body continued around and back into the water. I sent a runner to get a dozen men with pikes to guard the rear railing, and watched it until they arrived.

The Halmans were chunking away, and Tadaos was aiming one himself, laughing and shouting with every round that exploded above the mass. It was good shooting and better loading, because the loader had to time the fuse so that it exploded just above the heads of the enemy. Too high or too low and much of the effect was lost. The millions of rounds expended in training were paying dividends. Mongols were dying in droves.

The gunners from our boat's company of troops had their three dozen swivel guns set up on deck, adding joyfully to the carnage. Their rounds were far more powerful than those of the peashooters. You could see rows of three and four horsemen go down, all killed by the same bullet!

I'd heard that in modern battles, a quarter-million rounds are fired for every enemy killed. We were averaging considerably better! In fact, I never saw anybody miss!

And everything we were doing was soon multiplied by twelve, since the men in the other boats weren't acting like old maids either!

Any sane army would have run away from us, but these people weren't that sane. A modern army might have dug in, but that hadn't occurred to these horsemen, and with luck, it never would.

I could imagine Mongol commanders in the rear hearing about the slaughter and not believing it! I could imagine them sending observer after observer forward and not having any come back.

Or better yet, going forward to see for themselves what the racket was and doing a bit of dying of their own!

It was likely, since our gunners always went after anyone who wore a fancy outfit or looked like he was giving orders. Besides a loader, each gunner had an observer whose job it was to point out good targets, and a boat gunner's helmet had "ears" on it pointing backward so he could hear what was being shouted at him.

After a few miles of this, we started running out of Mongols, so Tadaos had the boat turned around and we went upstream for some more gleeful mayhem. The troops quickly remounted their swivel guns on the port railing and reloaded. There were so many arrows stuck to the inside of the port parapet that they had to get out their axes and clear away the gun ports before they could mount their weapons! The men on the port peashooters, who had been dying of frustration up to this point, got ready to get their inning in.

The RB7 *Invincible* was coming downstream at us, followed closely by the RB12 *Insufferable*, so we had to stay a little farther out in the channel and try not to shoot holes in them.

The sun was well up now, and shining in our eyes, but we didn't need accurate shooting at this point, we just needed shooting! Even at a gross yards, we could hardly miss that mass of enemy troops.

I went to the starboard side and looked over. Since it was only sheet metal over wood, there were thousands of arrows stuck in the ship's armor. But I guess we had judged the metal gauge right, since none of them penetrated all the way.

On the opposite shore, people on the walls of Sandomierz were waving at us, cheering us on. But sightseeing, I wasn't doing my job. I turned to go back down to the control room when a plane flew over. One of the oversized message arrows thunked into the deck. I picked it up myself and waved at the pilot. He wagged his wings and flew off.

Downstairs, I read the message.

"Praty gud!" it read. "Bot they mak a bridge 7 mil downstream of U. Lambert." So Count Lambert was finally learning how to read and write! A pity about his spelling, though.

I checked the situation board and found that we had no boats between Sieciechow and Sandomierz. There should have been, but nobody nearby wanted to miss out on the action here. I sent a message to Tadaos to turn downstream again and radioed RB17 *The Ghost of St. Joseph* to follow us.

The RB21 *Calypso* reported that another concentration of Mongols west of Brzesko had been spotted by a plane, and wanted to turn back and investigate. With the planes flying, we really didn't have to keep up a steady watch for breakthroughs from the boats. Permission granted.

As we proceeded downriver, it was soon obvious what Lambert had seen. Along the shore, a long line of small boats was being lashed together, gunwale to gunwale, and ropes and logs were being fastened on top of them to form a roadway. All the boats on the east bank were supposed to have been destroyed, but I guess that hadn't happened. Once completed, they would swing that pontoon bridge into the current and fasten it to the opposite shore. At least that looked to be their plan.

I called for Captain Targ, who commanded the company of troops we had on board.

"I need three platoons with axes," I said.

"Good, sir. The boys down below have been looking for something to do. It's no fun for them, sitting there while everybody else gets to play," he said, grinning.

"Such a rough life. Bow landing, you know the drill. And move some of your gunners up to the bow."

"Aye, aye, sir."

Piotr sent a message to RB17 *The Ghost of St. Joseph* to get their troops ready to take out the downstream half of the bridge. I went to Tadaos, who was pulling Mongol arrows from his deck and saving them.

"Most of these are long enough for me to shoot," he said. "I suppose you'll be wanting the flamethrower warmed up."

"No, we do this one with axes," I said. "We'll give it one pass to soften them up, then we put some troops ashore at the middle and cover them as we go upstream. The *Ghost* will take the first half of it."

"You sure about that, sir? I think now's the time for the flame-throwers."

"It's a little late to change things. I've already given orders to the *Ghost*."

"As you will, sir."

We'd drilled this maneuver last summer, but most of the men were new. The knights had been through it, though, and that should be enough.

We went into them with our escort right on our tail. This bunch of Mongols hadn't been fired on before, I think, because they didn't seem to take us very seriously until we opened fire. Then it was a little late for them.

The river embankment was twenty yards from the shore and pretty high just here, higher than the boat, actually, and not too many of the Mongols made it over the top. A few tried to outrun us, and we were going pretty slow, but not quite *that* slow. There wasn't much for the *Ghost* to clean up.

We made a U-turn and headed back to the middle. Of course, playing administrator was about as frustrating as sitting below, waiting for something to happen. As we approached our touch-down point, I decided *what the hell!* and ran down to join the landing party. It had been years since I had swung a sword in earnest, and rank hath its privileges.

I slipped the lanyard of my sword over my wrist as I approached Captain Targ.

"Do you have room for an extra man?" I said.

"Always room for one more! Or eighty more, for that matter."

"I see. All six platoons, huh?"

"I left the gunners up top, but we're so low on ammunition that they don't need loaders or spotters. They can take their time because they don't have enough bullets to shoot fast anyway."

"But surely you had the standard thirty-six thousand rounds in your carts," I said.

"Maybe a mite more than that, sir, but we just did one hell of a lot of shooting. We're down to a gross rounds per gun right now, and that's counting the boat's stores besides our own."

"I didn't realize consumption was that high. We should have conserved ammunition."

"What for, sir? We couldn't have used it better than we did! When every round kills an enemy or three, they're doing what they were made for!"

Before I could reply, the boat touched the shore and the front drawbridge dropped. We all rushed out and through the knee-deep freezing mud. What with my goose-down padding and all the excitement, I'd forgotten how cold it was. We started chopping up boats, lashings and any Mongols that showed signs of wanting to be alive.

The guns above were ready to give us covering fire, but it wasn't needed. Those few of the enemy who had gone over the hill were still going.

The captain and I were at the end of the line going out, and there wasn't much for us to do as we walked slowly along the riverbank, keeping even with the paddle wheel of the boat. The two hundred men in front of us were chopping everything up into tooth picks and hamburger. One of the troops ahead of us stopped to cut the purse off one of the Mongol dead, and this annoyed Captain Targ.

"Hey, you asshole! You know the doctrine! We don't pick up loot until the battle's over!"

As a general thing, he was right, of course. Countless medieval battles had been lost because the troops had stopped to loot instead of staying in formation. Our rules were that we didn't loot until afterward, and then all loot was divided up evenly, no matter who did the looting. But first you had to win, dammit!

But just now, there wasn't any enemy opposition and we really didn't have enough to do.

"Captain, maybe he's right. Detail a platoon to take the Mongol purses. Tell them not to bother with weapons and jewelry, but let's see what we get," I said.

"Done, sir. Blue platoon only! Start looting! Purses only! Pass the word!"

While he was giving orders, I picked up one of the purses myself. It was full of silver and gold, almost half and half, and must have weighed four pounds! I was holding everything this bastard had been able to steal in three years of looting Russia! Yet in a way, it made sense. While he was pillaging, he had to carry everything he gained with him. It wasn't as though there was a bank he could have deposited it in.

Doing some crude mental calculations, we must have killed a half-million Mongols this morning! If every one of them had two pounds of gold on him, that was ... well, given a fifty-to-one exchange rate, silver to gold, and a six-to-one rate, zinc to silver, that was ... more than I could work out in my head. But maybe I shouldn't have worried so much about the deflated currency. If something wasn't done, we were about to see one bodacious inflation!

I picked up eight more purses and was musing on this when all hell shut down for payday.

Chapter Sixteen

I saw my error as soon as it happened. The riverbank being taller than the boat, our gunners couldn't see over it. They didn't see the horde that was coming until it was on top of us. I should have put observers up there. To add to our problems, while our helmets offered excellent protection, you couldn't tilt your head back in them. The helmet and beaver clamped into a ring around the collar of the breast and back plates. The helmet could turn sideways, but not up and down. The only way to look up was to tilt your whole body. Most people rarely look up in any event.

I think the reason that we weren't all killed was that the Mongols stopped at the top of the embankment to let off a flight of arrows. This got our attention.

It also got me an arrow in the eye.

I staggered back, scattering the gold and silver I'd picked up, tripping over the wreckage of the pontoon bridge and falling into the freezing mud. For a moment, I couldn't figure put what happened, except that I couldn't see out of my right eye, and my left was blurry. The pain came a bit later.

I struggled to get up, but kept falling back into the slippery wreckage. I could hear the shouting and fighting around me, the peashooters and the swivel guns firing, but I couldn't seem to get untangled. I broke off the damn arrow and could see with my left eye. I guess it was only that the shaft was in the way.

I was on my left side, and suddenly I was surrounded by legs and boots. But those weren't army uniforms! I tried again to get up and something unseen bashed into me, knocking me down again into deeper water and mud. I fumbled for my pistol, brought it up and aimed at a huge gold belt buckle a yard away. The gun fired, but what with the slippery mud and all, it flew from my hand. There wasn't time to reload it anyway.

Someone slammed into my side and we went down in a heap. I managed to get hold of my sword, which was still tied to my wrist, rolled over onto my knees and jabbed someone with red pants in the groin. He went down, but I got another bash on the back of the head from somewhere. But while that helmet restricted visibility, it sure protected you! I don't know how many times that ring around my collar saved my life.

Then I heard an army rallying cry! I saw three pairs of red pants go down as a group and then suddenly I was being lifted up into the air by strong arms under each of my armpits.

"Can you walk, sir?" It was Captain Targ.

"I think so. How goes the battle?"

"Time for a strategic withdrawal, sir. Or in nonmilitary parlance, let's run away!"

"Okay. But don't leave any of our men behind! Not even if you know they're dead!"

"Right sir. Standard doctrine. Fall back to the boat! Don't leave our own men! Pick up our dead! Pass the word!"

The gunners above us were keeping most of the enemy from getting to us, but there wasn't anything they could do about those already on top of us. We were hard-pressed to keep up any sort of line, and in that damned mud, a saber had the advantage over a rapier. You couldn't get enough traction to lunge!

Fortunately, most of our men had axes and I had my sword. It was only the captain and his knights who had serious problems.

With only one eye, I still did my share. I think I must have killed a half dozen of the bastards, taking a dozen hits that would have killed me had I been wearing lesser armor. The stuff got in the way, but it was worth it.

In minutes, we weren't fighting in the mud anymore. We were fighting on top of the enemy dead, and that's treacherous footing. The Mongol sabers bounced off our armor, but many of them were armed with a spear that had a long, thin, triangular point, and that thing was a killer! Carried by a man on the run, or thrown at short range, they could punch right through our armor, and most of our serious casualties were caused by them.

Yet discipline and training held true for us. Our lines tightened up, our dead and wounded were put aboard and soon we were safe. I was next to the last man off the shore, and I would have been the last, except for the captain.

"My honors, sir. This is my company, and I'll be the last man off!"

He'd earned it, so I clambered aboard and let him follow me.

As Tadaos pulled the boat away from the shore, a medic took me inside and I was the last man to be hustled up to sick bay, even though I wanted to see what was going on topside. Medics have no respect for the wishes of a wounded man. They're all mother hens who are convinced that they know best.

He got my helmet off and *tsk-tsk*ed at my right eye.

"Have I lost it?" I said.

"No, sir, it missed the eyeball. But it stuck in the bone just to the right of it. You're going to have a scar, I'm afraid, but you'll see again. You were lucky."

"I would have been a damn sight luckier if the arrow had missed!"

"There is that, sir."

"Well, open that surgeon's kit! Get the arrowhead out, clean the wound, and sew it up! Didn't they teach you anything in medic's school?"

"I never sewed up an eye before, sir. In fact, I've never sewn up anything but dead animals in training."

"Well, boy, now's your chance to learn! First, wash your hands in white lightning, and then wash around the wound as best you can."

"Yes, sir."

After a bit, I said, "You got that done? Then get the pliers out of your kit and pull the arrowhead out. Better get somebody to hold my head still. It'll hurt, and I might flinch."

"You, sir? Never!"

"I said get somebody to hold my head and stop acting like I'm God! That's an order!"

"Yes, sir. You're not God. Hey, Lezek! Give me a hand! Hold his head!"

"Now the pliers," I said.

I don't know if I yelled or not, but I saw the most incredible visual display and I think I might have blacked out for a few moments.

"It's out, sir," he said, holding the bloody thing so I could see it with my good eye. The right one still wasn't working, somehow.

"Good. Throw it away. That kind of souvenir I don't need. Now get a pair of tweezers and feel around in the wound for any bits of broken bone or any foreign matter."

This time, I know I screamed. Having somebody feeling around inside of your head without anesthetics is no fun at all!

But he took his time at it and seemed to take out a few chunks of something. I wanted to tell him to leave *some* of the skull behind, but I thought better of it. I couldn't see what was happening and so I had to trust to the kid's judgment.

"I think that's all of it, sir."

"Thank God! Now, clean it all out again with white lightning. Pour it right in."

By now, the area was getting numb, and I didn't scream. I wanted to, you understand, but I could hold it in.

"Okay. Now get out your sterile needle and thread and sew it up. Use nice neat little stitches, because if my wife doesn't like the job you did, she will make your life not worth living. Believe me. I know the woman."

"Yes, sir. Try not to wince so much. It makes it hard to line the edges up."

"I'll try."

He put nine stitches in there. I counted.

"That's it, sir."

"Well, bandage it up then, with some peat-bog moss next to the wound!"

"Yes, sir."

Without adhesive tape, the thing had to be held on by wrapping gauze around my head and under my chin.

When he was done, I sat up.

"Well. Good job, I hope. Thank you, but now you better get around to the other men who were wounded."

He looked around the room. "No sir, I think the surgeons have taken care of everybody."

"The surgeons!" I yelled. "Then what the hell are you?"

"Me, sir? I'm an assistant corpsman."

"Then what the hell were you doing operating on my head?"

"But, you ordered me to, sir! It was a direct order from my commanding officer! What was I supposed to do? Disobey you?"

"Then what were you doing with a surgeon's kit?"

"Oh, they had extra of those at the warehouse, sir, so they handed them out to some of the corpsmen, just in case."

"They just handed it to you?"

"Yes, sir. It's nice to know what some of these things are for."

I found I couldn't wear my arming hat over the bandage, but I could get the helmet on.

Before I could leave the sick bay, the chief surgeon came up to me, his armor hacked in a dozen places. I could see by the insignia and the fact that he carried a mace rather than a sword that the equally battered man standing next to the chief surgeon was the company chaplain. In any modern army, both of these positions would have been given noncombatant status, but in ours, every man was a warrior. This Sir Majinski was banner of the orange platoon, besides his medical duties.

"The butcher's bill, sir," he said.

I looked at it. Eleven dead. Twenty-ten seriously wounded, and I wasn't on that list. Fifty-one with minor wounds. Had I done it Tadaos's way, with flamethrowers, these men would all be alive and sound.

"Sorry about the incident with the corpsman, sir. I kept an eye on him while he was working on you, but I had a man with a sucking chest wound on my table, and I thought I might be able to save him. But the corpsman meant well, and he did a fair job."

"Well, give the corpsman my apologies. The man with the chest wound, could you save him?"

"No."

I checked in with Tartar Control. The battle near Brzesko was up to three boats now, and the battle across from Sandomierz was still raging, with a dozen boats still butchering Mongols. But it wasn't the same dozen. That group, out of ammunition, was heading back upstream to East Gate to rearm. I knew the supplies we had there and it wasn't going to be enough.

In the history books I read when I was a boy, some said that the Mongols had invaded with a million men. Others said that this was impossible, that the logistics of the time couldn't have supported more than fifty thousand. But if the estimates that I'd made and those I was getting from the other boats were anything like correct, we had killed more than a half a million Mongols in the first morning of the attack! Furthermore, they showed no signs of thinning out! In any event, the numbers involved were so much higher than I had expected that I had vastly underestimated the ammunition requirements.

On the other hand, they were showing absolutely none of the tactical brilliance that they were supposedly famous for and that I had feared. So far, they were easier to kill than dumb animals. Not that they could be expected to stay that dumb.

Then too, some of my actions had been pretty dumb as well, and it was my duty to see that my last set of stupid mistakes was not repeated.

> RB1 TO ALL UNITS. WE HAVE ENGAGED THE ENEMY IN HAND-TO-HAND COMBAT AND LEARNED THE FOLLOWING:
>
> 1. WHEN PATROLLING A RIVERSHORE ON FOOT, PLACE MEN AS OBSERVERS ON TOP OF THE RIVERBANK TO WATCH FOR ENEMY COUNTERATTACKS.
> 2. ENEMY HAND WEAPONS ARE LARGELY INEFFECTIVE EXCEPT FOR A SPEAR WITH A LONG, THIN, TRIANGULAR POINT. THIS WEAPON IS CAPABLE OF PENETRATING OUR ARMOR WHEN CARRIED AT A RUN OR THROWN.
> 3. WHEN FIGHTING ON RIVER MUD, THE RAPIER IS NOT EFFECTIVE DUE TO THE LACK OF TRACTION DURING A LUNGE. OFFICERS ARE ADVISED TO ARM THEMSELVES WITH AXES UNDER THESE CIRCUMSTANCES.
> 4. WHEN TAKING OUT A PONTOON BRIDGE BEING CONSTRUCTED ON A RIVERSHORE, FLAMETHROWERS ARE MORE EFFECTIVE THAN AXES.
> GOOD HUNTING—CONRAD.
> OUT.

Was that worth the deaths of eleven men? Or the maiming of dozens of others? I swear that I was never meant to be a battle commander.

But something had to be done about the ammunition situation, and there was only one place to get more ammo. Our other units. We sent out radio messages ordering all units to send one-sixth of their swivel gun ammunition to East Gate, and for the Odra boats to send three-quarters of their peashooter and Halman ammunition in addition to this. I hated to strip the other units, but as the captain said, the ammunition couldn't possibly be spent better than it was right here.

I also ordered that all reloading equipment and supplies be transported from Three Walls to East Gate, along with any ladies who knew how to operate it.

I went back up on deck. We were heading upstream again to the fighting at Sandomierz.

"How did the battle go, Baron Tadaos?"

"Well, sir, since we was out to destroy the bridge, I guess you have to say we won. It's gone."

"We got the whole thing chopped up?"

"The *Ghost* did all right, but it wasn't attacked. We only got about half of our half done. But after we pulled out, the *Ghost* took out the last quarter with a flamethrower. That bridge burned real good. So did the Mongols."

Captain Targ came up. "It was quite a show, sir. Mongols don't like burning to death. A lot of them jumped into the water and drowned in preference to it."

"A good thing to know. Captain Targ, you saved my life today. If you hadn't killed the Mongols around me and pulled me out of that wreckage, I'd be a dead man. I owe you."

"No sir, you don't. I was just paying an old debt."

"Debt? What debt? Should I know you from somewhere?"

"I didn't expect you to recognize me, sir. You only saw me once and that was in the dark, plus I was only ten years old at the time. But I'd hoped you would remember my name."

"I'm sorry, but I still draw a blank."

"My father told me that if I could do you some personal service, I should tell you that once you threw bread on the waters, and that it has come back to you tenfold. Well, it isn't really tenfold. If I've saved your life, well, you once saved the lives of my entire family."

"I remember now. When I first got to this country, I was lost in a snowstorm, and your father let me in to the warmth of his fire. Doing that saved my life, I think."

"Perhaps, sir. But the next summer, my father's fields were flattened by a hailstorm. We would have starved to death that next winter except you came by and gave him a purse of silver. So now perhaps that debt is paid."

"In full, with compound interest, Captain. There were two of you boys, weren't there?"

"Yes, sir. Wladyclaw is a banner with the elevendy-third."

"And the rest of your family. Are they well?"

"Yes, sir, or at least they were as of a month ago. But my father wouldn't evacuate and that region is probably overrun by the Mongols now. There's no telling what's happened."

"I'll pray for them." It was all I could say.

Chapter Seventeen

"What are those things?" Tadaos said, as we cruised by the fighting near Sandomierz. What with the restrictions on ammunition, we were shooting now only on the closer, downstream leg of the circuit. We had ammunition left for one pass, so we wanted to spend it well.

"Darned if I know," I said. There were four of them, and they looked sort of like big door frames without the doors or the walls, either. They were maybe three stories tall, and had a sort of teeter-totter mounted on the cross beam. Ropes seemed to be coming from where each seat should have been.

"Maybe they make a playground for giants," Captain Targ joked.

We got our answer shortly when fully two gross men picked up ropes that were hanging from the near end of one of the teeter-totters and pulled, all at once. A rock bigger than a man flew in an incredibly high arc, and landed a few dozen yards upstream of us, kicking up a cold, drenching spray.

"It's some kind of Mongol trebuchet," the captain said.

"They could be big trouble if they get the range right," Tadaos said.

"True," I said. "Captain, have your men target on those catapults, once we get in close."

"Right, sir."

Another rock came flying, and another. The rate of fire on those catapults was remarkable. They were shooting as fast as they could drag up rocks!

They were set up on a hill for better elevation, and they were shooting at us from three gross yards away without difficulty. I had the feeling that their ultimate range might be a good deal more.

A second one got into action as we turned in to make our run.

Then a huge rock crashed into RB4 *The River Belle*, directly in front of us. Three more fell into the beach area right on top of the Mongol troops, but that didn't slow their rate of fire. It was as though they didn't care if they took casualties!

Tadaos and I were on the foredeck as I watched through my telescope. He was out of Halman bombs, and there wasn't a good target for his Molotov cocktails, so he had his bow out. He'd scrounged hundreds of Mongol arrows and was politely returning them to their rightful owners.

Our troops opened fire on the catapults about the time that the other boats started to take them seriously. The Mongols had to be close together to pull simultaneously, and bunched up like that they were dog meat for the swivel guns. Chunks of wood went flying from the uprights as well.

"It looks like it was a paper tiger," I said.

"Yeah, until they get brains enough to mount them things on the other side of the hill," Tadaos said. "Oh, shit."

"What?" I said, still looking through my telescope.

There was a huge crash and the deck bounced under me, throwing me off balance, tumbling me to the deck. I looked to my left and there was a yard-wide hole in the deck right next to me, right where Tadaos had been standing.

"Tadaos!" I shouted.

"Yes, sir?" he said from my right.

"My God! I thought you were dead."

"I saw it coming in time."

"Then why didn't you warn me?"

"There wasn't much time, and you was safe enough where you was. Could of been trouble if you moved."

Then a grappling hook with a leather rope attached came flying at me. It caught on the parapet, between two merlons. I got my sword out in time to lean over and slash open the face of a man who was climbing up the side of the boat.

"Captain! Get all your men on deck!"

"They're learning," Tadaos shouted as he drew his sword from over his left shoulder. "They're maybe a little slow, but they're learning."

Four platoons of troops ran up on deck and fended off what turned out to be a concerted boarding attempt. Once, the Mongols actually made it on deck, and had to be expelled with a pike charge. Things were interesting for a while, but then Tadaos came to me.

"We can handle things up here, sir, but I'm worried about that hole in the bottom. That rock went right through, you know."

"Well, I guess I am the best man for that job," I said. After all, I'd designed these boats. Who better to fix one? So I changed hats from battle commander to steamboat repairman.

That rock had gone through the top deck, through a double bunk on the middle deck, through the middle deck, through the cargo deck and through the bottom a half yard below that! I had the feeling that if it had hit me on the way, I wouldn't even have slowed it down!

The most serious damage was to the bottom, of course, and even that wasn't catastrophic. The volume between the cargo deck and the bottom was cut into dozens of watertight compartments, and only one of them was flooded. It would have been a different story had we been hit in the paddle wheel or the boiler. But there was no way to armor against two-ton rocks, so there was no point in worrying about it.

Except for the ones in the bow, the watertight compartments were all identical. The boat's dining room had three trestle tables that were just the right size to fit in the bottom of these. One of my better ideas. I got together a couple of crewmen and we lifted the floorboards, sank a table, and nailed it in place with all of us standing in the knee-deep water to hold down the table.

We put a portable pump down there and one man was left working it. It leaked some, but he could keep up with it. We stopped a moment to admire a job well done, when another rock came crashing through not four yards away, taking the corner off a war cart before it went through the bottom. Blood dripped through the ragged hole from the deck above.

"Do you remember what we did here," I said to the man next to me. He said he did.

"Well, do it again over there."

I went up to Tartar Control and discovered that we had a third killing ground going north of Czersk. Four boats were on it and the one near Brzesko now had six. All the rest were in transit to or from East Gate, to get more coal and ammunition.

The Mongols were completely inexperienced in dealing with us and our weapons, and paid heavily for the lessons they learned. Yet it was equally true that we were inexperienced with them. But with the radios, we could pass fighting tips around, while fighting in three separate groups; the Mongols had to go through each learning experience three times. And we charged full tuition to each and every one of them.

I got back on deck just in time to see the RB10 *Not For Hire* take a rock square on her paddle wheel. She was dead ahead of us and even as she slowed, Tadaos was getting a towing line ready. Using one of the Mongol grapnels as a monkey's fist, a line was tossed to her by one of the experienced boatmen in the crew just as we stopped alongside. Within a minute, Tadaos was calling for full-speed ahead and we resumed our way to East Gate. As we towed her home, I caught glimpses of the *Hire*'s crew dismantling the wreckage, preparing to rebuild. We were taking casualties, but we weren't giving the bastards any trophies.

RB1 TO ALL RIVER UNITS. THE ENEMY HAS A CATA-
PULT THAT LOOKS LIKE A TEETER-TOTTER MADE FOR

GIANTS. IT CAN THROW A HUGE ROCK FOUR GROSS YARDS, WHICH CAN DAMAGE A BOAT. IF YOU SEE ONE, DO NOT ATTACK UNTIL YOU HAVE TWO OTHER BOATS TO BACK YOU UP. THEY NEED A LARGE NUMBER OF MEN WORKING CLOSE TOGETHER TO OPERATE THEM, SO THEY ARE EASILY SLAUGHTERED BY OUR SWIVEL GUNS WHEN THEY ARE MOUNTED ON A HILL. THE PROBLEM IS THAT THEY ARE WILLING TO REPLACE MEN AS FAST AS WE BUTCHER THEM. IF THEY GET SMART ENOUGH TO MOUNT THEM ON THE OTHER SIDE OF A HILL, WE WILL BE ABLE TO REACH THEM ONLY WITH HALMAN BOMBS AND RIFLE GRENADES. ANY OTHER USE OF BOMBS IS NOW FORBIDDEN, TO SAVE AMMUNITION. IF THEY ARE HIDDEN BY A HILL, THEY MUST HAVE SOMEONE ON TOP OF THE HILL TO AIM THE CATAPULT. TARGET THIS MAN. CONRAD. OUT.

Of course, I wasn't the only one handing out advice, not by a long shot. Some ideas were brilliant, some were dumb. But a cumulative learning process was taking place.

Darkness fell as we passed Cracow, still safe on the west bank of the Vistula. Piotr's crew was radioing the boats, reminding them that we had now lost our air cover, and we would have to go back to patrolling until dawn. Fortunately, the Mongols seemed to have had enough for one day and were breaking contact. We couldn't follow them, so it was a quiet night.

There was only a platoon of boatwrights at East Gate, but they were our *best* boatwrights, and they had plenty of eager if unskilled help. Because we had called ahead, an entire paddle-wheel assembly was waiting for the *Hire*, and a crane swung it into position even as the troops were running on more ammo, food, and coal.

The patches in the bottom of the *Muddling Through* were inspected and secured with lag bolts. Linen caulking was pounded in the cracks and we were pronounced good enough. They gave us some boards and nails, and we were told to patch the upper decks on our way back to the fighting. Just then the boatwrights had better things to do.

Our badly wounded and dead were taken to an improvised hospital and morgue in the boat factory. I should have had something better planned, but I hadn't expected such heavy losses. I'd thought that our boats would be invincible!

We were almost ready to leave when I saw a Big Person come galloping in hauling a cart full of swivel gun ammo and four terrified troops. The carts were three yards tall and lacked brakes, springs, and a suspension system; they were never intended to move at the speeds that a Big Person was capable of. But she stopped it in time and gave me a "Hi there!" posture.

"Hi there, yourself!" I said. "Are you Anna?"

She said YES, so I gave her a big hug.

"You see? I told you they needed you! But I've got to run, love. See you in a few days. Don't scare these boys too badly!" I ran to my boat and went back to the war. I hoped she hadn't noticed my wounded eye.

I sent a message to Duke Henryk that night, telling him that we were holding the Mongols at the Vistula, but we could not do it forever. I begged him to advance now with whatever forces he had. He did not answer.

FROM THE AUTOBIOGRAPHY OF SIR VLADIMIR CHARNETSKI

Count Conrad's instructions had been quite clear. Duke Henryk was at Legnica with his own men, including my father and brothers. Count Conrad had sent him a written apology for not being there, along with six crews of radio operators who worked out of those little seven-man Night-Fighter carts. Duke Henryk was not pleased with us.

Duke Boleslaw was a fifteen-year-old knight who had resolved to defend eastern Poland. He was not on good terms with our liege lord Henryk.

If we dropped back to Legnica, as Duke Henryk wanted, we would be abandoning all of our factories and forts to the enemy. Our women would have to try to save themselves without our help, and the Mongols had long experience taking cities that were defended by both men and women. With women alone, well, I had to side with Count Conrad.

Yet if we fought alone, we would be a third separate force defending Poland. It was necessary that we make contact with Duke Boleslaw and join forces with him. But it was also necessary that we do so in such a manner that he supported our efforts as well as we supported his.

A combined strategy was necessary, and the young fool had rebuffed our earlier attempts at diplomacy. He had heard too many stories about knightly prowess and heroic deeds, and he could see no advantage in saddling himself with a "band of peasant footmen," no matter how large.

Myself, I think Conrad a fool for not using Countess Francine as his emissary, at least on the second try. That woman could talk a hungry dog away from a dead pig. But a young husband is often a fool when it comes to his new wife.

As it was, I left Hell with the biggest Christian army in all of history at my command, and I didn't know where I was going. All I knew was that Duke Boleslaw was somewhere between Plock and Sandomierz, and that somehow I had to join forces with him and work out some sort of strategy.

I had over two dozen of Anna's daughters, and I put a dozen of them with good riders to search for Boleslaw, men who were scions of the old nobility, men who Duke Boleslaw would not dare scoff at.

The other Big People were needed to run messages along my sixteen-mile-long train, and to lightly screen our flanks. We went on without stopping, and normal horses could never have kept up with us. My old Witchfire, now long in the tooth, was safely in the barns at Three Walls, and my love Annastashia was with our children not far away from him.

I had pulled a few strings and seen to it that my mother, my sisters, and sisters-in-law, along with all our peasants, were also at Three Walls, since I judged it to be our strongest fortification. Rank has its privileges, and I meant my family to be as safe as they could be.

We had practiced this business of continual motion last winter with six dozen carts, and had continued in circles for a month without mishap. Of course, that was with better trained men, men that had been winnowed out to remove the weak and the stupid. With this last class, well, they had been given only four months' training and we hadn't washed out anybody, except for those who had died. Still, their officers had been well trained, and we'd hoped that this would be enough.

Supplies of wood had been waiting for us along the roads since last summer with remarkably little pilferage. Supplies of water were provided. Crews of greasers went down the lines of moving carts, greasing the ball bearings in the wheels. The rails were new, the bridges intact, and we made six dozmiles a day on foot.

Some of the men had a hard time sleeping on the move, but experience had taught us that when they got tired enough, they would sleep.

By dawn of the second day we had passed Cracow, and still I had no word of Boleslaw.

Chapter Eighteen

FROM THE DIARY OF CONRAD STARGARD

The battle was not going as well as it had at first. As Tadaos said, they were learning.

They took out their first riverboat with a tree. During the night, they had chopped almost through the trunk of a huge pine tree right on the riverbank, then made a demonstration around it.

When the RB14 *Hotspur* attacked, they dropped that tree right across her deck, which nearly smashed her in half. Then they swarmed up the trunk and overpowered the crew.

By the time the RB12 *Insufferable* got there, the Mongols were learning how to use the swivel guns. After an exchange of gunfire, I ordered the *Insufferable* to burn the *Hotspur* with its flamethrower, and she went up quick. I pray to God in Heaven that all our men were dead before that happened.

They had mostly stopped using arrows on us, but they were still using the catapults, and still mounting them on hilltops. We kept on mowing down their crews and they kept on replacing them with a seemingly complete disregard for the lives of their men.

The RB21 *Calypso* got snagged on an underwater obstruction directly in front of one of the catapults. She took more than a dozen direct hits before her crew was taken off by the RB10 *Not for Hire*. By that time, the *Calypso* was completely out of ammunition, and her crew burned her before they left.

We got to avoiding the catapults as much as possible, and at full speed, zigzagging, it wasn't likely for a boat to be hit. It took a very tempting target to get one of our boats to slow down and stay near one spot, a temptation like a concentration of twenty thousand Mongols.

And seeing this, the enemy provided us with targets just to sucker us in! They were willing to spend ten or twenty thousand men just to kill one of our boats with less than three hundred men aboard! Madness!

Then they learned the best way to take out a riverboat, and we lost six boats in front of Sandomierz in less than an hour. Instead of rocks, they started throwing sewn-up ox hides filled with burning oil. The seasoned wood of our boats went up quickly, and usually we weren't able to save many of the crew. They were hurting us.

Yet we killed as many of them that day as we had on the first. I knew the ammunition we were using up, and I knew the conditions under which we were using it, mostly firing into packed crowds at pointblank range! Even the most conservative estimates still came out that we had killed over a million enemy troops! Yet they still kept coming!

We got to spraying our boats with water, inside and out, and this helped some. Wet wood burned more slowly and sometimes it took three or four fire bombs to destroy one of our boats. Fighting an oil fire with water is the wrong thing to do, but we didn't have any alternative. Sometimes enough oil could be flushed off the deck to save a boat. Sometimes not.

But the battle was on, and nobody ever suggested that we should quit. Even if we lost the Vistula, if we could kill enough of them, the rest of the army might have a chance.

By midnight of the fifth day, we were down to nineteen boats.

We couldn't patrol much that night. All of the boats had to go back to East Gate to replenish supplies, and our crews were exhausted, physically and emotionally. At dawn, we found three bridges more than half completed across the river, and we lost four more boats taking them out. The enemy had found a target that we couldn't refuse.

But after that, they were back to throwing rocks at us. Our best guess was that they had simply run out of oil.

Yet there seemed to be as many Mongols as ever, despite the fact that there were long stretches of riverbank strewn with their dead. Near Sandomierz, the enemy dead were more than ten yards deep in some places, and still they kept coming, like lemmings to their deaths.

We were hardly patrolling north of Czersk at all, since our boats were generally more than half out of ammunition by the time they got there. Our strategy, if it could be called that, was no longer to hold the Vistula. We knew we couldn't. It was simply to kill as many of the enemy as possible, and that was easier to do near our base.

Every night, I sent a message to Duke Henryk, begging him to advance with whatever men he had available. And every day, I waited for his reply, in vain.

Interlude Four

I hit the STOP button.

"Tom, I just can't believe the numbers of Mongols he's fighting."

"Believe it. At the time, those tribes of herdsmen had a population of over eight million, of which three million counted as fighting men. It wasn't as if they had to leave most of their men home to run the factories. Many of the Mongol warriors were on garrison duty, but they got most of their front-line troops from their conquered subjects. Most of those men Conrad was killing weren't Mongols. They were Iranians, Bactrians, Chinese, Russians, and what have you. Conrad mentions that they didn't seem to care if they lost men. They didn't. The troops they were losing were subject populations that were just surplus to them. Throwing them at the Poles was just another way of killing them off. Conrad's estimates were too conservative. All told, he killed over two million men at the Vistula.

"Those Chinese catapults had crews made up of prisoners, many of them Polish peasants. I suppose it's a good thing that Conrad didn't know the truth. He couldn't have done anything but what he did, but it would have been rough on his conscience."

"Wow. I'd always thought that the Mongols won so often because of superior tactics and strategy."

"It didn't take much to have tactics superior to those of the Europeans of the time. Like the Japanese of the same period, Westerners simply never trained as groups. It was all part of the mystique of knighthood. All their training was purely individual training, and one to one, the Europeans were inferior to no one. But their only group tactic was to get in a line and run at the enemy, mostly all at the same time.

"Also, it's a normal human thing to praise your enemy to the skies. It makes you look better if you win and not so bad when you lose.

"I don't know how many times I've heard Americans praise the fighting ability of Germans, for example, despite the fact that in all the time that there was a country named Germany, the Germans won only one small war, fighting little France alone, while losing a lot of big ones that they were foolish enough to start. In fact, the Germans were lousy fighters and their strategy was always absurd. It just feels better to say that you conquered a race of heroes than to admit that you blew away a bunch of damn fools."

"Huh. Another thing. Why didn't the Mongol delegation look Mongolian?" I said.

"Because the Mongolians were originally a Caucasian people, not an Oriental one. They only became Oriental after the conquest of China, thirty years after the time of this story, in our timeline, when for a hundred years, five or six generations, every Mongolian man came home with a dozen Chinese wives. A thing like that changes the bloodlines pretty thoroughly. The Mongol of later centuries was racially and culturally a totally different animal. Devout pacifists, most of them."

"Oh."

I hit the START button.

Chapter Nineteen

FROM THE AUTOBIOGRAPHY
OF SIR VLADIMIR CHARNETSKI

Finally, we know where we are going! My riders didn't find Duke Boleslaw's army, but Count Lambert's flyers did. They were proceeding up the Vistula from the north, and it looked as if we could meet up with them near Sandomierz.

When we were within a day of getting there, I collected a dozen of the Big People and set out ahead of my troops to talk to the duke. We got there at dusk, and were eventually escorted in to see the young man.

"Who were you, again?" Duke Boleslaw said.

"I am Baron Vladimir Charnetski, your grace. We haven't met, but we are related. Two of my aunts married two of your uncles, and one of my second cousins married two of your aunts, once removed, one on your father's side and one on your mother's, after the first one died. Surely you remember your Aunt Sophy and your Aunt Agnes. Well, they're my aunts as well."

Reminding him of our family ties seemed like a good idea. Actually, it was no big thing. I occasionally think that I must be related to everybody. Coming from a vast family helps, sometimes.

"You are the nephew of my Aunt Sophy? I haven't seen the old girl in years! How is she? And what of my Uncle Albert?"

"Just fine when I saw them last, a few months ago. They have thirteen children now, with another on the way."

"Thirteen! How is that possible? Two years ago, they had only nine!"

"Twins, your grace. Two pairs of them."

"No! That's amazing! And my Aunt Agnes?"

"Not so good, your grace. She's had a bad cough for almost a year now, and we're all worried about her."

"I shall include her in my prayers. But look, things are rushed just now, Vladimir. What can I do for you?"

"I think it's more what I can do for you, your grace. I am Hetman of Count Conrad's army. I have a hundred and fifty thousand men coming to join your forces."

"That was true, then? It wasn't some kind of silly joke? He really does have that many men?"

"Of course, your grace! Who could joke about such a thing? Anyway, they'll be here in a day and you can see for yourself."

"Here in a day? That's disaster!"

"How can that be, your grace? We're on your side, after all."

"It's disaster because I can't feed the men I've got now! The food merchants have not come! The cowards have all run away! Even the peasants have gone, and they've taken most of the food with them! I can't feed the twenty-five thousand men I have now! How am I going to feed a hundred fifty thousand more?"

"Oh, don't worry about that, your grace. We have food for a month with us, and all the grain we could ever need at the granaries in the Bledowska Desert. In fact, I can easily feed your entire army. I can have tons of grain here in a few days. Until then, we can feed your men and horses with what we have with us, but more food can be on its way here in an hour."

"How is this possible?"

"Easy. I brought a radio and a radio operator with me. We can send a message in a few minutes to the granary. They have mules and carts there. Why, four dozen carts a day can feed all your men and animals well. It has to come by rail instead of by boat because the boats are busy right now." I sent one of my men out to attend to it.

"Yes, I'd heard there was a battle going on at the Vistula. That's Conrad's riverboats, isn't it?"

"Yes, your grace, and Count Conrad is with them. They are slaughtering incredible numbers of the enemy, but it doesn't look as though they can hold out much longer. They say that tomorrow or the next day, the enemy will break through. Already, more than half of our men on the rivers are dead."

"Half dead? And still they fight?"

"Yes, your grace. They'll fight until they are all gone, every last man of them. I know. I trained them."

"On boats, perhaps. But what can footmen accomplish on a battlefield? Everybody knows that battles are won by men on horses! A footman can do nothing but get trampled."

"Wrong, your grace. Horsemen can do nothing against a mass of trained men with pikes! A pike is six yards long and can knock a knight out of the saddle before his lance can touch the footman. Believe me! We've practiced the very thing many times in the last five years. Furthermore, I have more than twenty thousand guns coming with my troops, and they can kill an enemy at a mile! What I don't have is a force of horsemen, but you do. If we can work together, we cannot be beaten!"

"Vladimir, we'll have to talk more on this. For now, do you swear that food supplies will be here by this time tomorrow?"

"I swear it by all that's holy, your grace."

"Then I'll believe that much at least. I must go and give orders that the last of the food reserves are to be handed out and eaten. That will give the men one good meal, and after that we are at your mercy."

Chapter Twenty

FROM THE DIARY OF CONRAD STARGARD

Of all the mistakes I've made, the most serious was to set the number of riverboats at only three dozen. We needed six times that number!

Of course, at the time, I wasn't sure if we would be able to use them at all. The river might have been frozen over, the water level could have been too low to get by some of the rapids, or any one of a number of things could have gone wrong. I don't know. I needed sleep, and there wasn't much of that to be had.

There came a time when we were the only boat north of Sieciechow, on a sector that hadn't been patrolled in days, and we found that the Mongols had completed a bridge across the Vistula. Thousands of enemy troops were rushing across it.

"Baron Tadaos, we've got to take that bridge out."

"Sir, we're out of Molotov cocktails and Halman bombs. We're out of peashooter balls. The flamethrower is exhausted. We have maybe a thousand rounds of swivel gun ammunition left and those troops outnumber ours by hundreds to one. How are we going to do it?"

"We're going to ram it. Captain Targ! Prepare to offload your men and your war carts!"

The captain gave a few orders that had his men scurrying, then ran up to me.

"We're going to attack that bridge, sir?"

"We are, but you are not. We're going to ram that bridge, and doing that will likely sink us. There is no point in your company going down with the boat. It would accomplish nothing, and you are needed elsewhere. You will get your men ashore and fight your way south to Sandomierz. Once there, you will join the garrison and help defend the city."

He stared at me for a long minute.

"Yes, sir. What about my wounded?"

"Take the walking wounded with you. The others will have to be left behind. There's nothing else we can do."

"Yes, sir."

I could see that he wanted to say more, a lot more, but he turned and went to obey his orders.

"Tadaos, I can handle the helm alone, but I'll need one man in the engine room. See if you can find a volunteer, a good swimmer. Then get the rest of your men ready to join Captain Targ."

He looked me straight in the eye and said, "Pig shit!"

Then he spat on my boots.

"Nine years I've been working for you and you don't know me any better than that? You might have taken command of this battle, and done some dumbshit things, but I am still master of this boat and baron of the whole damn River Battalion, or what's left of it anyway! Three-quarters of my men are dead now, and you expect me to turn around and run away? This is *my* damned boat and this is *my* damned duty station and I will damn well stay here until we've won or we're dead! And if you think that any man of mine feels any different, you can damn well ask them yourself!"

Then he turned his back to me and put a new string on his bow, his hand shaking with anger.

I stood there, not knowing what to do. Then I turned to the helmsman, a young kid who looked to be fourteen.

"Get out of here, boy."

"No, sir." His face shield was open and he was crying, tears running down his cheeks. "No, sir," he repeated and continued to stand his post, though the tears must have blinded him.

I turned and went below.

"Baron Piotr, get your men together. I'm going to take out a bridge by ramming. You and your men are going ashore with Captain Targ."

He didn't get up from the map board.

"Yes, sir. We heard something about that. But the fact is that we really don't know whether the boat will sink or not. Ashore, well, we wouldn't be able to do that much good for Sandomierz, since most of us here have been sitting at desks and radio sets for years. We are way out of training. But if the boat does stay afloat, we're going to be needed here to continue coordinating our efforts. We still have eleven boats on the river, after all. So, begging your pardon, sir, but we're staying."

"Damn you, Piotr, that was a direct order!"

"Sir. I am a Radiant Warrior, blessed by God to do His holy work. I am not going to run away now."

I looked around the room. All of the men were trying to look busy.

"This is mutiny!" I shouted.

"Yes, sir, I suppose it is," a mousey-looking radio operator said. "But it's really for the best, sir. Our place is here."

"Damn you all," I shouted and went down to the cargo deck.

One of the crew was flooding the odd-numbered watertight tanks, to give the boat more weight, he explained, and never mind about the buoyancy. He wanted to make sure that we hit the bridge as hard as possible.

"It'd be a shame to waste our last blow at the bastards, wouldn't it, sir?"

The troops were jamming the war carts up against the forward drawbridge, again to increase the impact.

Captain Targ came up to me.

"I regret that I have to report a mutiny, sir. I was afraid that this might happen, but the men won't leave. We're down to less than four full platoons now, and they've seen too many friends die to run away at this point. It would be like dishonoring the dead. Anyway, if the boat hangs up on the bridge, you'll need us to repel boarders, so it's for the best."

"God damn you all to hell! But that bridge still has to go!"

"Of course, sir. Speaking of which, we'd better all get up on deck or we'll miss the show. Tadaos won't be waiting for orders, you know. All platoons! Report on deck! Pass the word!"

"You are all crazy people!" I shouted.

"Yes, sir," a warrior said as he brushed by me, heading for the stairs. "I suppose we are."

I got on deck when we were less than three-gross yards from the bridge. We were going full-speed downriver and the helmsman had us aimed dead center.

The bridge was built rather high for such a temporary thing, and the top of the roadway was higher than the deck of the boat. It was built on wooden tetrahedrons made of oversized telephone poles that looked to be simply set on the river bottom, with the roadway strung on ropes above them.

There were thousands of men and horses on it, rushing across, and while some of them were shouting and pointing at us, they still kept coming. There were men getting on the bridge the moment we hit.

The impact was enough to knock us all over, and we all went skidding across the splintered deck. As I got up, I saw that we had not punched a hole through the bridge, as I had expected. We had actually tipped it over!

The part of it that was right in front of us was already in the river, and the roadway was caught by the current. On both sides of us, like water breaking over a dam, the long flexible bridge was pulled slowly over on its side.

The water was filled with thrashing horses, but with fewer men than you would expect. Not that many of the desert-bred Mongols could swim. Those few that did make it to shore didn't live long. The captain already had the swivel guns in action.

But the bridge was still in one piece and we hadn't gone through it. Tadaos got us into reverse and we backed off the wreckage.

A crewman ran up from below and reported to Tadaos, who turned to me and said, "The bow is smashed up, but we're still afloat. Maybe you ought to see about repairing the damage, sir."

So I went down to play steamboat repairman, again. On the way, I stopped to tell Piotr to radio the other boats that a bridge could be taken out by ramming. He had already done so.

The next morning, after the other boats had taken out four other bridges and lost two of their number doing it, it became strangely quiet, all along the Vistula. Some men thought that we had actually won and the enemy had given up. Others were sure that it was some kind of a trick. The planes reported that the Mongols were concentrating in a dozen groups, each a few miles east of the river, but not going back any farther. It was eerie and quiet for the first time in a week. Even the catapults were unmanned.

Then, the morning after that, an even stranger thing happened. All at once, along the whole river as far as we could tell, enemy troops led their horses down to the frozen banks of the river. Holding on to the horse's tail, they got the animals swimming across the icy waters of the Vistula, pulling the rider behind them.

We steamed through them, drowning hundreds, but they were like lemmings and we couldn't begin to stop them all.

Tadaos looked at it in disbelief.

"If they could do that, why didn't they do it a week ago?"

"There's your answer," Captain Targ said, pointing to the west bank. "Every horse had a man behind it when it went into the water. Only maybe half of those men are still there when they come out."

"Good God in Heaven, you're right! They are deliberately throwing away half of their army just to get across! Who could order such a thing? Why do they do it? Don't they realize that we no longer have anything to fight with?"

We all shook our heads and watched half of the enemy army die.

I don't know. Maybe they ran out of food. Maybe they just got impatient. It's likely they never realized how close to the wire we were. The only thing sure was that the Battle for the Vistula was over and the Battle for Poland had begun.

FROM THE AUTOBIOGRAPHY OF SIR VLADIMIR CHARNETSKI

We set up a system where each platoon "adopted" up to ten of Duke Boleslaw's troops, at least for dining purposes. Later we had to up it to twelve. More of them were coming in every day, and many had had a hard time finding us.

The printshop in Cracow made up thousands of little signs that said where our camp was; one of the Big People ran them to Eagle Nest and the planes were soon dropping them on friendly troops who looked lost. It helped, but as it turned out, it also told the Mongols where to find us. Maybe that wasn't so bad. We wanted to find them.

Grain was arriving daily from the granary, the first batch brought in by a dozen Big People the first day. They'd gone out and taken over the first dozen carts from the slow moving mules, mostly to show Duke Boleslaw that there was nothing to worry about.

Yet for three days there was nothing to do but wait. Patrols were sent out, but they found little. The area was evacuated, since the refugees that had been through a week ago had finally convinced almost every noncombatant to leave.

In hours, we'd set up what amounted to a very large city. Carts were hauled a set distance apart and tarps were zippered over and between them for roofs, just like in a training exercise. Hammocks were slung both under the carts and between them. Cookstoves all had their proper place by the streets, and latrines were dug as per the manual. Oh, everything was covered with freezing mud, but that was only to be expected. After the training we'd put our men through, it was hardly noticed.

Everything was just perfect except for Duke Boleslaw, who couldn't comprehend any sort of tactics except for charging at the enemy and killing them all gloriously.

After days of discussion, persuasion, and pleading, I finally had to threaten to cut off his food supply if he didn't let us take part in the fight. Couching it that way, where he was doing a favor for the people who were feeding him, he came around a little.

The plan we came up with, and after vast trouble got our knightly horsemen to agree with, was that they would locate the enemy and entice them into a trap.

They would charge gloriously in, slaughter droves of the enemy and then pretend to run away. They would lead the Tartars into a huge V-shaped formation of war carts, who would open up on the enemy with their guns. After twenty minutes, the horsemen would come back and finish the Mongols off. Thus, Boleslaw's knights would get both first blood and the kill, while we foot soldiers would be content with an assist. I had to use hunting terms with them because their hunting was organized, even if their warfare wasn't.

One problem with this, as far as the knights were concerned, was that it involved running away from the enemy. I had to convince them that it was a legitimate ruse of war and really a very clever thing for them to do.

I even promised them a beer while we were shooting up Mongols. Actually, I thought that there was a fair chance that they would *have* to run away, since all reports from the Vistula said that we would be vastly outnumbered, but I couldn't tell them that. I just wanted to make sure that they ran in the right direction.

Another problem was in being able to identify friend from foe. This was difficult enough in a hand-to-hand combat, especially since the riverboats had reported that the Mongols had drawn troops from all of their vast realm, and some dressed not too differently from Polish knights. At a distance, from the perspective of a gunner a half mile away, the problem was serious. Foreseeing this difficulty a year ago, I had caused to be made fifty thousand surcoats, each white with a broad red vertical stripe running up both the front and the back. They were easily identifiable at a great distance, and quite nicely made, since our knights insisted on going into battle looking their best.

The knights all admitted to the advantages of wearing identifiable clothing. The trouble was that they all had their own family devices and colors, and these were a particular point of pride with them. Many had taken vows to never fight without their family colors, and so felt honor-bound to refuse to wear the surcoats I'd given them. Days were spent squabbling over this point, until the duke at last ordered all his men to wear the red-and-white surcoats, *over* their own surcoats if necessary, but to wear them or leave the battle. At that, a few of our Knights actually went home, but not many.

Then we got word that the Mongols had crossed the Vistula, and two days after that, that they were camped five miles away.

Chapter Twenty-one

Late in the afternoon on the day before the battle, Duke Boleslaw called together all of his leaders, barons and above. This meant that my army was grossly underrepresented, because a conventional baron often had as few as half a dozen knights whereas mine each commanded a battalion of nine thousand men. But there was nothing I could do about it, so we went.

I'd had a big map made up of the area, and after the duke made a short, boisterous speech, I was surprised that he let me come up and give a presentation outlining the situation. Many of these men were not good with maps, but most of them had been on patrols throughout the area and were able to understand the situation.

I showed them how to get from here to there, where our ambush would be set up, what their "retreat" route should be. I stressed the importance of a good night's sleep, and a hot meal in the morning. And I repeated my promise of a beer if the ambush worked out well, having shipped in forty thousand gallons of beer for the purpose. These men had been dry for over a week and I think the beer was a serious inducement.

A priest said mass and we all went to communion. I think every man of mine went into battle in a State of Grace. There are no atheists on the battle lines.

It was dark when Baron Ilya came to me. The weather that had been perfect for the past week, a rare thing at this time of year, was turning bad. Thunder and lightning were crashing in the distance and it looked likely that we would be fighting tomorrow in a cold spring rain. The lightning had been raising hell with the radios since the day before, but fortunately, they had already done their jobs.

I was with the duke and a few of his friends, boys as young as he was, telling them the story of how Count Conrad and I had once chopped up a caravan of Teutonic Knights and rescued a gross of children that otherwise would have been sold into Moslem slavery. The story went over well, since despite the fact that the Teutonic Knights were nominally the vassals of Duke Boleslaw, they had not come to the battle, saying that they had to defend the northern borders, which was bullshit. The duke vowed that if we beat the Mongols, we would fight the Teutonic Order next. I had the boys in high spirits by the time the last Crossman raced over the hills with shit on his breeches. Two against seven, and they were vanquished without putting a mark on us!

"Sir, may I speak to you for a moment?" Baron Ilya said.

"Certainly. Is it something that can be discussed before these fine knights?" These boys were more proud of their knighthood than they were of their higher titles. Knighthood, after all, had to be earned, while their baronies and all had been inherited.

"I don't see why not, sir, since it's about the invasion. You know that I lead the battalion of Night Fighters. For four years, we have been training and learning to fight at night, in the dark. Well, it's a dark and stormy night out there, and now's the time to put that training to use! Let me take my battalion out there and shake them up a bit! Me and the boys can be back in time to help out with the battle tomorrow, but give us our chance tonight."

I was about to say, "Certainly, go see what you can do," but the duke was talking before I could get my mouth open.

"Just what is it that you plan to do, Baron?"

"Well, your grace, we'll probably surround them in the dark, send in creepers to take out their sentries, then roll grenades under their tents and so on. After that, we'll give them a good shelling to cover our men as they come out, and maybe slaughter their horses while we're at it. We'll get some of the bastards and cost them a night's sleep if nothing better."

The young duke was getting progressively more horrified as Ilya spoke, but Ilya wasn't sharp enough to realize it. Or maybe he was just too bull-headed to care.

"What a disgusting thing to even talk about! Do you think for a moment that I would allow such a dishonorable thing to be done under my command? I absolutely forbid this cowardly act you propose, and I tell you that you better see a priest and confess again if you want to be in a State of Grace for tomorrow's battle!"

"A State of Grace! I tell you that I am a Radiant Warrior and personally blessed by God!" Ilya exploded. "And cowardly? I want to go alone with only nine thousand men against half a million and you call that cowardly?"

I had to stand up between them to make sure they didn't come to blows. "Ilya, you damn fool! Shut up!" I pushed him toward the door of the tent.

"Forgive him, your grace. He's normally a good man. He's just overwrought. I'll take care of this." I followed Ilya out.

As soon as we were out the door, he said, "Sir—"

"Shut up! Keep your damn face closed until we get back to our camp!"

Thunder was crashing overhead and the rains had started.

Once there, I said, "Don't you have brains enough to not shout at a duke, for God's sake! And especially a duke who could wreck the whole battle plan if he gets a hair up his arse? Didn't your mother teach you anything?"

"I never had a mother. They said the stork brought me."

"I can believe that, judging from your manners! I've worked for almost a week convincing that kid that we're not a bunch of crude peasants and you had to prove otherwise in half a minute!"

"Sorry, sir. What about the raid on the Mongol camp tonight?"

I took a deep breath, letting my anger subside. "Can you do it so that no one from this camp sees you leave and come back?"

"In this weather, sir? Easy! The duke's sentries will never see us."

"Then do it. But don't get caught, or the duke will hang us both!"

"Don't worry, sir. It's just like stealing a pig."

AS TOLD BY BARON ILYA THE BLACKSMITH

"So like I was saying, we got us permission to make a little night raid, even if it was sort of an underhanded one. I got the boys out of the sack, fed, and called together. We'd been sleeping during the day to stay in shape, and doing night guard duty until we'd done more than our share by the night before. I'd timed the thing just right.

"The camp was quiet when we left, pulling our small night-fighter carts. See, most of the troops fight out of big, forty-three man platoon carts, but in the dark, there's no way that you can keep track of that many men around you. The most is about six, and you've got to know who your own men are, because everybody else is likely the enemy! So we use a small lance-sized cart, and right then they was unloaded of everything but the gun, ammunition, and grenades that each one carried. We don't use pikes or halberds. In the dark, them weapons ain't worth firewood! But we was pretty good with the knife, the garrote, and the grenade.

"I thought we was clear of the camp when we came on an outlying sentry, and you know it had to be one of Boleslaw's men.

"'Hold! Who goes there?'

"'Baron Ilya,' I says. 'Beer run.' It was the first thing that came into my head. Never mind that I had nine thousand men coming up behind me.

"'Beer? There's two dozen big carts of beer in the camp!'

"'Yeah, but that's what our hetman promised you horse jockeys. Now we're going out to get enough for the foot soldiers, too.'

"'What, all that beer for us alone? Well, carry on then.'

"I don't figure that man ever knew he had a creeper right behind him and a garrote over his head. I sure would have hated to do him in, but I did promise Vladimir that nobody would see us leave. If he reported that I went on a beer run, well, wouldn't nobody take it seriously.

"We had scouts ahead planting markers in the ground, sticks split so the white side showed toward us. There wasn't no problem finding the Mongol camp. The only surprise was how big that sucker was! It was fully four miles across and they had fires going all around it. No way we could surround this thing the way I told the duke.

"'Fire line, two yards apart, a gross yards from the pickets, pass it on.' I says. That would put us a quarter way around the camp, and the carts split off by companies to either side of me, forming wings a mile and a half long. The carts were tipped up on their sides and the guns mounted. They wouldn't be needed for a while, but it's always a good idea to be ready. The signal strings were strung up along both wings, and I waited.

"I got my telescope out and looked over the enemy sentries. Dumbshits, the lot of them! They was sitting around the fires, staring at the fires and talking. A captain with any brains posts his men so the fires show in the enemy's eyes, not your own. Those men were about to get a very expensive education in night-fighting.

"'Plan eight, red and white flares. Pass the word,' I whispered to both wings and to the sentry behind me who was sorting out the companies.

"It was a while before we got settled into position, but I wasn't worried none. The thunder and rain covered most everything. We was being quiet mostly out of habit. Them sentries weren't looking for trouble, but that wasn't going to help them none. Trouble had just come looking for them!

"It would have been nice if I could have gone in with most of the other men, but we'd proved time and again that the leader had best stay back and direct things, so that's the way I had to play it. That's one of Count Conrad's big problems. He always has to do everything hisself, and there ain't nobody can do everything, not and do it right.

"I got four tugs on the right-hand string, saying that the right wing was ready, and a few minutes later, the left-hand string pulled four times.

"I gave both strings three long, slow pulls and watched as the first-string creepers went out. These were the one best lance from each platoon, and we had a lot of contests to see who that lance was. They figured it was an honor to be the ones that went out ahead of the others and killed the sentries real quiet like.

"I saw the men in front of me in position, but I gave it a few more minutes to make sure that everybody else was ready. Then I lit off a small, red rocket. Count Conrad had made these things as a festival toy, but once I saw one, I knew it was just the thing to signal men in the dark.

"If any of the Mongol sentries saw it, they were looking at the rocket and not the men behind them. Just like a machine, six of my men came up behind six of theirs and slipped garrotes over their heads. The wires were pulled tight and most of them heathens didn't hardly even kick around. Those that did got knifed, but most of them got to die without getting their clothes bloodied. The sentry fires were smothered, usually by piling dead Mongols on them and stuffing the edges with mud and dirt, and it was time for phase two.

"I pulled the signal strings again and five more lances from each platoon went out, leaving only the gunners behind. I put a big white rocket in the launcher to be ready in case of any commotion, but I rested back with my telescope for about an hour and let the men do what they were trained for. They were going through the enemy camp, wreaking any silent mayhem they could do, and that was a lot. Those boys went out with six garrotes each, and they all complained later that they could have used more.

"There was a lot of knife work, too. You take sleeping troops a tent at a time, cut every throat at the same instant without a sound, then go on to the next tent. The trick is to get men on their stomachs laying all around the tent, ready to go under it. Then one man walks in the front door, calm as he can, and lights a pocket lighter. Before the sleepers know what's happening, they all have an extra mouth and the light goes out. It takes training and practice, but any job worth doing is worth doing right. I could see quick flashes as tents lit up for a moment and then were dark.

"There were enemy troops up and around, but our men was all walking natural and they weren't much noticed. Those Mongols must have had fifty different kinds of people there, and didn't none of them speak the same language. They all figured that if you was in the camp, you must be on their side, so they each had to learn different on their own. It stayed quiet for the longest time.

"One of the rules was that the most important men in the camp usually had the biggest tents, and these were usually in the center of the camp. When there are more than a dozen in a tent, it gets pretty hard to kill them all without somebody on one side or another making a noise, so doctrine was to frag the big tents. Course, the big ones often had sentries of their own, a sure tip-off that you was in officer country, so the sentries had to be taken out first, but we were pretty good at that sort of thing. When a man's upright, a garrote's the thing to use.

"You could always roll a grenade under a tent, but the effect was better if it was up off the ground. The best way was to slit the tent, put in the grenade dangling from a string with a fish hook on the end and with the wick hanging outside, and then light it with your pocket lighter when the signal went up.

"It was still awfully quiet down there and I checked the traveling clock we had with us. Yeah, it had been over an hour, and it was one of Conrad's double-sized hours at that. Some of the boys would be getting real antsy about now, so it was time for the fireworks.

"I lit off the big white rocket flare, which exploded pretty white streamers over the enemy camp so nobody could miss it.

"In a few seconds, there were explosions all over the Mongol camp, and most especially in the center of it, I was pleased to note.

"I sat back for another two-twelfths of an hour watching the mayhem through my telescope. The boys were really ripping them up. Each man had had two small four-pound grenades in his pack, as well as a big twelve-pounder, and didn't none of that ordinance get carried back to our firing line.

"As the first of our men got back, puffing and running with the big white crosses they'd opened up on their chests so our gunners would know not to shoot them, I started pulling on the signal strings again.

"The gunners generally let loose with a few rifle grenades first, in part to start some additional fires to shoot by, but mostly because they didn't get to shoot them very often, except for dummies, and they're kind of fun.

"A few fires were started near a horse park and that attracted some gunfire until the surviving horses stampeded through the Mongol camp and out of sight.

"More and more of our men were making it back, but the Mongols themselves hadn't acted like we was here yet. One of my worst nightmares had the enemy and our men running out all mixed together, and the gunners having to shoot them all down or be killed themselves. But that didn't happen. The enemy was real slow on the uptake. Me, I figure that was caused by the way we killed most of their officers, but there ain't no way to prove it. Only it figures, you know?

"We were almost all back, those that were coming back,

anyway, before the invaders got together enough to attack us. There was thousands of them on horseback, all yelling and screaming and running into each other, since they had the muzzle flashes coming in at them and that will blind a man or beast in the dark.

"Then we started doing jerk-fire shooting. That's where each gunner fires just after the man to his left does. This lets him aim by the muzzle flashes of the guns that just went off, so the field is almost perfectly lit up. But the men out there that you're shooting at look like they're jumping and jerking around real funny. Conrad explained it to me once, but I never did figure out what he was talking about.

"From out in front of it, when you're being shot at, it's just plain scary. It looks like there's these big bright moving things streaking from your right to your left, and there isn't a horse that will stay around it. Them that wasn't dead took off and their riders went with them.

"After that, they tried charging us on foot, but we shot that one up just as bad or even a little worse. There was dead bodies as thick as a carpet from their camp to almost our lines. I tell you that a man could have walked on dead Mongols the whole way and never stepped on the ground, they was that thick.

"But we were getting low on ammunition and dawn wasn't that far away. If they knew how few of us there was, they could have walked all over us, and anyhow, I told the hetman that nobody would see us coming back. I signaled a pullout.

"Slow burning flares were stuck into the ground in front of our positions, to maybe make them think we was still there. Then we pulled out in the reverse order that we came, and some of the gunners kept on firing right up to the end. We were halfway back, walking in the rain, when I got the butcher's bill. Four hundred fifty-five missing and likely dead, and damn few wounded. Well, in that kind of a fight, if you were hurt bad, you just didn't get out. We lost a whole lot less than I thought we would, but even so, odds were that a lot of those men still out there were friends of mine.

"That same sentry was there when we got back near camp.

I guess the duke's men weren't much on relieving the night guard.

"'You didn't get the beer!' he says.

"'Naw, the place was closed.'

"'Damn shame. Maybe we'll have some left over for you.'

"'You'd better.' What a dumbshit, I thought."

Chapter Twenty-two

FROM THE AUTOBIOGRAPHY OF SIR VLADIMIR CHARNETSKI

I talked to Baron Ilya in the cold rain at dawn. He reported a successful mission and requested more ammunition, most of his being exhausted. I put his little carts in back of the north line as a backup in case we were attacked there on the wrong side. He could scrounge ammunition from the carts near him, but I didn't want to do anything official about replenishing him, not when I had just disobeyed a direct order from the duke.

The radios were still picking up nothing but static, so I had all but two of them packed away, and their crews put on the battle line. I didn't know what was happening on the Vistula or in the rest of the country, but I told myself that it wasn't important now. This day's business could be done with horns and signal flags. The worth of all that I had done in the last five years would be decided today in the time of a few hours and the space of a few square miles.

We ate a hot breakfast in the dark, and the camp city was quickly taken down. Everything not essential to combat was packed neatly on the ground. The carts were empty except for arms, ammunition, and a light lunch.

I led the men in the sunrise service, even though we couldn't see the sun, and we moved out.

I'd picked the spot for the ambush carefully. It was a long, low valley with a small creek running down the center. The hills were gentle enough so that our war carts could be easily pulled over them, but they provided enough of a backdrop so that the carts would not be too obvious against a skyline. The valley averaged a mile wide and was ten miles long.

As each war cart got into position, the top was taken off, spare pike shafts were set into the armored side of the cart, and the yard-and-a-half wide-armored top was slung out to one side as a shield for the pikers. The four great, caster-mounted wheels were unlocked from their fore and aft traveling position and locked spread out to the sideways moving combat position. Pikes and halberds were broken out and distributed. Six gunners climbed in each cart and mounted their weapons. The thirty-six pikers and axemen snapped into their pulling harnesses and tugged the cart into its final position. Well coordinated, this took less than a minute. Then they stood and waited in the rain.

Our war carts stretched more than six miles along on each side of the valley and flared out at the end like a funnel mouth, two miles across. Sentries were posted behind us and the Big People were scouting to insure that we wouldn't be taken unawares. We were all in position by midmorning, and then there was nothing to do but wait.

Duke Boleslaw's horsemen had left at dawn, and I was worried about them. They were such a disorganized mass that I wasn't sure whether they could all stay together enough to get a decent charge at the enemy. But there was nothing I could do but wait and worry.

I was worried about Count Conrad as well. I hadn't heard from him in days, what with the problems with the radios, and in this rain, the planes couldn't fly safely, so I lacked that source of information as well. Until the day before, I had always known what was happening. Now, just as all things were coming to a climax, I was suddenly all alone. It seems strange to say that, since I had about me the finest and largest army in Christendom, but it was true.

After an hour of tense waiting, I saw one of our planes flying low toward us from the north, and then I saw another right behind it. Soon, there were twenty of them, and they circled low over the valley. Then they proceeded to land!

This was crazy! Planes landed only at Eagle Nest! Anywhere else and they couldn't take off again! Not unless we built a catapult on the spot. Furthermore, they had landed in the very place where we were expecting a horde of Mongols to come charging in at any moment! Those planes were a big sign that said "Mongol, run away!"

I had my Big Person, Betty, run me down to the first plane that had landed, its propeller still spinning and its engine making enough noise to scare away a saint.

"What the Hell are you doing here?" I shouted.

The engine stopped and Count Lambert got out, wearing his gold-plated armor.

"Baron Vladimir, fortunately I couldn't hear that, but you must learn to speak more politely to your betters," he said.

"But my lord, you have landed right in the middle of an ambush! The Mongols could be coming in any time now!"

"No, it will be another half-hour at the least. We saw them fighting Duke Boleslaw's men three or four miles from here. But have your men move these planes if they are in the way. Don't worry about hurting them, they'll never fly again. Be careful of the engines. They're expensive and they can be salvaged."

All of this made no sense to me, but I galloped to our lines and gave the necessary orders to get those planes hidden. By the time I got back to the count, a squire had ridden out leading two dozen war horses, all saddled and ready for combat. This crazy stunt had been planned!

"My lord, what is all this about?" I said.

Lambert put on a red-and-white surcoat and swung into the saddle. "About? Well, you could hardly expect us to miss the final battle, could you? For over a week now, we've been in the air, watching you and Conrad garner all the glory while we could only look on! We have taken some heavy losses doing it, too!

You see those twenty planes there? Well, there were forty-six of them to start!"

"That many? What happened to them?"

"Three crashed on landing at Eagle Nest. Two were seen flying too low over the enemy and were brought down by arrows. One flew into a thundercloud and we found the pieces later. The rest, we don't know. They just didn't come back."

"My God. I didn't realize it was that bad, my lord. But why leave the rest of them here? Surely you can't fly them out of here!"

"No, of course not. But don't you see? They're not needed anymore! They've done their job! The Mongols are all here. The army is here. The whole affair will be settled right here! If we are to get our share of the glory, we have to get it now! As to the planes, well, we have wood, glue, and cloth in abundance. We can build more later."

"But, but does Count Conrad know of this?"

"Who gives a damn about Conrad? Look, boy, Conrad is sworn to me, not me to him! But just now there's a battle to get to. The plan's still the same? Lead them through here, then come back in a bit for the kill?"

"Yes, my lord."

"Good!" He waved to his mounted aviators. "Let's go! *To war!*"

And they rode out of the valley.

Maybe the planes weren't needed, but as I saw it, things were still very much afloat. Who could tell what we would need and what we would not! I was almost glad that the radios weren't working. I would have hated to have to report *this* piece of insanity to Count Conrad!

We got the planes cleared away and hidden, and then it was wait and worry time again.

It was approaching noon, and I was wondering if I should feed the men when an outrider on one of the Big People came and reported that the battle was coming our way. I signaled "Ready" and "Hide," and could see the lines tighten up, the pikes drop, and the flag poles go down as soon as the message was relayed.

After a while, I could see our horsemen coming in exactly as planned, if a little late. They were in surprisingly good order, all things considered, and Duke Boleslaw himself was at their head, surrounded by his youthful group of friends. He was going a bit slower than a full frightened gallop, I suppose to insure that all of his men could keep up. A few Mongols had gotten out in front of him, but he wisely ignored them.

He came right down the middle of the valley, splashing over the little half-frozen creek twice just to keep going in a straight line. The kid was doing good! And after him came the vast horde of the enemy, which outnumbered Boleslaw's forces by at least twenty-to-one, galloping in a ragged mob and not noticing in the least the army waiting for them! It was working!

My station was at the mouth of the funnel, and as soon as the last of the Mongols went through, I advanced both our wings to seal it off. As soon as the duke's men were out of the trap at the other end, my second in command, Baron Gregor Banki, would close the small end and open fire, which would signal us to do the same, and the war would be nearly won!

The ends of the wings had more than a mile to go to close the gap, so this took a while. As I followed them in, another outrider reported that Count Conrad was arriving with what was left of the river battalion, forty-one war carts out of the two hundred sixteen he'd started with! I sent the man back with an invitation for Conrad to plug the gap in the center. After all that they had done, those men deserved the honor.

This delayed things a bit, but there wasn't an enemy in sight and I knew we could afford the time. I mounted Betty and rode around to my liege lord. I could safely leave my post because now there wasn't a single thing for me to do! When the shooting started, everybody would join in. I was no longer needed.

Count Conrad had a dirty bandage over his right eye and he looked horribly tired and old!

"My lord, it's good to see you! You look like you need this!" I threw him my wine skin. It wasn't exactly a regulation part of the uniform, but rank has a few privileges.

"Thank you." He took a long pull. "Things go as planned?"

"Perfectly, my lord. We're only waiting for Gregor to close his end and start shooting. It should be any time now."

"Good. We're out of ammunition. Can you supply some?"

"Of course, my lord!"

I gave the orders and runners started coming in with crates of swivel gun rounds. As we waited, I told my liege about Baron Ilya's night raid, and about Duke Boleslaw's reaction to it.

"You did right," he said. "At least, that's what I would have done."

Then I had to tell the count about his air force, or rather his lack of one.

"Damn," he said, looking more weary than ever. "If we live through this, I swear either I'm going to get control of Eagle Nest, or I'm going to build another one."

When Conrad's forces were supplied, we still hadn't heard from the small end of the funnel. Then horsemen started coming at us, but they weren't all Mongols! There were Polish knights mixed in with them, and soon a vast, slashing and hacking free-for-all was going on right before our eyes! Something had gone very, very wrong.

The signal flags started wagging, sending the same message to us around both sides of the ambush:

BOLESLAW HAS NOT LEFT THE TRAP. ONE OF HIS YOUNG FRIENDS FELL TO A MONGOL ARROW. BOLESLAW TURNED BACK AT THE LAST INSTANT AND WENT TO AID HIS FRIEND. THE DUKE'S HORSEMEN ALL FOLLOWED THEIR LIEGE BACK INTO THE MONGOL FORCES. THEY ARE NOW ALL MIXED TOGETHER. WE HAVE CLOSED THIS END BUT WE CANNOT SHOOT WITHOUT KILLING OUR OWN MEN. BULLETS GO RIGHT THROUGH ENEMY AND THEN CONTINUE THROUGH OUR MEN WHO ARE BEHIND THEM. WHAT SHOULD I DO? GREGOR BANKI.

"That's a good question he asks, my lord. What should we do?" I said.

"I don't know. What can we do? Nothing, that's what! We just have to let those crazy knights get themselves killed."

"Do you want to take command, my lord?"

"Me? No. This is your show. You do what you think is best. I screwed things up enough on the river. Now it's your turn."

"But I had heard that you had killed vast numbers of the enemy," I said.

"Perhaps, but look around you. Of the men I led into battle, not one in five is still fit to march. How can that be called a victory? I made mistakes, many mistakes. You have command here, Vladimir. Try to do better than I did."

"Yes, sir."

I signaled "Defend Yourself," "Give Aid," and "Stand By," which meant they should not let themselves be hurt, they should help out where they could, and then they should wait for further orders. What else could I tell them?

A half-hour later, I told them to break out lunch and eat in rotation, one lance per platoon at a time.

FROM THE DIARY OF CONRAD STARGARD

In front of us, like on a movie screen, the Polish nobility was slugging it out with the Mongol horsemen. Our men were hopelessly outnumbered, but they were giving a good account of themselves. They had some advantages.

They were generally bigger and stronger than their adversaries, and had much better arms and armor than the enemy. Most of them had been equipped out of my factories, and the poorest page had at least a full set of chain mail, doubtlessly a hand-me-down, but better than what many knights wore ten years ago. The Mongols, on the other hand, were wearing whatever they could steal or scavenge off of various battlefields, and many of them had no armor at all.

The Polish horses were considerably larger and more powerful than those of their adversaries, and in shock combat, this counted for a lot.

But mostly, the western knight was trained to fight as an individual, both on the tourney field and in battle. This was often to their disadvantage in combat with the more sophisticated easterners, but it wasn't that way today. The Mongols were showing none of their vaunted organization and discipline. If anything, they seemed more disorganized than we were. Perhaps Ilya's men really had fragged every Mongol officer.

Furthermore, our men could come to our lines when tired or thirsty or wounded. Any Mongol who got close enough to offer a clear shot was killed.

Our men had some advantages, but they weren't enough to offset a numerical disadvantage of twenty-to-one.

One by one, the pride of the Polish nobility was dying.

Chapter Twenty-three

The slaughter in the cold rain went on for hours, and watching it and not being able to do anything to help was one of the most frustrating things that I have ever done. It was equally rough on the men of the army who were looking helplessly on.

A group of women came by driving mules that were pulling a standard army tank cart filled with beer. They filled all our cooking pots with it.

"Compliments of the Sandomierz Whoremasters Guild," one saucy wench said. "Just be sure and save half of it for them fine young knights out there doing all the fighting!"

"What is the Whoremasters Guild doing with an army tank cart?" I asked.

"Oh, they was just sitting around, going to waste, when all them handsome knights was thirsty," she said. "We figured we'd do us a public service, being in that business, you know. Servicing the public, that's our job!"

"They? How many of my tank carts did you take?"

"Oh, there was maybe two dozen of them, and the mules wasn't being used either. But *your* carts? Then you must be that Count Conrad they talk about. You're the size they tell. Say, you ain't mad about this beer, are you? I mean, it ain't like we stole it to sell or something."

"No, I guess I'm not mad, and I suppose the men need a drink. But look, once you share out the beer, come back with that thing filled with water, all right?"

"Right-o, your lordship. Say, why don't we never see you around any? A man your size would be a fun one!"

"I'm happily married. But by the same token, what are you doing being a prostitute? You know the army is always hiring women as well as men. You could get a good job and maybe find a real knight of your own."

"What? Leave the guild? Say, my master'd whup me for even thinking about it!"

"You don't have to put up with that sort of thing! No whoremaster ever dared beat a member of the army!"

"What? Not whup me? Then how'd I know he still cared about me? Whoops! The cart's four places down already! Got to run, your lordship! *Ta-taaa!*"

And with that, she waved and ran away. I don't think I'll ever understand some people.

Well, at least I could understand the men around me. They wanted to go out there and kill somebody! Some of them had been training for this day for years, and now there was nothing they could do! We had over twenty thousand swivel guns pointed at the enemy, and they were useless! A bullet fired would go right through the Mongol it was aimed at, and kill some Christian who happened to be fighting behind him! It was all my fault, too. I made those guns too powerful! I'd had visions of Mongols charging at us six ranks deep, and our guns ploughing furrows through them. I never imagined anything like this!

One of my men looked up at me from the ranks in front of my cart and shouted, "Dammit! Do something!"

He was as insubordinate as hell, yet he had expressed the common feeling, and I had to answer him.

"Do what? What can we do? If we advance, we'd only squeeze them closer together, and our knights need room to fight in! If we shoot, we kill our own men as well as the enemy!"

"They're dying anyway!" another man yelled.

"Then better they should die at Mongol hands and not ours! If the knights would just get out of there, we could end this in minutes! This is their decision! There's nothing we can do!"

That didn't satisfy anybody, but there was nothing they could answer. I looked away from the slaughter and saw a strange thing.

A knight rode along the backs of our carts, not in the trap at all. He wore gold-washed chain mail of good quality but of the old style. His barrel-type helmet was gold-washed as well, with trim that looked to be solid gold. He was staring at the war carts and guns like a country peasant visiting the city for the first time. But what really caught my notice was his horse. It was pure white, but aside from that, it was absolutely identical to my mount Anna! The same gait, the same facial features, the same everything!

I had my face plate open when I said, "Can I help you, sir?"

He looked at me and I thought for a moment that he was going to fall off his horse! After a bit, he said in very broken Polish, "What...what this all is? Guns and plate armor! Here! Now! How?"

Now it was my turn to be startled, for he spoke with a strong *American English accent*!

"Just who are you?" I asked.

"I am Sir Manuel la Falla," he said.

"*In a pig's eye!*" I said to him in Modern English.

He almost fell over again, but a commotion out on the battlefield distracted me from talking further with the man.

Count Lambert was coming toward me with the battle behind him. There was a Mongol spear in his gut, one of those sharp, thin, triangular things that could pierce our armor. He was swaying in the saddle, and his horse was staggering as well. As I watched, horse and man collapsed to the ground not a hundred yards in front of me.

I jumped down from the war cart and pushed my way through the pikers. Tapping two of the front-rank axemen and motioning them to follow me, I vaulted over the big shield and ran to Lambert's aid.

I swear that my only intention was to drag my liege lord back to safety. I never meant to cause what happened. But that strange, crazy foreign knight, whatever he was, ran out after me, waving at the lines to advance and shouting *in English!*

"Come on you apes! Over the top! Up and at 'em! Chaaaarrrrrge!"

Somehow, the man had gotten one of our red-and-white surcoats. I suppose they thought he was obeying my orders, for I was out in front of him. They couldn't have understood a word of what he said, but his meaning was clear and *it was what they all had wanted to do for hours!*

From a hundred thousand voices came a roar!

"FOR GOD AND POLAND!"

All along the lines, a hundred and twenty thousand pikers and axemen went up and over the shields and staged an impromptu infantry charge on three times their number of cavalry!

Interlude Five

Tom hit the STOP button.

"Yeah, that was me! I think I led the biggest infantry charge in history, right there!"

"To me it looked like a damn fool thing to do!" I said. "An infantry charge on cavalry? That's unheard of!"

"It was when I did it, but it happened another time maybe three hundred years later, during one of the wars between the

English and the Scots, for about the same reason and with about the same outcome.

"You see, it was getting late in the day, and if the thing wasn't settled by sunset, those Mongols might have broken out. All those horsemen on both sides had been fighting for at least eight hours without a break, and the Mongols hadn't gotten much sleep the night before. And a horseman has it all over a footman, *providing the horse can move!* Once those pikers got them pushed back and jammed together, they were dog meat!"

"Hey, if you'd just gotten there, how did you have the time to figure all that out?"

"Well, I got there late. That was obvious, so I did a one day switchback so I could be involved in the whole battle. I was with Duke Boleslaw when he rode out that morning! I was there for the whole thing! Of course, I was taking stim pills to keep up with those youngsters, but that doesn't count. I *am* over eight hundred years old, after all. Then when Conrad went over the shield, I was back by his lines. I dismounted and led the charge."

"So you're pretty proud of yourself, huh?"

"I saved the day! There's only one thing wrong, though. The background scenery isn't right. That place doesn't look like Chmielnick at all. I know that area! That looks like it's about twenty miles west of Sandomierz, and the battle wasn't fought there!"

"Well, it was fought there now!"

I hit the START button.

Chapter Twenty-four

FROM THE DIARY OF CONRAD STARGARD

I stared in horror at the men running past me. The Mongols still vastly outnumbered us, and what had started so well would now end in absolute disaster! All because of Duke Boleslaw's stupidity and that crazy foreigner, our army would be destroyed, our country overrun, and our families all murdered! I yelled, I shouted but no one paid any attention. With all the noise and every man shouting, I doubt if any of them heard me. There was nothing I could do, and again, I was helpless.

But there was something I could do for Lambert, so I did it. I went over to him.

In falling from his horse, he had rolled clear of the animal, but that was the most expensive roll in his life.

"Ah, Conrad. I see that you have your medical kit with you as always. It seems that I need it for a change. Damnable thing! The first time in ten years I get a chance to get into a fight and this has to happen!" Lambert gestured toward the spear in him.

"See? You should have left the fighting to me. I only got an arrow in the eye." I ripped open and laid aside his red-and-white surcoat, unlatched his breastplate, and pulled it off. The Mongol spear came with it, dripping with blood and gore. Then I opened his gambezon and shirt, and surveyed the mess. There was a gash in his stomach as wide as both my hands, and deep.

"What? That little hole in my armor and that mighty slash in my gut? How can that be?"

"It was when you fell, Lambert. The spear spun around in there. The edges on those damned things are sharp."

"Well, that's it, then, and a sad ending it is! Done in by my own horse and my own peasant!"

"My lord? How so? I know your horse was wounded. I saw it stagger."

"He wasn't wounded. He was drunk! A half hour ago, I went to our lines for a drink. One of my own peasants, only he's a knight now, came out and gave me a well needed beer. When I asked for some water for my horse, he said they had none, though they had plenty of beer. I hated to see Shadowfax suffering, for he had served me well this day. I was in too much of a hurry to take him down to the stream, so I bid the man give my horse some beer, and he did, using his own helmet as a horse bucket. It was strong beer, and that was my downfall."

"My lord, this wound . . ."

"I know. I can see it. There's shit mixed in with the blood, so my gut is cut open. It will fester and I'm a dead man. Still, it's not a bad way to die, on a battlefield. Better than growing feeble and blind and impotent with old age, and that's all I had to look forward to. It was getting so sometimes I could only take one wench a day, and the virgins were getting hard to service. No, this is for the best."

"Shall I find you a priest, my lord?"

"In a while, in a while. I have some time left. I can feel it. I'm glad you're here. There are some things I want to talk to you about. I was right about your origins, wasn't I? You really were sent here by Prester John to save us from the Mongol invasion, weren't you?"

What could I say? "Of course, my lord. You alone had it figured out from the beginning." I lied, but it was a good lie.

"I knew it! But tell me, why did he only send one man?"

"Well, my lord, there was only the one invasion."

"What! Oh, ha-ha! Ooooh!" Suddenly his face went white. "Oh. It's like the old joke. It only hurts when I laugh. Well. Then there's my estate. I'm minded to give my daughter my lands in Hungary, which are twice as large as those in Poland, and richer, though not so well run, but I don't want you to be saddled with a liege lord who is whoever she marries. I haven't had time to pick the man! He might not treat my peasants properly or even service the girls at the cloth factory as they deserve, and that would be a shame and a waste! So I'm giving my Polish lands to you. Don't look so surprised or say anything. I've thought this out and that's the way that I want it. I've had it written all up and Duke Henryk himself has approved it."

"Thank you, my lord," Even though it didn't mean anything, it was a nice thought. I'd never inherit that land. As soon as the Mongols broke through our footmen, I'd die right here next to Lambert. Still, it was a nice thought.

"Just take good care of my vassals and my peasants, and see to it that the girls are well loved. They need that."

"We all do, my lord."

"That's God's truth! But do you swear it?"

"On my honor by all that is holy, my lord."

"Good. Well, be off with you, then. You've got a battle to fight. And if you see a priest, send him by. I'll spend my time getting my soul together. Be off now. No. Wait. You better take these. I won't be needing them anymore." He gave me back the binoculars I had given him on the first day we met. I took them. It would have been rude to do otherwise.

"Good-bye, my lord Count Lambert Piast, and may God bless you and love you."

I stood up, tears in my one eye, and looked out at the battle-field. The fight was a good ways away, more than a mile, and I started walking toward it. I heard a familiar whinny behind me and turned around.

"Anna?"

She nodded YES. She was looking at my wounded eye.

"Yes, I got hurt a bit, but it's all right. I'm glad you're here! But come on, girl, there's work to be done!"

I mounted and we rode to battle.

A half-mile later, I saw the strange, gold-clad knight back on his white horse, fighting two Mongol horsemen who had some-how slipped through the line of Polish footmen. I didn't know who or what he was, but he was wearing one of our surcoats now and he seemed to be on our side. I drew my sword and we galloped to his aid.

I was almost there when one of the Mongols threw one of those deadly spears at him. At a dozen yards, it flew straight through his eyeslit and the point punched its way out the back of his helmet!

I caught one Mongol unawares and chopped his head off before the other saw me. The second was just recovering from his deadly throw, and I got in a blow on his horse's neck. One does not have to fight fair with one's social inferiors.

He spilled on the ground and I took his right arm off at the shoulder on the next round. That was enough. Let the bastard bleed to death.

I dismounted near the strange knight. I was sure he was dead, but head wounds are sometimes surprising. People have recovered from the damndest things. I had to pull out the spear before I could remove his helmet and I had to put my foot on that helmet to pull the spear out.

There was no breathing, no pulse. The spear had made a ghastly hole where his left eye had been and I think it had severed the spinal column as well. He was dead. There was something familiar about the man, but I couldn't place him. The weird thing was his haircut. He was completely bald back to the top of his head. Even his eyebrows and eyelashes were gone, yet there were little cut-off hairs laying loose all over his face.

The white horse was acting shocked and nervous. From down here, it was obvious that she was a mare. "Are you one of Anna's people, like this girl here?" I said. She didn't respond, but then I remembered her rider speaking English. I repeated my question in that language, and she nodded YES, exactly as Anna does.

"Then I think it would be best if you came along with us. Your friend here is dead. There is nothing we can do for him," I said in my rusty English.

She nodded YES.

Interlude Six

I hit the STOP button.

"Tom, are you all right?" I said. He was staring fixedly at the screen, his eyes bulging, and he was making gurgling sounds.

"What? No. I'm not all right, you idiot! I'm dead! Don't you realize that we just saw me die?"

"But you know that this is some kind of alternate reality. It's not exactly real."

"It's exactly as real as the reality around us! Is that some *third* me who died out there? Or am I going to go back there later, subjectively, and die there in my own future?"

"Damned if I know, but if I were you, I'd never go to thirteenth-century Poland again!"

His hand was shaking as he pushed the COMM button and ordered a double martini. A naked serving wench brought it in instantly and he gulped it down. Then he sent her back for another, and she was out of the room and back in so fast that she must have passed herself in the hallway. Of course, that sort of thing happens all the time around here. I ordered a beer and she made a third trip.

"It didn't really happen that way," he said, staring at a blank wall. "That spear only glanced off my helmet. I saw it coming and I ducked!"

"It looks like this time you forgot to duck. Tom, why weren't you better protected than that?"

"I was! I always am! I wear a bio-engineered fungus coating called a TufSkin."

I was familiar with the stuff. I wear it myself, like most people. It's not only a cheap insurance policy but it makes shaving a breeze.

The stuff isn't noticeable, but it has these billions of tiny interlocking plates made of crosslinked tubular graphite, the toughest substance known. If you are hit from the outside, on impact and in microseconds, tiny muscles interlock those plates and give you an armor equivalent to a quarter inch of tool steel. Of course, when it does that, it shears off your hair in the process, but that's a small price to pay!

Tom was still talking in a dazed sort of way. "The only place it can't cover is the eyes, but the helmet I was wearing should have sensed that spear coming and slammed shut the eyeslits! Or I could have blinked! I should have been completely safe!"

"I guess this time there was some sort of mechanical failure."

His face was still white as he said, "But there wasn't one! My God, is the whole universe shredding apart?"

He hit the START button.

Chapter Twenty-five

FROM THE AUTOBIOGRAPHY
OF SIR VLADIMIR CHARNETSKI

Looking through my telescope, I saw a knight who I think was Count Lambert fall on the field, and another man who I am sure was Count Conrad run out to aid him. Surely there could be no other knight of his size!

But then I saw that Count Conrad was leading a charge against the Mongols, and doing it without my orders! He had, after all, left me in charge, and one of his first rules of leadership was unity of command! If he wished to take command, that was his prerogative, but he had no right to do so without notifying me!

And why in the name of all that is holy had he left the carts and gunners behind? It made absolutely no sense! Even if the pikers could encircle the Mongol horsemen, what could they do to harm them? They might skewer the first few ranks, but by that time, the enemy formation would be hundreds of yards thick! And completely unharmed! This was madness!

But there it was, and there was no way to call those men back now. If I countermanded his order, the results would be pure chaos! Some pikers would be out in the field and some of the carts would have no one but gunners to defend them. There would be gaps in our lines of footmen, and the Mongols could bypass them, cut through those unsupported gunners with ease and escape our trap. Already, I saw two Mongols riding behind our footmen, and a single conventional knight charging at both of them. My people have sometimes been called fools, but no one has ever dared question our courage.

There was nothing for it but to back my liege lord up, and hope that there was some reason for this insanity. I ordered "All Footmen Charge," and mounted Betty to follow them out.

FROM THE DIARY OF CONRAD STARGARD

When I got to the battle lines, I was astounded! We weren't losing at all! Our lines had been six men deep when we started, but as we closed with the enemy, the circumference naturally got smaller, and since we had started out in a long thin oval, the ends were naturally thicker with men than the sides, which pushed the mass of horsemen inside into something of a circle.

As I got there, our men were twelve to eighteen ranks deep, and as pressed together as a Macedonian phalanx! I think that if it were not for their clamshell armor, many of our front rank men would have smothered to death. Certainly, most of the horses died that way. They were squeezed so hard together that they could not breathe.

The enemy horsemen were packed so closely together that they could not get out of the saddle! Their legs were pinned in! Who could have imagined such a thing!

There were men with halberds and short axes milling around the periphery, wanting to get at the Mongols, but not knowing how.

Then one man wearing a turban wrapped around his helmet and wielding a short axe screamed and ran right up the backs of the outside row of pikers! He climbed to the top of the men and then actually ran down on the tops of the packed rows of pikes at the enemy! Shouting a war cry that sounded like the howling of a wolf, he leaped to the back of a Mongol horse that was so penned in that it could not move.

"*El Allah il Allah!*" he screamed again, in vengeance fifteen years delayed.

He stretched high as if he was chopping firewood and hacked into the neck of the rider. He swung a second time, though it surely wasn't necessary, and the Mongol's head flew loose. Then he stepped to the haunch of the next horse and repeated the performance!

Seeing this told our men what to do! A human wave of axemen ran up on top of the pikers, then across their shoulders and heads to get at the enemy! A lot of pikers might have had bruised backs, but I never heard any complaints. In minutes, ten thousand axemen and swordsmen were *running on top of* five hundred thousand Mongol horsemen, butchering them without thought of mercy.

It was over in less than a dozen minutes, and none but the Christian horsemen were left alive. A half-million of the enemy had been killed in this battle and the army's losses were almost nonexistent, a few broken legs and sprained ankles, plus one case of what looked like a heart attack.

Then it was over and a strange silence came over the battlefield. The pikers were still pushing forward, since they knew nothing better to do. The axemen on top of the enemy just looked around dumbfounded, seeing nothing else to kill and awestruck at the carnage that they had created. And they all stood there, breathing.

Then someone started singing one of the army songs, the one that one day would be the Polish national anthem.

"Poland is not yet dead!

"Not while we yet live!"

Then the song was over and someone started in on "*Te Deum.*" The men backed off and the Mongol horses slumped to the ground, asphyxiated or exhausted. Most of our warriors went to their knees as well, and gave thanks to God.

The war was over.

Hetman Vladimir came by and we discussed the cleanup. Our wounded to go to one place, our dead to another. Some men were detailed to collect booty, others to get supper going.

"And the Mongols?" he asked.

"Put their money and jewelry over here, their weapons and anything else valuable over there," I said, pointing. "Their bodies on that rise for burning, and their heads on that hill. I want a real head count, so stack them neatly."

"Yes sir. What about the Mongol wounded?"

"Once you've put all their heads on that hill and their bodies on that rise, you can give medical attention to any that request it."

"Right sir, no prisoners. I just wanted to make sure."

"Well, what could we do with a Mongol prisoner? They have no secrets to tell us. We can't keep them, guarding and feeding them forever. If we let them go, they'd have no choice but to rob and murder their way home, so that's out. The horde would never trade Christians for them. They look on one of their men who was taken prisoner as one who has failed in his duty! They want him killed! Best to just kill them now and be done with it."

"Yes, sir. I doubt if there are any of them left alive, anyway." He started giving efficient orders and I wandered on.

I saw by his mace that a priest was standing near me and I remembered Count Lambert. At first he was hesitant to go two miles away when there were so many who needed his services right here, but I dismounted and offered him Anna to get him there in a hurry.

She gave me an "I don't like this" pose.

"Look, girl, the war is over and Lambert needs a priest. I'll be okay. I have your white sister over here and she can take care of me as well as you can. But I'm the only one who can speak her language, so I can't lend her out. You understand, don't you?"

She was still sulking when she rode off with the priest. I mounted the white Big Person and rode about the field. There was a vast silence about all of us, as if a mass were being said and we must not speak. Men were working diligently at the tasks assigned to them, but they spoke only when absolutely necessary, and then in whispers. Something had happened that was vaster than all of us, something great and, somehow, holy.

The gunners had not participated in the final kill. A gunner stood to his gun no matter what happened. I told them to stand down and report to the field for duty. They passed the word and soon were helping get things in shape.

Beyond the north line, I came upon our battalion of Night Fighters, with sentries posted but most of them fast asleep in the rain and mud. I looked up Baron Ilya and got him out of his hammock.

"Ilya, you slept right through the battle."

"Our orders was to guard this flank, sir. We done that."

"You missed quite a show."

"Yes, sir, but so did they, last night. We did our part."

"Maybe more than that. But get your men ready to move. I want you to go back to the Mongol camp and see if you can secure it, since you have the only well rested men we've got."

"Yes, sir. That's an odd horse you're riding."

"Odder than you think. I've found another Big Person."

"There were *two* of them? Amazing. But for now, sir, I need your permission to strip ammunition out of these abandoned carts if I'm going to see about that camp."

"Granted." God, but I was tired.

Then I went back to my own cart, set up my old dome tent, and got my first full night's sleep in a week.

The next morning, after a breakfast of fresh horse meat, I found that the radios still weren't working, but I got the battle report. The amount of booty taken was fabulous. Every single man in my army was rich, and there was doubtless far more to be had once we cleaned up the killing grounds on the east bank of the Vistula. Some accounting would be necessary, but I think that the danger of inflation was very real.

Somehow, I would have to make sure that, while the troops were well rewarded, the economy was not ruined. I did not want to happen to us what happened to Spain after the conquest of the New World. There, so much gold poured in that even the lowliest Spaniard saw no reason to work. Farms and orchards were abandoned because if you were rich, why should you go out and do grunt labor? But within a few years, they discovered that there was nothing left for their money to buy and that the land had been wasted. Spain never did recover.

Our losses were surprisingly light. Out of the whole land army, there were only some six hundred dead or missing. Half of the Night-Fighter casualties were still alive in the Mongol camp when Ilya's battalion returned. Some had retreated in the wrong direction in the dark and some had been knocked unconscious by their own grenades and what not.

But after the Mongols pulled out in the morning, our stragglers had taken over the Mongol camp themselves! The Mongols had left behind only their most severely wounded and the surviving Polish girls they had captured on the way in.

The stories the girls told our men were so brutal that all the Mongol wounded were killed, despite the fact that most of the girls had actually been killed by us, in the course of the fragging. It had never occurred to us that the Mongol officers would have slave girls with them. In our ignorance, we had slaughtered more than three hundred young ladies, our own people.

But while the army's losses were small, the traditional forces were another matter. Duke Boleslaw of Mazovia was dead, as was the Duke of Sandomierz. Out of the estimated thirty-one thousand men that followed them, less than four hundred were left alive, and most of those were severely wounded. Virtually every nobleman from the duchies of Mazovia, Little Poland, and Sandomierz was dead!

A new age was coming to my country, but the flower of the past was gone.

The next morning, some of my depression had worn off and I was feeling a bit better. I saddled Anna and went to have a look around, with the white Big Person tagging along. That was another problem that would have to be worked out somehow. Anna wouldn't leave me and the new mount had no one that could talk to her but me. Yet it seemed a shame to waste the services of a Big Person.

Baron Vladimir had ordered Count Lambert's aircraft sent back to Eagle Nest. When I got there, the last of them was pulling out, strapped to the top of a war cart with the wing dismounted and roped next to the fuselage. The pilots who had flown them were dead, every last foolish one of them.

The Christian knights were being buried, each in his own

grave, with a dog tag on each wooden cross and another on his arms and armor, neatly bundled for return to his family. Someday, we'd send a crew of stonecutters here and have proper tombstones made.

It was too wet to get a decent fire going, so the Mongol dead were being piled naked in a huge common trench, along with the dead horses. Even the horses had been stripped. Baron Vladimir had apparently felt that a half million horsehides was a prize well worth taking. If he could get them salted down in time, they'd keep the army in boots for many years. I doubted if we had salt enough to do the job, even at Three Walls. Likely, we'd have to send men to the mines and get the mines going besides.

The heads of the Mongols were stacked separately, as I had ordered. A crew was putting them up on stakes made of old lances, in neat squares a gross heads to the side, for easy counting. Good. I wanted to make sure that no one ever doubted what we had accomplished here. Those heads were a fitting monument to this battle.

In a day or two, the cleanup would be done, and we could go home. Well, some of us. A contingent would have to be sent to loot and clean up the mess we'd made on the east bank of the Vistula. Likely, Baron Tadaos was starting that already. If only the weather would clear up so we could use the radios again. But the thunder and lightning went on and showed no signs of stopping. It seemed unfitting, somehow. Victories should happen in fine weather.

Finally, we found Baron Vladimir.

"Good morning, my lord. The sleep seems to have done you good. You're looking better. Have you had a medic examine your eye lately?"

"No, but I suppose I should, at least to change the bandage."

"Most of them are down at the field hospital, at our old campsite, my lord."

"I'll go there next. But for now, I want you to set up a meeting for me with the troops, captains and above, for late this afternoon, at six. There are some things I have to tell them."

"Done, my lord."

"Is anything coming through on the radios, yet?"

"I'm afraid not, my lord."

"Then perhaps you should put a dozen men on Big People and have them spread the word of our victory. Our wives are doubtless worried and Duke Henryk should be informed. Tell the duke that I advise sending at least his foreign troops south to King Bela."

"I'll see to it, my lord."

"Good. Then I'll see you at six, if not before."

The medic said that my wound was healing well, and it looked like the eye was uninjured. The only problem was that when he removed the bandage, I couldn't tell the difference. My right eye was blind.

Perhaps it's odd, but somehow it didn't bother me. After all the death I had seen and caused, well, maybe losing the eye was some sort of penance.

The day wound on and it was time for my talk.

I stepped up on the makeshift podium in front of my captains, komanders, and barons.

"Brothers!" I said. "I wish that I could address the entire army, and not just the officers, but you all know that it would be impossible. Talking to the almost eight hundred of you is about all my lungs can handle. I am therefore going to ask you captains to each give a similar talk to your men, so I'll thank you to take notes."

Notebooks and real lead pencils dutifully came out.

"Thank you. First, I want you all to know that riders have been sent to tell your families that you are safe, so they can stop worrying about you.

"Next, I want to praise you all for the magnificent victory you have won. For the first time in all of history, the Mongols have been beaten. In the last fifty years, those murdering bastards have defeated over fifty armies, and most of those armies outnumbered the Mongol invaders. But we went at them outnumbered twenty to one, and we killed them to a man!"

"Over a hundred major cities in China, Asia, and Russia have fallen to their rape, murder, and plunder, but not one major city in Poland has been lost, and all because of you men! The slaughter you worked has saved the lives of millions of your countrymen, and millions of other Christians, besides, for had we lost, the Mongols would not have stopped with Poland. They would have gone on to take Germany, France, and even England, Spain, and Italy. By stopping the Mongols here, you have saved all of Christendom! Your children and grandchildren and their descendants will be singing your praises for a thousand years!

"To honor you for this mighty deed, we are changing the name of our organization. No longer will we be simply 'the army.' From this day onward, we will be known as the 'Christian Army,' the defenders of all Christendom!

"The Mongol plan was to hit King Bela of Hungary at the same time as they invaded us. We don't know yet if they planned to take the Hungarians from the east, or from the north through Poland. If the second, you have saved Hungary along with Poland. If the first, if the Mongols actually had enough men to make both invasions at the same time, we have at least saved the many thousands of Christian Knights who are still with my liege lord Duke Henryk at Legnica. I have this day sent a message to my liege urging him to release those fighters to help King Bela. It may yet be that a victory to the south will happen, and part of the credit for that victory will be due to you.

"Then there is the matter of the booty you have earned. You all know that it is fabulous! Though it will be awhile before it can all be properly accounted and a fair distribution made, I think I'm safe in promising every man below the rank of knight at least a thousand pence! The knights will get twice that, and captains eight times that amount! So you are all rich!

"But you won't get a chance to start spending it immediately. There's still work to be done. The River Battalion killed far more of the enemy than were killed here on this plain, and there are too few of them left to do the looting, let alone the cleanup. But there at least we won't have the sad job of burying our own men!

"And now I want to talk a bit about the future.

"We have won a great victory here, but don't think for a minute that the Mongols have gone away forever. These marauders that we have killed had descendants, and if we don't do something about it, in twenty years our own children will have to try and repeat what we have done here. And next time maybe the Mongols won't act as stupidly as they have in the last few weeks.

"Yes, I said that we have defeated a stupid enemy! They lined themselves up on the east bank of the Vistula and let us cut them down like a farmer cuts down hay! They set up a stupid night guard on their camp, and let Baron Ilya's battalion of Night Fighters go in and kill fifty thousand of them, including most of their officers! And without those officers, the Mongol troops rode stupidly into a trap that got the rest of them slaughtered.

"Well, next time, they won't be so stupid! Next time, they will have learned something from the hard lesson we gave them, and next time they might win!

"Next time, we have to be far stronger than we were here. Next time we must have more troops, better weapons, and better defenses!

"So don't think that you can retire from the army and go back to whatever it was that you were doing before the Mongols and I came along. You can't! There's work to be done!

"I have bought up most of the land for five miles on both banks of the Vistula. We are going to build a fort like the one at East Gate every five miles along the river, all the way down to the Baltic, and on both sides! And after that, we'll build them up the Bug as well! Every one of those forts will be manned by a company of our men, so the army will not be disbanding. We will continue to grow, and you all can continue to look forward to promotions, for not only will we have to build and man the forts, we will have to vastly expand our manufacturing facilities to equip them.

"The Christian Army that we all belong to will be a permanent organization. In the same manner that the Church defends the souls of all Christians, we will defend their bodies. We will do our work in the realm of the physical just as the Church does its work in the realm of the spiritual. We will be doing God's work, and every one of you will be needed.

"Yet no man will be forced to stay in the army. Once we have finished with the cleanup, any man who wishes to leave may do so. I simply promise any man who leaves that he will regret it later, when he is a peasant and his old friends are knights and barons!

"In times to come, we will not only be defending Christendom, but we will eventually be able to take the war to the enemy. Millions of souls in the Russias and elsewhere are now living under the Mongols' brutal tread. We are going to go out there and free them, and make proper Christians out of them besides!

"I promise you all interesting times!

"That's about it. Have a talk with your men and then get a good night's sleep. Like I said, there's work to do!"

Interlude Seven

The tape wound to a stop.

"That's it? There?" Tom said.

"What do you mean?" I asked.

"But it didn't end there! Not when I was alive!"

"Tom, I know that this thing has been quite a shock to you. You need to unwind, to relax for a while. Then things will be clearer for you. Look, let's have a few more drinks, then take a steambath and maybe invite in a few of the wenches. After that a good rubdown and some more girls and I know you'll feel better."

"You think I'm crazy, don't you? I'm not! Something Conrad has done, or something about him has shattered the temporal continuity of all creation! Can't you understand that *I* built the first time machine and *I* don't understand what is happening!"

"Tom, I don't understand what's happening either, but I do know that a drink and a wench never hurt anybody. Come on." I took him by the hand and led him out of the room.

Appendix to The Flying Warlord

CONRAD'S ARMY

ORGANIZATIONAL STRUCTURE OF A TYPICAL COMPANY

1   Captain
6   Knight Banners, called "banners"
36   Knight Bachelors, called "knights"
216 Warriors, in three grades
       72   Squires
       72   Pages
       72   Warriors, called "grunts" when in basic

This was the plan, but such things rarely work out. Always there were people in school, people on indefinite leave, extra people temporarily assigned. The above represented a never-to-be-attained ideal.

In addition there were the wives and children. Warriors were encouraged to marry, and often met their wives in basic training. On being knighted, a man had the right, with his wife's permission, to have a "servant," a euphemism for a second wife. This was as permanent a relationship as marriage, and was attended by similar ceremonies, though it was not sanctified by the Church.

A servant had all of the rights, privileges, and duties of a wife, and her children were considered to be fully legitimate, but she was slightly inferior to the first wife socially.

A banner could have two servants, and a captain three. Higher ranks could have more in proportion, although relatively few took full advantage of this privilege.

As with any primitive people recently receiving proper sanitation and medicine, the population exploded. Families of nine were the average, and a certain Captain Sliwa was famed for having thirty-nine children and four happy wives. Aside from the rhythm method, contraceptives were unknown. Conrad was unconcerned. The population of thirteenth-century Poland was only three million. The land could easily support fifty million. Furthermore, there were vast tracts in Russia and the Ukraine that had been denuded of people by the Mongols, and after that there was always North America, Argentina, South Africa, Australia, and New Zealand; areas with climates suitable to North Europeans. And of course, the problem would eventually take care of itself. Education and a higher standard of living always cut the birth rate.

In addition to the above-listed line personnel, the typical company was supported by a number of auxiliary organizations, with the following typical staffing. They are listed as so many "men," but most positions could be held by either male or female personnel:

Chaplain's Corps—three men
> Usually a pastor with two assistants, these priests were responsible for the Church, the library, and the school. School teachers were often qualified line personnel who taught on a part-time basis.

Communication Corps—six men
> Responsible for the radios, the telegraph, and the mail within the company and all cartage and shipping outside of it.

Accounting Corps—three men
> Responsible for all financial transactions between companies, outside suppliers, etc. Also handled payroll and kept individuals' bank accounts.

Medical Corps—one man

Medical Officer also had 12 trained part-time Corpsmen for emergencies. Responsible for the general health of the company, and also for sanitation inspection.

Commercial Corps—four men

Operated a general store that sold all sorts of products to anyone who came in. They also had a catalog sales operation and would handle the sale of farm produce from neighboring, nonarmy farms on a commission basis.

The Inn—twelve men

Personally owned by Conrad and the basis of his personal fortune. These inns were generally a smaller version of the Pink Dragon Inn.

Observers—fourteen little old ladies

These were a group of older people whose job was to sit in the towers and to keep a lookout in case anything bad happened. Equipped with telescopes and intercoms, each was usually somebody's grandmother. It gave them something useful to do, a place to live, and a modest income, while freeing up warriors for more strenuous duties. They usually had two-person cottages on top of the towers and spent their days and nights gossiping. But those towers were also equipped with machine guns, and on certain rare occasions these people were known to use them.

Many of the above positions were filled by women, and throughout the army there was no limitation as to how far a woman could rise. Women received combat training of a less vigorous nature and their armor was much lighter. However, women were excluded from combat except for guarding castle walls when the men were away. Also, women were forbidden to do strenuous work for the four months prior to childbirth and the two after it. Because of this last and because most women were pregnant half the time, few of them rose high in the hierarchy. As in most countries, a woman's status was largely determined by her husband's.

The family was vitally important to the army and was kept together at almost all costs. If shift work was necessary, then husband and wife were kept on the same shift regardless of the needs of the army. Further, their children went to school on that shift. If one spouse was assigned to a school, the other was also assigned to the complementary school. Vacations were always assigned to the entire family at the same time. Retirement was always announced for the family as a whole. This last was true even when it conflicted with the wishes of the individual.

One of the results of this policy was that single individuals were often promoted faster than their married counterparts. It was simply easier to move them around and promotion often comes with motion. Single ladies sometimes rose quickly and high.

Pregnant women and those with minor (under five years old) children worked fewer hours than normal and they were paid at half the usual daily rate.

The typical company had its own castle or buildings and was the basic unit of the Christian army. A person's company was his home, and except for promotions or when new companies were being formed, a person was rarely transferred out.

Even then, new companies were usually formed by a process of "budding." A banner, six knights, and thirty-six squires would be sent from a single company to three-month-long schools for promotion. Then in the following four months they acted as drill instructors for two hundred sixteen basics who had survived the first part of their training. Training completed, the basics and their instructors became a new company and left as a group for their new assignment.

Even in basic, where the attrition rate was high, a serious effort was made to break up groups as little as possible. Support personnel were generally assigned to a company on a permanent basis.

Other things were done to generate a team feeling. Everyone ate the same food in the same dining hall. Except for insignia, their military clothing was the same. Housing was allotted on a square yard basis proportional to the number of people in the family, although higher ranks were stationed higher up in the building.

The unit was a company in the commercial as well as the military sense. Each company usually had agricultural, commercial, and manufacturing interests as well as military duties, and each company was treated as a profit center, for accounting purposes. Economically, they competed freely with each other and with nonarmy organizations. In addition to their pay, individuals received a quarterly bonus proportional to their rank and the company's profits. Profits were determined in the usual manner and were split between the army's general fund and the company's personnel. Each company was thus externally a capitalist entity in a free enterprise system, although internally it was a socialist institution.

The company, then, was the home of about three hundred families, or about three thousand people, living in a set of buildings that looked like a castle, but was in fact an apartment house with a church, a school, a store, an inn, factories, and usually farms. They tried to make it a nice place to live.

As in a modern navy, every adult had both a combat occupation and a noncombat occupation. Rank was often but not always the same in both. When they were different, pay and status went according to whichever was higher. One lived with or near one's combat unit, no matter where one worked. Uniforms had a large arm insignia for combat rank and a small collar design for noncombat rank.

The banners often had several noncombat occupations. Companies often required an executive officer, purchasing agent, sales officer, military training officer, agricultural officer, manufacturing officer, etc. And anything else that the captain felt was best. He did not actually command the support personnel attached to his unit. These corps each had their own separate hierarchies. However, the radio operator who did not take a captain seriously was a fool. The captain's job was to decide what was to be done and who was to do it, and he had limited judicial functions, but it was intended that a good captain should spend most of his time idly observing the operations of his company.

FIELD GRADE OFFICERS

A Komander	ran a	Komand of	6 companies	with		1,500	Men
A Baron	ran a	Battalion of	6 Komands	with		9,000	Men
A Kolomel	ran a	Kolumn of	6 Battalions	with		54,000	Men
A Count	ran a	County of	6 Kolumns	with		324,000	Men
A Hetman	ran a	Division of	6 Counties	with		1,944,000	Men
A Duke	ran an	Army of	6 Divisions	with	11,664,000		Men

Of course, it was never anything like this neat. While the companies were remarkably stable, the upper command was in a constant state of flux. During its first thirty years of existence, the Christian Army expanded from nothing to over twelve million fighting men, plus their wives and an ungodly number of children. Countless changes were made as the structure tried to accommodate new technology and rapid expansion. It got so that warriors often did not know who their field officers were, but then, it was not important that they know. Their captains knew and that was enough.

But despite the growing pains, there were never more than six ranks above captain and an officer rarely had fewer than four or more than ten subordinates.

Except in time of war, komanders rarely took direct control of their komands. Instead, they functioned as staff officers for their barons. These seven officers, with a rump company, generally had a castle, but spent most of their time touring their thirty-six odd companies, either in a riverboat (if all of their battalion was on a river, as many of the earlier ones were), or a set of traveling cars pulled by the Big People (as Anna's progeny were called). Each komander had a specialty (agriculture, military training, etc.) and acted as a counselor to the banner in charge of that function within a company. The baron counseled the captain. The emphasis was on training rather than on reprimands, although ass-chewings occurred.

These visits lasted a day or two, happened to a company four to eight times a year (at the discretion of the baron, who was supposed to allot more time to problem children), and were always on a surprise basis. On rare occasions, the baron might take direct control of a troublesome company and spend a month there with his komanders straightening things out. The usual technique was to have the unfortunate captain and banners stand silently by while their stand-ins directed their subordinates. I mean a banner literally had to stand beside a komander, keep his mouth shut and take notes. That evening, he was permitted to ask questions. An embarrassing procedure, it rarely had to be repeated on a company.

This constant traveling encouraged the use of multiple wives. The members of an inspection team each took one or two of their wives with them on their endless tours, leaving other wives home to take care of the children. The wives provided companionship of course, but most of them were skilled managers in their own right and helped to spread knowledge and new techniques within the battalion.

When an organization was sufficiently large that a kolomel was not in charge, the counts and kolomels functioned in a similar manner to the barons and komanders, visiting their counties on a regular basis.

The head of an organization (be it the Chaplain's Corps, the Regular Army, the Wolves, the Eagles, or whatever), always had a large staff with sections in charge of inspection, engineering, auditing, etc. Each organization published a magazine, usually monthly.

THE CHAPLAIN'S CORPS

The Chaplain's Corps was in an awkward position in that it was subordinate to both the Pope and to the army. It survived by turning a blind eye to various army practices, such as the custom of multiple wives and not taking prisoners in combat. It maintained a college for novitiates in the Sudeten Mountains and did not accept candidates unless they had survived basic training. In combat, chaplains fought along side the men of their company, although they used a mace rather than an edged weapon since the Church forbade the shedding of blood.

THE TRAINING CORPS

The Training Corps was the only organization that did not maintain stable companies. Instructors were constantly being cycled back into the field and were normally there on a temporary duty basis only. However, the upper echelons were stable and kolomels acted as if they were captains. The Training Corps had a huge base near Three Walls, popularly called "Hell." It maintained the following schools:

BASIC TRAINING

This school accepted anyone aged fourteen to thirty who presented themselves at the door, and army policy was to provide free transportation to anyone who wanted to enlist. Enlistment was not for a fixed term of years. Any member of the army could quit at any time, except in a combat situation. Well, you could quit during combat, but your superior was then required to shoot you.

Women were accepted for training as well as men and more girls applied than boys. Perhaps this was because girls are more adventurous, or that this was a place where one could find a husband who would become a knight, or that here was where a woman could develop her own self, without having to be a peasant or a rich man's toy. Or a combination of the above. In truth, it is impossible to properly raise children and maintain a career in any culture. Many doubtless intended to travel single careers, but Mother Nature generally won out.

Basic training was extremely rigorous, with only about half of the male candidates surviving the first eight months, after which things eased up. Many candidates washed out for physical, emotional, or intellectual reasons, but eight percent actually died in training. Female training was less demanding physically, but equally rough on mind and spirit. About two-thirds of the girls graduated and actual deaths were rare.

These factors resulted in a sexual imbalance within the entire army, women outnumbering men by even more than could be accounted for by the knight's multiple wives. Yet to correct the problem, the army would have had to either reject some female candidates for arbitrary reasons, which seemed unfair, or to make the girl's course more demanding, which seemed impossible. Then, too, many men claimed that there was no problem at all and that the surplus of ladies was a good thing.

A candidate washing out was generally permitted to retake the course after waiting a year.

KNIGHT'S SCHOOL

This was a three-month-long course that prepared people for the first level of command. When a man attended, his wife attended the parallel school for women, while the kids were being taken care of by their home company. The emphasis was on training rather than on weeding out the unfit. Virtually everyone graduated, but one's grades counted toward one's next promotion.

BANNER'S SCHOOL

Like the knight's school, one grade up.

CAPTAIN'S SCHOOL, KOMANDER'S SCHOOL, BARON'S SCHOOL, KOLOMEL'S SCHOOL, COUNT'S SCHOOL

Each step up the ladder had its three-month-long course and was required for permanent promotion. There were no schools above those listed, though, as there were never enough candidates to maintain permanent classes. And anyway, who would teach in them?

THE REGULAR ARMY

This was the largest full army organization. Its combat-mission was to defend the country in the event of invasion and to maintain a vast number of forts strung along the borders, rivers, and other strategic (and not so strategic) positions. These forts usually housed a full company, were generally placed about five miles apart, and were connected by railroads. Each commanded about twenty-five square miles, which land was owned by the army and farmed extensively. Also, each fort contained some light-to-medium industry. Depending on the season, people worked at farms or factories. Except for military training, which occupied one day a week, army personnel stayed productive. There were never any of the time-wasting activities that predominate in the usual modern army.

THE CONSTRUCTION CORPS

This large organization was responsible for building the countless forts, bridges, dams, canals, and whole cities that the army required. Since much of the work was repetitious (the forts were all virtually identical), whole companies were specialized in the various phases of the construction of a single type of building. Once the legal department had acquired the land, and engineering had approved the site, a company of railroad builders would extend a line out to it. Then a site-preparation company might spend a week there and move on. On their heels would come a company of foundation layers who would move in and do their job in another week. In this manner, forts would pop up along a river on a weekly basis, each to be manned by a new company of Regulars fresh out of Hell.

Although the Construction Corps had no direct combat role (aside from its own defense), it was actually the most aggressive unit in the army. When invading enemy territory, army policy was to move slowly and build forts as they went. Territory taken was taken permanently.

Construction Corps companies lived in hundreds of rail-mounted mobile homes, which were set up in precisely the same way each week, to give some feeling of continuity. They could knock down their installation, move it five miles and rebuild it, complete with a dining hall, a church, a school, a store, and an inn, all within half a day.

Winters were often spent logging, not so much because of the need for lumber (most construction was in concrete), but for land clearance. In the twentieth century, forests have become precious, but in the thirteenth, eighty-five percent of the known world was forested. The wilderness was the enemy. The army needed vast amounts of agricultural land to feed its growing population, and a Mongol can't hide in a potato field.

THE WOLVES

The Wolves were the army's only full-time combat unit. Composed almost entirely of the sons and daughters of the old nobility, their role was to guard the construction corps when it operated in enemy territory and to raid the enemy, keeping him off balance.

The lowest rank in the Wolves was a knight and companies were led by a komander. Wolf bases were few and large, with six companies of Wolves and a support company of regular army.

This support duty was hated and the Regular Army tended to use it as a punishment detail.

THE EAGLES

The Eagles were the air force and were the most prestigious unit in the army. Flying wood-and-canvas planes for over twenty years, until magnesium was available, their casualty rate was high. Yet always there was competition to get in.

The Eagles recruited young people (fifteen was the maximum age of entry) who had completed the first eight months of basic training. They maintained their own schools and had their own aircraft factories. Although most of them spent most of their time in building and repairing aircraft, it was a point of pride with them that every Eagle, man or woman, was a pilot and flew regularly.

Their combat role was to patrol the borders and to work with the Wolves in harassing the enemy.

TRANSPORTATION AND COMMUNICATION CORPS

This was the most profitable unit in the army, as its services were unique and available to civilians as well as military users. It maintained steamboat lines on all navigable rivers, even on many outside of Poland. It maintained the railroads and supplied most of the transportation in the entire country. It maintained a complete postal system. It took care of the telegraph system as well as the radio system. Radio was strictly a communication device until after Conrad's death. Conrad felt that home radios, televisions, telephones, and private automobiles were detrimental to civilization and refused to let them be developed.

The Transportation and Communication Corps maintained ocean ships and eventually developed and totally controlled world shipping. It also made a bundle publishing the reports of its Explorer Force, which often made for fascinating reading.

LEGAL CORPS

The Legal Corps was concerned primarily with criminal law within army jurisdiction, but it did handle civil matters occasionally. It had its own school and publishing house. It provided circuit-court teams consisting of a judge, four lawyer-prosecutors (they took turns), a recorder, and a bailiff. These teams stopped at each company about once a month and heard any serious cases. (Captains had the authority to handle minor offenses.) Higher courts handled appeals.

The usual sentence was a bad conduct discharge and a term of years in a prison coal mine, which was run by the Legal Corps.

Attached to the Legal Corps, but largely independent, was the Detective Force. Each detective was paired with one of the Big People, and their arrest rate was excellent. The Big People's sense of smell was particularly important in this work. They made a bloodhound look like a dog. Warsaw and Katowice had their own uniformed police forces, but there were no other police forces in Poland.

MEDICAL CORPS

Besides providing a medical officer to every company in the army, the Medical Corps maintained a number of company-sized hospitals and a major teaching facility.

COMMERCIAL CORPS

Maintained stores at every army installation, as well as some in major civilian cities. It also ran a catalog sales operation out of its single huge warehouse. It bought and sold commodities, maintained the huge granaries in the Bledowska Desert, and eventually maintained trading posts around the world.

WARSAW CORPS

In our timeline, Warsaw was not built until the sixteenth century. But like every modern Pole, Conrad had to have a Warsaw, so he built one. This was a city of almost half a million people, larger than any city of the time outside of China.

Its primary function was political, though few people living there would have believed that. Conrad wanted to so impress the sovereigns of Europe that they would be eager to join his planned Federation of Christendom. What he built would have impressed even a jaded twentieth-century American. It was part university, part palace, and all World's Fair.

The city had no manufacturing facilities and little direct trade. Tourism was the biggest industry, with education running a close second.

The transport system consisted of eight moving slide-walks, seven of which were circles a third of a mile in diameter. The eighth was a mile across, enclosing the others. Each of these walks consisted of many bands, each a yard wide, each of which moved three miles an hour faster than the one before it. The center band of the longest walk moved at thirty-six miles an hour, was eight yards wide and was equipped with benches and food-vending kiosks. Vertical transport was handled by elevators of the *pater nostra* variety.

With this system, it was possible to go from any point in the city to any other point in less than twelve minutes.

The transportation deck was covered by a sixteen-yard-high ceiling and amounted to a vast mall, with stores, restaurants, and theaters.

Above the mall was an outdoor park and garden.

Outside of the big walk were a gross of company-sized buildings, each two gross yards long and seventeen stories tall, arranged like cooling fins, where most of the inhabitants lived. Each had its own dining facilities, church, and school. Young children did not have to be exposed to a big city environment. Many of these companies were home companies. Some were for transients.

Each of the smaller circles contained a single large building. The center one held the tallest, the cathedral. This was twice as high inside as the recently completed Notre Dame, and contained eight times the volume. You couldn't hear a sermon beyond the tenth row, but the place sure was impressive.

The palace had room for a senate and legislature, the private chambers of King Henryk the Pious, office space, and lots of room for visiting firemen.

Three of the circles contained institutes of higher learning. The

University taught the usual subjects of the time—law, theology, the classics, etc. The Institute taught sciences and engineering. The Academy taught art, music, and drama. Soon, this was where the nobility of Europe came to be educated.

One circle contained a sports arena that was covered once structural steel became available, and the last circle had a major hotel.

Surrounding the city and subordinate to it was a power plant and nine company-sized forts. These companies were primarily engaged in providing fresh foodstuffs and included a huge bakery and a bodacious dairy. Tunnels connected these installations to the city proper.

South of the city was a modern zoo, with lions and tigers and bears, and attached to it was an international village, with Chinese pagodas and Burmese stupas and Javanese temple dancers and Indians and Batu warriors.

All told, Warsaw was an incredible place.

THE MANUFACTURING CORPS

With a greater population than any other unit in the army, the Manufacturing Corps was not really a military organization. After the Battle of Chmielnick, early in the army's history, it was never once called to active duty. Furthermore, more than half of their workers were not actually members of the army, but were civilian employees. These employees got the same pay and benefits as their military counterparts and they did not have to participate in basic training and military exercises. On the other hand, they did not receive the twelve-year bonus, and promotion was faster for army personnel.

The Manufacturing Corps was responsible for mining, heavy industry, and a fair amount of medium industry, the borders with the Regular Army being pretty vague as to who could do what. There were many Regular Army companies that had their own coal mines and one Manufacturing Corps company produced musical instruments.

Much of the Manufacturing Corp's facilities were located in a mile-wide strip over the Upper Sileasian coal basin. This amounted to a city of over six million people that was over four dozen miles long and under one roof. Sprawling and brawling, Katowice was considered by many to be a greater wonder than Warsaw.

Others thought it a vision of Hell.

THE MILITIA

There was a major bonus, equal to all the money that a person had received up to that time, paid after twelve years of honorable service in the army. A man's wife(s) was also given a bonus at that time. At this point, certain less-than-acceptable personnel were eased out. Most had the option of remaining in and letting their eventual bonus increase.

A person accepting his twelve-year bonus was effectively retiring from the army. Since many people joined at the age of fourteen, this often happened when they were only twenty-six and a second career was expected. But a person never totally left the army. He could be called back in the event of an emergency, in theory at least. Oh, he could always quit, but that would mean giving up the prestige of his rank (it was customary to bump a man a grade on retirement), giving up his eventual rights to an army old folks' home, giving up his right to return to the army if things didn't work out, and possibly giving up the friendship and use of his favorite Big Person. And, in fact, the Militia was almost never actually called up.

The army had various offers to relieve a retiree of his money. Whole towns and small cities were built, all of them with public utilities like sewage systems. A man could buy a farm or a condo and office or shares in a factory. Many men left as a group to work on some commercial venture. If a knight bought into Militia property, he knew that his children would have schools and churches. Since his wife(s)'s money was also involved, be assured that most men stayed in the Militia.

In order to pay for essential services, Militia towns charged their residents certain taxes and fees. These were the only taxes that existed within the entire system.

THE PINK DRAGON INNS

Throughout Conrad's lifetime, the Pink Dragon Inns were not exactly part of the army, but rather were Conrad's personal property. They were the basis of his considerable private fortune. Every army installation of any decent size had one attached to it and thus they had a large captive audience. But in their defense, it must be said that they were extremely clean, cheerful, and inexpensive. Waitresses were always attractive and single, although the requirement for virginity was dropped after the first decade, and they were remarkably well paid. Permanent personnel had pay and benefits identical to those in the army and when the inns were transferred to the army on Conrad's retirement, the transition was hardly noticed.

THE WORK DAY

In the Middle Ages, the normal work day was dawn to dusk, which in a Polish summer could be eighteen hours. As soon as clocks became available, Conrad cut this to twelve, but with artificial light, the twelve-hour day, six-day week became the standard. The day started at dawn with a short, obligatory sunrise service. The Regular army stayed as much as possible with a day shift only, but many units worked around the clock, especially those with expensive capital equipment. The entire city of Warsaw ran non-stop, even the universities, and night was like day in Katowice.

RECREATION

The army was by no means all work and no play. Every company had an inn. There were bands of traveling entertainers, some under army contract but most operating independently. Athletic competition was strongly encouraged, especially when it was related to military training. Whole companies fought mock battles with each other and the betting on these was so heavy that the battles themselves sometimes got out of hand.

Less vigorous competitions also took place, with chess and music being the most popular. The ability to play a musical instrument was considered to be a standard accomplishment, and only a clod couldn't play at least a recorder.

Children's needs were carefully attended to, with nurseries, playgrounds, and youth centers. Scouting was popular.

All personnel got a paid two-week yearly vacation. Once there were enough Big People to go around, it was possible to rent a railroad car set up as family living quarters and go touring. Many companies operated as tourist traps.

THE ARMY'S BETTER HALF

All of the above really describes the activity of only half the army. The army was composed of two distinct intelligent species. Anna's progeny, the Big People, were a breed of genetically engineered horses. The products of a technology vastly beyond Conrad's Poland, these beings were in many ways superior to humans.

Their eyesight, hearing, and sense of smell were phenomenal and they possessed full use of a magnetic direction-finding sense that humans have but can't use. They didn't need sleep. They could eat anything organic, up to and including coal. They could run at thirty miles an hour all day long. They were immune to all diseases and seemed to have no fixed life span, apparently living forever.

They were all female and could reproduce voluntarily by parthenogenesis. It was only necessary to ask one to have babies and she would do it. A litter was always four. They were sexually mature and full-sized in four years. They could understand Polish, but not speak it.

Most astoundingly, they possessed a sort of racial memory. At around three, they started to remember everything their mother knew up to the time of their conception. The process was completed in about six months.

The Big People were less intelligent than the average human and were completely unable to handle higher mathematics or other systems of abstract thought. Given a concrete problem, on the other hand, they would often do as well as humans. Their ability to travel from point to point was near perfect, and their memory seems to have been eidetic.

They had a very amiable, placid temperament, except in combat, where they were absolutely deadly. Ordinarily, they were happy to go along with just about anything, although they expected to be treated politely. They were gregarious and they liked being around humans even more than their own kind. They liked being talked to and for this reason got along very well with children.

Anna was very taken with a sermon she heard and became extremely religious. Her daughters, being her identical twins in both mind and body, followed suit. Among the other trials and problems faced by the Chaplain's Corps was the necessity of baptizing, confirming, and giving sermons to beings who looked like horses. They gave silent prayers of thanks for the fact that no Big Person was ever observed to sin, so it was not necessary to confess them in pantomime.

The Big People were considered full members of the army, with all privileges. They were paid as warrior basics and when they spent their pay at all, it went mostly on sweets and jewelry. They had full legal rights and their testimony was admitted in court.

There were too few Big People at the time of Chmielnick to have much impact on the battle, but in the years that followed they became increasingly important. The Wolves had first priority to their services and then the Transportation and Communication Corps, who used them to carry the mails and pull railroad cars. Once they knew the route, a rider or driver was unnecessary. Because of their night vision and ability to see into the infrared, they were used as pilots on boats and ships. Big People showed no interest in aircraft and refused to board them. Some Little People claimed that this was obvious proof of their wisdom.

Eventually, there were enough Big People so that some could be spared for agriculture. Within a few years they had taken over ninety-five percent of all farmwork, which they preferred. Pulling a plow was no different than pulling a railroad car and you got home every night. Spending all night weeding? Hey, that's grass, our favorite food. Humans had little to do but make the decisions, keep the machinery fixed, and help out with the harvest.

When the Big People population approximately equalled that of adult Little People, they were asked to stop reproducing. Thereafter, the two populations were kept about equal and a one-on-one relationship was the most satisfying to all concerned. Big People were often "adopted" into human families, attending church and amusements with them, and taking vacations at the same time.

For fear that they might be mistreated, Conrad had asked the Big People to never leave the army and none of them ever did. Many followed their best friends into the quasicivilian Militia, but after the death of that person, they always returned home.

FINANCES

The army never taxed anyone and it refused to pay taxes. It supported itself by selling its products and services. Most of its production was consumed internally and most of its people spent most of their pay on army-supplied items, so there was little need for external money. Most of what was spent went to the purchase of land, and the army never sold any of the vast tracts it conquered from the Mongols.

Poland had large reserves of zinc ore, but zinc, as a separate metal, was unknown in Europe in the Middle Ages. Conrad developed a production process, but kept it an absolute secret, more tightly held than that of gunpowder. He cast a coinage out of it, used this coinage internally within his organization, and declared it to be equivalent to the existing silver coinage. Since he was always willing to trade it evenly for silver, people naturally believed him. This was brilliant from the standpoint of economics, but had the disadvantage of making zinc a rare metal. He had to keep secret the fact that brass was a zinc alloy and to charge absurd prices for galvanized iron.

Pay scales stayed absolutely constant throughout the period under discussion. All other prices fluctuated and generally went down, but not these. The army pay scale eventually became the "gold standard" of the world. Zinc coins with their actually increasing value became the standard coinage everywhere. This had the result of vastly increasing the army's wealth, since valuable goods could be purchased with cheaply produced coins. Furthermore, it was rarely necessary to redeem these coins with goods in return, since they often stayed circulating in the local economy. A similar thing happened to American paper money in 1945-60, when Europeans, desperate for a stable currency, took to using American dollars. Those "eurodollars" never were returned and the United States economy got a major boost. The amounts involved were several times those spent on the Marshall Plan.

Salaries were automatically banked on a bi-weekly basis. When you wanted your pay, you went to Accounting and got it.

DAILY PAY RATES

Warrior .... 1 penny
Page .... 2 pence
Esquire .... 4 pence
Knight Bachelor .... 8 pence
Knight Banner .... 16 pence
Captain .... 32 pence
Komander .... 64 pence
Baron .... 128 pence
Kolomel .... 256 pence
Count .... 512 pence
Hetman .... 1024 pence
Duke .... 2048 pence

By the standards of egalitarian twentieth-century America, where superiors are often paid only ten percent more than their subordinates, the rate of these increases might seem excessive, but remember that the Middle Ages were well convinced that rank hath its privileges. If an army baron was noticeably poorer than a traditional baron, the prestige of the army would suffer. Also, remember that these moneys represented "spending cash." One's necessities (food, clothing, housing, etc.) were provided free by the army. And lastly, Conrad never once drew his own pay. His personal expenses and his extensive charities were paid for out of his profits from the Pink Dragon Inns. Further, many higher officers imitated his comparatively modest style of living and did not draw their full salaries.

POLITICS

Democracy never developed in the army except in the Militia. At first, this was because Conrad felt that his countrymen weren't ready for democracy and later, after his retirement, because nobody really felt the need of it.

Militia towns were each governed by an elected counsel, although the elections were weighted. Warriors got one vote, knights got two, captains four, etc. These counsels eventually formed a Grand Counsel, but its decisions were purely advisory and it never was very powerful.

But there are other ways than elections for the will of the people to filter up to government, and the army used questionnaires. Twice a year, all personnel filled out an extensive form and answered questions about everything imaginable. The last one was always "What should we have asked about, but didn't?" These forms were tabulated quickly and taken seriously. The results were published in the *Army Magazine* in a few months along with Conrad's commentary. He never bound himself or his successors to follow the recommendations of his subordinates, but he always tried to justify his position when army policy was contrary to army opinion.

RELIGION

Most of the people in the army were Roman Catholics, and it often seemed that Catholics were promoted faster, but other religions were never forbidden. Jews were particularly welcome because they were happy to work on Sunday when everyone else wanted off.

Much to the annoyance of the Pope, the army refused his orders to slaughter a surviving pocket of Catheri heretics, but rather talked them into moving bodily to a protected area in the Ukraine, where they remained.

The army never ceased in its efforts to reunite the various branches of Christendom. On one occasion they hosted delegations from the Roman, Orthodox, and Coptic Churches at an isolated site where they could hopefully resolve their differences. With nothing accomplished after three years, the frustrated site komander put all of his charges on a diet of potatoes and water and refused to let them leave until such time as there was a uniform doctrine of faith. Even that didn't work and there was no end of flak from the Vatican.

TECHNOLOGY

Army technology was, by the standards of the main timeline, extremely spotty and inconsistent. Electronics was well developed because of Conrad's training in that field. They had radar before they had a reliable diesel engine, and their aircraft had solid-state computers while still made of wood and canvas. Astronomy was retarded and medicine was primitive, except for the universal cure given them by Conrad's uncle. Chemistry was behind but rationally organized so that progress was steady. Manufacturing techniques were superlative, with many factories being almost completely automated in Conrad's own lifetime. Agriculture too was well developed and as the Big People did most of the work, human input was limited to supervision, specialty harvesting, and research. Transport was both primitive and efficient. The Big

People could only run at thirty miles per hour, but things ran smoothly day and night and except for intercontinental service, the mails traveled about as fast as they did in twentieth-century America. Physics was totally developed but completely Newtonian. The very existence of atomic power was unknown and research in that direction was discouraged. Conrad wrote a secret book on the horrors of atomic war and set up a tiny group of scientists to police the field. Their technique was to recruit any researcher who stumbled onto the forbidden knowledge.

INHERITANCE

The inheritance of position was not permitted in the army and even Conrad's legitimate children got nothing.

The inheritance of wealth was never actually forbidden in the army, but for several hundred years, Conrad's dislike of the system resulted in those with considerable inherited wealth being socially snubbed as those who "couldn't make it on their own." Eventually, this practice declined. So did the army.

THE STAR LINE

It eventually became obvious to Conrad that promotions within the army were being made largely on the basis of seniority. To a certain extent, this was good, since the average age of his men was so low. But it had the effect of keeping bright young people out of upper management and he feared a repetition of the Russian system, where only old men run the country. Also, there was the problem of eventually picking his own replacement.

His solution was to set up a secret organization whose function was to single out outstanding young people while they were in basic, and to observe and guide their careers.

Only about one person in two thousand got this special treatment, and that person never knew that he or she had been so honored. But a casual acquaintance would suggest that he apply for advanced training at Warsaw and, by golly, it would be approved. A star found himself transferred fairly often, to broaden his background. Promotions happened more quickly, even though his superiors didn't know what was happening.

Even his love life was molded and many were channeled out of inadvisable marriages, finding themselves in situations where the only available partners were of their own caliber.

Not everyone responded to this sort of nudging, but enough did to populate the upper echelons with some very competent people.

Conrad decided that he would retire at the age of seventy-five and that his successor should be between thirty and thirty-five. He should be technically competent, emotionally mature, and a born leader. Also, he had Krystyana, Cilicia, and Francine pass on his selection as well, since he knew that it was helpful to be handsome. At seventy, he settled on a vastly surprised twenty-nine-year-old komander, let it be known that the boy was anointed, and spent the next five years teaching him the ropes. The result was a remarkably smooth transition of power.

LIFE OUTSIDE THE ARMY

The Christian Army eventually became the largest organization in the world, and the only real fighting force, but by no means was it the *whole world*. Even at its peak, it never comprised more than ten percent of the population of Europe, nor more than three percent of the population of the planet.

Most civilian populations belonged to the army-sponsored Council of Peoples, originally called the Federation of Christendom. Any group of more than fifty thousand were allowed to join, providing that they guaranteed to support the army's three basic rights:

THE RIGHT OF DEPARTURE

Any person had the right to leave the country where he was living and go elsewhere. This effectively outlawed slavery and all other forms of involuntary servitude. A person could even run out on his debts. In the case of a criminal, that person had to be guilty of a crime by army law before the army would return him. It was only necessary for a refugee to set foot on army property to obtain army protection, and this was not just real property. Stepping on the shoe of an army knight was sufficient to invoke this right.

THE RIGHT OF TRANSIT

Both army personnel and civilians had the right to cross national borders for peaceful purposes. A country had the right to refuse people only on an individual basis, and only with cause.

THE RIGHT OF PURCHASE

The army had the right to purchase property in any country, after which that land was under army jurisdiction and no longer subject to the laws of the local country. The army paid no taxes.

In addition, the army often demanded of a country that was applying for membership a strip of territory around that country's borders that was typically five miles wide. This land was then turned over to the regular army, which fortified it and farmed it. Besides being profitable to the army, these border zones deterred aggression and, in the event of a war, made it obvious who the aggressor was.

In return for the above, the army guaranteed the national borders of any member state and would itself make war on any aggressor. It provided an arbitration service between member states that was also available to individuals. Aside from this, any country was allowed to do anything it wanted within its own borders, to have any sort of government and social institutions. But because of the right of departure, any government that was particularly oppressive found itself rapidly depopulated, soon losing its most energetic citizens.

In the thirteenth century, large nations did not exist in Europe. Few members had more than a million people. The army encouraged bilingualism, teaching Polish in the free schools available in every member country. The result was that many people were actually members of two cultures, their own local people and a worldwide civilization.

Conrad's historical branch never attained the bland homogeneity that the modern world is tending toward. There were interesting times.

LORD CONRAD'S LADY

volume five
in the
Adventures of conrad stargard

I would like to thank Phil Jennings, Tomasz Kamuzela, Bill Gillmore, and Debra S. Haberland for their kind help in proofreading this book and for their many valuable suggestions for improving it.

However, any overt sexism and male chauvinism noticed in this work is totally the fault of Bill Gillmore, and all complaints should be directed to him at the Dawn Treader Bookshop of Ann Arbor, Mich.

—Leo A. Frankowski

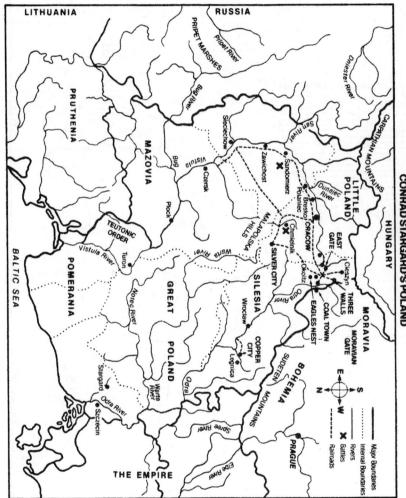

CONRAD STARGARD'S POLAND

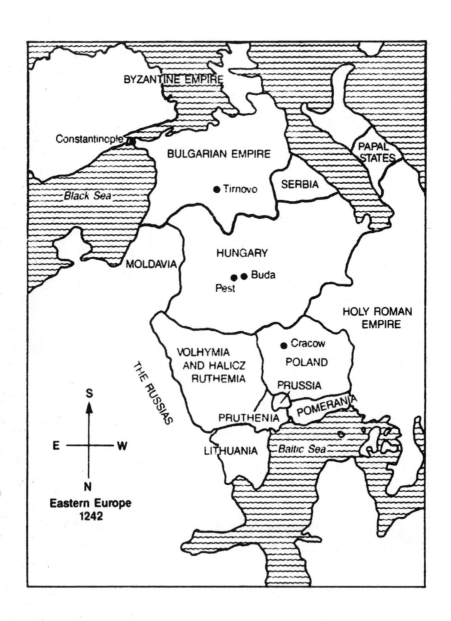

BYZANTINE EMPIRE

Constantinople

BULGARIAN EMPIRE

PAPAL
STATES

SERBIA

Black Sea

● Tirnovo

HUNGARY

MOLDAVIA

● ● Buda
Pest

HOLY ROMAN
EMPIRE

VOLHYMIA
AND HALICZ
RUTHEMIA

● Cracow
POLAND

THE RUSSIAS

PRUSSIA

PRUTHENIA

POMERANIA

S

E ——→ W

N

LITHUANIA

Baltic Sea

Eastern Europe
1242

PROLOGUE

On the lush African plain, at two and a half million years B.C., two small brown individuals were sitting naked on a small hill. To all outward appearances they were a pair of type twenty-seven proto-humans.

"There's blood on your leg," he said.

"I'm menstruating. The antifertility vaccine is wearing off. It's been a hundred and eighty years, and the shot was only supposed to last a century."

"Yeah. My shots are wearing out, too. My eyesight is going bad, and my joints hurt a lot in the mornings."

"We're getting old," she said. "Just like people used to grow old before technology."

"They'll never find us, you know. If they were looking, they would have been here by now."

"What did we ever do to deserve this?" she said.

"*I* didn't do anything. *You* dumped the boss's cousin into the thirteenth century when the guy didn't even know about time travel."

"Shut up! I don't want to talk about it again."

"Well, there's something we ought to talk about. We're getting old. Before too many more years, we won't be able to take care of ourselves anymore. If we stay with the protos, they'll treat us the same way they treat their own parents when they get too old to be useful. They'll just abandon us," he said.

"So?"

"So we have to do something about it! We have to make sure that there's somebody around to take care of us when we get really old. See, my antifertility shots have worn off, too. For the next few years you can still have children, and I'm still fit enough to take care of you and them. If we raise them right, they'll take care of us when it really gets bad."

"You're such an asshole. Do you think I'd have children and raise them to live in this environment? To be savages two million years before any other real people exist? No way."

"Will you say that when you are starving to death because you have no teeth to chew your food with? By then it'll be too late to do anything about it!"

"You're also a damn coward," she said.

Chapter One

FROM THE JOURNAL OF COUNTESS FRANCINE

Everyone seems to be keeping diaries now, and I suppose I should do so, too, though mine will be written in French so that the maids can't read it. Perhaps writing will help me take my mind off the horror of my situation.

I sit here in my husband Conrad's city of Three Walls on the tenth of March, 1241, looking out from a tower window on the area that he calls his killing field. He named it thus because it was used yearly as a place to slaughter the surplus wild animals on his extensive lands here in southern Poland. It is a part of what he calls his game management program.

The field still earns its name, though in a far more gruesome way, for the beasts now concentrated on the field below are an *entire horde of besieging Mongols!*

My husband trained all his men into a mighty army and took them to the east to defend the land against the Tartar invaders. In so doing, he left the defense of his cities to the women, and we are less sure of our abilities than we pretend to be. Why he left our strong walls to fight hundreds of miles away is a matter of dispute among us. For mine own part, I think that if he wanted to find Mongols, he could have saved himself the trip.

We wait here, not knowing if our loves are alive and not knowing how long we ourselves may yet live.

My reader, if any there might chance to be, will therefore forgive me if I write on more pleasant times in more civilized places.

My childhood was a pleasant one, for my grandfather was a bishop, and to be a bishop in France means to be wealthy and powerful. This was all the more true because his diocese was centered on the wealthy city of Troyes, and it stands astride the major trade routes between Flanders, where the cloth is made, and Italy, where the world's cloth is dyed and finished. Two great fairs were held there every year, and Grandfather got his share of it.

My mother was his only child, and since my father held the very high post of Grandfather's privy secretary, we lived in the palace as part of Grandfather's household.

Grandfather's palace was a vast and beautiful place, as full of color and statues as the great Cathedral of St.-Pierre, which stood just across from our courtyard. Our palace was much larger and far more sumptuous than the palace of the Count of Troyes, though of course the count had other palaces and castles in the countryside.

Suffice it to say that until I was nine years old, I had four servants, and my mother had twice that number. My days were spent in pleasant amusements and in learning from my tutors the arts of reading and writing and sewing.

We were very happy until two great tragedies struck us within a year. The first was that the Church declared that all members of the clergy must be celibate. They may not marry, and further, they had *never been* married! This meant that both my mother and I were illegitimate, for my father was also an ordained priest.

This ruling was none of my grandfather's doing, and for a time he was able to protect us from this calamity.

Then, within the year, my wonderful old grandfather died of a plague. Since my mother was no longer born in wedlock and my father was but a priest who was living in sin, there was no inheritance for us. The new bishop had no desire to associate himself with the sinful life of his predecessor, so my father was turned out of his job, and we all were turned out of the palace. We had neither friends nor influence, for although my father was a learned man, his family was of no great means or prominence. For a long time we were at great strife to get enough food to eat.

At long last my father secured a position as a professor at the University of Paris, so we made the long, hard journey to that city. Being a mere university professor was of course a position far below his previous one of secretary, and we had to subsist on whatever the students felt like donating after they heard his lectures. Somehow, my mother was able to make a sort of home for us in our single rented room above a tavern and across the street from a brothel. I was able to continue my education by attending free of charge my father's lectures and those of his fellow professors, for they made this arrangement with each other. Thus we lived until my fourteenth year, for my father considered our location to be convenient for him. He taught classes in a room that the university rented above the brothel.

Then my dear father died, and our situation became dire indeed. Many told me that I had become a great beauty, and I was much noticed by the students and the young guildsmen of the city. Yet being poor and without a dowry, I got no offers, or at least no offers that a virtuous young woman could accept. Indeed, the most persistent of my followers was the owner of the brothel, and his proposal was for a position that I did not desire. Such a life is sinful, dirty, and short!

Then I met a young student who had recently taken Holy Orders and would soon be returning to his native land of Poland. He asked my mother for my hand, and at first she turned him down, for a priest could not possibly marry. It was this fact that had caused all our difficulties in the first place! But he persisted and proved to her that the Gregorian reforms that forbade the marriage of the clergy had not yet been ratified in Poland and, further, that they were not likely to be. Thus, my mother blessed our marriage as the best that I could do without any dowry at all. The very day of our small wedding, she left us to join a convent, being tired of this world and its pain.

As the rent was not paid on my mother's old room, I spent my wedding night with my new husband in his bunk in a student dormitory. Nothing took place that night, but I put this down to his shyness, considering that there were other students in the same room. And truthfully, I was not precisely sure at that tender age just what should have taken place, anyway.

It was early spring, and we left the next morning to go to Poland on foot, for my young husband was almost as poor as I was. We traveled all spring and summer across France, over the many Germanys, through Bohemia, and into Silesia, that westernmost of Polish duchies. We made the trip barefoot for lack of the price of shoes, and indeed we were often hungry, yet as I look back on it, we had a good time. We were young, we were in love, and we were traveling through a world that was forever new.

Yet our love was not physical in the carnal sense of the word. John did not seem to want to talk of it, and I decided that he did not want to burden us with a child until such time as he could properly support it. This made his actions seem pure and noble to me, and of course I did not press him further.

At length, in the fall, we got to the city of Wroclaw and reported to the bishop there at his palace. Compared to that of my grandfather, it was an inferior place, yet for two ragged and barefoot travelers, it seemed sumptuous indeed!

The Bishop of Wroclaw was a pompous old man, with a character far different from that of my beloved grandfather. He acted not at all pleased with his two new ragged guests. Indeed, we seemed to embarrass him. He gave us each a new set of cheap clothes and sent my husband on to a new post within days.

This was at the new town of Okoitz, which Count Lambert was then just starting to build. When we arrived, there was nothing but a clearing in the woods with a half-finished wooden wall and a few huts built against it. And in this we had to survive a cold Polish winter!

My husband still did not properly consummate our marriage, yet it seemed to me that to endure pregnancy and childbirth in those difficult conditions would be dangerous indeed and that poor John was again sacrificing his pleasure for my own welfare. I loved him all the more for it.

Count Lambert, on the other hand, had no such inhibitions. His wife stayed on their other lands in Hungary while the count merrily swived every unmarried peasant girl in the village, and did this somehow without a bit of complaint from their parents! In truth, my husband never chastised him for his actions, either, in part because had we been sent away by the count, we might have had a hard time finding another parish that would take us in. Though the marriage of the clergy was legal in Poland, yet was there much prejudice against it.

And so the years went by at Okoitz. In time, a large wooden church was built adjoining the count's rustic palace, and we had a decent enough room adjoining the church. Our situation became comfortable and secure, and I began to yearn for a child. Also, the count's example with his eager peasant girls convinced me that physical lovemaking must be as enjoyable for the woman as for the man, and it was a pleasure that I still had not partaken of!

After many long, tear-drenched conversations, my "husband" finally admitted that his abstinence was not the result of the nobility of his mind. It was the result of the inability of his body! He couldn't properly play the man's part in the game!

There was no one with whom I could talk this problem over. Indeed, the women of the village all came to me with their difficulties, but as the wife of the priest, I wasn't supposed to have any troubles of my own. I had to be sweetness and light and wisdom, me, an aging virgin of seventeen! Slowly I decided that I was perhaps not a married woman at all, for by the laws of the Church and of the state, a marriage must be consummated to exist.

Then Sir Conrad came to Okoitz out of the east, burdened by some geise that he might not tell of his origins. All the town was buzzing about his prowess as a warrior, for he had single-handedly rid the county of an entire band of outlaws that had been murdering the people and stealing the cattle.

Yet when first I saw Sir Conrad, I thought that I was looking on a messenger of the Lord! He was incredibly tall and handsome, with a true hero's litheness of body, with fine, broad shoulders and—dare I write it?—the most lovely posterior I had ever seen! And there was about him such an astounding aura of wisdom and learning and kindness that my heart went out to him in that instant. In truth, I remember that I let out a little squeal of delight, despite the fact that my husband, John, was in the room with us.

In the months that followed, I tried to convey to Sir Conrad that I would be eager to do anything that he desired, but such was his sense of honor that he would not even think sexual thoughts about a woman that he thought to be married. And since Count Lambert let Sir Conrad make full use of his peasant girls, there was no need for Sir Conrad to look farther afield. Not to mention the fact that those girls were all years younger than I.

Sir Conrad had an almost magical horse that could run at an amazing pace for hours on end. It could answer questions by nodding or shaking its head, and it never soiled its stall but went out in the bailey like a well-trained dog. It was astoundingly gentle to all, even the smallest child, unless it felt its lord was in danger, at which time it became the most deadly of beasts! I greatly admired this animal and often visited its stall.

Sir Conrad was a great master of all the constructive arts, and he built for the count great windmills and an entire cloth factory. He brought with him hundreds of types of seeds that grew into vastly productive food plants and radiantly beautiful flowers. He knew a thousand songs, and I was sure that he thought them up on the spot, though he denied it. He could dance a dozen new steps, and I thrilled to be in his arms for his waltz, his mazurka, and his polka. He could tell a thousand wondrous stories of lands and times far, far away. Many were the nights that he talked until midnight of the adventures of nine-fingered Frodo or of Luke Skywalker. He loved children and was always telling them some new story or teaching them some new game or making them some new toy. He was a master of the sword, the chessboard, and the pen. How could I help but love him?

For all this work, and to encourage him to continue it, Count Lambert gifted Sir Conrad with a vast tract of lands in the mountains to the south of Okoitz. Sir Conrad went to these lands with a half dozen of the count's peasant girls, and I feared at the time that he was leaving my life forever.

He returned monthly, but not to visit me. He did it in feudal duty to the count, to oversee all the new construction at Okoitz. I watched from a distance and hoped.

My relationship with John was steadily deteriorating, and it got so that I could hardly bear to be in the same room with him, let alone the same bed. Yet such was as it had to be, for while we had food, clothing, and shelter, we had very little money. I wanted to leave John and again try my luck in France, but in years of scrimping I had hardly saved a small handful of silver pfennigs. To travel takes money, and to establish oneself in France takes even more.

Things finally came to a head with John one winter's night. I left our room the next morning and found that a merchant's caravan was leaving Okoitz immediately. They were going east instead of west, but it might be long before another caravan came by, and I leapt at the chance to leave, no matter what the direction. Of course, I did not tell John or anyone else that I was going.

One of the merchants mentioned that there was a new Pink Dragon Inn at Sir Conrad's new industrial town of Three Walls. I had heard long before that the waitresses at these inns could earn more money than at any other trade, no matter how sordid. They required that a woman be beautiful and a virgin, but I qualified on both those counts. They required that a waitress wear a costume that consisted of little but high-heeled shoes and a loincloth, but the barbarians of this backward land have no shame for their bodies, and indeed, the only way to bathe among them is to sit naked together in a sauna, so I was well used to exposing my body in public.

I left the caravan and spent the night in one of the barns at Sir Miesko's manor. I hid because I was well known to that good knight and did not want him to be able to tell John of my whereabouts. In the morning a small caravan left for Three Walls to deliver food, and I went with them.

The Pink Dragon Inns were all that they had promised to be, and in the first week there I made over forty pfennigs, almost as much as a belted knight with horse and armor would have been paid by a caravan. Further, my food, room, and such little clothing as I wore were provided me free, and all that I earned could be saved. All this for the light and pleasant work of serving beer and being decorative! I was wondering if I really needed to return to France at all when my "husband," John, found me.

Interlude One

I hit the STOP button, popped the tape, and looked at it. There was nothing unusual about it. It looked completely authentic. So why had that guy acted so strangely when he'd handed it to me? He'd just walked up, put this tape in my palm, and walked silently away.

I rubbed my temples and pushed the call button for one of Tom's naked virgins. She was in before my finger was off the button, and I ordered some Blue Mountain coffee and something for a hangover. Last night's bull session had turned itself into a weapons-grade binge.

The girl was back immediately, doubtless having literally passed herself in the hallway. You do that sort of thing when you have a time machine handy. Whatever they used for Alka-Seltzer around here worked fast. I sipped my coffee and considered things.

Item: A lot of very weird things were going on. The temporal structure of all creation seemed to be shattering, even back here in 60,000 B.C. The supposition was that Conrad had something to do with it, although nobody had the slightest idea how, including Tom, and he had been one of the inventors of the time machine.

Item: Tom had agreed to meet me here this morning and hadn't done so. That was odd. With time travel, if you didn't want to go someplace at a particular time, you could always go later and still get there on time. Tom always kept his appointments, even when he was five years late, subjectively. I'd written him a note already and put it in my letter box, and his reply hadn't popped immediately out of the other side of the box the way it was supposed to. There was nothing in those boxes but a timer and an ejection mechanism. Not much there to go wrong.

Maybe he just wanted me to watch this tape first.

I looked up at the girl who was awaiting further instructions.

"Do you have any idea what is going on?" I asked her.

"No, sir."

"Then sit down and watch this tape with me."

"Yes, sir."

I hit the START button.

Chapter Two

It was a bitterly cold night, and John's hair and clothes were rimed with frost. He had lost his hat, and his eyes were red and shot through with blood. In front of everyone, he grabbed me and demanded that I return to Okoitz with him immediately. When I managed to free myself from him, he pulled out his belt knife. I was frightened and hit him on the head with a stool. I swear before God that it was never my intention to kill John, or even to seriously harm him, yet it happened.

Sir Conrad was called to the inn, since he was lord of the city. He rarely frequented his own inn and was shocked to find me there.

Yet on hearing the tale, he said that I was not guilty of the murder of my husband, for it was an accident and done in self-defense, but that Count Lambert alone had the right of high justice.

On returning from Okoitz, Sir Conrad told me that Count Lambert had said that since a priest had been killed, my case came under canon law rather than civil law, and the matter would have to be taken up with the Bishop of Wroclaw.

Now, it is normally desirable for a criminal to have her trial brought before the Church. The penalties demanded by the clergy are usually far less severe than those handed out by the local lord. But in my case I felt this change of jurisdiction was for the worse, for the Bishop of Wroclaw did not like me, but Count Lambert certainly did. With John dead, I knew I could easily enter the count's bed, were I willing to share that honor with a dozen peasant girls!

Also, the Church moved very slowly on legal matters, and many years could go by before I might be free to return to France. I spent the uncertain months of winter working at the inn, saving my money.

In the spring, Duke Henryk came to Three Walls to see the wonders that Sir Conrad was building in his factories and furnaces. The duke was a robust old man of seventy, with an outside that was as hard as the crust of good French bread and an inside that was just as soft. The duke made me an offer that I couldn't refuse—more money than I was currently making, his considerable protection from any Church prosecution, and duties that involved only serving the duke himself. I left Three Walls in the duke's company.

Thus I spent the next five years as the personal servant and confidante of the most powerful man in Poland, and in the process learned much about the politics of this new and somewhat barbarous land. I learned who wanted what and for what reason, who hated who for no understandable reason at all, and, sometimes quite literally, where all the bodies were buried. As opposed to the feuding nobles of England, Italy, or even France, Polish nobles were less likely to go to war with one another than to resort to poison, a trap, or a knife in the dark. Perhaps this was because the Polish fighting man was often a member of a large, extended family and was ever ashamed to kill his own cousins, who might be on the opposing side. Family loyalty often took precedence with them over mere oaths of fealty.

My duties to the duke were not well defined. I simply did whatever he wanted me to do. Since he wanted me to continue dressing much as I had as a waitress, my legs and breasts were rarely covered, save in the coldest weather. Indeed, it started a fad, a clothing style that many of the ladies of the court followed, at least to the extent of baring their breasts. Almost none of them adopted the short dress, feeling that naked legs were a bit much.

I always traveled with the duke and was privy to his many secrets. Indeed, an old man will always tell everything to an adoring young woman! One of the strangest things that I learned was that Sir Conrad was not a native to our own times but rather had come here somehow from the far future! Just how this was done was a mystery even to Conrad himself. All that I can think is that the future must be a grand place indeed, for if Conrad was but an ordinary man from that time, as he has so often insisted to me, what must the exceptional men be like?

I usually slept in the duke's bed, to comfort him. However, like my late "husband," the duke was incapable of actual sex, though seventy-five years on God's earth certainly gave him a fair excuse!

Eventually Duke Henryk raised me to the peerage, making me the Countess of Strzegom, with a nice manor house and a few hundred peasants. I am not ashamed of anything I did with that fine old man, and I certainly do not regret my years with him.

The duke did not die of old age, as all expected, but rather by a cowardly assassin's crossbow while he was sleeping at my side in Wawel Castle.

The duke had long and carefully trained his son to wield the sword of power, and young Duke Henryk easily stepped into his father's position. Yet the younger Henryk was not his father's puppet but did things in his own style. The very day of the assassination, all the ladies of the court were wearing dresses that covered everything but their faces and hands, knowing the new duke's displeasure with the old bare styles. Though young Henryk was absolutely honorable in all things, I knew it would not be wise for me to remain at court.

Sir Conrad—or rather I should say Baron Conrad, for Count Lambert had enlarged him—was in Cracow, and gifted the new duke with four of his marvelous horses, that they might protect him against assassins. While testing these horses, I persuaded Baron Conrad to let me go with the party, riding apillion. When we were racing through the fields, an attempt was made by three crossbowmen to kill the new duke, and Baron Conrad drew his wondrous sword and killed all the assassins while the duke's bodyguards took their lord to safety.

There was something unbelievably exciting about the chase and the fight with the assassins, bouncing behind Conrad and holding him tightly while he dealt death to the attackers. When we dismounted in a secluded wood to see if we could identify the bodies, well, to state it simply, I seduced him. I suppose I should be ashamed of myself, but in truth I was then twenty-six years old, and that is a perfectly stupid age at which to be a virgin. And how could I ever regret the wonderful pleasure that he gave me and that I had so long been denied!

Baron Conrad was then not maintaining a harem in the manner of his liege lord, Count Lambert, but was contenting himself with a single woman, a dancer from the far east who wasn't even a Christian. I had met Cilicia often, and she was a pleasant enough person, but I thought that I would have little difficulty displacing her in Baron Conrad's heart. I traveled with him to Three Walls, part of the way on his new steam-powered riverboat, an almost magical contrivance.

Yet he would not dismiss the foreign girl, but tried instead to make us join together into a single household! A foolish attempt—of course it did not work. My love, so wise in all things technical, is like a little boy when it comes to solving the far simpler problems of people. He needs my help so much and so often!

But at the time I could accomplish nothing with his other paramour, Cilicia. She seemed to think that she had prior claim on him, and indeed she was again pregnant with another of his children. After a month of trying, I left for my own estate.

Conrad contrived to visit me there at least once a month and often twice. And always I gave him a warm welcome. I wanted more, much more. I wanted a proper marriage and children by him, but I settled for what I could get.

In his own way, he was generous with me. I remember best the time when forty men and as many loaded mules came to my manor gate and announced that they were my birthday present. Since they were from Conrad, I bade them do as they would, and they fell to it with a will. One band of them put glass in every window of my manor, on frames with hinges that could open out and with screens of a coarse metal cloth that fended off insects in the summer but let the breezes through.

Another band took the roof off my highest tower and mounted there a small windmill and a huge water tank with a new well below it. Yet others dug pits and trenches in the kitchen garden and buried clay pipes and even a small stone room. My kitchens were rebuilt with a big copper stove and sinks with running water, but my favorite was the bathroom, with hot running water and a huge porcelain tub large enough for two! We used it often together, Baron Conrad and I. For years I spent much of my life waiting for his return.

Then, just prior to last Christmas, Count Lambert did a remarkably stupid thing. His wife, whom he had not seen in twelve years, died in Hungary, and his daughter, a girl of fourteen summers, came north to live with him. The count decided that Baron Conrad would be the perfect match for the girl and *ordered* Conrad to marry her. This at a time when Conrad was making final preparations to defend the land from the Mongol invaders! Conrad refused, saying that he had never met the girl, and anyway, they didn't even speak the same language. Count Lambert became incensed and ordered Conrad off his lands. Conrad, disgusted, packed his saddlebags with gold and headed west like a knight-errant in a story, without so much as a change of underwear.

Fortunately, he stopped at my manor on his way, and I was able to talk some sense into my poor little dumpling. Count Lambert wanted him to marry his daughter, and to be sure, young Duke Henryk wanted Conrad to marry *somebody* and to stop living in sin with a Mohammedan. I suggested that he marry Cilicia, knowing full well that it was impossible. This made Conrad say that he could never become her sort of heathen and that he had been a failure at trying to convert her to the true religion. Therefore, no priest of either persuasion would ever marry them, nor a Jew either, for that matter.

I then suggested that he marry me. This would satisfy the duke, and Count Lambert would no longer force the issue if it could not possibly bear fruit. Conrad decided that a small wedding would be all that was needed and that things could go on pretty much as before, with nothing changed but one small ceremony. I, of course, knew all the players in the game, and I knew that nothing of the kind would take place. But a wise woman always knows when to keep her mouth shut!

In the morning he asked me to be his wife, and I consented with all my heart. His proposal was particularly welcome since I had twice missed my time and knew that I was heavy with his child.

We rode to Cracow to talk to the duke, who, after all, was my legal guardian, and he gave us his blessings, along with a promise to have a serious talk with Count Lambert. Conrad was enlarged to count, since a mere baron could hardly marry a countess. We had a beautiful wedding in Wawel Cathedral, and all the nobility of Poland attended it. Indeed, there were so many that the heralds could find room in the cathedral only for barons and above, and my husband's party was almost excluded for being mere knights! He solved this problem by enlarging his entire party to baronies.

Our marriage has had no time to be blissful, for my husband has spent the months since our wedding almost exclusively in preparation for war with the invading Mongols. Conrad is facing grave political difficulties as well as military ones, yet despite the fact that I am far more adept than he at anything concerning people, he will not let me help him with politics.

The duke has invited many foreign knights to aid us against

the Tartars, and he bade all the fighting men in Poland to rally to him near Legnica, where provision has been made to support so large an army. The dukes of Sandomierz and Mazovia have refused to do this, as it would involve abandoning their own lands and peoples to the Mongols and then having to reconquer them again. Further, the nobles of Little Poland were also loath to abandon their estates and start the war by retreating hundreds of miles to the west. They left Duke Henryk as a group and swore to serve under Duke Boleslaw of Mazovia, despite the fact that they had once sworn fealty to Henryk.

And Conrad, with the biggest and finest army of all, though none will credit it, felt that he could not follow Duke Henryk either, since much of his force was with the riverboats on the Vistula River, and these could hardly go west overland to Legnica. There were flying machines that flew from Eagle Nest, near Okoitz, but they could not fly from Legnica, needing the catapult to launch them. Further, Conrad's huge land army needs the railroads that have been built for the purpose along the Vistula. They cannot fight efficiently in the west. And lastly, Conrad was loath to abandon his factories and cities to the enemy. My love therefore felt obligated to disobey Duke Henryk and rather go to the aid of young Duke Boleslaw of Mazovia, who was leading the Polish forces of the east.

But Duke Boleslaw is a boy of fourteen who has heard too many tales of knightly prowess and sees no need of saddling himself with "a lot of peasant infantry."

If ever there was a blood-soaked need for some adept political maneuvering, this is the time! Further, I seem to be the only person about with the political skills necessary to unite the military forces of this confused and barbarous land.

Yet Conrad is so naive and helpless at all things political that *he does not even realize how stupid he is*! I could not persuade him to let me smooth his path. He treats me like a pretty child who needs protection rather than as the one person who could solve at least some of his obvious problems. A few weeks ago it got so bad that he even had a guard posted at my door "for my protection," he said, but in fact to keep me from going to Duke

Henryk and Duke Boleslaw and bringing them together as the old duke certainly would have done.

Three weeks ago my love marched out with the largest and finest army in Christendom to seek the Mongol foe. I stayed behind, almost as a prisoner, when I should have been aiding our efforts. Being six months pregnant didn't help, either.

And two days ago the Mongols found us! We beat off their first two attacks with our swivel guns and our grenades, and the field below is dark with their bodies. Now they are camped beyond the range of our guns, more of them than we can count with our telescopes, and they are building huge siege machines to close with us.

Conrad has not come, and we know not whether he is alive or dead. But if he be alive, he must come soon, for if he is late, it is we who will be dead, and our children with us.

Chapter Three

FROM THE DIARY OF CONRAD STARGARD

Two hundred miles from my home the weather was still foul, the lightning and thunder went on without rest, and the cold drizzle had been replaced with sleet. The troops were nearing exhaustion, but three days after our battle with the Mongols, the cleanup was just about completed. By actual count, 216,692 of the enemy had been killed, and that was in our base-twelve numbers. In the base-ten numbers that I had grown up with, we had done in more than half a million of the bastards here. Their bodies had been stripped and buried twelve deep in long trenches, but their heads were set on stakes and lances in neat squares, a gross skulls to the side. There were more than two dozen of these squares stretching across the battlefield, quite a monument to Polish arms.

A ghastly sight—I'd had it done so that no one could ever doubt what we had accomplished here, so that no one could ever say that we had exaggerated.

The booty taken was equally vast. Each of the enemy had carried an *average* of five and a half pounds of gold and silver, three years worth of plunder in the Russias. There were no commercial banks available to looting Mongols, so they had to carry their spoils along with them. It was easy to see why most medieval troops were so eager to break ranks and loot. That much gold and silver was easily six years' pay. My troops, of course, were better disciplined. We would share out the loot in an equitable manner once it was taken home and counted.

Just how I was going to do that in such a manner that my entire army didn't quit and retire was a problem I hadn't solved yet. There was so much money suddenly available that it could ruin the economy with inflation, the way Spain was ruined after the conquest of the Americas. I'd have to think of something.

Since our supplies of food and ammunition were partially exhausted, each of our war carts could carry about an additional five tons, yet it took two gross of the things to haul the gold and silver alone. Another six gross carts were needed to carry the captured weapons and other gear that looked worth saving for trophies if nothing else. Each of these carts would go back toward Three Walls with a platoon of forty-three men to pull and guard it.

Most of the enemy horses had been killed in the battle and in Ilya's night raid the evening before. Baron Vladimir had felt that a half million horsehides was a prize well worth taking, and he had had the animals skinned before the carcasses were buried. Salting them down would have to wait, since we'd have to get the salt mines working again first. For now the skins were just stacked on the field, with a prayer that the cold weather would hold and they wouldn't rot. Near those stacks was a huge pile labeled "scrap iron," junk arms and armor that nobody would want to hang on a wall. The forges could always use scrap. We'd be back for it eventually.

There were perhaps sixty thousand horses still alive, mostly Mongol ponies but also some of the war-horses used by the conventional Christian knights who had been massacred on the field while we had stood by helpless. After I had discussed the matter with some of my officers, it was decided to simply let them all go free. Untrained for the job, they wouldn't have been much use as cart horses even if suitable harnesses had been available. The truth was that they would only slow us down. There was no way for us to take care of them and still get the rest of our work done. When the peasants returned, they'd find a use for the Mongol ponies. Most of the Polish war-horses were either branded, or had had their ears punched with identifying marks, so they could eventually be returned to the families of their owners.

Each fallen conventional knight's arms and armor were carefully bundled along with his jewelry and personal effects, and one of his dog tags served as a label for its eventual return to his heirs. Each Christian body was properly buried with the other dog tag on a lance to mark the grave, but nothing of value was actually buried with the body. This was standard army policy, for history shows that the bejeweled dead are never allowed to rest in peace. Someday we would set up proper tombstones. Someday.

For now there was still a much bigger cleanup job to do. Far more Mongols had been killed on the eastern bank of the Vistula than had ever crossed it, perhaps as many as five or six times as many. There was probably a far greater booty to be taken, and certainly a far bigger mess to be cleaned up before the weather turned warm and rot and disease started to spread. But at least there we wouldn't have to do the sad job of burying our own people. Our casualties had all been on the riverboats, and most of them, those who hadn't gone down with their boats, had already been taken to the army city of East Gate.

I sent Baron Vladimir east to the Vistula with two-thirds of our men, there to get over to the east bank and take care of the cleanup there. That was about a hundred thousand men, eleven of our "battalions." I'd once read that God was on the side with the biggest battalions, so I'd made ours almost as large as a modern division just to be safe.

Just how Vladimir was to contact the boats to cross the river was a bit problematic, since the weather was still foul and the radios still were not working. Our spark-gap transmitters and coherer-type receivers were very sensitive to atmospheric disturbances. We'd been out of touch with the rest of the world for almost a week.

I left with the other third of our land forces, which included all our industrial workers. It was important to get our factories going again as soon as possible, since we had lost most of our riverboats and were out of some kinds of ammunition. We were taking back to Three Walls our booty, along with fifteen aircraft engines. Nine reasonably intact planes had already been sent ahead to the boys at Eagle Nest.

The pilots of our *entire air force* had deliberately crash-landed along with my former liege lord, Count Lambert, in order to take part in the final battle with the Mongols. They had taken part, all right, and had died to a man, along with most of the other valiant but undisciplined conventional knights. They had vainly spent their lives and accomplished nothing. *Idiots,* the lot of them!

One should not think badly of the dead, but *by God* I wish those planes were still flying! They could have kept our communications intact. As it was, what with the weather making our radios useless, I didn't know what was happening in the rest of the country. I had sent couriers to Cracow, Three Walls, and Legnica, but so far none of them had returned. Was Duke Henryk still waiting at Legnica for the rest of the foreign troops to arrive? Had the Hungarians been invaded at the same time we were? How bad was the destruction on the east bank of the Vistula? Was my wife, Francine, alive and well? I had no way of knowing.

Baron Vladimir pulled out at dawn, and I left with my own troops shortly afterward, leaving two companies behind to care for our pitifully few wounded.

I was riding the new white Big Person I'd found on the battlefield. Anna, my usual mount, wasn't at all happy about this, but the new bioengineered horse understood only English, and so I was the only person in this century who could use her properly.

Big People were too valuable to waste, so I lent Anna to one of the scouts who was screening our force. There were few enough Big People to do the job. I had only ten out of our total of thirty-three, and that's a thin screen for a force of over fifty thousand men, especially when there were who knows how many Mongol stragglers around. We'd spotted a few. The job couldn't be done with men on ordinary horses, since once we got on the railroad, our men could pull a war cart six dozen miles a day at a walk, far faster than any war-horse could travel.

I wished that the white mount's rider was still alive. There were a lot of questions I wanted to ask that man. In the few moments that I'd been able to talk to him, he had spoken with an *American English accent*! Further, if he was riding a bioengineered horse, he must have had something to do with whoever it was that had built the time machine that had brought me to this century. He had to be some kind of observer at the battle, or even a tourist, but he had been killed by a Mongol spear before I had had time to get some answers out of him. I'd like to know just why I was dumped into this brutal century! There can't be that many time travelers around. Would I ever get another chance to talk to one?

It took all our men to haul the carts over the half-frozen fields, but we got to the railroad track south of Sandomierz around noon, and once on it we could go much more quickly. Further, riding on iron tracks, it takes only a dozen and a half men to pull one of our big war carts, and they can pull it easily even with the rest of the men riding on or under the cart, slung on hammocks, sleeping. This let us travel day and night without stopping. The men all had full plate armor, although it was common practice to leave the helmets and leg armor in the carts while pulling.

Cookstoves were slung from the rear of each cart, with the cooks walking behind as they did their work, and dinner was being prepared when a wounded rider on one of our Big People came galloping up to me. I recognized him as being one of the couriers I had sent out, the one who had gone to Legnica. His right side and leg were drenched with blood, and he didn't waste time conveying any message to me from my liege lord, Duke Henryk.

"Lord Conrad, *Cracow is burning*!" he said before he fell unconscious from the saddle.

Chapter Four

I stopped the five-mile-long column that I was leading, turned
to the captain of the leading company, and shouted, "Dump the
booty on the ground! Dump it, I say! We have to lighten the
load and go as fast as we can. Dump it and then get your men
going at double time. *Cracow is burning!*"

He looked at me aghast, and it was a moment before he could
comprehend what I was saying. Dump an unimaginable fortune
on the ground? Victory had been turned into defeat? How was
that possible? But discipline and training took over. He turned
and obeyed orders. Men scurried off the carts, the big lids were
taken off the six carts that the captain commanded, and thirty
tons of gold and silver were dumped on both sides of the double
track.

A banner had the wounded courier hauled onto a cart, and
a medic bent over him. A new man was appointed scout and,
with the Big Person, was added to our screen. Actually, it wasn't
necessary to make a new scout. We had twice as many scouts as
we had mounts for them, a fact that made sense once you realize that Big People didn't need sleep, but us Little People did.
But there wasn't another scout present, so I let the man have
his promotion.

As the new scout started to ride out, I called to him and had him
come back. Instead of joining the screen, I had him ride back toward
Sandomierz and tell Baron Vladimir about the attack on Cracow.
This action turned out to be one of my major tactical errors.

"Get the pullers moving!" I shouted. "They can run while the other half of the men dump the load. Throw out everything but weapons, ammunition, and four days' food. *Double time!*"

The men on the carts behind were staring in unbelief at what the first company was doing, and I realized that this was an order that I would have to give personally to each officer. They wouldn't have believed it otherwise! I signaled DOUBLE TIME, PASS THE WORD and rode down the long line of troops and carts, shouting orders.

After a bit, one of my captains asked, "The radios, too, sir? And how about these airplane engines?"

"Hell, yes! They're not doing us any good now, are they?" There were a dozen radios with the companies farther up the line, enough in case the weather cleared.

"Just figured I should ask, sir."

I was already on my way as the expensive set went flying to smash on the siding of the railroad.

It took an hour to get the job done, and the carts were more strung out than I would have wished, but fourteen hundred *tons* of gold and silver were scattered out beside four miles of track, along with three times that weight of fancy swords, decorated armor, and other booty. Four hundred tons of surplus food were dumped as well, but we were running to Cracow.

I ordered the last company in my column to stay there and guard what we had abandoned. They didn't like it, but they did it.

Running at double time, the men pulling have to be changed every quarter hour, but the carts don't stop. Everything happens at a run, and each man is relieved when his replacement catches up with him. There were ladders on both sides of each cart to let a man climb up even when it was moving, but the warriors rarely used them. Once you knew the trick, you could step between the spokes of one of the huge wheels, let it carry you up, and then step from the top of the wheel to the top of the cart. Pity the man who trips and falls, but don't stop for him!

In practice sessions we'd been able to keep this up for an entire day and a night with fresh troops. These men were far from fresh, having started out nearly exhausted, but they did it, anyway.

We ran nonstop for the rest of the day and ate two meals literally on the run. As dusk fell, the lanterns were set out at the ends of the carts, and we pushed on into the night. I ordered a midnight breakfast since, as the Eskimos say, food replaces sleep.

I sent three of our scouts forward to find out anything that they could. I desperately wanted to go myself, but I couldn't. My place was with my troops.

The pace was deadening, mind-numbing, absolutely exhausting, but to drop back to a walk would delay our arrival in Cracow by a day. How many of our countrymen could be killed by a Mongol horde in a day? Thousands? Tens of thousands? We had to push on, no matter what the cost, for the price of anything else was more than I dared pay.

And it was costing us, how much I didn't know. Most of my men had had only four months' training, and many of them couldn't keep up the pace. Men dropped and lay where they fell, and more than once I felt my mount jump an obstacle on the path beside the track. I could only hope that we didn't trample anyone. As men began to fall and not get up, officers at the rear of the column started abandoning carts and moving the men forward to replace our losses. These abandoned carts would make Baron Vladimir's job of reaching us that much harder, but there was nothing else we could do.

The Night Fighters used a smaller war cart than did the rest of the troops, pulled by a seven-man lance rather than a forty-three-man platoon. With only four men pulling, they were having a hard time keeping up with the other, more efficient full-sized carts. Over Baron Ilya's protests, the Night Fighter Battalion was disbanded, the carts put off the road, and the men distributed to the other five battalions as replacements.

It wasn't as hard on me as it was on most of the men, since I was one of the few who were mounted. I felt guilty about it, but I didn't lend out my mount, since it was my job to be alert for any emergency. Easing the pain of one of my men could get thousands of them killed if we were ambushed and I wasn't ready to give quick orders. Yet it was still vastly tiring, and I was older than most of the men under me.

Extreme fatigue always gets me first in the eyes, and now, what with the wound I had gotten from a Mongol arrow, I had only one eye left. It felt like there was sand in it and that the sand had been there forever. At night, since there wasn't much to see, anyway, I closed my eye, held on to the saddle, and trusted to the incredible night vision of my new white mount.

We were all exhausted, the men worse than I, but I knew that once the battle was joined, we'd be awake enough. God always has a last supply of adrenaline for a man when his life is on the line.

It was gray dawn and the towers of Brzesko were on the skyline to our left when the first scout came back to report. Cracow was indeed burning, and the outer walls had fallen to the enemy. The lower city was filled with fighting, but Wawel Hill, with the castle and the cathedral, still seemed to be in friendly hands.

As a hint of the sun came over the horizon, I had the semaphores signal SAY YOUR VOWS ON THE RUN. We had all sworn to repeat our vows every morning, but I wasn't going to let anything slow us down. I could hear the troops near me gasping for breath as they chanted:

"On my honor, I will do my best to do my duty to God and to the army. I will obey the Warrior's Code, and I will keep myself physically fit, mentally awake, and morally straight."

The Warrior's Code:

"A Warrior is: Trustworthy, Loyal, and Reverent; Courteous, Kind, and Fatherly; Obedient, Cheerful, and Efficient; Brave, Clean, and Deadly."

They meant it, too.

Most of the towns and castles along the Vistula were set right on the river to make them easier to defend. Our new rail lines had to swing out and around them, to the north at Brzesko and Cracow. After the scout reported, I sent him to Brzesko to see how things stood there. He reported shortly that the castle and town were a smoking ruin, with no one there left alive. We pushed on.

I couldn't understand how all this was possible. Until the big battle near Sandomierz we had had aircraft patrolling the skies and riverboats on the Vistula. How could they have possibly missed an entire Mongol army? We had lost the planes through sheer vanity and stupidity, but what had happened to the riverboats? There had been at least nine of them left when I had parted company to join the land forces. They were equipped with lights and didn't stop for the dark. The railroad paralleled the river. Why hadn't I seen a single boat all night long?

Dear God, just what the hell was going on?

It was midmorning when we sighted Cracow, although we'd first seen the cloud of black smoke above it an hour before. The railroad was a mile north of the city walls, and the land intervening was a suburb of burned-out cottages, orchards, and smoldering barns. Not the sort of terrain where we could easily use our war carts. Furthermore, the fight was going on within the walls, in the city itself, where the narrow, twisted streets would make the carts useless. I stopped at what would be our center once we got into position. When the tail end of the line was about as far from the city as the front, I had the semaphore operators signal ALL STOP, FULL ARMOR, ABANDON CARTS ONE GUNNER EACH, and HOSTILES TO THE LEFT. That meant that we were also abandoning our swivel guns, with one gunner left behind on each cart to guard them. The guns had to be mounted on the carts to operate, but we couldn't get a significant number of carts into the city, anyway, and I didn't think the Mongols would be defending the wall against us. Not their style. I hoped.

My men were each armed with halberds or six-yard-long pikes as primary weapons and axes or swords as secondaries. All were in full plate armor, proof against Mongol arrows. Despite their fatigue, discipline was still good. In less than two minutes my entire command was lined up and ready. I signaled ADVANCE.

What with the broken terrain, I did not dare order double time. The men were tired, and we would soon have gotten scattered. Also, away from the carts we were down to bugle calls for communications, and there was no point advertising our existence. It wasn't likely, but maybe the Mongols didn't know we were here yet.

We spent two dozen quiet minutes getting to the city wall, but those minutes were not pleasant. This was the first time we had seen what the Mongols do to a civilian population. It hurts me to write about it, to even remember what I saw. Forced by necessity, I can be as hard and as brutal as the situation requires, but for the *love of God* I cannot comprehend the needless murder of helpless civilians, the senseless torture of women and children. Why would any rational beings do it?

The atrocity that burned most deeply into my soul was in a small hamlet. A young woman had been stripped naked and nailed by her feet to the lintel of the door frame of her cottage. Around her were the mutilated bodies of what must have been her aged parents and her four children. The youngest of them might have been a year old, her head bashed open on a rock. The woman's belly had been torn open from crotch to breastbone, and dangling amid her slashed intestines was a six-month-old fetus. She was still alive, barely.

I dismounted and went to her. She seemed to want to say something, and I bent close to her to hear.

"Kill me," she whispered. "Please kill me."

The laws of God and the Church make no provision for mercy killing. To grant her wish would make me a murderer, fit only for hell. Yet despite the fact that I knew that God would damn my immortal soul for the act, there was nothing else I could do.

"A place waits for you in heaven," I said, the tears running down my face. I drew my sword and cleanly slit her throat. "Though a place no longer waits there for me."

Nor was that the only atrocity that I saw on that walk to Cracow. I do not know why an army would want their enemies to hate them. I do not know why they would want to turn fifty thousand tired troops into fanatics bent on their destruction. But they did, and we were!

The city wall was an old, crumbling, useless affair only three stories tall. The city hadn't been seriously attacked for hundreds of years, and the city fathers had been slack in their duties. There were enough hand-holds on the old bricks and stone to let my warriors climb up them, especially since wall climbing was part of the training they'd been through. And up they went, without waiting for orders to do so. The troops had seen the same atrocities that I had, and there was no stopping them now. Nothing would stop them until either all of the enemy were dead or every one of the warriors had died trying to kill them!

The warriors were moving, and I could see that they would be uncontrollable until the city was theirs or they died in their armor. Not that I wanted to control them. They knew what to do!

This meant that I had no further duties as their commander and was free to join in on the fun. I headed through the increasingly heavy rain for the nearest city gate, the Carpenter's Gate as memory served, since I wanted to have a Big Person under me in the battle, and while these bioengineered horses had some amazing abilities, wall climbing wasn't one of them. I hoped that this new mount was as good as Anna in a fight.

The upper city, Wawel Hill, was in the hands of the nobility, but the lower city was governed and defended by the commoners. Each city guild had its own gate, tower, or section of wall to defend, and each of these defenses had been named for a particular guild.

The wall was lightly guarded by Mongol archers, with more arriving every minute. The troops ignored them, and some had a half dozen arrows sticking in their armor as they went over the top. Pikes and halberds were tossed up to them, and they made quick work of clearing the ramparts. I saw one halberdier take the heads clean off two of the enemy with a single sideways blow and then stop and stare at what he had done, unable to believe it.

"Yes, Yashoo, I saw you do it, too!" a man beside him shouted. "Now come and help us with these other ones!"

The Carpenter's Gate was ours by the time I got there, and I just rode straight through. Some of the officers had been training for battle for five years, and now they finally had a chance to put that training to use. They were in high spirits, and the mood was infectious, doubtless aided by the giddiness that is caused by the lack of sleep. Seeing the men now, no one would have believed that they had been awake for two days and had spent much of that time at a dead run. Some of our troops were laughing and a few were crying, but none of them were holding back.

Most of the Mongols were on horseback, but they soon learned not to attack our ranks. I saw three of them charge splashing through the puddles at a dozen of my warriors, or at least charge as best they could in the narrow winding streets of the lower city. Rather than cowering from the horsemen as the Mongols had obviously expected, our men fairly leapt at them. Grounded pikes skewered horses and riders! Axes and swords swung no more than once each, and all three of the enemy riders were dead before they hit the ground. None of the good guys were injured.

"Hey! That really works!" one knight shouted. "Let's go find some more of the smelly bastards and do it again!"

They left at a trot. I went over and inspected the fallen enemy soldiers. None of them had been wearing armor, though even in the rain it was obvious from the wear patterns on their clothing that they owned chain mail and had left it back in camp. My guess is that they had planned to spend the day murdering the seven thousand women and children who lived in the lower city. Encountering fifty thousand of the best-armed, best-armored, and best-trained troops in the world hadn't been part of their daily game plan!

It was soon obvious to me that if I was going to accomplish anything, I was going to have to get out ahead of the foot soldiers. That wasn't easy to do in those tangled streets. Mongols were soon abandoning their horses and taking refuge in the buildings. Seeing this, our warriors started a house-to-house search. Some were using impromptu battering rams, but a quicker technique was more often used. This was for an armored man to run at a barred door full tilt and at the last instance to flip around and smack the door flat with his back. This usually took down any ordinary doorway, and six of his friends ran through right on top of him. If it didn't work the first time, they'd try it again with two men flying backwards. There's something about good armor that gives a man the feeling of indestructibility, and he'll willingly take more actual abuse while wearing it than he would without.

I finally got ahead of most of my men and into a section of the city that was burning fiercely. The smell was enough to make me want to vomit. I might have done just that, but I thought about the results of heaving inside a closed helmet and somehow held it in. Like all the other old cities in Europe, Cracow had no sewage system. For hundreds of years people had been dumping their garbage and shit directly into the streets, and now the mess was going up in flames along with the wooden buildings around it. Actually, a good fire was what this place really needed.

Urban renewal, medieval style!

I got past the worst of the fires and into a section that was mostly burned over. One of the few buildings standing was the Franciscan church and the monastery attached to it.

There was a fight going on in front of it, a crowd of Mongols attacking a band of monks in brown cassocks. We galloped to their aid, my mount and I, and as I approached, I saw that the man leading the monks was my old friend and mentor, Bishop Ignacy.

Just as I reached the fray, a Mongol horseman swung his sword, and the good bishop went down!

Chapter Five

We chopped into the fight, my Big Person and I. I took the head off one of the Mongols and the arm off another before most of them noticed that I was there. My mount was not being a slouch, either, being every bit as good as Anna and doing at least as much damage as I was. Thunder rippled across the sky but couldn't drown the crash of sword on shield, the popping squish of a human head trampled beneath a horse's hoof.

Once the enemy noticed us, though, things got a bit hairy. I was soon surrounded and had to spend most of my effort fending off their blows rather than delivering my own. But they'd never seen a horse that could fight like mine, and she did in four of them before I could score again. Yet every time a Mongol went down, another was all too eager to take his place. I began to realize that I was growing too old for this sort of thing and that getting ahead of my own troops was maybe not such a good idea.

The cavalry came to my rescue in the form of my captain of scouts, Sir Wladyclaw, the oldest son of my good friend Sir Miesko. He was riding one of our Big People, one of Anna's progeny, and was slewing and slithing as I had done before I had become the center of the Mongols' attention. Didn't the idiots ever put out sentries?

He soon made it to my side, and while we were still surrounded, at least now I didn't have to try to watch my own back. We were soon fighting to good effect, and I think that I killed six more Mongols before things quieted down. That wasn't enough to extract full vengeance for what these bastards had done to that woman in the hamlet, but it was enough to get me a good honor guard into the hell I'd earned for putting her out of her pain.

"Well met, Captain Wladyclaw, and thank you! How did you manage to find me?"

"I didn't, my lord. This is Anna! She's been looking for you and disregarding everything I've wanted to do since we got through the city gates!"

"Well, thank you, love." I scratched Anna's ear the way she liked it. Then I saw that there was still a crowd of Mongols in front of the monks. "Whoops! There's more work to do. Let's go! *For God and Poland!*"

In the course of our fight we had drifted a gross yards from our starting point, and so we had time to get up to speed before we hit them again. Big People were larger than the usual war-horses and far more powerful than a little Mongol pony. We struck the Mongols like a pair of bowling balls, and they flew like a rack of pins. Then we were back to hacking and slashing in earnest, the blood and raindrops splashing around us.

I soon realized that the monks were not behaving like innocent victims. They were handing out as much as they took in and were tolerating an unbelievable amount of punishment in the process. They were swinging long iron maces since a man of the Church wasn't allowed to shed blood, but all the swords except mine were dulled to clubs by that point, anyway.

Then I saw Bishop Ignacy cave in the skull of the last standing Mongol and suddenly all was quiet. We dismounted, and both of the Big People started going about calmly stepping on the necks of the fallen Mongols. They always do that sort of thing, but I'd just as soon not watch.

"For this timely aid, much thanks, my son! You know, I've always wanted to say something like that," the bishop said, laughing.

"You are most welcome, your excellency. But tell me. Did I or did I not just see you go down before a Mongol sword?" I asked.

"You did, Conrad."

"Then how is it that you are standing before me? One miracle in a lifetime is enough, after all."

"There's nothing miraculous about it. I am standing now simply because I stood up again after he knocked me down! Oh, I see what you mean." He folded back the cuff of his wide sleeve to reveal a set of our regulation combat armor underneath. Looking about, I realized that all the monks were similarly attired. "The Lord said that one should turn the other cheek, my son, but he never demanded that one's cheek must be naked."

"How did you get that armor? Why are you wearing a monk's cassock instead of your bishop's robes? And why are you down here instead of up in your cathedral?" My head was buzzing.

"We got the armor by going to Three Walls and paying for it. The Church is not poor, after all. I am in the lower city because I judged that Wawel Hill would hold but that I would be needed down here. As to the cassock, well, the ladies often spend years embroidering a single one of my formal robes, and it would be rude to ruin one. Is anything else troubling you, my son?" he said patiently, standing in the rain.

"No, Father."

"Then you had best get about your business. This day's work isn't done yet. Go with God, my son!"

We mounted up and rode out.

Captain Wladyclaw and I rode through the town, taking out the enemy as we found them until we got to the Butcher's Gate by the waterfront. Quite a few enemy horsemen had apparently had their fill of fighting real warriors and were streaming out of the city.

"There's the place for us," Captain Wladyclaw shouted, pointing with his saber. "Every one of them that gets out now is one more that we'll have to catch later on!"

"Right you are! *For God and Poland!*"

We hacked our way to the gate and then turned to defend it, not against an aggressor from the outside, as is usual with city gates, but against aggressors from the inside who were trying to escape. The gate was a tunnel a dozen yards long and just wide enough to allow two men on horseback to fight while guarding it. A convenient killing ground.

The first Mongol to follow us through plunged out of the rain and into the relative darkness of the gate without realizing that we were there. Captain Wladyclaw got a lance into his horse about the time I split his greasy head open with my sword. Our eyes were accustomed to the darkness, while those of the enemy weren't. The second enemy's horse tripped over the remains of the first, but the end results were similar. The Mongols weren't expecting anyone to be trying to stop them from leaving, and in that dark tunnel a fair number went down without getting a chance to draw their swords.

A proper Christian knight would have been horrified at what we were doing, but my forces didn't believe in fighting fair. You were either out there to kill the bastards or you shouldn't be fighting in the first place. Anyway, I kept seeing in my mind that mother nailed to the door frame of her house, and I didn't feel very merciful.

Soon, however, the dead men and horses in front of us were warning enough for all but the absolutely stupid, and things started to slow down. In a few dozen minutes, my sword arm was getting sore and the dead before us were piled up saddle high. Mongols had taken to dismounting in order to climb the pile of their dead, and a Mongol on foot is dog meat to a warrior mounted on a Big Person. Nonetheless, we were being slowly pushed back out of the city gate for no other reason than that we couldn't climb the dead bodies, either. Eventually we were out in the rain again.

During a lull I said, "You know, Captain Wladyclaw, that gate is so packed that it will be hours before they can get a horse through it, and a Mongol on foot isn't much to worry about. What say we see how the other gates are doing?"

"Whatever you say, my lord. You're the commander." Anna smashed in the skull of another Mongol footman, and such had become our casualness with killing that it didn't break our conversation.

"Have you seen me command anything lately? The fight in the city is so scattered that no one could possibly keep track of it, let alone give any sensible orders. But as your brother in arms, I suggest we try the next gate east."

"Done, my lord, or brother in arms, as you would have it!" he said with a smile.

At the next gate we found two of my other scouts with exactly the same idea that we had, and with much the same results. We wished them well and continued on around the city. We found a lance of our own foot troops guarding the third gate we came to.

"Sir, our captain said we was to guard this gate, but there ain't nothing happening here. Any chance we could go back in and join in on the fighting?" the knight in charge said.

"Sorry, but you're needed right where you are. The Mongols have been trying to break out of a lot of the other gates, and we've been bottling them in. If they try it here, you'll have your hands full."

"But there *ain't* no Mongols hereabouts, sir!"

"Your job is here. Do it!" Captain Wladyclaw and I rode through the gate and back into the fight.

Soon we were in another free-for-all, a bloody chaos of swinging and stabbing with the city still burning around us, despite the rain.

The only water available was in a few wells, enough to provide some not particularly safe drinking water but totally insufficient for fire fighting. In the quieter areas civilians were trying to save their homes, but they didn't have much chance of success. Aside from the churches, most of the buildings in the lower city were made of wood and had roofs made of straw. What's more, they were built right next to each other with no space in between, and the upper stories overhung the narrow streets below so that the fires could easily leap the narrow gap between two city blocks. The rain helped a lot to slow things down, but the place was still a firetrap. I didn't see how anything could stop the fires but running out of fuel. That's to say, running out of city.

In one burned-out area I was pleased to note that my Pink Dragon Inn was still standing. My chief innkeeper, Tadeusz, had spent some of our fabulous profits giving the inns in the more important cities brick walls and tile roofs. I suppose he had done this more for reasons of prestige than for fireproofing, but the result was the same. Since the inn was so big that it took up an entire city block, it was isolated from the flames that had burned all around it.

I dismounted and beat on the door.

"We're closed for the duration of the battle," came a muffled voice from within.

"You're not closed to me! I own the place!" I shouted back.

A peephole slid open, and then the door was unbarred. The rotund shape of Tadeusz himself filled the doorway.

"My lord Conrad! I didn't know it was you!" He was shocked by our appearance, a reasonable thing since we were both drenched with human blood.

"Very little of the blood is our own," I assured him. "Can you spare us a quick meal? We haven't eaten since daybreak."

"Of course, my lord, of course. I'll get it myself, since the waitresses and cooks have all been sent to shelter on Wawel Hill. There's none here but the bartenders and a few old guards, and they're all on the top floor with crossbows. Come in, come in, my lords, and you'd best bring your mounts in with you. They'll be wanting food and drink, too, yes, of course." He barred the door behind us.

"We're not particular about what we get so long as we get it fast," I said, leading the group into the kitchen. I put a bushel of fairly fresh bread in front of each of the Big People, and Captain Wladyclaw set out two buckets of clean water for them. We sat at the cook's worktable, which Tadeusz proceeded to cover with fifty kinds of preserved foods, most of them of the rare and expensive variety. We didn't give it the attention it deserved but just wolfed down the calories as fast as we could. We both passed up the wines that were set out for some big glasses of small beer. Fighting is thirsty work, and the job wasn't done yet.

The innkeeper was still setting out food when we got up to leave.

"You're leaving so soon, my lord?"

"There's work to do. Look, move all this stuff and as much else as you need to the front door. Thinking about it, I have fifty thousand hungry troops out there, so you'd better get some help and empty out your entire cellar. When any of my men comes by, feed them near the door. Don't let them stay in or you might have problems getting them out. They're all so tired that they'll fall asleep if they sit down. And give them only one jack of beer each. I don't want them drunk!"

We headed back to the war.

Two blocks down we hadn't found any Mongols, but I ran into Baron Gregor, my second in command. "So how goes the battle?" I asked.

"We seem to be winning, sir, and I think that our casualties have been light. I wish I could be more definite than that, but this is the most chaotic battle I've ever heard of. I don't even know where most of our units are!"

"I don't think anybody does. I've seen a lot of Mongols escaping out the city gates. You might try and get some of our men to guard each one of them."

"I'll see to it, sir. A few men on the walls wouldn't be amiss, either. You know, this is a situation where the radios would really have come in handy."

"Yeah, if the damn things worked," I said. "You go east along the walls, and we'll go west. When the gates are all guarded, we'll meet somewhere along the wall at the other side of the city. Oh, yes. You can stop at the Pink Dragon Inn for a quick bite to eat. Pass the word on that one."

"Right, sir."

We headed back to the gate through which we had last entered. Captain Wladyclaw came with me, since he was still on Anna and she wasn't about to leave my side. Had a human acted that way, I would have busted him for insubordination, but with Anna, well, what could I do?

We got to the gate with a platoon of troops we had picked up on the way. Enemy troops were streaming into the portal, and we had to fight our way to it for the last gross yards. We got there to find the bodies of the lance of men I had met on our way in. All seven of them had died where I had left them. I should have reinforced them at the time. Another sin on my already blackened soul.

The platoon seemed to be holding pretty well, so I went on to the next gate, sending the next platoon I came across back to reinforce the first. This went on for one of our long, double-sized hours before I again met Baron Gregor. I sent him to continue his way around, inspecting and manning the walls while Captain Wladyclaw and I went outside the city to see how things were going there. It was dusk when we got to the dock area to find that one of our riverboats, the RB29 *Enterprise*, was just pulling in. I saw Baron Tadaos on the bridge.

"Baron Tadaos! What happened to your *Muddling Through!*" I shouted.

"Burned, sir!" he shouted in the darkening gloom. "Burned along with four other boats and the whole damned city of East Gate. I came here looking for help!"

Chapter Six

Good God in heaven! A *third* Mongol army?

"Tadaos! We have a third of the land forces in the city now. You collect up as many troops as you can hold and take

them to East Gate. I'll follow as fast as I can with the rest!"
I shouted.

"I'm low on fuel, sir!"

"Then tear down these docks if you have to, and those buildings, too, if you need more wood. But get there!"

"Yes, sir!"

The nearest city gate was the one Captain Wladyclaw and I
had left stuffed with Mongol corpses, so we had to race on to
the next. Damn! I should have had brains enough to mount a
signalman on one of the Big People and keep him with me, but
I simply hadn't thought of it. When the men were concentrated
in war carts, there was always a signalman handy in every sixth
cart, so there was no point wasting a Big Person on one. Now
the situation had changed, and I hadn't been bright enough to
change with it. My stupidity was wasting precious time!

Once in the city, I soon found a bugler and had him sound
BREAK OFF FIGHTING, MAN THE WAR CARTS, and EAST GATE IS
BURNING. The first two were standard signal tunes that most
of the men knew, or at least the officers did, and they could
inform the others. The last required the use of a special code
that the signalmen had worked out. Our bugles could play only
seven notes, but if one played two or three notes in rapid suc-
cession, there were enough combinations to cover each letter
of the alphabet as well as the numbers and punctuation marks.
Messages were spelled out in a sort of code. It took a man with
perfect pitch to play and understand the code, and many of the
signalmen couldn't do it. Fortunately, the man I'd found was one
who could, and there were enough others like him to get the
message passed around.

Soon bugles all over the city were repeating my orders. Men were
scurrying to find dropped weapons—many had abandoned their
pikes as being unmanageable in the narrow, crooked city streets—and
making their way to the Carpenter's Gate. We raced across town to
get to the carts ahead of them, but it occurred to me that I'd better
tell the people still on Wawel Hill what was going on.

I went to the Inner Gate and shouted to the guards, "East Gate
is burning! The army is going to have to pull out of here and

go to their aid. I think we've killed most of the Mongols in the city, but you people will have to do the final mop-up yourselves. Do you hear me?"

A gray-bearded man in ancient armor stuck his head out of a small window and looked down at me. "We hear you, Count Conrad, but you must realize that there are few here save women, children, and the aged. The noble knights all went off to fight the enemy in the field! Their ladies all just went off somewhere, I think to find a safer place to weather the invasion. Most of the young guildsmen fell defending the outer walls, those that did not leave months ago to join your army. Many of those that were able to get here after the lower city fell have died defending Wawel Hill. Women have been manning catapults and crossbows, and children have been bringing ammunition to them. We have nothing left to 'mop up' with!"

"You'll just have to do the best you can," I shouted back. "Good-bye and good luck!"

I heard him swearing at me as we left, but what else could I do?

We went through the city, out the Carpenter's Gate, and back to the war carts. Few of the troops had gotten there yet, and most of the cart guards were asleep. They'd decided that one man awake out of six was sufficient, and I really couldn't fault them. A minor attack had been beaten off earlier in the day, but aside from that it had been quiet. I let them sleep, since it would be good to have at least a few men who were well rested.

More of our men were arriving all the time, though most of them were staggering badly in the rain and gloom. Few of them were actually wounded, but running and fighting for two days straight is about all any normal man can take.

I waited in the rain and dark for an entire hour and then decided that we had to go.

"But only half the men have gotten here yet, sir!" Baron Gregor objected. "There's only about two dozen men to a cart, and that many could never pull nonstop to East Gate. They wouldn't have anyone to relieve them."

"You're right, of course. Well, move the men up to the first carts. Get a full platoon on each cart and have them move out at a quickstep. As more men straggle in, we'll fill more carts and have them catch up with the rest at double time. You'd best stay here and see that the job gets done."

"Sir, that'll make a mess of the whole command structure! Nobody will know who's in charge."

"Structure be damned! East Gate is burning! Just make sure that there are six knights and a knight banner for each cart, and a captain for every six of them. The field-grade officers can sort things out among themselves as we're moving. It's not as though anybody can get lost on a railroad!"

"Yes, sir. What about the wounded?"

"Send the walking wounded back into the city to help out there. Set up a camp for those badly hurt right here."

"Yes, sir," he said, and started shouting orders. The first cart moved out in minutes, with Captain Wladyclaw acting as point man.

Even doing a quickstep was torture for the men, but we pushed on into the night. At around midnight I got word that we now had an even gross of companies in the column, and I hoped that they would be enough to handle whatever was happening at East Gate. By this point each of the men had been able to get a few hours' sleep while riding the carts, and I figured that they could take it. I gave the order to go double time.

I found myself dozing in the saddle, but fortunately a Big Person doesn't need to sleep at all. We pushed on, changing pullers every quarter hour.

I wished that there was some word from Baron Vladimir, but none had come. Had he encountered still more Mongols? Had the courier failed to make it through to him? This business of not knowing what was going on was nerve-racking. I'd often heard of the "fog of war," but I never would have believed that it could take so much out of a commander.

If the Mongols had gotten to East Gate, had they gone beyond it? Were the boys at Eagle Nest under attack? The girls at Okoitz? And what about my people, my wife and children at Three Walls? Had all of southern Poland been overrun?

And what of East Gate? Was it still standing? It was our

strongest fortification next to the city of Three Walls. It had six towers surrounding the castle, each nine stories tall and made of reinforced concrete, with a dozen swivel guns on top of each one. A low two-story wall connected the towers, and while that wall wasn't tall enough to stop footmen with ladders, no horse could ever get over it. Then six dozen yards inside those defenses was a concrete castle that was as strong as I knew how to make it. The walls were six stories high and protected by six more towers, each eight stories tall. The whole complex bristled with guns and had all sorts of nasty tricks to play on an attacker.

How could such a fort be taken by an enemy with only horses and arrows? How could a completely concrete structure possibly be on fire? To be sure, the fort was manned by women, but they were all properly trained and highly motivated. Much of their ammunition had had to be transferred to the riverboats during the Battle for the Vistula, but a great deal was still left to them. They were up to their armpits in refugees, but the captainette in charge should have been able to handle things. With that strong a fort, all she had to do was close the gates, and then she could laugh at the enemy. The walls were too tall to be scaled and too strong to be battered in.

Well, outside of the walls was the huge Riverboat Assembly Building, and it was made of wood.

A cold feeling went through me. Our casualties during the Battle for the Vistula were much higher than I had expected them to be. The castle had been filled to the rafters with civilian refugees, so I had the loft of the assembly building converted for use as a hospital. Those wounded men were at the mercy of the enemy, and the Mongols didn't know what mercy was!

We pushed on through the night and into the morning. The men were staggering with fatigue, and I found myself dozing off in the saddle, dreaming strange dreams and suddenly jerking back into reality, unsure of whether I had dreamed or was hallucinating or was actually trying to survive in an alien environment. I saw my pregnant wife, Francine, naked with her feet nailed to a door frame, her belly horribly slashed and her throat cut open by my own sword. I saw my children by Krystyana and Cilicia murdered on the ground, their tiny heads bashed open on the rocks. Eventually the nightmares of my dreams of torture and the nightmare of my tortured reality fused into a living horror that went on and on forever. Yet when I was sure that I could go no farther, when I knew that I must fall off my mount and sleep forever, I looked and saw the troops gasping, running, staggering, splashing on the muddy boards beside me. If they could go on, then so could I. I drew strength from their dedication and pushed onward.

It was well past noon when we got to East Gate. The Riverboat Assembly Building was gone, reduced to a few blackened stumps sticking up from rain-soaked foundations. The *Enterprise* was at the docks, next to four hulks burned to the waterline, and the city was guarded by my own troops.

A sentry waved us through, but I stopped to talk to him.

"What's going on here, warrior?" I asked.

"We got here at dawn by riverboat, sir. Everybody was dead."

"Dead? How many Mongols were involved? Which way did they go?"

"I don't much know anything else, sir. I've been standing guard ever since we got here, and nobody's told me nothing. Maybe you'd best talk to Baron Tadaos. He's back on the boat, I think."

I told the men in my relief column to pull into the railroad yard and rest, and once there most of the men pulling just lay down in the cold spring rain and fell asleep. Those on the carts were already sleeping.

Captain Wladyclaw was near at hand. I told him to get fresh scouts out on Big People and to find out what he could.

Baron Tadaos was in his cabin, debriefing a young corpsman who was crying and shaking in his chair. The man's clothes were badly burned, his hair was mostly gone, and there were blisters on his hands and face.

"Come in, sir, and sit down. There's some terrible things happened here," Tadaos said.

I sat, grateful to sit on something that wasn't a saddle. "Maybe you'd best tell me the story from the beginning, Baron."

"Yes, sir. I got here yesterday around noon and saw the boat house was burning. I'd put off my company of troops with you almost a week before, so I was down to the boat crew and the signal group under Baron Piotr. Mongols was all over the place, but we docked between two of the other boats that was here. See, half my boats was in port for lack of repairs, fuel, and ammunition. We only had a dozen rounds for each of the guns, but I figured that we'd see what help we could be, anyway."

He was interrupted as an armored boatman came in with a big tray heavily laden with food and drink. "We found a storeroom in the castle that hadn't been broken into, sir. You haven't eaten since yesterday, and I promised your wives that I'd take care of you, sir."

He set the tray on the desk and left without another word.

"I can only pray that the girls are still alive somewheres. I guess we all need to eat. Dig in, gentlemen," Tadaos said.

"But like I was saying," he said with food in his mouth, "we left three gunners on the bow to do what they could, and the rest us went out with swords and pikes. I was even out of arrows, so I left my bow behind. Never did see it again.

"We joined up with what was left of the boat repairmen, the crews of the other boats, and the medics that was taking care of the wounded in the hospital here. A lot of the walking wounded was with us, too, but we was still way outnumbered. Them Mongols being on horseback didn't help none, neither. We lost us a lot of men, and they pushed us back to the boats.

"Only by then most of the boats was on fire, except for this one on the end, the *Enterprise*. The engineman on the boat had brains enough to have a head of steam up, and we had no choice but to push off and look for help.

"I didn't like doing that, since all five of my wives was in the castle, or so I thought, and it felt like I was murdering them and the kids, too. But it was run for help or die right there for no good reason, so we ran.

"Those damn radios of yours haven't worked for a week, but when we got to Cracow, we saw that it was burning, too. That's when I ran into you. Doing what you said, we collected up four companies of troops, all of which I could get aboard, seeing as how they didn't have no war carts, and we ripped down the docks and a dozen sheds nearby to fuel our trip back here. It damn nearly wasn't enough. I'd already given the order to start tearing down the boat when the lookout spotted East Gate, and we made it on our head of steam with the boat still intact. Just as well, since this just might be the last boat we got left!

"The place was empty when we got here first thing in the morning. Empty of living people, anyhow. You could see where there'd been a fight in front of the boat house, and our boys sold their lives pretty damn dearly, let me tell you. But there wasn't no fight around the castle. There was just a massacre, I think the worst massacre the world has ever seen! I just come back from there, and what I saw would make the worst sinner in the Christian world fall down and cry!

"There must be twenty or thirty thousand people dead in there, sir, and every one of them women or children or a few old gaffers. Ain't a one of them could have done the Mongols a bit of harm, but the filthy bastards murdered them all, anyway. Shit, sir, I ain't got words bad enough for them . . . them . . . whatevers."

Chapter Seven

The baron was crying, and I let him have a few moments to get a hold of himself. After a while he continued.

"Sir, I didn't find any of my people, but there was so many dead in there that I knew we'd be weeks sorting them all out. I figured my family was done for, but then some of the troops found this young feller, and what he says is that it wasn't our people who was murdered in there. I mean that they wasn't army families. He says that all them women and kids was the families of nobility from Cracow, Sandomierz, and points in between! But maybe you better hear about it straight from him."

"Maybe I'd better, Tadaos. How about it, son? Are you up to repeating your story for me?"

"Yes, sir. I think so, sir. I was a corpsman working in the hospital that was set up in the loft of the boat house, I mean the Riverboat Assembly Building."

"Relax, son," I said. "You're among friends here. Just tell us the story the way it happened. And tell me, how old are you?" It was maddening to take all this time listening, but unless I knew what had happened, I wouldn't know what to do next.

"Yes, sir. I just turned fifteen. Anyway, I heard my captain telling one of the banners that he had just come back from the fort and that they couldn't give us any help. He said that the women's army contingent there was pulling out with all the commoner refugees in the whole fort. He was pretty mad about it, but he said that there was nothing he could do to change things. He didn't command the stupid cunt in charge of the fort. Excuse me, sir, but that's what he called her."

"Yes, yes. But *why* was she abandoning her post?" I said. A captainette was the woman left in charge of an installation when the men went off to war. It was an unusual position in that it was temporary in nature. For example, Captainette Lubinska, who had been in charge of East Gate, was ordinarily in charge of the accounting section there, and during normal times she had no authority at all outside of accounting. But once the men went off to fight the enemy in the field, she was in absolute charge, subject only to a clearly defined chain of command that ended with me. She even outranked the six baronesses that ordinarily lived at East Gate, for example, and they were expected to obey her orders.

The reason for all this was that men rarely chose their wives for their ability as battle commanders, and it was important to have the most competent woman in charge, no matter who she had married.

But nobody except me and Baroness Krystyana could have legally ordered Captainette Lubinska from her post.

"Sir, I was just overhearing somebody else's conversation, and my captain's at that, even though he was pretty loud about it. He said that Count Herman's wife came up with a few dozen bodyguards and a large group of other noblewomen, and the captainette wouldn't let them in. She said that fort was full and that these new refugees would have to continue on down to Hell, I mean the Warrior's School, thirty miles away, for shelter. But the countess talked the captainette into coming down and talking to her, and then the countess said that the fort wasn't your property, sir, so it wasn't army property. The fort really belonged to Count Lambert, her brother-in-law, and Count Lambert wanted her to take it over and shelter there, since it was the strongest fort in Poland, and everybody knew it."

"That wasn't true," I said. "Count Lambert paid for the fort, but I was to see to the manning of it. He wouldn't have changed that without talking to me about it. I can't believe that he would ever have given anything to the countess. He hated her! Not that we'll ever know for sure. Count Lambert died days ago on the battlefield west of Sandomierz."

"Yes, sir, but she got the captainette to believing her, anyway. They went into the fort. Then an awful lot more nobility kept coming, and the countess turned every commoner out the fort to make room for them. Some of them went on to Hell, or the Warrior's School, I mean, and some went up to the hills to take their chances up there."

"And this happened three days ago?" I asked, trying not to vent my anger at the captainette. It was really all my fault for appointing that woman to so important a post in the first place. I'd had a bad feeling about her, but I'd done nothing about replacing her.

"I think four, sir. Then about noon yesterday, I was outside taking a breather, and I saw about a hundred old-style knights ride up in chain mail and all. I thought it was kind of funny because they were all riding little horses, but their leader spoke real good Polish to the sentry, and their shields were all painted with Polish arms. Anyway, the leader said that they had word from Cracow, and I heard the countess yell that they should be admitted. I saw the gates go up and the drawbridge go down, but then my break was over and I had to get back to tending the wounded. I didn't think much of it at the time, but I guess I should have. That must have been how the Mongols tricked their way into the fort.

"Then, about a half hour later, one of our men came up shouting that the place was crawling with Mongols, that they were streaming in on us from the south. We all armed ourselves, but my captain said I was to take care of the wounded, since some of those men were badly hurt. I was the only corpsman left behind. I didn't like it, but orders were orders. I could hear screams from the castle and shouts from the fighting down below. All the wounded who could move had gone down to join the fight, even some guys with only one arm, but there were still more than two dozen of them up there that were helpless.

"A while after that, one of my patients started shouting that the building was on fire, that we all had to get out somehow. From the smoke and the smell, I could see he was right, but there were so many of them and only one of me! I picked up one of the men who was near the stairway and carried him down to the ground floor and outside, but the fighting was so bad out there that he was killed by a Mongol arrow before I got out the door.

"I went back up, and the fire had gotten real bad. Men were crying to me, begging me to not let them die by burning to death. One man, a captain with his legs both messed up, he grabbed me by the arm. 'You know what you've got to do!' he says, and I said that I didn't. He says, 'You can't let all these men die by fire! That's the worst possible way to go. It's so painful that any man doing it would die with a curse on his lips, and then what happens to his soul? You've got that axe, boy. Use it! And use it on me first!'

"Then he starts singing 'Te Deum,' sir, real loud, and the rest of the men starts singing with him, those who were conscious. I'd armed myself when everybody else had, and my axe was sharp and new in its sheath. I'd never used it, not till then, anyway.

"Sir, I chopped that captain straight across the neck, and it took his head almost off. Then I went down the line of wounded men and did the same to almost every one of them. They kept on singing until I was done. Some of those men I killed were already unconscious. Some of the others gritted their teeth as I came up to them, and a few nodded to me that it was okay, what I was doing, but only one of them said I shouldn't do it.

He was Robby Prajinski, and I knew him because he was from my own village. He screamed and begged me not to hurt him, so I didn't. I just went to the next man. I guess the fire was real bad, because I couldn't see so good. Maybe it was the smoke, or maybe I was just crying, but I hit every one of those poor men square, sir, even the last one where the floor burned out under us. He was singing until I hit him. I guess that's where I got these burns.

"I lost my axe in the fall, and I could hear Robby screaming somewhere, but I couldn't find him in the fire. I got outside somehow, and all of our men out there were dead. I was thinking I should go back in to try to find Robby, but my clothes outside my armor were burning. It was like the Mongols didn't see me somehow, because I made it into the river, and that put the fire out. I drifted downstream for a while, and I was kind of surprised that I floated in my armor. Maybe it's the goose-down in the gambesons. Anyway, I crawled out, and I guess I mostly slept until the sentries found me."

I buried my face in my hands, unsure whether I was crying as much as the young corpsman was.

"You did what you had to do, son. Fate put a horrible job in front of you, but you did your duty, and you did it well. May God bless and forgive you," I said. After a bit I added, "You did right, son, but maybe you'd better go to confession. There are a number of chaplains around here somewhere."

"Yes, sir." The boy got up to leave, and Tadaos put some more food in his blistered hands before showing him out.

"Take care of him, won't you," I said to Tadaos.

"Will do, sir. Now, before you leave, do you have any spare ammunition? We'd stripped most of the ammo from the fort for the fight on the river, and it seems like the Mongols burned all the rest of it they could find."

"We can give you a few dozen cases. You're going to see what you can do about patrolling the river?"

"There's nothing much else I *can* do, sir. That, and there are still three of my boats unaccounted for, and I mean to find them. Baron Piotr's getting downright antsy about it."

"Piotr still lives, then?"

"Yeah, he was one of the lucky ones."

"I'm glad. Well, good hunting." I stood to leave.

"You too, sir."

It was now late in the afternoon, and if we left within the hour, well, there were a dozen targets for the Mongols within two dozen miles of here. We'd probably get wherever we were going before dawn. I ordered that all of our Night Fighter companies be re-formed and put in the front of the column, that all of the relatively fresh men who had come in by riverboat be put on the line behind them, and had the two companies in the worst shape left behind to man this installation and start cleaning it up. While I had been talking to Tadaos, eight more companies had come up from Cracow. The city was now secure, even if most of the wooden buildings in the lower city were totally burned down. At least there were no Mongols about, or rather, no live ones.

But there was no word from Baron Vladimir. Two-thirds of our army might as well have vanished from the earth for all I knew.

Baron Gregor just about had things reorganized when Captain Wladyclaw galloped up.

"It's definite," he said. "The entire Mongol force somehow regathered into a single body, and then it went east. There was some fighting at Sir Miesko's manor, but it did not fall to the enemy, or at least it hadn't when one of my scouts saw it through a telescope an hour ago. He said that a bunch of crazy old ladies were up in the towers there with swivel guns and a few gross Mongols were lying dead around them, while the other living enemy troops were keeping at a respectable distance. But he said that the bulk of the Tartars had turned south and are heading for Three Walls, sir."

Three Walls! My wife, my children, and most of my ex-mistresses were at Three Walls. My first impulse was to take my entire force there at a double time, but Baron Gregor talked me out of it. Or rather, he shouted me out of it.

"Sir, these troops are simply not physically capable of running all night long three nights in a row! Nobody could possibly do that. Furthermore, at a quick march, where the men can get at least some sleep, our forces can get to Three Walls by dawn. Getting there sooner won't accomplish anything except telling the enemy that he is about to be attacked! It makes sense to send Baron Ilya ahead with his Night Fighters to see what they can accomplish, but the rest of our men are best off being fresh to fight at dawn.

"Three Walls is even stronger than East Gate here was, and Baroness Krystyana's in charge there. You know that girl even better than I do, and you know she wouldn't fall for a Mongol ruse the way that silly twit of a countess did here!"

"Yeah, I guess you're right, Gregor." I swung into the saddle.

"And another thing, *sir*! Every man here has gotten at least some sleep in the last four days except you. Have you gone crazy? Do you think you can direct a battle with half your brain not working? Do you think we'd trust our lives to someone who was about ready to keel over? Now, you get off that goddamn superhorse and stretch out on one of the war carts! Go to sleep! We'll get you to the war on time, never you fear."

"But ..."

"But nothing! Shut up and soldier!"

"Yes, sir," I said.

Chapter Eight

My second in command was shaking me awake. "It'll be dawn in half an hour, sir."

Sleeping in well-fitted plate mail is fairly comfortable, sort of like relaxing in a good contour chair. I threw off my old wolfskin cloak and shook my head to clear it. "What's been happening, Baron Gregor?"

I sat up on the moving cart, and Gregor, riding beside me on the white Big Person, put a bowl of soup in one of my hands and a mug of beer in the other. Not quite what I needed. *God,* but I wished that something was available with caffeine in it.

"We're about three miles from the hedge at Three Walls, sir. The rain stopped just after you started snoring, and a while later the radios started working after a fashion. Duke Henryk *still* has not pulled out of Legnica. Baron Vladimir has arrived at Cracow and is advancing on us. The transmission was pretty poor, and that's all we have been able to find out about him."

"The duke's conventional knights wouldn't be of much use to us, anyway. Look at the fiasco they caused at Sandomierz. I can't see waiting for Baron Vladimir. He'll be days getting here. What about the rest of our installations?"

"Okoitz, Coaltown, Eagle Nest, and Copper City are all safe and sound. They haven't been bothered. The boys at Eagle Nest say that they have one aircraft rebuilt and ready to fly. A second should be ready later this morning, sir."

"Good. Tell them that I want that plane flying over Three Walls as soon as possible. We need all the surveillance we can get."

"Yes, sir. The granary in the Bledowska desert was taken by the Mongols—we only had a platoon guarding it, and it was never meant to be seriously defended—but the Mongols left it intact. They probably considered it useful booty, to be used later. Sir Miesko's manor was hit, but the attack was squashed by a hundred lady schoolteachers under Lady Richeza. Our ladies at Three Walls have beaten off two serious attacks, and the Mongols have laid siege to the place. Your wife tells me that a siege tower and some wheeled catapults are being built just out of swivel gun range."

"Francine is well, then?" I finished the beer and started in on the soup. It had a lot of meat in it, but very little grain and no vegetables. It was Lent, but the men fighting to defend their country had been given dispensation to eat meat by the Bishop of Wroclaw. When we had thrown out some of our supplies to lighten the load, the troops had kept the foods they craved the most, and two weeks on a high-protein diet had not made up for the lack of meat in the weeks before that.

"She said she was, and she sends you her love. I sent her yours, of course, but I didn't see any sense in waking you. So far, casualties at Three Walls have been almost nil. An arrow hasn't much force left by the time it gets to the top of a seven-story wall. The catapults are something else, however."

"Yeah. Especially if they're like the ones they used on us in the riverboats. We'd better hurry."

"We'll get there at a walk in time for an attack at gray dawn. There's no point in getting there sooner than that," Gregor said.

"Oh, I suppose you're right. Do the Mongols know we're coming?"

"Possibly not. Baron Ilya's Night Fighters did a pretty fair cleanup job while you slept. The Mongols seem to have a real general in charge. At least they left plenty of sentries and scouts out. 'Course, they still haven't learned not to do sentry duty sitting around a campfire, but the thought was there. The last bunch Ilya taught that lesson to weren't in any shape to pass on the education they got! He had the horses slaughtered as well as the men so that none of them would find their way back to the enemy camp and tip our hand. I think our scouts took out all of theirs. When a Big Person starts to sniffing on the trail of a Mongol, you just know there's going to be bloodshed, and those girls can really fight in the dark!"

"So Captain Wladyclaw gets another feather in his cap, and Ilya'll be harder to control than ever," I said. "What do you know about the enemy positions?"

"Best as we can tell, they're all camped on the killing ground, this side of the kitchen gardens, on the place we used to use for a parade ground. There's some wells down there, and they probably figure that the big hedge of Krystyana's roses offers them some protection."

"Nice. Better wake all the men and get some food in them."

"The cooks have been at it for an hour, sir. During the night I had all the cart wheels greased so they're real quiet."

"Good. Make sure that the men stay that way, too. Semaphores and hand signals only from now on."

"Right, sir."

"And give me my mount back!"

It was still dark as we approached the city. I was in front of our silent column to make sure that things were the way I thought they were. The double-tracked railroad went through a simple gate before it entered the killing ground.

This gate was never intended as a military defense; its main job was simply to keep animals in. Nonetheless, I was surprised to see that it was manned by our own Night Fighters. Baron Ilya was there waiting for me.

"I got maybe a company of my men just inside the gate in Mongol outfits, sir, so's they wouldn't know we was here. I just wanted you to know so's you wouldn't shoot them down."

"Okay. I'll signal you just before we start the attack, and you pull those men behind our lines in a hurry. Once things warm up, the gunners won't be too choosy."

"Right, sir."

Baron Gregor had a man using hand signals to split off our troops, sending a column of war carts in each direction on our side of the rose hedge. Save for the snap of branches as the big carts were pulled through them, the columns were silent as snakes. We could hear the Mongols a dozen yards away from us on the other side of the hedge, but we didn't hear them give any alarm.

As each cart reached its assigned position, the men quietly took the big armored lid off the vehicle. This was slung on spare pike-staffs six yards to the side of the cart to act as a shield for the men pulling it. At the same time, the pins were pulled from the casters of the big wheels, the wheels were turned at right angles away from the line of march, and the wheels on the armored side were locked in that position. The carts were pulled sideways into battle.

Harnesses were attached to the armored side of the cart, and the pikemen tied them to the ring on their backplates with a slipknot. Gunners quietly mounted the pinions of their guns into the "oarlocks" built into the sides of the carts. They lit the ignition lamps in the base of each gun, loaded them, and set out their spare ammunition. Cook-stoves and other nonessentials were set on the ground. Pikes and halberds were handed out, and men checked each other's arms and armor.

Having been practiced hundreds of times, the conversion from transport vehicle to war machine took only minutes, even in silence and nearly total darkness. Some of the halberdiers had to be reminded to get in front of their shields, since this wasn't their usual position, but Baron Gregor had briefed the captains on our plan of attack.

Six hundred carts take a long time to move two miles quietly in the dark and over unprepared terrain, even when everything is well coordinated. At any moment the Mongols could find us sneaking up on them, and a well-planned surprise attack could be turned into a bloody chaos. But despite my sins, God was still on our side.

At the first hint of dawn I saw my troops lined up and ready, stretching a mile on each side of me. I called to Ilya in a stage whisper, and a few hundred ersatz Mongols poured quickly through our line, heading back to where they had stowed their armor.

Still using hand signals, I gestured ADVANCE, and every captain passed it on.

The hedge was five yards high and thickly tangled with long, sharp thorns. The seed package had claimed that a hedge of these Japanese roses was proof against man and beast, and for once the seed company hadn't lied. I think it gave the Mongols a false sense of security. No man or animal smaller than an elephant and bigger than a mouse could possibly go through it, but good steel could!

Thirty-six hundred halberdiers started making toothpicks out of two miles of Krystyana's roses. The hedge had been only two yards thick when we'd planted it seven years earlier, but it had somehow spread to a dozen yards and more in some places. This surprised me, and perhaps it gave the enemy more time to get ready for us, but I think they wasted a fair amount of time trying to figure out what the strange noise was, so it all balanced out. We finally broke into the clear, and the gunners opened fire.

We went across the Mongol camp and trampled it flat in the process. It was huge. Judging from the size of the enemy camp near Sandomierz and the known number of men that had been in it, there must have been two hundred thousand Mongols here, yet at first the resistance was surprisingly light. No more than five thousand men came against us, and many of them were obviously wounded. They went down quickly, and I signaled CEASE FIRE.

A panicky thought shook me. Had the bulk of them somehow escaped our trap? All my forces were facing Three Walls. Were the Mongols behind us, waiting to hit our unprotected rear?

Anna came up to my side, carrying the protesting Captain Wladyclaw with her.

"Captain Wladyclaw! I'm glad you're here. Look, we aren't finding enough Mongols in front of us! If they're to our rear, we're in big trouble. Get your scouts way behind us and get word back in a hurry if we're walking into their trap instead of springing our own. Here," I said, dismounting. "Take the white person with you as well and put another man on her. I'll ride in on the carts."

"Yes, sir, but Anna has stopped obeying me again."

"Anna, if you love me, go with Wladyclaw and help protect my back." She hesitated a minute and then galloped back through our lines.

Chapter Nine

A while later we topped a rise, and I saw where the missing Mongols had gone. They were pulling a dawn attack of their own. Lovely! If they were getting set to attack, their minds would be off defense. The war carts went ahead at a quick-step. We were still two miles from the main wall as the sun came up. We recited our morning oaths as we advanced.

Except for one week of the year when we thinned our stock of wild animals, the lower portion of the killing field did duty as our parade ground and as pasture for our dairy herd. The evidence was that the Mongols had slaughtered our cows, but they'd soon pay for them in full. Fortunately, this was not our prize herd, or they would have made me *mad*!

We were advancing over the very ground that many of my officers had practiced on for five years. We knew every hill and rock on it. What's more, there is a certain psychological advantage to fighting on your own home turf.

Three Walls was built where I had found a number of minerals in a boxed canyon. I'd given it its name because God had already built three of the city walls for us, and we only had to build the fourth. Since that time we had added a second wall made out of bricks that doubled as a housing unit outside the first wooden one. Eventually a third wall, concrete this time, was built outside the second, and now most people thought it was named for the three combination wall and apartment buildings we'd built there.

We topped another rise, and I could see a commotion ripple through the Mongol ranks. They knew we were here, and they knew that they were caught between the proverbial rock and the hard place, with the walls of the city to their south, impenetrable hedges to their east and west, and seven ranks of armored men coming shoulder to shoulder at them from the north! Further, there were 3,600 guns pointing in their direction, and if they didn't know what that meant, they were about to learn.

The Mongols had built four huge catapults mounted on wheels, along with a wheeled siege tower that looked to be eight stories tall. The catapults were built fairly close to the ground, and were pulled along by men with ropes as well as pushed forward by men leaning into long poles, without needing much in the way of direction by the Mongol officers. The officers were there anyway, though, keeping all four catapults in a neat, straight line, a dozen yards behind the siege tower.

The siege tower was being moved in much the same way, except that many long ropes were attached to the top of it as well. Directed by a wildly gesticulating officer at the top of the tower, men were pulling on these ropes to keep the ungainly structure from toppling over. The great wooden machines moved slowly toward the city wall as we advanced on the enemy.

Our ladies manning the swivel guns on top of the wall were

firing constantly at the enemy troops who were laboring to get the machines into position, and were killing them in droves—but as soon as a man fell, he was replaced by one of the seemingly inexhaustible Mongol reserves.

Suddenly, the siege tower started to tilt forward, toward the wall. The men on the ropes behind the tower strained to keep it upright, while the officer at the top directed those pushing and pulling it forward to continue at their task. The effort was well coordinated, and the front two wheels were actually lifted slightly into the air, with all of the weight of the siege tower on the rear two wheels, as it continued inexorably forward.

I could see what the officer in charge was trying to do. Some castles have big clay jars buried around the walls that will be crushed when any great weight rolls over them and will stop or tip over a siege engine. If the officer could get his machine past the hidden jars that had just been crushed by the front wheels, it would be in position to attack our walls. The only problem with his plan was that we didn't have any such jars planted.

I'd never really studied a modern sewage treatment plant back when I had the chance, but I had once helped to install a single-family septic system. Needing to do something with the sewage generated by the four thousand families living in my city, I had simply scaled up that single-family system by a factor of four thousand. Three Walls had a tile field that covered almost a square mile, which made the kitchen garden above it one of the most fertile in the world. There was also a bodacious septic tank that was as long as our outer wall. It went from hedge to hedge, and was thirty yards wide and ten deep. And the roof of the tank wasn't any stronger than it had to be.

Watching them through my binoculars, I could see that the Mongols were racing hundreds of men into the moving tower, all of them eager to be among the first to attack the women on our city wall. The Mongol officer looked supremely self-confident until the rear wheels of his siege tower encountered the holes that had been punched into the roof of the septic tank by the front wheels.

With a certain calm deliberation, the huge siege tower dropped three stories into the dark gray muck below. Many of the men pulling from the front were dragged down with it, and those at the back, pushing on the long poles, were suddenly catapulted into the back of the tower, to slide helplessly down into the slime with the others. Then the tower started to tip sideways, and fell with apparent slowness onto the tightly packed horsemen who were escorting it forward. I saw the face of the officer in charge, looking vastly annoyed as he and they and it went through the roof and sank out of sight.

Smelly gray muck splashed over the catapults and those propelling them forward, but with a stoic lack of imagination, they all continued their advance, thinking perhaps that it can't happen here.

It could. Simultaneously, with military precision, all four catapults broke through the roof of the septic tank and sank out of sight, along with most of the men propelling them.

A cheer went up from our ranks, and from our ladies guarding the city wall.

"A rough way to die." One of the pikers laughed. "Drowning in sewage!"

"Laugh all you want to," another said. "Odds are we're the ones that are going to have to fish out and bury them smelly farts."

"Would you do it for five pounds of gold and silver? That's what every one of them bastards carry! I tell you I would!" a third trooper shouted.

"I believe you! 'Course, in your case, nobody could smell the difference!" a fourth yelled.

My men were outnumbered at least eight to one, and they were on foot while their enemies were mostly mounted. Yet not a man of them seemed to have even considered the obvious possibility that they might lose! Considering their spirit, I thought that it was an unlikely possibility, too!

An airplane came and circled overhead. He didn't drop any messages, so everything must have looked okay to the pilot.

A few squadrons of Mongol horse archers rode past our line and let fly at us. I ignored them. Best we save our ammunition until we were firing at point-blank range into crowds of them. Their arrows couldn't do us much damage anyway.

Through my binoculars I could see the occasional puff of

smoke from the swivel guns atop the wall, but I could also see that Krystyana hadn't fired her wall guns yet. Smart girl! She was saving her best for the last.

The wall guns were cast into the two yards of reinforced concrete that made up the first story of the wall. Imagine a shotgun with a bore you could stick your leg into or a primitive sort of breech-loading claymore mine. The muzzles were still covered over with their thin coating of plaster, a surprise that was yet to be presented at the party.

The field narrowed as we marched south, and the carts on the ends had to drop out and follow behind. This caused no confusion because we'd practiced on this very field so many times before.

A half mile from the wall the Mongol general must have decided that a breakout was in order, for at least half their horsemen formed up and charged our line. It was time. I ordered FIRE AT WILL, and the bugles played it along our whole line.

Our swivel guns let loose, and noise and smoke covered the field. Through patches of clarity, you could see where single bullets had plowed rows through the Mongol ranks, killing three or four of them at a time. Very few of that first wave got through to hit the pikers and axemen, and I don't think any horseman who got into our pikes lived to try it again.

This was exactly the sort of fight I had envisioned from the beginning, the sort we had armed and trained for. And it was working beautifully. The men were elated! After the huge losses we had suffered on the riverboats, after the helplessness the troops had felt watching the conventional knights being slaughtered west of Sandomierz, after the confusion of the battle at Cracow, after seeing the senseless slaughter at East Gate, and after all the mind-numbing running and pulling in between, finally, at last, something was working perfectly!

Naturally, somebody started to sing, and the troops along the entire line picked up the tune.

> *Poland is not yet dead!*
> *Not while we yet live!*

I could see that up on the wall, despite the fact that they were both pregnant, Cilicia and Francine were manning swivel guns right next to each other, firing down at the enemy. And I saw that two of Krystyana's sons—my own children!—were running ammunition to them. I waved, and they all waved back.

But you don't kill a quarter of a million men in a minute, and we kept advancing as best we could, but no longer at a full quickstep. Going over the fallen enemy and making sure they were really dead slowed us down. Our center was soon bowed back as the edges advanced more quickly, and we had them surrounded. I had to order the wings to slow down so we wouldn't be shooting through the enemy troops and back into our own.

About then Krystyana decided that it was time for the wall guns, and all nine dozen of them let loose at once. The effect astounded even me, and I'd designed the bloody things. Suddenly, everything within two gross yards of the wall was either very dead or trying very hard to get that way! Bits of shrapnel and dead Mongol were blown as far as our own troops. The enemy still standing were stunned and made easy marks for the swivel guns.

Then one knot of horsemen turned as their leader pointed directly at me. Suddenly, some three hundred men and horses wheeled and charged straight for my cart! Everything had been so beautiful, but suddenly things didn't look too good.

The gunners tore into them, and many riders went down. The Mongols knew that they were all dead men, but they wanted vengeance for their own deaths, vengeance in the form of *my* life! They kept coming, and as their ranks thinned, I saw in the center of them two faces I recognized. One was that of the Mongol ambassador, and the other was General Subotai Bahadur himself.

Standing in the center war cart, I drew my sword and waited. There was nothing else I could do.

"Thank you, our Lord, for these thy gifts, which we are about to receive, from thy bounty, through Christ, our Lord, amen," one of the gunners on my cart said. I didn't know if he was being sacrilegious or just thanking God for the targets, so I kept my mouth shut. It was pretty dry just then, anyway.

The two older Mongols seemed to be leading charmed lives, or perhaps the gunners were reluctant to shoot a man with white hair and wrinkles when there were so many younger targets available, but in the end they were the last two left alive. Together, their horses jumped my cart's big shield and came down directly on top of the pikemen. As they leapt from their dying horses toward the cart, a wounded piker caught Subotai in the gut with a grounded pike. I don't know which of the three us was most surprised, but the old general was suddenly airborne. He actually pole-vaulted right over my head!

The ambassador landed in the cart between two startled gunners and swung his sword at me. I parried it and gave him a slash to the forearm. His hand and sword went flying. He pulled a dagger with his left hand, and I took that one off as well.

He said, "Damn you, Conrad!" and slumped to the bottom of the cart.

I looked at him and decided that we could use a Polish-speaking prisoner. I put tourniquets on his stumps.

The roar of gunfire slowed to a rattle and then to occasional pops. Slowly, it stopped completely. Troops looked wide-eyed over the smoke and the smell of the carnage, not quite ready to believe that it was finally over. Slowly, the truth dawned.

Victory! The tops of the walls and towers were covered with our women and children, cheering for us and for themselves. Baron Gregor had the men unleash themselves from the carts, and they walked to the wall, axes and pikes in hand so that they could chop up the fallen enemy and make sure that dead Mongols stayed that way. A brutal business, but a necessary one. There was no exchange of prisoners with the Mongols, and any who escaped would have to rob and murder their way home just to stay alive. Best to kill them clean here and now.

The prisoner I had taken was another matter. I had one of our medics sew up his stumps and left orders for him to be guarded.

Actually, our medics outnumbered our wounded, and we had less than a hundred killed. A remarkably one-sided victory.

I climbed down from my war cart and joined the others streaming toward the now open city gate. As I passed our wrecked septic tank, I saw a number of warriors around it, pikes in hand. Quite a few Mongol troops were floundering around in the wretched stench below us.

"Do you think they'll want some prisoners?" one of the warriors asked a friend.

"They didn't say nothing about wanting none," his friend answered. "Anyways, it 'ud be easier to catch them some fresh ones than it would be to clean these bastards off." And with that, he reversed his pike and used it to hold one of the dog paddling Mongols under the stinking grey mud.

"I guess you're right," said the first, reversing his pike.

I just shook my head and walked on until I ran into my second in command.

"Give the men leave to enjoy themselves until tomorrow morning," I told Baron Gregor, "except for two companies that you don't like. Somebody had better stay on guard. We'll be needing some radio operators as well."

"Right, sir."

"Try to get through to Baron Vladimir and tell him the news. Have him send half his men back to where we dumped all that booty and bring it here. The rest of his men should stop at East Gate and clean the place up. Send a scout to him if the radios aren't working. And I want the planes to fly over all of the country that they can and make sure that there isn't yet another Mongol army out there."

"Right, sir."

"Can you think of anything else we have to do?"

"Not offhand, sir, aside from spreading the word about this victory."

"Then after you get those messages out, go see your wives. I'm going to mine right now!"

I went back to my old apartment in the first wall through the cheering crowds of soldiers and their dependents. I smiled and waved back, trying to be the good politician, but my heart wasn't really in it. I had been going on my own adrenaline for weeks, and now at last it was leaching out of me. I felt incredibly tired, drained, and weak. I was sick of war and blood and dirt and saw nothing glorious about wallowing in them. What I really wanted to do was get out of this filthy, stinking, blood-soaked armor, take a long, hot bath, have a stiff drink, and kiss my wife, and not necessarily in that order.

I went up to my rooms and found both Francine and Cilicia waiting for me. Inwardly I groaned. The last thing I wanted now was more confrontation, and the Chinese symbol for an argument is two women under one roof.

They both smiled at me.

"We have decided," Francine said. "When we were shooting at the Mongols, we decided that we should share you. We both love you, and you love both of us, so we can make it work."

This statement surprised me as much as a new Mongol army. I sat down to take it all in. The horse really had learned how to sing!

The war was over, and now we'd have to get busy and build the peace.

Chapter Ten

FROM THE JOURNAL OF COUNTESS FRANCINE

Once I heard that our men were coming, I was no longer afraid. I knew that Conrad would never let us be harmed. Captainette Krystyana allowed me to operate one of the swivel guns, even though there were other women who were better at it than I. She said that seeing me in battle would encourage Count Conrad. I suppose that it was for the same reason that she put Lady Cilicia at the gun next to mine.

There is something about fighting in the company of others that gives one a strong sense of camaraderie, and I wonder if this isn't the reason why men like to do it so much. Certainly I could no longer hate Cilicia when she was shooting at the same murderers that I was.

"He loves both of us," she said to me during a lull in the fighting. "And we both love him."

"What you say is true. We can't help ourselves. Truly good men are hard to find," I said.

"Many of the women here share a man. Couldn't we do the same?" she said.

And so it was that after Conrad had rescued us from the Mongol horde, we both gave him a warm welcome. Knowing him well, we had a warm tub of water waiting for him, and together we stripped off his filthy, blood-drenched armor and clothes.

He had not had the chance to change his clothing for two weeks, and his outer clothes were spattered with so much blood and gore that they were stiff and hard even after we removed the metal from them. We didn't even consider having them laundered, but sent them out to be burned!

With one of us at each side of the tub, we washed him down like a little baby, and he loved it. We scrubbed him and rubbed him and even made little baby noises at him. We had to change the water twice before we got him really clean, and he drank an entire pitcher of cold beer while we did it.

Our love had been through a half-dozen fierce battles and had only one small injury. He didn't tell us then that this wound had cost him the sight in his right eye.

We hesitated in giving him a really proper hero's welcome, for we were both in our sixth month and feared to harm our children. Before he got there, we had debated what to do and had finally called in one of the maids to attend to his needs. The poor girl was disappointed, though, for once we got him out of the tub and dried, he went into his chamber and fell sound asleep on top of the covers. He didn't wake until noon the next day, and by then I was gone.

Leaving the maid to attend to Conrad in the unlikely event that he awoke, Cilicia and I dressed in our best and went down to join the army in its celebration. It was important that we make an appearance among the warriors. We first went and sang a mass at the church, as many of the men were doing, though Cilicia sat quietly through it, not being a Christian.

Then we went to join the party. The ladies had brewed vast quantities of strong beer for the occasion, and it was being consumed with gusto. We were both dying to find out all that happened, and Baron Gregor was most helpful. Baron Ilya was even more so, for I think that he is the only one of my husband's barons that does not have even one wife, so we had him to ourselves. As he talked on about the fighting on the riverboats, the battle near Sandomierz, the burning of Cracow, and the murder of the people at East Gate, the full horror and magnitude of the slaughter came to me.

And also the priceless opportunity that all this represented!

Think! Almost the entire nobility of the duchies of Little Poland, Sandomierz, and Mazovia had been killed. And not only the fighting men but most of their wives, children, and grandparents had died as well. In all of eastern Poland, there was no one left with the strength to defend the land except my husband, Conrad!

And there was no one left alive to inherit it all!

By himself, Conrad had defeated the biggest invasion Christendom had ever suffered, and he had done it almost without losses, except for his riverboats and aircraft. His huge land army was completely intact.

Those three duchies needed Conrad's protection, and I intended to see to it that they got it in the traditional manner! The few surviving nobles and freemen of eastern Poland were going to make Conrad their duke. Dukes! With the right persuasion, they'd make him the duke of all three duchies!

To do that, I was going to have to speak to all of them, and I'd have to do it before Duke Henryk got off his slovenly rump in Legnica! He hadn't fought for eastern Poland, and I was not about to let him reap the prize of victory.

First I went to Baron Gregor and told him of my plan. He was very enthusiastic about it and agreed to stop sending messages to Duke Henryk. He felt that it could be disastrous to tell the duke actual lies, but he thought it might be possible to convince his grace to stay in Legnica for another week by slight misdirection. I left that to the good baron and got myself ready to go to Cracow.

You see, the only way to talk to every one of the scattered people of eastern Poland was to use Conrad's magazine. For years everyone had relied on it for the news, and it had a perfect reputation for always telling the truth. Yet it hadn't occurred to anyone to use it to persuade.

The magazine was printed in the Franciscan monastery in Cracow, and Baron Gregor said that the monastery still stood, even though the buildings around it were in ruins. I intended to be there by dawn.

My condition was such that I could not safely mount a horse, but Conrad had had a number of railroad carriages built. One of the smallest was light and fast, though it carried only five people. I had two of my maids pack for themselves and me and went to the stables. Luck was still with me, for I found Anna there.

She was in surprisingly low spirits, and I had to take her to her "spelling board" to find out what the matter was. It took an hour to get the whole story out of her, but it was time well spent.

Conrad had found another mount like her, but white in color, and this person could not understand Polish as Anna and all her children could. She could only understand the English of the future that my husband came from. Conrad, acting with stupid male practicality, had kept the new mount to himself and had been ignoring Anna just when she felt he needed her most.

I had long admired Anna, and now she really needed a friend.

"Oh, you poor baby," I said to her. "So Conrad went running off to battle, first on a riverboat without you and then on this new white hussy. Shame on him! To do such a thing to his oldest and best friend. As soon as we get back, I'm going to scold him for what he has done to you. But right now there's something that we must do that is very important for him. I mean, he's been a bad boy, but we are still his ladies and we must take care of him, yes?"

She nodded yes.

"We have to go to Cracow and get the monks there to print a special issue of the magazine. This will tell everybody that Conrad should be the new boss. Can you get us there by morning if you push that new little railroad cart?"

She nodded yes.

It took some struggling to get the cart out of the building, for there were no attendants about. Everyone seemed to be at the victory party.

"My lady, you shouldn't be doing such heavy work!"

"Oh!" I was startled and looked to see a young officer standing in the limelight. "You're Sir Miesko's son, aren't you?"

"I have that honor. Captain Wladyclaw of the scouts, at your service, my countess," he said, bowing deeply.

"I'm so glad you're here, Sir Wladyclaw. Can you get this carriage on the track?"

"But of course, my lady. Yet what do you want with it?"

There was nothing to do but take him into my confidence and explain the whole thing to him.

"Well, if Baron Gregor approves the plan, then so do I," he said. "Lord Conrad *should* be a duke, or better yet a king! But I think that he would not approve of his wife going all the way to Cracow unescorted, especially as there could be a Mongol or two still hiding out there. However, my men and I are free at the moment and would be honored to do the task."

"But Sir Wladyclaw, that would make you miss the victory celebration."

"It matters little, my lady, since my own men have their wives at the Warrior's School and not here. I myself am yet a bachelor, and there are six hundred platoons of young men in earnest competition for the regretfully few single ladies at Three Walls. Also, if we do not go to Cracow in your service, we will likely have to spend tomorrow burying dead Mongols, a task worth avoiding if it can be done with honor. So you see that it is you that do us the favor, Countess. I shall have a lance or two of scouts here before your servants arrive with your luggage."

The captain was always true to his word, and we were on the road in minutes, the captain with ten scouts, all riding Anna's children, and in Anna's carriage two of my maids and myself.

Conrad must have designed the carriage with Anna or one of her identical children in mind. Its wheels were placed under springs, with some sort of oil-filled pot that Conrad called a "shock absorber." Suffice to say that it ran with remarkable smoothness.

Conrad called this sort of carriage a "convertible," since the railroad wheels had very thick flanges that permitted it to be driven on ordinary roads as well as on railroad tracks.

At the back, there was a sort of lower half of a horse collar that perfectly fitted Anna's neck and shoulders. This let her push the cart without being encumbered with a harness, and the cart was so low to the ground that she could easily look over it. Pushing this collar to the left or right permitted her to steer the cart when it was *off* the railroad. Also, this arrangement permitted the passengers to talk to the person pushing it, and Anna and I still had a lot to talk over, one girl to another.

Later in the evening, when conversation was starting to ebb, Sir Wladyclaw rode to the side of the carriage and begged leave to introduce his men to me. I was of course delighted to meet them, for besides its being good politics, I enjoy meeting with young people, and these were all very young men.

It was rather like holding court, save that we were all moving down the railroad at a pace that no ordinary horse could keep up for long. They couldn't all line up at once, since some must needs ride "point" and others "flank." I resolved to have Conrad explain these strange terms to me, but just then I did not want to expose my ignorance to Sir Wladyclaw.

Somehow it was necessary to shift men to and from various positions before each could meet me, but this had the advantage of letting me speak at length with each of them.

Or rather I should say shout, for our speed was such that the wind was strong.

It also allowed my maids to size them up at length and to speak of them in a most immodest manner when we were between visitors. It has always been my custom to let my servants speak as they will when we are alone, for one learns much from one's subordinates. The girls were quite pleased with Sir Wladyclaw's men, and for good reason. Not only was each a fine specimen of young manhood, but each was also from a very good family. I found that while I did not know any of them personally, I knew friends and relatives of every one of them. We spent some pleasant hours discussing mutual friends. When the lengthy introductions were at last over and Sir Wladyclaw was again at my side, I spoke to him of this.

"But of course, my lady. A scout must be a well-traveled man or he will get lost trying to find the enemy or even his own army. The work is vigorous, so he cannot be too old. He must be a born horseman who can spend days in the saddle without tiring. That was necessary enough in the days of ordinary horses, but in these modern times, why, a Big Person can run for days without stopping. Who else but a nobleman could have this experience? Oh, think not that I'm being snobbish! Both of my own parents were born commoners, for my father was knighted on the battlefield for valor, not because his father was noble. But the fact remains that I got my first horse when I was four years old, and I made my first visit to Cracow when I was six! A commoner simply doesn't get the benefit of the sort of upbringing that I got. And some of my men were better off than I, since their fathers, grandfathers, and uncles were all widely traveled horsemen. What I am trying to say is that when we formed up the scouts, we knew that we would have very few Big People for the first few years. We had to get the absolute most we could get out of them. That meant that we needed the best horsemen we could possibly find, and I think we did a very good job."

"You did indeed, Sir Wladyclaw," I said. "But you said that there would be very few Big People *for the first few years*. There are less than three dozen of them at present. Surely they can never be numerous!"

"Though it pains me to disagree with so gracious a lady, I fear I must do so. There are but two dozen and ten adult Big People now, counting the new white one that Lord Conrad found, but there are also two gross, six dozen, and four young ones growing up right now. Further, in the next month or two, nine dozen and eight fillies will be born, assuming that we haven't lost any Big People in the war. A few are missing, you know. In two years' time we shall be able to equip an entire company with Big People, and in twenty years they could well outnumber all the Little People in the rest of the army!"

"Then you can expect considerable promotion as your little command expands," I said.

"That is my hope, my lady. Indeed, I voluntarily took two demotions in grade in order to get this post, and I don't think I'll regret that choice in the long run. Also, it means that the men under me will be promoted as well, and I have chosen them for command ability as well as for horsemanship."

"But you haven't explained why they're all so handsome!" one of my maids said.

"But they're not," Sir Wladyclaw said. "You only think that they are because of your essential lechery, my young lady, and I love you for it!"

"Well, you haven't done that yet!"

"Patience, my love. There was a slight matter of an army to train and a Mongol horde to vanquish first. But now that these trivial chores seem to be accomplished, I shall devote myself to honoring my noble mother's dearest hope, the getting for her of some grandchildren. It is my earnest intent to spend as much of my time as my lords permit in the next few years in the granting of my dear mother's wishes. The assistance of healthy young ladies is earnestly sought!"

"I don't know if you're serious or not," she said.

"Alas, it is a thing known to but a few. But we shall study the matter with deliberation as soon as my lords and your lady permit."

And with that, our gallant Sir Wladyclaw rode out to inspect his men. The girls were both giggling at the exchange, and in truth I was smiling about it, too, me, a pregnant woman of thirty.

To be sure, much of what he had said was surely nonsense, but he had said it with a smile on his lips and a twinkle in his eye. More importantly, he was fit and lean and strong. He was clean and polished and remarkably sexy. He had a good mind, a decent education, and a proper attitude on things. Indeed, he was a young man who would go far in this world.

Chapter Eleven

At first light we went through the bloodstained gates of Cracow, which Conrad and Sir Wladyclaw had completely stuffed with dead Mongols, if the tale could be believed. We could have found rooms at Wawel Castle, but it was not convenient to the Franciscan monastery, and I was beginning to find walking difficult. Also, there is a great deal of time-consuming ceremony at the castle, and I did not want to waste a moment on anything but the task at hand. Thus, we proceeded directly to the Pink Dragon Inn and obtained lodging there. Oh, the innkeeper said that the place was completely filled with people whose houses had been burned, but on realizing who I was, he quickly agreed to clear the rooms necessary for my party.

We ate a remarkably spare meal, even for Lent. There was only oatmeal porridge and new beer, for the inn's huge cellars had been completely cleared to provide a quick lunch for a twelfth of my husband's army. Even rare wines that had been aging in the bottle for *three entire years* had been given away, for Count Conrad had said "Empty out your entire cellar," and the innkeeper had taken him exactly at his word. A sad loss.

We then went to the monastery, arriving as the monks were chanting Prime. Soon the new abbot was with me, for the old one had died in the fighting. This new man, Father Stanislaw, had been in charge of the print shop, and he, too, fell completely in with my plan. There was much anger in Cracow at Duke Henryk, for that nobleman had once sworn to defend the city but now had failed to do so, or even to come when the city was under siege.

To be fair to Henryk, the nobles of Cracow had so disagreed with his battle plan that they had left him as a group and gone to fight the Mongols under the leadership of Duke Boleslaw of Mazovia. But the nobles who had done so were now almost all dead, and the commoners have a short memory about such things. The abbot said that to a man, the people of Cracow wanted Conrad for their duke.

The abbot had supplies on hand for a "print run" of twelve thousand copies and set aside all other work to get it done.

Together we talked of an entire issue that treated nothing but the recent war with the Mongols, as opposed to the usual format, where there were a dozen short articles on everything from current events to cooking recipes. We would have a dozen or so witnesses of the various battles each tell their story, stressing how it was that Count Conrad had saved all of Christendom. Near the end there would be an article stressing the danger that eastern Poland was in without a properly confirmed duke to defend it. Then there would be an appeal, hopefully by Bishop Ignacy, for all the freemen and nobles of the duchies of Little Poland, Sandomierz, and Mazovia to meet and elect Conrad duke. Or maybe even king.

The story of the battles had yet to be written, and several monks were put with Sir Wladyclaw and his men to get some of it down on paper. I left to secure Bishop Ignacy to our cause, but as I boarded my carriage, word came that a riverboat had come to port. I had Anna take me there immediately for fear that the boat might leave before I had a chance to talk to the captain. The magazine would have to be delivered, after all.

The boat proved to be the *Enterprise*, with Baron Tadaos himself commanding. This was a stroke of luck, for he commanded all the boats on the river and knew more of the river battle than did any other man.

The baron gave me a warm greeting, and he, too, liked my plan of making Conrad Duke of eastern Poland. He promised all assistance in delivering the news but would not take the time to write the story of the river battle. His duty, he said, was to patrol the rivers and search for his several missing boats. However, he lent me Baron Piotr for the task of writing the history of the Battle for the Vistula, as he called it, and I had to agree that this intelligent young man was certainly up to the task.

As I drove Baron Piotr to the monastery, I said, "You realize that it is important that as much credit as possible must go to Count Conrad himself. You know that if Conrad himself were writing the tale, he would praise everyone but himself, but we must see to it that the truth is told."

"My lady, the only way that Conrad could have done more than he did would have been for him to have killed every single Mongol with his own sword! I shall praise him to the stars, not because you have asked but because he deserves it," the baron said.

Leaving Piotr in the care of the monks, I went to Wawel Cathedral in search of Bishop Ignacy. He was important to my plan because he was so well known and loved. He wrote a sermon every month for the magazine and thus had great influence in the country, indeed in the world, for many copies of the magazine found their way to all the countries of Europe! He was very patriotic and had long worked for the unity of Poland.

Thus, I was very taken aback when, having explained my plan, I found that the bishop was less than totally enthused by it.

"My lady, I have my doubts as to the wisdom of all of this."

"But your excellency! Eastern Poland lies defenseless! Only Conrad has the power capable of defending it."

"I quite agree with you, my daughter, but Conrad would defend it in any event, whether he were duke or commoner."

"But the people want him for their duke!"

"I don't doubt it. Furthermore, they're right. He'd make a fine duke!"

"Then, your excellency, why do you oppose this plan?"

"I am not opposing it. I simply have grave doubts. You seem to forget that I am Conrad's confessor. I know the man very well, perhaps even better than you do. I have no doubt that he would be very good for the country. Indeed, since Duke Henryk controls most of western Poland, were Conrad to control the east, Poland would once again be a united country, could they but agree. And I think that they would. I tell you that Conrad could be made the first King of Poland for a hundred years!"

"Then why do you doubt him?"

"I don't doubt him! Conrad would make a great king, but would being the king make a great Conrad? Do you think that he would be happy with such a position? I don't! Do you know, when once I suggested the throne to him, he said that it looked very stiff and uncomfortable and that he had a fine, soft leather chair in his office that tilted back and suited him. When I suggested the crown, he said that a crown was nothing but a hat that let the rain in. You may want Conrad's enlargement, and the people of Poland may want it, too. But does Conrad want it? I doubt it! He wants to be free to work on his technical devices, and he considers them to be far more important than the fleeting glories of temporal power."

"Your excellency, I cannot believe that any man in his secret heart would turn down absolute power."

"Conrad has very little of this 'secret heart,' as you call it. Indeed, he truly wears his heart on his sleeve, most of the time, to his considerable pain. True, he likes power, but power to him is a very different thing than it is to you. The power he glories in is the power of a white-hot spray of liquid steel pouring from one of his furnaces or the thundering power of one of his huge engines turning at great speed. He cares nothing for the brutal power that permits a king to put some offender to death. He doesn't dream of crowds chanting his name. He avoids crowds as much as he can! He does not want the honor of sitting at the high table of a banquet. He makes excuses and tells lies to avoid banquets altogether! He has dreams, yes, but his dreams are of great cities gleaming white in the sunshine with not a bit of trash in them, of steel tracks that crisscross all of Europe, connecting every hamlet, of mighty ships traveling swiftly to far lands with neither sails nor oars. That's what *power* means to your man! Not sitting on a gilded chair wearing a golden hat."

I was much taken aback by all the bishop had said, for there was more than a grain of truth in it. Yet I was not about to let half a country slip through my fingers.

"You speak the truth, Father. I realize now that when the seym, the local parliaments, meet and they choose Conrad as duke, he will refuse them. After all, they can't *force* him to become a duke. But think of what this will mean, your excellency! Without Conrad, they must then choose someone else. If they are all met together and have already decided to choose a single man, Poland is united! The eastern half, anyway, or all of it if they then choose Duke Henryk, who is Conrad's only real competition. Father, you have changed my reasons for what I'm doing, but you have not changed my intention to do it! Doesn't Poland need to be united? Won't you help me with this plan?"

"Hmm. On that basis, where we would only be using Count Conrad's current popularity as a device to get the people together, yes. To that I would lend my support."

"We need more than your support, your excellency. We need your active help and leadership! With so many of the noblemen dead, I think that you alone would have the prestige to call together all the seym here to Cracow and have them come. Or do you think that Sandomierz would be more centrally located?"

"Sandomierz is not only more central, my daughter, it is also intact! Surely you have noticed that lower Cracow is a smoldering ruin. No, I'm afraid that we must definitely choose Sandomierz."

I left the good bishop working on his proclamation and his sermon and had Anna drive me back to the inn. And then I went to sleep.

Chapter Twelve

FROM THE DIARY OF CONRAD STARGARD

I woke to see that it was broad daylight outside. The second thing I noticed was that I had an attractive young lady in my arms and that she wasn't one of my wives. I thought about it a bit and decided that they had probably provided me with this substitute since they were both in advanced pregnancy, and that it would not be gallant to look a gift lady in the mouth. Of course, if she were not here with my wives' permission, there could be fireworks, but what the hell. I had been two weeks and more without, and that's an absurd amount of time!

So I found out that her name was Mary and that she was one of Cilicia's new maids. I had never known Cilicia to have a maid before. She was picking up Francine's bad habits already. I told Mary that all this was wonderful and topped her for the better part of an hour. About fifteen years old, she was an enthusiastic and healthy girl, if not particularly skillful. At least she wasn't a virgin.

Then I began wondering what the army was doing.

Promising the girl that I'd see her later, I threw a cloak over my bare shoulders and walked over the catwalk to the second wall. The few people I met gave me a smile and a nod, but left me to my mood. The three walls, which doubled as apartment buildings, were connected with narrow, lightweight wooden bridges at each floor that let you go from one apartment building to another without having to go all the way down and then up again. They were built such that if the first wall was taken by an ·enemy, the catwalks could be easily knocked down and the fight could be continued from the second or even the first wall. Fortunately, this had not proved necessary against the Mongols, but every little bit of safety helps.

I got to the fighting top of the outer wall and saw that the cleanup job was well under way. A start was being made at repairing the septic tank. Dead Mongols were being stripped and decapitated, with the bodies being hauled away for burial somewhere out of sight. In the distance, heads were being stuck on poles lined up on both sides of the railroad tracks. Different from what we had done before but just as effective. Maybe even more so, to someone traveling down the track. I wondered if anyone had calculated just how long a double line of a quarter of a million heads was. I did the arithmetic in my head and came up with six dozen miles! Perhaps Baron Gregor was in for a surprise.

The dead Mongol horses were being skinned, and a fair number of the young and healthy ones were being butchered. Many of them were being salted down. Krystyana always was a tightfisted little manager.

Things were being done, they didn't need my help, and I found this to be good. I went down to the showers, which were empty at this hour, and then to the dining room. I was surprised to find that lunch was already over, but I wanted a breakfast, anyway. I hadn't had an egg in two weeks, and I not only ordered six of them, over easy, I had the cook go out to the chicken coop herself and get some that were absolutely fresh. I had them make me some fresh biscuits, too. Rank hath its privileges, and for a day or two I intended to wallow in them!

Yet still I missed a cup of coffee, and no amount of wealth or power could get me one. Most modern Poles prefer tea, but I had developed a taste for good coffee during my college days in Massachusetts and had kept with it after going home. An expensive habit, but worth it.

After eating, I went to the church, feeling guilty for not having gone there yesterday as soon as we had won the battle. Even with most of the people working on the cleanup, there was still quite a crowd in the church, most of them silently praying, giving thanks. There was a long line of people waiting for a chance at the confessionals, one of the things I had introduced to this century. They were standard in my own time, and the priests here had accepted them almost without question as a convenience. My own soul was blackened almost beyond redemption, and I knew that soon I would have to go to Cracow to see my own confessor, Bishop Ignacy. I prayed for an hour and it helped.

My next stop was to the Big People's barn. All of them were gone except for the new white one. Out on patrol, I supposed. I needed to talk to the white person, anyway. I took her over to the big letter board so she could spell out words and answer my questions. The Polish alphabet isn't quite the same as the one used in English, but they are similar enough to get by. Like Anna, she knew that she was a bioengineered product of a civilization in the distant past. Like Anna, she hadn't the slightest idea how a time machine worked. She knew her former rider only as Tom. If he had a last name, she hadn't heard it. In fact, she had absolutely no new information for me at all, except for her name. It was Silver. I should have guessed.

I told her that she was on the payroll now and that she was welcome to swear allegiance to me. She didn't know what that was, so I put it off until later. Somewhat disappointed, I went back to my apartment.

I never developed as close a relationship with Silver as I had with Anna. She didn't like to come up to the apartment and listen in to the conversations, since she couldn't understand them. She couldn't develop friendships with the local children the way Anna did, for the same reason. And I was now a far busier man than I had been ten years earlier. I just didn't have as much time to spend with her as she deserved. I hired two young boys to stay with her and try to teach her Polish, but she proved absolutely incapable of learning the language. A bad situation, but I didn't know what to do about it.

Back in my apartment, I passed Cilicia in a hallway. She smiled and gave me a quick kiss, but she knew enough about my moods to know that I needed to be alone.

I went to my office and told Natalia, my secretary and Baron

Gregor's first wife, that I didn't want to be disturbed by anything less than Duke Henryk or a new Mongol army. I closed the door, and if I had had a telephone I would have unplugged it from the wall. I had some thinking to do.

For the last nine and a half years I had been busy building the seeds of an industrial revolution and building an army to defend Poland from the Mongols. The second objective was now accomplished, for we had given the greasy bastards the soundest beating that they had ever gotten. They'd be a generation sucking their wounds before they dared try us again. By that time, we'd be invincible. We'd likely be attacking them!

As for the first objective, well, there were a lot of improvements still to be made in our technology. Indeed, many had been made in the last few years and had been shelved because we were so involved in war production that we didn't have time to mess with them. The idea that war encourages technology is a myth. War encourages war production and very little else.

The alchemists had come up with an improvement on our method of making sodium bicarbonate, an important chemical in the production of glass, medicines, and the biscuits I had just eaten. The old method mixed salt water (sodium chloride) with carbon dioxide from heated limestone (calcium carbonate), and ammonia from our coke ovens. This yielded sodium bicarbonate and ammonium chloride. The problem was that we couldn't find much of a use for the ammonium chloride and didn't get all that much ammonia from the coke ovens. This greatly limited the amount of the stuff we could produce.

Zoltan's improvement was a way to take quicklime, calcium oxide, and combine it with the ammonium chloride to get all the ammonia back, which we could then recycle. We were still throwing away the calcium chloride. Well, it melted snow, and eventually we came up with the idea of using it as a dehumidifier as part of an air-conditioning system. But mainly, now there was no limit to the amount of glass we could make! Within a year, glass would be cheap enough to use for making canning jars.

Some experimental work had been done on electricity, too. We now had a varnish that was a fair insulator, provided that the voltage was low and you didn't expect much flexing. We had plenty of copper, and all the new towns I had built were very compact, so they could be easily defended. If we put a generator within each city, we wouldn't have to send the electricity very far, so using a low voltage made sense. It eliminated the need for ugly power towers that couldn't be defended, and for half the year we could use the waste heat from the generators to heat our buildings. The usual modern method of doing things wastes about two-thirds of the energy in the fuel in generation and transmission losses. With my system, much of this waste was eliminated, at the price of having a power station next door.

Electric lights would be nice, and although I didn't know where we could get tungsten for the filaments, Tom Edison made a decent light bulb using a carbon filament, simply a baked thread. It's easier to make a low-voltage light bulb than a high-voltage one, since the filament gets shorter and thicker. And once you have a light bulb, you have solved most of the problems in making an electronic tube.

Well, we'd have to work on it.

Nonetheless, the big job ahead of us was simply to do more of what we had been doing.

The simple fact is that mass production is necessary to produce goods and services in sufficient quantity to maintain a decent standard of living. Mass production cannot exist without mass distribution. The larger the market you are serving, the more specialized and efficient you can make your productive machines and processes.

It was critically important that we build more railroad tracks so that industrial and agricultural products could get from place to place more easily.

The failure to emphasize the importance of transportation is one of the Russians' greatest failings. Karl Marx, in his nineteenth-century evaluation of the world economy, lived much of the time in a British industrial area. He not only was never a railroad man or a seaman, he seemed to think that these things were unimportant. All his thoughts were on the making and consuming of things.

As a result, orthodox communistic thinking stresses production and treats transportation as a necessary evil.

This philosophical bias has resulted in an inadequate transportation network in Russia, and this in turn is one of the causes of that country's incredible inefficiency.

The railroads were a top priority, but the more I got to thinking about it, the less important a railroad engine seemed to be. Pulling carts with mules, as we were doing now for civilian transport, was a hundred times more efficient than using pack mules in caravans, which was the only competition. It takes almost as much manpower to tend one of our primitive steam engines as it takes to tend a string of mules. More important, in twenty years we'd have so many Big People that we could use them to pull the carts. Then we wouldn't have to expend any manpower at all! The motive power would also be the driver. A Big Person can pull a ten-ton cart six hundred miles in a day. That ought to be fast enough for anybody. Pulling one cart at a time, we wouldn't have to bother with railroad hump yards and all that sort of time-consuming nonsense. And Big People don't consume nonrenewable resources or pollute the environment the way mechanized transport does. Best to leave mechanically powered transportation to the rivers and oceans.

Then there was the problem that in the last half year we had multiplied the size of the army by a factor of six, to 150,000 men. This was accomplished by giving them an abbreviated course at the Warrior's School. They had learned to handle weapons and take orders, but they hadn't been taught to read, write, or do arithmetic.

This necessary expansion was a tremendously big bite for us to take, and I rather wished that it was possible for us to chew it up. At present, though, we had housing and permanent jobs for only about twenty-five thousand families. More housing and more factories and more farms were obviously needed. But the only thing I could see to do for now was to at least temporarily discharge everybody below the rank of knight who hadn't worked for us before. Then, in time, those who wanted to come back in could finish up the Warrior's School course, and if they passed, they could come back into the army.

No! Stop! Dumb idea. We might need those men again at any time, especially if I had judged the Mongols wrong. Rather than discharging them, I had to form them into active reserves. That would mean regular pay, regular practice sessions, a reserve command structure, and a dozen other headaches. And doing all this while they were scattered all over the country! I'd have to delegate the authority on this one, since I certainly didn't want to bother leading it myself. I wondered if Baron Vladimir would want the job.

The reserve force would have to be a temporary thing, designed to phase itself out as the men came on as full-time workers or retired after ten years or so.

Construction was going to be the big game on campus for quite a while. I had long dreamed of building a line of company-size forts along the Vistula and the Bug as a defense against Mongols, and a similar line along the Odra and the Nysa against the Germans. Oh, except for the German Teutonic Order, the Germans hadn't given us much trouble lately, since they were mostly involved in conflicts in Italy and with the Pope, but from a historical standpoint they repeatedly invaded us, and it was just smart to be ready for it.

We had already built a good working model of a standalone fort, the one at East Gate. It had been taken by a combination of trickery and stupidity, but there had been nothing wrong with the design that I could see. It was easily defensible and looked like a castle, but actually it was mostly an apartment building for two gross families. It was really a small town, with factories, a school, a library, a store, an inn, and everything that such a community needs. Two gross families is about the right size for a town, too. At that size, you have enough neighbors to have somebody interesting to talk to and there are enough of you to support a full set of community services, but you are not so big that people get lost in the crowd. Three Walls, for example, was already too big. Despite the fact that everybody was well taken care of, we were getting a crime problem. I don't mean relatives getting into fistfights, either. That sort of thing will always be with us. No, I mean real organized crime, like that fair-sized theft ring we broke up a year ago. In a town of under three hundred households, things like that aren't likely to happen. Everybody knows what's going on!

Each fort would be situated on twenty or thirty square miles of land, and that land would be farmed by the troops. In the off-seasons there would be light industrial work available to keep them busy. They would spend one day a week in military exercises, but mostly they would be a working community.

I had long been toying with the idea of a factory that would build large precast concrete sections that could be shipped by railroad or boat and assembled on site into a fort. They'd have to go up fast, since I wanted to get the army back up to its present size in a hurry. To house an additional hundred thousand men and their families in four years, I'd have to throw forts up at the rate of two a week!

And there wasn't only the concrete to think of. There was plumbing, wiring, power plants, heating systems, weapons, schoolbooks, and beer steins. I got to sketching out what was required, and it was very dark before I quit.

We were going to have to build a factory that built factories that made the components of the forts, which were themselves partly factories! I wrote a note to Natalia to have all drafting and engineering personnel relieved of all military duties and back at their desks immediately. I needed help!

I woke up in the sunshine again, with the same girl in bed with me. I had missed the sunrise service two days in a row! There was some cheering going on outside, and I went to the balcony to see what it was all about. The women and children from East Gate were back! Not the nobles who were murdered there by the Mongols, but our own people who had left the fort two or three days before that. The women and children had wandered around in the hills for a week before they had found their way back here.

I got some proper clothes on in a hurry and went down to

the mob scene below. Understandably, the men whose families had been missing were delighted to find that they were safe and sound. They were hugging and kissing and laughing and crying, sometimes the same person doing all four at the same time. What annoyed me was the fact that the captainette who had brought the dependents in was being carried around on some of the men's shoulders as though she were a hero.

I got over to them and wrenched her down. "You stupid bitch!" I shouted. "You're under arrest!"

"But what for, sir?" one of the men asked.

"What for? For dereliction of duty, for abandoning her post, for treason, and for contributing to the murder of twenty thousand women and children!" I shouted.

Then suddenly everybody was quiet.

Chapter Thirteen

Three Walls still didn't have a jail, so I had a blacksmith put leg shackles on her and followed the two knights who took our prisoner to the storeroom we used as a lockup when necessary. The room was already in use for the handless Mongol ex-ambassador, but I had her thrown in with him. He stank the way all Mongols do, but I didn't owe her any favors. I was on my way back up when I realized that I was going to have to judge the case.

You see, "count" is a judicial title, like "judge" or "justice." A man holding it had the right of high justice within his realms. That is to say, he could hold a trial for a major crime and punish the offender as he saw fit. His word could have a man hanged. I had held the title of count since the Christmas before, but that meant that I was count of Francine's tiny county of Strzegom, where there never was much crime. Here, at Three Walls, I had remained Count Lambert's baron despite my right to use the title of count. Up until a week ago, that is. When Count Lambert had been killed by a Mongol spear and I had inherited his lands in Poland, I had also inherited his responsibilities. I couldn't fob off my serious criminals on him anymore. I was it!

I went back up to my office to ponder this latest problem. For years I had been ducking my legal duties by having somebody else do them. On Sir Miesko's recommendation, I'd appointed Baron Pulaski to be my judge. The baron had four subordinates, a court recorder, a bailiff, and two prosecutor-defenders. These last two took turns. They went around my extensive and scattered estates, hearing cases and writing up their recommendations to me. I almost invariably went along with them or, in the case of serious offenses, handed their recommendations up to my liege lord, Count Lambert. In time he got to following their recommendations as well.

But they really didn't have any official sanction for their existence. Since they normally tried trivial matters and only conducted hearings on serious ones, nobody had seriously complained about it. But Captainette Lubinska's crimes were hardly trivial. Whether I tried her or had Baron Pulaski do it, I would be setting a precedent.

After some hours of agonizing over it, I decided that the baron was more competent a judge than I was, and he was certainly more unbiased. Furthermore, I didn't want to spend the rest of my life being a trial judge. I had better things to do than sit on a gilded chair deciding if some poor bastard deserved to die. If my liege lord, Duke Henryk didn't like it, he could start by telling me so.

If, indeed, he still was my liege lord! The last I'd heard from him, he was damning me for failing to go to Legnica and join his forces there. For all I knew, he considered me to be an independent duke now.

The simple truth was that the military forces that obeyed me were vastly superior to his, and I controlled quite a bit more money than he did, although as a good socialist, I had difficulty thinking of all this vast wealth as being my own. Actually, I could probably declare my own independence and make it stick!

Not that I'd want to.

I could see no advantage to independence and quite a few disadvantages. Being part of a greater whole, I could expand my industrial and agricultural revolutions as fast as necessary simply by doing it and paying a fee or buying land if it was required of me. A little persuasion was all that was usually needed. As an independent king, or whatever, I'd have to fight a war every time I tried to open up a new market. Insanity!

I sent a runner to find Baron Pulaski and ask him to come have a talk with me.

My designers and draftspeople had all shown up at dawn and had spent the morning getting their work area cleaned up and ready to go. It had been more than a year since we'd used it, what with the war and all. Most of them were back in civilian clothes and feeling a little unusual about it.

"I'm not going to enforce any dress codes around here," I told them, "but if you have to go out to the field or even to the shops, I'll expect you to be in uniform. You're still in the army, after all. Now then, we have some factories to design, and we'll need at least the foundation drawings finalized in two weeks so the troops can start on them as soon as they finish cleaning up the mess we made on the Vistula. Now here's what we need . . ."

Once I got them going, I went back to my "manager" office, called for my secretary, and asked if there were any messages. She brought in a stack as thick as my arm, sorted as to what they wanted. An efficient lady.

Baron Gregor wanted to release all his men who had been workers at Three Walls to get the factories going again. He was particularly worried about the ammunition situation. I wrote "granted," with a note that all men who had served in the Construction Corps should be sent under Baron Yashoo to East Gate to rebuild the Riverboat Assembly Building. Since almost all these workers had at least a half-dozen new subordinates who had gone through only four months of training, these subordinates would be assigned to other knights at no more than a dozen new men each.

There were six dozen letters of congratulations and then a request from a priest that in the future all Mongols should be baptized before they were beheaded. Denied. The bastards didn't deserve to go to heaven.

There were a lot of requests for discharge, mostly so the men could search for their families. Denied, put your request through channels. There wasn't much to worry about, since most army personnel had their dependents at army installations that had not been attacked, and nobody had gotten killed at any of them.

I made an exception in the case of Captain Targ, whose family was far to the east, near what would be Zakopane. I owed him a serious favor, since he had saved my life, and I thought this was a good way to pay it. I sent orders to his baron that he and his brother should be given indefinite leave and lent horses if they wanted them. I really meant to do him a favor, but I guess it didn't turn out that way. The two brothers headed east, crossed the Vistula, and were never heard from again. Their family was also among the missing.

Lady Natalia came in after a while and asked me if I wanted my dinner brought up, but I decided that the men should see that I was still alive, and we went down to the cafeteria, not that there was any "cafe" to justify the name.

The chow lines there were absurdly long, worse than what happens when the communists try to sell six refrigerators in Warsaw. I told Natalia that she should put out the word that the cafeterias would have to be restricted to dependents, officers of the grade of captain and higher, and men who had originally worked at Three Walls. All others would have to eat at their war carts, though the cooks could draw on the stores here. Natalia and I, of course, took cuts in front of the line. RHIP.

The next week was spent in meetings and similar boring but important trivia. The aircraft had found no trace of other Mongols, even though we all knew that there had to be a lot of stragglers hiding out there somewhere. Francine was in Cracow playing hostess to some political nonsense, but she seemed to be having fun and staying out of trouble. I supposed that she needed to get away from it all for a while after the tensions of the war, and I let her have her own way. The cleanup at Three Walls had been completed, and the original workers from each of my other installations were sent home to get things productive again. Getting things back to normal seemed to take as much work as getting us on a war footing had.

Then Baron Vladimir arrived.

I gave him a hug when he got to my office. "God, Vladimir, it's wonderful to see you! What took you so long?"

"What took me so long, my lord? I think that the problem started when I was entirely too efficient in getting across the Vistula. You recall that as we left the battlefield west of Sandomierz, you were to return the booty here to Three Walls, and I was to take the larger group of our men to cross the Vistula and clean and loot the killing fields there. We found no riverboats running, but we found two of those river ferries of the sort you invented so many years ago, during that delightful journey we made with our ladies to the River Dunajec. You know, the sort that uses a long rope to force the river itself to carry one back and forth. Three dozen big river barges were available at Sandomierz, as was a good supply of rope, so we quickly built three dozen more of the things. By dint of efficient organization and hard work, I was able to get my entire command across by midnight.

"Now I have a question for you, my lord. What ever possessed you to entrust so important a message as the fact that Cracow was burning to an absolutely untrained peasant? The silly fool had never before in his life been more than six miles from the village in which he had been born! He had never been on a Big Person before. He had never even seen one! Is it any wonder that he never thought of telling her who they were trying to find? He had not the slightest concept of geography, and he couldn't have read a map even if he'd had one! He couldn't read, period! Is it any wonder that he missed us in the dark and rode all the way to the Crossman city of Turon? He was two days finding us! Why did you do this thing to me? Two-thirds of your men missed out on half of the war!"

All I could do was to bury my face in my hands and say, "*Mea culpa, mea culpa, mea maxima culpa.*" Through my fault, through my fault, through my most grievous fault.

"Baron Vladimir, I'm sorry. At the time he was simply a man on a Big Person, and I didn't even think about what I was doing. A courier had come in badly wounded with the news about Cracow. One of the officers assigned a man to ride the Big Person and help out our flankers. Then I realized that you must be told as soon as possible, and so I changed the man's orders. I never stopped to think about how limited, how restricted the average peasant is. I'm sorry."

"And I accept your apology, my lord. You made a mistake, but as it turned out, no great harm was done. You had sufficient forces with you to handle the problems that happened to come up. My men could have given you more power, but they could not have given you more speed. Yet it could have turned out otherwise! The Mongols might have caught you strung out on the road with your men half-armed and armored, with your pikes stored for transit, and your guns unmounted. They could have met you with locally superior forces and wiped you and all of your men out! You were lucky. But while I was waiting to see you—"

"They made *you* wait?"

"The Baroness Natalia is sometimes overly protective, my lord. But while I was waiting, I heard the tale about Captainette Lubinska. She made a mistake as bad or even worse than yours, and she didn't have your luck! Now you plan to have her hanged for it. Do you realize that she was born a peasant girl on a farm just outside of Cieszyn, where Count Herman's wife held sway for so many years? For all of Lubinska's life, the countess was an authority figure whose word was not to be questioned. Then, one day, the countess lied to her, usurped her authority, and ordered her away from her post. Is it any wonder that she obeyed the countess's orders even if they weren't exactly legal? What did the captainette know about the law? She was only a peasant, for God's sake!"

"Again you shame me, Vladimir. Look, I've turned the matter over to Baron Pulaski. Why don't you speak to him, and also speak at her trial?"

"All right, my lord, if you wish it. But remember, the right of high justice is yours now. You may delegate the duties, but not the responsibility!"

"You are entirely too right. For now, though, what happened once you got the word about Cracow?"

"Well, once I got the message out of the peasant—he hadn't slept in days and was babbling—we had to drop everything and recross the Vistula. The railroad tracks are on the west bank only. I sent troops south in battalions at a walk until the rest could catch up. After that we went to double time. When we got to the company you left behind to guard the booty, we absorbed them in our van, since they were fresh by then, and eventually left our hindmost company on guard. At Cracow I left a battalion to secure the city and relieve the wounded you left behind there. We had just arrived at East Gate when we got the word about your victory here. As per your orders, we cleaned up East Gate and sent men back to the dumped booty to pick it up. Half of my men are now on the way back to clean up the killing grounds on the east bank of the Vistula. Also, I sent a battalion west to the salt mines to dig and bring back all the salt they could. We'll need it if we're to save the horsehides we've taken. The rest of them are here now with your booty and what we collected at East Gate."

"What booty at East Gate? We lost there!"

"Many of those women and children had jewels and money secreted about their persons, my lord. Perhaps the Mongols were in too much of a hurry to search them all properly. But for whatever reason, there was quite a lot of it, and policy is that the dead should never be buried with anything of value, not if you want them to rest undisturbed."

"You're right, of course. Is there any chance of returning the money and jewels to their next of kin?"

"No, my lord. Only a few of them could be identified. We never thought to issue dog tags to noncombatants."

"Well, we can hardly keep it for ourselves. Looting Mongols is one thing. Robbing the Christian dead is quite another. Perhaps we should donate it to the Church."

"That was to be my suggestion, my lord."

"Well, get some rest and see your family. There's a meeting at one tomorrow that you should attend, and then I guess you'll be going back to the Vistula."

"I can delegate the cleanup, my lord. I have a trial to attend first."

Interlude Two

I hit the STOP button, leaned back, and stretched. Tom still hadn't gotten here. I was almost to the point of worrying about him, but not quite.

"It's getting to be lunchtime, don't you think?" I said to the nude girl snuggled next to me.

"Yes, sir."

"Well, why don't you get me a couple of salami sandwiches, a side of onion rings, and a cold Budweiser. And get anything you want for yourself."

"Yes, sir."

An untalkative girl, but she was pretty and obedient, and I guess you can't have everything. Nice outfit, too. She was back almost immediately. She spread my lunch out on the control desk and stood waiting.

"Aren't you hungry? Why don't you eat?" I said.

"Yes, sir." She brought in a bowl of something that looked like custard and spooned it quickly down.

"Is that all you're eating?"

"Yes, sir."

"Don't you want anything else?"

"No, sir."

I shrugged. Well, she was pretty young, and kids that age can survive on nearly anything. I put it down to some sort of fad diet.

I sat back, put my arm around her, and hit the START button.

Chapter Fourteen

Captainette Lubinska's trial went on for five days. I managed to scrupulously avoid it, except when I was called in to testify as to exactly what orders she had been given. Baron Vladimir spoke at length in her behalf, but when the sorry affair was over, a jury of her peers, twelve captains and captainettes, found her guilty. According to the code of military justice that I myself had written, the punishment was death by hanging, and that's exactly what Baron Pulaski sentenced her to, to be carried out first thing in the morning.

My own rules required a speedy sentence, provided that the case could be reviewed in time, since to keep a condemned prisoner waiting for months or years, as is often the modern practice, seemed to be unnecessarily cruel to the criminal. Enough time for the condemned to say a good confession, go to mass, and spend a night in prayer was all that could be morally justified. Also, much of the reason for punishing someone is as an example to others, and if the thing drags out for years, people forget what the crime was all about. The hanging, when it finally happens, becomes a simple, needless murder by the state.

Baron Vladimir came to see me that evening. He repeated all the arguments he had made before, and also said that much of the fault for the incident was mine, for I had put a weak and stupid peasant woman into a position that was too far above her.

"My lord, if you loaded ten tons of iron onto the back of a mule and it collapsed, would you blame the animal? Would you kill it for having failed in its duty?"

"We're not talking about a dumb animal here, Vladimir. We're talking about a human being!"

"True, my lord, and I would not be arguing so strongly if it were only a dumb animal you were abusing, though I would still call your failings to your attention. You are my liege lord, and I am obligated to give you my best counsel, even and *especially when you don't like it*! Furthermore, the difference between a dumb animal and a dumb peasant is less than you may think. We are knights, you and I. Our function is to protect the peasants, not to hang them for *being* peasants!"

So that was the crux of the problem. Baron Vladimir was a traditional member of the old nobility, while I was a man born in the twentieth century. Vladimir was a good friend and a valuable subordinate, but his world outlook was very different from mine. And he hadn't stopped explaining things to me yet.

"We were put here by God to protect women, my lord, not to kill them for having feminine weaknesses! I say again that the fault is yours for putting her in the position that you did, for elevating her far above her station, and for trusting a woman to do a man's job. You had men who were sound of mind but could not join us in the field. Baron Novacek, for one. He may not have hands, but he could have commanded East Gate and done a good job at it. Why you insisted on having all your women's companies led by women is beyond me."

Why indeed? It had seemed good for morale, and it ensured that a man wouldn't take advantage of a female subordinate, but the main reason was my twentieth-century belief in equality. If women were doing the defending, they should lead the defense as well. Now it seemed that I was equalizing the captainette right out of her life.

I let Vladimir continue until he started repeating himself, then I said, "Baron, I don't know what I'll do about this mess yet, but whatever I do, it won't be done lightly. Tell me, that courier who missed you in the dark near Sandomierz. What did you do to him?"

"Him, my lord? Well, he was incompetent as a scout or mes-senger, so I could hardly leave him with a Big Person, but he had done his best within his limitations. I let him sleep while we recrossed the Vistula and then put him back down in the ranks as a pikeman. It doesn't take much brains to do that job, simply courage, strength, and obedience, things that a peasant is often good at."

"But you didn't punish him?"

"Would I punish a fish because it couldn't fly? *Peasants are stupid!* You can't expect one to do a nobleman's job."

"I see. To change the subject, what about you, Baron Vladimir? You've done a wonderful job these last six years with the army. Have you done any thinking about what your reward should be? About what you want to do now?"

"Hmmm. I've had some thoughts, my lord, or perhaps I should call them dreams. I have saved much of my salary over the years, and I'll get my share of the booty. I wonder, well, there is the castle you got from Count Lambert, the one Baron Stefan used to hold. You've never used it for much of anything. Would you consider selling it to me?"

"No, but I'd give it to you if you wanted it. You've certainly earned it, and as you say, it's just going to waste. Or better still, how about the new castle I built for Count Lambert at Okoitz? It's a dozen times larger and comes stocked with a renewable supply of attractive young ladies."

"A portion of me is tempted by Okoitz, my lord, but my better parts say that I'd be happier with my wife and family without the count's fabulous harem. You see, what I want is to live in the old traditional way, with the wife and children that I haven't seen enough of these past years. My oldest boy is eight years old now, and he has seen very little of his own father. I don't want to live as Count Lambert did, and I certainly don't want to live like you! Further, I think that there are a lot of the peasants on the lands that you've gotten that prefer the old ways as well. With your permission, I would gather together those peasants that would swear to me and take them from these mines and factories of yours."

"Permission granted, old friend. From my standpoint, you'll be relieving me of some of my malcontents. The castle is yours, along with as much land as you can find men to farm it."

"And a bit more, some forest for a hunting preserve, my lord?"

"Fine, so long as you don't go and reintroduce wild boars and wolves on it. And the people you talk into joining you, well, don't get *too* traditional on me. I'm going to insist that they have schools, stores, and modern farming methods."

"Of course, my lord. I never intended to throw out any of your *improvements*! It's this business of changing jobs all the time, and promotions, and not knowing the grandsons of your grandfather's friends that troubles me. I don't know quite how to put it, but it's as if things have gotten like a river that is running too wide and too shallow! I want to go along in a deep, old channel, where the human things go on as they always have and always will. Glass in the windows and flush toilets and good steel plows are fine things, and a man would be a fool to not use them, but it's the human factors that I worry most about."

One of the failings of the communists was that they had a vision of the future that they thought was good, and they tried to make everybody conform to their ideas of goodness. To my own mind, well, it's a big world and it takes all kinds of people to fill it. If some peasants prefer a lifestyle that I would find oppressive, well, as long as nobody is forcing anyone, I say let them do as they wish. I don't need *everybody* on my bandwagon.

"Then you shall have it as you want it, Baron. Just remember the ancient right of departure. Some of the children of the men who swear to you may not feel the same way as their fathers. But I'm not minded to lose your good services entirely. If you wish to live in a feudal manner, then you must do feudal duty to me. What I want you to do is to command the active reserve forces of our army. You see, this time we had warning about when the enemy would attack, but next time we might not be so lucky! Now, my plan is . . ."

We talked for hours about what the reserves should be, and when we parted, we were in agreement.

At least about the army.

As he left, Vladimir said, "Do you know yet what you are going to do about the captainette?"

"No."

I left word that I must be up before dawn and sent notes to

both Baron Pulaski and Baron Gregor that the execution must not take place without me. God forbid I should cause a woman's death because I overslept.

Then I tried to sort out the problem of Captainette Lubinska. I sent away the servant girl I found in my bed, and I tossed and turned for half the night. On the one hand, Lubinska was legally guilty of abandoning her post during time of war, and that had started a chain of events that had ended in a terrible massacre.

On the other hand, Vladimir was right. She had been put in a situation where she was in way over her head. But then, every person in the army had been thrown into deep water, including Vladimir and myself. A lot of people had died because they were too weak or too stupid to perform the task before them. A lot of people had died because they had a problem that nobody, no matter how strong or brilliant, could possibly have solved. I saw one boatman get squashed flat when a two-ton rock came down on him, and where was justice then? Nowhere, that's where. But had he lived, he wouldn't have had to stand trial for not stopping that rock.

So why do we try anybody?

It has often been argued that a person is the result of his heredity and his environment, that we are what we were made to be and therefore are not responsible for our failings.

Well, if human beings are just things that were made, then it doesn't matter if they are punished or not. It only matters whether they act as desired. If a pot was made badly, throw it out! It's not the pot's fault, but that doesn't matter. The whole idea of guilt doesn't come into it at all. Once you think about it, you have to conclude that *people don't matter at all* unless you grant them a moral sense, unless you grant them a soul. Maybe that was the root cause of many of Stalin's atrocities.

I gave up trying to sleep. I put on some clothes and walked to the church. I sat down in a pew, but soon I was on my knees.

Well, then. You can say that God made people and everything else. It's all His problem! Let Him solve it! Why should we poor fallible mortals ever judge anybody? What right do we have to judge His work?

Except that we all know that if nobody was ever punished for doing anything, crime would soon be so rampant that nobody would be safe. Many people would live by stealing, and people would be murdered every time somebody got angry. Life would hardly be worth living in such an environment. Like it or not, we sad, confused, and fumbling mortals have to do something about criminals. We have to do it for simple, practical reasons. We can't blame it on God, and we can't let Him do the punishing, since He waits until the sinner is dead before doing the job of judging him, and that's a little late by human standards if we want to have a safe society.

Good. This was getting me closer to the mark. Forget about the moral reasons for punishment. They rest on sandy ground. We have to punish wrongdoers in order to (A) stop them from hurting the rest of us again, that is to say, in group self-defense, and (B) as an educational mechanism to convince others that they should not imitate the wrong-doer.

So. Were we going to hang Lubinska because she was likely to abandon her post again and get another 21,000 women and children killed? Of course not! Well, obviously, she should never be trusted with an important post again, but we wouldn't have to kill her to accomplish that. Discharging her or busting her down to the lowest rank would be sufficient. Certainly she presented no further danger to society.

So we must be killing her as a teaching aid. Well, would it be an effective teaching aid? By this time everybody knew how and why she had screwed up. Everyone realized now that to abandon a post can cause a great tragedy. Would one more death added to 21,000 make any difference? No. It would be insignificant.

Then what were we gaining by hanging her? Were we providing ourselves with a sacrificial lamb to cleanse the guilt from our hands? A scapegoat? I never could go along with that strange bit of theology.

Actually, you couldn't blame the captainette for the deaths of all those people, not directly. The Mongols had killed them, and we had killed the Mongols. Case closed.

The Mongols had been let in by Count Herman's wife, and they had killed her for it. Again, case closed.

The captainette had believed the wrong person as to who should be in charge at East Gate. She had believed her traditional boss instead of me. She had been given her command by me, and I had done it because Baroness Krystyana had recommended her.

Night was fading into gray dawn when I finally knew what I had to do. Somehow I was immensely comforted by the certainty of it.

There was quite a crowd in front of the outer wall when I got out there. The sun was about to peek over the horizon, a gallows had been built, and a lot of people were standing around it, including all of my barons who were at Three Walls. The Lubinska woman was near the scaffold, attended by a priest and two guards. I went to her and said quietly, "You're not going to die this morning." Stunned and unbelieving, she looked at me and said nothing.

Baron Vladimir led us in our morning services, and a priest, not the one attending the captainette, said a very quick mass without a sermon. The people were expecting Captainette Lubinska to climb the scaffold, but she didn't.

I did.

Chapter Fifteen

FROM THE JOURNAL OF COUNTESS FRANCINE

The job of writing the articles for the magazine was done in but two days, and work had already begun on the casting of the drums of type to print it. But then the time seemed to drag, for there was much work to be done in the casting of type and the printing of the half gross of pages that the magazine would contain, and none of it could be done by me.

It would be a plain magazine, for there was no time to carve the woodcuts that usually adorned its pages, except for a few old commercial messages that were used to fill otherwise blank space. Since there was no time to contact the merchants and obtain payment from them, you may be assured that all the "ads" that we used were from my husband's factories.

Indeed, it seemed for a time that the cover, too, would be blank, until a friar named Roman came down from the cathedral and painted three lithographic blocks for the purpose. He was a merry man, grown pudgy and red-nosed from drinking too much wine, but he was a fine artist for all of that. The cover he made had on the front a fine portrait of Count Conrad in his armor and with our battle flags flying behind him, and on the back a lively scene of our gunners shooting at the Mongol enemies over the heads of our footmen. Further, all this was done in inks of three colors, the first cover that had been done so. I think that some may have purchased the magazine only to have the fine artwork!

I persuaded the abbot to give his men dispensation from the saying of their prayers eight times a day so that they might spend the time in work, and I made arrangements with the inn that they should be fed as they worked at the machines that Conrad had built for them. The monks were at first much taken aback by this, for the waitresses of the inn did their work, as always, nearly naked. Yet there were soon far more smiles on the monks than scowls, and I bade the waitresses to continue as they had. I was something of a heroine to these young ladies, for I had once been of their number and now was of the high nobility. I suppose that my success fed their dreams. Yet when they asked that I dress in their fashion and help serve, I must needs turn them down. My waist had grown too large with pregnancy, and anyway, Conrad would certainly not have approved! Still, I was tempted.

The monks worked from before dawn straight through to the dark of night, but still, the job would be a week in the doing, and always I feared that Duke Henryk would arrive and take the whole thing into hand himself.

I took myself to Wawel Castle and spent the day there talking to any that I could meet about the seym that was soon to be held in Sandomierz. All that I met, the old and the infirm, were enthusiastic for Conrad's enlargement, yet there were very few of the nobility there. All too many were gone or dead.

The city council *came to me* with the plea that Count Conrad should be their duke and protector, and we talked long as to how this could be accomplished. They then sent representatives to every incorporated city in eastern Poland to plead for our cause, and they did this at their own expense, as well! Not that I was in lack of funds, but when those tightfisted burghers had their *own* money involved, you can be sure that they would give it their best effort!

While I was thus employed, Sir Wladyclaw was also busy. The weather was now fair and the radios were at last working properly, so his men were no longer needed as messengers. Keeping only one at his side, he sent the others about the countryside in search for Mongols and, when time permitted, to tell the gentry of the victory won by Count Conrad and of the seym to be held at Sandomierz. They found no large groups of the enemy, and we were growing daily more certain that victory was truly ours, but more than once scouts brought back heads barbered in the strange Mongol fashion as proof of their prowess!

I sent occasional messages to my husband, telling him that I was well and that I was helping to organize a meeting of the seyms of eastern Poland, since because of my association with the old duke, I knew so many of the people in this area. I never exactly told him that the feeling here was that *he* should be duke of all three duchies, for fear that he would decline the offer before it was even made to him. Bishop Ignacy was entirely too accurate in his estimation of my husband! When the time came, I wanted him to think that the nomination was entirely spontaneous and that it was his duty to accept it.

Until the time was right, I wanted him to stay in Three Walls, doing his little engineering things!

He *should* come to Sandomierz, I told him in the messages I sent, for he did have lands that he had purchased along the

Vistula, and thus he was obligated to come, but to be there a little late would cause no harm, I said. My intent was that when he got there, the matter would be already settled. Once he was duke, he would find reasons of his own for remaining duke. I knew it as I knew him.

When the print run was almost done, a scout brought back from the army camp west of Sandomierz a list of the Polish nobility that had survived the battle there. To publish a list of those who had died would have taken a book three times longer than our entire magazine, though we promised that such a magazine would be published in the future. For now, all that we could do was add eight pages with the names of the living. *So few!*

At last the printing was done, and all the monks fell to the task of combining the pages and binding them together. I was able to get many of the town's folk to help with this task, and as soon as a stack of finished magazines was ready, one of Sir Wladyclaw's scouts was there to take them to all the towns and hamlets of eastern Poland. Of course, we were careful that none were sent to the west for fear that Duke Henryk would hear of it.

The riverboats helped distribute the magazines as well, for Baron Tadaos now had three at his command. Two of them had been found up a small creek, intact but devoid of their crews. There was evidence of a fight, but what exactly had happened there was something that we would probably never know. The baron had found men to operate them and ammunition for their guns, but what he was happiest about had nothing to do with men or arms. His many wives and their children had been found, and all were alive! Indeed, they were helping him operate his boat.

Sir Gregor sent me a message that said that our radio operators at the duke's camp at Legnica told of sickness there and that the duke was taken ill with it. He was not likely to die, yet he would not be fit to travel for at least a week. The message ended with a request that we should pray for the duke's recovery, and indeed I did pray for his health, but that it be returned to him later. *Much later!*

Once, in our long fireside conversations at my manor before we were married, Conrad had told me of a land in which once he had lived where all the leaders were chosen every few years by all the people. He talked of candidates for office shamelessly putting up great pictures of themselves and hanging many posters with slogans on them as though they were so many cattle to be sold at auction! At the time I laughed at the thought of the old duke thus pandering himself, but as I later thought on it, I could see the necessity of it all.

It took far less time to print the covers, which were done on a separate machine, than to print all the pages of the magazine. Since the facilities and supplies were available, I persuaded Friar Roman to make some posters as Conrad had once described. Some were just the front cover of the magazine, with my love's portrait. Others boldly said, "I want Conrad for my duke!" Many thousands of these were made, though at a price for the friar's services. I promised that after I had my child, I would pose for him in any manner that he wished while he painted me. Well, perhaps it would be fun.

I wanted to get to Sandomierz well ahead of the crowd, to set the stage, as it were. Soon we were on the road again, my maids crowded out of the carriage by stacks of posters and magazines and riding apillion with two of Sir Wladyclaw's Scouts. None of those involved seemed to mind the arrangement in the least.

The captain felt that an escort of five would be safe enough, but I persuaded him to bring all his men to make a better appearance as we rode into Sandomierz.

The city of Sandomierz had been under siege, but it had not been taken. The city council had long looked to the strength of its walls, which were well built and defended. These people were among the few burghers that had purchased sufficient guns and armor from Conrad's factories. Further, they had heeded his thoughts and the suggestions that he often wrote in the magazine and had been ready when the Mongol hordes had come against them. Thus, while the suburbs had been devastated, all that was within their walls was safe. Also, those who had been on the walls had been treated with a view of the major battle of the war, at least in terms of the number of enemy killed. It was here that the riverboats had made their greatest slaughter, and dead Mongols had been heaped up on the bank opposite until they were twenty bodies deep! Even as we arrived, battalions of my husband's men were still stripping and burying the dead, for Conrad was afraid of the pestilence and disease that follow battle. The heads were all up on pikes, a huge monument to Polish arms. Also, the Mongols had looted widely in the Russias, and he wished to see this wealth back in Christian hands.

On arriving, I went directly to the inn. It had been doing very good business, but for months the innkeeper had not been able to deliver its profits to Conrad. I drew on these funds at need, in part to rent most of the rooms at the inn itself. Thus, when an important person could not find lodging in the town, I could offer it to him as a favor from Conrad. And surely no decent man could speak publicly against his host!

We spent much of the next week talking to all who would listen, which was practically everyone, about the upcoming seym and about Count Conrad. It was easy to persuade the town's people to adorn their storefronts and homes with our posters, for it seemed to them that to do otherwise would be to slur the man who had saved their city! They all knew that had Conrad not killed the Mongols west of the city, they and all they had would be gone. And once a burgher had Conrad's name and face on his home, he could hardly say anything but that he favored him! Thus, as the first notables came to attend the seym, it must have seemed to them that the matter was already settled. Not many men will go against their neighbors once the matter has been decided!

Further, I hired men who could read well in public to stand in the squares and read the magazine to any who would listen. Thus, we told our story to everyone, including the majority, those who could not read at all.

The good Friar Roman had also written some poems in Conrad's honor, and we were able to find minstrels who put those poems to music. Soon they became all the rage, and other minstrels began to write songs of their own in his honor just to compete!

All things were going beautifully, and I was having a wonderful time.

Chapter Sixteen

FROM THE DIARY OF CONRAD STARGARD

"There will be no hanging this morning," I said to the crowd from the vantage point of the scaffold. "The right of high justice is vested in me and me alone. Baron Pulaski, you and your jurors did your jobs properly. By the letter of the law, Captainette Lubinska is guilty of abandoning her post in time of war, and the punishment for that is, and ought to be, death by hanging. But the ultimate responsibility is mine, and I choose not to permit the sentence to be carried out, despite her guilt. Perhaps this guilt is mitigated by the fact that she was lied to by a woman who once was her liege lord's wife. Perhaps it is softened by the way she got her charges safely back here to Three Walls.

"But the real reason why I will not hang her is because her death would accomplish nothing. She is not guilty of causing the death of those twelve thousand, five gross, ten dozen, and five women, children, and old men who were murdered at East Gate. The Mongols killed them, and our army killed the Mongols. All but one, the one in fact who tricked Count Herman's wife into letting the enemy into the fort! That man is now my prisoner, kept alive because we might one day need a messenger who can speak both Polish and the Mongol tongue. He'd probably prefer death to imprisonment, since both of his hands were cut off in the fighting.

"If any of our fellow Poles is guilty of the tragedy at East Gate, it must be Count Herman's wife. She was the one who improperly took charge of the fort and then allowed the Mongols in. Well, the Mongols killed her for the favor, and she's in God's hands now.

"Captainette Lubinska's crime was therefore one of bad judgment, and if her judgment was bad, she never should have been given such an important post in the first place. I should have relieved her when I saw that she was acting erratically. I gave her the position because she was recommended to me by Baroness Krystyana. So.

"For exercising very poor judgment while in command of a major post, Captainette Lubinska is busted to the lowest grade and is to be given only the most menial of duties for the next five years. After that time she may never again be promoted beyond the third level.

"For recommending a person of poor judgment to an important post, Baroness Krystyana will be demoted to the lowest level for a period of one month during which time she shall be given the most menial of tasks. After that month, she shall be returned to her present position and pay grade.

"For believing Baroness Krystyana and for failing to replace Captainette Lubinska at a later date, Count Conrad Stargard will be demoted to the lowest level for a period of one week, during which time he shall be given the most menial of tasks, and after which he shall be returned to his present position and pay grade.

"I have spoken. It is done."

My proclamation was met with stunned silence. Well, if punishment is supposed to be an educational procedure, I think that these people were being properly educated. At least I was making them think!

For the next week I worked in the kitchen, washing dishes, while designing a dishwashing machine in my head. The job involved using a whole new set of muscles, and I came home every night just a bit stiff. And you know? It felt good!

Krystyana was less gratified working the tub beside me, but then, she always was feisty!

Soon people started coming down to the kitchens so that I could solve their problems. I referred them all to Baron Gregor, since Baron Vladimir had left for the Vistula. I was a lowly worker, and it wasn't fair to expect much from a warrior basic.

Soon I had to post my secretary to fend off these people so that I could attend to my proper duties, the washing of dishes from dawn to dusk, with a timed lunch break.

On my last day of playing bubble dancer, when Krystyana was out feeding the chickens, Natalia let one visitor through to me. It was Warrior Lubinska.

"You shouldn't be doing this, sir. You humiliate yourself."

"There's nothing humiliating about honest work. Actually, I'm rather enjoying it. It's good therapy. Anyway, you shouldn't call me sir. My army rank is now the same as yours. How about 'my lord,' since it would take the duke to change my civil rank."

"You should have hanged me."

"Nonsense! If you had deserved hanging, I would have done it. You got what you had coming, nothing more and nothing less."

"No, that's not true at all."

"Well, what *is* true is that you were ordered to do menial labor, and you're not doing it. Take off your jacket and roll up your sleeves. You can help me with these dishes."

I did my clumsy best at talking her out of her depression, but after a few hours of working next to her I could see that I hadn't helped much. I think that much of her problem was what I'd heard called "survivor's guilt," the strange, irrational guilt that a survivor feels after almost everyone has died but her. Lubinska wasn't the only one feeling it. There were reports from the field hospital we'd set up near the battlefield west of Sandomierz that a number of the surviving knights had committed suicide. But what could I do? I just didn't know.

When our work shift was over, I told her to buck up, that things would get better. The words were phony, but what else could I say?

The next morning I was told that during the night Lubinska had tied one end of a rope around one of the merlons on the outer wall. She'd tied the other end around her neck and jumped.

Since she was a suicide, there was no mass said for Warrior Lubinska, and she didn't receive extreme unction. They couldn't bury her in hallowed ground, so they buried her alone, a bit away from the Mongols.

It was bad being a battle commander, but being judge was far worse! I was never trained for this kind of thing. I had no aptitude for it. I just couldn't take it! I had no business being a count.

As soon as Duke Henryk was well, I intended to ask him to make me a baron again and take back the right of high justice. That is, if he'd still talk to me. He hadn't answered my last dozen letters and radio messages, but I guess he was still pretty sick.

The next day I was informed by Francine that it was time for me to show up at the seym in Sandomierz. It seemed like a tedious thing to do, but good citizenship requires that you vote whenever you have the chance, and I supposed that I should set a good example. Anyway, it would do me good. I needed to get away from things for a while.

When I asked her, Cilicia wasn't interested in going. She had always been a quiet and stay-at-home type when she was pregnant. I was getting ready to set out alone at dawn when Captain Wladyclaw showed up with a dozen of his men to give me an escort, an honor guard, he called it. I thought it a silly waste of manpower and told him so. But they were already at Three Walls, and their proper post was in the east, looking for Mongol stragglers, so they might as well go back east in my company. The captain also said that my wife had insisted that I wear my fancy gold-plated parade armor, which my smiths had once made for me as a Christmas present. I'd worn it at my wedding, but I hadn't touched it since. The captain was fairly adamant about it until I relented and changed out of my practical combat armor. But if I hadn't, Francine would have acted hurt, and that can get hard to take.

"Your wolfskin cloak sets well against that gold armor, my lord," the captain said.

"More importantly, it's warm. We've wasted enough time already. Let's ride," I said.

Big People can run as fast as a modern thoroughbred racehorse, the difference being that they can do it with big armored men on their backs instead of little jockeys, and they can keep it up all day long instead of for a single mile.

We went nonstop until we got to East Gate. Baron Yashoo had

the new Riverboat Assembly Building more than half up. In the past seven years we'd cleared more land than we'd used lumber, and what with the new sawmills, it had made sense to saw and stack the wood for proper seasoning. Baron Yashoo was drawing on our lumberyards. I complimented him on his progress, and we were on our way again in minutes.

I wanted to make a stop at Cracow to see Bishop Ignacy and go to confession, but Captain Wladyclaw said that he thought that the bishop was at Sandomierz attending the seym, and anyway, Lady Francine was waiting for us. I saw no point in arguing with him, and we rode on.

Running along the side of the railroad track, or on it sometimes, we made good time, arriving just after noon. Our railroad tracks were far straighter than the twisting trails that passed for the roads that covered most of Poland. The girls could really stretch out and move! After a few weeks of being in a city, it felt good to have a fine mount like Silver between my legs. I was smiling as we went through the city gates, and the crowd there was lively.

I supposed that it was natural for people to cheer for a visiting general, a patriotic sort of thing for them to do. It was a few moments before I realized that they were shouting "Duke Conrad!" at me, and a few more before I saw my name and pictures of my face plastered over everything in sight.

All I could think of was that as duke I'd have a hundred times as many court cases to worry about. I'd have to go through the agony of the Captainette Lubinska affair six times every week from now until forever! No way did I like or want that sort of life-and-death responsibility.

No!! Not me! No way, gang!

The crowd was soon so packed that we couldn't move except in the direction in which we were heading, and instead of going to the inn, as I had expected, we were forced toward the main square of the city.

"Captain Wladyclaw, just what the hell is going on here?" I shouted at him.

"They seem to be taking us to church, sir," he said, pointing to the great Church of St. James across the square.

"That's not what I mean, and you know it! What's with all these posters and pictures and people calling me duke?"

"Well, they need a new duke, and there's nobody else left! I'm afraid that you're stuck with the job, sir."

"No! No, I won't do it!" We were being slowly moved toward the church, the crowd acting like some fantastic undertow pulling me to my doom.

"Sir, I believe you've already been elected."

"The hell I am! They can't elect me without my permission."

"I'm not sure of all the legalities, sir, but by tradition, the seym doesn't need anybody's permission to meet and hold an election. Certainly not yours."

"That's not what I mean, and you know it! They can't make me! They'll have to find someone else!" I swear that everybody was smiling and cheering except me. Dammit! Wasn't it enough that I had helped wipe out the Mongol invasion? Did they have to saddle me with a job I didn't want just because I'd helped them?

"Who, sir? I tell you that all of the normal candidates were killed by the Mongols!"

"Duke Henryk! He'd be great for the job." Not only did everybody want to cheer for me, they insisted on touching me, patting my mount, and pawing the legs of my armor. I was getting a sort of claustrophobic feeling.

"They'd never have him, sir. Don't forget that he abandoned eastern Poland to the Mongols and hasn't gotten off his rump in Legnica since."

"He's been sick! Anyway, his conventional knights couldn't have accomplished anything important except getting themselves killed. Legnica is a good place for him. And them!"

"He *says* he's been sick, sir, but none of these people have seen it. He's a villain in their eyes, whereas you have saved all of their lives. If your forces are far superior to his, all the more reason to want you!"

"Nonetheless—"

"Nonetheless, we're at the church, sir. You'd best dismount and greet your wife."

"I'm not through with you, Captain, but this mess is more her fault than yours!" I swung out of the saddle into the crowd and pushed my way up the church steps.

The captain came up behind me and removed my helmet. I turned and stared at him, wondering why he had done this strange thing.

"But sir! You can't wear a hat in church!" he said.

I just shook my head and went on.

Francine was standing in front of the Romanesque portal.

"Welcome, my hero, my love!" she said.

"Like hell it's a welcome! It's an abomination! I know that this is all your fault, and I won't do it! Get somebody else to be the damn duke. Not me!"

She turned me toward the altar and began walking slowly toward it. "But you must, Conrad, if only for a little while." She spoke in a low voice, and I had to bend my head to hear her.

"What do you mean for a little while? Being a duke is a lifetime job with no retirement benefits!" I followed after her. It was that or lose her in the crowd.

"It is until you abdicate, my only love," she said softly.

"Abdicate? Then why do it in the first place?"

"Because Poland needs to be united, that's why. For the last hundred years, Poland has not had a king. It has been nothing but a collection of independent duchies where the people happen to speak the same language. Right now, for the first time in a century, the people of Mazovia, Sandomierz, and Little Poland are willing to unite under one man. Only one man. You! They would never do that under Duke Henryk, even though the western half of Poland swears fealty to him, for they think that he has betrayed them. They would never pick some distant relative of one of the dead dukes, since that would give a huge political advantage to the new duke's home duchy, and the other two duchies would lose out. It has to be you! But only for a little while, my love. Then, when things settle down, you can work out an arrangement with Duke Henryk, and Poland can be united under a single man. The land will again have a king!"

"Yes, but surely, if I talk to the seym, I can sell them on some other guy—"

"But nothing! Do you know anyone else who could be trusted with such a temptation? Is there anyone else but you who would willingly give up power when the time comes? Go ahead! Name me one man!"

I pondered for a minute, and the slow procession to the altar stopped. "Bishop Ignacy! He could be trusted."

Francine tugged me by the sleeve and got me moving again. "Nonsense! The bishop is a good man, but if he held the eastern duchies, he would put them under the control of the Church. Admit it! The eastern duchies are still exposed to the Mongols. Consider that you have defeated an enemy army, but you have not yet defeated their nation! Poland needs a war leader, not a churchman, in power."

"Yeah, I suppose so. What about Baron Vladimir?"

"I tell you that no man but you could be trusted. This much power would tempt any other man."

"Then why trust me?"

"Because you don't want to be duke in the first place! Your very arguments defeat themselves. Darling, this is your duty to your country. You must not fail Poland!"

I'm a ponderer by nature. I can usually come up with the right answer, but it takes me a while. I never was one of those glib, fast-talking sorts who can sell farm machinery to Mongols. I'm not really quick thinking on my feet in a confusing situation. As I was trying to sort this one out, Francine knelt down at the communion rail, and so I just naturally knelt down beside her, out of habit, I suppose. As I did so, the Bishop of Plock put the ducal crown of Mazovia on my head! The crown of Sandomierz was quickly put right on top of that, and the crown of Little Poland was promptly placed on top. I was stood up, wondering how the Church that I had trusted could do this thing to me. I was turned around, and everyone in the big, crowded church started cheering. I tell you, it was annoying!

Chapter Seventeen

I stared at the shouting crowd, and it was all that I could do to not scream right back at them. I took the crowns from my head and looked at them. Someone had modified them so that they all interlocked into the silliest-looking thing imaginable. I handed the contraption to Francine.

"Here! You wanted it! You take it!" I said. She was so shocked that for once she didn't have anything to say.

"But you *must* keep it!" the bishop said, horrified.

"The only thing I *must* do is die, and I have *some* say-so as to when that's going to happen! And as for you, your *excellency*, there are fourteen tons of gold and jewels that I was going to donate to the Church. You're not going to get them now! I trusted the Church, and you went and pulled this shit on me!" I turned from him and looked to the back of the church. "*Silver! Come here to me!*" I called out in English.

Somehow she heard me above the crowd and came straight in. Silver didn't have Anna's religious side, and the church was just one more building to her. The people had been taken aback by my taking off the crowns, and even more so by my speaking in a strange, harsh foreign language, but they got out of her way as Silver came straight up the church aisle.

I mounted up and rode out.

At the church door Captain Wladyclaw was still standing there, dumbfounded. I took back my helmet from him and said, "As for you, Wladyclaw, you have been telling me lies all day long. If your father wasn't one of my oldest friends, I'd have you court-martialed! As it is, well, you'd better stay far out of my way."

The inn was almost empty when we got there. Everybody except the innkeeper seemed to be out in the streets, cheering. The door of the place was big enough to ride through, and that's just what we did.

"My lord!" The innkeeper looked up at me, shocked and afraid.

"Right! I want your best room. Send up a meal for me and my mount. And bring up a pitcher of beer, a pitcher of wine, and pitchers of anything else you have around!"

He knew better than to argue and led the way to a room marked DUCAL SUITE. I ripped down the sign, dismounted, and told Silver that no one but the innkeeper was allowed in.

She nodded YES.

Someone else's things were in the room, but the innkeeper just picked them up and went out with them. To hell with him, whoever the last tenant was!

The innkeeper returned quickly with four nearly naked waitresses carrying food, six pitchers of potables, and fresh sheets. I had to tell Silver that the waitresses were okay before she'd let them in.

"What's this stuff?" I asked, pointing at one of the pitchers.

"You said to bring some of everything that I had, my lord. That is from a barrel that was sent to me years ago from your inn at Cieszyn. It's called 'white lightning,' but no one liked it. Still, you said . . ."

I poured some into a glass. It had been clear white when I'd made it nine years ago, but it was a golden amber now. I tasted it and smiled for the first time in a while. Nine years of storage in an oak barrel had done amazingly good things to it.

"Good. Now go out and find me a block of ice! This stuff is just what I need!"

The innkeeper made the sign of the cross and left. The waitresses scurried about, changing sheets and towels. This suite had its own bathroom, a rarity. Finished, they hurried off after their boss, frightened.

I started in on a monumental drunk.

I was too upset to sit down, and so I paced the room with a

glass in my hand. A waitress came in with some ice, cut from the river during the winter and stored in one of my icehouses. I put some in my drink and told the girl to sit in the corner and be quiet, since I might want something else later.

After a while I was over being absolutely angry and could think again.

Now, what was I going to do about *this* mess? Unifying the country was certainly important, but dammit, I'm an engineer, not a politician, and certainly not a hanging judge! All I wanted was to be left alone to do my job, the truly important job of getting this country and this century industrialized. I had neither the talent nor the ability nor the inclination to wander about the countryside playing God in a gold hat!

There was some commotion out in the hall, but I ignored it. Everybody I knew was smart enough not to argue with a Big Person who had her orders, especially one who didn't understand Polish!

I'd played at being a battle commander, but only because it was absolutely necessary. Without my army, my training, and my weapons, we'd all have been killed! But I hadn't been very good at it. In fact, I'd screwed up a lot of times and had come through on sheer luck. Well, that and the fact that the enemy was even dumber than I was. Some recommendation!

What to do about the election? Well, I could take the job of duke and then delegate away all the power. Set up men in each duchy as my deputies and let them do things their way.

Right. And in ten years' time the men I had delegated would effectively be dukes, and all their cronies would be counts and barons. Eastern Poland would stay feudal and backward. Peasants would stay peasants, and the infant mortality rate would stay such that half the kids born wouldn't make it to their fifth birthday, and it would be all my fault.

It got louder outside the door. I sent the waitress out with the message that if they didn't quiet down, I'd have the entire inn cleared. It quieted down.

Damn them all! Or I could take the job and do to these duchies what I'd done to Baron Stefan's barony: put in schools where there weren't any, subsidize the new farming methods, and bring the people into the industrial sector as fast as possible.

Except that eastern Poland doesn't have the natural resources that Upper Silesia has. This area never would be heavily industrialized. Damn.

Since most of the nobility was dead, probably most of the land would escheat back to me if I were duke. I could just parcel the land out to anyone who wanted to farm it and make the area a land of yeoman farmers. That might be the best bet. But to do it, I would be involved with lawsuits with every fifth cousin of the previous owners. Thousands of lawsuits! It would be a full-time job for the next twenty years, and I'd never get the chance to work on electric lights.

Well, if I did take the job, the first thing I'd have to do was to take a survey of just what lands and properties were mine. Probably a good job for Baron Piotr, with Sir Miesko's help. The school system under Father Thomas Aquinas probably had information as to which major family had what. We'd pulled all the schoolteachers west in February, so they were all still alive.

No, that would have to be the second thing I'd have to do. Everything east of the Vistula was probably destroyed, and there was a lot of work in disaster relief to be done. At least there was plenty of money to work with, but that was yet another problem to solve. How to divide up the booty we'd taken without inflating the economy to destruction?

There was a writing desk in the suite, with paper, ink, and some of our new steel pens. I started taking notes but was hampered by my armor, which I was still wearing. Army-issue combat armor can be gotten into or out of in a hurry, but this gold stuff I was wearing had dozens of straps and buckles. I had the waitress help me out of it, and the gambeson as well, since I was hot. The inns were always overheated because of the waitresses' costumes, or rather, their near lack of them. Taking off the gambeson had me down to my long johns, but what the heck. I was still wearing a lot more than the girl was.

Actually, she was a pretty little thing, if still a bit frightened. She was about fourteen, fair and bare, with long, straight blond hair, a nice body, and nipples so small and pink that you could barely see them. And she was a virgin, the inn's rules being what they were. I told her to relax and have some wine. I wasn't going to hurt her.

I went back to my notes, and started making up a PERT diagram of all the things that had to be done assuming that I actually accepted the job of duke. After a while I noticed that the whiskey pitcher was empty and sent the girl out for some more. She took an empty mead pitcher with her as well.

Eventually the job started to look possible. I'd have to swear fealty to Duke Henryk as soon as possible, with the price tag of a nationwide system of courts in the modern fashion. He'd be in charge of it, and I would never get involved. Would the military courts be under him? I wasn't sure if that would be good, since I'd be keeping command of the army, of course. I put a star next to it, as I had on all the other problems I didn't know how to answer.

The three Banki brothers would each be put in temporary charge of a duchy, say, for two years, until things settled down. They'd each have to have a list of instructions limiting their power. We really didn't need any more conventional counts or barons, for example.

Halfway through the second pitcher of whiskey, I started to feel very tired. I went over to the bed, crawled under the covers, and fell asleep.

I awoke to find the waitress in bed with me, and, yes, she had taken off the shoes, stockings, bunny hat, and loincloth that were her uniform. At least I think she had done it. I didn't remember being responsible. She was snuggled up under my arm and seemed contented enough.

I had only a slight headache, and heavy drinking always makes me horny. I woke the girl up, and she smiled.

Somehow, during the night I had decided that I had to become a duke, and as such I could do anything I wanted, at least until I swore fealty to Henryk. I didn't know if I had taken the girl the night before, but I rolled over onto her and did so now. She seemed to be waiting for me to do it, and eager.

As it turned out, she'd been a virgin when I'd started, but not for long thereafter. Good, though. Some fine natural talent there.

"Thank you, your grace," she said when we were done. "I always hoped my first one would be a hero."

"Well. You're welcome, uh, what was your name?"

It was Sonya, and after a bit of talking I gave her a job in my household as a maid, since I'd just deprived her of her job as a waitress. She no longer qualified.

I got up and stretched. I would have to tell the world that I'd take them up on their job offer, but I was in no great hurry to do so. First a bath and breakfast. I sent Sonya down to get some food and checked on Silver. She was still doing guard duty, and the innkeeper had seen to it that she had been unsaddled, fed, and rubbed down. Her saddle and bags were there beside her in the hallway. I took my saddlebags into the room and drew an oversized tub of hot water.

Sonya came back and joined me in the tub without asking. Soon she was scrubbing me down, and I found myself enjoying the pampering. She washed my hair, cleaned my fingernails and toenails, and even shaved me, saying that she had always shaved her father. A very well-trained young lady! Up until now I'd always resisted the notion, but maybe having a personal servant wasn't such a bad idea, after all. Efficiency isn't everything!

After being toweled off, I was sitting nude and letting myself get completely dry when two other waitresses came in with our breakfast. The food and service were good, and I found myself wondering if I didn't want three or four servants instead of only one. Later, perhaps.

The sun was coming through a window, and I said my Warrior's Oath, which impressed the girls no end. Then they helped me into one of my best embroidered outfits, buckled on my sword, and kissed me good-bye. All three of them. I went out feeling fit to face demons, dragons, and even a politician or two. Someone had saddled Silver, but I didn't ride out as I had ridden in. I was no longer mad at the world.

Chapter Eighteen

My wife and a few dozen dignitaries were waiting for me in the common room of the inn. They all looked at me apprehensively, more than a little frightened.

I turned to Francine. "I take it that these gentlemen are what is left of the authorities of the eastern duchies?"

"There are many others, my love, but these men are the most powerful."

"Well, then," I said, "if you still want me to be your duke, I'm minded to take the job."

That got them all cheering. I really must have had them worried.

"I hadn't planned to be your leader, and you really should have asked me about it first. Be that as it may, I'll do it because the job needs doing. You understand that if I'm going to do this, I'm going to do it in my own way. I am not going to maintain three courts full of unproductive people as my predecessors did. I'm not even going to have one of the silly things. The proper function of government is to provide law, order, and security. It is not constituted to provide amusements for idle people. Agreed?"

The bishop who had crowned me stood up and looked about to see if anyone objected to his speaking first. No one did. "Your grace, we shall be content to follow you in whatever manner you choose to lead. We all know by your past actions that what you will do will be good."

"Where I come from, they call that a blank check. Thank you." I got out the notes I'd made the previous night and found that I could read most of them, except for the last page or so, where the scrawl became drunkenly illegible. I read them to the group to let them know what I had in mind, leaving out the part about my swearing to Duke Henryk.

"There are still a lot of points that have to be worked out, but in general, that's the program I have in mind. Do I hear any objections? No? Then I'd best get on with it."

Francine stood. "Then if you are to be my duke as well as my love, would you please take these back?" She handed me the three crowns, and I took them. That got another round of applause.

All my inns had a radio transceiver and a post office, although the posts had been shut down during the war and were not yet working again. I sent messages to many of my key people, asking them to come to Sandomierz. Then I sent to the granary in the Bledowska desert, ordering all carts available to be filled with the new grains and shipped north and east. Spring planting was almost upon us, and I doubted if there was any seed to be found east of the Vistula. The millions of Mongols who had been through surely would have eaten everything they could find.

Next I rode to the ducal palace to take possession of the place. I could have done everything from the inn, but that would have lacked class. Also, it would have cost me money in lost revenues, since while the rooms of the inn could be rented out, those of the palace couldn't. At least not now. In the future, once some more efficient government buildings were up, all the old palaces and castles around might make very charming hotels. An interesting thought, anyway.

The palatine of the ducal palace was a venerable gentleman who had been working there all his life. He showed me around, and it wasn't bad at all. I'd visited the place a few years before, but as a mere baron from a distant duchy, I hadn't gotten the grand tour. It was a smaller version of the castle on Wawel Hill, which I also owned now, thinking about it. It was built of red glazed brick, and a fine collection of old weapons, furs, and tapestries gave it a certain barbaric splendor. There was indoor plumbing, though, and glass in the windows. Except for adding some radios, there wouldn't have to be much in the way of needed changes.

I made some, anyway. I had lunch and fired the cook. I think that if the last duke could stand the cooking at his palace, he must have gotten his taste buds chopped out in a tournament. I figured that anybody who could ruin roast mutton couldn't possibly be retrainable. He was replaced by the cook at the inn. In the same message to the innkeeper, I explained about Sonya and had her sent over along with my clothes and armor, and the barrel of nine-years-in-wood whiskey, which was declared to be my own private stock. All other innkeepers were to inventory their supply of the stuff and reserve it for my own exclusive use. RHIP. While I was thinking about it, I sent a message to Cieszyn, ordering the cook who had helped me make that first batch to run off another six thousand gallons of it and store it in oak casks. I promised to call for it in nine years.

Baron Wojciech was the first of the Banki brothers to arrive, since he had been in charge of the cleanup on the battlefield directly across the Vistula from Sandomierz.

He came into my chambers at the palace with a cloth-wrapped package under his arm and looked admiringly at the tapestries, the furs, and the brightly painted wood carvings.

"You know," he said, "saving the country must pay pretty good. Someday I'm going to have to try that myself, sir! Or I guess I should call you your grace now."

"Sit down and have some mead," I said, pouring. "Wojciech, you can call me anything but an atheist, and you did your share in saving the country!"

"Thank you, your grace. I have a present for you, or at least a present I can give back to you." He unwrapped the package to display my pistol, the one I had lost during my fight at a pontoon bridge on the other side of the Vistula. It had been polished and cleaned and was only slightly rust-pitted. It had my name engraved on it, since the smiths always seemed to do that sort of thing whenever they made anything for me, along with a note as to who had made it. Advertising, I suppose.

"Thank you. I see that you provided a new belt and holster."

"I didn't know if you'd thrown the old ones away, your grace."

"Just as well. I left them on the *Muddling Through*, so I suppose they were burned when she was. I take it that you like this palace?"

"Of course! It's beautiful, your grace!"

"Good, because you have a present coming, too. This palace is going to be yours for the next two years. I want you to run the Sandomierz duchy for me as my deputy."

"Thank you, your grace! I'm honored. Yawalda is going to be thrilled! I know she will fall in love with this place."

"Well, don't get too attached to it. Remember, it's only temporary."

"Yes, your grace. I'll be able to choose my own subordinates?"

"Within reason, yes. You'll have a battalion of regular army troops under you, but it's going to take some sorting out, since most of the warriors have farms or businesses to get back to. I want to keep three battalions of full-time fighting men together, though, in case we're attacked again. That's one here, one at Cracow, and one at Plock. Your brothers will have the other two. Baron Vladimir will command in time of war, and he'll have about a dozen battalions of part-time active reserve forces to back you up.

"Still, I don't think we'll be bothered for a while, and your main job will be to get every farmer who wants it seed, tools, and all the land he can farm. We can give them credit on supplies, and there should be more than enough land, what with all our losses to the Mongols."

"There were more losses than you know about, your grace. The Mongols took the city of Sieciechow, on the east bank of the Vistula, and I don't think that they left a single man, woman, child, or domestic animal alive. They just murdered everybody, even the cripples and the priests. We even found somebody's pet dog nailed to a church door. And the young women . . . You don't want to hear about what they did to the young women! And there were worse things. You know those big Mongol catapults? Well, it looks like all the people that were pulling the ropes on them were Polish peasants! Many thousands of them were killed by our own guns, it looks like."

I put my face in my hands. "Oh, my God! I was there! We killed them ourselves! We thought that they were Mongols. Those catapults were destroying our riverboats! What else could we do?" I was crying. At the time, we'd been laughing at the way they died so easily, the way single bullets would take out whole rows of them. Would there be no end to my sins?

"You didn't know, your grace. You couldn't know. And even if you did, like you said, what else could you do?"

"Nothing, Wojciech! There wasn't a damn thing we could do. But I'll tell you this! Once we get things squared away around here, in a few years, we are going to go out east and get those filthy bastards. We are going to hunt them down and kill every Mongol in the world!"

"Good, your grace! I'll help you do it! I've seen the figures on the number of Big People that will be available in ten years, and with them we can chase the Mongols right off the edge of the world."

"That we will! Or right into the sea of Japan, anyway!"

"Just don't forget me when the time comes. Don't forget that I was the one who had to bury those poor peasants."

"I won't. Tell me, what are things like in the east?"

"Empty, your grace. I think that there were three million Mongols who invaded us, and what they didn't eat, they fed to their horses, and what their horses didn't eat, they burned. You know, I think that's why they had to cross the Vistula so badly during the war. They had eaten everything on the east bank, and it was either cross over or starve! There are a few of the scouts who claim to have even found the remains of half-eaten humans, but you couldn't prove that by me. Just the same, folks are scarce over there. In the weeks that I've been on the east bank, I don't think I've seen over a thousand of our own people, except for the army. We put them all to work, you know, digging graves, mostly. We pay them, of course, and feed them, which is more important. But there are so few of them left!"

"A lot of people believed us when we told them to run to the west. Most of them will be returning. It's important that we repopulate that area. If we leave it empty, somebody else will move in. Maybe some of the warriors we'll be discharging will want land there. Write up an order for me to all commands, telling them that there is land east of the Vistula free for the farming. We can give them credit on tools, seed, and so on."

"Yes, your grace, but our people won't need credit. The booty hasn't been counted yet, but I can tell you we're all rich! I think there was more gold left on the banks of the Vistula than ever crossed it."

"Indeed? I would have thought that the Mongols would have looted their own dead."

"They did, your grace, but I think only on the sly, you know? I mean, there wasn't much to be found on the bodies on the tops of those piles, but there were dead men two dozen deep in some places! They never got to the ones at the bottom."

"Wow. It looked like they were piled that deep when we were shooting them, but I'd convinced myself since then that it couldn't possibly be true. Well, get yourself settled in and send for your wife and family. I'll be leaving here in perhaps a week, and you can take this chamber for your own then."

The next few days were spent getting organized. Word came that two Big People had been killed in the war, both while carrying couriers from the battlefield near Sandomierz. Judging from the mess we found around their bodies, they and their riders had spent their lives very dearly, but they had spent them nonetheless. Jenny and Lucy were gone, and they would be missed.

Of their remaining sisters, ten Big People were assigned to the postal service, and the mails started to move again. Six other Big People were assigned to the Detective Corps, since crime was on the rise in the wake of the social disruption of the war. The rest of them were assigned to the scouts, since I was still worried about our borders, and the few planes we had up couldn't be everywhere.

Captain Wladyclaw was sent to patrol the eastern marches, a good place for him. I got the feeling that he was more attached to my wife than to the army, and nonsense like that belongs in *The Three Musketeers*, not in Poland. He was promised the twenty Big People that would be coming of age in the fall, but for now he was just going to have to make do with what he had. I kept Silver, of course, and Anna seemed to have attached herself to Francine, so I let them stay together. And there were still four Big People with Duke Henryk.

I'd never thought to stockpile farm machinery, war production being what it was, and major orders for plows, cultivators, and harvesters were placed with the factories.

The last of the booty was finally sent to Three Walls, and Baron Piotr was put in charge of counting it. Working with the Moslem jeweler we'd picked up years ago, he simply had it all melted down, refined it into bricks of pure gold and silver, and then weighed it, except for some pieces that were judged to have sufficient artistic merit to be worth saving. Silver City, the zinc smelting and casting works in the Malapolska Hills, was put into full production making coins. We'd decided that the men should be paid in standard army currency rather than in actual silver and gold. One currency around was enough.

Jewels were sorted as to size and type, and some wooden warehouses were thrown up to store the war trophies. Just how those fancy swords and armor were to be divided was still unclear. Was it worth sending the entire army back to Three Walls just so each man could take his pick?

After much discussion, we decided that each warrior should be paid his back pay and one thousand pence as an advance on his share of the booty. Knights would be paid two thousand, and so on up the line. Not that they *had* to draw that much immediately, but they could.

A major headache was determining which men wished to stay with the army and which wanted to return to the semi-civilian life of the reserves. And after that there was a major reshuffling of personnel to make up the three battalions of troops that we were keeping on a full-time basis.

None of this concerned the people who worked at my factories, of course. They were aboard forever!

There were crowds of refugees that needed to be fed on their way home and thousands of lost or orphaned children that needed taking care of.

The details kept us up night after night.

Francine was being very quiet and subdued, realizing that she had overstepped her bounds by far in conning me into taking the dukedoms. I finally got it through to her that had she let me in on the plan from the beginning, there wouldn't have been any problem. But you shouldn't surprise a guy that way!

Anyway, she didn't say a word about Sonya. Whether this was because she thought it normal for a nobleman to have a servant or because she was just afraid of another row, I don't know.

Sonya had shown up at the palace in a waitress outfit, and my only comment was to tell her to get rid of the rabbit ears. She worked that day topless, not having her other clothes with her, and the next day all the rest of the women working at the palace were doing the same, even Francine's maids. Old Duke Henryk, the father of the current duke of that name, had in his last years ordered that all of his palace serving wenches should bounce around bare-breasted, and I guess the local girls figured that old Duke Henryk's styles were back. While I never told anyone that she should work with her top off, I knew better than try and stop women when they pick up on a new fad. I just passed the word that the style should be restricted to unmarried girls over twelve or so, and then only in warm weather, saying that there was nothing pretty about a girl who was freezing to death. A bit of sanity returned.

In a week the worst of the trivia seemed to be beaten down, and it was time to go to Plock. I invited Francine along, since I knew that some politicking might be needed there. Plock hadn't been hit by the Mongols, and the German Crossmen had their main base of Turon not far away. If I was going to have any resistance, I'd be getting it there. Then I changed my mind. Plock might be the most politic place to go, but I was way overdue for confession. We went instead to Cracow and Bishop Ignacy.

Chapter Nineteen

FROM THE JOURNAL OF DUCHESS FRANCINE

In the early morning we were set to visit Plock, the capitol of Mazovia, when Conrad abruptly changed our destination. Baron Gregor was removed from my carriage to take the horse ridden by his brother, Baron Wiktor Banki. This worthy knight was put into my carriage to join me, my maids, and that annoying little trollop Conrad had picked up for a servant. The others were told to follow us along the track, but Conrad insisted that we should run to Cracow immediately. The other four carts of our party, being pulled by ordinary horses, might be able to get there by sundown if they could find a change of horses, but the Big People could run us up to Wawel Castle an hour before dinner. Conrad laughed off the idea that we wouldn't be safe without a bigger escort, saying that his sword was better than most, and anyway, the Mongols were all dead or gone. Of course, he was wrong.

Conrad had made such a horrible scene at his coronation that I refuse to write about it! It was all I could do to convince the leaders of the three duchies that he was still suffering from the war and get them to wait on him the next morning. Fortunately, by then Conrad had gotten his wits about him and had done the sensible thing. After accepting the crowns, he went about taking control of Sandomierz with a wise program of ignoring the existing power brokers who had elected him, since he no longer needed them, and putting the whole place under the control of his own trusted men, his army. Those men would follow him into hell—or go there alone if he commanded it! I was so proud of him that I didn't complain about his new blond-haired chippy.

Sometimes he is absolutely brilliant, and at other times such a total fool! Or could it be that the whole scene in the Church of St. James was just an act to get them to accept his new program absolutely and without question? Could he actually be that astute? So many times he has done such seemingly dumb things, yet always he ends up on top. No! It was impossible! He was just lucky! I think.

He wasn't so lucky when we were attacked on the road. Conrad was a few gross yards ahead of us when two Mongol warriors rode out of the bushes a gross yards from the road and attacked him in the early morning. Baron Wiktor had his sword out as soon as he saw them, and vaulted to the top of our carriage to defend it. But from there he could accomplish nothing, for Anna had already gone alone to Conrad's aid, and the Mongols were putting all their efforts to the killing of my beloved husband!

Anna screamed a warning, but Conrad was far ahead of us when the fight started. She raced to his aid, but before she got there, it was all over. The first Mongol threw one of those deadly spears at Conrad, the sort that all the warriors I had met complained of. At close range, those spears could puncture even our best armor.

Conrad turned in the saddle and slashed the spear in half as it flew at him! His second blow came downward at the spearman's neck, and head and arm came off the rest of the body in a single piece. He then wheeled his mount and charged at the second Mongol, who was shooting arrows at him. Two of the missiles struck my love in the chest and stuck there, but he paid them no attention. He simply charged straight in and knocked them over, man and horse! As the enemy started to get up, dazed, a last blow of that amazing sword chopped through both helmet and skull, and suddenly all was quiet.

"Well done, your grace!" Sir Wiktor shouted as our carriage coasted to a stop. "I have heard of your prowess often enough, but that's the first time I've ever had the chance to see it."

It was the second time I'd seen my love in battle, and it affected me this time just as it had before. I wanted nothing more than to take him into the bushes and love him on the spot, the child in my womb notwithstanding! A glance at the maids told me that the effect was universal, and the new blonde was chanting, "Yes. Yes. Yes," with a silly grin on her face.

Duke Conrad dismounted and called to Baron Wiktor, "Come help me round up their horses! The people behind us were worried about spare mounts. Now we can leave them some. Francine, get out your writing kit and write them a note that we can leave behind."

There wasn't much time lost in getting the enemy horses, since Anna and Silver cooperated nicely in rounding them up. Soon Conrad came to the carriage with two large purses filled mainly with gold. He looked at the arrows stuck in his golden breastplate as if he had noticed them for the first time, and pulled them out.

"Well, there's a mess for the jeweler to worry about. And here's some booty that we won't have to share with the whole army! What do you say to an eight-way split, for Anna and Silver deserve a share as well."

And that's just what he did. The maids were ecstatic! They each got four years' pay.

The horses were tied to the track along with my letter to Baron Gregor, the dead Mongols were left for the others to dispose of, and we were back on our way to Cracow in minutes. And still I wasn't sure. Was he that lucky or simply that good?

Finally I asked him about it as he rode along by my side. He said with an almost perfectly straight face, "My strength is as the strength of ten, for my heart is pure."

So I still didn't know! He wouldn't tell me pure *what*!

At Cracow the carriage was taken from the track at the station, and Anna pushed it slowly through the burned-out cottages of the suburbs. It was a sorry sight, yet the first greenery of spring was on the land, promising the healing of old wounds. At the city gate, Conrad left us to go to the bishop's palace on Wawel Hill, and we followed slowly afterward, for to push the carriage over a plain road without iron rails made Anna's task more difficult.

The guard at the inner gate at Wawel Hill gave us a joyful greeting, saying that Conrad had gone before and that Duke Henryk was here as well. Baron Wiktor and I were more than a little apprehensive as we went to Wawel Castle, for confronting the duke was a thing that neither of us looked forward to. Yet it had to be done, and it was better that we should do it before Conrad was through with Bishop Ignacy. There was no telling what my love would do if the situation was left to him alone.

As we entered the ducal chamber, Duke Henryk was sitting behind the desk that he had used so many times before, that he himself had once ordered made in imitation of the one Conrad had given to the bishop. But it was a chamber that had been promised to Baron Wiktor by my husband, in a castle that no longer belonged to Henryk!

"Welcome to Wawel Castle, your grace," Baron Wiktor said.

"You bid *me* welcome, Wiktor? To my own castle?"

"Yours no longer, your grace. The seyms have elected Conrad duke of Little Poland, and of Sandomierz and Mazovia as well."

"The nobles of Cracow all swore fealty to *me*," Henryk said. I could see that this would go as badly as I had feared.

"True, your grace," Baron Wiktor said, "but since that time, you abandoned the city to the Mongols, and the men who swore to you have been killed almost to a man. The nobles and burghers who are left would never obey one whom they think has betrayed them, and Conrad is now duke."

"So I have been told by the churlish louts, may their souls be damned! I never abandoned Poland!"

"Yet you were not here when the city was attacked, your grace. Duke Conrad was."

"He was here in disobedience of my orders! I told him to come to me in Legnica!"

"He could not obey you, your grace. Your battle plan was foolish, and he had to obey a higher power."

"What higher power? *I* was his liege lord!"

"Your grace, can you possibly have forgotten the night five years ago when you and he and I, along with three dozen others, stood vigil in the mountains? Can you have forgotten that morning when God Himself put a holy halo about each of our heads and blessed the work that we were going to do? Can you have forgotten that you yourself knelt before Conrad and were knighted by him into our Holy Order of the Radiant Warriors?"

Duke Henryk was cringing before the baron's onslaught. I

was surprised to see Baron Wiktor standing up to the duke so forcefully, so masterfully. There was more to the man than I had suspected, and he wasn't through with the duke yet!

"You must have forgotten, for when the time came for us to do the work that God had ordained, you went and came up with a silly battle plan without even consulting with the man who headed your own order. You had a fine time writing and consulting with every king and duke in Christendom, but you had never a word for the man with the finest army in the world! The man whom *God chose* to do the job! So you sat and hid in Legnica while Conrad fought the war without you, and now you have the gall to sit in his castle as if the spoils of that war were yours to take!"

"There was sickness in our camp. The foreign troops were slow in arriving. We could not advance," the duke said weakly.

"The sickness could have been avoided had you heeded Conrad's book on camp sanitation. *We* had no sickness! And to hell with the foreign troops! *We* didn't need them!"

"Well, the foreign knights have now been sent to Hungary to aid our allies in accordance with my agreement with King Bela. More than half of my own men went with them as well."

"Good, your grace. We no longer need them. What remains to be seen is whether or not we need *you* any longer, either!"

"You threaten me, Baron Wiktor?"

"No, your grace. I merely suggest that when you meet with my liege lord, Duke Conrad, you assume a properly grateful attitude. He, not you, saved the country, and he, not you, commands here. Remember that he now controls half of Poland, and he could take the other half by force at any time if he was minded to!"

"I . . . I will bear your words in mind, Baron Wiktor. If you'll excuse me, Duchess." And with that, Duke Henryk left the chamber, his back bent.

"Baron, you were magnificent," I said as soon as the door closed. I couldn't resist throwing my arms around him!

"I merely spoke the truth," Wiktor said as he disengaged himself and sat behind the desk. "Duke Conrad has made me his deputy here, and I would have failed him if I had let someone else usurp that power. Please be seated, my duchess. Our lord can't be too much longer with his confessor."

Chapter Twenty

FROM THE DIARY OF CONRAD STARGARD

My session with Bishop Ignacy was one of the longest that we ever spent together, and the vespers bell rang long before we were done. We had supper sent up to us, and my confession continued well into the night. With most priests, confession is a fairly short, perfunctory affair, but it is never so with Bishop Ignacy. I was deeply troubled, and he took all the time that was necessary to dig into all the bloody, crowded doings of the last month.

In the end he gave me his usual scolding about my sexual affairs, but absolved me completely for all that had happened in the course of fighting the Mongols, and for the Lubinska business as well. I felt clean for the first time since we had headed out for war. Clean, but still I bore scars within that would always be with me.

When we were through, I said, "By the way, what did you think of those inquisitors that I had sent to you, Father?"

"What inquisitors? I have met no one from the Holy Inquisition."

"Well, the day before we marched out to war against the Mongols, two members of the inquisition came to speak to me."

"And what did they have to say?"

"I'm not at all sure, Father. You see, neither of them could speak Polish, and I can speak neither Italian nor Latin. Furthermore, they had apparently been forbidden to speak of the matter with anyone else but me, so they could not explain the thing to our translator. Also, you have forbidden me to talk about my transportation to this century with anyone but you, Father. Therefore, I made sure that they had a good map to Cracow and directions on how to get here and told them that they should talk to you. Now you say that they never got here."

"Well, that's reasonable enough, seeing as how you probably gave them one of your 'army maps' with south at the top and everything else topsy-turvy. No wonder they got lost! Everybody knows that *east* belongs at the top of a map! After all, the Garden of Eden was in the east, and we are all descended from Adam and Eve, who lived there. Since we are descended from the east, it must be above us, and therefore it belongs at the top of the map. It's perfectly logical!"

"Yes, Father. So you haven't seen them?"

"No, and by this time I think it unlikely that they will arrive. They have either been killed by the Tartars or they are going back to Rome in disgust! Now I will have to write a formal letter of inquiry, explaining what little I know of this matter and asking what happened to the inquisitors."

"Yes, Father. Could you please ask them to send someone who speaks the language next time?"

"Good night, Conrad."

A sleepy castle page showed me the way up to the suite that had been reserved for me, the duke's apartment. I found that Francine was already asleep, but Sonya was waiting up for me, good little servant that she was.

In the morning, bathed and shaved, I was having breakfast, when Francine joined me.

"Good morning, Francine. You slept well?"

"Yes, my love, though perforce alone." Sonya brought us some more sausages and hotcakes, and I could tell that Francine was trying to ignore her. She had accepted Cilicia and had offered me her own maids on occasion, yet she didn't seem to like me having one of my own, somehow. Oh, well. Women are strange. It was best to ignore the situation and wait for the horse to sing.

"Well, you were sleeping when I got back. I didn't see any point in waking you."

"You took so long in confession?"

"I had a lot to confess. Millions of people are dead because of me," I said.

"And many millions more yet live because of your diligence and prowess. Have I ever told you how much the whole of Christendom owes you?"

"Hmph. I'm just a man who's trying to do his job."

"Then there is more work yet for you to do, my love. Duke Henryk is in the castle."

"And we're in his old room. I guess I'll have to have it out with him today, though I can't say that I'm looking forward to it."

"Much of the way has been cleared for you, my love. Baron Wiktor and I talked long with him yesterday. There is much to the baron that I had not seen before."

"He's a good man, though his brother Gregor is the truly wise one of that bunch. That's why I'm giving Gregor command of Mazovia. Sonya, would you please go to Duke Henryk and ask him when it would be convenient for him to talk with me today? And, uh, put a dress on first. Henryk has this problem with feminine skin."

"Wait!" Francine said as Sonya was about to leave. "Is that wise, my love? *You* command here, and you should tell him when it would please you to meet. And if it pleases you to have your wenches nearly naked, you should not change your custom to suit a visitor."

I shook my head and said, "Okay. We'll compromise. Sonya, ask the duke if he would join me here for dinner at noon and don't bother dressing up for the occasion. After that, tell the cooks to have a meal for two sent up at three sharp and remind them that I fired the head cook at Sandomierz. You know my tastes in food."

As she left, I said, "Satisfied?"

"With you, always, my love. You might want to dress in one of your army uniforms to remind the duke of your bond with him and the fact that you head the Order of the Radiant Warriors."

"As you will." It takes so little to keep her happy sometimes.

I spent part of the morning with Baron Wiktor, getting things organized in Cracow, and then saw a delegation of the city fathers.

They wanted me to redesign the lower city for them, since it had mostly been burned to the ground. Yet at the same time, they wanted to start rebuilding immediately, without waiting to install sewers and water mains. And once we got into it, they didn't want a new street layout, either, since that would mean that all the existing building plots would change, and who would know who owned what? Somehow they wanted me to bless it and make it all better, but not to change anything!

My own private thought was that it would be easier to simply build a new city. As for the old one, well, there had been a half yard of organic fertilizer on the ground there for centuries. If they would put a plow to it, they'd have the richest farmland in the world! But I couldn't tell them that, so I told them to think over what they really wanted and promised to meet with them later.

I knew that in the end what we would do was come up with some new building codes, requiring fireproof materials for the walls at least, and plan to put in the utilities later in a piecemeal fashion, the way things are normally done. It would be more efficient to build from scratch, but there wasn't time. The people of Cracow had to have a place to live *now*. But best for them to come to that realization for themselves.

I had Natalia make a note to tell the factories to get into full production of all building materials as soon as possible. She was Baron Gregor's wife and would soon be leaving me to join him at his new post in Plock. She was trying to train one of the other girls to take her place, but she had been with me for nine years, and training a replacement to know what I wanted without being told every little thing wasn't easy.

It was a pleasant spring day, and I had lunch set up on one of the battlements that served as a balcony. I was surprised to see that the duke also wore one of our red and white army dress uniforms, probably for the same reason that I did. Francine had been right again.

"Welcome, your grace," I said. "Have a seat."

"Thank you, your grace," he said, looking pale from his recent illness. "I want to start by offering you my apology. I formulated a poor battle plan without your advice and consent. I ordered you to follow it even though you knew that it was foolish. And in anger, I have not answered your many letters and messages. For these things I ask your forgiveness."

"I accept your apology, your grace. I, too, need to apologize, since I deliberately disobeyed your direct orders. But let's just say that these unpleasant things never happened."

"Done. And since we now are both of the same rank, wouldn't equals speech be more appropriate?"

"Right you are, Henryk. Much has happened since our last meeting. It's been almost half a year." Sonya and three of the castle servants brought in our food and set the table. While it was a warm day for the season, it wasn't run-around-in-half-a-bathing-suit warm, and I could see her tiny nipples harden up in the breeze. I waved her back into the building with the other servants.

"True, Conrad, and that is entirely too long. Where should we begin?"

"Well. I suppose that you have heard that Count Lambert fell fighting the Mongols. I was there, and before he died, he told me that I was his heir and that you had approved it. Is this true?"

He looked down at his plate. "Oh, yes, you inherit his lands and much more besides. Did you know that Lambert's brother, Count Herman, also died?"

Lunch consisted of breaded chicken, deep-fried in a pressure cooker a la Colonel Sanders, with French fries and coleslaw. And bottled beer with some fizz in it. No coffee or Coke, alas. Henryk didn't seem to know how to handle the chicken, so I picked up a drumstick to show him that eating with the hands was proper for this exotic dish.

"No, I didn't, although I knew that Herman's wife was dead."

"Count Herman died of the sickness that struck my camp at Legnica. Now, do not tell me about your book concerning camp sanitation measures. I am well aware of it. I had my own knights follow your suggestions to the letter, but I was unable to control the foreign troops that well. They insisted on doing things as they always had, and disease spread among them the way it always does. And then, of course, my own men caught it. As best as I can determine, Count Herman died just a few hours before his brother did, and the count's wife was killed a half day before that. Therefore, Herman inherited his wife's share of their estates, and Lambert inherited them before his death. This means that they all come down to you. You are now Count of Cieszyn as well as Count of Okoitz!"

"Wow. I'd certainly never expected that," I said.

"It is also possible that you have inherited Lambert's extensive Hungarian estates as well, since his daughter has not been heard from since she left, and I understand that the fighting in Hungary has been fierce. I do not think that they were hit with as many Tartars as you were, however. The number of enemy heads on pikes along your railroad tracks would be unbelievable had I not seen them with my own eyes."

"I wish I could help the Hungarians out, but my foot soldiers would be almost helpless without the railroads, and there are none in Hungary. You know, I once tried to get King Bela to let me run a line down into his country and to put some steamboats on his rivers, but he refused me permission to do it. As to the heads you saw, well, they represent not one in twelve of the Mongols we killed. Before you go back west, we must visit the major battlefields here. Then I'll show you heads!"

"We must do that. As to King Bela, well, if he lives out the war, he will be less arrogant in dealing with you. But these are all trivial matters compared with what we really have to talk about. You know that my father spent his life trying to unite the country, and that I have done all that I can to continue his work. I now hold all of western Poland, except for the seacoast of Pomerania. You hold all of the east except for what is held by the Teutonic Order—"

"The Crossmen were sworn to my predecessor, in theory at least, and they'll damn well swear to me or leave bleeding!" I said.

"Well put! I think together we would have little trouble getting the Pomeranians back into the fold, as well. And we must be together!"

"Indeed. I agree."

"Good. Well, then. I came here to offer you my oath of fealty, Conrad. You will be the first king of Poland in a hundred years!"

"Hmph. And what if I don't accept your oath?"

"What? How can you say that? After all this, you mean to humiliate me further?"

"Not at all. I'm just saying that under certain conditions *I* would be willing to swear to *you!*" I said.

"Do you actually mean that? Why? You have the power now, not I! Why would you do such a thing?"

"Because I don't *want* to be a king! I'm not even very thrilled about being a duke. I'm a technical man, an engineer. I have no training in law, or politics, or sovereignty! I don't like sitting in judgment over other human beings. I don't even like sitting at the high table of a banquet! Sovereignty is a job that you have been training for all of your life, and you're welcome to it! I want to be free to get back to work at developing industry here, and I want you to take over all the other trivia for me."

"You would be a craftsman and call the crown trivia?"

"Yes, because it is! In the long run my job will be far more important than yours."

"Well, if that is truly your wish, then so be it. But a moment ago you said 'under certain conditions.' What conditions did you have in mind?"

I pulled out a list from my breast pocket.

"Well, first off, I'll stay in charge of the army. My forces will be the *only* military forces in Poland, and all other forces will be either disbanded or merged with the army over the next six years. I'll pay for the army myself, but that's the only thing I'll pay for. There will be no other taxes on me."

"Granted, although disbanding the feudal levies will be no easy feat. What else?"

"I'll have to stay Duke of Sandomierz, Little Poland, and Mazovia. Frankly, the people here wouldn't have you directly in command, and these areas will be underpopulated for some time, anyway. But I don't want the dukedoms to be hereditary. If they were, there's a good chance that your heirs and mine would come to blows, and that's best avoided now."

"You mean that I would be your heir?"

"Yes, insofar as those parts of the duchies that are not settled by the army are concerned. You, or your heir, will inherit the fealty of those lands and peoples that remain under the conventional nobility. The army will keep its own lands and choose its own leader, although I haven't worked out how yet," I said.

"Then, of course, I completely agree. Next?"

"Primogeniture. This business of dividing the country up between the sons of the last king has got to stop. An equal division among the heirs of lesser titles is fine, but the country, once united, must be indivisible."

"I had planned such a change myself. Granted. Next?"

"The lands that I have inherited border on Little Poland. I want them combined with my duchy here."

"Very well, although bear in mind that the law in each of the duchies of Poland is different. There will be a certain reluctance to change on the part of the people living there."

"That's another thing. I want a single, simple set of laws that is the same throughout the land. I want that law to be administered by carefully trained and very honest men, and not by the local lord of the manor. We need a system of police and judges and courts that honestly and fairly enforce the law, not the barbaric hodgepodge that we have now."

"Now, that will be a hard thing to do. People resist changes even when they are for the better. Furthermore, it will be expensive."

"I'll be responsible for the salaries of the people involved, if necessary, but the rest is your job. You write the laws, and you administer the system. Only check with me before you publish those laws. I don't demand veto power or anything like that, but I do want to have a chance to give you my advice."

"I will agree to this in principle, although we both know that it will be many years in the doing. What about your army? Will these laws cover it as well?"

"If a warrior breaks a civil law, he will be punished by the civil courts. There will be military laws as well that the warriors will be subject to, but civilians won't. I'll worry about military law."

"Good. Next?"

The meal was over, and the servants cleared the table. Sonya brought in desert. Ice cream! Excellent, despite its lack of vanilla flavoring. You know, there are advantages to occasionally firing a cook!

"I'm going to be building forts all around the borders of the country. I'll pay for the land I need, but once bought, it will be army property, under army control and not taxable by anyone. Okay?"

"Very well. Anything else?"

"Well, there's Copper City. For years I've been running it and sending you the profits. The bookkeeping involved is annoying. I want it made mine entirely."

"I hereby grant you title to Copper City. Is that the last request?"

"It is."

"Good. Then the matter is settled, though we shall have to put it all in writing, of course. Since you dictated the terms, why don't you see to getting some fair copies made. Then there is the matter of your oath of fealty. We will want to do it again with all of your officers and my nobles present, but let us swear to each other now, while the sun is yet high."

And so together we raised our right hands to the sun and swore. And Poland again had a king. Or so I thought.

Chapter Twenty-one

Francine hit the roof when she found out that Henryk was to be the next king instead of me. She ranted and screamed for hours, not listening to a word I said, until I finally just left the room

and went down to the Great Hall, which was the closest thing
to a tavern that was immediately available. I just can't *tolerate* a
screeching woman! When I came back that night to sleep, she
was still at it, shouting at the top of her lungs, with her servants
cowering in the corners. It seems that she had now found out that
Henryk had started out by offering fealty to me and that I had
turned him down. Castle servants talk too much! After another
hour of this I left again, to find that Sonya had arranged another
room for me at the other end of the palace. Women are so much
nicer *before* you marry them!

Dammit! I never promised to make her a queen! I never
promised anything except seeing to her needs, and a throne was
hardly necessary for her well-being. In fact, history proves that
a throne is a very dangerous possession. Too many kings—and
queens—have failed to die peacefully of old age in their beds.
Anyway, all this political and social aggrandizement was her idea,
not mine. I mean, I'd gone along with making her a duchess,
hadn't I? Wasn't that enough? What did she want to be? Empress
of the known world?

The next morning Sonya told me that she had a friend who was
looking for work. I interviewed the girl over breakfast, a pretty,
well-built redhead who had come dressed for the job. On Sonya's
suggestion, she showed up for her job interview wearing nothing
but her freckles. I hired her as a second body servant. At least
with servants you can fire them when they get out of line.

I never should have gotten married.

I spent the day doing administrative stuff, writing a set of
building codes for the city fathers of Cracow and making a deal
with them on building materials. I sold them bricks, hardware,
lumber, and so on at wholesale prices and gave them three years'
free credit on it. They would worry about parceling the stuff out
to the citizens at retail prices and collecting payment for it. The
actual construction work was up to them. I wouldn't be involved.
Later, in a year or two, we'd worry about water mains and sewers,
and by then, what with their profits on the building materials,
they would be able to afford the utilities. A backward way to do
things, but there wasn't really much choice.

A few days later Francine was calmed down enough to at least start out civil at a banquet that Henryk had insisted that I attend.

Nine years before, on the day after I had first met the then Prince Henryk, we had both joined a party hunting wild boar and bison. The regalia required for this sport included a shield, and he had been a bit offended by the motto on the bottom of my heater, which was the first line of the yet to be written Polish national anthem, "Poland is not yet dead!"

We had talked about it, and I had promised to paint it over if and when he finally got the whole country united. Our new armor was so good that a fighting man didn't ordinarily need a shield, and I hadn't used mine in years. Henryk had found it somewhere and had it brought into the Great Hall, along with brushes and a collection of paint pots. He told the story to the gathered notables and invited me to keep my word. There was nothing for it but to put down my knife and fork, scrape the old motto from the shield, and publicly paint on it "Poland is alive and well!"

It was mostly a party joke, and I mugged up my part in it to suit the occasion, the way I had to do every Christmas for the peasants in imitation of my old liege lord, Count Lambert.

This bit of buffoonery miffed Francine no end, since she felt that since I was now a duke, I should be a somber ass as well.

Later, when somebody mentioned that Henryk would be my heir for the three eastern duchies, she got downright livid! She flew totally off the handle again and was literally frothing at the mouth before we got her out of the hall.

And she accuses *me* of making scenes in public! She accused me of robbing my own children, by which she doubtless meant *her* own children, yet to be born.

At this point I had about a dozen others by various fine ladies, but I don't think that she figured that those kids counted. Personally, I have always done my best to treat them all the same. Playing favorites wouldn't have been good for them.

To my way of thinking, saddling a kid with any sort of an inherited lifetime job would be one of the worst possible things you could do to him. "Well kid, here's your role in life, written down on these here computer punch cards, ha, ha! Live out your only earthly existence precisely in accordance with the pattern that is given you from the high mountain! Make sure that you fit the cookie cutter exactly, baby!"

Bullshit! What a horrible thing to do to a little child!

A kid deserves a good education and a lot of love, and on top of this, I figure that all my kids started out with a pretty good set of genes. Beyond that, you owe it to him to see to it that he has a chance to grow in the directions that suit him best, and that goes double for the girls!

And damn all these Dark Ages attitudes! I had done the best thing possible for my children, for Poland, and for me!

I didn't see Francine for the rest of the week, and to hell with her. I had two new girls to take care of me. Young ones! And what they lacked in skill, they made up for with cheerfulness, obedience, and enthusiasm.

Sonya mentioned that she had another friend looking for work.

"Sonya, just why is it that you and your friends are so eager to do the dirty work around here?"

"It's not all that dirty, your grace."

"You know what I mean. Some places that I've been, the young ladies would have been insulted if you offered them work as a domestic servant."

"Then in those places the young women must all be fools, your grace."

"What do you mean? Come on, you know I'll never get angry at an honest answer."

"Well, it's a great honor to serve so high a lord, and a great pleasure to serve one who is so kind and so virile."

"The truth, Sonya."

"That is the truth! Or at least part of it, anyway. The rest is that, well, you have a *very good record*, your grace! Nine years ago Count Lambert sent you out to your new lands with five simple peasant wenches. Now, after staying with you, *every single one of them is at least a baroness,* and they're all rich besides!

A poor priest's wife is now a *duchess* because of you! I've only been working for you for a few weeks, and I'm already wealthy from my share of that Mongol booty, as are both of Duchess Francine's maids and even your horses! I tell you that any woman who wouldn't warm your bed or clean your chamber pots would be a damn fool who wants to stay poor!"

"Hmph. You know, I've never thought of it that way, but I suppose that a young person has to look out for herself."

"Of course, your grace. And a bright girl takes care of her friends as well. You can never tell when you might need a return favor. Did you want to see Kotcha?"

"Why not?"

And then there were three.

Well. Baron Wiktor was settling into his new job nicely, and before long we had things reasonably under control. Within a week it was time to visit Mazovia and get that business over with.

Duke Henryk—well, he wasn't crowned yet—suggested that he go along and that we visit the battlefields on the way. It seemed like a good idea at the time. Francine still wasn't speaking to me, so I left her behind.

We loaded our entourages, Big People and all, onto one of the three steamboats I had left on the Vistula, Baron Tadaos's *Enterprise*, and headed downriver. A few months ago, there had been three *dozen* of them! Not one Vistula boatman in four dozen was still alive. There were so few river boatmen left that the boat was "manned" largely by the baron's many wives. Training boatmen was another thing to worry about.

Tadaos proudly demonstrated his favorite bit of war booty, a huge leather-covered recurved Mongol bow that he claimed was better than the English longbow he'd lost when his old *Muddling Through* had been burned.

We stopped at each of the major killing fields on the way, told the story of what had happened there, and watched Henryk being properly impressed by the huge squares of mounted human heads. The ants and carrion birds were still having royal banquets, feasting on flesh and eyeballs. An ugly sight, but better the Mongols should do that duty than us. Anyway, it wasn't as though we had invited the bastards here.

At the first such stop Henryk mentioned the big pile of Mongol weapons and equipment that was stacked there.

"That stuff?" I said. "That's what was left after we sorted through it. The best trophies were all taken to Three Walls to be divided out among the warriors as spoils. This pile will be taken back as scrap metal when we get around to it. If you or anybody here wants to pick through it, feel free."

The duke's pride wouldn't let him touch it, but most of his men picked up a sword and a dagger or two. Our servants all did likewise. Even Sonya got to wearing a dagger on her loincloth for a few weeks until she decided that it was silly. I passed the word that if any of the returning peasants wanted any of it for their personal use, they should feel free. It's not as though we were short of scrap iron. Weeks later, Baron Novacek, my sales manager, was angry about these gifts, and he sold much of what was left at a healthy profit.

The next day Henryk and I were standing apart from the others on the top deck of the boat as we were approaching Sandomierz. Tadaos was taking us carefully past the wreckage of yet another Mongol bridge.

"Henryk, when were you planning on having your coronation?"

"I am not sure, Conrad. In a year or so, as soon as the Pope confirms it, I suppose."

"The Pope? What does he have to do with it?"

"Well, everything! Poland is a papal state, after all."

"Poland is a *papal state*? You mean like all those little countries in Italy? I've never heard of such a thing!"

"Well, as a mere baron, you have never had to pay Peter's pence. It is no small tax, I assure you."

"But I still don't understand. You mean to tell me that Poland is subordinate to Rome? When did that happen?" I asked.

"Why, almost at the beginning, more than two hundred years ago. At the time it was a wise political move, since we were being invaded by the Germans and it gave us a certain moral force against them that we lacked up until then. Now it has become more of a tradition than anything else, although I reaffirmed our status with Rome a few years ago for much the same reasons that my ancestors had. It gives us moral support against the Germans. In theory, Poland is a member of the Holy Roman Empire as well, though neither my father nor I have ever paid taxes to Frederick II. I suppose that he could crown me as easily as the Pope, but talking Gregory IX into it will be an easier job. It is better politically as well, what with all the troubles that Frederick has been having. I would prefer to be associated with him as little as possible, even though I married one of his nieces. He has been excommunicated more than once, you know."

"I guess I don't know. I've never paid much attention to world politics."

"By our agreement, it is all more my worry than yours, Conrad. If you really want an education in it, talk to that wife of yours."

"Whether we ever talk again remains to be seen. I never thought that she'd react to our agreement the way she has."

"And that is all more your worry than mine. But if I may make bold a suggestion about your domestic life, I would say that you should leave your wife at home, as I customarily do and as my father did before me. That way, when you do get back, you will be warmly welcomed, and when you are away, you will be unencumbered with emotional baggage that you do not need."

"I'm afraid that Francine will never make a contented housewife. She'd rather be a world power."

"Again, my friend, it is your problem, though it might solve itself once she has a child in her arms. It often has a calming effect on them. If that does not work, I remind you that the Church allows you to beat her so long as you do not use too big a stick."

"I don't think that I could do that. The customs were a little different in my time. Back to this business of your coronation. Do you really think it's wise to let the Pope, or any other power, for that matter, crown you? If he can make you a king, can't he unmake you as well? And as to your paying this Peter's pence—that's in addition to the tithing you do, isn't it? Well, Poland has just saved all of Christendom from the greatest danger that ever threatened it! It seems to me that our military services should be taken in place of that money. We saved France and the rest of the wealthy countries to the west from total destruction. Let *them* pay Rome's bills!"

"Those are two very interesting suggestions, Conrad. I particularly like the idea of getting out from under the taxes. They would double on me, you know, since our agreement has you paying no taxes to me and someone would have to pay the Peter's pence on the eastern duchies. I think I will do it! At the worst, Gregory will scream too loudly, and I might have to back down. But it is certainly worth a try."

"If you did get off that hook, you could afford to pay for the new legal system, couldn't you?"

"I suppose I could, but first let us see if it can be done."

"And what about my other suggestion? What if *I* were to crown you?" I said.

"Now, that would require more thought, Conrad. Politically, it might be dangerous. Yet I must say I like the concept."

The boat had made the usual U-turn and was coming upstream to the landing at Sandomierz. Doing it any other way was just about impossible with a stern-wheeler.

"Well, you think on it, Henryk. For now we just have time to visit the battlefields west of here if we are still to get to the palace for supper."

I went with Henryk and his three guards to the battlefield, since we were the only ones on Big People. Everybody else went directly to the palace.

A city of round Mongol felt tents had sprung up on the old battlefield, housing not only the remaining sick and wounded and the troops attending them, but also the arms and property of the Christian knights who had fallen there. So far not much of it had been retrieved by the heirs of the dead.

By accident, I came across the gold-plated armor that I had once given to my former liege lord, Count Lambert. Since I was his heir, I gave orders that the armor should be sent to my jeweler for repair and then on to Baron Vladimir. Vladimir had worn that armor as my best man at my wedding a half year ago, and it had fit him well. It seemed proper that he should have it now.

Back in Sandomierz, Baron Wojciech still had everything well in hand, and Yawalda was glorying in her role as vice duchess. Watching my old lover preside made it one of the least boring banquets I'd ever attended, almost worth the time it wasted. The former peasant girl was doing her new situation up proud!

Yet the burghers of the city treated Henryk with a certain aloofness and seemed not totally pleased with my subordination to him. It wasn't as strong as it had been at Cracow, where more than one citizen had thrown garbage and dead cats at the duke, but you could tell that at best they had a wait-and-see attitude.

The next morning was spent going over the killing fields opposite of Sandomierz, and I pointed out the place where my stupidity had earned me an arrow in my right eye. But by this time the huge squares of human heads, the massive piles of rusting arms, and the vast stacks of salted-down horsehides were getting a little boring, and I was glad that our grisly tour was over.

Baron Gregor and Natalia were eager to push on to their new post in Plock, and aside from the wreckage of a few more Mongol bridges, the rest of the journey was uneventful.

The people of Plock had been warned of our coming, and they had the city decked out with flags, banners, and colored bunting. Some of Francine's annoying political posters had found their way here as well. Plock had been bypassed by the Mongols, and the city itself was entirely unharmed. Yet every fighting man in the entire duchy who could afford a horse had ridden south under the banners of young Duke Boleslaw, and most of them had died with him when he had foolishly stayed on the battlefield instead of leaving the enemy to my army, as had been planned. It was a city of women, children, and old men, and they were truly glad of our coming.

A battalion of army troops had arrived a week before, and they were cheering us, too. Judging from the color of their eyeballs, it looked as though they had spent their time and half of their back pay on drink and in the comforting of too many young widows. But I suppose that they each deserved a hero's traditional welcome. They'd certainly earned it.

I really don't like having people cheer at me, although I try to act the part. Henryk, however, seemed to be enjoying it immensely. Good. That was part of being king, and he was welcome to it. I let him make most of the speeches to the crowd, and when my turn came, I just thanked them for making me their duke and told them that Henryk would be the next king and that Baron Gregor would be my vice duke here. That seemed to make everybody happy, although in the mood they were in, that mob might have cheered if I had said that I was giving the country to the Mongols!

The palace at Plock had much in common with the others I had in Cracow and Sandomierz. One had the feeling that the previous dukes had competed with one another for status symbols, and had done a lot of imitating in the process. Natalia was delighted with her new home, and Baron Gregor seemed contented with the rewards of his faithful service to me.

I spent the usual week helping Gregor get settled in, and Henryk was a great deal of help as well. I'd thought that he would be treated coldly, as he had been in Cracow and Sandomierz, but not so. Perhaps it was because the battles had happened so far away from this city and because, since Mazovia had never been subordinate to Henryk, he could not possibly have ever betrayed it.

In any event, it was finally looking as though I would soon be able to get done with this time-wasting political stuff. I was eager to get back to my proper job at Three Walls.

Then suddenly all bets were off.

A breathless lookout ran in and announced that the Grand Master of the Teutonic Order was approaching the city gates with a thousand knights and men-at-arms behind him. The Crossmen were coming!

Chapter Twenty-two

FROM THE JOURNAL OF DUCHESS FRANCINE

So it was that because of my arrangement of the situation and Baron Wiktor's adroit handling of Duke Henryk, the duke became convinced that his only hope of survival lay in his unconditional submission to my husband. Through hard work and no small a dose of good luck, the stage was properly set for Conrad's final enlargement to King of Poland.

Oh, I knew that he would make his usual objections to this advancement, but I also knew that just as he soon found reasons of his own why he must needs remain duke, once it was thrust upon him, he would also convince himself that he must remain king. Men are really such simple beings, and so easily manipulated.

Conrad insisted on quietly conversing with Henryk at a meal alone with him, so I was not able to attend, yet I was not worried. All things had been so well managed that there could be only one possible outcome from their meeting. And better that they should think that they had done it all by themselves. It saved bruising their fragile masculine pride.

Thus, you can imagine my abject horror at finding out that they had managed to do the exact opposite of what was sensible! Despite the fact that Conrad not only held the will of the people but had vast, almost unheard of wealth and a huge, efficient army and Henryk had none of the above, somehow they had decided that Henryk should be king and Conrad but a vassal.

And my stupid dumpling of a husband was dull enough to be pleased with the arrangement!

And these two, both the bumpkin and the shyster, had sworn on it! Oh, not publicly as yet, but with too many servants present to silence them all without notice being taken of it.

Is it any wonder that I was annoyed?

Then after Conrad gleefully gave me his disastrous news, he tried to convince me of his brilliance in doing it! He kept making no sense at all until he finally lurched out of our chambers.

I then tried to get the entire story out of the servants that were present. Of course, the bare-titted hussy that he euphemistically calls a personal servant was completely useless to me. She knows how long she would last without Conrad's protection! The others were castle servants, left over from the time when Henryk ruled here. It didn't take me long to show *them* where their kasha was salted!

Thus it was that I found out that Henryk had started out by offering fealty, as was to be expected, but my stupid, doddering husband had refused it! After Conrad returned and I explained it all to him, he again left me to spend the night with his blond trollop.

I am becoming convinced that my mother was right. The pains of this world are too much for a woman to bear, and the only sensible course is to retire to a nunnery.

Why am I tortured like Tantalus, to have all that I desire but a hand's length away, only to always have it wrenched away when it is seemingly within my grasp? What great sin have I committed that I should be treated by God in so cruel a manner?

Yet still, I strived to be a peacemaker, and when I was formally invited to a banquet with Conrad and *that duke*, I decided that it would be seemly to go. Perhaps some small thing could be rescued from this debacle.

Such was not to be. At the feast Henryk taunted my husband, making him act the clown, the buffoon to him. And Conrad willingly did it! He louted before the mob and Henryk, too. Conrad, whose armies could have stomped this entire castle flat without taking their hands out of those *pocket* things of theirs!

I was mortified. And no sooner was this ugly scene over than some simpering courtier pranced up and casually mentioned that Conrad had also given away our own children's birthrights. They were to be disinherited in favor of Henryk! The child in my own womb was to be cast out before it had even had the chance to draw its first breath.

So now Conrad and Henryk have gone north to make a mess of things in Mazovia, to alienate the population and probably get themselves into a stupid, useless war with the damned Teutonic Knights!

And I sit here alone, abandoned by all save the servants, my guards, and the courtiers.

A nunnery. There must be a decent nunnery somewhere in Poland!

Chapter Twenty-three

FROM THE DIARY OF CONRAD STARGARD

Damn. I had to face yet another high-anxiety situation, and this was likely to be a big one. I had been bumping heads with the Knights of the Cross since the first day I got to this century, when one of them had bashed me on the head for not groveling properly. Later I'd caught seven of them taking a gross of children south to sell as slaves to Moslem brothels, and when we had put a stop to this molestation of children by cutting down most of the Crossmen, I had been forced to fight a Trial by Combat with their champion to stop the Crossmen from repossessing those kids.

Plus, well, I knew my history well enough to know that having those Germans on Polish soil would cause seven hundred years of misery for my country. Not only were they completely obliterating several Baltic peoples now, they would continue their bloody expansionist ways forever!

Several of the most murderous battles of the entire Middle Ages were fought against them, and once they were defrocked by the Pope and had become a secular Protestant group, they became the duchy of Prussia that was eventually to unite Germany under a military dictatorship that was one of the root causes of World War I. And World War II was started when Hitler invaded Poland to forcefully take the land bridge that separated Prussia from the rest of Germany.

Added to all this, my father and uncles had been resistance fighters in Poland during World War II. I grew up hearing first-hand about all the unspeakable atrocities committed by the Germans. I mean, the Russians are by no means pleasant, but they are sweetness and light compared to the Nazi Germans. Germans are not a lovable people!

Furthermore, while they had sworn fealty to Duke Boleslaw of Mazovia, they had failed to come to the aid of my predecessor when he had called on them to join in the defense of the country against the Mongols. All they had done was to send a puny five-hundred-man force to Henryk at Legnica, and he had been forced to bribe them to get even that!

I now had the opportunity to remove these evil people from the map of the world, and you can bet that I was going to do everything in my power to do it!

"Battle stations," I shouted. "Baron Gregor! Get the gates closed and your men and guns on the walls!"

Within moments, bugles were blowing and men were scurrying about, finding their arms and armor, readying themselves, and finding their proper positions. It wasn't as well rehearsed as most of the army's maneuvers. In fact, we had never gotten around to actually practicing it yet at all. Chaos and confusion were sucking up precious minutes.

But God was still on our side, for the Crossmen had been spotted from the cathedral tower two miles from the city and were advancing only at a walk. The troops managed to get the gates closed in time, but just barely.

I was as late as anyone, since the only armor I had with me was the damnable gold parade stuff that Francine had insisted that I wear, and it takes forever to get into it. I was panting as I joined Henryk and Gregor at the Northern Gate. Henryk was wearing the golden armor I had given him years ago, but Gregor was wearing the much more practical cloth-covered army combat armor.

The Grand Master was just coming into view, riding at the head of the miles-long column. He was easily spotted since his surcoat was more highly decorated than were those of his men, although it was done in the same drab black and white as the others. Under their garb, I noticed that they were all wearing old-fashioned chain mail, being too proud to buy better armor from my factories. Not that I would have approved the sale.

"That's not the same Grand Master I met at my Trial by Combat," I said, looking through my binoculars.

"No," Henryk replied, squinting through a telescope of the sort that all my officers carried. "Herman von Salza died peacefully two years ago, in his sleep."

"There's very little justice in this world," Baron Gregor said.

"There is even less than you think. The filthy blackguard coming toward us was sent by me to aid the Hungarians not a month ago. He could not have gone there and still be here now! It seems that he has broken yet another vow," Henryk said.

"Wonderful," I said. "Unless these bastards have changed their ways recently, none of them will be able to speak Polish. Does anybody around here speak enough German to act as a translator?"

"I do," Henryk said. When I looked at him in surprise, he added, "My mother was German, after all, and I had to learn more of the language to speak to my wife. I'll talk to them, but I think that talk is all we should do with them today. I would rather that this did not come to a battle, Conrad. If we must fight them, let us try to do it on their soil, ruining their property, not ours."

"A good thought, and the army could use a few more months' rest after fighting the Mongols," I said. "The problem is that their property *is* my property. I *am* their liege lord, after all."

"True in theory, Conrad. In practice, I have some doubts. Well, wish me well."

The German column had stopped in front of the closed city gate, and Henryk shouted down at their leader. An exchange in German started that went on for some minutes while the rest of us on the wall waited around, wondering what was being said. All I could tell was that the words were getting louder and harsher. German seems to be a great language for being rude in.

Finally Henryk took pity on us and said, "Mostly, I've been discussing his failure to go to the aid of King Bela as promised. He wasn't expecting to find me here."

"Well, when you get around to it, tell him that I am prepared to accept his oath of unconditional fealty."

"He will love you for it," Henryk said dryly, and then started shouting in German again. The Crossman column continued to advance, crowding against the city wall and spreading to both sides of the gate. There were more than twelve hundred swivel guns on the wall, mounted in holes hastily drilled into the parapets. That much at least had been done during our week here. Every gun that could be brought to bear was pointed at the big black crosses that the Germans wore on their surcoats. Nice of them to provide us with cross hairs.

The unintelligible conversation went on for the fair part of an hour. I was beginning to wonder if I shouldn't send out for refreshments when Henryk turned to me.

"He says that he doesn't need to swear fealty to you because he is here in Poland by a perpetual written treaty with the late Duke Boleslaw's uncle, the previous Duke Conrad I of Mazovia. That man still lives, you know, but he's prematurely senile. Poor fellow, he's only fifty-four, but he can't even feed himself, let alone say a complete sentence."

"I'd like to see that treaty," I said.

"As would I. They say they have it with them and invite us to come down and examine it. Are you minded to risk it, Conrad?"

"Don't do it, your graces!" Baron Gregor said. "Those Crossmen can't be trusted under ordinary circumstances, and just now it would be to their advantage to see both of you dead."

"Hmph. Henryk, what say we invite a delegation of them inside the city. We can sit down with them someplace comfortable, have a meal, and try to talk out our problems."

"A noble thought, Conrad, but it is best to meet a Crossman in the open and to be upwind of him. The rules of their order forbid all bathing, shaving, and whatnot, you know. If rumor can be believed, they don't even wipe their arses. Also, they have more strange dietary restrictions than the Jews, which they adhere to rigorously, in public at least, so it is nearly impossible to feed them without giving offense. I ate their food once, and I would not willingly repeat the experience. Enough said?"

"So there is no excuse that you could make to get a few of them inside here."

"None that would not convince them that we were planning treachery. Dishonest people assume that all others are like them."

"Then you figure that we should go out there and trust them?" I said.

"Well, the first part of that, anyway. We really must see this document that they have. But their very presence here proves that they are oath breakers, so keep your sword loose in its sheath."

"Okay. Let's do it, then. Baron Gregor, I'd like to have six companies of troops ready at the gate to come to our rescue, and make sure that the gunners on the walls are alert!"

"Right, your grace."

I tightened my armor, loosened my sword, and went down the steps with Henryk behind me. I ducked and went through the small door that was opened for us in the main gate, and faced my adversaries. As luck would have it, I was downwind of them, and Henryk's advice about their lack of bathing proved to be entirely too true. The small door was closed behind us, and despite the fact that we were out in the open, I felt claustrophobic. I glanced at Henryk, and he started talking to them in German. After a while they handed him a rolled-up piece of parchment, which he unrolled and studied silently for a while. Then, without a comment, he handed it to me.

"It's an obvious fraud," I said. "First off it's written in German! A Polish treaty, granting lands on Polish soil, would be in Polish, not in some foreign language. Then, there is no date on this 'document'! Anything official has to have a date. And worst of all, there is not a single signature on it. And not a single seal! It's preposterous, and I can't even read what it says."

"Well, I can," said Henryk, "and I assure you that the content is as absurd as the format. It purports to give the Teutonic Order permission to do as they please to the inhabitants outside our borders, whether they be Christian or heathen, and grants them Polish lands equal in area to those that they conquer from our neighbors. Furthermore, it states that all such lands taken or granted become their property, subject only to the Holy See and the empire. They no longer admit to being your vassals, or the other Conrad's, either. What is your reaction to that pile of barley?"

"You can tell them that I am waiting for their abject submission to me, and barring that, that they have one year in which to leave my lands and all of Poland. After that, I will kill them all and put their heads up on pikes, as I have done with the other people who have recently invaded my land. Tell them that exactly." There was no point in prolonging the conversation, and anyway, the smell of these bastards was getting to me. At least the Mongols didn't stand upwind and breathe in your face! On the improbable chance that they *did* swear to obey me absolutely in all things, I planned to send them back to the Holy Land where they had started from and tell them to kill rag heads. I just wanted them *out*!

So I stood there while they screamed gibberish at one another for a quarter of an hour. I envied the UN people with their headsets and their real-time translations, but Henryk seemed to be doing his best, and I didn't want to break his stride.

Eventually he turned to me and said, "They don't seem to have grasped the extent of what you have done with the Mongols. What say you have some of your people give a delegation of theirs the tour that you just gave me."

"Fine, just so long as I don't have to do it myself. Their stench is overpowering me!"

After another long babbling match, with more gutturals than could have been manufactured by three dogs fighting over a dead pig, Henryk said, "Good. They will have twenty men ready to go tomorrow."

"Done," I said, though that meant that we'd have to spend days hosing their stench out of one of our only three riverboats. "I presume that you will be escorting them, your grace."

"I seem to be stuck with the task, your grace, being the only one handy who speaks German. Sovereignty is a demanding profession."

"And one that you are welcome to," I said.

That evening Henryk came to my quarters.

"You know, Conrad, fighting the Crossmen is not going to be as straightforward as beating the Mongols. The Knights of the Cross are in theory a religious order, and they have papal sanction. Certain factions in the Church are not going to be pleased with us when we kill them. Then, too, Emperor Frederick II has conferred on them an imperial charter, and he won't love us either if our plans go well."

"Are you saying that we should back off on them?" I asked.

"No. I think that we have to get rid of them or they will be a thorn in our side forever. But I think you should know that this is an issue where for the first time in a century, the Pope and the emperor will agree on something. We may well have a further war with the empire on our hands, as well as papal sanctions against us. I for one would not like to be excommunicated."

"Nor would I. Well, then, I'd say that you have your work cut out for you. You must see what you can do about gaining support for our cause in the Church and in foreign courts."

"How right you are, Conrad. And you must see to it that not all of your forces face the east. The next war may come at us from the west!"

The next morning they went away, the Crossmen and the king, and I was able to get another boat the next day, the RB47 *Millennium Falcon*. Later, as I was pulling into East Gate, I got a radio message from Henryk.

CONRAD. THE CROSSMEN ARE BOTH FRIGHTENED AND ADAMANT THAT THEY WILL NOT LEAVE. I ASSUME THAT YOU WERE SERIOUS ABOUT GIVING THEM ONE YEAR TO GET OUT, FOR THAT IS THE ULTIMATUM THAT I HAVE GIVEN THEM. HAVE I DONE RIGHT BY YOU?—HENRYK.

After thinking about it a bit, I had them send back:

HENRYK. FINE BY ME, BUT GIVE THEM UNTIL THE FIRST OF JUNE 1242. THAT WILL GIVE MY TROOPS TIME TO GET THE SPRING PLANTING IN. CONRAD.

Thus, I had a year before I had to worry about any more military or political nonsense, and I was eager to get back to some simple, sensible technical problems. At the time I didn't think it would take much to throw out the Crossmen, not when I had an army that had kicked shit out of the Mongols! Of course, I screw up pretty often.

The Riverboat Assembly Building had been completed, and work was under way on the construction of four new steamboats. Two of our existing Vistula boats were doing patrol and transport duty, but the third had been fitted with a derrick and was engaged in salvaging what it could from the boats that had been lost in the war. Already, the engines, boilers, and all the major hardware needed for the boats under construction were on hand and being rebuilt, and more salvage was coming in every day. Plenty of seasoned lumber was available, and the boatwrights were sure that we could replace our war losses by late fall.

East Gate was now manned by a company of regulars, most of whom worked as boatwrights and the rest as mule skinners on the railroad.

My first inclination was to go straight to Three Walls and dive into some refreshing engineering work, but on reflection I realized that it was important that the folks at the other installations see me. Best to make as fast a tour as possible. I sent my entourage to my home by mule-drawn carriages while I went out ahead alone on Silver.

My first stop that morning was at Sir Miesko's manor. His wife, Lady Richeza, had been instrumental in starting and running the school system, and when the war had come, she had invited all the lady teachers in eastern Poland to weather the Mongol advance behind the strong walls of the manor. Most of them were still there, since commercial transportation had only recently resumed operation.

She said that her husband was in Hungary, fighting the Mongols for King Bela, and that I would know better than she where her older sons were, since they were all members of my army. I assured her that her boys were all well, and she served me a nice dinner. During the meal, she and her fellow schoolteachers proudly told me every detail concerning how the Mongols had attacked the manor and about how the ladies had shot them all down with the swivel guns that Sir Miesko had provided in such abundance.

They got quite animated in the telling of the tale, pantomiming themselves in battle with a degree of showmanship surpassed only by Baron Vladimir when he was a young man! It is surprising how much bloodthirstiness lurks in the heart of the gentlest of schoolteachers. After dinner they proudly displayed the booty that they had taken, the sacks of gold and silver as well as saddles, arms, and bloodstained armor. They had decided to keep it and divide it up among themselves, since the school system was more than well enough funded. They even had the enemy heads up on pikes in the gruesome army fashion!

It was mid afternoon before I could bid these charming, learned, and remarkably brutal elderly ladies good-bye and ride to Okoitz.

Chapter Twenty-four

Okoitz had been the seat and home of my liege lord, Count Lambert, and I had built him a magnificent castle there in return for six years of output from the cloth factory that I had designed for him. Lambert had been a libertine and cocksman par excellence, though in a very friendly sort of way, and the girls "manning" his factory were remarkably loving and giving. The biggest Pink Dragon Inn I owned was at Okoitz, having been enlarged three times over the years. You see, this was where the boys came to meet the girls working at the factory. And why were so many girls eager to get work at the cloth factory? Because this was where the boys were, obviously!

The castle had room for the hundred peasant families that farmed the land in the area and worked at a part-time sugar mill in the winter. There was also room for the six hundred attractive young ladies who worked at the cloth factory and the hundred-odd servants, cooks, and repairmen who did all the work needed to feed so many people and keep the place livable.

But all these people together occupied only half the living space at Okoitz. On certain occasions Count Lambert liked to invite all the nobility in the county over for a festival, and to make this possible, there was rather posh living space here for an additional thousand people.

The count was inordinately proud of his castle, but no sooner had it been completed and furnished than he had been killed and I had inherited the place.

The problem was, What to do with it?

I toured the town, starting with the factory, looking at it with new eyes. The machinery was mostly of wood and at least eight years old. I had been pretty proud of it when I had first designed the place, but now, compared with my other installations, it was behind the times. Everything was very labor-intensive, and for a good reason. Every time I had suggested some improvement to Count Lambert, he had always found reasons why it should not be done. The truth was that he didn't give a damn about efficiency, but rather he looked at every job eliminated as one less girl he had in his fabulous harem! Eventually I had stopped trying to sell him on improvements altogether. The factory was far superior to its competition, anyway, even though there were a dozen similar operations going now in Poland alone, owned and operated by men Lambert had proudly shown through his factory.

But now, while I certainly didn't plan any reductions in the work force, there was always the need for more production, and the local herds had increased such that during the last two years the county had actually been selling raw wool to outside buyers. New factories were definitely in order—two new factories, one for linen cloth and one for wool. The old one was made of wood and lacked proper foundations, anyway. It was showing signs of rot.

Okoitz was built above the huge Upper Silesian coalfield, one of the biggest in the world, and there was already a working mine on the property. Steam-powered factories were obviously the way to go.

Of course, developing the new machinery would have to be done here, where the problems involved with working with fibers could confront the designers directly. Designing at a distance, as the Russians usually do things, is inefficient and can lead to disaster. This meant that we would have to build a machine shop here first. Not a production shop, but a research and development shop.

So why not move the entire R&D section from Three Walls to Okoitz? Three Walls was getting overcrowded, and we were starting to run out of building space there. R&D was probably the easiest group to move, and it would give us something to do with all the extra space we had in the castle. My own household was outgrowing my old apartment at Three Walls, since everybody seemed to be sprouting body servants, and Count Lambert's vast apartment might suit me very nicely. Yes.

All this was going on in my subconscious mind as I toured the factory. My conscious mind was mostly on the hundreds of sexy young ladies who were working the machines. They were all flirtatious and tended to wear as little as the temperature permitted. Another good reason for moving R&D here was that the apprentices who made up two-thirds of the teams would surely appreciate the scenery hereabouts. I certainly did!

Mulling through my thoughts, I tried to have supper quietly in the big cafeteria, but the manager of the factory, a Florentine named Angelo Muskarini, insisted that I give a speech to those present. There was nothing for it but to oblige him.

"Thank you," I said when the girls and farmers had quit screaming at me. "As you doubtless all know, the war is over, and the good guys have won!" This brought on more cheers. When they died down, I continued. "The important fact for all of you ladies to know is that except in the river battalion, our losses were small, and that if your favorite young man has not gotten back yet, he will likely be coming here soon." More cheers and bouncing up and down.

"I suppose that you have all heard that my liege lord, the noble Count Lambert Piast, died honorably in the defense of his country. You also know that I was named his heir. I simply want to say that I intend to make very few changes around here, and those will all be for the better. We will be expanding our cloth-making operations, since for the last two years our shepherds have actually been selling raw, unprocessed wool to foreigners, to be spun and woven in foreign lands instead of here. To counter this trend, we will be hiring more workers and making better, more efficient machinery for you to work at. This will mean putting a new group of intelligent young men to work here to design and build the new equipment, but I expect that you fine ladies can keep these poor lads from getting too lonely!" Again, more cheers.

"Perhaps, if you make them welcome enough, we'll move all of our research groups here. Well, we'll see. There is one other major change that I would like to make, however. Up until now you fine ladies have been working for cloth, not money. That is to say, you have been working on a barter system. What would you think about being paid in money instead? Then you could buy cloth, at special prices, if you wanted to, but you could also buy anything else you wanted as well." The reaction was mixed. Some cheered, but they were probably doing that out of habit. Most didn't do anything, since this was a new thought for them.

"Well, you think about it, and we'll talk it over again when I return in a few weeks. You might want to elect four or five representatives to negotiate for you. Also, what would you farmers think about my dividing Lambert's farmland up among you, thus having your own land doubled, paying taxes or a fee on it to pay for what you and your families eat here in the cafeteria and then selling your crops to the kitchens here for money? I'm not saying that we *have* to do it this way, but I want you to think about it. That's about it. I want to finish my dinner now, even if it has gotten cold. I'll be back in a few weeks."

Of course, a lot of the girls had all sorts of questions, and they had no qualms about shoving the peasants aside and putting their scantily clad young bodies out in front. After a while I tried to get away and pleaded fatigue, but four of them sort of invited themselves to talk further with me in Lambert's old chambers. They were all pretty. A plain girl wouldn't have dared to be that pushy, fearing rejection.

There is a limit to how many times a man can say no, and I passed it. I was bleary-eyed the next morning and told myself that I was getting too old for this sort of thing.

I met Muskarini for breakfast and told him about the rest of my planned changes. Lambert had been running the entire factory on a barter system. Wool and flax were provided by his vassals, and like the workers, they received a portion of the finished cloth in return. The problem was that wool comes in various grades, of different values. The long wool from the sides of the animal is far more valuable than are the short hairs that grow on the legs. And some sheep grow much finer wool than others do. The workers had various skill levels in different crafts, and we produced hundreds of grades and types of cloth, again worth all different amounts. The accounting required by all of this was so ridiculously complicated that I doubt if anybody really knew what was going on.

There was a very good reason why Lambert had done things in this strange way. By the terms of his separation with his wife, he had to send her one-half of all the money that he took in. Not half of his net income but half of the cash that he grossed. When he had made this agreement, it had been reasonable enough, since most of what little money Lambert got he received from selling his surplus agricultural products, what was left over after he and his peasants had eaten most of it. His old castle had been built for him by his people out of local materials. His smiths made many of the things that he needed. Cash money was just something with which to buy occasional luxury goods from the merchants, not something that was needed for life itself. Also, Lambert's wife had very extensive estates of her own in Hungary to support herself with, so she wasn't hurting.

But all this changed when I built him a productive factory. He could hardly pay her one-half of the gross cash worth of the products of his factory, since the cost of materials and labor was well over half the sale price. Running the clothworks with a conventional accounting system would have put him quickly out of business. Indeed, for several months, until he came up with the barter solution to his problem, he was very difficult to work with!

I was under no such liability, and I wanted to know what was happening financially, so I ordered the factory changed over to a sensible money system. We would buy our wool and flax with money, pay the workers with money, and sell all our output for money. Well, we'd offer special discounts to our workers and vendors to keep them happy, but it would now be an account-able system.

Muskarini was not at all pleased with my changes and came up with all sorts of ridiculous reasons why we couldn't convert to a cash system. This made me suspect that he had his hand in the till somehow. After two hours of arguing with the man, I told him that he would do it my way or I would send him back to the garret that I had found him in nine years before. That quieted him down some. On leaving him, I went to the inn and sent a message ordering a team of accountants and time-study men to descend on this place, ASAP!

I saddled Silver to get to my next stop, Eagle Nest, before lunch. The medieval world had no great collection of restaurants available to travelers, and you generally had to time your trips around the hours when food was served at the manors and factories if you didn't want to miss a lot of meals.

As I was leaving, one of the girls who had spent the night with me was waiting by the drawbridge. She smiled and reminded me that Eagle Nest was an all-male institution, and didn't I really want some companionship tonight? I decided that if I didn't give her a lift, she'd probably hitchhike there, putting herself into all sorts of danger. At least that was how I rationalized it to myself. I pulled her aboard and set her on the saddle bow. She was the prettiest of last night's group, with incredibly soft skin for so slender a person and the longest legs I've seen this side of a Hollywood musical. Her name was Zenya.

I found that I rather liked having a girl sitting in front of me, where we could talk easily, as opposed to having her behind, riding apillion. I resolved to have a saddle made up with a more comfortable seat for a woman up front.

The boys at Eagle Nest were always enthusiastic, bustling about wherever they went, and their mood was infectious. They had eight planes flying now, and many more were being built. Their eager-beaver attitude toward whatever they were doing was a joy to watch. It was such a pity that I was going to have to slam them down hard!

On being told that all the aircraft were brand-new, except for the engines, I said, "But there are the nine planes that were still intact after crash-landing on the battlefield at Sandomierz. They were sent here immediately after the battle. What happened to them?"

We asked around, but no one had any knowledge of them. They had received the thirteen engines that we had hauled back with the booty, but whole planes? No, sir!

What bothered me worse than losing the planes was the fact that each of those planes had been strapped to the top of a war cart that had been manned by a full platoon of warriors. Where were all those men?

I sent a dozen messages out, trying to locate them, but had no luck. A company and a half of men had simply disappeared! We never did find them, their equipment, or the airplanes, either. It remains a mystery that is told late at night around the fires, and the story grows a bit with each retelling.

Interlude Three

I hit the STOP button and started fumbling with the keyboard, trying to call up the Historical Corps records on just what had happened to all those men and all that equipment. I wasn't that used to the system, and it took me quite a while to get what I wanted.

The naked girl at my side looked on without saying anything, so I explained to her what I was after. She just said, "Yes, sir."

She was a cuddly little thing and seemed to enjoy my light petting, but she didn't have a lot to say. I mean, she didn't actually encourage my roving hands, but she didn't object any, either.

Eventually I dug out what I was looking for.

"Those men were caught in a Mongol ambush," I told her. "They were going without a cavalry screen, and those planes on their war carts made it hard to get their weapons out. They were killed to a man. Then the Mongol commander had their armor and equipment sent straight back to the east, and the bodies hidden. If the Mongol craftsmen can figure out the guns and planes, Conrad is going to have some serious problems on his hands!"

"Yes, sir," she said.

I hit the START button.

Chapter Twenty-five

FROM THE DIARY OF CONRAD STARGARD

Since the war was over, the boys were back at their usual two shifts, going to school in either the mornings or the afternoons and working in the shops or flying on the opposite shift. I couldn't address them all until after the evening meal.

"Gentlemen. First off, I want to thank you for your dedicated service in the war that together we have just won. While a final head count is not yet in, I think that I am safe in saying that over two million Mongols were killed on the banks of the Vistula by our riverboats, and those boats could not have done half that job without your accurate scouting and reporting of enemy positions. I think that it is fair to say that a million of the enemy owe their timely deaths to your own very good work! That's more than were killed by the regulars at Sandomierz, Cracow, and Three Walls combined!

"Furthermore, the land forces were able to defeat the Mongols that got over the Vistula with relatively light losses. That would not have been true had there been another million enemy troops fighting against them. We could have been totally defeated! And had the Christian army lost, Poland would have been lost. The fifty thousand or so knights that waited with Duke Henryk at Legnica probably would not have fared any better than Duke Boleslaw's conventional knights at Sandomierz. You deserve much of the credit for saving all of Christendom!"

They spent some time cheering. I let them go on until they wore themselves out. Then I told them the other half of the story.

"On the other hand, your performance was far from perfect. First off, you totally missed the entire Mongol army that skirted the Carpathian Mountains and entered Poland by crossing the rivers where they are scarcely more than mountain streams. You got so involved with patrolling the Vistula that you didn't bother looking south of it. You not only did not find them, you made the near-fatal mistake of assuming that they could not be there!

"Worse yet, you did not sit on Count Lambert when he got the stupid idea of landing at Sandomierz to take part in the 'final' battle with the Mongols. True, he was your liege lord and you were required to follow him, but it was also your duty to give him good advice, and there you failed him completely! You failed him, and he and two dozen of your classmates died because of your failure. They died uselessly, because of one man's vanity and your pusillanimity. And then, since we had no aerial reconnaissance, Cracow was burned because of your failure! East Gate fell because of your failure! Three Walls was attacked because of your failure!"

A look of dark horror was spreading over the boys. I stopped and let my words sink in. Then I continued.

"The trained warriors of the Christian army would not have failed in this fashion. Part of the training they get clearly defines their duty to both their subordinates and their superiors. They know what courage, and honor, and duty really are. And you must learn!

"Therefore, Eagle Nest, with all who work and fly here, is going to be absorbed into the Christian army. Starting one year from today, no one over fourteen years of age will be allowed up in a plane who has not completed the full one-year course at the Warrior's School. This means that in the next two years every one of you is going through that school, and if you want to swear fealty to me and not have to give up flying forever, you had better pass the course! That includes the instructors as well.

"The Warrior's School will be starting up again in two weeks. I will expect half of those of you who are over fourteen to be at it. In the future, no new student will be accepted here without first being a warrior. That's all that will count, besides good eyesight and physical fitness. Eagle Nest will no longer be a haven for those of noble birth. Anyone who can qualify will get in. And it will no longer be an all-male organization. Qualified young ladies will be flying within the year.

"I am Conrad, and I taught you that air is strong! Believe what I say!

"On the plus side, this means that all of you boys and men will soon be drawing a regular army salary, and your various benefits will be brought in line with theirs.

"Oh, yes. You will also be getting a share of the rather extensive booty that the army took, so if not exactly rich, you are all at least quite nicely off. I'd like to speak to the instructors tomorrow morning for about a half hour to discuss scheduling. Good night!"

I had jerked the boys around pretty severely, and I didn't want to sit in on the inevitable bull sessions that would occur while they absorbed it all. I went immediately to the small room that was always reserved for me there. Zenya was waiting for me, of course, but I firmly resolved to get at least some sleep that night.

My next stop was Coaltown, where things were booming nicely. The coal seam there was one of the most massive in the world, being fully two dozen yards thick. Once our miners had penetrated through the substantial layer of limestone above it and the layer of clay between the coal and the limestone, they had just been going in any which way. It didn't seem to matter to them, since wherever you dug, you were digging through coal.

We set up a more rational system of exploitation. Surveyors transferred a true east-west line down to the bottom of the main elevator. Then the miners cut a barrel-vaulted chamber, two dozen yards wide and a dozen yards high, through the limestone, leaving the clay on the floor. Every four dozen yards they started a cross-vault to send shafts at right angles to the main one. The limestone was sent to the cement plant.

When these miners got a gross yards east of the shaft, another group started harvesting the clay for the brick works. And this group was followed by coal miners, who could work with a stone ceiling over their heads, which, being vaulted, wasn't likely to cave in. Not only did this prove to be an efficient way to get the minerals out, it also left behind these huge, cathedral-like rooms and tunnels that sure looked to be useful for something.

The next day I went to Copper City. Here the Krakowski brothers had things well in hand, and production was going full swing. They were delighted that the city was now army property, though in fact it didn't actually change anything immediately except for some accounting procedures. In the long run, though, it meant that we didn't have to get Duke Henryk's permission to change things, and that speeded things up a bit. Mostly, I had asked for the city because I had been pretty sure that I could get it at the time. Greedy of me.

Then we raced back to Three Walls and got there on the evening of the fifth day since leaving East Gate. At last I could get down to being an engineer again!

Zenya had just sort of tagged along during the trip, and I really couldn't just leave the girl in what was to her a foreign city. Once back at Three Walls, she sort of fell in with my other three servants and proved to be outstanding at giving back rubs. A week passed before Sonya asked me if she shouldn't be put on the payroll like everybody else. By then I had gotten so used to having her around that I went along with it. Yet the whole affair nagged me. Had I hired her, or had *she hired me*?

Francine was still staying in Cracow, and that was fine by me. She could come back when she was ready, but I'd be damned if I was going to beg her to come home.

Despite my firm intentions to do technical work, my next four days were spent doing managerial stuff. There were the plans for the new standardized factories to be gone over and approved, and then the plans for the factory that would make the precast concrete structural members for the standard factories. The bills of materials had to be carefully scrutinized, since we would be putting these buildings up at the rate of one per week for the next two dozen years or so. Little mistakes can become big mistakes when you are working with those sorts of numbers.

And each of these structures was more than just a factory. Each housed a complete company of workers and their families, with a school, a church, a cafeteria, and many of the usual things that a stand-alone company needed. Well, since they would be built right next to each other, they could share facilities on certain things. They didn't each need a separate general store, for example, and inns were built only at the rate of one for every two companies, although they had to be larger, of course. Rather than having one medical officer per company, they were grouped in clinics that each served six companies, so that there were always two doctors on duty at any time of the day or night.

We were really planning a huge industrial city, and except for some land set aside for hobby gardening, there would be no agricultural work being done. But at the same time a city environment needs things that a country place can do without, and each factory had a gymnasium and a swimming pool.

The factories were to be built on both sides of the Coaltown-East Gate railway, which would be expanded to four tracks and roofed over in the course of construction. In the future, bad weather wouldn't slow down interfactory transportation.

Each company-sized factory/housing complex was to be seventy-two yards long, three to six stories tall, and a half mile wide. It would be a strip with housing on the outside, then community services, and then a factory at the middle that abutted the covered railroads. All this would be under a single roof, and it would rarely be necessary to go outside in the cold Polish winter.

Building one a week, on alternate sides of the road, we would be constructing a long strip city, a mile wide and growing a mile longer every year. It would be called Katowice after my hometown in modern Poland.

A more difficult job was scheduling just what each of these factories would produce and making sure that they had the machinery and skills to produce it. There were many crowded product sections in our existing system, and much of the job would consist of moving them to Katowice and enlarging and modernizing them in the process.

After a few years, once we had at least three companies producing a given product, we would be able to use a system where the captain of each company would have almost complete control over what his group would be making and how they would make it. Functionally, it would be a free enterprise system. But free enterprise doesn't work well when there is only one producer and only one consumer, and for start-up, that would be the situation. Most of what would be produced would be needed for building these factories and for the concrete forts we would start putting up next year. We had specific requirements, and it would have to be regulated from the top. It was a massive scheduling job, but at least there wasn't much politics involved. It was such an audacious project that people got a kick out of just jumping in and doing their best.

Chapter Twenty-six

I was going over the truly bodacious amounts of steel reinforcing rod that would be needed, and subconsciously worrying about how I was going to fairly divide up the booty without causing inflation, when a visitor arrived.

I wouldn't have been disturbed this way if I had still had Natalia working for me, but the new girls weren't as sharp as she was. Four people were trying hard to replace one, and they were doing a poor job at it! I didn't realize what a treasure I had until I lost her.

Anyway, this guy was standing at my drawing board, trying to get my attention while I was doing arithmetic in my head. He was covered with rings, brooches, necklaces, and other jewelry, a thing I have never liked on a man. Personally, I wore almost none at all, except for the brass on my dress uniform. And the solution hit me!

It was vitally important that each of the men get his fair share of the booty. I couldn't possibly cheat them and keep the army intact. Yet having that much spending cash dumped on the market would be equally disastrous. The answer was jewelry! Every man would get a new dress uniform with the epaulets, buttons, buckles, insignia, sheaths, dirk handle, and sword guard in solid gold. With a little creativity we could probably get three or four pounds of gold on the lowest warrior basic!

And then there would be a glorious medal for being a member of the Radiant Warriors, bigger than a man's hand, and various other medals for valor and participation in various battles. The women who manned the forts would get similar decorations, along with a nice dress uniform, which we didn't have as yet for the women, and the Big People would be decorated as well! And there should be something nice that a warrior could give to his wife, say, a necklace or a belt—or, better yet, both! They would get the booty, but not in the form of inflationary cash. Uniform doodads would stay off the market, because the men would have to come in dress uniform on certain occasions, and it would be embarrassing to show up wearing mere brass.

I was smiling insanely when I looked up at the fellow and said, "Can I help you?"

"Well, yes, your grace," he said, confused by my grin. "I am Baron Zbigniew, and I was vassal to Count Herman of Cieszyn. I have been told that you have inherited his estates. Is this true?"

Would you believe that what with all the things going on, I had completely forgotten about the city that I had inherited? I dropped my pencil and bent the lead point.

"I *knew* I forgot something! Forgive me, Baron. Yes, I now own Cieszyn and those lands that were held by both the count and his wife. There has been so much happening lately that I have not had time yet to do everything. Look, for now have one of the secretaries put you up in the noble guest quarters, and we'll discuss the matter tonight at dinner."

"Yes, your grace." The baron limped away on crutches.

When he was gone, I said to my lead architectural designer, "Do you know of anybody who would want to be my representative in Cieszyn?"

"Why not Komander Wrocek, sir? I served under him in the war. He is a member of the old nobility, so he knows the game, and he lost his leg at the fight in Cracow, so he won't be of much more use to the regular army. He should be up and around by now, I expect."

"Not a bad thought, Josep. Betty, go to records and get me Wrocek's file. Then check through the files and get me the names of all the officers, captain and above, who were permanently disabled in the fighting. Sitting at the high table and presiding might be just the job for them. There are going to be a lot of posts like this to fill once the knights get back from Hungary."

I tried to get back to what I was doing, but other things were nagging me. I sent a message to my jeweler, telling him to see me, and another to Francine:

> MY DEAR WIFE, IF YOU DO NOT WISH TO JOIN ME AT THREE WALLS, WHAT WOULD YOU THINK OF BEING MY REPRESENTATIVE AT CIESZYN? CONRAD.

Francine answered back within the hour:

> MY DEAR HUSBAND, YOU ROB ME OF THE CROWN OF POLAND, AND NOW YOU WANT TO STUFF ME INTO A BACKWATER PLACE LIKE CIESZYN? MAY YOUR DEAR SOUL ROT IN HELL! FRANCINE.

I deduced by this that she was still unhappy. And now every radio operator in the army would know about it. I was angry at her, but I wouldn't hire a new maid this time. I was already one up.

So I sent to Komander Wrocek, who was recovering at Wawel Castle, offering him the job at his old rank. He was delighted and promised to come within two weeks, as soon as his doctors let him free. Another message was sent telling my accountant at the Pink Dragon Inn in Cieszyn to go to the castle and see what he could do about figuring out the finances there.

By then the afternoon was over, and it was time to meet the baron for dinner. More and more, lately, I found myself taking my dinner away from the cafeteria, and many of my breakfasts as well. Mostly it was my new servants' fault. They made eating so damn decorative! Yet I made a point of always eating lunch with the other people in the cafeteria just so I wouldn't get out of touch.

I explained the arrangements that I had made, and Baron Zbigniew was agreeable, though he looked disappointed. I decided that he probably wanted the job for himself. When I talked with him a bit, he admitted it.

"I'm sorry, Baron, but the fact is that I barely know you. I hope that you can understand that I need an old and trusted friend in such a critical position. Your services will still be needed, of course. Komander Wrocek will need all the help he can get. He lost a leg at the Battle of Cracow, you know. How did you happen to be injured, incidentally? The Mongols?"

"I only wish it had been an honorable war wound, your grace, but the sad truth is that I had no sooner gotten to Duke Henryk's camp at Legnica than my horse slipped on the ice and I went down on an iron spit that was loaded with a duck that was roasting next to a cooking fire! The damned thing went right through my leg and into my horse. It nailed us together, and after they put the poor beast down, they had to cut it—and the saddle!—in half to get the carcass off me. And all the while I had to lie there half in the snow and half in the burning coals, and me not a Radiant Warrior!"

It occurred to me that *on the average* he must have been reasonably comfortable, but I didn't say it. "Horrible!" I said.

"Yet I tell you that the pain of the wound was nothing compared to the mortification I felt while everyone stood around trying to figure out how to get us apart, and the squire who owned the duck screamed at me the whole while. The entire infamous affair took hours to resolve, and I am sure that the foreign knights were taking bets as to how it would work out. Then the damned surgeons thought that my leg would have to come off, but I wouldn't allow that. It seems to be healing well enough now, though."

"Oh, you poor fellow! While you're here, you might want to ask one of our army doctors to have a look at it. They're better than most."

"I'll do that, your grace, but I doubt if there's anything they can do to mend a man's broken pride! The greatest war in history, and *I missed it because of a roast duck!*"

The girls seemed to like him well enough. At least I noticed one of Cilicia's maids sneaking into his room that night. My household seemed to be developing the morals that Count Lambert's had had. Yet Lambert's dying wish had been that all the ladies would be properly loved, and I had promised him that I would do my best to see it so. It wasn't any of my business, so I pretended that I didn't see her.

The next morning I got a double-sized research crew going on light bulbs: a glassblower, a machinist, and four apprentices. They didn't have a good source of electricity yet to power it, but there were plenty of problems to be worked out first. How to blow a glass bulb around a fragile baked thread. Coming up with a metal wire that would be wetted by molten glass and have a similar coefficient of thermal expansion so that the glass wouldn't crack as the bulb heated up and cooled down. Developing decent hardware, like a screw base and a light switch. And harder yet, making a good enough vacuum pump.

An electric generator was a separate problem for a separate team. I designed what I thought would be a decent DC generator and had them get to work on building it. I knew full well that we'd go through a dozen models before we got something good enough to go into production with. Generators were one of those things that I studied in school and had seen working but had never had a chance to design. It was another one of those specialized things that a generalist like me never got involved in. It would be years.

Then there was plumbing. We were casting our pipes out of copper. This required making the walls much thicker than was necessary to carry water, but we couldn't dependably cast them any thinner. Modern copper pipes are drawn, stretched into shape by pulling the copper alternatively between outside dies of the sort used to draw wire in order to make the copper pipe longer, and inside dies in order to stretch the metal to a larger diameter with thinner walls. Simple enough machinery, in theory at least, and it seemed likely to drop the cost of pipes threefold. I got another team on it.

Yet another team was put to work on some better wiredrawing machinery.

Teams were also assigned to develop a clothes washer and a dishwasher. One group got going on a sewing machine, although privately I considered it to be a very long-term project, since it was so complicated.

I wish we could have worked on power hand tools, but that looked impossible to me. For a long time to come all powered installations would have to be permanently mounted. We didn't have any rubber or plastic with which to make an extension cord!

I thought about getting a few teams going on new weapons and developing some of the things that had been invented just before the war but too late to get into production, but I decided against it. For one thing, we had more arms and equipment of the old style than we had men to use them. New weapons would require new tactics and new training, with a lot of man-hours required. We were already so superior to anybody else in the world that making us better was simple overkill. And mostly, in twenty years, there would be as many Big People around as there were Little People. We wouldn't be mostly infantry then; we'd be almost all cavalry. Best to wait a few years and then start working slowly on some good cavalry weapons and tactics.

A relaxing week slid pleasantly by before I got a message from my team of accountants at Okoitz. Angelo Muskarini was under arrest!

Chapter Twenty-seven

Sonya wanted to go and visit Okoitz, so I took her along, even though taking a woman to Okoitz was on a par with hauling coke to Coaltown.

I got there to find Muskarini chained up in a storeroom. He was a mass of bruises, his teeth were loose, and both eyes were blackened shut.

"Resisting arrest?" I asked.

"No, sir," said my senior accountant. "He just made us angry."

Well, my accountants were not the mousy sorts who live on American television. They were warriors first, bookkeepers second. Of course, they shouldn't have beaten the man up. I'd talked to my detectives on the importance of using the minimum possible force, but it had never occurred to me that the accountants needed the lecture as well.

After we stepped into the hall and away from the cell, I said, "You shouldn't have done that. It's not nice to beat up someone who can't hit back."

"Sorry, sir. But this dog turd was robbing his own liege lord of a fortune!"

"Can you prove it?"

"Of course, sir. I can show you the figures. Muskarini has been stealing nine parts per gross of the entire factory output ever since the first year he got here. It was no accident. He was very consistent about it, and Count Lambert doubtless thought that it was a normal production loss."

"That must be a lot of money."

"One gross, eleven dozen, and four *thousand*, a gross, nine dozen, and three pence, sir."

I whistled. They were talking base twelve, and that came to almost a half a million, the way I was brought up. "Has this money been found?"

"Yes, sir, and then some. The figure I mentioned was just on the missing finished cloth. We think he might have been getting kickbacks on the dyes and other supplies that were bought by the count. That was what much of the beating was about. Finding the money. He was keeping it in the dye supply side shed. He had the only key to the place."

"Hmph. You know, he couldn't have stolen that much alone. He would have had to have accomplices. No one man could possibly have carried out that much cloth and not been noticed. After all, hundreds of people work around here, and many of them were Count Lambert's knights."

"We know, sir, but he won't talk about that."

I went back into Muskarini's cell. He knew I was there, even though he couldn't see me. "Well, Angelo. What do you have to say for yourself?"

"I didn't steal that money, your grace. It was mine."

"Yours? Almost half a million pence was yours? Look, I was there at the beginning, remember? You were absolutely penniless, starving to death in a garret in Cieszyn! I hired you as a gift for my liege lord. How could you have gotten such wealth? You'll have to tell a better lie than that before I believe it!"

"Count Lambert gave it to me, your grace. He did, I swear!"

"No, Angelo. The count was very generous about a lot of things, but not money. Lands, yes. Women, yes. Money, no!"

"But he did, your grace. That wasn't nine parts per gross I got. It was six percent! The count, he gave me that much as a bonus. See, I was only being paid one hundred pence a year, plus room and board. Once the factory was working well and making fabulous profits because of my knowledge and labor, I asked the count for a substantial raise, and he wouldn't give it to me. I kept on asking him, and he kept on turning me down. But he was giving cloth out easily enough. You certainly got enough of it! So I asked if I could have a share of the cloth we made, and he said that would be possible. He asked how much I wanted, and I told him six percent, figuring we would settle for some much lower figure, since he'd been so stingy with me so far. But the count said that six percent would be fine, and he went in to his latest lady. I could hardly believe my ears, but he agreed to it! I swear that this is true on the grave of my own mother!"

"Hmph. Then how did you turn that cloth into money?"

"Why, I sold it to merchants, your grace, the same way that everybody else does."

"*The same way that everybody else does?*"

"Yes, your grace. Many of the girls here sell cloth to the merchants. That's how they are paid, in cloth. Oh, some of the workers come here for just a season and go home with a full hope chest, but some of the ladies have been working here every year since we started. They are our skilled workers, and we couldn't possibly manage without them. Now, you can't expect a lady to save cloth for nine years and never need a penny in real money! Of course we all sold to merchants, and Count Lambert never said a thing about it. We have a regular exchange set up, with fixed prices, and a girl draws her back wages in cloth according to what a merchant wants to buy. It was our cloth, after all. We'd earned it!"

"You know, Angelo, that story is almost believable. But tell me, why did you keep your money hidden?"

"Your grace, if you had such a fabulous sum, wouldn't you worry about thieves?"

"It would have been safe enough in the count's strong room, especially what with the new locks I installed there for him."

"Yes, your grace, but then he would have seen how much I had earned working for him. You see, I had the feeling that he didn't know how much six percent of gross was. I didn't want to remind him."

"Hmph. And that's why you spent hardly any of the money, so the count wouldn't know that you were rich?"

"Of course, your grace. In a few more years I was going back to Florence, a wealthy man, a merchant of substance!"

"Hmph. Knowing the count as I did, I almost believe your story. Almost. The real problem is that even if every word you've told me is true, you were still robbing Count Lambert. You say that you had a verbal contract with him, and I admit that verbal contracts were the only sort that Lambert would make. But for a contract to be binding, there must be a meeting of the minds. If Lambert didn't know how much you were getting, there was no contract. You were stealing, nonetheless!"

"Your grace, you can't believe that! You wouldn't have me killed!"

"No, I probably wouldn't, but *my* contract with Duke Henryk has him worrying about all legal matters. Your life is in his hands, not mine."

I went out and told the accountants to call in Baron Pulaski and have him hear the case. Then they would send the results to Duke Henryk for his determination.

My immediate problem was to find a replacement for Muskarini. Something that he had said gave me hope, though. There were women here who had more than six years' experience in cloth making. I went through the factory looking for them, since of course there were no personnel records. Soon I had five possible candidates for the job, and I was told of three more on the night shift, whom I sent for. Then I took them into one of the guest rooms one at a time and spent about a quarter hour talking to each them. And you know, there wasn't the slightest doubt in my mind as to who was best qualified for the job of running the whole factory.

One young lady was twenty-two. She seemed to know everything I did about cloth making and quite a bit more that I didn't. She was currently in charge of the linen-weaving operation, but she also knew what was happening everywhere else. She had taken full advantage of the educational opportunities at Okoitz and could read and write adequately as well as keep accurate books. And when I hinted about getting together for the night, she very politely turned me down. That impressed me considerably! So once I had seen all of the other candidates, I promoted her. But not at six percent of the gross.

Needless to say, the workers were happy about drawing their money in cash and not having to bother with the clumsy subterfuge of barter. The merchants were also happy, and we never had any serious problems with workers abusing their right to buy at below-wholesale prices. At least none that we found out about.

Months later Duke Henryk decided that Muskarini was defrauding Lambert even though it was likely that Lambert had agreed to the six percent bonus. Muskarini had been paid at a hundred pence a year, an absurdly low figure for a skilled worker being employed in a managerial position. Henryk decided that four thousand pence a year would have been a more honest wage and awarded Muskarini 35,000 pence in back wages. The balance of the money was rightfully Lambert's and therefore mine as Lambert's heir.

Then he banished Muskarini, saying that he wasn't the sort that was wanted in Poland. A knight was assigned to escort him over the German border, Hungary still being at war.

I'm glad that I didn't have to make that decision.

The summer passed pleasantly. Cilicia and Francine both had healthy boys, although Francine still would not come home. She spent her time visiting Cracow, Sandomierz, and Plock, playing the grand duchess and not bothering the Banki brothers too much. She was drawing money for her expenses from the Pink Dragon Inns, but not in absurd amounts. I let her be.

Baron Vladimir was getting the active reserves going and complaining that he had even less time at home than before. His biggest headache was that virtually all our men at or above the level of knight were working in the factories or in the regular battalions, and almost all the men in the active reserves were those who had come to us last fall and who had had only four months of training. He had almost no senior officers. He had a huge army of nothing but warrior basics and was forced to hand out temporary promotions to inexperienced and often illiterate men.

Baron Vladimir demanded and got back his old Big Person, Betty, so that he could cover the country properly. I suggested that he delegate most of the work to regional "barons," but he had to do things in his own fashion.

Over a thousand of my factory workers swore fealty to Vladimir, deciding to be peasants again, which was far more than I had expected. But I had given my word and gave Vladimir land enough for all of them. Anyway, very few of them were highly skilled workers. It takes all kinds. My father told me that.

As new Vistula riverboats were put into commission, officered largely by men from the Odra boats, they had plenty of business. Not cargo so much, since trade was still recovering, but passenger travel. Everybody wanted to visit the battle sites, and Baron Novacek, my sales manager, hired tour guides to tell people the stories for a price. He made an absolute killing, selling to the tourists "absolutely genuine Mongol war relics," the junk arms and armor that I thought would be melted down for scrap.

Duke Henryk made the tour five more times, impressing foreign dignitaries. I was glad that I didn't have to do more than smile and have a meal with them when he brought them around. Usually Henryk let me get away with serving them in my apartment, with my household, or even letting them serve themselves informally in the cafeteria, since he knew how I hated formal banquets. On rare occasions he felt that formality was necessary, and then we did it his way. Fair is fair. Anyway, the girls liked banquets when they didn't happen too often.

The Pruthenian children Vladimir and I had rescued from the

Crossmen were all adults now, and they all spoke Polish well, but some of them still remembered their native tongue. Henryk borrowed a dozen of those who were bilingual for a diplomatic mission to the Pruthenian tribes. He also asked for and got my Mongol prisoner, why I don't know or care. I was glad enough to be rid of the smelly bastard.

Baron Piotr came up with a decent trophy-distribution program for our own troops. The stuff was sorted according to quality and put into separate warehouses according to army rank. There was a big warehouse filled with lower-quality stuff for the warriors, a smaller one with nicer things for the knights, a much smaller one for the captains, and so on. Then each man was issued a chit that let him go to Three Walls any time in the next year and take his pick. New rooms were opened up over the months so that those who came late didn't get things that were too picked over. The system assured that the higher-ranking men who had been working in the army for many years got the better gimcracks and that there were some things left for the lowest-ranking men.

Coming up with 150,000 sets of eighteen-carat military decorations was no small feat, and production lines were set up to stamp and cast it all during the summer. Many workers were shocked at the thought of working in gold instead of their usual iron or copper, and all sorts of proposals were tossed around to make sure that none of it was stolen. Aside from carefully sweeping up after each shift and making everybody dust off thoroughly before leaving the area, none of these plans were put into effect. And you know? As close as we could weigh it, not one pound of gold was stolen!

Besides an average of five and a quarter pounds of gold military jewelry, the lowest man in the army got 6,200 pence in cash. Barons got thirty-two times that amount, but then, people in the Middle Ages were well convinced that rank had its privileges. All of this was paid in our zinc coinage, of course. I kept the actual gold and silver.

Even these large amounts were arrived at only after a certain amount of mathematical chicanery. Piotr and the accountants decided that I deserved to be reimbursed for my expenses incurred because of the war. They arrived at the figure they did by taking the gross income of all my lands and factories for the last nine years, plus the value of the lands I had been granted or had inherited, and subtracting from that the value of my current nonmilitary properties. The difference between these two must be what I had spent on the war, they claimed. It came to two-thirds of the gold and silver we took!

Then they awarded shares of the booty to the conventional horsemen who had served under Duke Boleslaw at Sandomierz, in accordance with their rank. Since over half of them were knights and one in seven of these were barons, the shares were large. Since many of them had died without heirs, much of this money escheated back to me as their duke.

A generous fund was set up to take care of the dependents of the army personnel who had died in the fighting or in training. And of course these dependents also inherited their share of the booty besides.

The value of the money and jewels taken from the Christian dead at East Gate was spent on aid to refugees and war orphans, and when this proved to not be quite enough, the balance was paid by the booty fund.

All of this dubious accounting was published in the first monthly issue of *The Christian Army Magazine*, along with an invitation to object to any feature of it that was felt to be unfair. Only four letters of complaint were received, and those complaints all concerned the war trophies, not the money. I felt a little guilty about it. I mean, it looked to me like I was being paid for the Pink Dragon Inns that had been burned down, but everybody seemed to think it was fair. Maybe by medieval standards it was.

Anyway, by the time all this settled out, I had these two huge stacks of metal bricks, one of gold and one of silver. Worrying about the difficulty of guarding it and the wasted man-hours that would involve, I had each stack cast into a single massive cube, except for 150 tons of the silver, which was earmarked for silverware.

Up until now we had been using brass forks and spoons, and

brass sometimes has a funny taste. I let it be known that I would be happy to hear about any good use for our precious metals, and quite a bit of it was used for things such as church vessels and medical equipment.

But most of it went to these huge solid cubes, which were put on public display at Three Walls. I felt safe, since they were too big to move without heavy machinery, and passersby would act as guards against that. People got quite a kick out of just walking up and touching them. From then on, no one ever doubted the army's credit!

And the jewels? Well, no one knew how to value them, let alone divide them fairly, so they just gave them all to me. I separated out the diamonds, which were useful industrially, and put the rest into a big, sturdy chest. Then, one day, I snuck out to the woods and buried them, very deep, with Silver as my only witness. She promised to show them to my successor after I was gone. Damned if I was going to waste good men guarding the stupid baubles!

In late summer, word came from Hungary. We had won the war! The Christian and Mongol forces had been fairly evenly matched, and they had slugged it out all summer long. Veterans returning from the south all seemed to make the trip around the battlefields in Poland, which was now running as a regular guided tour, and they were generally astounded at the number of Mongols we had encountered. Apparently, the main enemy force had been sent to Poland, and only a small one to Hungary. Bulgaria hadn't been invaded at all despite the fact that the Mongols had promised to do so. In my timeline the Bulgarians had paid tribute to the Mongols for a century.

Most of Lambert's knights came back from Hungary alive and well, including Sir Miesko and both of Sir Vladimir's brothers. They had plenty of stories to tell and occasionally even a bit of booty to back it up. Yet be that as it may, knights returning from Hungary bought an *awful* lot of Baron Novacek's absolutely genuine Mongol war relics!

Chapter Twenty-eight

Construction was the big game on campus, as usual. Double-tracked rail lines were laid north to Plock and beyond, and west to a few miles from the Holy Roman Empire. A road east from Sandomierz was sent as far as the Bug River, and another went from the Vistula to the salt mines. I seemed to own those mines now, since none of the former owners could be found, and in such cases, as in modern times, the property goes to the state. Only now I was the state. The old works manager at the mines was gone, too. A pity. He had been rude to me once, and I was looking forward to firing the man.

The Reinforced Concrete Components Factory was completed, and soon it was providing structural sections for our ambitious building plans. To a certain extent the factory built itself, since at first it was nothing but a vast field with foundations, plumbing, and concrete molds built into the ground. As these molds were completed and prestressed concrete members were cast into them, the first use of these pieces was to put up the walls, pillars, and ceilings of the building itself!

Housing for the workers went up at the same time, and within a few weeks the first additional factory was erected, a major cement plant. A continuous casting operation for steel reinforcing rods went in next, and after that it all became routine. Plumbers followed the masons, and window glaziers came next with carpenters on their heels, putting in the doors.

The new R&D machine shop at Okoitz was built of brick to match the existing castle and the inn there, although the roof was of prestressed concrete. When I had sketched the shop, I had also sketched out the additional cloth factories to be built eventually, mostly to make sure that everything would fit well and look nice. Because of some snafu, these sketches were detailed and given by mistake to the construction captain sent to build the machine shop. So while he was there, he also put up both new cloth factories. Not that we had any machinery to put in them. It hadn't even been invented yet, let alone built!

I am personally convinced that much of this happened because the construction workers *liked* being stationed at Okoitz, living in the noble guest quarters and being available to all the cloth factory's eager young ladies, and thus they did what they could to prolong their stay. Oh, I couldn't prove it, but nonetheless I gave that company all the dirty jobs for the next two years.

I suppose I shouldn't have let three months go by between visits, but a man can't be everywhere.

We wouldn't be able to start building forts along the Vistula until the next year, but the three battalions in the eastern duchies were busy preparing for it, clearing the sites and putting in foundations, wells, and septic systems. Winters were spent logging, mostly to clear the land for farming. As the saying went, a Mongol can't hide in a potato field.

The first electrical generator worked, and the third one worked very well indeed. At first we couldn't find any graphite for the brushes, but the name told us the way the oldsters had done it. Brass brushes, and I mean something that looked like what you could clean a floor with, worked just fine. We got it working one week before a merchant came up from Hungary, riding right through a war zone without even noticing, with twenty-two mule loads of graphite.

The electric light bulb team was having less luck, and the tubing team was running into problems because the copper they had to work with was too brittle. I knew that this meant that our copper was too impure, for pure copper is very ductile.

This set of circumstances naturally got us involved with electrolytic refining, where pure copper is plated out of crudely smelted bars in a copper sulfate bath. This pure copper worked well in the new tube-drawing machines, although die wear was a big problem and a lot of work was still needed to improve our lubricants.

On the bottom of the refining tanks an annoying black sludge kept building up, and I wouldn't let them throw it away because of my pollution-control rules. The team took some of the sludge over to the alchemists to see if they could find any use for it. They could. The sludge was nineteen parts per gross silver and seven parts gold. The rest of it seemed to be some metal that the alchemists had never seen before, but they promised to work on it. We didn't have a copper mine at all. We had a gold mine that also produced silver and copper!

Very quickly, we were selling electrolytically refined copper exclusively and quietly buying back our old stuff whenever possible. The silver and gold in it were worth more than the copper! Admittedly, I had a surplus of silver and gold just then, but I wanted it nonetheless.

Mass producing electrical generators made them inexpensive enough to use them for other things, besides. Putting graphite electrodes on either side of a bath of salt water generates sodium hydroxide, which is useful in making good-quality soap and is a basic chemical starting point for thousands of other things. The process also generates hydrogen and chlorine, which can be combined immediately to produce hydrochloric acid, or the hydrogen can be burned as fuel and the chlorine can be used for bleach, in paper-making, for killing bacteria in water, or for killing things in general. The same chlorine that is found in all modern city water supplies makes a very effective war gas.

It occurred to me that I could get rid of the Teutonic Order without having to get any of my own men killed at all. It struck me that there was a certain justice about killing Germans with a gas chamber.

I worked on it and other things for the war.

Our school system now covered all the lands that Henryk and I held and went quite a way beyond them, to include virtually all the Polish-speaking people in the world. In addition, there were a few schools in Germany, Hungary, and the Russias, mostly training bilingual teachers for our next phase of expansion. The plan was to educate the children of the surrounding countries to be bilingual in Polish rather than to produce schoolbooks in every single different language, a daunting task since there were five thousand different languages in the world and we had grandiose dreams. Most foreign languages weren't all that standardized, anyway.

Teacher education was still a far cry from the standards of the twentieth century, but it had come a long way in the last ten years.

The school system was completely self-supporting, since each school also had a post office and a general store that sold everything that my factories made. The schools outside the range of the railroads and riverboats lost money because of the high cost of transportation, but those within it more than made up for this deficit. In fact, it sometimes proved difficult to keep the schools from showing a profit.

The army system of weights and measures was well on its way to becoming universal, at least within Poland. We never forced anyone to adopt it, but anything bought by the army was bought in our units. If a farmer wanted to sell us food, he had to sell it in terms of our pints and pounds and tons.

Our transportation system handled things in terms of carts that were two of our yards wide, six yards long, and a yard and a half high, the same size as our war carts. They had a weight limitation of twelve of our tons. We had a standard-sized case that was a yard wide, a half yard deep, and a half yard high. Six dozen of them fit neatly into a cart and incidentally made a comfortable seat for two. Upended, they were the right height for a workbench, and our cases sometimes did double duty as furniture. If you wanted to ship something that did not fit conveniently into a cart or a case or a standard barrel, shipping charges were much higher, and most of our users soon adopted our standards.

Our glass containers were rapidly being accepted, and we made them only in certain fixed sizes. Jars were made in sixth-pint, half-pint, pint, two-pint, six-pint, and twelve-pint sizes, and that was all, except that the larger sizes also came in a small-necked version. Each had dimensions such that it fit conveniently into our cases, and if you wanted to buy from us or ship something in glass containers, you had to use our system of weights and measures. This also made it easy for consumers to compare prices.

Our construction materials—bricks, boards, concrete blocks, glass, and so on—all came only in standard sizes. If you wanted to build a comfortable and inexpensive house, you had to use our system.

There was surprisingly little resistance to this gentle coercion, and one city council after another voted to adopt the army system of weights and measures.

We had a better than average harvest in 1241, and the granary in the Bledowska desert, which had been almost emptied in the spring and summer to provide seed and food, was now half-refilled. At this point virtually all the grains grown in Poland were of the modern sort, descended from the few grains I had brought here in seed packages ten years before.

Potatoes were now a major item in the diet, as were corn, tomatoes, squashes, peppers, and many of the other vegetables that had come originally from the New World. All the old vegetables were still on the menu, of course, and many people were starting to believe me when I said that a healthy diet was a varied diet. The children were growing up bigger and stronger than their parents, and the infant mortality rates were approaching modern levels, outside of the old cities at least. Someday we'd get decent water and sewer systems in them. Someday.

On the downside, tooth decay was on the rise, especially among the children of the wealthy, and I began to regret that I had been instrumental in increasing the amount of honey and refined sugar available. Now I had to sell people on the advantages of brushing regularly and restricting the use of my own products. Dentistry. I would have to do something about dentistry.

Decent eyeglasses were being made and sold. I got into it when one of Krystyana's kids turned out to be nearsighted and I started to need reading glasses.

The never-ending work of animal breeding was still going on, and to encourage it Count Lambert had started a system of county fairs, with prizes for the best laying hen, the best milk cow, and so forth. The prizewinning animals were auctioned off, often at fabulous prices. I expanded Lambert's system of both fairs and prize herds and usually bought the best available at each county fair, often at huge prices. My buyers had fairly strict guidelines.

A sore spot was that a wealthy merchant from Gniezno, who always boasted about the quality of his table, was observed to regularly purchase prize animals to slaughter and eat just so he could brag about how good his meat was. This bastard was even slaughtering prize milk cows for their meat! I wrote him, politely explaining the purpose of the prize herds and the improvements that had been wrought because of them, but he went right on doing what he had been doing. When I had him banned from the auctions, he had his subordinates do the buying for him. So I contacted my accountants and suggested that this was a man deserving of a beating. Even then they had to work him over twice before he stopped his annoying practice.

Another example of the creative use of accounting, I suppose.

My sheep herds were expanding yearly, and for the last seven years all the males in the main herds had been culled from the prize herd. Improvements in both the quality and the quantity of the wool were manifest, but since my best sheep could produce *three times* the wool of the average sheep, there was obviously a long way to go.

The same was true of the dairy herds, except that there the best was five times better than the average. Do you begin to see why I was so annoyed at having prize animals butchered?

Our best chickens were laying five eggs a week, and some breeders were starting to ignore ducks and geese. They simply couldn't compete with the chickens in either egg or meat production. I tried to reverse this trend, but I had also shown them how to compute profits on livestock, and they knew.

Pigs were getting shorter-legged, bigger-bodied, and faster-growing. They were still hairy, though. Not only did they have to live through the winter in unheated barns, there was a big market for pig bristle, a market that is satisfied by plastics in the modern world.

My wild aurochs herd was now up to three hundred animals that had outgrown all three of the valleys that I had them in. We were feeding them a lot of grain to keep them going and culling half the bulls each year, selecting for size and meat production if not for placid temperament. Something would have to be done before too long. I needed someplace to fence in a *big* area for them. I checked with the Banki brothers, and Wiktor pointed out an area north of where Sieciechow had been that might be suitable. At least there were very few trees there and almost no people at all left. I sent a surveying team out to look at the possibility of walling it in. We had found out the hard way long ago that ordinary fences didn't impress not very domesticated aurochs much. They walked right through them! It took a thick masonry wall, built wavy in the Thomas Jefferson fashion, four yards tall to do the job. *Huge animals!*

In October another milestone was reached. From that point on our profits from our commercial services—that is to say, transporting passengers and goods as a common carrier, the mails, and Baron Novacek's mercantile enterprises—were higher than our profits from selling the output from our entire factory system. Much of the reason for this was that we didn't pay tolls, while the other merchants did when they weren't using our railroads, plus our communication system let our buyers know quickly about prices here and there.

The conventional merchant would buy goods, pay heavily to take them somewhere, and hope to be able to sell them for more than they had cost him. Since this was an inefficient way of doing things, they generally tried to make profits of from one hundred percent to five hundred percent to make up for their occasional losses.

We usually had the goods sold before we bought them, and our transportation costs were very low. Everywhere our railroads and riverboats went, people got more for what they had to sell and paid less for what they wanted to buy, and we made a whopping profit doing it. Of course, the merchants howled about it, but their shouts of anguish impressed neither Duke Henryk nor me. And we were the law. A lot of merchants gave up and came to work for us.

We moved my household and the R&D teams to Okoitz in the fall, and the researchers were soon finding uses for the large empty buildings that were scheduled to one day be cloth factories. To quote Parkinson's law, "Work naturally expands to fill the time available to do it in," I would like to add one of my own:

"Building space is consumed in direct proportion to its availability, regardless of what, if anything, has to be done there."

There would be hell to pay when I threw the researchers out to make way for production machinery. I could see them kicking and screaming for days, trying to protect their precious little territories.

Nine R&D teams were set up to work on the various steps of producing cloth, and some progress was made fairly quickly. Some of the most complicated-sounding things worked right off, and some of the most trivial seemed to take forever. What worked on linen almost never worked on wool, and vice versa. You never can tell about research.

As time went on, an increasing number of researchers were foreigners, since a lot of bright kids throughout Europe were reading our magazines and wanted to get in on the action. We let them in—once they survived the Warrior's School.

Baron Piotr went to Okoitz with us both as a member of my household and as a floating member of all the R&D teams. Whenever the teams ran into math problems they couldn't handle, they took them to Piotr. He was good as a general idea man, too. He stayed head of the mapmaking group, but now he rarely went out into the field. This got the mapmakers moved to Okoitz as well, with their lithographic machines set up in the new cloth factories.

The ladies at the cloth factory gave the R&D people a warm and friendly welcome and soon got to referring to them as "the Wizards." The guys liked the title, and the name stuck.

Chapter Twenty-nine

FROM THE JOURNAL OF DUCHESS FRANCINE

Childbirth was not as bad as I had been led to fear it would be, but it was certainly painful enough. The midwife had convinced me that at thirty I was too old to be having a first child, and indeed she had me quite worried, but my son and I came through our ordeal alive and in good health.

I secured a wet nurse for him immediately so that my nipples would not become unlovely. Within a month, by fasting and exercise, I fit well into my old dresses, but more months passed before I felt myself shapely enough to keep my bargain with Friar Roman. In all, he did four nude paintings and gave two of them to me. I put them away, to look at in my old age, I suppose. Soon I could ride Anna without pain or danger, and a fast run through the countryside, often in the company of the delightful Sir Wladyclaw, became my greatest pleasure.

Conrad did not ask to come to the christening, and so I did not invite him. Baron Wojciech stood in his stead, and Duke Henryk became my son's godfather. I arranged it thus so that Henryk might be more inclined to see that my son one day got his patrimony. We named him Conrad to remind my husband of his duty to our child.

Yet in truth I did not not want to see my husband. My anger at the way he treated our child was such that years must go by before the hurt was eased. Instead, I put my mind to the problem of assuring my son's future. After much thought, it occurred to me that if I could do some service to Duke Henryk, some service greater in value than the three eastern duchies, he might be prevailed upon to see to it that my son was properly enlarged, as was his birthright.

Conrad and Henryk were preparing for an utterly stupid war with the Knights of the Cross, a war that would surely get them into a further war with the entire Holy Roman Empire if Emperor Frederick II ever stopped fighting with the Church long enough to get back to Germany.

War with the Crossmen will put them in the bad graces of the Church as well, for the Teutonic Order is legally a branch of the Roman Catholic Church. Already I am sure that the real reason why the Vatican was delaying granting Henryk the crown of Poland was this planned war against the Church!

Well, the death of Pope Gregory IX and the fact that Celestine

IV died after only two weeks in office haven't helped much, either. Rumors from Rome have it that the factions in the College of Cardinals are so bad that they may be years electing another Pope, and until they do, poor Henryk will have nothing to cover his head but a hat! Not that he's earned anything better.

The color change was on the trees before a suitable opportunity presented itself to ingratiate myself with Henryk. Sir Wladyclaw scouted the eastern frontiers with his men, and often they went well beyond the borders in search of our enemies. One day, he told me that Prince Daniel of both Ruthenias, our neighbors to the east, was vassal to the Mongols and not at all pleased by the situation.

It was an audacious thought, but I wondered if I could persuade this Prince Daniel to throw off the Mongol yoke and swear fealty to Duke Henryk. Surely the Mongols had learned to fear my husband, and word of his protection might be enough to keep Prince Daniel safe. If I could manage it, surely Henryk would be deeply in my debt. Perhaps enough for him to feel obligated to do right by my son. At least it was worth a try.

Sir Wladyclaw agreed to help me in this endeavor, for it was his task to protect our frontiers, and what better way to do that than to put a friend across the border in place of an enemy.

I left my baby with his wet nurse and one of my maids at Wawel Castle and rode out in the early dawn. I was accompanied by Sir Wladyclaw and a dozen of his men, three of whom spoke Ruthenian, and we rode secretly to the city of Halicz and the court of Prince Daniel.

It was a journey of two days, even for our Big People, for we dared not ride along the railroad tracks for fear that word of our mission would get back to Conrad. We had to travel by slow and winding forest trails where our mounts could not make their best speed. And once we got into Ruthenia, the trails were even worse than those in Poland.

Indeed, just before we stopped at Przemysl for the night, the trail was covered with a black grease that was at once sticky and slippery. The point man and his mount slipped in it and went down in a dreadful heap, though fortunately they were unhurt save for the grease and dirt. We all wondered at what this strange liquid was and who had dumped it there. It certainly made a mess by splashing on my dress and Anna's barding, and the knights accompanying me were spotted with it as well.

But of course, with their camouflaged armor and barding, a few spots made little difference.

I was delighted to find that there was a Pink Dragon Inn in Przemysl, and the innkeeper there, once he was made acquainted with who I was, was most helpful. He was easily sworn to secrecy, he made us most comfortable, and he was even able to show my maid the way of removing the spots, using lighter fluid. He said that everyone using that trail was afflicted with the greasy mud, for it had always been there.

We reached the court of Prince Daniel the next evening and were given by him a warm welcome. Sir Wladyclaw and I were placed next to the prince at the high table, and I was delighted to find that he spoke excellent Polish, as did many of his subjects.

Prince Daniel was a robust and fascinating man of about my husband's age, full of vigor yet with a sharp wit and a good sense of humor. He told us of many of his hunting experiences and of some of his adventures fighting the Mongols. Sir Wladyclaw was able to equal or even top a number of his tales, and I told of the Mongol attack on Three Walls, of how I manned a swivel gun, and of how Conrad's army slaughtered the Tartar horde at our feet.

"I've heard of these guns of yours, but of course I've never seen one," Prince Daniel said. I knew that he had been forced to send men with the Mongols against Poland but that he had not gone himself. Yet it was not politic for either of us to mention this unfortunate fact.

"Then you must come to Poland, my lord. My husband's factories make them by the thousand," I said.

"Now, that might be difficult, your grace, for you see, I am vassal to the khan and thus unfortunately an enemy to your people, at least in theory."

"How sad. I would much rather have you for a friend," I said, and smiled.

He smiled back and said, "You understand, of course, that

things are not always what one would wish." He looked about, afraid that he might have said too much in public. "But we must talk more of this later. For tonight, we must be soon abed, for we wake early tomorrow for a stag hunt. I am very proud of my kennels here. My huntsmen and I would be delighted if you and your fine gentlemen would join us."

"We would be honored, my lord."

That night I cautioned Sir Wladyclaw and his men to not take first honors in the hunt by getting to the kill first, as they could easily do riding on Big People. Some huntsmen are easily offended in this way.

Hunting with dogs is rarely done on my husband's lands, for neither he nor Count Lambert before him liked the sport. A pity, for it is exciting to chase the dogs across the fields, to race to the kill, and then to share the roast venison in the evening. Conrad is such a bore about some things.

One does not hunt deer in armor, as one does with wild boar or bison. Fortunately, Sir Wladyclaw and his men had their dress uniforms with them, and they made a bold show in their new red and white garb, so covered with gold. They were proud to tell how all their decorations had been made from booty taken from their enemies, and many Ruthenians looked on them with envy, for these people had to pay gold to the Mongols, whereas we had gotten it from them!

The hunt was beautiful, and the dogs tore the throats from two stags by dinnertime. After a light lunch brought out by the stewards, I found myself separated from the others and in the company of the prince. This was not at all by accident, for we had both been trying to arrange it so all morning.

"You ride so beautifully, your grace. Never before has a woman kept so close to me in the hunt. Why, I almost think that you could have beaten me to that last kill if you had really tried."

"I could only follow your example, my lord. But surely you have more interesting things to talk of than my poor horsemanship."

"Indeed I do, my lady. You spoke truth last night when you said that I should see your country. I would dearly like to do so, but I fear both spies in my court and the fact that I could be arrested in your land as a spy myself. Yet I have heard many wondrous things about what your great husband accomplished this spring on the battlefield and the wondrous machines that he has on the rivers and even in the air. It is true, isn't it? He can really fly?"

"He has men who can pilot machines that can fly, my lord, though he does not do it himself. He says that he's too old, though his last liege lord, Count Lambert, was older than Conrad and flew a great deal."

"I would like to see these things for myself. Can you think of a way that it could be arranged?"

"You must be of a size with one of the knights that accompanied me here, my lord. If you and my party and, say, four of your men were to ride out to one of your other estates, no one would think it strange. We could even let them think that we would be lovers if you thought that wise."

"That would be a delightful thing, my lady, did I not fear the fact that your husband is called the fiercest fighting man in all the world. And in truth, my wife is no simpering lily, either! I think it would be best if we kept our pleasant relationship platonic."

"I quite agree, my lord, with much the same regrets as yours," I said with a sad smile. "Well, then, once our party is out of sight and in some secluded place, you and your men could trade horses and costumes with five of mine. In the armor of a Radiant Warrior, no one would recognize you. Indeed, you could keep your visor down if you wished. In addition, these mounts we ride are very special. They can go like the wind, and no one in Poland would question a man who rode one. We could go there and be back in a week, my lord."

"You seem to have this well planned out, your grace."

"Indeed, I have thought long on it."

But then we had to join the others, for the master huntsman rode up carrying the droppings of a large stag in his hunting horn for the prince to examine.

And so it was that Prince Daniel got the grand tour of the battlefields, saw our aircraft, and rode on a steamboat. He was astounded almost as much by the Big People. I was able to show him some of my husband's factories, with their huge moving machines and white-hot spraying steel. We toured East Gate, and he found that starting the next spring, Conrad would be building a fortress like it every week. Yet what impressed him most was the three million Mongol heads he saw up on pikes.

"These are not all the Tartars we killed, you know," I said. "About half a million more were drowned in the Vistula when they tried to swim across, and they were so weighted down that most of them never did float up. There's still a fortune in booty lying for the taking on the bottom of the river."

"My God!"

So over a week passed before we were again in Ruthenia. Prince Daniel wanted to talk to his nobles and councilors, but I knew that he would throw off the Mongols and swear fealty to Duke Henryk could he but work out a suitable treaty with us.

He invited me back in a month, and of course I would be there. While back in Cracow, I sounded out Henryk, and he approved in principle of what I had done.

More importantly, I got his solemn written word, in his own hand and sealed, that if I was able to arrange a suitable treaty, my son would be given his rightful inheritance, or one even more valuable. Also, Henryk agreed that it would be best if Conrad did not know about my role in these affairs or about our agreement as well.

Again we went to Ruthenia, and again we brought back Prince Daniel incognito, but this time to meet with Duke Henryk. I introduced the two leaders, and they soon were engaged in animated conversation. I wisely remained silent, for men do not like women to intrude on what they consider "man's talk," even when it is we women who make all the arrangements, set the stage, and even determine what is to be said.

A formal treaty was eventually signed by all interested parties, including my husband, and my son had regained his birthright!

In the winter, when all had been finalized and troops had been sent to Ruthenia to aid in its defense, I met again with Duke Henryk, who gave me a privy letter that confirmed our original agreement.

"Francine, that was a fine job you did with Prince Daniel. Because of you, an enemy has been turned into a friend, Poland now has a buffer state between herself and the Tartars, and I have gained a doubling of my territory, if not my income. It is going to take us a few years to absorb all of this, but in a year or two I am minded to send you north to talk to Prince Swientopelk so that you can talk him into giving us his duchies of East and West Pomerania!"

Chapter Thirty

FROM THE DIARY OF CONRAD STARGARD

My own personal life remained pleasantly tranquil, even though, or perhaps because of the fact that, Francine stayed away. I hadn't even seen my son by her, but I was not about to force her into coming home just so she could make me miserable. She stayed in the east, and I spent most of my time in the south. When I went to Cracow to see my confessor, Bishop Ignacy, she was always elsewhere. Twice I went to Sandomierz and Plock to check on things, but she wasn't there at the time. Even when Duke Henryk and I hit twelve cities, one on each day of the twelve days of Christmas, she managed to be somewhere else. All that I could figure was that she had an efficient spy system.

Cilicia, on the other hand, remained all sweetness and light. She continued teaching dancing, mostly as a hobby, I think, and continued to manage her string of dance studios at a considerable profit, though God knows we didn't need the money. But her real interest was now in our four children and in the other three dozen or so kids in the household.

These weren't all mine, not by any means. At least a dozen of them were orphans left over from the Mongol invasion. There were some where we knew the mother and nobody was exactly sure about the father, but nobody much cared. When in doubt, I was always happy to confess to just about anything at a baptism. I'd never let a kid be hurt over a little thing like pride, even when the mother wasn't up to my usual standards.

Piotr and Krystyana were still in the household with their six kids, and others came and went as the need and the inclination required. When it came to my household, I ran a very loose ship, and I liked it that way. About my only rules were that kids had to stay out of my office and nobody could permanently enter my household without my invitation. Well, there were some kids who sort of temporarily attached themselves to us for years, but what the heck. As a general thing, a pleasantly disorganized chaos reigned, and any time I needed rejuvenation I had only to sit down on one of the couches in the living room, and there were a couple of kids on my lap and generally a pretty girl under each arm. A good life.

During our Christmas tour Henryk mentioned an offer that he'd gotten that he didn't want to refuse. The Russian principalities to our east were Volhynia and Halicz Ruthenia, and they had a combined area that was at least as large as that of Poland, if not larger, although because of the Mongols, they no longer had anything like our population. They were Russian to the extent that the people there were mostly Greek Orthodox Christians, and their political and social ties were more with the east than with the west.

"Russia" in the modern sense, with its huge uncaring bureaucracy and its brutal central control, would probably have been better called the Muscovite Empire. Politically, it is a Johnny-come-lately, not one of the ancient nations of eastern Europe. It simply didn't exist in the thirteenth century. Moscow was now a small backwater village.

To the north, there is a major city-state called the Republic of Novgorod, which is run by an oligarchy of wealthy merchants, about the way that Venice is in Italy.

In the south, there is a Russian people who would one day

be called Ukrainians and who consider their capital to be Kiev, even though Kiev had been massacred by the Mongols a few years ago and still was almost absolutely empty. Before that time it had been a fairly ordinary kingdom, with nothing particularly offensive about it.

In addition to these two large states, there were a dozen or so minor duchies and principalities scattered around the east, all of whom, like their big brothers, were either paying tribute to the Mongols or had been depopulated by them, or sometimes both. Certainly there was nothing about the Russias of the thirteenth century that you could hate.

The prince of both of these principalities of Volhynia and Halicz Ruthenia was a man named Daniel, and he had come to Duke Henryk with an interesting proposal. Prince Daniel offered to swear fealty to Henryk, to become a Roman Catholic, and to encourage his people to do so as well. He would even pay what taxes he could, but in return he needed protection from the Mongols. Henryk wanted to know if we could guarantee that protection.

Well, I had been planning to fight the Mongols again anyway, and having more allies hardly ever hurt anybody. From a strictly practical standpoint, we didn't need any more land at all. We were currently seriously overextended, trying to digest what we already had. This was one giant bite more. Yet I agreed with Henryk. It was too good an opportunity to miss, although I couldn't help wishing that it had come along five or ten years later.

I said fine, I could spare Daniel three of our nine-thousand-man battalions of regulars when they graduated in the late spring, as well as my force of scouts mounted on Big People, all as a permanent force there. I could give him some air cover, and I could get an additional fifteen battalions to him in ten days if there was another invasion, but I needed some things in return from Daniel.

I needed land along the Bug and the San rivers for the construction of forts against the Mongols. A five-mile-wide strip on both sides of each river was to become army property.

I wanted some land granted to me near the town of Przemysl, because I happened to know that there was an oil field there.

In my time, the first oil wells in the world had been drilled in these fields, and that told me that it couldn't have been a difficult drilling job. I needed that oil as a lubricant, for kerosene lamps, and for aircraft fuel. The wood alcohol we were using wasn't all that energetic on a per-pound basis.

In addition, I wanted the same rights to buy land in the east that I had in western Poland, and I wanted the same rights to transport goods without paying tolls. I wanted the Polish legal system, once it was organized, to be put in effect in Ruthenia the same as it was in the rest of Poland. Ruthenia was to become a permanent part of Poland, individual Ruthenians would have the right to join the Christian army, and under no circumstances was I to be taxed by anyone.

Henryk was agreeable to my demands, said he'd keep me posted, and sent an ambassador to Daniel to finalize the deal.

We kept busy working all through the winter, for although the men in the army were all wealthy now, we never slacked off on the twelve-hour workday or the six-day workweek, one of which, on the average, was always spent in military training. I had no trouble enforcing this, since good men like to work when they know that they are working on something important.

The deal with Prince Daniel didn't work out exactly as planned. He wouldn't go along with combining the legal systems, saying that his people had different customs than ours did. Instead of getting land and drilling rights near Przemysl, I got the whole city and much of the surrounding area. It seems that this land had once been part of Poland and the people there were still ethnically Polish rather than Russian, so Daniel gave the land back to us, or rather to me as Duke of Little Poland.

The right of the Christian army to travel duty-free across the principalities, even when we were engaged in commercial pursuits, became the Right of Transit. The right of the army to do recruiting was enlarged to the traditional Polish Right of Departure. Every man, except for convicted criminals, could leave his present job or condition without anybody's permission. And the right of the army to buy land and then not pay taxes on it became the Right of Purchase.

This meant that the political body we were forming would be more of a federation than a union, but I could live with it. I signed the treaty Henryk and Daniel had formalized.

As soon as the treaty was signed, still in the winter, a volunteer battalion of active reservists with regular army officers was called up to stand guard in the new territories until late fall, mostly to demonstrate good faith to Prince Daniel. There were a lot more volunteers than places available, and the officers in charge could pick the best. Mostly, the troops spent their time putting in a rail line along the west bank of the River Bug and another up the San, but they were ready if the Mongols wanted to start trouble. In a few months three battalions of regulars who would be graduating from the Warrior's School would go east to back up the reservists and keep my word to Daniel.

I'd kept the boys at Eagle Nest posted on the need for a longer-range observation plane to patrol the borders of Ruthenia and let Daniel know that we were doing our part. Aircraft engines were now sufficiently dependable that a second one was an asset rather than a liability. They came up with a big (for us) two-engine job that could stay up for five hours and had a range of six gross miles. An interesting plane: The pilot lay prone and looked mainly downward, just what was needed for an observation plane when the enemy had nothing in the sky. This also made for a very small frontal area. It was our first plane that could take off without the aid of a catapult, and it even boasted retractable landing gear. The boys wanted to call it the *Eagle*, but I wouldn't let them do it. I said that the eagle was the person flying it, and the name stuck. From then on, our air force was known as the Eagles.

Duke Henryk sent me a copy of his proposed code of laws with a note stressing that it was only a rough draft and that he was asking for comments from many others besides myself. There was a criminal code with clearly defined penalties for various clearly defined crimes and a civil code with long sections on inheritance, land use and ownership, and contracts. I spent a few days going over it and wrote him a lengthy commentary. This was the sort of thing where getting it done right was far more important than getting it done quickly. Any errors would be very expensive for someone. In many cases it was literally a matter of life and death.

My main objection to Henryk's laws was in the field of punishments. He called for the traditional medieval corporal punishments, such as whipping, branding, and beheading. In the twentieth century, the western governments punish people with use fines and various terms of incarceration. The eastern governments have a different theory, one that I can't help but agree with. It is felt that a criminal is one who has caused damage to society and who is therefore in debt to society for the damage that he has done. This debt must be worked off, normally with a term of hard manual labor. There are several advantages to this theory. One is that the criminal is often a mentally ill person, and hard work is often very good therapy. Another is that society benefits from the work that is done rather than being harmed again in feeding and guarding the criminal, as in the western system. It took work, but I finally talked Henryk into starting a prison coal mine and using work rather than whippings.

By spring it was obvious that the killing inflation I had so feared wasn't going to happen. Most of the surplus cash either stayed in my bank drawing interest or, rather "damages," to get around the Church's strange thoughts on usury or was spent on things like buying farmland from me. Then *I* sat on the money, and things smoothed out.

As soon as the snows melted, work was started on a second Reinforced Concrete Components Factory, this one built next to the new Riverboat Assembly Building and set up to build parts for "snowflake" forts like the one at East Gate. In a little over a month we started on the first of several thousand fortified army towns.

There wasn't any problem finding the oil fields. The stuff was running out of the ground! We didn't do any drilling at all at first but simply channeled it into some storage tanks. Why it hadn't caught fire sometime in the past was beyond me.

At East Gate we started production on a new sort of riverboat. It consisted of nothing but an engine and some crew's quarters on the back of a long, low barge. Inside the thing were two gross copper oil drums, piped together to haul crude oil from the fields at Przemysl. On the way up it was designed to carry deck cargo, such as concrete structural members. And that was all. No guns, no Halmans, and no passengers. Strictly a civilian cargo vessel. An oil refinery was started at East Gate as well.

Finally, with spring planting done, it was time to clean the Teutonic Knights out of Mazovia. In my time, despite the fact that they were theoretically a branch of the Church, they had spent the winter of 1242 attacking the Christian Republic of Novgorod and had been beaten by Alexander Nevski in the famous Battle on the Ice. Well, Alex was spared both the trouble and the fame in this world. Here, the Crossmen had spent the winter recruiting more fighters and reinforcing their city-castle of Turon, which means "thorn," appropriately enough.

They had seen what we could do in a field battle but figured that they could stand siege against us. Nice. I'd been counting on that.

My people were all looking forward to the war, for the Crossmen never had worried about making themselves popular. They still made a practice of butchering entire villages and sparing only the adolescent children who brought good prices on the Moslem slave blocks. When I suggested that a single battalion would suffice to handle the Knights of the Cross, I nearly had a mutiny on my hands. Everybody wanted to go!

I didn't want to upset our production schedules, so I forbade the industrial workers to attend. They screamed, bitched, and cried, but I wouldn't back off. There were plenty of men working their farms, and the war would take place during the slack period between spring planting and the first hay harvest. Even so, there were too many volunteers, and I finally had Baron Vladimir set up a competition such that only the best fighters from each unit in the active reserves were allowed the privilege of going and risking their lives. It's strange the things some men will do for prestige.

Chapter Thirty-one

I took three battalions of reservists to the war, along with three of regulars, and made Baron Vladimir hetman in charge of all of them. This was far more troops than was required, but the pressure on me to let everybody go was pretty strong. Captains and barons were coming up with the damnedest reasons why it was necessary for them to participate even after I said that any booty taken would go first to defray expenses and that the rest would be divided out among the entire army. They didn't care. They still kept calling in old favors and trying to go.

Since it wasn't really going to be much of a fight, I took my four maidservants along, with plenty of creature comforts in a big rail car. Cilicia insisted on coming, too, and brought with her a troop of over fifty dancers and a dozen musicians. She knew of Duke Henryk's plans to invite many foreign observers, and she figured that they would want entertainment.

Over her fifty-megaton protests, Krystyana was left home to take care of the kids. Piotr wasn't going, and, well, somebody had to do it.

We had riverboats enough on the Vistula to carry two battalions with their war carts, but I wasn't about to commit more than a quarter of them to the war, not when they were making such profits providing civil transportation! Also, the boats were needed to transport construction materials for our extensive building program. Anyway, if the troops wanted to go that badly, let them walk!

And walk they did, nonstop in the army fashion, all the way to Plock and beyond to the edge of Crossman territory, where the railroads stopped. From there they were ferried downstream to Turon, where we found the city packed with German knights and the gates closed to us.

At first there was no opposition at all. A platoon of scouts scoured the countryside and found nothing but peaceful peasants, whom we left alone. Turon had no suburbs, being a military installation, so we had a clear field of fire all around the walls. We surrounded the city, dug fortifications, and set up housekeeping. Then we waited two days for Duke Henryk to arrive.

You see, Henryk was planning to make as much political hay out of this battle as possible, and he wanted as many foreign observers around as he could get. On the southwest side of the Vistula, across from Turon, we built a good-sized tent city for them, set up a river-crossing boat, and assigned two companies of complaining warriors to guard the place and cook for our guests. The numbers of delegates arriving surprised even Henryk. Poland was big in the news, especially since our magazines were still the only newspapers. Many people wanted to see what we were doing for themselves.

Duke Henryk arrived on schedule with his two young sons, Henryk III, a fine boy of thirteen, and Boleslaw, who was going bald at the age of eighteen, as well as their mother on a rare outing from her estate. But his dozens of delegations of observers straggled in, and another week went by before they had all gotten there.

Rather than let my warriors stand idle, I had half of our forces out preparing the beds for railroads while we waited, and construction companies were confidently extending the railroads downstream along the Vistula while the "war" was going on.

The tent city soon became a regular international village, with six separate groups coming from various states in the Holy Roman Empire, two from various factions in Bohemia, three from Hungary, two from Pomerania, and three from the various Danish principalities. Twenty men were sent up from Tsar Ivan Asen II of the Bulgarian Empire. A group arrived from France, personal emissaries from Louis IX, and even some Castilians from Spain.

There were delegations from all the tribes of the Pruthenians: Sambians, Natanoians, Warmians, Pogesanians, Pomeranians, Haitians, Galindians, and Skalovians. The Lithuanians came, headed by Prince Mendog, and the Lusatians were there, too. There was a delegation from Novgorod, headed by none other than Alexander Nevski, who doesn't look at all like he did in the movie. Furthermore, he was a noble prince, not a stalwart yeoman, as the old Russian motion picture would have it!

We even got a Welshman, a Scotsman, and an Irishman.

Prince Daniel was there with two groups from the Ruthenias, and Prince Swientopelk of Pomerania showed up in person. This surprised certain people, because it was claimed by some that he had engineered the assassinations of two Polish dukes. Duke Boleslaw the Pious and Duke Przemysl came, both of Great Poland and subordinate to Henryk, as did Duke Casimir of Kujawy, a small, still independent Polish duchy.

The Church was well represented by Bishop Ignacy of Cracow, plus the Polish bishops of Plock, Poznan, Wroclaw, Lubusz, Wloclawek, and Kamien, and the Archbishop of Gniezno, along with hundreds of minor clerics. Ignacy had even brought a printing press with him and was running off a four-page daily newspaper. The world's first!

In short, everybody who was anybody in eastern Europe, and most of the rest of Christendom besides, was there or was represented, except for the Mongols. No, let me take that back. The handless Mongol ambassador I had given to Henryk was there as well, in a steel cage with a double door like an air lock. Henryk wasn't taking any chances with him.

There were so many delegates that we had to enlarge their camp twice, stripping tents from my troops and making the warriors double up. Four more unhappy companies were added to guard and cook for them.

The foreigners wandered around everywhere, inspecting the steamboats and the artillery, talking to the troops, and even visiting the Teutonic Knights, who were still holed up in their city.

While everyone was there for the nominal purpose of watching a battle, Henryk had countless meetings called every day, and every night was spent in feasting, drinking, and politicking. Cilicia's dancers were the big hit of the event, and two temporary Pink Dragon Inns were running on a standing-room-only basis. Baths and massage parlors were running at all hours of the day and night.

Henryk bought two dozen of my surplus aurochs bulls, and though not fully grown, they dressed out at over a ton of meat each. They took three days to roast whole over an open fire, but he served one up each day, and that was but a single item on a large menu. The beer, wine, and mead vendors were making a fortune! And this despite the fact that many delegations were providing potables free.

My troops were coming over the river to join this festival at every possible excuse, of course. It became a major headache for Hetman Vladimir to see that Turon remained properly surrounded. Yet the Crossmen never poked their heads out of their walls. At least not that we heard of, anyway. With so many foreigners coming and going from Turon, it was likely that there were Crossman spies among us. Not that it mattered.

While all this was going on, I had the six siege cannons I'd had made hauled up from their special barges and located out of crossbow range of the city-fortress of Turon, pointing at the two main gates, where they could be seen by the delegates. They each had a bore of half a yard and were six yards long. They were low-tech muzzle-loaders, since I wasn't in any hurry about rate of fire and didn't plan to ever need them again after this battle. But they fired a round iron ball that weighed over half a ton, and I didn't imagine that any brick city wall could stand up to them for long.

Then six huge mortars arrived, each with a bore of one yard and a four-yard-long tube. They were set up in plain view of the delegate camp, as close to Turon's walls as we dared put them. A system of racks and hoists allowed them to be loaded quickly, for here I needed a high rate of fire. The men tending these monsters wore a uniform that consisted of black boots, a black pair of pants, and a black hood, which when wet could double as a gas mask. They swaggered around stripped to the waist, a bit of showmanship on my part. Mostly, I wanted the identity of these picked men to be kept a secret.

Their ammunition was placed along the river embankment and constantly guarded. If one of these rounds should leak, it was the duty of the black guards to roll it into the Vistula, for cool water can absorb large quantities of chlorine, and the river's turbulence would soon dilute the poison to a safe level.

And still the warriors waited, for Henryk wanted the conference to continue a while longer. He made a point of introducing me to everyone, of course, and I sat in on many of the meetings, but in truth, such things bore me. The only interesting thing to me was that almost all the visitors spoke Polish, mostly from reading our magazines. My plan to make Polish a world language was working!

And with everybody important at the camp, it was inevitable for my wife to come, too, since she loves the smell of political power. She'd been there a week before I ran into her as I was on my way to yet another meeting, this one on fixing a date for the proposed All Christendom Great Hunt chaired by Sir Miesko.

"Well," I said, trying to be friendly. "There really is a Duchess Francine. Have you been well?"

"Yes, your grace." She looked at me strangely, coldly.

"And you have to speak so formally to your own husband?"

"It seemed fitting, Conrad."

"So. And my son. He too is well?" I tried to smile, but it didn't come off.

"Yes. He's in good hands in Cracow."

"I suppose that you were right in not taking him into what is, after all, a war zone. I'd like to see him someday."

"Of course, my husband. You can see him at any time."

"And you. Will I be seeing you again? Will you be coming home, as most wives do?"

"Yes, I'm sure I will, in time."

"In time. Well. When that time comes, be sure and let me know. There will always be a place for you."

"Thank you, my husband," she said stiffly.

"You must keep in closer touch, then."

"Yes, my husband."

I turned and left. She was as cold as a killing frost and just as unsympathetic. Whatever had happened to the warm, loving woman I had married? Just because I didn't want to be a king, that didn't mean that I no longer wanted to be a husband! Yet she was still a beautiful woman for all her stone-cold features and stone-rigid bearing. I felt the old urges despite the fact that I had brought my servants to the war.

Days later I went to see Bishop Ignacy, and after confession I asked, as usual, about the Church's inquisition concerning me.

"Oh, I'm afraid that there won't be anything happening on that for some time, Conrad. You see, the College of Cardinals is deadlocked on the selection of the next Pope, and nothing much will happen until such time as they resolve their differences. It could be quite a while from what I hear."

"So the whole Catholic Church stops until they get around to doing something, Father?"

"Not in the least! People are being christened and married and buried. Souls are still being saved. The only difference is that nothing new will happen. No high offices will be filled, and no changes will take place until we have a new pontiff. You know, I've never understood your anxiety to get this matter of your inquisition finished, Conrad. After all, if they decide that you are an instrument of God and a saint, well, you cannot be canonized until after your death, anyway, so why hurry? And in the unlikely event that they decide that you are an instrument of the devil and should be burned at the stake, why, isn't it better to put off that unhappy event as long as possible? Surely there is nothing of the suicide about you!"

"I'd just like to have the thing settled, to not have it hanging over my head, Father."

"Very little in this life is ever settled, my son. It's like that story you once told me about the little people. 'The road goes ever on.' One can only live life. Soon enough God will decide it is time for it to be 'settled.'"

"I suppose so, Father. To change the subject, have you been to see the Crossmen?"

"No, but many other churchmen have. After all, you have vowed to kill them all, and you have a reputation for carrying out your vows with a vengeance."

"Oh, they'll all die, all right, as soon as Henryk has milked all he can out of this conference."

"It is remarkable how well you two dukes are getting along, how well your abilities complement each other."

"He takes care of the law and the politics, and I handle the army and the factories. Neither one of us wants the other's job. It's a good partnership, Father, and I think the world will profit by it. But back to the Crossmen. I'm going to kill them, so don't try again to talk me out of it. You already know my reasons, and I've heard all of your objections. But I don't want any innocent bystanders killed with them. I still have nightmares about the Polish slave girls that we killed when we raided the Mongol camp at night, or even worse, the Polish peasants we slaughtered when they were forced to work those Mongol catapults. I want to know that there is no one in Turon except members of the Teutonic Order."

"But surely they have had plenty of time to get out."

"Well, maybe they can't get out, or maybe they think the Crossmen will win, or maybe they think this will be an ordinary battle where plenty of people survive. You've seen those big guns I've had made. Do you think that one of those half-ton balls will stop and see what uniform they're wearing before it smashes everyone before it?"

"If you wish, I will visit Turon and examine it. Mind you, I won't do any spying for you. We've talked over my opposition to this war often enough. But I will do what I can to prevent injury to the innocent."

"Good, Father, because I want you to convey an offer to the Crossmen for me. I will pay them one thousand pence in army currency, silver or gold, as they desire, for every noncombatant that comes out of the city on the day before the battle. I'll pay an additional one hundred pence to each person as they leave. I'll even pay the Crossmen one hundred pence for every domestic animal, as well, and guarantee that all these people and beasts will be fed and housed well at my own expense until the issue is settled. If you wish, I will pay the Church for their upkeep, and you can see to it that it is properly done."

"That is a generous offer, Conrad."

"I'm just trying to save my soul, Father. Those siege cannons aren't the most deadly weapons that I have. Anyway, I'll be getting most of it back as booty once I win the battle."

"Very well, Conrad, I'll see what I can do, and I'll get the archbishop involved in this as well. However, I notice that you are again calling your weapons of war 'canons.' A canon is a law of the Church, and while your strange use of the term was funny at first, the joke has gone stale. I want you to stop it."

"Yes, Father."

"On another matter, you have not been living with your wife. This is not good. You were joined together by God, after all."

"Father, she is still angry because I did not make her the Queen of Poland. I didn't do that and I won't do that, because I don't want to be the king. Henryk is far better qualified than I am, and anybody sane can see it! I've asked her to come back and told her that there will always be a place for her. What more can I do?"

"You could be a bit more vigorous in your invitation, my son."

"You're saying that I should use force?"

"The Church allows it, within reason."

"The Church allows it, but God doesn't demand it! I'm not going to beat her or shackle her to the kitchen stove. Good men didn't do that sort of thing in my time."

"Well, think on it, my son. Meanwhile, I shall see what can be done with the Teutonic Knights."

The bishop returned to me the next day with word that the Crossmen had accepted my offer and he had worked out with them a system where there wouldn't be much cheating. They also offered me their war-horses on the same terms at a thousand pence a head, with the understanding that they could get them back at any time by repaying the money should the battle prove

to be protracted. I went along with that. There was no point killing dumb animals, I'd be getting the money back, and we could
probably train most of those chargers to pull railroad cars. From
the Crossmen's point of view, the Church would be taking care of
their horses at my expense until they were needed, but let them
have their dreams.

The time was dragging slowly, and the troops were getting
antsy. Finally, I talked to my partner about it.

"Henryk, I don't want to rush you, but it's been more than
three weeks now. Do you realize that I am paying the salaries
of over fifty thousand men while many of them sit idle every
day?"

"Yes, Conrad, and I well know how you hate waste. But this is
not time wasted. Prince Swientopelk is starting to come around.
The Baltic seacoast could be ours! What would you think of having not one but *two* seaports, one at the mouth of the Vistula
and one at the Odra?"

"It would be fine, and I've often dreamed of building oceangoing steamships. We could buy and sell abroad, explore the
world, and spread the faith. We could even find coffee and
rubber! But we could not start doing it for years yet. We
have commitments that will take us years to fulfill. We are
too overextended now to even consider further expansion at
this time. You know that."

"But the iron is hot now, Conrad, and it might grow cold in
five years. We need not promise to do much until then. Just some
little show of support might be enough. Your reputation alone
could do it. Have I ever told you that putting those Mongol heads
up on pikes was a stroke of genius?"

"Not in so many words, and thank you. But what can I tell
my men? When can we start the battle?"

"A week, Conrad. Can you give me another week?"

"A week. Very well, I'll hold them back until then. But a week
from this morning I'm opening fire!"

Chapter Thirty-two

The next week was simultaneously hectic and boring. A few dozen people tried to put their mark on history by playing the peacemaker. They ran back and forth between me and the Crossmen and Henryk, carrying absurd peace offers. None of us took these fools seriously, but none of us wished to appear to be unreasonable warmongers, either. My best offer to them was that if the Crossmen would go back to the Holy Land, where they'd started from, and never come back, I'd call the whole thing off, let them march out with their weapons and treasure, and let them all live, besides. Their best offer to me was less polite.

Bishop Ignacy did a good job getting the noncombatants out of Turon. There were over 500 of them, servants, stable boys, and prostitutes, mostly. He also got us 1,900 horses, all of them in very good shape. It turned out that the Crossmen had sent most of their chargers away before we got there and had kept only the best, because of a lack of hay to feed all of them during a protracted siege. There were a remarkable number of dogs, cats, and caged birds that I paid for, but I drew the line at "pet" rats and mice. They figured that it had been worth a try.

At just before noon on the scheduled day we opened up on them with our swivel guns, shooting just enough to teach them to keep under cover. Half our guns were available for targets of opportunity, but each one of the other half had its own assigned target: a window, a doorway, a space between two merlons on the wall. They were bore-sighted and packed between sandbags, and in the course of the day, by trial and error, they got their targets down pat. This was to teach the Crossmen the art of not being seen. All through the next night the sandbagged guns fired occasionally at random, teaching the same lesson at night: Stay down! The few slit windows in the outer walls were soon plugged up tight with timbers by the defenders, nicely sealing the entire structure, which was the purpose of the exercise. This stopped the bullets, because this year we were firing cartridges with far less gunpowder than last year's. Six inches of pine could stop our rounds cold. I didn't want to put holes in anything. Quite the opposite.

The random firing continued the next day, except when the gunners actually had a target, an increasingly rare event. Around noon we took a few trial shots with the mortars, using dummy rounds loaded with sand. They did very little damage, but they let us know that our aim was good enough. Small-arms fire continued into the second night, and I was sure that by then the garrison was very low on sleep. An hour before midnight the small-arms fire slackened off.

It was a sultry night and almost completely calm. It would work tonight if it was going to work at all. I had the small-arms fire stop completely and allowed the Crossmen a quarter hour to get to sleep.

Then we opened up with the mortars, firing as fast as their crews could load them, one round a minute each. This continued for only twelve minutes and then stopped. They were out of ammunition, which relieved me. Having that stuff sit around for weeks in the sun and in public made me nervous.

The mortar rounds were a yard in diameter and two yards high. They were made of a thin iron shell with a blown-in glass lining. When the shell struck, the glass broke and the pressurized liquid chlorine inside was released. If the lining broke in the course of being fired, it didn't matter, for the metal shell kept it together long enough to get the poison into the sleeping city.

The delegates were encouraged to watch the shelling, and when it was over, I told them that I thought that we had just won the battle. When they asked me how that was possible, I told them that wars were ugly things and it was best to get them over as soon as possible. Then I suggested that they all go to sleep. Nothing else should happen until morning.

The army troops couldn't sleep, however. At first they stood to their guns with slow flares lit in front of them in case the Crossmen came pouring out of the city. Then they were all standing on top of their war carts in case something far more deadly than enemy troops came pouring out. More of the deadly gas might have leaked out than I had calculated. Chlorine is heavy stuff, almost three times heavier than air. I figured that it should fill the city up to the top of the walls, like soup in a bowl, and hug the ground until it was absorbed by the dew.

The warriors heard a few shouts and screams from the Crossmen, but soon the city was quiet. They had a boring night, but I hadn't told them to come.

I was still across the river, safe from the chlorine. I went back to my big railroad car to sleep. At the doorway of my car a foreign knight waited, standing in the yellow torchlight.

He was dressed in old-fashioned chain mail, though it looked to be washed with gold. There was quite a bit of solid gold on his outfit as well. And there was something very familiar about the man.

"What can I do for you?" I asked.

"I think it is time that we had a talk," he said in Polish but with a strong *American English accent!*

He was identical to the man I had seen killed on the battlefield a year ago, except he had all his hair. He had to be somehow connected to the time machine that had brought me here over ten years earlier.

"Yes," I said. "I would like that. Won't you come in?"

"Thank you," he said, entering and nodding to my servants. "Perhaps it would be best if you dismissed your people."

"Very well." I motioned them all out, and they obeyed.

"Good. I think *here* would be best." He went to my stand-up clothes closet, opened the door, and walked through. The closet was standing along the wall of the car, and there was nothing on the other side of it. In fact, I had just walked past that wall, and I *knew* that nothing had been set up on the other side of it. Yet when I looked into the closet, there was a modern living room in there! It had wall-to-wall carpeting, electric lights, and comfortable-looking leather furniture. There was even a cheerful fire going in a fieldstone fireplace. This was impossible!

I went to the side of the closet, moved it away from the wall, and looked behind it. The back of the closet was solid, and the railroad car didn't have a hole in it. Yet from the front, you could see ten yards into it!

But I wanted to get some answers out of this man, and I dared not turn coward now. I took a deep breath and stepped in. The door closed behind me with a solid click.

"Have a seat, cousin," he said in English. "Surely you recognize me. I'm your rich American relative, Tom Kolczykrenski. I put you through college, remember?"

I sat. "Yes, I remember now, but what are you doing here? And what is *here* doing here?" I said in my rusty English.

"This room, you mean? Well, you must understand that when you control time, you control space as well. They're really all part of the same thing, you know."

"No, I don't know."

"Then you will soon," he said. A very beautiful young woman came into the room completely naked, carrying a tray with drinks on it. "Have a martini. I'll bet it's been years since you had an olive."

"Thank you." For ten years a thousand questions had been racking my brain, but at the moment I couldn't think of a single one. "What can I do for you, Tom?"

"Well, it's not what you can do for me but what I can do for you that matters here. You see, in a way it's partly my fault that you were dumped into this barbaric century, and now finally I can do something about it."

The girl left the room, and my eyes followed her.

"Yes, Conrad, my tastes are pretty much like your own. But she's not what we should be talking about. Do you want to ask questions, or should I just tell you about what happened?"

"How about if you talk, and I'll ask questions as they come up."

"Good enough. More years ago than I like to think about, working with two partners, I invented a time machine. That's how we got rich in the first place, you know, playing the stock market with next week's *Wall Street Journal* in our hands. After a while, subjectively, we all grew up a bit, and we each started working on our own projects. I spent my time building a fine, rational civilization in the distant past, where it wouldn't upset our present at all, and Jim did something similar, but with a different slant on things, being a psychologist.

"But Ian's main interest was history, and he runs something called the Historical Corps, which is writing the definitive history of mankind. The Red Gate Inn that you got drunk in so many years ago was one of Ian's installations. He usually places inns over his time transporters, since strangers aren't much noticed around one. It was some of his people that screwed up, with your drunken help. Instead of finding the rest room, you managed to go down one flight of steps too many and fell asleep in a time transporter. You went through a series of open doors that never should have been open, and even if they had been, the site director should have noticed it on his readouts. But screwups happen, and nobody noticed you at all. More snafu happened at the thirteenth-century end of the line, and you weren't seen sneaking out of the inn."

"What happened to the people who screwed up and sent me here?"

"Oh, they were punished, never fear. Punished more than they deserved, actually. We seem to have lost them a few million years ago in Africa. The search goes on, though."

"So it was all an accident? But if you have time travel, why couldn't you go back to the time I came out of the inn and put me back into the time machine?"

"Because of causality. You were not noticed until I went to observe the Polish defeat at the Battle of Chmielnick. I didn't see you until you had been in this century for almost ten years! I saw you with what was, for this time, advanced technology. That was a fact, and you can't change established facts, or so we thought at the time, anyway."

"At the time?"

"Standard English is not well suited to talking about time

travel. We use a few extra tenses to cover it all properly, but there isn't any point in teaching you a new language right now. Suffice it to say that we had been operating for eight hundred subjective years on certain principles that always worked. That's eight hundred years of my own life, as I lived it. Our medical people are quite advanced, you see. Anyway, we *knew* that you couldn't change the time stream. We *knew* that time was a single, linear continuum and that nothing we could do could possibly change it. Furthermore, from the very beginning, we were very careful not to change things. We didn't want to play God, after all. My partners and I are pretty staunch individualists, but we're not *crazy*! We never tried to see what would happen if we killed off our grandfathers, for example. We're not murderers, after all. Anyway, my grandfathers are both very fine gentlemen, and I wouldn't dream of hurting them."

"So you're saying that you knew that you couldn't change the past, so you never tried to?" I said. "That's ridiculous!"

"Is it? Tell me, what would happen to an engineer at your old Katowice Machinery Works if he started spending all of his time and the company's money working on a perpetual-motion machine?"

"Why, they'd send him to a mental institution if they didn't fire him first."

"Right. And what if the boss of the outfit started working on the same project?"

"The same thing, I suppose, although they might take more time doing it. Everybody knows that perpetual-motion machines are impossible. They violate the second law of thermodynamics!"

"True. And what if, say, the U.S. government started a major research effort to develop perpetual motion?"

"This is a stupid line of questions. No government would ever do anything like that! The second law is absolutely correct. We've been using it for a hundred years, and it's always right!" I shouted.

"Fine. Then what if I told you that it was possible to build a machine that took in tap water and produced electricity and ice cubes?"

"I'd say that you were lying."

"You'd be wrong. Such a type two perpetual-motion machine is quite possible, and in fact this 'apartment' that we're in right now is powered by one. After all, we're in a temporal loop here, so there's no place we could possibly put a radiator. Without our 'impossible' power source, it would get pretty warm in here after a while. What I'm trying to tell you is that cultures all develop blind spots, things that they don't even think about because they *know* the truth about them. Your blind belief in the absurd second law is a case in point. Something similar on a bigger scale stopped the ancient Romans from developing science at all, but that's another story. Suffice it to say that for a time we fell into the same mental trap, until you shook us out of it."

"It was all my doing?" I asked.

"Correct. You came along and threw all our theories right out of the window! Do you realize that you have created an entirely new world here? That you have not only duplicated most of the eastern hemisphere but that in some places you have shredded it? Made dozens of worlds? And that the shredding in some cases went back for thousands of years?"

"Huh. I think I follow you except for these 'shreds' going backward in time," I said.

"They can do that if you are taking information, artifacts, and people from several parallel timelines back down to what had been a single line. When that happens, you shred the past, and oscillations can be set up."

"Oh. Okay. So then the other thirteenth century, the one in my own past, still exists? I was worried about that," I said.

"You should have been. You have caused us no end of trouble and damage. I managed to give you sufficient wealth for you to survive comfortably until we could pick you up. You didn't have to tear a hole in the whole universe!"

"Tom, all I did was try to survive. If I've hurt you, well, I never asked to come here. The fault is yours, not mine."

"You're mostly right. But you could have just left for France and lived a pleasant life. Western Europe was fairly peaceful in this century. You never had to build factories and steamboats!"

"You're saying that I should have abandoned my country to the Mongols? That I should have stood by and watched half the babies born die because of a lack of simple sanitation? What kind of a man do you think I am?"

"I know *exactly* what kind of man you are, Conrad. You're a hero, and you do the things that heroes do. Anyway, we're getting a handle on the time-shredding problem, and things are starting to settle out."

"I still don't understand this multiple shredding that you're talking about. What did I do to start things coming apart?"

"We don't understand it all that well ourselves, and the math is such that even *I* have trouble following it. You see, the world we know isn't just one single world. It's a finite but astronomically large number of worlds, lying close to one another like the pages of a book. These worlds interact with one another and tend to keep one another identical. Philosophically, they are normally one single world with slight variations. As a crude analogy, think of a book that has been left out in the rain and then dried. The pages are wrinkled and dimpled, but they still fit into one another fairly well. That is to say, to a certain extent they interact with one another. What you did was to make two pages pop apart from each other and get some different dimples, to be slightly different from each other. Going down the page, in the direction of the normal direction of time, they continued to separate and become more different. It isn't just one page, though. You seem to have taken half the book with you! In some places, especially around the battlefields, several pages came apart, although they are starting to converge now."

"Somehow, this smacks of the Heisenberg uncertainty principle."

"Uh, sort of, as a theory, although most people misunderstand Heisenberg. He was not saying that a thing can be and not be at the same time. He was only saying that there are limits to what we can know. One of the philosophical stupidities of the twentieth century was the confusion of what we think we know with what actually is, but that's not what we should be talking about now. Yes, there is a divergence principle. Small changes happen all the time between the pages of that ruined book I was talking about. A coin comes up heads or tails, a seed is eaten by a bug or grows into a tree, and so on. It even happens all the time in our own human experience. Have you ever been *sure* that you had your keys in your pocket, only to find out that they were still on your dresser? Well, some of the time you really did *both* put them in your pocket *and* leave them behind.

"You see, there is also a convergence principle operating here, analogous to the force that is trying to force the pages of the ruined book into the same shape. The vast majority of differences are soon smoothed out. In the end, the small changes settle out and make no difference at all. The time line is not so much a monolithic pillar as a rope made of millions of fibers that are all going in the same general direction.

"*Except where you are concerned.* There's something about you, cousin, that makes you different. We don't know what it is, but with you, things don't settle out. The first split that you caused happened a month after you got to this century, when you had to decide whether to abandon a child in a snowy woods or try to save her, even though it looked impossible. Well, you did *both.* And that's the point where you split the world in half!"

"I remember that. I didn't know if it was a boy or a girl, and I christened her Ignacy," I said.

"Right. Now, before we go any further, there's something I need to know. Conrad, I can take you home now. If you want, you can be back at your desk at the Katowice Machinery Works tomorrow morning. Do you want to go?"

Now, that was a kick in the head! Did I want to leave this brutal world and go back to my safe little home? I had to think about it, and Tom was silent while I thought. The serving girl refilled our glasses and left in silence. There was my mother there. How would she take my loss? Yet there were so many people here that needed me, people that I loved. And while I really don't care much about material things, could I go back to standing in lines at the government stores after my loyal troops had slaughtered millions of the enemy? Could I give up my wife and servants, my world-shaping plans, and go back to designing nothing but machine tool controls? Did I really want to become unimportant again? No, by God, I did not!

"I think that I have a better life here, Tom. I'll stay. But try and do something for my mother, okay?"

"I'll do better than that. I'll give her back her son. You see, when you split the world in that snowy woods, you split yourself, too. Your mundane, less heroic self, the one who obeyed his employer and abandoned a child to freeze to death, did not make out as well as you did. I found him in poor straits in Legnica, and he was most eager to go home to his mother. He can warm your chair at the factory and tell himself that it was all some crazy dream."

"Well, that's settled, then. But look, Tom, I have a battle to conduct soon, and the morning is not far away."

"We have all the time we want. It's my stock-in-trade, after all. When you go out that door, not a minute will have gone by in the world outside. Why don't you stick around for a while longer. There's more to discuss, and I'd like you to have a medical checkup while I'm here. If you're tired, there's a spare bedroom with a modern bed, and the wench will get you anything you need."

"Can I have a cup of coffee in the morning? You can't imagine how many times I've dreamed of a cup of coffee."

"We stock the best."

"Then I'll stay, cousin."

I was deadly tired, and in my years in the Middle Ages I had never gotten around to making a really decent box spring mattress. The girl came out a poor third in my priorities, but then, I really hadn't been offered her.

Chapter Thirty-three

Tom was gone the next morning, but he'd left me a note saying that he would be away for a while. The girl served a gorgeous breakfast with maple syrup and real Jamaican Blue Mountain coffee. After that, there were books to read that I hadn't written myself, a good stereo system, and a fine videotape library. Heaven after so many years in the wilds.

I tried repeatedly to strike up a conversation with the serving girl, but no luck, aside from getting her name, which was Maude. She was always smiling, but it was the fixed, artificial sort of smile that you see on a salesman or waitress, not a show of genuine pleasure. At first I thought it odd that Tom should choose such a strange person for a companion. Eventually I realized that she was not a companion in the ordinary sense but just another accessory in this place. She was certainly pretty and very useful, but she seemed to have about the personality of a tape deck. Still, I tried hard to be nice to her, even if she did seem to be emotionally handicapped. As the days went on, I discovered that she responded best when I treated her like Anna, my old mount, with lots of compliments and friendly banter. In time I even tried scratching her behind the ear the way Anna liked, and she smiled with a sort of twinkle in her eye that told me that she was really happy. Although she stayed naked, even of pubic hair, she never made any overt sexual advances, and while I thought that she would not reject mine, I felt it best simply to keep it friendly.

I spent seven days with her in the strange, windowless sealed-off apartment, reading up on all the bits of technology that I had needed and had forgotten or had never learned, listening to good music, and watching all the movies I had missed. It was a marvelously restful vacation, and it gave me time to think.

I got to considering the events of the past ten years, and it slowly sank into me how incredibly successful I had been in modernizing medieval Poland. I had started a primitive country on the way to industrialization and had done it without coercion, without fanaticism, and almost without pain. Looking back, I think we all had a good time doing it.

Compared to the bloodshed and suffering that Russia or almost any other country went through in turning a nation of peasants into a modern society, what I had done had been astoundingly easy and painless. I had gotten us going in ten years, not the fifty or seventy-five years that all the other nations had needed in trying to modernize. And I had done it without any outside help but a pocketful of seeds and the little knowledge that I had in my own head.

I had formulated no dogma, told no one of my long-term plans, and made as few speeches as possible. That is to say, I had made no promises. I had just gone ahead and done the best I could, and that had made all the difference.

When other people tried to change the world, Lenin and his crowd, for example, they started by publishing grandiose promises, outlining their program and claiming that all sorts of wondrous things would come of it if everybody went along in lockstep. They claimed that soon everyone would work only a few hours a week, because these silly academicians thought that work is something that nobody would want to do. Yet with their program, everybody would have free food, free medical help, free vacations, and so forth. They would move mountains, though nobody seems to have asked why a mountain should want to be someplace else.

Well, people are smart enough to notice after a while that magic doesn't happen. If you want more things, you have to make and distribute more things, and that means that at least for the first few generations you have to work harder and more efficiently.

I just offered people a low-paying job with long hours and hard work and did what I could to make that work seem meaningful to them. Once a good man or woman sees that what he is doing is good and important, work becomes a pleasure, one far more enjoyable than any silly game or amusement. The only promise I made was that we would all eat the same, and I didn't really even promise that. I just did it, and enough people responded to get the job done.

I never tried to get everybody into the program. I just took on those who wanted to help and never wasted any energy on the rest. In so doing, I made very few enemies, and I never had to set up a huge, expensive, and hated police force to coerce those who didn't want to take part. The guilds, the nobility, and the Church all went their own ways with my blessings, except for those few occasions when they got in my way. My father told me that it takes all kinds, and I've always believed that.

I never published a vast scheme of things, so I was never blamed for anything when things didn't go right. I made a lot of mistakes, but very few people noticed them, while my successes were fairly obvious.

I am convinced that the reason why things have gone so well is not so much the things that I have done but rather the things that I haven't done.

I've just been an engineer, a simple man with a job to do.

Tom returned one day in time for supper, which was a pile of fresh Maine lobsters with all the trimmings. The apartment had a time locker that was used as a sort of refrigerator. It not only kept things fresh, it could keep them alive. The girl was an amazing cook, even if she couldn't carry on a conversation.

"Where have you been, Tom?"

"Nowhere. I just went into stasis for a few days to give you a small vacation in a bit of the modern world."

"Thank you. I've really enjoyed it, but it's time to talk some more. A few days ago you said that you couldn't come to get me until after the time you saw me at the Battle of Chmielnick. Well, I wasn't at the Battle of Chmielnick. There wasn't any Battle of Chmielnick! I was at the Battle of Sandomierz, and when I was there, I saw you get killed. There was a Mongol spear that went right through your eye and out the back of your helmet. You weren't breathing, and you didn't have a pulse. Do you want to explain these things?"

"It's like I said, the shredding around the battlefields was the worst. Yes, that really was me, and I really did die. It was a me from some other subjective timeline, I hope, although it could possibly be a me from my own subjective future, so I avoid that time slot. As to whether the Mongols were killed at Sandomierz or Chmielnick, well, in a thousand years it won't make any difference. Maybe the historians will argue about it, maybe not."

"Isn't it confusing with a lot of you running around?" I said.

"No more than it is for you. There was one of *you* at Chmielnick, after all. And none of this shredding was ever noticed until you came along."

"Is that why you waited a year after the battle before talking to me? To wait for the shredding to settle down?"

"Yes, of course," he said.

"Then why do you come now on the eve of another battle? Won't that cause problems?"

"This thing with the Crossmen isn't a battle, it's an execution, and they were all dead before you got back to your trailer. But now, if you are through with that chocolate éclair, we'll give you a medical checkup."

In a side room that had been locked before there was a thing that looked like Spock's coffin, with an attached keyboard. In it was a frightening number of mostly concealed tubes, needles, and little knives.

"Are you sure that you know how to work this thing?" I said.

"Relax. It happens that among other thing, I'm a doctor of medicine. In nine hundred years you become a lot of things. Get in."

I didn't love the idea, but I'm supposed to be a hero, so I got in. The lid came down on me, and it got dark, and then the lid came up, and I got out.

"There, that wasn't so bad, was it?" Tom said.

The first thing I noticed was my eyesight. I could see as well as I could when I was a teenager. I put a hand over my left eye, and I could see out of my right. I wasn't half-blind anymore!

"It turned out to be easier to regrow a whole new right eye rather than trying to repair the severed optic nerve. And from there it was only a matter of hitting another button to regrow them both," Tom said. "Your arthritis is gone, along with your hemorrhoids, and so is a small cancer that you didn't know about. Your immunizations have been updated, and I've done a general rejuvenation treatment on you. You look the same, but your ladies will be able to tell the difference."

"Wow. I feel great! You did all that in a few seconds?"

"No, it took me three hours to set it up, and inside the machine's time field you spent four months on the program, or your body did. There wasn't any point in boring your mind with the procedure, so I shut that down for the duration."

"Huh. Well, thanks, Tom."

"No charge. All part of the service. You've been a pain in the ass, but the trouble you've caused has been the first decent challenge we've seen in centuries. What's more, what you have done is very important. Think about it. A whole new world! A whole doubling of the human experience! As time goes on, this branch will develop its own arts, its own sciences, and its own technologies. What new music will they play, what new insights will they have, what new things will they build? I tell you that there are glorious possibilities here, and we intend to explore them! Maybe we'll even try to split one off for ourselves."

"Well, don't rush it, Tom."

"We never have to hurry. Well, now, do you feel ready to go back to the world you've created?"

Maude left the room, and I said, "In a minute. Just a few more questions. What is it with this servant of yours? She's one of the strangest women I've ever met."

"Well, that's why! She's not a woman. She's a bioengineered creation, just like that neohorse I gave you. They were designed in the same studio and have much in common chemically. She's not a modified human if that's what you're worried about. I'd never allow anything like that. Her equivalent of DNA was built up entirely out of simple chemicals, and she was designed to be attractive, industrious, and completely contented with her lot. Human servants are naturally resentful, doing a demeaning job. Wenches work out much better."

"She has a lot of Anna's traits? Racial memory and all that?"

"Oh yes, along with multiple births and a similar sensory apparatus. She doesn't need a neohorse's remarkable digestive system, though, being designed for a civilized environment, and she can talk, of course, whereas if a horse talked to one of our field researchers, it could get him into trouble. But basically, the two designs are similar except for outward appearance."

"Interesting. I suspected something like that. Another thing.

Once my life was saved by some golden arrows coming down out of the sky. Was that your doing?"

"Who else?"

"Who? God, of course."

"Don't be absurd. There's no such thing."

"You're so sure of that? Maybe that's why you can't change the time stream. Have you ever thought of praying?"

"I'm not even going to answer that one, Conrad."

"Huh. One last question. The afternoon before I rode your time machine, I met a girl at a seed store, a redhead. She was supposed to meet me that night, but she didn't. What happened to her?"

"Somehow I knew you'd ask that. She wanted to come, but her installation director got word of a surprise inspection the next day by the assistant secretary for agricultural research. Her whole outfit spent the night cleaning the place and waxing the floors."

"Huh. I'd forgotten what bureaucracies were like."

"If you say so. Don't you know that they do the same thing at your factories before you show up?"

"Perish the thought! I'll put an end to that! Oh, yes. You've been telling me what a wonderful person I am. Could this wonderful person have a present or two to take back with him?"

"Like what? You want the wench?"

"No, I've got plenty of those, and mine are real. Anyway, I doubt if you have one who can speak Polish."

"True."

Maude came back and was waiting attentively.

"Then I imagine that she'd be pretty lonely in Poland. But how about some of that coffee?"

"Fine, I'll have her get all you can carry."

"Thank you. And how about some reference texts, an encyclopedia, for example? And I'd give a lot for a *Handbook of Chemistry and Physics*."

"Are you sure that it would be wise, Conrad? You've made remarkable progress here, mostly because your people have had to think out and solve their own problems. This has put practical working people in charge of things. But when one culture tries to learn from another one, the sort of people who succeed and take control are the academic, unworldly sort, and history has repeatedly proved that it is easier and quicker to invent it all for yourself. I mean it! The United States developed a world-class technology in the fifty years between the Civil War and World War I. It took Japan, Russia, and a dozen other places seventy-five years to do the same thing by copying them, and they had a much harder time doing it. You are progressing just fine on your own."

"If you say so. How about some modern farm animals? Or even just some prize sperm?"

"Same thing. You'll do it better on your own!"

It was a polite no but a no just the same. Well, I tried. Maude came in casually, lightly carrying two huge leather suitcases, almost trunks. I peeked inside one of them, and it was full of freeze-dried instant in vacuum cans. Yet when I picked up the suitcases, it was a strain. That little girllike thing was incredibly strong!

"Well, good-bye, Tom, and thank you again. Keep in better touch from now on."

"Good-bye for a while. I'll be keeping an eye on you, don't worry."

And so I stepped back through the looking glass, or at least my closet. My last view was of the wench smiling at me with that special twinkle in her eye. I closed the door, and when I opened it again, there was nothing there but my clothes.

I called my servants in and went to bed. And yes, the girls could tell the difference in my rejuvenated self! All of them. Several times.

In the morning the weather was still dead calm. I had Sonya bring me a cup of boiling water to show her how to make instant coffee. But packed between two big cans inside the second suitcase was a copy of *The Handbook of Chemistry and Physics.* Maude certainly had a lot in common with Anna and was not the automaton that Tom thought she was. Nice kid!

After enjoying my coffee, I crossed the river. We waited until the sun was fully up, and then I had the siege guns blow down both of the main gates. It took only one round from each of the guns.

It wouldn't have taken even that, but the other gunners weren't about to go through the battle without firing a single shot.

The delegates watched all this through the telescopes that Boris Novacek had provided them with—at strictly retail prices, at my insistence and over his earnest objections. Boris figured that we could get away with charging double.

A greenish-yellow gas flowed stickily through the shattered gates, and the gunners ran for high ground as they had been taught. It flowed down the road, through a gutter, and was eventually absorbed into the cool waters of the Vistula.

We waited until the middle of the afternoon, and then Baron Vladimir sent in a few volunteers. They came out saying that the place stank but that the Crossmen were all dead.

They weren't quite right.

After we entered, a group of Teutonic Knights in chain mail and black and white surcoats started shooting crossbows at us from one of the towers. They wounded two men, though not seriously. As he was being carried away, one of them mugged, "What? True belted knights shooting crossbows? How unchivalrous!"

We all laughed.

Then we just fell back and called in the artillery. The gunners had fun knocking down the tower. They were taking bets as to which crew would hit it first. Number six got it on the second round. They still weren't much on accuracy, but what they hit stayed hit.

Then we looted the place. It stank with chlorine but also with the stench of ten thousand unwashed bodies. I decided that the city-fort wasn't worth keeping.

Once we secured the Crossmen treasury, including the money that I'd recently paid them, we allowed the delegates in to look around. They all acted suitably impressed.

After that it was a matter of hauling out the enemy bodies for burial. The churchmen present wouldn't hear of us beheading the Crossmen and putting their heads up on pikes, so we helped them give the bastards a Christian burial. It wasn't the huge cleanup job that we had had to do after the Mongols. After all, we now outnumbered the enemy by almost five to one. There were almost enough of us to act as pallbearers. By dusk the job was completed.

All of this got me an unbelievable amount of flak.

The high churchmen were horrified not so much by the fact that we had killed them but at how easily their feared military monks had been slaughtered. I said that I'd planned it that way and that I was happy that I hadn't lost a single one of my own men.

The military men among the delegates said that this massacre of good knights was an offense against military honor. I said that there wasn't any such thing as military honor. War is just organized killing, and while a butcher is not necessarily evil, he's no great pillar of mercy, either. Warfare as a sport was out.

And my own troops were the angriest of all. At least they acted that way, knowing me well enough to know that I wouldn't have them shot for speaking up. They had marched all the way to Turon and then had done nothing but wait around. There hadn't even been a fight. I told them that "they also serve who only stand and wait" and furthermore, I'd only wanted to take a single battalion here. They'd invited themselves along, and if they didn't like the party, tough!

But as a sop to them, I told them that I didn't plan to haul all the siege gun ammunition back, and if they wanted to try shooting down the Crossman fort at dawn, after the sunrise services, they were welcome. This got a betting pool going immediately.

The delegates were all still there in the morning, and they watched the target practice. The fort was gone before the ammunition was.

Brick walls are cannonball-degradable.

Eleven thousand four hundred and three Crossmen were killed, and that's in decimal. The accountants figured it out that way because most of the delegates weren't up on the new math.

The treasure taken didn't cover the costs of the war, so we didn't have to worry about dividing it up. We so outnumbered the enemy that you had to be a knight or better to rate a Crossman sword to take home, and many of the men got nothing but a surcoat or a bit of chain mail. But I got the Grand Master's sword and armor to set up in my living room, and his battle flag for my wall.

The delegates monopolized the riverboats for a few days, going home, and again the army had to wait. Before the boats were free, the construction people got the railroad built down to where Turon had been, and I told the troops to march home. Single file, because there was other traffic on the road.

One battalion of regulars under Baron Josep was left to take command of the former Crossman territories, and they were soon complaining about the lack of adequate housing. That summer they actually had to rebuild Turon out of used brick.

Dammit, I can't be expected to think of everything.

As things were closing down, Francine came to me. She wasn't as icy as she'd been before.

"Conrad, this is a wondrous thing that you have done here, to kill off a great power so casually. All of these great men from so many places, they all respect you and love you and fear you all at the same time! Even Henryk feels that same confused way. They have the honors and the titles, but it is *you* that truly have the power!"

"I'm still only a man trying to do my job, Francine."

"You are far more than that. *You* are the master builder! *You* are the great mover and shaker of all of Christendom! It is *you* that really control and command all things!"

"If you say so. I take it that you are ready to come home now?"

"Of course, my love!"

Within six months Duke Henryk had treaties with Pomerania, Kujawy, nine separate pagan Pruthenian tribes, the kingdom of Hungary, and the Bulgarian Empire, the terms of which were essentially identical to those in our treaty with Prince Daniel of the Ruthenians. Even the pagans said they were willing to become Christians just so long as I didn't get mad at them.

And three months after that, since the Church still didn't have a Pope, King Bela of Hungary, Tsar Ivan Asen of Bulgaria, and I got together and crowned Henryk King of Central Christendom.

And after that I had an *awful* lot of steamboats and railroad tracks to build.

Interlude Four

The tape wound to a stop. I looked at the wench at my side and wondered just what I had been doing. Enjoying myself with a woman? Making love with an alien? Petting a dog? Whatever it was, I felt uneasy about it. I peeled myself away from her.

"Picking up another bad habit, son?" I looked up, and Tom was there.

"Why didn't you tell me about these servants, Tom?"

"Why didn't you ask me? There are all sorts of things going on around here. For your future reference, all entertainers are human, all servants are constructs, and when in doubt, ask them. If you're worried about offending her, don't. Wenches don't get offended. If you really want to, you can use her sexually. She's physically capable of it, and she'll enjoy it as much as she can enjoy anything. They're not very emotional, you know."

"So she's more of a machine than an animal or a person?"

"If you want her to be. She doesn't really fit into any of the usual categories. She's a chemical construct, self-replicating, servant, household. I suppose she's an animal, but a conventional biochemist wouldn't recognize any of the things she's made of. She's simply a perfect personal servant, to be used and ignored. That's not why I'm here."

"So why are you here, and where have you been?" I said.

"Actually, I've been gone for over a hundred years, subjective, getting a handle on what Cousin Conrad has done. I gave him the garden-variety explanation, and I let you get it off the tape to save time. At nine hundred, I might not have all that much time to waste."

"You're as healthy as one of your biocritters, and I have a better academic background than Conrad," I said.

"You'll still have to go back to school to pick up on it. For starters, we used to think that the universe had eleven dimensions. Lately, they've proved the existence of four more."

"Damn. And here I thought I was ready for management."

"Don't worry about it. In another ten or twenty years you will be, son."

"Wonderful. Anyway, I'm glad that Conrad worked out so well. It was quite a story."

"True. But stories never really end, you know. Not when you have a time machine."

EPILOGUE

On top of a windy cliff in Africa, at about two and a half million B.C., two long-lost members of the Anthropological Corps were sitting and chewing on dried meat as well as their few remaining teeth would allow.

"My eyesight is getting a lot worse," he said.

"Yeah, but my periods have finally stopped," she answered, turning her back to him.

"Then it's finally too late to do the sensible thing."

"The cowardly thing," she said.

"Stuff it," he said, turning his back to her.

"Yeah, stuff it."

There was a shimmer in the air in front of him, high above the valley floor, but his eyesight was so bad that he hardly noticed it.

Only when the shimmer resolved itself into a tall, athletic young man and that man started to walk toward him on the clear air did he finally take notice.

"Look," he said.

"Look yourself," she said, unmoving.

"No. I really mean turn around and look."

"What?"

"Turn around, dammit! I think they've finally found us! Can you see him, too?"

She turned and stared at the blond young man who was smiling as he walked through the clean air without visible means of support. There was a lot of gold trim on his well-fitted red-and-white dress uniform, an outfit that would have looked more at home at a fancy costume ball than high above the ancient African plain.

"He's there," she said, "but he's not one of ours."

"Who cares, just so long as you see him, too, and I'm not crazy! I mean, who cares who saves us or how he does it, just so long as we're saved!"

"Sorry we took so long," the smiling young apparition said, his polished black boots resting on nothing, a few feet from the edge of the cliff.

"You're not one of us," the woman said.

"No, I'm from one of the alternate branches. I'm here on loan, lending a hand. Shall we go? I can have you home in a few moments." He reached out to them.

Fearfully, hesitantly, they reached out and took his hands.

CONRAD'S QUEST FOR RUBBER

volume six
in the
ADVENTURES OF CONRAD STARGARD

Prologue

FROM THE DIARY OF CONRAD STARGARD

February 10, 1246

We destroyed the Teutonic Order four years ago, and since then things have gone remarkably smoothly, especially when you compare them to the first ten years that I spent in this brutal century.

It wasn't easy to survive after I was accidentally shipped here from the twentieth century. I had to prepare Poland for an invasion by the Mongol Empire, and then I had to direct the war after we were invaded.

There were some tight spots, but we managed to win.

Now we are at peace. For the first time in a century, Poland is united, from the Baltic Sea to the Carpathian Mountains, and from the Odra River to the Pripet Marshes. What's more, it had all been done peacefully, voluntarily, and even eagerly, once the kings, dukes, and princes saw what my cannons could do. Furthermore, Poland, Ruthenia, Hungary, and Bulgaria have joined together to form the Federation of Christianity.

Our school system is being extended throughout Eastern Europe, as is our system of railroads, our uniform system of measurements, and our uniform coinage.

We've seen interesting times, but thank God they are over. I haven't had to kill anyone in over three years, and it feels good.

Sitting in my leather chair behind my nicely carved desk, I could see by the numbers before me that the factories were running at full capacity, the army was expanding at an optimal rate, and our concrete castle-building program was right on schedule.

Sweet success.

As I sat patting myself on the back, a young woman, one I didn't recognize, walked into my office. She had huge green eyes, flaming red hair, and a full set of matching freckles. None of my wives, friends, or current servants had such stunning coloration.

Without saying a word, she stamped the snow from her felt boots, shook the melted drops from her heavy, fur-lined cloak, and hung it up on a wooden peg near the door.

"Excuse me? Should I know you?" I asked.

"Probably not, your grace, but we *have* met." She spoke Polish with a Hungarian accent. She took off her felt overshoes, and then her slippers, and set them all neatly against the wall under her cloak.

"You are not being very helpful."

"Your grace, I hope to be *very* helpful," she said as she took off her belt. She rolled it up and put it in one of her boots, then started unlacing the front of her white woolen dress.

"This must be somebody's idea of a joke," I said. "You have to be a prostitute hired by someone from accounting."

"I am not a prostitute, and nobody hired me," she said as she dropped her dress to the floor. She stepped naked out of it. She was obviously still in her early teens, but she had little of the baby fat that so many girls her age are afflicted with. Instead, she was blessed with the firm, trim body of an athletic woman of about five years older. Not to mention remarkably large, firm breasts. Or the dusting of freckles all over everything. I tried not to let my normal male reactions show, and was glad of the desk in front of me.

She hung the dress on another peg before continuing. "In fact, I'm still a virgin, and people have told me that I am an attractive one."

"Your face and body are more than adequate, but your character is very much in question," I said as coldly as I could manage. "I am not a teenage boy who becomes irrational at the sight of a few square yards of female skin. I want to know why you think you can get away with approaching me so boldly, and I want to know your name."

My hopefully stern admonition had no apparent effect on the girl. She came around my desk and sat on my lap. She gave me an inexpert kiss, with her lips too hard.

"My lord, I have the right to be bold with you because you are my proper liege lord. You rescued me at a tender age from death, outlaws, and a winter blizzard. It is only proper that you should now enjoy the flower of my maidenhood."

The whole situation had me stunned, flabbergasted, and thoroughly confused. Especially that last statement.

"I still don't understand. What is your name?"

She kissed me again in the same inexperienced fashion. Part of me wanted to explain to her the proper way of doing things, but most of me didn't want to change the subject.

"My name is the one you gave me when you christened me in a snowy woods. I'm Ignacy. You really *must* remember me now."

Ignacy! Now I remembered. While escorting a merchant through the forests east of here—what, fourteen years ago?—we were attacked by a highwayman with a black eagle on his shield. Defending ourselves, we killed him and his henchmen, and my mount accidentally trampled a young woman in the process.

Later, I'd found a baby in the outlaw's camp. I christened it in case it didn't survive the rest of the wintry trip to shelter and brought it with me to Count Lambert's castle, here at Okoitz.

Only then did I find out that I had christened a girl with a boy's name.

And *this* was what that tiny bundle had grown into?

"I remember now. I also recall that you were adopted into a peasant family, that your new father soon died, and that your stepmother then married a blacksmith."

"Yes, your grace. She told me that his name was Ilya, and that Count Lambert had forced them to marry. They never did like each other, and she eventually ran away to Hungary with another blacksmith more to her liking."

"Remember that I was there at the time. She was not actually forced to marry Ilya, although Lambert was generally too persuasive by half," I said. "None of which explains why you are sitting naked on my lap."

"This is Okoitz, isn't it? And the custom here is for a maiden to be taken first by her lord, isn't it?" She kissed me yet again and managed to wiggle herself around such that she was straddling me as I sat upright in my chair. Her body and breasts were pressed tightly against me, and my resolve to treat this event as an annoyance was weakening.

"It was Lambert's custom to bounce every peasant girl within arm's reach, if that's what you are referring to. But Lambert has been dead for five years, and you are not a local peasant girl. You were raised in Hungary, judging from your accent. And thinking about it, I believe that you are legally still the daughter of Ilya the blacksmith, who has since become Baron Ilya. You and he are thus both members of the nobility, not the peasantry."

I was wearing an old embroidered velvet outfit rather than one of my usual military uniforms. The almost annoying young lady was busily undoing the strings on my codpiece.

She said, "You are trying to wiggle out of this on a legal technicality, and I won't have it! Ilya isn't my father. My father was the highwayman Sir Rheinburg, and you killed him!"

"If Sir Rheinburg was your father, and if he legally married your mother, then you are a member of the German nobility and not a peasant. However, it is by no means certain that he was your father. Rheinburg had two men-at-arms with him, and either of them could have been married to the woman who was killed. Or there may possibly have been a fourth man involved somehow. We don't know. What we do know is that your mother and probably your biological father were dead, that you were adopted, albeit informally, into a family, and that later your stepmother legally married Ilya. She never divorced Ilya, even if she left him for another man. No, there's no way around it. You are stuck with being a baroness, and you are not acting like one."

It took me a while to say that, since while I was talking, she had continued with her program of kissing and disrobing me.

"I've been planning for this day for years, and you're *not* going to talk me out of it!"

The conversation continued for a while longer, but there is a limit as to how long any normal man can stay firm in his noble intentions. I bowed to the inevitable before I committed the sin of Onan.

Much later, as she was leaving, I said, "Well, Baroness, I still think that you should go and at least meet your father. He's stationed at Three Walls, a half day's ride south of here."

"I'll think about it, your grace."

And then she left without asking my leave and without saying a good-bye, much less a thank-you.

Baron Piotr was just approaching my office door as the disheveled girl walked away.

"What was that all about, your grace? I'm sure that I've never seen her before."

"I'm not really sure, but I think I was just raped."

He pondered that a bit before answering. "Remarkable. Still, she doesn't seem to have caused you any permanent damage, sir. What disturbs me is that a total stranger could enter your castle and make it all the way to your inner sanctum without being stopped or even identified.

"You know, your grace, I think we are getting entirely too lax about security around here. What if she had had different designs on your body? Putting some extra holes in it, for example. What then? I notice that you aren't even wearing your sword."

"Hmm. Yes, you're right. I must have left it somewhere."

"I noticed that you weren't wearing it at lunch, either. Your grace, you must remember that you aren't just a backwoods knight anymore. You have become one of the most important men in the world. There are people who feel that they have good reason to hate you, and men in your position have been assassinated for reasons that no one has ever figured out. The death of Duke Henryk the Bearded is a recent example."

"Okay, okay, I'll make a point of always wearing my sword from now on. Enough said."

"No, not quite enough, your grace. You need a bodyguard, or better yet, a number of bodyguards such that there are always at least two of them awake and on hand at all times."

"Piotr, that would be a royal pain in the butt, and I am not royal enough to have to put up with it. I won't do it. Also, I am not at all sure that bodyguards make a man any safer. They make him stand out when there is safety in anonymity. And bear in mind, the Duke Henryk you mention was murdered by one of his own bodyguards. So was Philip of Macedonia, Alexander the Great's father."

"You have very little chance at anonymity, your grace, being at least a head taller than anyone else in the city. As to the rest, I expect that guards have saved a hundred rulers for every one they have killed."

"Piotr, the only really nice thing about being a 'ruler' is that you get to do what you want. I want no bodyguards."

"Yes, your grace."

Chapter One

FROM THE JOURNAL OF JOSIP SOBIESKI

written January 15, 1249,
concerning my childhood

My name is Josip Sobieski. I find myself sitting in a cave just south of the Arctic Circle, with nothing to do for the next three months. In hindsight, this will doubtless seem a wonderful adventure, especially to someone who has never been here. Presently, I find it to be a deadly bore. To while away the hours, I have resolved to record the events of my life. I expect that future readers, if any, will find my experiences a fruitful example of what *not* to do with the only life God has given them.

In 1230, when I was five years old, my father became a baker at Count Lambert's castle town of Okoitz. Thus, I had the rare privilege of being personally on hand at the beginning of what was to become the most remarkable story of our age.

Lord Conrad came to our town on Christmas Eve, in 1231, although he was called *Sir* Conrad then. I first became aware of him when I saw him sitting at the high table during a feast. It would have been hard to miss him, since even seated he was a head taller than Count Lambert, who was himself a very big man.

He was the talk of the town, having fought and defeated the evil Sir Rheinburg and all his men, killing each with just a single blow. With the other boys, I watched while four suits of chain-mail armor were taken to the blacksmith's for repair, so we knew that every word of the story was true.

He was a strange man, much different from the other knights and noblemen who made life at Okoitz interesting. For one thing, he was always making something, either showing the men how to build the mills and factories that Okoitz soon became famous for, or carving some toy for the boys of the town, or sometimes even things for the girls. With his own hands he carved me a spinning top that, once you learned how to do it, would flip over and spin for a time upside down! I still have that toy and keep it as a treasure, although I've never been able to figure out exactly why it works.

For another, he took little pleasure in the usual knightly enjoyments. Once, when Sir Stefan brought in a bear, for baiting, Sir Conrad didn't even know what bearbaiting was. Once he found out, he was furious, calling the sport cruel. Rather than let the bear be torn apart by the castle dogs, he killed it himself, with a single stroke of his mighty blade, and he cried while he did it. And then he fought Sir Stefan over the matter, and I think he might have killed that knight had Count Lambert not intervened.

Sir Conrad didn't like cockfighting either, and soon the peasants at Okoitz stopped doing it, rather than risk offending him.

While all of the other adults considered small boys to be little more than nuisances, to be ignored at best and spanked at worst, Sir Conrad seemed to like us, to actually enjoy our company. He almost always had time to stop and explain things to us, to tell us some of the thousands of stories he knew, and to teach us our numbers.

Furthermore, he paid our priest, Father Thomas, to teach us to read and write, every weekday morning during the winter.

The fathers of most of the boys were peasants, farmers who had little to do during the winter, so having their boys in school was no hardship for them. My father was a baker, and bakers must work hard almost every day of the year. If they wish to take even Sunday off, they must work twice as hard on Saturday, or the people of the town would go hungry without bread. Even then, someone was needed at the bakery to keep the fires going, since most of the people brought their meals in a pot to our ovens for cooking.

This meant that my help was needed every day in my father's bakery, for children naturally help their parents at their work. My parents had six children, and my father felt that the boys, at least, should go to school.

My older brother and I felt guilty about sitting in school while the rest of the family had to work longer hours. We would have preferred working, but our father's word was law.

Every afternoon, when we all worked together after school, he always questioned us minutely about everything that was said in class. At the time, we thought that he did this to assure himself that we were not wasting the time spent there, but much later we realized that this was his method of absorbing the new learning for himself and for his wife and daughters. Since we boys were responsible for repeating to him every single word that was spoken in class, we did not dare be inattentive.

Both Father Thomas and Sir Conrad praised our diligence. They should have praised our father.

As interesting as Sir Conrad was, his horse received even more attention, from us boys, at least.

Anna was a huge animal, even bigger than Count Lambert's

favorite charger. But while Whitefoot was dangerous to be near, ever eager to nip off an ear or to crush a rib cage, Anna was the most gentle of creatures, provided that you treated her politely.

Well, she kicked Iwo's father when he whipped her to get her back into her stall after Anna left it to relieve herself outside. Anna was very clean in her habits, and never soiled her stall.

He did not hit her hard, and with most animals of that size you have to hit them just to get their attention. With Anna, on the other hand, all you had to do was ask her, and she was happy to do just about anything for you. And to be fair, she didn't kick the man very hard, for he lived and was able to go back to work in a few days.

Later, when we asked her about the incident, she said that she had objected to being sworn at as much as being struck, and that in any event, it wasn't polite to interrupt a lady while she was attending to private matters.

You see, we boys soon discovered that Anna could understand the language perfectly, and although of course she couldn't speak it, she would nod or shake her head to answer yes or no to any question asked her. It sometimes required a lot of questions to get the whole story out of her, but that was generally our fault and not hers.

She was as intelligent as any of us boys, and we considered her to be much smarter than most of the grown-ups around.

Also, like her owner, Anna seemed to positively like children. I think that much of it was because grown-ups think they are much too busy to bother taking the time a conversation with Anna necessarily took, assuming all the while that they were among the minority who believed what we told them about her. We children were delighted that someone as big as her would take the time to fully answer us.

And, perhaps, we really did have more spare time than the older people did.

We soon learned that she was a good friend to have. Whenever a grown-up was spanking a child, or even shouting at one in public, Anna would walk over and stare at the adult doing the spanking or shouting. She never made a sound or actually did anything. She just stood close by and stared at them, and that was generally enough. Having this huge animal stare at you was very intimidating, and any urge to chastise the less fortunate soon evaporated.

We boys speculated that if someone tried to do actual harm to one of the children of the town, Anna's response would have been more active and indeed deadly. Since no one in memory had ever been that evil, we were never able to confirm our suspicions.

Still, we were glad she was there.

Some of the peasants complained to Count Lambert about this habit of hers, saying it was unholy, but Lambert just laughed at them. He said that *everything* with eyes has to look at *something*, and that "something" is usually the last thing that moved. If being looked at troubled the peasants, the cause of it must be their own guilty consciences. He said that they were well-advised to seek out the priest and go to confession!

In all events, my parents were never forced to endure Anna's staring, since to my memory they never had to severely chastise any of their children, and in turn, none of us ever wanted to displease them.

Simply put, they were good parents, and we were good children. I think this made us unusual.

At the time, our cheerful obedience seemed quite ordinary to my brother and sisters and me, and I occasionally questioned other friends of mine as to why they wanted to get into the various sorts of mischief they always seemed to be involved with. They could never satisfactorily explain their motivations to me, nor, in truth, could I explain mine to them. To anger my father seemed as silly to me as eating dirt. I simply had no desire to do such a thing.

Strange to say, one of the boys in the town, Iwo, actually did just that, once. He went into the bailey, sat down on the ground, and proceeded to eat dirt for no obvious or conceivable reason. His father was angry and spanked him. On this occasion, Anna was tardy in going over to stare. She was as mystified as the rest of us.

But my story is not about Iwo, and he came to a bad end, anyway.

A few years later he ran away, and somebody eventually said that he was hung in Gniezno, although they didn't know why.

Sir Conrad left in the spring with Anna and some girls. (A boy of seven generally has little interest in girls, except, perhaps, for occasional target practice.) He went to build the city of Three Walls on the land that Count Lambert had given him, and we were all sad to see both of them leave. They returned for a few days almost every month, and over the years, Anna saved many a boy from the beatings that most of them undoubtedly deserved.

A different kind of beating happened during the first Christmas after Sir Conrad left us. I remember it clearly with all of my childish impressions still attached.

The story circulated that Sir Conrad found a caravan bound for Constantinople that was owned and guarded by the Teutonic Knights of the Cross. He found a gross of pagan children that the Crossmen were planning to sell to Jews and Moslems, who must have been terrible people, we imagined, although we had never met one. We children understood that something bad would then happen to the young slaves, but no one would tell us exactly what that bad thing was.

Conrad beat up the Crossmen guarding the caravan and saved the children, because he was a hero. Then he took them back to his city, gave them to good families, taught them how to speak, and made them into good Christians, people said.

The Crossmen didn't like him doing all this, so they came to Okoitz, a thousand of them, and Sir Conrad came here, too, for a trial by combat. It seemed to me that everybody else in the world came as well, and all of them needed bread to eat, so we bakers hardly had time to sleep at all. Whenever I looked outside the bakery, which wasn't very often, all I could see was that everything was packed solid with people. My whole family had to sleep in the bakery, since Count Lambert had lent our house out to a bunch of other people we didn't even know.

There was a kind of festival going on then at Okoitz, not that I got to see much of it. But when the trial by combat between Sir Conrad and the bad guy happened, well, my father made sure we closed the bakery in time for all of us to go and see it.

Sir Conrad and Anna beat up the bad guy and chopped his head off. They chopped his horse's head off, too, because it was crippled.

Then a bunch of the other Crossmen went out to kill Sir Conrad, when that wasn't allowed, and God made a miracle happen! Golden arrows came down from the sky and killed every one of them in the heart! I was there and I saw it myself, and so did two bishops and the duke and everybody else.

They say that after that, nobody ever tried to bother Sir Conrad again. No Christians, anyway.

The town of Okoitz was constantly changing, all through my childhood. From the time we first got there, when our town was nothing at all except a clearing at the side of the road that went from the Vistula to the Odra, something was always being constructed.

My father's bakery was almost the first thing built, since people need to eat before anything else can happen. Then the outer wall was built, with the houses and stables each side by side against it, and the blockhouses at the four corners. Then the church and Lambert's castle went up, and most people seemed to be happy with the thought that the job was finally done.

That was when Sir Conrad arrived, and all the men of the town were soon out chopping down trees with which to build a huge windmill, the likes of which no one but Sir Conrad had ever seen. A big cloth factory went up, and a lot of girls came to work there, and then they made a second huge windmill, until everyone said that if they kept on building, there wouldn't be any room left in the town for the people!

But soon they started on Lambert's new castle, which when completed turned out to be three times bigger than the whole rest of the town, and much taller, besides, so they had to make it outside of the walls themselves. It was four years in the making, and long before it was done, my family and even the bakery was moved inside it.

All of this civic growth was good for my father's business. He was forced to take on apprentices and even journeymen from outside of our family to satisfy the needs of his growing number of customers.

When a second baker came to town with Count Lambert's permission, my father wasn't worried about the competition, but instead they immediately formed a guild in the manner of the big city guilds, to do proper charity work and see to it that there was employment and plenty for all.

With father now a guildmaster, our family prospered. My sisters began to receive substantial dowries when they were married. My brother and I soon realized that one day there would be a considerable inheritance for us and a respected place in the community. He liked the thought of all this, but I was of mixed mind about it.

Oh, I was pleased that my family prospered, but it was obvious that to do well, a baker had to stay in one place. All of my life, the interesting people I saw and occasionally was able to meet were those who traveled, who went to strange places and saw strange things. I heard magic, faraway names like Cracow and Paris and Sandomierz, and I wanted to see these mystical places. I yearned to go with those far travelers, to join with the caravans of merchants, soldiers, and priests who were always coming and going from our gates.

I wanted adventure.

And my father, whom I loved and wanted to obey, would not even discuss the matter. We were bakers, we always had been bakers, and we would always be bakers. Nothing more could be said.

Chapter Two

FROM THE JOURNAL OF JOSIP SOBIESKI

written January 17, 1249,
concerning October 10, 1240

In the fall of 1240, the call went out. It was time to prepare for war. Together with my brother and my father, and the last fifty-five other sound men from Okoitz, I made the day-long walk to Baron Conrad's Warrior's School, commonly known as Hell.

I had long wanted to make the trip. All of the other boys of my age from Okoitz had joined the army the year before, as soon as they turned fourteen. Their letters to me bragged about how they would be knighted by the time I got there and how I would have to serve under them, do their bidding, and polish their boots!

I had begged my father's permission to go with them when they were leaving, and my brother had been begging for two years, but while father had always been so generous with us in so many ways, on this subject he was absolutely unshakable.

We were a family of bakers, he said, not warriors. We fed people. We did not kill them. In time of war, if our country and our liege lord needed our help, we would of course go, but only when we were absolutely needed.

Ironically, my mother and sisters had been issued weapons and armor over two years before, and they trained for one day of every week to defend Okoitz when we men finally went out to face the enemy.

To me, it had seemed strange and unfitting that my youngest sister, only two years older than me, should be war-trained when I was not, or that my mother should wear a sword over her broad left shoulder when my father had none, but there it was.

My father was a man of peace, and in the family, he ruled. He had kept us at our normal work for as long as possible, but now Mother ran the bakery with the help of my sisters and a dozen other women, and we men walked away through the first snow of the year to answer the call.

We men were all in our oldest, shabbiest clothing, for we had been warned that we would be issued uniform clothes, and that anything we had with us would be thrown away. The women were dressed in their best to see us off, and the difference in clothing was somehow unsettling.

All of us, the men as well as the women, were soon crying at the shock of this first sundering of our family. My people had never before been parted for more than a few hours, and now we would be separated for months even if all went well.

If it didn't, we might never meet again.

Strangeness, the seeing of new things, the hearing of new sounds, the sampling of new smells, does odd things to one's sense of time. A day spent in the bakery, doing the same things I had done on countless other days, went by in a seeming moment. A year spent in mixing dough, baking it, and selling bread seemed to go by even faster.

That first day away from home—walking over a trail I had heard about all of my life but never seen, except for the few hundred yards of it visible from the gates of Okoitz—took forever.

Even years later I can remember with crystal clarity the shape of bare oak branches, the flecks of rust on the railroad tracks we walked beside, the squish of wet snow beneath my sodden birchbark shoes.

I can close my eyes and see the white clouds forming from my breath, smell the tang of fresh-cut pine trees, and feel the cold breeze against my back. Yet of my father's old bakery, where I had worked for years, I find I can remember very little.

An odd thing, memory.

A long walk has healing powers, I was convinced of it, even though I had never been out of sight of my hometown before. Not accustomed to hours of walking, I was sore and tired, yet I felt less lonely and depressed by the time we arrived at the Warrior's School.

A friendly guard at the gate directed us to the Induction Center, where they gave us a meal, warned us a bit about what to expect, and found us a place to sleep for the night. In the morning they had us line up and raise our right hands to the rising sun. They led us through the army oath:

"On my honor, I will do my best to do my duty to God and to the army. I will obey the Warrior's Code, and I will keep myself physically fit, mentally alert, and morally straight.

"The Warrior's Code:

"A Warrior is: Trustworthy, Loyal, and Reverent. Courteous,

Kind, and Fatherly. Obedient, Cheerful, and Efficient. Brave, Clean, and Deadly."

We were told that we would be repeating that oath every morning for the rest of our lives. My father said nothing, yet I could see a bit of doubt in his eyes.

I had heard all sorts of descriptions of the Warrior's School, but none of them prepared me for the unbelievable number of people we found there, or for the organized confusion that prevailed.

People in apparent authority were constantly shouting incomprehensible things at us, talking so quickly, in so many strange accents, about such unfamiliar things, that it seemed almost as though they spoke some foreign language. When they did say something simple, something we could understand, it was such a rare event that we did not at first react to it, and then the shouting got only louder and longer.

We spent two days standing in long lines, something none of us had ever done before, interspersed with numerous embarrassing interruptions as we were washed, shaved, deloused, fed, inspected by a half-dozen medical people, and, finally, after being naked for an entire day in a huge, cold building, issued uniform clothing.

We were a vastly changed group when at last we were counted off, assigned to our companies, and taken to our permanent barracks.

As it happened, my position in the line was such that I was the last man in one company and my father was the first in the next. My father shouted protests at this separation of his family, but the captain in charge was too tired and harried to pay any attention to him.

I felt a twinge of both panic and anguish at being thus separated from my father and brother, since in the course of our induction we had somehow parted company from all of the others who had come with us from Okoitz. Indeed, it was the first time I had ever been separated from my male relatives.

For the first time in my entire life, I was friendless.

I was dazed and confused as I obeyed the shouting captain, and walked away at the end of the line. Everything was so strange, so different from anything I had ever seen before.

For all of my life up to that point, for as long as I could remember, I had always been surrounded by people that I knew. An unfamiliar face had been a rare thing, a person from some distant land whole miles away from where things had such a comforting familiarity.

Now, as I looked around, I could see not one single person I knew. We had walked a long way through this weird place, with many twists and turns, and I was soon lost. I didn't know where I was. I didn't even know why *I* was.

We stopped in front of a building that seemed to stretch out to the horizon in both directions, a mile long, at least. The captain told us his name was Stashu Targ, and that we were the Third Company of the Second Komand of the First Riverboat Battalion. I promptly forgot everything he had said. He pointed to the number written above the doorway behind him and read it to us, twice. I forgot this, too, just as quickly. I had seen too many new things this day, and my mind simply could not take in anything more.

I think that the others around me must have been in the same sad shape that I was, for when the captain stopped talking, we all just stood there, dumb.

Then a knight came up with a pen and a horn of indelible ink and wrote the number above the door on the back of our left hand, one of us at a time.

"This is where you live," he said patiently to each of us. "When you get lost, come back here."

I nodded mutely. It was as though I was surrounded by a fog, and that fog would not lift for months.

I did what I was told, and they kept me amazingly busy. We marched in step with one another for many mind-numbing hours. We endlessly repeated the same awkward motions with pikes, knives, and axes, until somehow they became less awkward.

We ate together, sang together, and prayed together. Over the weeks, we were armed and armored, but we were all disappointed when we were issued axes as our secondary weapons rather than swords.

Captain Targ explained that the sword was a hard weapon to master. Skill with one took years to develop, and we had only four months before the Mongols would arrive. On the other hand, everybody had chopped firewood. We already knew how to use an axe.

The problem, as far as we grunts were concerned, was that an axe is a peasant's weapon, whereas the sword was the weapon, even the symbol, of a nobleman.

Sir Odon said that we would learn about swords after the war, when we all came back for the other eight months of the Warrior's School. Furthermore, our primary weapons were the two-yard-long halberds that the first lance used, the six-yard-long pikes that the second, third, fourth, and fifth lances carried, and most important, the swivel guns that the sixth fired. Swords, axes, and knives were really unimportant.

We grunts would still have been much happier with swords than with the axes we were given.

Somehow, though I was never quite sure when or how, I learned how to take care of my equipment, how to answer properly to my superiors, how to fight with my weapons. I felt my muscles getting bigger, my hands getting harder, my waist getting smaller. They had to adjust my armor three times to fit the changing me.

They yelled at me, gesticulated, and swore at me as no one ever had before, but eventually I ceased to be troubled by it. They chewed my ass so many times that after a while all they could get was scar tissue.

What I did not ever do was find my father, or my brother, or indeed anybody at all that I had ever known before. I searched, but I never found them.

In school, back home, they had taught me a bit about probabilities, and I tried to compute the possibility of finding my family and friends. At Okoitz, I must have known—what?—two hundred men? Here in Hell, they told me there were a sixth of a million of us. If I saw a hundred men outside of those in my own company every day, how long should it be before I saw a single familiar face? I worked it out again and again and rarely got the same number twice, but it seemed that it could not possibly take as long as it was taking.

The company kept records on those of us who belonged to it, but there were no central records for the entire army. There was no one who could tell me where in this huge city—the largest in Christendom, they told us—my father and brother were.

They had tried to keep such records once, but as the army grew, the task became impossible. Sir Odon said that maybe after we won the war, we would have time for such things. I did not find this to be comforting.

I often wrote to my mother, and I was sure she was writing to me, but the mails were all fouled up. Delivering them was one of the things the army did in times of peace, and I could understand we had other priorities now. In four months I got only two letters from her, and neither of them seemed to contain any answers to my questions, like "What is my father's address?"

The fact that she had my address meant she must have gotten at least one letter from me, and surely my father must have written to her as well! All I could think was that perhaps my questions had all been answered in some earlier, undelivered letter.

Yet all things fade, including the loneliness in my heart and the fog that surrounded my head. Slowly, I began to take notice of the other men in my lance, in my platoon, in my company. I began to realize I had new friends now, and in some ways they were better than those I had left behind.

At least they were more interesting, none of them being bakers.

The fellow in the bunk above me, Zbigniew, had worked on Lord Conrad's ranch, where they had a large herd of slightly domesticated aurochs. He had been one of the Pruthenian children Lord Conrad had rescued from the Crossmen.

The guy in the bunk below, Lezek, came from the neighboring ranch where all of Anna's children were raised until they reached their fourth year.

At that age, they somehow "remembered" everything that their mother had known up to the time they were conceived, even though there wasn't a stallion involved in their procreation.

Unlike people and just about everything else in the world, Anna and her children had offspring whenever they wanted and did it without the help of the opposite sex. In fact, the opposite sex didn't exist for their species, a thing that made most of the men in my lance claim to feel sorry for them.

You see, sex was a subject that was often discussed among us, though I suspected my lance mates had as little real knowledge of the subject as I did.

In any event, Lezek was impressed with the fact that I had known Anna herself since I was six years old, and he questioned me for days about every incident I knew of concerning her. Even though his father had worked with the Big People for years, no one he knew had actually talked for any length with Anna herself.

While there were only twenty-nine adult Big People at that point, there were three hundred sixty-four young ones at the ranch, managed by a young woman named Kotcha, whom I vaguely remembered. Once, she had lived a few doors down from my family's house.

Lezek said that in ten years there would be twenty-four thousand adult Big People, and ten years after that everybody would have one. I'm not sure if anyone believed him, but that's what he said.

The other three men in our lance were less talkative, since none of them spoke much Polish. Fritz was a German who came from a farm not far from Worms. He could read and write our language well, since he had been reading Lord Conrad's magazine every month for five years, but his pronunciation still left much to be desired. He had come to join our army, he said, because the chances of rising in the world were better here than anyplace else, and that being a farmer was mostly a matter of walking behind a plow and staring at the ass end of a pair of oxen for most of your life. And anyway, he had more brothers than his father had farmland for them to inherit.

Kiejstut was a Lithuanian who had come because he heard that the army would arm, armor, and train him to fight Mongols. A year earlier, Mongol raiders had killed his father and one of his brothers, kidnapped his youngest sister, and burned down his entire village. He wanted vengeance, even though he was by nature a rather quiet, reserved, even shy person, one who was always careful not to give offense.

The sixth member of my lance was Taurus, a Ukrainian whose family had once lived north of Kiev. He was the only one of his large family who was still alive. Hatred and bitterness seemed to radiate from him. I never once saw him smile, and I never heard him laugh, not until we saw combat and he started killing Mongols. Sterner and far more exacting than our knight, Sir Odon, he was always quick to chastise the rest of us for any slackness during our training, and even for any levity.

Our training went on for four months, and at the time it seemed forever. Sir Odon said that we were getting only a special short course, and if we wanted to stay in the army, we would have to come back here sometime and take another eight months of this.

We all groaned at the thought of an additional eight months in Hell. Almost as an article of faith, we soldiers complained about everything we did or had done to us. This was even true of those grunts (for that was indeed what they called us) who did not come from Lord Conrad's lands, about three-quarters of those in my company.

I had noticed these generally older men when we were first joined together to form our company. Mostly, they were less healthy than the rest of us, thinner, and poorly fed. Also, it seemed to me that some of them were mentally duller than the people I had grown up with. Now they were wearing the first pairs of leather boots that some of them had ever owned, and almost all of them had put on healthy weight, but they still felt obligated to complain, so they did so.

Privately, I think they were impressed by the wealth of the army, and that most of them had resolved to stay in, if they could possibly manage it.

At the end of February, when final preparations were being made, when weapons, ammunition, preserved food, and everything else we would need for the months ahead was being issued, one of the warehouse workers handed me a white leather kit with a red cross on it.

I asked what it was.

"It's a medical kit," he said. "We usually hand them out only to people who have completed the surgeon's course, but someone had too many of these kits made up. The captain said to hand them out to one man from each company, just in case you need it."

I said that I was in the fifth lance, so I'd had the first-aid course, but that was just to help the wounded until somebody got there who knew what he was doing. I didn't know anything about really fixing people!

"Everybody who does already has a kit. Keep it. Clip it on your belt, just in case."

I did as I was ordered, and I quit wearing my smaller first-aid pack since everything in it was also in the big medical kit.

I soon discovered there were advantages to wearing the kit, since real medics were rarely sent out to do the dirtiest jobs, such as cleaning the latrines. Once I had the kit, people assumed I was trained in its use, and thus my life became a bit easier. No one ever asked me if I had taken the proper course, so I was never even tempted to lie about it.

Our company was part of the River Battalion, the men who would be manning the riverboats on the Vistula. This intrigued me, since I had often heard of boats, but had never seen one. In truth, I had never even seen a river.

We wouldn't be actually operating the boats, of course; that was the job of another group entirely. We had only to ride along, we were told, and to obey the orders of our knights and captains, who had vast experience on the dozens of steam-powered boats the army had.

Well, my knight, Sir Odon, was the same age I was, but had joined the army a year earlier, and I don't think he had vast experience in anything. My captain, Sir Stashu, looked to be perhaps eighteen and was no gray-bearded repository of wisdom, either, but I kept my mouth shut, as my father, a wise man, had taught me.

Grunts bitched about everything, but we learned that there were a few topics of conversation that could get you chosen to shovel out the garbage, or to wash a few thousand dishes, and that among these was the inexperience of our leaders. They knew it themselves, and preferred not to think about it.

Chapter Three

FROM THE JOURNAL OF JOSIP SOBIESKI

*written January 19, 1249,
concerning February 15, 1241*

At last, we said our final Sunrise Service in Hell, and we marched out to war.

Well, we had to pull our war carts behind us, there were only two railroad tracks to pull them on, and there were a sixth of a million of us troops to move out. An hour went by before we finally left Hell, and we were near the front of the line. Our doubled column was over sixteen miles long! Even at a brisk walk, it took almost six hours for us to march by!

Once we finally got on the tracks, it wasn't all that hard to pull the big cart, even loaded as it was with the tons of guns, pikes, and all the other material we needed to fight with. Counting our six knights and the knight-banner who led us, there were forty-three men in our platoon.

Our cart could be pulled by eighteen of them, with the rest of us riding aboard, resting, eating, or even sleeping. This let us continue onward right around the clock, doing over six dozen miles a day without ever once breaking into a run.

The six carts of my company pulled off the main road when we got to East Gate and left the main body of the army to go on without us.

A great crowd of civilians was leaving the dock area. There must have been thousands of them, mostly peasants, but with a scattering of well-dressed people as well. They were all walking back the way we had come; refugees who would shelter at the Warrior's School, we presumed.

I had heard much about the castle that had been built at East Gate, how it was made entirely of reinforced concrete, and I was eager to examine it closely.

I never got the chance for we were marched straight onto our boat, the RB1 *Muddling Through.* The tracks went right up to and over the big drawbridge at the front of the boat and right into the cavern of a hold that made up most of the lower deck. We could hardly see the huge boat as we went aboard it.

The drawbridge door was closed behind us, leaving us in the dark, and our riverboat pulled out immediately to let the next one up to the dock to be loaded. It was like being locked up in an oversized barn, filled with six war carts and the almost two gross of men of my company.

We soon found out that we were riding in no ordinary steamboat, but in the craft that held the commanders of the entire river flotilla, all three dozen boats. We had two army barons aboard, as well as Sir Conrad, now Count Conrad, himself.

Captain Targ didn't want his troops getting in the way of all these high personages, so he had us stay down below on the cargo deck, just in front of the engines. The second deck had the radios and the war room, called Tartar Control, as well as the kitchen and the sleeping rooms for the officers.

There was a fighting top above that, and a few hours after we were aboard, the sixth lance of each platoon was sent up there with their guns. So were the fourth lances, who acted as loaders for the swivel guns, and the third, who acted as spotters.

My own fifth lance acted as corpsmen, assistants for the surgeons, and we wouldn't be needed until somebody got shot. This meant we had to stay inside, cooped up without even a window, until somebody had the courtesy to get decently wounded so we could go outside and do something.

That night I was one of the few men below who couldn't sleep. I was standing near the stairs with my helmet off when a tall man walked by with a line of white circles down the armor on his back. I snapped to attention.

You see, the army used a color code for the numbers of its lances, platoons, companies, and so on. One was red, two was orange, three was yellow, four was green, five was blue, and six was purple. The buttons on our uniform jackets used these colors to define where we were in the army's organization.

The top button was your position in your lance, the second, your lance's position in your platoon, the third was your platoon's place in the company, and so on. The buttons on my jacket went, from the top down, orange, blue, blue, yellow, orange, red, green, blue, and red. This meant that I was the second man in the fifth lance, of the Fifth Platoon, of the Third Company, of the Second Komand, of the First Battalion, of the Fourth Column, of the Fifth County, of the First Division of the army.

The leader of any group used a white button in that position. That is to say, Sir Odon's buttons were the same color as mine, except that his top one was white. Captain Targ's top three buttons were white.

On our armor, which zippered together, there were big spots, a different shape for each color, running down the chest and the back, painted in the same colors as our buttons. Otherwise, we all looked the same in armor, and with the faceplates closed, you couldn't tell who was who. Once you got used to it, you could spot your friends quickly.

Also, if someone was impersonating a warrior, before long his button colors would get him caught by someone who knew he wasn't who he was supposed to be.

So when I saw a line of nine white circles on the man's back, I knew he had to be Lord Conrad himself. I came to attention, as I had been taught, and he stopped, turned, and looked at me.

"I know you, don't I?" He said, "Yes, you are Josip, the son of the baker from Okoitz."

I said that I was, and that I was surprised so great a person as he was had actually recognized me.

"I am just another man, Josip, not much different from you. I think that mostly I remember you because of your surprise and your laugh when I showed you that top I made for you."

I said that I had been six years old then, but yes, I remembered it, too. I said I still had that toy, carefully stored away, and that if I ever had a son, I would give it to him.

"It feels good to be appreciated. But tell me, Josip, is there anything I can do for you now?"

I said there was, and explained to him that I had been on the boat for twelve hours now, and they said that the boat was on a river, but I had never in my life actually seen a river. Could I perhaps have permission to go up and have a look?

"You never . . . ? I'm sorry, but I sometimes forget how restricted the life of a commoner can be. I'll do better than just let you topside. I'm doing an informal inspection just now. Come with me, and I'll give you the threepenny tour of the *Muddling Through*."

And with that he took me all around the boat, starting with the engines, where the engineer had forbidden us troops to go. But who would dare stand in the way of Lord Conrad, or even the lowly grunt who was accompanying him?

I was surprised to discover I already knew the baron who was in charge of the radio room. He was Piotr, whose parents had the room two doors down from my father's. Eight years older than me, he had once been one of the "big kids," although he had been the smallest "big kid" at Okoitz, and now I was a head taller than he was.

He said he remembered me, but somehow I don't think he really did. He was just being polite. Truthfully, I doubt if I could remember any of the little kids there who were eight years younger than I was!

The dawn was breaking before we finally got all the way up to the fighting top, and at last I saw what a river looked like. The Vistula was as beautiful as they had always told me it was.

That morning, word went out that those of us below could go up topside, one platoon at a time, whenever there wasn't a battle going on. I'm sure that order came from Lord Conrad.

I was below at noon, when all of the guns above us started shooting, not just the three dozen swivel guns my company manned, but the steam-powered peashooters that quickly spat out thousands of small iron balls, and the Halman Projectors that threw bombs high over the enemy. It went on for an hour before my lance was called up to the ready room. After a few minutes we were needed up on the fighting top.

The gun smoke was so thick you had to gag, and after the darkness below, the sunlight was blinding. The noise could make a man go deaf, and the number of arrows being shot at us was simply unbelievable. They were stuck all over the deck and looked almost like wheat ready for the harvest. We found that we had to walk with a sort of sliding motion, breaking off the arrows as we went, to keep from tripping over them.

All of the men on deck had arrows sticking out of them, a frightening sight! But we soon realized they were all right. Our armor was of plated steel, heavily waxed and covered with thick canvas. It was proof against the Mongol arrows, although those missiles tended to stick in the wax and canvas.

What I had taken at first for convulsions was in fact the men laughing about the whole situation!

A gunner signaled for help, with an arrow in his upper arm that was squirting blood. Somehow, it had managed to slide up his brassard and get under his pauldron. Not a deadly wound, but it needed tending. Fritz and Zbigniew helped him below, his loader took over shooting the gun, and the spotter took over loading the twenty-round clips into the gun, and then reloading the empty clips from the ammunition boxes.

I had nothing better to do, so I felt free to stand behind them and act as their spotter. It gave me a chance to see what was going on.

A great mob of Mongols was on the bank, crowding right down to the shore. They were trying to kill us with their arrows, which were obviously ineffective. We, on the other hand, *were* hurting them, hurting them badly.

Three dozen swivel guns were each shooting twenty rounds a minute into a packed crowd of men and horses, and you could see where individual bullets were killing three and four of them in a file at a time. The two peashooters on that side of the boat were spraying away, taking out Mongols in horizontal ranks. And the Halman bombs were bursting above them, each explosion knocking down a circle of the enemy a dozen yards across!

The enemy was being shot so fast that no attempt was made to remove the dead and wounded. Those that fell were just left there to be trampled, to bleed, and to die.

And the fools kept coming! They made no attempt to run away, or to hide behind something, as any rational creature would, but instead were actually *climbing on top of their own dead in order to get at us*!

I tell you that in some places they were sitting on horses that were standing on three and four layers of dead men and dead horses!

And once there, there was nothing they could do. Their arrows couldn't really hurt us, and when some of them went into the water to get at us, those that didn't freeze immediately soon found that the sides of the boat were six yards high, and made of smooth metal that couldn't possibly be climbed.

In our months of training, we had been repeatedly told that we were facing the craftiest, best organized, and best led enemy in the world. That day, it seemed to me we were simply slaughtering a mob of idiots with less brains than a herd of sheep.

Then the loader on the gun next to me got an arrow in the eyeslit, and I had to leave off watching the war and go to his aid. He was on his back and not moving. I needed help to get him below.

Looking about, I saw Taurus was shooting a gun three places down, and laughing and screaming insanely at the Mongols the whole time. He was shouting what could only have been the names of his family and friends who had fallen to the Mongol onslaught of the Ukraine.

I thought that he was somehow living in Heaven and in Hell at the same time. I knew that while he had both bullets and Mongols to shoot them at, I would get no help from Taurus.

Then Sir Odon saw my need and ran over to help me. Together we picked the wounded man up and carried him down the steps to the surgery.

Later, we found out that our gunner lived, and he was back at his gun the next day.

This sort of slaughter went on for days, and we were all amazed there were so many Mongols. One night I spoke briefly to Lord

Conrad again, and he admitted to being as astounded by their numbers as everyone else was. His biggest worry was that we would run out of ammunition before Batu Khan ran out of warriors.

Then the Mongols started to get a little bit smart, or maybe, as some said, their engineers finally caught up with their frontline troops.

One of our planes, piloted by Count Lambert himself, someone said, dropped us a message telling us that the enemy was building a pontoon bridge along the riverbank, downstream of us.

We went there with another boat following us, and they ordered us to get ready to land and chop the thing up with our axes right after we gave them a pass with the guns.

All of us except the gunners poured out of the drawbridge in the front of the boat, with the fifth lance of each platoon taking up the rear, as usual. We had to be behind the other guys in order to see them when they got wounded, and get them back to safety. Not that we didn't do our share of the fighting, you understand.

The first lance, made up of the biggest men, always went in first with their halberds, and we went in last to pick up the pieces, whether we were with our pikes, towing a war cart behind us that was full of gunners, as in a field battle, or when we just went in with axes, like now.

The Mongols had broken and run away after our gunners had done their job on them, which made me figure that their engineers must be a lot smarter than the average run of the enemy—say, about up to the level of a flock of ducks.

There wasn't much for us to do, since the guys up front had already chopped up everything that looked like it might have been a part of a bridge, or a bit of a Mongol.

There were a lot of dead bodies lying around, hacked up and bloody and stinking worse than anything you could possibly imagine. It wasn't just the shit that had been shot out of the guts of so many of them.

During training, we'd been told that Mongols never bathed, that they put their new clothes on the outside and then let those on the inside just rot away, but we hadn't believed it, not until we had to walk through all those dead bodies.

By this time everybody had gotten used to seeing dead people, but the stench of that beach got at least a dozen of the guys heaving their breakfast out, and that was a very bad thing to do when you were wearing one of our helmets, which covered your whole face. Think about it, if you really want to.

We had one guy whose visor hinge got jammed, and he darned near drowned before Zbigniew got the thing freed up.

There was a lot of gold on that beach. Every dead body seemed to have a big pouch full of the stuff. I didn't dare touch any of it, since doctrine was that you had to win the battle first before you started to loot. And even then you couldn't keep what you picked up, since all of the booty had to be brought together and counted before it could be fairly shared out.

Still and all, the temptation certainly was there. One of the men yielded to it, picked up a Mongol pouch, and got yelled at by Captain Targ. Then Lord Conrad said we might as well pick up a few pouches, just to get an idea of how much loot there actually was, and the captain gave the job to my platoon.

So I had about *fifty pounds* of gold and silver in my arms when all hell burst loose over the top of the riverbank.

Chapter Four

FROM THE JOURNAL OF JOSIP SOBIESKI

written January 20, 1249,
concerning February 21, 1241

At that point the river had a high bank, higher than the top of our boat, so the gunners and other people up there couldn't see over it to warn us about what was coming.

The other thing we had going against us was the fact that our helmets fastened to our breastplates and back armor with a rotary coupling that let you twist your head sideways but not up and down. It was a good system, most of the time, since a bash on the head wasn't likely to break your neck.

But in this instance, with the enemy suddenly above us, well, most of us didn't even know they were there until they shot us.

Actually, the Mongols did us a favor of sorts with that first volley, since it got our attention, and their arrows, like I said earlier, weren't usually all that deadly.

We soon found out that they had a spear with a long, thin point and sharp edges that was sheer murder.

Thrown at close range or carried at a run, that thing could punch right through our armor, and then right through the man who wore it, just about anywhere they put it. Once they had one of those spears in a man, they would jerk the spear sideways, and a little hole on the outside left a big, deep slash inside.

Had they just charged at us straight off, they could have killed most of us before we even knew there was a battle going on.

Even then, I was slow on the uptake, I am ashamed to say, because at first I had a hard time throwing away all that gold. I mean, here in my arms I had more money than my father could have made in twenty lifetimes of hard work, and while it was probably only a few moments before I threw it down and pulled my axe from its sheath, those were some long and important moments.

They came at us on foot, jumping down from the bluff, breaking their fall on the sloping sand and smashing into us. I had my axe out in time, but I didn't have a chance to swing it before this smelly individual knocked me over and ended up on top of me. He couldn't use his sword any more than I could use my axe, and he thought of his knife before I did.

I felt his knife hit my left side and bounce off my armor twice before I got my own knife out and did unto him as he was trying real hard to do unto me. He had armor, but it wasn't nearly as good as the stuff Lord Conrad's factories make. I had to stick him four times before he gave up and died.

I threw his body off me and tried to stand up, but before I was upright, some other Mongol ran into me and sent me skidding across a patch of ice and into the muddy water by the river.

What with the goose-down padding we wore under the armor, I hadn't much noticed the cold up until then, but when the water seeped in, it was ungodly cold. The Mongol next to me noticed it, too, or maybe he was just afraid of drowning, but he lost interest in me and tried to get back on dry land.

That was his big mistake, because I still had my knife in my hand. Still on my back, I caught him in the back of the knee, and he went down. I crawled over and got him in the neck before I stood again, picked up somebody's axe, and looked around, trying to figure out where I could be of the most use.

The gunners were blazing away, shooting those Mongols who were still on top of the bluff or just starting down, but they were afraid of shooting those in our midst for fear of killing their own men.

Down below we were outnumbered maybe two to one, and the Mongols, a whole lot more agile than we were, were swarming all over us. Our troops looked like clumsy bears being attacked by a fast and deadly pack of wolves.

It was our armor, you see, that made us slow and half blind.

It also made us almost indestructible, and I saw men take a dozen hits and keep on fighting as if they didn't notice them. In one case, I'm sure he didn't.

Taurus was swinging his axe like a madman, screaming insanely, running at the enemy and chopping down everything in front of him. I think he was seeing every Mongol as one of those who killed his family, and he was laughing at every throat he cut, every skull he smashed.

He certainly didn't need or want any help, and I had the idea that it wouldn't be safe to stand next to him; he might not know friend from foe until after the battle was over.

Some of the old fireside stories told of the times the Vikings invaded Poland and how they all got killed for their trouble.

One kind of Viking was called a berserker, men who went absolutely crazy during a battle. Looking at Taurus, I couldn't help thinking he must have some of that berserker blood in his veins. It was possible, because hundreds of years ago the Ukrainians had lost to the Vikings instead of killing them all, as we Poles did.

A Mongol in baggy pants singled me out, shouted some war cry, and ran at me with one of those deadly spears. Luck was still with me, for he slipped on the muddy ice and landed facedown at my feet. I chopped down, catching him in the middle of the back, between the shoulders, and he stopped moving. I looked back out at the fight.

A dozen of our men had formed up in a circle. They didn't seem to need help, and anyway, getting in there through the crowd of Mongols surrounding them looked impossible.

Then I spotted Captain Targ and Lord Conrad struggling in the mud, trying to get up while a dozen Mongols were trying to put them down. I was needed.

The tactics they taught us at the Warrior's School said that fighting fair is fighting stupid. If you do not kill the enemy as fast as possible, he will kill you instead, and your mother told you to come home alive. Fighting to win always seemed very sensible to me, despite all the glorious fireside stories I had heard about knightly honor, valor, and courtesy.

I killed three of the enemy surrounding my leaders by chopping them in the back before they knew I was there. Then suddenly, entirely too many of them noticed me, and it was my turn to need help. It came in the form of Fritz and Zbigniew.

Soon we were fighting on top of the dead, or nearly dead, bodies of the slain, and we were getting the upper hand. Those of the enemy who were still alive were falling back, or at least had become less aggressive about attacking us.

Then another band of Mongols came toward us, riding on horseback along the riverbank. With pikes, we could have taken care of them easily, but our pikes were stored in our war carts, back in the boat! Faced with fighting horsemen with only peasant axes, well, I was grateful when Captain Targ called for a retreat!

We made it back on the boat in good order, taking with us our wounded and our dead, more of both than I thought we had lost when I was fighting.

Even Taurus made it back, I think because he got turned around in the fight and found Mongols between himself and the boat. He didn't hurt any of us, but only because two men ran away and one man threw himself flat on the ground when they saw him coming.

Sir Odon had to hit him and take the axe from his hands before the captain allowed him on board. At least Taurus hadn't stripped himself naked, the way they say the Viking berserkers did.

The next-to-the-last man in was Lord Conrad, and I saw that he had an arrow in his eyeslit. I helped him up to the surgery and gently took his helmet off.

"Have I lost it?" he said, referring to his right eye.

I told him the arrow had missed the eyeball, so it was likely he would see with it again, but the arrow had stuck in the bone to the right of it, and there would probably be a scar. Still, he had been lucky.

"I would have been a damn sight luckier if the arrow had missed!"

I had to agree to the truth of that statement.

"Well, open that surgeon's kit! Get the arrowhead out, clean the wound, and sew it up! Didn't they teach you anything in medic's school?"

I tried to explain that I wasn't qualified, that I had never sewn up an eye before, that in fact I had never sewn up anything but some small dead animals in training, but it seemed he was adamant about me doing the job, and doing it immediately! I looked desperately around for help, but both of the surgeons were working on men who were far more seriously wounded than Lord Conrad. High rank has its privileges in most places, but not in an army surgery.

"Well, boy, now's your chance to learn! First, wash your hands in white lightning, and then wash around the wound as best you can."

What could I do? I had been given a direct order by a very superior officer! I had no choice but to obey.

When I finished with the washing, he said, "You got that done? Then get the pliers out of your kit and pull the arrowhead out. Better get somebody to hold my head. It will hurt, and I might flinch."

I could not believe that the greatest hero in all of Poland would ever flinch and tried to say so, but he shouted me down.

"I said get somebody to hold my head and stop acting like I'm God! That's an order!"

Shocked, I agreed that he was not God and called Lezek over to hold his head still.

"Now the pliers," he said.

The pain must have been horrible, for while he did not cry out, he did pass out for a few moments. When he came to, I told him it was out, and showed him the bloody arrowhead.

"Good. Throw it away. That kind of souvenir I don't need. Now get a pair of tweezers and feel around in the wound for any bits of broken bone or any foreign matter."

I thought of keeping that Mongol arrowhead myself, as a conversation piece, but orders were orders, and I gave it a toss. I found the tweezers and went to work. This time he cried out, although he did not pass out. I felt around in there as gently as I could, and found a few small bits of broken bone, which I removed. Then I told him I was done.

"Thank God! Now clean it all out again with white lightning. Pour it right in."

I still felt awkward about all of this, but what could I do but follow orders?

"Okay. Now get your sterile needle and thread and sew it up. Use nice neat little stitches, because if my wife doesn't like the job you do, she will make your life not worth living. Believe me. I know the woman."

I had heard tales of Lord Conrad's lady, and I had no desire to be her enemy. I carefully made nine neat little stitches, and when I was done, you could hardly see where the cut was. Then I bandaged him up, wrapping the clean gauze around his head and then under his jaw to keep it in place.

He sat up and said, "Well. Good job, I hope. Thank you, but now you better get around to the other men who were wounded."

I looked around and told him that it wasn't necessary, the surgeons had already taken care of everybody.

"The surgeons!" he yelled. "Then what the hell are you?"

I told him I was in the fifth lance, an assistant corpsman.

"Then what the hell were you doing operating on my head?"

I tried to explain that he had ordered me to do all that I had done. That I had been given a direct order by my commanding officer. What else could I have done but obey him?

"Then what were you doing with that surgeon's kit?"

So I explained how they had had these extra kits at the warehouse, and how they handed them out to some of the fifth lancers, just in case we needed them.

"They just handed it to you?"

I said yes, and thanked him for showing me what one should do with many of the things in the kit. It had reminded me of my boyhood at Okoitz, when Sir Conrad always seemed to have time to explain things to us.

But he just turned away from me with a look of exasperation on his face. I thought about the way Sir Conrad had always had a lot less patience with adults than he had with children, and I supposed that I was finally growing up.

Nonetheless, I beat a hasty retreat down to the lower deck.

Lezek followed me, giggling.

Chapter Five

FROM THE JOURNAL OF JOSIP SOBIESKI

written January 21, 1249,
concerning February 26, 1241

We got back to East Gate every second or third day, to load up on more coal, food, and ammunition, and to put ashore our dead and our seriously wounded.

The fighting was getting grim. The Mongols were becoming a lot less stupid than they had been, and we were starting to take serious losses.

The Mongols killed their first riverboat by luring it close to shore, and then felling a tall pine tree on it. They swarmed over the tree and eventually killed everyone in the crew. They were learning how to use the guns when Lord Conrad had another boat set the captured boat on fire with its flamethrower.

Their engineers all seemed to have black hair, yellowish skin, and funny-looking eyes. Lord Conrad said they were Chinese, from a place called China on the other side of the world.

They started setting up a sort of Mongol catapult. The things had a long arm with a big rock at one end and maybe two gross of their men pulling ropes on the other. They worked a lot better than you'd think, throwing rocks weighing over a ton for hundreds of yards.

One day when I was resting down on the cargo deck, a rock came through the fighting top, through two bunk beds in the officers' quarters, through the second floor, through our war cart not a yard from where I was lying down on top of it, through the cargo deck floor, and down through the bottom of the boat a yard below that!

I'd made the mistake of removing my armor before lying down to rest, so I got sprayed with about two dozen big splinters. I was never in danger of dying, but it took the surgeons over an hour to patch me up. And it hurt.

Lord Conrad got the bottom fixed before we sank, but just when he was done, another rock came all the way down through the boat not three yards from where the first one hit!

I tell you, warfare was starting to get dangerous!

We managed to keep our boat afloat, but had we caught a rock in the boilers, or on the paddle wheel the way some boats did, we would have been wrecked just like so many of the others.

Usually, the boatmaster could get his boat on the west bank before the thing sank, or sometimes another boat was near enough to be able to help out, so most of the men were saved. Most, but by no means all.

Sir Odon said it was possible to swim in armor, and he had done it himself, but he didn't think that a man could last long in the freezing water of February. It didn't make much difference to me one way or the other, since I had never learned to swim.

We got to avoiding those catapults, except where they started building a bridge in front of a bunch of them. As long as we could keep the Mongols on the east side of the Vistula, we knew eventually we would beat them. We didn't dare let them across, so we didn't dare let them get a bridge built.

Then the Mongols came up with their best idea yet, only maybe I should call it their worst one. They got whole cowhides, sewed them back together, and filled them with oil and lard. They lit them on fire and threw them at us with their catapults. When they hit a boat, it usually burned to the waterline. We lost more than half of all our boats to those firebombs, and all too often their crews were burned up with them.

In front of Sandomierz, where the enemy tried again and again to build a bridge, I saw six riverboats get hit by those oil bags and burn right down to nothing. Each of them had over two gross of our men on them, and only one of the six was able to beach itself on the western shore. You had to cry, looking at it.

Then, as suddenly as the firebombs started, they stopped. The best anybody could figure out, the Mongols must have just run out of oil and lard.

We were running out of almost everything, too.

Finally, there came a time when there were only about a dozen or so riverboats left on the Vistula.

We were out of the wood alcohol and pine resin stuff they used in the flamethrowers, out of bombs for the Halmans, out of iron balls for the peashooters, and almost out of ammunition for the swivel guns. We had even run out of Mongol arrows to shoot back at them.

Almost everybody on board had at least one wound, and out of my company we had more than six dozen men gone, either dead or wounded so bad they couldn't possibly fight.

We had some coal for the engines and food enough to eat, but that was about it.

And we were all tired. Deep-down-right-to-the-bone tired, so tired that even sleep didn't seem to do much good anymore.

That was when we found a completed bridge all the way across the Vistula, with thousands of Mongols racing across the top of it, getting to the west bank we had protected for so long.

Most of us were down in the cargo deck finishing lunch when Lord Conrad ordered everyone ashore, except for one volunteer to take care of the engines. He said he was going to take out the bridge by ramming it and this would likely sink the boat, so there wasn't any sense in getting everybody killed.

Except by then, well, there weren't any of us that had much sense left!

Leaving the boat? Abandoning ship when so many of our friends had died to preserve her? How could we do such a thing?

I looked at the men around me and said that maybe the boat wouldn't sink. Maybe the boat would get hung up on the bridge and we would be needed to clear the decks of the enemy. The others around me nodded. What I said seemed like perfect sense to them.

Then someone said that if we pushed all the carts right up tight to the front of the boat, the boat would hit the bridge with a much more solid blow, and a bunch of the guys immediately started packing the big war carts tight up against the bow.

One of the engine crew said if we flooded some of the water-tight compartments below the floor, we would make the boat heavier, and it would hit harder, so they started doing that, even though we all knew that doing so would make the boat even more prone to sink.

To all of us, it was no longer important whether we lived or died. The important thing was to knock down that bridge, and then, if we were still afloat, to defend the boat from the Mongols.

Lord Conrad and Captain Targ were shouting at each other. I'm sure I heard someone say "Mutiny!"

Then our captain said, "Of course, sir. But for now, we'd better all get up on deck, or we'll miss the show. The boatmaster, Baron Tadaos, won't be waiting for orders, you know. *All platoons! Report on deck! Pass the word!*"

"You are all crazy people!" Lord Conrad shouted.

Sir Odon said, "Yes, sir. I suppose we are." Then he hurried up to the fighting top, and I was right behind him.

The bridge was tall, much taller than any of the other ones we had destroyed. I guess they had cut the logs thinking that the water was deeper here. Anyway, it was higher than the boat, and the roadway was made out of ropes that ran at the top of the logs.

There were I don't know how many thousands of Mongols up on that bridge, moving across as fast as they could. They saw us coming, they were pointing at us and shouting, but they never stopped moving. I saw men and horses getting on that bridge right up until the moment we hit it.

And hit it we did! Only we didn't punch a hole through it, the way I thought we would. We knocked it right over! Those big logs must have been just sitting on the bottom, because the ones right in front of us just went right over, Mongols and all! Then the water sort of caught the rope roadway and dragged it downstream, which just naturally pulled down the whole rest of the bridge with it!

There were all those thousands of Mongols splashing in the water, but none of them splashed around for long. Somebody said they came from a dry country called a desert, and they couldn't swim one bit better than I could!

Well, a few of them got near the western shore, so the gunners used some of their last bullets to get rid of them. I think most of the horses swam away, though.

It took us the rest of the day to get the boat fixed up.

Then things got quiet for a few days, and some of the guys said that the Mongols must have quit and gone home. The captain said that the enemy had pulled back from the river, but they weren't headed home yet, so we just paddled slowly around, waiting.

Then a really strange thing happened.

Early one morning, all along the river as far as we could see, the Mongols rode their horses down to the riverbank. They each got off, grabbed their horse's tail, and made the animal swim out into the water. And those horses swam all the way across the Vistula with the men behind them!

Our boat went right through them, drowning I don't know how many. Hundreds, maybe thousands, but not all that many compared to the huge numbers of warriors that were in the Vistula that chilly morning.

I heard somebody say that if the Mongols could do that, why hadn't they done it weeks ago, before we had killed so many of them on the riverbanks and on all those bridges we took out?

Then somebody else said to look carefully at the horses getting out of the water. Only about half of them still had a man behind them. All the rest of them must have drowned and sunk to the bottom in their armor.

That meant we had just seen half of the entire Mongol army drowned! They wanted to get across so bad they were willing to see half of their men die just to do it! And I mean half of the men they had left, after we had spent a week killing them by the thousands!

We were all dumbfounded, including, I think, Lord Conrad. The best anybody could think up for an answer was that maybe they had run out of food for themselves and their horses. There were millions of them, after all, and that many people and animals must eat an awful lot.

Later that day, when the insane enemy advance was over and the banks of the Vistula were again empty, Captain Targ told us we would be going ashore soon, to join up with the rest of the army that was getting ready to fight the Mongols, west of Sandomierz.

This time, no one thought of disobeying orders.

The Battle for the Vistula was over.

The Battle for Poland was about to begin.

Chapter Six

FROM THE JOURNAL OF JOSIP SOBIESKI

*written January 22, 1249,
concerning March 7, 1241*

They collected all the riverboats they could find, and together we disembarked in the cold rain, all of the men from the River Battalion who could still fight.

There were only nine boats left, nine out of the three dozen we had started out with.

There were only forty-one war carts to be pulled away from the shore out of the two hundred sixteen that had been loaded aboard at East Gate.

There were only sixteen hundred twenty-nine of us left out of the nine thousand men who had marched out of Hell to war, and almost all of us were wearing bloodstained bandages.

My lance had been surprisingly lucky. All six of us plus Sir Odon were still alive and upright, if not exactly well, but we were no longer together.

We had lost our platoon leader, and our war cart itself was smashed in the fighting, so the fifth platoon had been split up, temporarily, to fill out the losses in the other platoons.

Only Taurus was still by my side. Captain Targ told me to keep an eye on him, and Sir Odon told me to hit him on the head if he went crazy again. They both said that he was a valuable fighting man, but we had to make sure he did his work only on the Mongols.

Taurus himself had been very quiet since that fight on the

riverbank. Days later and late at night, when the others were asleep, he asked me to tell him just exactly what had happened. When I told him, he just nodded, as if he was trying hard to absorb it all.

Then, on another night, he had me go over it all again, and this time he was counting on his fingers the number of men he had killed. He asked me to add this to the number that he guessed he'd killed when he had been shooting the swivel gun, since his own arithmetic wasn't very good. I came up with a hundred twenty-one.

He nodded, and he almost smiled.

It had been a hard morning's work, pulling the heavy war carts mostly cross-country in the freezing mud, and it was near noon when we finally found the rest of the army, west of San-domierz.

I had the luck to be pulling on the very last cart in our column, and in the sixth file, so when we joined the rest of them, the man standing next to me, on my right, was from a different battalion. He had been there all day long and could tell me what was going on.

To know what was going on is a rare thing in the military. Usually, you find out only much later, and then what they would tell you had happened didn't seem to have much in common with what you had actually seen going on.

The first thing we found out was that the other battalions hadn't seen any action at all, except for the Night Fighters, and they were asleep somewhere. The army had been mostly waiting for the Mongols to cross the river, when all the while, the River Battalion was trying to stop them from doing just that.

They all had plenty of ammunition, whereas we were down to two bullets per gun. They quickly shared with us, and soon their other companies were helping out the rest of what was left of the River Battalion.

The entire army was there, although most of it was over the horizon, lined up in battle array, surrounding a long, shallow valley that they said held the whole Mongol army. We had the honor of plugging the hole they had ridden in through, chasing the noble knights of three duchies who were pretending to flee.

"Or pretending to be pretending!" Somebody laughed. Many commoners have a less-than-worshipful view of our traditional nobility.

Our noble knights were supposed to run out the other end of the valley, some other battalion would close off the hole, and then the whole army would advance and destroy the Mongols.

Of course, the other end of the valley was eight miles away, so things took a bit of time, but soon we would be getting the order to advance. We ate a hasty lunch and waited.

An hour later word got back that our noble knights had not left the trap after all, but outnumbered ten to one, had decided to take on the Mongols by themselves.

I nodded, yes, that sounded like every noble knight I had heard about in every fireside tale. Nitwits, the lot of them.

Much later we could see the horsemen fighting and slowly working their way toward us.

These Mongols were just like the ones we had been seeing for weeks, in motley clothes and armor and riding undersized ponies. Only their red felt hats, with the peak pulled forward like they said the elves wore, were anything like a uniform.

The noble Poles were almost all wearing Lord Conrad's plate armor, but they wore it polished and on the outside rather than in pockets sewn in canvas overalls, the way the army wore it. It was pretty worn that way, but they said it took an hour to buckle each piece on separately, and it took more man-hours to keep it shiny than a regular soldier could spare.

One surprise was that all of the nobles out there were wearing identical red-and-white surcoats, which just had to be the army's doing. By themselves, that bunch couldn't agree on what kind of air to breathe.

The fight spilled into the big fields in front of and slightly below us, and it was just like being at the biggest tournament anybody ever told tales about. I don't think that such a sight was ever seen by mortal men before, and here we had perfect front-row seats, figuratively speaking.

Our people were mostly riding big warhorses, chargers, and that gave them quite an advantage over the easily knocked-over Mongol ponies. Our men had better armor and were bigger and stronger, too.

But nothing could offset their problem of being outnumbered ten to one.

Our knights were tough, and they fought hard, but one by one they were falling. The fight went on far longer than anyone would have imagined, but anyone with eyes could see that it was a losing battle.

And there wasn't anything we could do to help them! The fight was so tangled, with individual horsemen fighting other individuals almost nonstop, that any shots we fired from the swivel guns were as likely to kill our own people as the Mongols.

A swivel gun bullet could go through six armored men, and even when you hit your intended target square on, the men standing behind him could be anybody!

Oh, every now and then a wounded man would come near our lines, and some of us would go out to him. If he was a Christian, wearing a red-and-white surcoat, we would help him to safety, and if he wasn't, we would kill him and let him lie, but it still wasn't much of a contribution to the cause.

I could see Taurus on my left getting more and more anxious, and I did what I could to calm him down, not that talking did much good.

A while later a pair of very pretty girls drove up behind our war cart with a huge, army liquid cargo cart full of beer! Since our dinner gear was still packed, we had nothing but our helmets to put it in, but the war wasn't affecting us much just then, and anyway, we drank it in a hurry. A helmet full of beer calmed Taurus down considerably, and I worried less about him.

The girls didn't stay, which was a pity, but I suppose it was just as well.

Most of the troops were angry about the way we were standing idle while our knights were dying out there, but I had mixed feelings about it.

I mean, it was their decision to be out there in the first place, and in the second, if any of them wanted to leave, we would have let them through our lines.

I think those knights were actually having fun, and if they were crazy enough to think they were accomplishing something, well, that was their problem. With all the guns we had pointed at the Mongols, we could have blown them away in minutes, if the noble knights would only have gotten out of our way!

And anyway, I really hadn't liked most of the noble knights I had met. Oh, some of them, like Lord Conrad and Count Lambert, were truly fine people, but so many of them were just a bunch of privileged bullies. They were rude, and sometimes they took my father's bread without paying for it.

And why the girls who worked at the cloth factory—most of whom were of my age—wanted those knights when they would have nothing to do with me, well, it was beyond me.

Finally, in the late afternoon, after hours of watching the bloody show, I saw Lord Conrad run out onto the field with a nobleman right behind him, leading the thousands of men in his army into the fight.

"It's about time!" the men all around me said.

We all shouted, "*For God and Poland!*" We slipped the ropes that held us to the carts, vaulted the big shield in front of the first line axemen, and charged out onto the field.

We weren't marching in step, of course, since we were running. But habits stick with you, and we kept pretty much in line.

The horsemen, almost all of them Mongols by this time, were shocked to see us running at them. Most of them turned and ran away from us, or maybe their horses did and the men went along for the ride.

A few turned and charged right back at us, but that was something for which the army had trained us well. Our men just lined up and grounded their pikes, and the men nearest the center impaled the horse front to rear. The other pikers around them went for the rider, and if he lived to hit the ground, he rarely lived to get up, since a dozen or more troops would mob him.

Like I told you before, fighting fair is fighting stupid.

I saw hundreds of Mongols die that way, but a few hundred

was just a few, compared to the huge numbers of people involved in that battle. Most of them ran away, or tried to, since we had them surrounded, even if they were a while finding it out.

It was a run of several miles, in armor, and we were carrying our heavy pikes, but we were trained for it. As we ran, the circle got shorter and shorter, and our lines, five men deep at first, got thicker and thicker. Eventually, there was a great seething mass of mounted men, I don't know how big around, and they were surrounded by a mass of army troops at least three dozen men deep, pushing them tighter into a circle.

I think that if it wasn't for the breast and back armor we all wore, none of our people toward the center of that mess would have been able to breathe. As it was, we found out later that most of the horses we had surrounded did die because they were squeezed too hard. At least they were dead without a mark on them.

But while we had the Mongols surrounded and pressed in, we weren't really any better off than before. We still couldn't get to most of them. Oh, the outer few yards of them were within range of our pikes, but most of the enemy still couldn't be reached.

Then one trooper figured it out. I think he must have been wounded, for he had a big bandage wrapped around his helmet, but he started screaming something that sounded like the howling of a wolf. He ran *right up the backs* of the men surrounding the Mongols and then *right over the top of them*, running on their pikes and their heads and their shoulders!

He ran onto the back of a horse that was so squeezed in it couldn't take a step. The Mongol riding it was so pinned in that he couldn't move his legs, either! The soldier with the bandage started swinging his axe like he was chopping wood, and he took the head off that Mongol in two hacks.

Then he stepped over to another Mongol and repeated the process.

The rest of us weren't slow once somebody had given us a hint, and Taurus, who had stayed beside me during the whole charge, was now out in front of me. We dropped our pikes, pulled out our axes, and ran on top of our own men to get at the Mongols!

The whole affair was over in a few minutes.

We all looked around at the blood and gore, amazed at what we had done. Then the men at the edges sort of relaxed, and the whole mass of dead men and dead horses sort of slumped under my feet.

Somebody started to sing, and most of the rest of the guys joined in, but me, I just sat down and took off my helmet. I put my elbows on my knees and my head in my hands.

I was tired. Very, very tired.

Taurus came over to me. He wanted to know how much was one hundred twenty-one plus eighty-four, but I was too tired to think.

I told him, "Too many."

Chapter Seven

FROM THE JOURNAL OF JOSIP SOBIESKI

written January 23, 1249,
concerning March 8, 1241

They told the River Battalion to stand down, go back to our war carts, pitch camp, and rest. There was still a lot of work to be done, but there were plenty of nearly fresh troops to do it.

The next day, we watched as the rest of the army cleaned up the battlefield.

The Christian wounded were cared for as best as we could. There were relatively few of them, and we actually had more surgeons than there were wounded people for them to tend.

The Christian dead, almost all of them noblemen, since the army had taken almost no casualties at all, were properly buried, their arms and armor neatly bundled for return to their next of kin, and such of their horses as were uninjured were simply set free, until they could be later collected up, sorted out, and returned home.

The Mongol dead were stripped, their arms and armor thrown into one pile, their purses and jewelry thrown into another.

After that they were all beheaded and their heads stuck up on broken pikes and lances, in neat squares a gross of heads to the side for easy counting.

They tried to burn the bodies, but with the rain that had been falling for days and the general lack of firewood locally, they gave up on it. They just dug a huge, long pit and threw the naked, headless Mongol bodies into it.

Not a very polite thing to do, I suppose, but it wasn't as though we had *invited* them to Poland!

The amount of booty collected was simply fabulous, but I had known how that would go since before that battle on the east riverbank. We were told that once the loot was all collected and divided out, we would all be rich.

I had to think about that, because I wasn't really sure just what "rich" meant. Did it mean I could have a castle like Lambert's?

But then who would live in it with me? Who would do all the work that it took to keep the place up? I mean, every man I knew was now in the army, and so every one of them would be getting at least as big a share of the loot as I was.

Somebody would still have to plow the fields, or we'd all starve, that was plain enough. And somebody would have to bake the bread, and I knew that that somebody would be my father and his family.

That had to be the way of it. If everybody was rich, then nobody was rich. All it meant was that we'd all have lots of pretty gold jewelry and things, but we'd still be working people all our lives.

I tried to explain my reasonings to the other guys around me, but none of them believed me. They called me a pessimist and went on talking about their big houses, their vast fields, and their numberless herds of cattle. In an hour they all had fine horses, beautiful wives, and dozens of even prettier servant girls.

As if the Mongols had brought a few million extra pretty girls with them from wherever it was they had come from!

Any fool could see they had brought the gold and silver they had stolen from the Russians, and their swords and other weapons, and that was about it.

Well, they had brought their ponies, too, and those that were still alive had all been relieved of their saddles and released for lack of anything better to do with them. We didn't have the harnesses we'd need to hitch them to our war carts, and anyway, they would have slowed us down. With men pulling the things, we could keep going around the clock, and no horse except Anna's kin could possibly do that.

I supposed that come spring, a lot of poor peasants would be using Mongol ponies to pull their plows instead of making their wives do it. That would doubtless be an improvement, but I wouldn't call it "rich."

But a pony wasn't of any use in a bakery, so I stopped thinking about it and went to sleep.

The next morning the battlefield was cleaned up. It is amazing how much work a sixth of a million men can do when they are organized properly.

One komand of six companies was being left on the battlefield to take care of the wounded and keep an eye on things, half of the rest were going back with the booty to get the factories going again, and the remaining seven battalions would be going east of the Vistula to see about cleaning up the mess we'd made over there.

A few million unburied dead bodies lying around can start a plague, they told us, and there was probably more gold over there than had ever been brought to this side of the Vistula.

And since the River Battalion knew where all the bodies weren't buried, we would be going back to show the rest what to do. Apparently, we would not be among the idle rich for a while yet.

The first problem we faced was that we couldn't find the riverboats to take us across the river. It seemed that the rains and thunderstorms of the last week had made our radios not work, somehow. The boats had to be out there, somewhere, but they didn't know we needed them.

Fortunately, someone found some big barges at the docks of Sandomierz and a lot of rope in one of the warehouses. With these things, they made up six of the sort of ferryboats that Lord Conrad had invented ten years ago.

The idea was that you tie a boat to the bank with a long rope, with the centerline of the boat at an angle to the river. The force of the river's flow will then push the boat across, the way the wind moves the sails of a windmill. Change the angle around, and the boat will go back again.

I know this works because they decided that the River Battalion should be the ones to work them. Since this was a task far preferable to stripping and burying dead Mongols, we took on the unfamiliar job with alacrity.

By night we had all seven battalions east of the Vistula. A company from the River Battalion was left with the ferryboats, but it wasn't mine.

We spent two days doing the dirtiest jobs imaginable, stripping, decapitating, and burying the Mongol dead. Once we had carried away the top layer of them, we discovered that the dead bodies below were packed so tightly they were stuck together!

We had to get a rope around each man and each horse, and then twenty men would drag the dead body out for another group to process while we went back for another corpse. Ugly work.

Then we got shocking news.

Cracow was burning!

We dropped what we were doing and recrossed the Vistula as fast as we could. Since we all had to use the same ferryboats, it was like trying to empty too big a bottle through too small a neck.

We worked quickly, but everything took so much time! Troops were sent south on the railroad in company-sized units, rather than waiting until we could move together.

Days before, when the first half of the army was heading south, they had lightened their loads when they heard about the Mongol attack on Cracow. They had thrown out everything they didn't absolutely need to fight with and took off at a run to save the city.

Scattered by the side of the road were tons of food, clothing, and even radios, but more important, tons and tons of booty. Fabulous amounts of gold and silver coins and precious jewelry were lying all about, and the last company in line had been left to guard it.

Every platoon had to take its cart with it, and these carts were difficult to remove from the railroad tracks. So when the troops from across the Vistula finally came along, the guard company, now rested, had left in their van, and the last company in each group had taken over the guard duty for a bit, until they in turn were relieved.

And since we were the people who were operating the ferries, my company was the very last one to head south.

So we were the ones who got stuck with guarding I don't know how many tons of useless gold. We completely missed the Battle of Cracow, the Slaughter of East Gate, and the Battle of Three Walls!

The world is sometimes most unfair!

It was weeks before we were sent enough men and carts to move all of the booty to Three Walls. We were allowed but one night there to have a beer and hear about everything we had missed before we were ordered back across the Vistula to finish up with the dirty cleanup job that had been interrupted.

Eighty thousand other soldiers were there with us doing the same dirty job, but that didn't make us feel any better about it!

The worst of it was when we got to those Mongol catapults, and saw all the bodies around them. Back when we were killing them, we had wondered at the way the Mongols didn't seem to care if we killed them or not, and at the way the catapult crews fell so easily, as though they had no armor at all.

Now we found the reason for it. The people pulling those catapults weren't Mongols at all. They were Polish peasants who had been captured and forced to help the enemy! Those had been our own people we were forced to kill!

And all we could do was bury them.

I don't think that I ever felt guilty about killing the enemy, but up until that time, I didn't really hate them, either. Now I learned to hate the Mongols, and hate them I still do.

After a week spent cleaning up the killing fields where the riverboats had wreaked such havoc, we split into smaller groups, back into the countryside, to bury the dead who had not taken the army's advice about evacuating the area.

The horror was not to be believed.

Not just the dead bodies of weaponless men, women, children, and even household pets, but the deliberate torture and then desecration of those people was what got to you.

I could almost understand an invading soldier raping an attractive woman. I could not forgive it, of course, but I could understand why a man might do such a thing.

But why would someone then tie the feet of that naked woman to a large tripod and start a small fire under her head?

What reason could a man have for nailing a small dog to a church door, and leaving it there in pain until it died of thirst?

Why would they cut out an old man's eyes and tongue, and then leave him in his home, when they had killed everyone else in the village and left them where they had fallen, so that by touch he would find those he loved, one by one, dead and cold?

We had given that old man water and food, and made him as comfortable as possible, but that night while we slept, he took Fritz's belt knife and plunged it into his own heart.

We buried him with the rest of the villagers and never told the priest that he was a suicide. To do so would have meant that the old man would not have been buried in the churchyard with the family he loved.

If God wants to punish us for that, He is free to do so.

But all things end, even the worst of them. At the end of April, Sir Odon, who was again our lance leader, told us he had wonderful news.

The River Battalion was being given preferential treatment for processing through the Warrior's School. While most of the army was being temporarily disbanded, and converted into reserve forces, we would be able to enroll in a month! Thus, we would be assured of being able to stay in the regular Christian Army indefinitely!

He was very excited about it, and soon got the others enthused as well. For myself, well, I was not sure what I wanted to do.

Anyone could leave the Christian Army anytime he wanted, except in an actual combat situation. My military experiences had, on the whole, not been pleasant, but they had not been boring, either, and surely the worst of the warfare was over.

They say that the only thing Lord Conrad ever promised anyone was that he would see interesting times, and Lord Conrad has always kept his promise.

But there was more than my wants to be considered. I still had not found my father, but I was sure he was still alive, somewhere.

I knew full well what his desires would be. He would go back to his bakery, and he would demand that I go back there with him.

I had never even thought of disobeying my father. Not before then.

Chapter Eight

FROM THE JOURNAL OF JOSIP SOBIESKI

written January 24, 1249,
concerning May 2, 1241

Sir Odon would not hear of my resignation from the army, not then, anyway. He said we had a month's leave coming—with pay—and after I had spent the time thinking it over, he would listen to me then.

For now, he was signing me up for the last eight months of the Warrior's School, and that was that.

We left our war carts at Sandomierz for the battalion that was forming up there to protect the duchy and heard the news.

Count Conrad was now Duke Conrad, and furthermore, he was a duke three times over! He was Duke of Mazovia, Duke of Sandomierz, and Duke of Little Poland, the area around Cracow.

It seems that most of the noblemen of those duchies had been killed in battle, and most of their dependents had been slaughtered by the Mongols who had tricked their way into East Gate, where they were sheltering.

There wasn't anybody else left to rule half of Poland, so now it was Lord Conrad's, and therefore, the army's, we supposed.

The people of Sandomierz were well-disposed toward the men of the army, and we spent a week there before we headed southward again, for home.

We had a remarkable time. We had not received any of our pay yet, much less our share of the booty, but the lack of money didn't seem to matter. Everything seemed to be free to members of the victorious army, and from the first, we got uproariously drunk.

I had been drinking beer all of my life, of course, and I'd often been a bit tipsy, but this was my first experience with drinking so much that I couldn't dance upright, or crawl a straight line, or even see the same thing with both eyes!

It was my first experience with another thing as well, and pretty little Maria was a wonderful instructor.

It was the first time I had ever felt, in a loving way, the incredible softness of a woman's breast, or the unbelievably welcoming smoothness of her lower parts.

Sometimes, lying abed in the late morning, we fantasized about a wonderful life together. She was recently widowed, she was fairly wealthy, and she owned what had been a thriving tailor's shop.

The laws were such that a woman alone found it hard to run a business. She needed a husband, but she needed more than just an agreeable young man.

She needed someone who could take over her property and manage it profitably, and I knew nothing about tailoring. I think that if my father had been a tailor, or if her dead husband had been a baker, I would have married Maria. We might have spent the rest of our days happy in Sandomierz, but such was not to be. After five delightful days together, the reality of our situations finally came home to us.

We parted the best of friends, and we have written each other ever since, although not often for she soon found a tailor from the first platoon of my own company who satisfied all of her needs.

She writes that they are still very happy.

I found the others of my lance just before they left without me, and we were lucky enough to get a ride back to East Gate on a riverboat, one of only three left on the Vistula. From there, the railroad mule carts from East Gate to Coaltown were operating again.

We went as far as Three Walls to collect our pay and a hefty advance on our share of the booty. They were handing out a thousand pence—three years' pay!—to any soldier who would sign for it. They still hadn't figured up how much we each had coming, since more loot was still trickling in.

While we were there, we stopped at a special army warehouse to select our share of souvenirs. I got a yak-tailed banner, two heavily decorated swords, and some jewelry that I planned to give to my mother and sisters. As things turned out, the fine young ladies of the cloth factory ended up with almost half of it.

Finally, I put my armor and weapons in storage, signed for two sets of class A uniforms, and caught a mule cart for Okoitz.

I had been writing my mother regularly, although for the last two months I hadn't been in one place long enough to have a return address. Without one, she couldn't write back to me, but at least they knew I was alive and well, and that I was coming home. Someday, the army would solve its problems with regard to the mail, but it hadn't done so yet.

My father and brother had been home for weeks, as were

most of the other men from Okoitz. Things were almost back to normal, but they gave me a big welcome home party anyway. More men than I could remember came up to shake my hand, and I was kissed and hugged by hundreds of women, and some of them were pretty.

When all of this was added to more drinking, eating, and drinking than was prudent, or even sane, well, it was the afternoon of the next day before I finally had a chance to talk with my father and my brother.

It seems that they were trained in a company near the northeast corner of the Warrior's School (my father never called it "Hell"), while the River Battalion was at the southwest corner. We were a mile and a half apart from one another, separated by what was actually, at the time, the biggest city in all of Christendom. It was little wonder that our paths had never crossed.

The same was true at the Battle of Sandomierz, where we had all fought, but were stationed five miles apart.

They were impressed by the fact that I had served in the River Battalion, for the stories about what we had done were told again and again throughout the rest of the army.

For my part, I was eager to hear once more about what had happened at Cracow and at the Battle of Three Walls, where my father and brother fought, side by side, and had taken part in the annihilation of the second Mongol army. In truth, I envied my brother for being able to serve with his own father by his side, and I told him so.

Late in the afternoon, my father suggested that I might want to take a few days off, to rest, before I resumed my job at the bakery.

At that point I had to tell them about how the River Battalion was being sent through the rest of the course at the Warrior's School, and how I was signed up to start there in three weeks.

My father's reaction was about what I had expected, or perhaps I should say, what I had feared. He became angry, and told me I was being a fool.

"You have the right to leave the army, and that is exactly what you should do. It is what you *will* do!" He said, "Why should you want to go and spend eight more months in stupid training when the Mongols have been totally defeated. Training to kill who? After what has happened to all the Mongols, nobody will ever again dare to molest Poland!"

I had to tell him I could not answer his questions, and that I wasn't really sure what I should do.

He said, "If you are not sure, well then, I am! You should obey me, as a good boy should always obey his parents."

He walked away then, which was just as well. I didn't want to confront him, but I didn't want to lie to him, either.

My brother just told me to take some time and think it all over carefully. Together, we went over to the Pink Dragon Inn, got roaring drunk, and tipped the lovely waitresses there more than they were used to, since he had as much surplus cash as I did.

Later, we found two willing girls from the cloth factory, and eventually spent the night with them in their room in the castle. In the arms of a lovely woman, I went to sleep that night thinking that being a baker at Okoitz might not be such a bad life after all.

After spending two weeks working in the bakery, I was no longer sure. In truth, doing again and again the same dull things that I had done for most of my life, I was bored, bored almost to death.

When I thought on the things I had done in the war, the friends I had known, and the things I had seen, there seemed to me to have been a certain . . . greatness about them. It seemed that somehow the army and the war had lifted me up to a higher level of being. That I had, for a short while, been like one of the heroes they told about in the old fireside tales or even like one of the ancient pagan gods!

When I thought of the friends I had made in those few months, I was amazed at the closeness I felt for them, and how much I truly missed them all, even Taurus's craziness and Kiejstut's sullen quietness.

I stood there, my face and hair dusted with rye and wheat flour, my arms buried up to the elbows in sticky bread dough, trying to be polite to Mrs. Galinski, an annoying lady customer.

Was this the way I wanted to spend the rest of my entire life? The only life God would ever give me?

No.

Better to live the full life for a year and have it end with my breast pierced through by a Mongol spear, than to have it slowly ground away to nothingness by the bitchy Mrs. Galinski!

I would not be a baker. I would go to the Warrior's School and see where life would lead me.

And perhaps my father would forgive me.

I talked it over first with my brother. He said if this was truly my wish, then he would do everything in his power to smooth the way for me with the family, and especially with our father.

He also said he was not being entirely altruistic in all of this, because it would probably mean that he would one day inherit the bakery alone, rather than having to share it with me.

I said that if he stayed here, working in the bakery, then he would have earned his inheritance, and he should enjoy it with my blessings. Furthermore, if he ever needed help taking care of our parents once they got old, he should feel free to call on me to help out with the expenses. We shook hands on it, and I've never regretted the decision we made that night.

I told my mother about our agreement, and I could see we had made her very sad. She left for a while and came back tearstained, but she said that if this was what I wanted to do, well, I was no longer a boy and must make up my own mind about what was right for me. She said she would miss me, but that I had her blessings. I could tell she dreaded breaking the news to my father as much as I did.

Indeed, I dreaded telling him so much that every day for a week I kept putting it off. I procrastinated.

I kept on procrastinating until the morning of the last day possible for my departure. Then I simply showed up at the bakery wearing my uniform.

My father looked at me, shook his head, and walked away without speaking to me. I looked for him for hours, but I couldn't find him.

I had to leave home without his blessing.

Chapter Nine

FROM THE JOURNAL OF JOSIP SOBIESKI

written January 25, 1249,
concerning June 4, 1241

As I suspected would happen, my entire lance showed up for the second part of our training, and Sir Odon didn't even say "I told you so" when I arrived at the last possible moment. We all looked at each other and smiled. Even Taurus smiled, the first time I ever saw such a thing. We all had the warm feeling that our family was together again.

The course of study in Hell was much different from the one we'd gone through a few months before. Then, there had been very little in the way of classroom work. Everything we had learned was to teach us how to kill Mongols and how to stop them from killing us.

Now things were different. Fully half of our waking hours were spent in the classroom. Many of the courses were on expected subjects, that is to say, military in nature. How to plan an ambush, how to arrange for supplies, how to take care of and repair weapons, clothing, and armor.

Some subjects were less concerned with immediate military operations, like military law and what constituted a legal order.

I was surprised to find that there are some orders that are actually illegal to obey, such as an order to kill an unarmed and nonviolent noncombatant.

If your commanding officer ordered you to do an illegal act, you were *required* to disobey, and if you were not actually in combat with the enemy, you were *required* to arrest your own officer!

You had to be deadly careful with that law, however, because if you invoked it, there would be a mandatory military court-martial that would be the end of someone's career, and quite possibly the end of somebody's life. Maybe yours, if you were wrong!

Other courses included map reading and mapmaking, mathematics, the operation and repair of steam engines, the operation and repair of radios, the construction of roads and bridges, and other suchlike things. They weren't trying to make us masters of all of these arts, but to teach us enough to get started and to know which manual to get to teach you all the fine points when you needed them.

But then there were a group of subjects I never thought would be important to a warrior. We took courses on both military courtesy and *social courtesy*. If you were invited to dine with the local baron, your manners had better not embarrass the Christian Army! We took courses in playing musical instruments and even in dancing, since a true warrior was expected to be as competent with the ladies as he was with the enemy!

Of course, the other half of the day was spent doing physical things, and it was as demanding as it had been before.

But even here, there were differences. For one thing, they finally issued us swords, and we spent at least an hour a day working out with them. The sword the army used was not the horseman's saber, but the long, straight infantryman's épée. It had very little in the way of a cutting edge and was primarily a thrusting weapon, but once you knew how to use it, you could even defeat a man in full armor. Once you were fast enough, and accurate enough, you could hit the cracks in his armor, his eyeslit, the places where one plate moved over another.

It was worn, not at the belt, but over the left shoulder. A leather tube was fastened to the epaulet to protect the *forte* section of the blade, and a long, thin knife sheath at the right buttock covered the tip. It came out quickly enough, although it took a bit of squirming (or a friend) to resheathe it.

Much time was spent studying unarmed combat, on the theory that a warrior was always a warrior, even if he was naked.

That, and they finally taught me how to swim.

Since there were many fewer people in Hell than there had been last winter, we ran the great obstacle course at least once a day. Last winter we were only able to get to it about once a week.

Lastly, there was much more emphasis on religion than before. If you didn't have a thorough grounding in Christianity before you went to Hell, you certainly got it there. This produced several problems for the men of my lance.

For reasons that I don't understand, throughout our first training session and the war that followed it, we had never talked much about religion among ourselves. Lezek, Fritz, Zbigniew, and I were all Roman Catholics, we had always lived where everybody was a Roman Catholic, and none of us had a clear idea about how anybody else could possibly be anything different.

We were surprised to discover that Taurus was a Greek Orthodox Christian. He'd been going to church with the rest of us because there wasn't one of his faith available, and he figured that it wouldn't do any harm.

Kiejstut was the quiet Lithuanian who spoke so little that it was easy to forget that he was there. It turned out that he wasn't a Christian at all!

He was some sort of pagan, and had been going to church with the rest of us because he was afraid of what we would do to him if we found out the truth! Once the truth came out, it took us, and the priest who was teaching the class, a long time to relieve him of his anxieties. It was only when I told him to relax, that we weren't going to eat him, that he finally did calm down.

Secretly, I believe he *really was worried about being eaten*! That either his tribe or some of those around his people actually did eat human beings. Or maybe his tribal shaman, or whatever they had, had told him Christians ate people, I don't know.

But when the priest asked him if he would like to take some extra study, and then be baptized a true Christian, he jumped at the chance.

Long before the school was over, we all went to his christening.

➤   ➤   ➤

We learned one very sad piece of news in the fall of 1241. Captain Targ was missing and presumed dead.

His parents had a farm west of Sacz, near the Dunajec River, and with Lord Conrad's blessings he and his brother, a platoon leader from another company, had borrowed a pair of conventional army horses and ridden east to visit them and see to their safety.

And that was all we knew.

They were never seen again. A lance sent out to look for them found nothing except the farm, which had been burned out by the Mongols, apparently in the early spring. There was no sign of Captain Targ's family, either.

With both our captain and our platoon leader dead, my lance felt that it was orphaned.

When most of the course was over, we all underwent an ordeal and a blessing. Sir Odon was included with us, since he had not yet performed this ceremony. After a day of prayer and fasting, with our souls in a State of Grace, we walked barefoot across a big bed of glowing coals. We were not harmed, being protected by God.

The others were perhaps more impressed by this miracle than I was, but then they had not seen golden arrows come out of the sky to kill four Crossmen who would have harmed Lord Conrad.

Then we did a night's vigil, praying on a hilltop outside the Warrior's School, and in the morning we looked down on the fog in the valley below. Each of us saw a halo, great rays, or horns of light, around the shadow of his own head, but not around the heads of the others. We had been individually blessed by God and were all knighted, and made Knights of the Order of the Radiant Warriors!

The next day, we were issued the army's new full-dress red and white uniform. We were amazed at the amount of gold that one wore on it.

There was a big, heavy medallion on the front of the peaked hat, and a band of solid gold below it. On the jacket there were golden tabs on the collar, huge gold epaulets on the shoulders, and solid gold buttons. Over it, one wore a belt with a solid gold buckle from which hung a fancy dress saber with a solid gold hilt and handle, and a matching dress dagger with matching gold trim.

Pinned to the jacket there was a huge and glorious gold medal, as big as your hand, announcing that we were members of the Order of the Radiant Warriors, and two smaller gold medals, one for the Battle of the Vistula and one for the Battle of Sandomierz.

Personally, I thought we should have been given a medal for the really tough job that we did, cleaning up the bodies east of the Vistula, but that didn't happen.

We even had golden spurs, like the French knights are said to wear, although ours had a rowel at the back, rather than the cruel spike they used. Not that any of us had been on a horse even once during our entire time in the army.

All told, we were to walk around with over *eight pounds* of gold hanging about our persons! I was relieved to discover that it was customary to wear this finery only at very special ceremonies and to otherwise leave our decorations locked up in the company vault.

Of course, we all planned to wear it home, at least once, and on any occasion when it was desirable to impress the ladies.

Once, I had told myself that the gold we got from the Mongols would only mean we would wear more jewelry, but somehow in the course of things, I had forgotten my own prediction!

There was one major sour point in all of this, however. Despite the fact that we had been knighted as part of our induction into the Order of the Radiant Warriors, and despite the fact that we had golden spurs, as only knights wore in France, and despite the fact that we had completed a course of study that resulted in the knighting of everyone else who had taken it before us, despite all of this, we were still not officially knighted, not as far as the army was concerned.

Sir Odon was still just a knight, not a knight-banner, as he had assumed he would be, and each of the rest of us was only a squire, at four pence a day, rather than a knight at eight.

"They hang eight pounds of solid gold on each one of us and then they are too cheap to pay us another four pence a day?" Zbigniew said.

We complained, but we didn't get very far, since everybody else was complaining about the same thing.

"It's the new policy," the baron's executive officer said to an angry crowd of us. "The graduates before you were promoted to knight because they would be immediately each given a lance of men of their own to train. Back then the army had to expand very rapidly to be able to meet the Mongol threat. But until we finish the training of everybody who took the short course just before the war, we will not be adding very many new members to the army. It only stands to reason that promotion will be slower."

Maybe it was reasonable to him, but it wasn't so to us. We locked away our new dress uniforms, put on our old class B uniforms, and went out and got roaring drunk.

We had orders to report for duty at East Gate in two weeks. Sir Odon, Zbigniew, and Lezek elected to go home on their leave, but there wasn't time for Taurus, Fritz, and Kiejstut to do so. They had, however, heard wonderful things about the girls of Okoitz, and I suggested they accompany me home.

We rented two rooms at the newly enlarged Pink Dragon Inn for the four of us, and I left them in the taproom staring at the nearly naked waitresses while I visited my family.

It was not a joyous homecoming.

Most of my family was eager enough to see me, but my father would not say a word to me. He came in, stared at me for a moment, then turned around and walked out.

It hurt.

I visited twice more during my leave, but nothing changed. My mother, my sisters, and my brother all promised to try to talk to him, but none of it did any good.

My friends had a marvelous time at Okoitz, and by joining them, I mostly had a good time, too. The ladies of the cloth factory seemed to think that being a Knight of the Order of Radiant Warriors certainly made one a true knight, and that anyway, any man who walked around wearing *eight pounds* of solid gold had to be worth spending some time with!

We discovered also that music was almost as good an aphrodisiac as wealth, and our new-taught musical skills did us yeoman service in the cause of Eros.

Since it was winter, the cloth workers dressed warmly enough at the factory, and they wore a long, heavy cloak to go between the castle, where they all lived, the factory, where they all worked, and the Pink Dragon Inn, where they all played.

But all of the Pink Dragon Inns were kept very warm because of the outfits their waitresses wore. Or rather, the outfits they pretty much didn't wear, since it consisted of little beyond high-heeled shoes and a loincloth.

As a result of the competition at the inn, the cloth workers usually wore only a very short skirt, with nothing above it. It was a lovely style, and well appreciated by all of us men.

Suffice it to say that for two weeks not one of the four of us ever slept alone, and it looked for a while as if Fritz was going to get married, although that affair soon fell apart. We were all happy when we left for East Gate, and would have been happier still if our heads had not hurt so badly.

Chapter Ten

FROM THE JOURNAL OF JOSIP SOBIESKI

written January 26, 1249,
concerning February 17, 1242

They had a brand-new boat ready for us at East Gate, but the river was frozen over, and the boat wouldn't be going anywhere for a while.

With nothing better to do, we spent a day inspecting the remarkable "snowflake" fort there. The outer walls were of reinforced concrete, seven yards tall and thick enough to stop any siege engine. The inner walls, twenty yards high, were actually part of a huge, hexagonal building that housed an entire company along with all of their dependents, as many as fifteen hundred people. The complex contained a church, a school, an inn, and a machine shop. All this was crowned by a central tower fully four dozen yards tall.

Properly manned, I did not see how any army could have possibly taken it. It had a reputation for invincibility, and that very reputation had been the cause of its downfall.

It had fallen during the war, when Count Lambert's sister-in-law had usurped authority over the fort, then used it as a refuge for the noncombatant nobility only. To make room for all of them, she had evicted the female commoners trained to defend the fort, and had then let herself be tricked by the Mongols into opening the gates.

Most of the men of the old nobility had fallen in battle, but their parents, their wives, and their children had been slaughtered here at East Gate. There were twenty thousand tombstones in the adjoining graveyard, but few of them bore a name. There was no one left alive to identify the dead children.

New orders soon reached us, and we spent the next six weeks sawing down trees along the Bug River, preparing the way to put in a railroad.

The Ruthenians were now allied with Poland, rather than with the Mongols, and the railroad would let our army get there as quickly as possible, to support them if or when the Mongols objected to the new arrangement.

The work wasn't what we'd hoped for, but it was temporary and somewhat interesting. I'd never done any outdoor work before, and climbing higher than a church steeple to cut the top off a huge pine tree certainly got your blood going! Evenings spent singing or playing our new musical instruments glow pleasantly in my memory like the coals of the fires we sat around.

We worked five days a week and did military exercises on the sixth, which was the usual routine in the peacetime army.

We came back to civilization rippling with new muscles, and the girls almost fought each other to get at us!

When the ice broke up, we were back at East Gate, and soon we were back on the water again, riding the *Spirit of St. Joseph II*.

Peacetime riverboats had a crew of only twenty-two, and even that many was because most of us were in training. Only two people on board really knew what they were doing, the captain and the engineer. The rest of us were there mostly to learn how to run one of these things. In the course of 1242, I worked every single job on the boat, from helmsman to fireman, plus ticket salesman, sanitary engineer, radio operator, waiter, cargo master, mail sorter, painter, repairman, purser, steward, and cook.

The boat's captain was not the same thing as an army captain. That is to say, the first was a job position and the second was a military rank. Our current captain was in fact a knight-banner, while our boat captain during the war had been Baron Tadaos.

Our boat was a standard army riverboat, just like most of those we had seen the year before, although it wasn't a command boat like the *Muddling Through*. We had two Halman Projectors, four peashooters, and mounts for six dozen swivel guns, although we carried only twelve of them on board.

But despite our military capabilities, we were operating like a commercial common carrier. We had cargo space for six standard cargo containers, which were the same size as our war carts had been, six yards long, two yards wide, and a yard and a half high.

The main difference between a cart and a container was that the containers weren't armored, and they were built much closer to the ground, being mounted on railroad trucks, rather than the huge, cross-country wheels we used on the carts.

A container could snugly hold twenty-seven standard barrels. Or it could hold exactly six dozen standard cases, which were each a half yard wide and high and a yard long.

Those cases were just the right height to make a comfortable seat for two, or, upended, they were the right height to make a support for a workbench. Over the years, a lot of our cases ended up as furniture in peasant cottages, since the deposit on them was only a penny each.

We would take cargo that wasn't packed in our standard containers, cases, or barrels, but we charged a lot more to do it.

The army was big on standardization. There were only eight diameters of nuts and bolts, for example, so that when something broke, it was easy to replace. Glass jars came in only six sizes, each about twice as big as the next one smaller.

Each kind of jar was sized so a certain number of them fitted into a standard case, with no wasted space, and when you bought a quart of milk in Sandomierz, it was exactly the same size as a quart in Cracow. This was something new, since up to a few years ago, every city and town had its own sizes for everything.

It once was necessary for a merchant to personally be on hand whenever he bought or sold anything. Now he could purchase a container of army-grade number-two wheat in Plock, and do it by mail or even by radio, if he was in a hurry. He could have it shipped to a purchaser in Gniezno, while all the time he stayed in Cracow, secure in knowing exactly what he had bought and sold.

Many fortunes were made by those who were quick to learn the new ways of doing things. Those of us who worked on the rivers often indulged in this sort of trade whenever we noticed that the price of a given commodity in one place was much different than it was someplace else.

For years we more than doubled our salaries doing this, but eventually some merchants in Poznan set up a service where they systematically queried some two dozen cities on the local prices of three dozen commodities and made this information available, for a price, to other merchants. After that, only modest profits could be made, since no one but a fool would pay much more than the Poznan price for anything.

We carried passengers as well, with two dozen cabins on the second deck, for those who could afford them, and seats on the fighting top, for those who couldn't.

We would cruise up and down the Vistula, and every five miles or so there would be a depot with a dock. If they had business for us, they ran some flags up their pole or some lanterns at night and, by a system of codes, we would know if they had something that we had room for, which we usually did. We heard about really important passengers and cargoes by radio.

Evenings aboard, we sold beer and wine to passengers in the dining hall, earning a bit more money on the side, and I have always liked listening to travelers' tales, or hearing the songs they sang, or the tunes they played on strange, new instruments. To get into a competition, pitting our skills on the recorder, lute, or krummhorn against theirs, was always a joy.

It was a pleasant enough existence on the whole, because we stopped at all of the big cities along the way and there was always something new to see.

My main claim to fame came when, annoyed at doing the laundry, I put the dirty clothes along with some soap in a leaky barrel that had all four bungs missing. I tied the barrel to the rear railing with a long rope and kicked it over the side.

The barrel filled with water, then tossed and turned as it was pulled along, washing the clothes. Eventually, the soapy water was washed out and replaced with clean river water, and the clothes were rinsed.

Two hours later I pulled the barrel on board, and the clothes were clean! Soon, every boat on the river was doing laundry that way, and they named the barrel after me. Now, whenever anybody on the river washes clothes, they get out their Josip Barrel.

As the summer of 1242 came along, the army was preparing for another war, this time with the Teutonic Knights of St. Mary's Hospital at Jerusalem, better known as the Knights of the Cross, or just the Crossmen. It was to be a set-piece battle, with both sides agreeing on the time and place.

Naturally, we wanted to get involved, but our pleas and petitions got us nowhere. Apparently, every outfit in the army wanted to go, and there were only ten thousand Crossmen who needed killing. That wasn't much more than a single one of our battalions.

Also, it soon became obvious that Lord Conrad was planning to try out some new weapons on the Germans. It was all kept very secret, but we hauled some monstrous cannons down to

Turon, where the Crossmen were holed up, along with some big canisters of something so poisonous that everybody but the fireman was required to stay up on the fighting top when we had it in the hold.

Lord Conrad and his liege lord, King Henryk, had invited "observers" from just about every Christian country in the world, and from a lot of those that weren't Christians, too.

We carried passengers from Hungary, Bulgaria, France, Spain, and Scotland, and that was just on our boat alone. There were three dozen other boats involved in the business, as well.

Mostly, it wasn't a war so much as it was a big political convention followed by an execution.

We weren't there when they shot poison gas into the Crossmen's fort, but they say there wasn't much to see, anyway.

We were by a few days later, after the big cannons had spent a few hours blowing down the brick walls, and again there wasn't anything to see. Where once there stood a fine, strong fortification, there was now only broken bricks and rubble.

Most of our troops in that "battle" never even got to shoot at the enemy, and we boatmen were so busy transporting the visiting dignitaries back to where they'd come from that our soldiers had to walk home, just as they'd had to walk there.

There wasn't any loot to speak of, either, and what there was didn't cover the cost of the war. Most of our knights got a trophy to hang on their walls, and that was about it. After fighting the Mongols, it was something of a comedown.

That winter, which we again spent logging, we looked into the possibility of transferring our lance from the Transportation and Communication Corps over to the Eagles, who built and flew all of the aircraft, but that proved to be impossible. We were already too old. They accepted only volunteers who had completed the Warrior's School and were fifteen or younger. An opportunity missed.

The next spring, 1243, our lance was given its own boat, of a totally new, special-purpose design—an oil tanker.

Oil wells had been drilled near Przemysl on the San River, and a refinery had been built on the Vistula, north of Sandomierz. Ours was one of three boats designed to transport crude oil to the refinery, and refined oil in bulk wherever it was needed along the Vistula and its tributaries.

Refined oil, in its various grades, was used in the new kerosene lamps, and as a replacement for coal on the steamboats, where it eliminated the need for a fireman, and, mixed with wood alcohol, as a very energetic fuel for the aircraft. Other products, like asphalt roads, were being developed.

The new boat's engines were the same as those we were used to, except they were oil-fired. The kitchen, mess hall, and living quarters were small, and the boat was only a single story high, plus the bridge, since there were only the seven of us on board. The rest of the boat was nothing but a collection of low-lying steel tanks, almost like a long, low barge that we pushed ahead of us.

We joked that our boat was lean, low, stripped down, and topless, and that her name, *The Lady of Okoitz,* was therefore very appropriate.

We had no mounted weapons at all, since we didn't have enough people to man them, and we were too flammable to put up a serious fight, anyway. Faced with an enemy, our orders were to run away.

At first we were delighted to have our own boat and the responsibilities it entailed, but eventually the job palled.

For one thing, we now made far fewer stops in our travels, and those stops were invariably at industrial sites, which rarely had much going on except for the same work that they had been doing the last time we were there. We met fewer young ladies, and our love lives suffered.

We no longer carried passengers, who had seemed to be a great bother back when we carried them. After they were gone, well, it had been a long while since I heard an entertaining traveler's tale.

Also, a bulk tanker was much more difficult to keep clean than an ordinary riverboat, and we not only had to spend long hours scrubbing it, but found ourselves being dirtier than we ever had been before. This, too, did not help out our love lives.

Even our music was starting to get flat and stale.

But most of all, our increase in responsibility was not matched with an increase in status and pay. We had all been mere squires for several years, and we often heard of the promotions of others with less seniority than we had. This was particularly painful for Sir Odon. We called him our captain, but in fact he was still a mere knight, and he desperately wanted to advance in the army.

Also, there were no longer any opportunities to make additional money on the side. No legal ones, anyway, and none of us were thieves.

Suffice to say, after three and a half years on an oil tanker, we were all heartily sick of it!

Thus, we were all most interested when, in August of 1246, Sir Odon found a new possibility of employment for our lance.

The Construction Corps had been building a series of company-sized forts just like the one at East Gate, throwing them up at the astounding rate of one a week. They were built five miles apart all along the Vistula and now stretched along the west bank from the headwaters to the Baltic Sea. They were all part of an invincible defense against any future attack by the Mongols.

A second group had begun putting forts of the same design along the east bank of the Odra, some said against a possible invasion by the Holy Roman Empire, who were rumored to be very angry at us for eliminating the Crossmen.

The construction project was continuing and expanding, with plans to eventually put forts on both banks of every major river in Eastern Europe, but more important to us was what was being built at the mouth of the Vistula.

Sir Odon said that a major seaport and shipyard was being constructed there, and the plans were to soon begin building oceangoing steamships.

Were we interested in seeing if we could get involved with this new endeavor?

Well, of course we were! Over the last few years, we had been up every tributary of the Vistula, and frankly, one river is much like another.

But to travel the high seas! To explore, to boldly go where no Christian had gone before! We had been reading about how the world was really round, a great ball in the heavens. What would it be like to be on the first ship to steam around it? Glorious!

We all got together in writing our application for transfer, carefully explaining why we were the best possible people to choose for this new endeavor. We wrote about how our lance had been working smoothly together for years without any of the friction that had disrupted so many other groups.

We stressed that we had experience with various kinds of boats and had thus proved we could take on and master new things. We talked about our military prowess, of the battles we had fought under the watchful eyes of Lord Conrad himself.

We wrote about all of the other skills we had, from baking bread, farming, and handling cattle, to living off the land in the trackless wilderness of Lithuania.

We told our varied ethnic backgrounds and how among us we had speakers of Polish, German, Ukrainian, Latin (Fritz had been an altar boy), Pruthenian, and Lithuanian, so we would be able to communicate with the inhabitants of many different areas.

We explained how we were all bachelors who could take long trips away from home without distressing any wives or children. We wrote and rewrote that application so many times that we were sure if they did not transfer us to the High Seas Battalion, they would at least have to give us an award for literature! Finally, we had Zbigniew write up the fair copy, since he had the best handwriting in the group.

Then we faced the problem of just who we should send this application to. Normally, when one wished to transfer, one applied to the personnel department of the battalion or corps involved. But in this case, as far as we knew, the organization we wished to join did not yet exist.

"If it is new, you just know that Lord Conrad will be involved with it," Sir Odon said. "He likes being in on the beginning of things. You know him personally, don't you, Josip?"

I had to admit I did, that I had been a boy at Okoitz when he first arrived in Poland. However, I had to stress that our last meeting had been less than pleasant, and I quite possibly had been responsible for putting Lord Conrad's eye out or at least causing him to lose the use of that eye.

"I read in the news that he regained his sight in that eye years ago," Kiejstut said. "Anyway, Lord Conrad is not the kind of a man who would hold a grudge over a little accident like that."

I said losing an eye was not a "little accident," and that I was still apprehensive about writing to so high a personage.

Sir Odon said, "Nonsense, Josip. The worst that can happen is that if he is still mad at you, he will throw the letter away without reading it, so the thing for us to do is to make up two copies, one to Lord Conrad with your name on the return address, and one to Baron Tadaos, who I heard was being considered for heading the ocean steamship command, with my name on it instead of yours."

"I heard that it was to be Baron Piotr, of the Mapmakers," Lezek said.

"Then we'll send him a copy of our application, too," Sir Odon said.

In the end, we sent off nine separate copies to nine different army leaders.

And then we waited for a reply.

And waited.

Chapter Eleven

FROM THE DIARY OF CONRAD STARGARD

January 4, 1246

One of the better things to happen to me when I was in school was that my father bought me a loose-leaf binder that had a full color map of the world printed around the outside cover, and a map of Poland on the inside front.

I always found most of my classes to be extremely boring, but staring out the window could get you asked questions at awkward moments, and falling asleep in class could be disastrous.

So instead of listening to my teacher, I studied my maps, pretending to go from this city to that country, to sail on a gaff-rigged schooner from Papua New Guinea to Tahiti in Polynesia, or to go by camel caravan from Timbuktu to Samarkand.

The names on the maps were better back then, before some dreary politicians erased the glorious lands of Tanganyika and Zanzibar and replaced them with Tanzania, before the Congo became Zaire and Madagascar was turned into the Malagasy Republic, a name that sounds like it means "bad stomach gas." Surely Siam has more magic in it than Thailand, and Ceylon, or better yet Serendip, was finer than Sri Lanka. And what ass made Iran and Iraq out of Persia and Mesopotamia?

But be that as it may, while I was only slightly better than average in most subjects, I became outstanding in geography.

I was sitting at my desk in my office, drawing a map of the world as best as I could remember it. I was deliberately vague about national borders, because those had all changed radically in the seven hundred years between this time and the time I was born into. Indeed, I generally left boundaries out entirely and just put the names of nations across the continents. And the exact paths of rivers wasn't worth being too specific about, either, since they can change considerably, especially around their mouths, which is all an oceangoing ship can find.

Of course, not all of the names on my map were those you would find on a map of the twentieth century. When I could, I used the more poetic titles.

I went to college in America, and that place has always been very special for me. I loved the land, and I loved the people who lived on it. But to build that magic place, they had to replace the native peoples who were already there, and I didn't want to see that happen, not again, not in this new time line. My plans for those two continents were such that in this time line, America would be a very different place.

Then, too, perhaps the Americas had been misnamed, for Amerigo Vespucci really didn't do very much and certainly not enough to get *two* continents named after him. Consider that the only other person to have a continent named after her was Europa, and she had to put up with being raped by a bull to get the honor.

On my map, the landmass to the south was called Brazyl, and the area of the Andes where the Incas had their civilization was named Hy Brazyl. To the north I put Atlantis, and the land of the civilized people of Mexico I called Hy Atlantis.

I'd been thinking about doing this for years, but the time for procrastination was over. At last we had gotten our technology to the point where it was possible to build oceangoing steamships, and a whole new Age of Exploration was about to open up.

Oceangoing sailing ships, of the sort used in my time line from the fourteenth to the nineteenth centuries, could probably have been built at almost any time since the days of the Ancient Egyptians, just as those same peoples had the materials and skills to make, say, hang gliders, if they had known that one could exist.

But it would have been extremely difficult for us in mostly landlocked Poland to use them, for while the ships could have been built easily enough, having the skills to sail them was another matter entirely.

In the old British navy it was reckoned that a boy had to start learning aboard ship before he was twelve years old if he was ever to master his craft, and even that assumed that older, experienced men would be around to teach it to him.

Getting from place to place while taking into account the winds, the tides, and the ocean currents, not to mention storms and all the other hazards of the sea, was no easy task, and often the very best of men were not up to it. In the early days of long voyaging, three ships out of four failed to return home, and in the fifteenth century, Portugal was almost denuded of men because of the horrendous losses at sea.

But a steamship was actually much easier to operate than one of the old square riggers. You didn't have to worry much about wind and tides. You just fired up the boiler and pointed it in the direction you wanted to go. It took many years to train a good topman, but you could teach a steam mechanic his trade in a year. Large numbers of men were needed to handle large sails, while only a few could keep a steam engine going.

And the bigger the ship, the less you have to worry about storms. There are limits as to how big you can make a wooden sailing ship, but those same limits don't apply when you are building out of steel.

Well, we didn't have our steel industry to the point where we could roll the thick plates necessary for shipping, but in the course of building hundreds of reinforced concrete fortifications, our concrete capacity had become huge, and with the new continuous casting plant, we were now making more steel re-rod than we needed. Ferrocrete ships were within our capabilities, and such ships can be built to be every bit as good as steel ones.

So. We were poised to go out and explore the world, to bring Christianity to the heathens, and to become fabulously wealthy in the process. The world out there needed us, it needed our products, and it needed our culture. And we needed it!

Right then, I could build electric hand tools, and with them I could double the productivity of our skilled men. But while I could build the tool, I could not make the extension cord to get the power to the tool! I didn't have a decent elastomer. I could build air tools, but I couldn't make a flexible air line. The sorts of machinery we could build were greatly limited because of our lack of rubber. Our surgeons' patients would have had fewer infections if only the surgeons had latex gloves. Fewer people would have frozen in the winter if they had rubber boots. Electrical installations could be simpler and safer if we had rubber insulators.

Rubber was only one of the hundreds of items that we needed and that weren't available locally. We needed world trade. We needed to conquer the seas. The trick was to do it in a safe and sane manner.

In the first twenty-five years of the twentieth century, humanity conquered the skies. It was done with amazing speed and for comparatively little money, but an ungodly price was paid in human blood. Worldwide, it is estimated that more than four thousand five hundred young men died during those years flying in experimental aircraft. That does not include those who died learning to fly, those who died in warfare, or those who died in accidents in production aircraft. Essentially, we lost forty-five hundred test pilots, people who tend to be among the brightest, the bravest, and the best.

It took humanity about the same amount of time to conquer space, but in that case, the work was sponsored by governments. In dollars, pounds, and rubles, the price of spaceflight was at least a hundred times higher than that paid for air flight.

But the cost *in lives* was a hundred times less!

In the first twenty-five years of spaceflight, fewer than thirty lives were lost. The difference was that the Quest for Space was organized.

I don't know how many lives were lost in the course of the original Age of Exploration, but I'm sure that it was in the millions. Throughout the period, the frontiers were lawless places where the worst of society went. Misfits, criminals, and lunatics; they threw away their lives, killing each other and the native peoples they found in their way.

Furthermore, a lot of things happened during those years that I, as a European, am not very proud of. The destruction of two fledgling civilizations in the Americas, the brutal things that were done to China during the Opium Wars, and the enslavement and transportation of millions of Africans were things that were as stupid as they were shameful.

And they were not going to happen while I was in charge!

Besides knowing in advance where we were going to go, and approximately what we would find there, we would have a trained group of well-equipped, intelligent, and competent men to do the exploring.

Contrary to the practice of most of the organizations in the army, where women competed on an equal basis with men, the Explorer's Corps had to be an all-male organization. Small groups of our people would have to spend years out in the wilderness, far away from help and hospitals. We didn't have anything like a birth control pill; a pregnant woman would have had a hard time surviving out there, and supporting one could get the rest of her team killed along with her.

These thoughts soon got me to sketching up a plan for recruiting, selecting, and training my future Explorer's Corps. I was so engrossed in my work that I didn't even glance at the man who walked into my office.

"I'm busy. Can it be put off until later?" I asked without looking up.

It must have been the sound of his sword being pulled from his sheath that startled me, because if I hadn't jerked back, his sword would have split my skull and scattered my brains all over my drawings! As it was, he cut most of them in half and left a big gouge in the top of my desk.

He hauled back for another swing while I groped for my sword and pistol.

They weren't at my waist! I had forgotten to put them on again.

I shouted for help, and as he swung, I dropped to the floor, sending my chair slamming against the wall. When I saw him climbing over my desk to get at me, I shouted again for help and crawled under it.

I saw his feet hit the ground where I had been sitting, saw him starting to crouch down to get at me, and I knew I was a dead man.

Then a shot rang out, my assailant dropped to the floor, and an acrid cloud of gun smoke filled the room. I crawled out from under the desk to find my wife, Francine, standing there with a golden pistol, engraved and bejeweled, smoking in her hand, and a look of disgust on her face. Behind her stood Baron Piotr and his wife, Krystyana, both bearing naked steel.

Before I could thank them, Francine said, "So. You were again *too lazy* to put on your sword."

Then she walked out.

I shook my head. "What could he have wanted?" I said, looking at the body on the floor.

"Obviously, he wanted your life, your grace. As to why he wanted it, well, he might have been a hired assassin, or a disgruntled nobleman, or a simple lunatic, but I doubt if we will ever really know," Piotr said, bending over the fallen assassin. "This one, whatever he was, is dead. But you really must do something about security around here. You must make up a restricted list of people who are permitted past the guards at the gates, and you absolutely must get yourself some bodyguards."

"Yes, I suppose you're right. Thank you for your help."

"I did nothing, your grace. You owe your life to your wife, the Duchess Francine, and she isn't around here all that often to protect you," he said.

"True enough. Why don't you make up that list you mentioned and make sure that the guards know everybody on it by sight."

"Yes, your grace. And the bodyguards?"

"Let me think about that."

"Don't think about it too long, your grace."

Chapter Twelve

FROM THE JOURNAL OF JOSIP SOBIESKI

written January 26, 1249,
concerning September 18, 1246

One evening a month later, Lezek was playing his flute, and the rest of us were drinking beer. Our boat was waiting its turn in line to be filled up with number two kerosene when Sir Odon came into the boat's mess hall with a vast grin on his face while holding up an official-looking letter.

"Ahem! 'To Sir Odon Stepanski, Master of the Tanker Boat *The Lady of Okoitz*, Vistula Patrol, et cetera, et cetera, and so forth.

" 'You are requested and required to report with your lance of men to the offices of Lord Conrad, Okoitz, at the first hour after sunrise, on Monday, the fifth of October, 1246, to discuss with him your application to the Explorer's Corps, currently being formed.

" 'Please be advised that your services will be required here for at least one week for further consultation and testing. Report with full kit. Leave your boat at East Gate without resigning your present command, since your group's appointment to the new corps has not yet been confirmed.

" 'Yours most truly, et cetera, et cetera, and so forth,' and it's signed by Lord Conrad himself!"

We all stood up and applauded, but then Lezek said, "But what's this about the 'Explorer's Corps'? That doesn't sound like what they'd call a steamship command."

"Whatever it is, it has to be better than hauling oil around the Vistula from one smelly place to another," Sir Odon said, and we all drank to that.

"True," Zbigniew said, "but what did you make of that business about showing up in 'full kit'? Do they mean 'full kit' like they did in basic training?"

"What else could they mean?" Taurus said.

"Then I have some problems. We haven't needed most of that stuff for years, and as for my equipment, what isn't missing is pretty shabby," Zbigniew said.

I told him that he wasn't alone, and the party broke up as we all went back to our rooms to inventory our equipment. When I got back to the mess hall, Sir Odon was sitting in front of a stack of requisition forms, telling Zbigniew what to fill out, and Kiejstut was on the front deck, waving the boats behind us in line to go around. We had no time to bother with number two kerosene. We had other things to do tonight!

We never found out just what Sir Odon said to the supply captain to get such good service, but three days later it took us three trips to the warehouse to pick up all of the new equipment.

Then it took us three and a half days to polish, sharpen, iron, fit, adjust, wax, and otherwise make usable and presentable all of our new stuff.

The armor was the hardest part, since after we put our plates into the new coveralls, we found that we were in much different shape than we had been. Mostly, we were thicker in the waist and narrower in the shoulder.

Three and a half years of working on an oil tanker had put us all in very poor shape. Besides getting generally dirtier as each year dragged by, we couldn't usually stop the boat while we did the prescribed one day a week of military exercises. We had been getting by with sporadically fencing with practice swords and occasionally doing a few jumping jacks on the foredeck.

Furthermore, the last few winters had been unusually warm, and the rivers had never frozen over. Because of this, we had spent them delivering oil rather than chopping down trees, a far more vigorous pastime.

Sir Odon vowed that we would do something about it! He cut our rations in half, took beer off our menu, and led us in four hours of vigorous exercise a day.

Annoying, but it was needed. There had been that line in the letter about a week of "consultation and testing," and none of us thought that Lord Conrad was going to ask us about how he should run the army. We had better be in shape for whatever they threw at us!

We had two weeks before our appointment, and we spent them getting in the best shape that we could. Then, in new, freshly ironed class A uniforms, with brightly polished shoes and hat brims, we were promptly on time for our meeting with Lord Conrad.

He was an hour late, but that is to be expected when dealing with so important an individual. Eventually, he invited us into his office and courteously bade us to be seated.

"Sorry about being late, gentlemen, but there was a problem at Szczecin that had to be taken care of first. Now then," Lord Conrad said as he opened a folder and took out all nine of the applications we had sent in, along with copies of each of our service records. "You seem to be very eager to leave the Vistula Patrol."

"In truth, sir, we are eager to do something a little more adventurous than delivering oil to oil depots," Sir Odon said. "Also, it would be nice to work someplace where promotion happened a bit quicker."

"Well, you can't expect promotions to happen on a yearly basis the way they did when the army was expanding to meet the Mongols," Lord Conrad said. "Still, your records are all good, and if you stayed where you are, I imagine that you would all be getting your own boats before too long."

"Yes, sir. But even that would not be ideal. We are a very good team, sir, and if we stayed in riverboats, the only way we could be promoted would be to break that team up. With a large, oceangoing steamship, on the other hand, it should be possible for us to be promoted and still stay together," Sir Odon said.

"I see. However, the personnel charts for that operation, the steamships themselves, were filled some time ago by Baron Tadaos. You are presently being considered for something different. The Explorer's Corps. The plan is that when we enter into a new area, a new sea or a new coast, we will put teams of trained men ashore at intervals of about four dozen miles, ideally at the mouth of a river.

"The team will spend a year or so exploring the area, finding out who lives there, learning their language, and teaching the local inhabitants some Polish.

"We need to know what kind of people they are, what sort of products they produce that might be of interest to us, what sorts of things we have that they might want, and so on.

"We will want to know what minerals and other natural resources are available there, what agricultural possibilities exist, and what the military capabilities of the local inhabitants are.

"We want to know as much as possible about their culture, as well. We want to know about the songs they sing and the dances they do. We want to know the stories they tell, and if they are pagans, we want to know as much as possible about their gods.

"And we will want the area to be mapped as thoroughly as possible.

"Each of our ships will be capable of carrying about a company of men in addition to the crew. That is to say, about three dozen seven-man teams. On a given cruise, it will put the teams ashore and then spend much of the year mapping the shoreline, measuring the currents and the tides, surveying the fishing and other resources, and generally being on hand to help out if any of the explorer teams gets into trouble.

"Does this program sound interesting, so far?"

Sir Odon glanced at the rest of us, sitting on the edges of our chairs, and said, "Yes, sir. We are very interested."

"Good. Now, if you find something of sufficient commercial interest at the site of your operations, and if the local inhabitants agree to it, we plan to build permanent trading posts whenever possible. The team that first investigates an area will make a percentage of future profits, and will obviously be the best choice for personnel to run the trading post. It could be a very lucrative proposition, with considerable possibilities for independent action.

"Our ships will visit those posts periodically, of course, for commercial and religious reasons."

"Yes, sir. You say religious reasons?"

"Yes. We are not going out into the world for crass commercial reasons only. Oh, if a thing cannot pay for itself, we could not afford to do it too often, but our main reason for going out and discovering the rest of the world rests on the fact that the people in most of the world are not Christians. We want to give them a chance to come to Christ."

"Uh, sir, I'm not sure that any of us are truly qualified to teach religion," Sir Odon said.

"Well, I *am* sure, and yes, you're not qualified. If all else works out, your team will need an additional member, a priest. But we'll worry about that later. You will be interviewed by a number of other people. My secretary will give you a list. But so far, you seem to be the sort of people that we are looking for," Lord Conrad said as he leaned back in his chair, becoming less formal. He looked at me. "You are the same Josip Sobieski who operated on my eye, that time during the Battle for the Vistula, aren't you?"

I felt my innards tighten up, from my testicles to my throat. I admitted that I was.

"Thinking back on it, it really was an amusing misunderstanding. I've remembered it often, reminding myself not to take things for granted. Assumptions seem to always get me into trouble. I think I might have been a bit rude to you at the time, and I'm sorry for that. Please remember I was under a lot of stress and pain, and forgive me, will you?"

I said there was nothing to forgive, and I was glad when I learned that the results of my clumsy efforts had finally healed.

"Well, there's no proof that it was your fault the eye went blind in the first place. The surgeon who watched the operation said he wouldn't have done anything differently from what you did. So like I said, thank you for helping me.

"Oh yes, one other item. Sir Odon, next time you want to change jobs, please consider that *one* application is usually sufficient. We really do read these things, you know, and it wastes a lot of valuable time to have eight different barons all reading the same application."

"Yes, sir. Sorry, sir."

"Very good. Dismissed."

We all walked out grinning ear to ear. True, there would be other people who would have to pass on us yet, but we were all sure they would merely confirm whatever Lord Conrad wanted, and we were sure that he wanted us.

Chapter Thirteen

FROM THE JOURNAL OF JOSIP SOBIESKI

written January 28, 1249,
concerning October 5, 1246

Lord Conrad's remarkably attractive secretary gave Sir Odon a list of people we were to look up, and a slip for the palatine authorizing rooms and meals for us while we were at Okoitz, which spared us the expense of staying at the inn.

We spent the rest of the day making appointments with the people we had to see. There was a medical doctor who would be giving us all a physical examination, since, if we got the job, we would be away from a hospital for years at a time. We had to be healthy to begin with.

There was a priest to see. We supposed he was to make sure that we were sufficiently devout to do God's work among the heathen. There were visits to three linguists, to make sure that between us, we really did speak all of those languages.

There were experts in agriculture, manufacturing, mining, geology, music, radios, mapmaking, and survival training, and finally a meeting with a certain Baron Siemomysl, the man who would be leading the Explorer's Corps.

After supper, the others retired to the Pink Dragon Inn, for a drink and a look at the scenery, while I dutifully made yet another visit to my family in the hopes that my father would finally talk to me.

My visit was just like all of the others I'd made over the years. Everyone was glad to see me, except for my father, who, as usual, walked out as I came in. I was almost used to it by now, like a dull toothache that has gone on for years.

I was feeling depressed as I walked back through the seemingly endless corridors and stairways of Okoitz, going to our assigned room, but I was cheered to find that the others were already back from the inn.

As expected, they had found suitable female company for themselves, and being truly decent sorts, they had invited along an extra girl for me.

It's good to have friends.

Most of the people we had to see were teachers, and their interest wasn't so much in deciding whether we could join the Explorer's Corps as seeing what we each knew about their own specialties, and what they would have to teach us to make us into useful explorers. Mostly, they were planning our curriculum, because, unbeknownst to us at the time, we were going to be spending the next eighteen months at the Warrior's School.

The exception was Baron Siemomysl, who could have sent us back to our oil tanker if he did not like us. But apparently he did, because by the end of the week, they gave our boat to some other bunch of deserving young warriors, and we went to Hell.

Only we didn't call it that anymore, and it didn't seem like Hell anymore, either. The section of that huge school we occupied was now a lot like the University of Paris, or so said some people who had been to France.

We spent a long army hour every day doing physical exercise, mostly working out with swords, axes, knives, or just fighting empty-handed. But the workouts weren't brutal anymore. They were just to keep our bodies in shape while our teachers worked over our heads.

The Explorer's School was planned to have two functions: to train future explorers, and then to organize what we learned about the world into something meaningful. But naturally, they had to do the one thing before they could start on the other.

The first class through the school was only of company size, three dozen lances, but then the first year, we would only have one steamship in operation anyway. To teach us, there were some five dozen instructors, so we got a lot of individual attention.

The school was fascinating. They taught us everything known about the world, and all of our textbooks were annotated by Lord Conrad himself. Pick a subject, and we probably had a course in it. We had geography, geology, cartography, genealogy, navigation, and mathematics at one end of the spectrum, and woodcraft, music, and primitive construction techniques at the other.

Linguistics was important, and courses were taught in how to learn a new language, since in most places we would be going, people spoke languages that no civilized man had ever heard spoken. Lord Conrad claimed there were over six thousand languages in the world, and that someday there would be books at the school on every one of them.

One language that we all had to learn was Pidgin. This was an artificial language, one made up by scholars. It was based on Polish, but was very easy to learn. There were only four hundred words in the whole vocabulary. Anything else you wanted to talk about had to be done with combinations of allowable words. Everything was absolutely simplified. There were no plural forms. You said one dog, two dog, many dog. Cases didn't exist, and neither did tenses. To talk about the future, you used present tense with the word "gonna." For the past, you said "was," and then talked in the present tense. There were no sexual forms. Boys, girls, and dinner plates were all "him."

There was never anything ambiguous about Pidgin. The word "we," for example, can mean "you and me, but not those other people." Or it can mean "me and my friends, but not you." In Pidgin, there were two separate constructs, "you-me," and "me-fella."

To give you some idea of what it sounded like, in Pidgin, the Lord's Prayer started out, "Me Papa, Him big fella, Him alla time on top . . ."

It sounded strange at first, but the beauty of it was that it was extremely easy to learn. You could actually hold a meaningful conversation in it after studying it for only a few days. They claimed that a foreigner could learn it faster than a native speaker of Polish, since he didn't have anything to unlearn.

We were encouraged to use Pidgin among ourselves to increase our fluency in it, and that had the effect of giving the Explorer's Corps its own secret language. It was useful when you wanted to say something in mixed company, and you didn't want the girls to know about it, whereas the ladies had to go hand in hand to the pissatorium to accomplish the same thing.

The Wizards, the research and development people at Okoitz, had come up with a totally new sort of radio. It had at least five times the range of the old spark gap transmitters and much better sensitivity than coherers or even the newer cat's whisker receivers. It used radio tubes, and a super heterodyne receiver. It had rechargeable batteries, and it was one-sixth the weight of the old sets, even with the dynamocharger.

The explorers were the first people to be issued them, and of course we had to know how to operate, repair, and even rebuild them. All of us. Specialization was not encouraged in our corps, not when we would have to spend a year in possibly hostile circumstances, with no possibility of finding a replacement for anyone.

Geology was one of my worst subjects, and I was vastly relieved to learn that each explorer team would be taking along a compartmented box with well-labeled samples of a few hundred of the most useful minerals in it. Once I have something in each hand for comparison, I can usually figure out what is what.

I was very impressed with the quality of both my fellow classmates and my instructors. They were all remarkably intelligent, enthusiastic, and decent people. I'd often thought that one reason why my own lance was so close-knit was that everybody else in the world was so much duller than we were. When I first had that thought, years ago, I thought I was being shamefully boastful, and mentioned it to no one, but on more mature reflection, since I was now twenty-one, I have decided that it was nothing but the simple truth.

About halfway through the course, we had an eighth member added to our team, Father John. He was two years older than the rest of us, and had been an ordained priest before he went through (survived) the army's Warrior's School. Like all priests in the army, he was still officially a member of the Chaplain's Corps, and only on loan to the Explorer's Corps. He had a certain quiet strength to him, and always pulled more than his share of the load, never claiming any special privileges. He was easy to get along with and merged well with the rest of the group. Even our drinking and womanizing did not seem to bother him, or at least he never scolded us, the way so many other priests did, and he would often show up for at least the start of a drinking session. Also, he played a very fine violin, which made him particularly valuable when we made music. He eventually became the confessor of each one of us.

Yet he was not lacking in zeal, and whenever he spoke about the future, when he would have a chance to convert the heathen to Christ, you could see a certain light come on in his eyes. It was a beautiful light, but sometimes it was also a frightening one.

Toward the end of the course, almost as an afterthought, we were issued firearms of a new and interesting sort. The powder charge in the old, heavy swivel guns was ignited by a "firecracker" wick at the back of the cartridge that was lit by an alcohol flame. This was good enough when you knew a battle was coming, but it could be very awkward when unexpected things started to happen quickly.

The new guns were handheld rather than mounted, and were much lighter, about ten pounds for the rifle and three for the pistol. Ignition was by a piezoelectric crystal in the stock which, when struck by a small hammer, put an electric current through a spark plug at the back of each cartridge.

The pistol was a single-shot, break-action affair, while the rifle had a seven-shot, spring-fed clip and a bolt action. We were issued new knives with the rifles, called bayonets, which fastened to the end of the barrel, making the weapon usable as a short pike. All told, it was a remarkably well-thought-out weapon system, and we were proud to be the first unit to be issued it.

Graduation involved both written and oral examinations, and a number of practical tests as well. One of them involved being dumped naked and alone in a forest in the early spring, and being expected to build yourself suitable shelter, to make yourself suitable tools, clothing, and weapons, and to find or kill sufficient food to keep yourself alive for two weeks. They actually weighed you before and after the test, and you lost points if you lost weight!

In the end, everyone in my lance graduated, and most of the others did, too. We had a nice commencement ceremony with everyone in our eight-pounds-of-gold uniforms, and they handed out illuminated certificates to us with our friends and parents watching.

Well, parent, in my case, since my father refused to attend.

Most important for Sir Odon and all his loyal men was the fact that with graduation, our long-awaited promotions had at last come through. I was now Sir Josip, at eight pence a day, and Sir Odon was now a knight-banner, at twice that, with the right to use a triangular flag on his cavalry lance, if he ever got one, or, indeed, if he ever got a horse.

This made for some unusual ranks in our charts. The lowest rank in the Explorer's Corps was a knight, and the lance leaders were all now knight-banners. In theory, we were organized in the usual six lances to the platoon, but since each lance would be acting independently, there were no platoon leaders. Lance leaders reported directly to the company commander.

And our company commander was not the usual captain, but Baron Siemomysl himself.

Still, nobody ever said that the army had to be absolutely consistent. In the Wolves, who are made up entirely of members of the old nobility, the lowest rank is also the knight, and platoons are led by captains.

The next day, we were loaded into six chartered riverboats for the trip north. The reason for this seemingly lavish excess of transportation was that each explorer lance had an entire war cart filled with its supplies for our upcoming adventure. That was eighteen cubic yards, a ton and a half per man.

Besides our personal gear, which included everything from our armor and weapons to a year's supply of underwear and toothpaste, we had a wide variety of preserved food, enough to feed us all for three years. The trip home might be delayed, or we might have to feed a hungry tribe in the winter.

We also carried a wide variety of trade goods—tools, weapons, jewelry, cloth of many varieties, glassware, needles, fishhooks, books, even toys and games.

In a special strongbox, each lance was equipped with a large supply of money, a quarter of a million pence, equivalent to ten years' pay for every man in the lance. Some of it was in gold, some in silver, and some in the army's own zinc coinage. Sir Odon was responsible for accounting for every bit of it.

We made the trip north to Gdansk, where our new ship, the *Baltic Challenger*, was completing its first shakedown cruise. We drank and sang and partied the whole way and had about as much fun as an all-male group can possibly have.

At one point we got the riverboat's regular crew so drunk that they couldn't stand, much less operate the boat, and then my lance took the thing over and ran it until the next morning, when the regular crew woke up.

Through the night, we had sent out dozens of strange, rude, or downright obscene radio messages, and the next day the regular crew couldn't blame it on us without confessing to being drunk on duty. They were in a lovely pickle when we finally bid them good-bye.

Chapter Fourteen

FROM THE JOURNAL OF JOSIP SOBIESKI

written February 1, 1249,
concerning May 10, 1248

The *Baltic Challenger* got back to Gdansk after her shakedown run the day after we arrived, and almost the entire Explorer's Corps was on the dock to cheer her in. Most of us got there early, and at first all we could see of our new ship was a dot on the horizon that our telescopes couldn't do much to resolve.

It was a clear day, and we could see across the Vistula Lagoon and far out into the Baltic. Quite a while went by before we realized that we were looking at her smokestack. The rest of her hull appeared to be below the horizon, and eventually the realization hit us that we were actually seeing proof with our own eyes that the world was indeed round!

In the course of an hour she both grew and seemed to rise out of the water, to become of respectable size, and although we were seeing her at her smallest, from head on, we grew increasingly impressed with the engineering feat she represented.

We had all seen drawings of her, of course, and knew her specifications by heart. She was five dozen yards long at the waterline and six dozen yards long overall. She was almost two dozen yards wide and three dozen yards tall, from her keel to the top of her radio tower.

Her speed was an incredible one and a half gross miles a day, so fast that if the world were all ocean, she could circumnavigate the globe in only four months! Her fuel tanks were big enough to let her do it nonstop! Her normal fuel was oil, but in a pinch, her boilers could burn coal or even wood.

Her nine long cargo holds could hold *two gross* containers, compared to the six that our standard riverboats could handle. What is more, the containers used were mounted on half nuts, and these rested on large screws that ran the length of the cargo holds. Cargo could thus be easily shifted while the ship was under way, and those containers needed at the next port could be made ready for rapid discharge.

She had evaporators aboard that used engine waste heat to produce fresh water for the boilers and for use by passengers and crew. The same evaporators also produced sea salt, a salable commodity.

She carried two steam launches aboard, and eight container-sized barges that could be towed into the shallowest water. The *Baltic Challenger* could take on and discharge cargo and passengers without needing any port facilities beyond a simple crane. A war cart could be put ashore without even that.

But seeing technical drawings and reading specifications, even if they were astounding, could not prepare us for the sheer immensity of the glorious machine in front of us. As she came closer and closer, she grew and grew, and I had to keep telling myself that *she was still far away*!

Finally, she turned into the lagoon, and we could see her whole majestic flank from the side. Her hull was bright red, and her topsides were white, except for the streamlined red smokestack with its white Piast eagle.

She was a magnificent sight, and as she backed into her stall between two huge docks, she towered over us. It became my urgent desire to run aboard her and examine her from stem to stern, like a wonderful new lover found after a long and lonely trip.

But such was not to be. My lady had many other lovers besides me, and most of them vastly outranked me in the army's scheme of things. Lord Conrad was there, high above me on the reviewing stand. He had with him at least two dozen of his barons, and his liege lord, King Henryk himself, beside him. There was a crowd of foreign dignitaries up there, too, and it was easy to imagine why they had been invited. If anything could impress a foreign government of our power and wealth, this incredible ship would do it!

Annoyingly, the men of the Explorer's Corps, the very people the *Baltic Challenger* had been built for, after all, were not allowed aboard until late in the day. Even then, we were put ashore within the hour, before we had seen a twelfth of what we wanted to see.

Our departure date was put back by three days while Lord Conrad and King Henryk took the foreign dignitaries, three of whom turned out to be kings in their own right, out on a pleasure jaunt.

Politics!

Still, there was much to see around the new harbor and the huge shipyard. The ferrocrete hull of the *Challenger* had to be built indoors, out of the weather in a dry dock that was necessarily much bigger than the ship itself. The woman showing us around bragged that the naves of six cathedrals the size of Notre Dame, currently being built in Paris, could be placed side by side inside the dry dock without crowding. The dock's great overhead crane, a masterful engineering work, could have picked any one of them up, and turned it sideways! Notre Dame had been eighty years in the building and was not yet finished, while the dry dock had been completed in less than two years.

In the dry dock, work had begun on the *Atlantic Challenger*, sister ship to the *Baltic Challenger*. They hoped to build them at the rate of two a year for the next five years, at least.

The entire corps spent a day with the master shipwright, while he explained the difficulties of making a huge ship out of steel and concrete, and what one had to do to be sure that it was all one, seamless piece.

The sheer scale of things at Gdansk and the precision with which such huge things were made so impressed us that we were almost tempted to apply to work there. Almost, but not quite.

➤   ➤   ➤

Finally, we were ready to get under way, and the plan was to explore the lands around the Baltic Sea.

Admittedly, it was not a very ambitious project, since the Baltic probably didn't need exploring, but they told us that you have to start somewhere. True, there were plenty of Christian ships already there, and while they were little wooden things, they were well-organized, with their own political setup: the Hanseatic League. There were plenty of Christian seafarers around who could navigate to any of the ports in the area, and indeed we did have two such pilots aboard, to advise Baron Tadaos, our ship's captain, but what can you do?

It wasn't my idea, anyway.

Looking at Lord Conrad's sketched maps of the world, the Baltic seemed to be so close and so small that we felt we would be like little boys camping out in their mother's herb garden, but ours was not to reason why.

Left to ourselves, the corps would probably have steamed off to Africa, where they say the people all have black skins, or to Hy Brazyl, or to some other romantic-sounding place shown on Lord Conrad's roughly sketched maps, but we were ordered to start with the Baltic, and being good, obedient young men, that was what we would do.

Next year, maybe we'd steam to China.

On the fourteenth of May 1248, we set forth at dawn to discover the world, but, like I said, just the Baltic this year. We left Gdansk and the ship headed east, to circumnavigate the Baltic, counterclockwise.

We had to feel a little sad about the first lance of the first platoon, because they were put ashore on the afternoon of the very day we left. So much for being far travelers.

They were going into the territory of a pagan tribe called the Sambians, about whom very little was known, despite the fact that they were only five dozen miles away. Regardless of appearances, it wasn't really a wasted trip, and we gave them a good send-off.

After that, we dropped off an average of two lances a day, one almost every morning and every night.

In one respect, our ship was not as specified. She did not travel at one and a half gross miles a day. She could do two gross miles per day, and thus, except for the continents in her way, she could go around the world in a single season!

She had performed almost flawlessly on her shakedown run, and never had a serious problem while we were aboard. The only piece of her equipment that failed was her depth gauge, an electronic thing that was to bounce a sound wave off the bottom of the sea and by timing the echo reveal the depth.

They had two manual backups, though. One used a man with earphones to judge the echo, and the other was a man with a weighted rope who stood on one of the wings and found the bottom by feeling for it.

It was primitive, but the pilots from the Hanseatic League trusted the method.

My lance was the sixth of the fourth platoon, and as it turned out, we got placed farther away than any of the others, at the north end of the Gulf of Bothnia. At least, it was called that on Lord Conrad's map, although nobody ever figured out who or what or where Bothnia was. One of life's little mysteries, since Lord Conrad said that he didn't know, either.

That was one of the truly fine things about our leader. Like all men, he was sometimes wrong, although he was much more often right than wrong. When he proved to be incorrect about something, he never tried to pretend that he hadn't said what he had said, or that he had really meant something different, or used any of the other face-saving bits of nonsense that so many leaders use. He would simply say that it looked as though he was wrong, he would correct whatever needed correcting, and then he would continue on with the task at hand.

We all admired his honesty.

My lance's turn had come at last, and we were ready early, standing and waiting for Baron Tadaos of the Oceangoing Steamers and Baron Siemomysl of the Explorer's Corps to decide precisely where to put us.

Since we had no idea what sort of reception we would get from the local inhabitants, we were fully armed, with our swords at our left shoulders, our bayonets belted at our left, our pistols belted at the right, and our rifles slung on our right shoulders.

We weren't in full armor, however, since there was always the chance of falling into the water. We made do with light, open-faced helmets, rather than the big war helms that attached to the breast and back armor we were wearing. We'd left off the arm and leg pieces, and stowed them in our cart with the war helms. Even so, it was a fair load, and I couldn't help wishing that our cautious leaders would either hurry it up or send for some chairs.

The weather was good, and for the last few days they had been towing the steam launch and its barge behind the ship rather than hoisting them in and out twice a day.

Once a decision as to our destination was finally made, they simply brought up our war cart in the elevator, Sir Odon verified that it was ours by checking the serial number, and the cart was lowered into the barge that was already waiting alongside, below the starboard wing. We followed our cart down to the barge, somebody wished us luck, and the launch took us ashore while the ship continued on its way without stopping. Our whole departure was completed in minutes.

We were towed into the mouth of a fair-sized river, the Torne, we were told, and after examining both banks, Sir Odon signaled the men in the launch to put us ashore on the west bank.

The launch crew went toward shore as quickly as possible, then turned at the last possible moment and cut their power. This maneuver left the barge going straight in until it bumped the river bottom a few yards from shore. Lezek and I quickly set out the ramp boards, and Fritz took a block and tackle to shore and tied the block to a convenient tree.

Taurus had the other block hooked to the cart, and by the time the rest of us walked dry-shod ashore, all was ready for us to pull the heavy cart from the barge to the land we were to explore. The job was quickly over, and we waved the launch good-bye.

That sort of smooth coordination was something all eight members of my lance always did. There might be some conversation while we decided what should be done, but rarely was an order given about who should do what while we were doing it. Sometimes hours would go by without anyone mentioning the work at hand. Mostly it was a matter of thinking about what we were doing, and always being ready to do the next logical thing. A well-coordinated group can accomplish three times as much as a random bunch of the same number of people.

So there we stood on the beach, slowly beginning to realize that we were on our own. Well, not quite alone, since we had been discovered by a few million mosquitoes, black-flies, and other things that must have been creations of the Devil, for God was too good to make such things. We pulled the barge as far ashore as we could without moving the forward block.

"I had expected some sort of welcoming committee," Father John said, swatting a bug. "A human committee, I mean."

"Or some people of some sort, anyway," Kiejstut said. "They had to have seen the *Challenger* out there."

"Maybe there just isn't anybody around here," Sir Odon said. "That would make for a very simple exploration report, and a very dull year. But for now, we should find a good campsite. Kiejstut and Taurus, you two go look for one. The rest of us will start moving the cart uphill."

Taurus checked his compass and said, "For reasons best known to Lord Conrad, my compass is pointing almost due east. I know the true directions because I got them from the compensated compass on the ship's binnacle. I have long been accustomed to them pointing east of north, but never this far."

The rest of us confirmed that, for whatever reason, our compasses agreed with Taurus's, and the scouts left.

The cart was too heavy for six people to tow on soft soil, but with a good block and tackle and plenty of trees to tie it to, we made fairly rapid progress.

Our scouts did us up royal when it came to a campsite. They found a flat shelf of land on the side of a big hill. From it, we could see and be seen for miles. There was a small, clean stream running beside it, and there was plenty of firewood available. Better yet, there was usually enough of a breeze up there to blow away most of the blasphemous mosquitoes.

But most important, there was a dry cave not ten yards from the campsite. It was a perfect place to store things, and would make us a good shelter if the weather got really bad, although it was a bit cold in there to be really comfortable.

"Unless we find a friendly town around here, I imagine that this will be our home base for the next year," Sir Odon said. "Keep that in mind when you build the latrine and the cooking area."

The rest of the day was spent getting the cart hauled up to the campsite and then getting things there set up properly, the tents pitched, and the kitchen made usable.

Most of the supplies that we wouldn't be needing immediately were taken from the cart and stored back in the cave. Father John cooked supper, while we used the cart lid to make a dining room table, and then set out some of the supply cases to serve as chairs.

After a good meal, we were all surprisingly tired, even though it was still light out. Sir Odon set up a sentry schedule, which had each of us standing for a quarter of the night, every other day. I wouldn't have to stand mine until tomorrow.

We had a small clock with us with the new temperature-compensated pendulum, but the normal army day starts at sunrise with the thick hand pointing left at the zero. The clock wasn't set because we hadn't been here at a sunrise yet.

Sir Odon hung the clock in the mess tent, facing north, lifting the weights but not starting the pendulum. He told the sentries to guess at the time until dawn, and then to start and set the clock.

The clock had a thermometer on it, and we were all reminded to record the temperature and the weather four times a day, to document the local climate.

There were twelve hours of the same length in the army day, measured from dawn to dawn, and those hours were twice as long, on the average, as the hours used by the regular clergy. The monks used twelve hours for their day, and then twelve more for the night, but since the length of day varies with the season, the length of their hours varied as well.

Chapter Fifteen

FROM THE JOURNAL OF JOSIP SOBIESKI

written February 2, 1249,
concerning May 26, 1248

I fell quickly to sleep, despite the fact that the sun was still up, and I slept soundly enough. Yet, I was still tired when Lezek woke me up, even though the sun was again well above the horizon.

Over breakfast I noticed that everyone had bags under their eyes, and I said that they all looked about the way I felt.

"Maybe it's got something to do with the air, this far north," Father John said.

"More likely, it was all the excitement yesterday, not to mention all the work of getting the war cart all the way up here," Sir Odon said.

"I don't think so," Fritz said. "We have often been a lot more excited than yesterday, when we didn't even get drunk or laid, and we've done more work than that on most days of our lives. I think we're all maybe a little bit sick."

"Well, we'll all have to be a lot sicker before we can let ourselves start sloughing off. First off, we need to look at the surrounding area, in case there's anything dangerous out there. For today, I want Lezek and Kiejstut to take the canvas kayak and cross the river. Then I want you to map the coastline east of here. Do as much as you can, but be back here by nightfall. Taurus and

Fritz, I want you to do the same thing on the coastline to the west. Besides mapping, I want you all to try to find some of the local inhabitants and try to make friends with them, if you can. Take some money and a pocket full of trade goods with you, for presents."

"Should we carry a full weapons load?" Fritz asked.

"I think one rifle for the two of you ought to be enough. But take the rest of your personal weapons with you. Father John and I will do some mapping and searching along the riverbank, heading north of here. Josip, you were complaining about the lack of fresh bread last night at supper, so you have the honor of making up some sort of oven today, and I will expect fresh bread with my supper tonight. Zbigniew, we won't talk about your sins, but you'll spend the day building a really sturdy latrine, a two holer, if you please, at the east end of the campsite. Questions? Then let's get to it."

Those going out each took a pouch of money, a bigger pouch of various trade goods, and a third belt pouch of dried food, mostly fruit, cheese, and meat. Armed with sextants, compasses, and sketch pads for mapping, they set out, trusting to the length of their pace for distance measurements.

Taurus took an axe with him rather than a sword, which I considered wise. A sword is good against an armored man, and against a man with another sword, but for all else, an axe is much better, and it's a useful tool besides. Of course, a sword is also a status symbol, and when I'm out in public, it's my weapon of choice.

The clock said it was a half hour past dawn when I started working on the oven. There was clay to be found in the stream, and there were plenty of flat limestone rocks around. With a bit of help from Zbigniew carrying over the biggest ones, I had the oven almost completed by three.

What you need to bake bread is a hot hole in a rock. The easiest way to make one is to build something like a very deep bookcase out of flat rocks, seal it up as well as you can with clay, and then bury everything but the front of it with dirt. The one I made was big enough to bake a dozen loaves at a time.

To use it, you build a fire inside each of the holes until the whole oven is hot enough. Then you put the risen bread dough in using a long paddle, and close up the front holes with some more flat stones. If you've done it properly, the bread will be baked, but not burned, before the oven gets cold. Knowing how to do this exactly right is called "skill."

I got some bread dough mixed and rising and then cooked lunch for the two of us.

My lunch partner refused to talk about whatever it was that he had done to merit spending the day building an outhouse, but he would talk about the outhouse that he was building.

Zbigniew's plans for the outhouse were a little on the grandiose side, a small log cabin made out of thin logs. It would be light enough to move when the shit hole filled up, but with all of the joints cut wedge fashion, it would be sturdy, especially since all of the joints were to be carefully lashed together.

I didn't think there was any hope of his finishing by evening, so once I got the oven built, and small fires going in each of the baking holes to slowly bake the clay and heat the thing up to bread-baking temperature, I went over to give him a hand.

By seven o'clock we had seen no sign of the others, and the sun was still disconcertingly high, but I put the bread in to bake, and since I was fussing about the kitchen, I cooked supper as well, a stew made of dried beef, carrots, and potatoes.

By eight o'clock the food was done and in danger of either getting cold if I took it off the fire, or of burning if I didn't. I called Zbigniew over to eat, since it didn't make sense to ruin our supper, even if the others were late. I told him I was worried about the other men in our lance.

"One team could have gotten into trouble, but not all three," he said. "The sun is still high. They have plenty of time."

I said it was after eight o'clock.

"Then there must be something wrong with that clock. The sun isn't anywhere near setting. Look. Just put the stew and this good bread you made into one of the empty cases, and it will stay warm enough for the others once they get back. For now, come and help me with the latrine. With two of us working, we might get it done before sunset."

I asked him again what he had done to offend Sir Odon, and this time, since I was helping him, he told me.

"You know that yesterday's latrine was just a small trench with a couple of flat rocks on either side of it. Well, when I used it last night, I found that it was infested with stinging ants, so I dragged the two rocks a few yards farther back and used them there."

I asked why Sir Odon should be angry about that.

"Because he used the latrine right after me. He could see the white limestone rocks in the dim moonlight, but he didn't notice the old trench, which he stepped in."

I laughed and said that was Sir Odon's fault, not his.

"I agree," Zbigniew said, "but Sir Odon thought I was playing the old outhouse joke on him, you know, where you pick up and move the whole outhouse back a yard, so the next person out there falls into the shit hole, which is usually about neck deep."

I laughed and said that Sir Odon sometimes takes himself too seriously, even if Zbigniew had tried to dirty his boots.

"But I didn't do it on purpose, and our noted leader wasn't wearing his boots."

I said that just made it funnier, and Zbigniew didn't answer. Then I said now we knew why Sir Odon wanted a really sturdy latrine. He wanted it to be too heavy for Zbigniew to move, without the help of his friends, anyway.

"I suppose you're right, but we'll have to wait a few months before we can do anything about it. We can't have him falling into a dry hole, after all."

Well, we had everything done except the roof when Sir Odon and Father John got back. I told them about the food in the box, and we made a fair start on getting the outhouse thatched by sunset.

The others had gotten back safely by then, and were complaining about the cold food when we joined them.

"Blame it on a broken clock," Zbigniew told them. "Josip cooked your dinner according to the clock that was set this morning. I just looked in on it, and it claims that it is half past ten right now."

"The nights are short, this time of the year, but that's ridiculous," Sir Odon said. "Leave the clock running and we'll see how far it's off at sunrise. Maybe we can adjust it. I take it that nobody found any trace of the inhabitants of this fair land?"

Two pairs of heads shook no, they hadn't seen anybody.

"I'm still feeling tired, for some reason," Father John said. "But it doesn't seem to have affected my work. We mapped two dozen miles of river today, and then walked the whole way back. That's quite an accomplishment."

Fritz and Lezek said that they had each done almost as much. I said I was as tired as I had ever been, and that I was going to sleep.

Sir Odon warned me that I had the fourth watch, and I made Fritz promise to wake me.

I woke with Fritz shaking my arm and the sun in my eyes. I jumped up and asked why he hadn't woken me on time.

"I *am* waking you on time," Fritz said. "You have had only three hours of sleep."

I said I was confused.

"Sir Odon's orders. Daybreak now happens four hours after sunset, no matter what the sun feels like doing."

I must have still looked befuddled, because he continued, "Look, just stay awake for an hour and then wake everybody else up, including me."

I got up, Fritz went to sleep, and the first thing I did was walk over to the clock in the mess tent. It said it was half past one.

I had breakfast ready for the others when I woke them at half past two. Sir Odon got up, went over to the clock, and reset it to zero.

Then he said, "Good morning, Josip. Thank you for getting breakfast ready."

I asked him to explain what was going on.

"Wait until the others get here. There's no point in going through this twice."

Once we were all together, he said, "Last night was clear enough for me to shoot a sighting on the North Star. We are very far north. In fact, we are only about four dozen miles south of the Arctic Circle. Also, we are only a few weeks away from the Summer Solstice. This means that in a few weeks' time, if we go just two days' march north of here, the sun will never set at all. We will be in the Land of the Midnight Sun.

"Furthermore, the nights here and now are so short that we will fall over dead of exhaustion in a few weeks if we try to sleep only when the sun is down. Therefore, until further notice, we will wake up four hours after sunset, since I think that we would have trouble falling asleep when the sun is still up. Sunset is now at eight o'clock, and the first sentry sets the clock."

"So that's why we were all so tired," Father John said.

"Of course. If you work eleven hours every day and sleep only one, you will be tired. The fact that we all did that without noticing it proves that people have a very poor sense of time."

Lezek said, "Lord Conrad once wrote that it was possible to build a clock so small that it could be worn on your wrist, but I've never heard of anyone who actually made one."

"We certainly could have used one these past few days," Sir Odon said. "Now then, I want to be north of here to see this Midnight Sun business. We've read about it, but we could be the first men in the entire army to see it. But before we can go, there are some things that must be done around here first."

"Then what should we do?" Father John said.

"I would like to see at least two more scouting patrols made, one to the northwest and one to the northeast, so we can be sure that there aren't any people around here. We need to get a medium-sized garden going, to see what varieties of plants can be grown here, and to get some fresh food on the table. We need to get a radio antenna up so we can report in, and the same pole might as well serve as a flagpole. Can anyone think of anything else?" Sir Odon asked.

"I think we will need a very sturdy door made for the mouth of the cave," Kiejstut said, "something strong enough to discourage a bear, since I don't want us to lose our winter's food supply while we're gone."

"Good idea. Any other thoughts? No? Then how about if

Josip and Kiejstut head northeast, and Taurus and Zbigniew go northwest. Fritz, you get started on a garden, Father John and I will take care of the antenna, and that leaves Lezek to worry about the door for the cave. You fellows on patrol, try to bring back some fresh meat, if you can do it without bothering the locals."

Kiejstut said, "What locals?"

"Just don't shoot somebody's cow. Well, let's get going."

Chapter Sixteen

FROM THE JOURNAL OF JOSIP SOBIESKI

written February 3, 1249,
concerning May 28, 1248

Due to some near fatal hangovers and a fouled-up railroad connection, Kiejstut and I had both missed the one-day course they'd given on the folding kayak. Fortunately, the thing went together easily enough. Folded, it looked like a six-yard-long bundle of sticks wrapped in canvas. You simply inserted three vaguely oval-shaped ribs in the right places, gave them a twist, and it popped out and became a lightweight boat that was pointed at both ends, and could hold three men in a pinch.

The double-ended paddles were strange, but easily mastered.

We crossed the icy cold river, beached the kayak, and hid it under some bushes. Then, packs on our backs, weapons loaded, and our hearts light, we headed out looking for adventure. What we found were mostly hills, small bushes, and a vast number of carnivorous insects.

"I am rigorously opposed to this business of being in the middle of the food chain!" Kiejstut complained, swatting at the bugs. "In my family, we always sat on the *top* of the chain."

I recommended chastising them for their lack of respect of his exalted station in life.

"Chastise them? I am already slaughtering them by the thousands! What else can I do?"

I suggested attempting to engage in a meaningful conversation with them, but his only reply was to throw a rock at me.

We had no luck in finding any people, but were more successful when it came to fresh meat. Kiejstut and I each managed to shoot a deer.

I was walking far in the lead when Kiejstut waved me to take cover. He had the rifle and lay down behind a bush while two small bucks slowly came within range. I stood behind a tree far to his right, watching and waiting. When they came within nine dozen yards, he fired, and his marksmanship was absolutely perfect. Shot through the heart, the buck fell backward without a sound or further motion.

The second buck sprang up and started running, and it had the bad luck to run straight at me. I was surprised, but I had the presence of mind to draw and cock my pistol. The animal didn't see me until it was only about a dozen yards away. It turned and offered me a perfect side shot. One does not often get the opportunity to brag about having felled a deer with a pistol, so I fired. The buck went down, but when I got to it, it was still alive. I drew my bayonet, held back its head, and cut its throat.

At that point we were more than a dozen miles from our base camp, and there didn't seem to be much sense in going on any farther. We each slung a buck over our shoulders, but they were heavier than they looked. It was soon obvious that if we tried to bring back both whole animals, we couldn't possibly make it to camp by dark.

I asked if he thought we should abandon one of the deer, or if we should leave our armor, weapons, and supplies behind.

"Sir Odon would have a fit if we abandoned any equipment, even temporarily. Remember that they made him sign for all of it. As to leaving our weapons, well, don't even think about it!" Kiejstut said, "You really should have let the second deer go. As it is, well, to throw one of them away would be wasteful and little children in Mongolia are going to bed hungry."

I had to agree that he was right, although shooting had seemed a good idea at the time. Anyway, both bucks were bigger than I had at first thought.

So we stopped, and I built a fire as much to destroy some of the mosquitoes as to cook lunch. Kiejstut started with the butchering. We cooked and ate one liver, put all of my trail food into my partner's pouch, and then put the second liver in my pouch. This meant that I would have a messy cleaning job to do once we got back, but then the original sin was mine.

Regretfully, we discarded all of the rest of the tripe, the heads, the feet, and even the skins, to get the loads down to a weight we could live with.

Even then, we nearly swamped the kayak bringing home the venison.

When we got back to camp, we found that Taurus and Zbigniew had also brought back a deer each, and they managed to bring back the whole animals. A surfeit of riches.

We spent the next few days gorging on hearts, brains, kidneys, and livers, and spent much of the time cutting most of the meat into thin strips. We built a smokehouse, and then salted and smoked the meat so it would keep. Fritz even made us some smoked sausages. We already had plenty of dried meat, but waste not, want not.

As we got the garden prepared and planted, a debate arose among us as to whether we should leave someone behind at the camp when most of us walked upstream to map the river. On the one hand, if someone or something despoiled our supplies and equipment, we could be in very serious trouble when winter arrived. But it was also dangerous to split our forces. The decision was finally made when no one would volunteer to stay behind and miss seeing the Midnight Sun.

We radioed the ship that we were leaving and put the radio away in the cave. If we got into trouble when we were away from the camp, it wasn't likely that those on the ship would be able to find us, so we couldn't really expect any help, anyway.

We placed in the cave everything we weren't taking with us, closed the sturdy door that we'd built, and locked it with one of the new combination padlocks. Then we all spent a few hours covering the entrance with rocks, burying the rocks with dirt, and finally planting a few small bushes in the dirt, as camouflage.

We left a small pile of trade goods outside on a big flat rock, mostly some knives, jewelry, arrowheads, and metal cups—as a gift—in case we were trespassing on someone's land.

After a total of five days at our base camp, we left with four weeks' worth of supplies in the heavy packs on our backs, heading north along the river.

Following four days' march, much of it uphill, the weather was getting colder, and we were marching through coarse, dirty snow left over from last winter. When we came to a split in the river, we took the west branch, since taking the other would have involved building a raft and risking the swift-flowing, icy white water.

Three days later we saw our first Midnight Sun, or at least some of one, for the sun was two-thirds hidden by the hills on the horizon.

Twelve hours after that, we climbed to the top of the highest hill around so as not to miss the amazing sight of a sun shining at midnight. But once up there, the day turned foggy and cloudy and there was no sun to be seen, Midnight or otherwise.

It stayed cloudy for five more days, and I thought we all would die of terminal frustration. But all things pass, even bad luck, and finally we had clear weather and a mountaintop, and we all cheered.

But now we didn't even have the sun to guide us, for instead of rising in the east and setting in the west, the way a proper Christian sun should, the silly thing just went round and round, above the horizon! Well, it went higher in the south, and it almost kissed the horizon in the north, but it was still most disconcerting!

We had trouble knowing when to sleep, until Father John pointed out that we could still use the sun as a clock, if we assumed that the face of the clock was lying on the ground. If your compass was pointed to the east at the clock face's zero, the sun told you the proper army time of day.

Think of that! Telling time with a compass!

The next day, things started to get more interesting. We were walking near the river when we saw a large herd of the same sort of deer we had been occasionally seeing in ones and twos through the trip. Now there were thousands of them, and they kept on coming!

There were so many that, while they weren't acting aggressively, they were starting to crowd us, and Sir Odon had us all climb a rock outcropping perhaps four yards high, to get out of their way. We were up there for about an hour, taking a forced break from the march, when I saw our first people.

I shouted to the others that they should notice the hunters, chasing the deer.

"Those men! They are not carrying weapons! They aren't hunters!" Kiejstut said. "They are herding the deer!"

Taurus said, "Whoever heard of such a thing? I never thought that deer *could* be herded."

I said they were herded every year, at Lord Conrad's Great Hunt, except that there, they had to be completely surrounded.

"These are a different kind of deer than what we have farther south," Zbigniew said. "The deer in Poland stay in small groups when they aren't alone. They mostly eat bushes and hide in the thickets and forests. The deer here eat mostly moss and grass and live in herds. Their faces look different, they have wider noses and bigger antlers. And unless all those deer are male, their females have antlers just like the males."

He jumped down from our rock, right down among the fast-moving deer. Then he lay down right on the ground and looked up at them!

"Get back up here, you crazy fool!" Sir Odon shouted.

Zbigniew climbed safely back up and said, "Sorry I scared you, sir. But you know, *most* of those deer are females, antlers or no antlers."

The herdsmen running on foot were followed by others, men,

women, and children, who were riding on sleds or sleighs. The sleighs were being pulled by deer!

"Using deer as beasts of burden! This has to be unique!" Father John said.

We smiled and waved at the people passing us, and they smiled and waved back, but they didn't stop. I had the feeling that they were doing something too important to bother with strangers.

When they were gone over the next hill, Sir Odon said, "Well, at least they aren't hostile. Come on, let's follow them, but at a distance, so we won't threaten them."

We followed, and there wasn't any question of us crowding them. Even at a run, we could barely keep up! Finally, hours later, we came upon their camp. Sir Odon and Father John left their weapons with the rest of us and approached the camp, staying in the open and bowing whenever any of the natives noticed them.

The technique seemed to work, for soon three of the locals, two older men and one mature woman, came out and bowed back, apparently in imitation of our leaders. They began to try to communicate with each other, but they didn't seem to have much luck. Seemingly, the natives spoke neither Polish nor Latin.

After a bit, Sir Odon called Fritz to join them, to try his German on the locals. Fritz came back after a short while and sent Taurus out to try Ukrainian. He was followed by Zbigniew with his Pruthenian, and then Kiejstut with his Lithuanian, but none of them had any luck. Fritz said that whatever they spoke sounded a little bit like Hungarian, but no one in our group spoke any of that language.

Lezek and I were the only ones in our lance who spoke no foreign languages, so we weren't sent to try to talk to the people.

While this was going on, small gifts were exchanged with the deer herders. We gave them a dozen small knives, some needles, fishhooks, and some glass beads for jewelry, since the woman already had some sewn into her coat. In return we got some fresh meat and some nicely made handicrafts, including some beautifully embroidered leather belts.

While our leaders continued to make progress, the rest of us pitched camp where we were standing and built a fire, since, despite the snow on the ground, there were still mosquitoes flying.

We cooked a meal, and the three locals were invited to come and join us. They were particularly taken with the dried fruit we had with us, and were given paper bags of it to take back with them.

Finally, they left with what we thought was an understanding to return after we all slept for a while. We posted no sentries, since that might show distrust of our new friends.

When we woke, four hours later, the locals had already packed up their camp and left. None of us could figure out why.

We followed them for three days, traversing three fords, heading due north where the river we had been mapping was now heading northwest. It eventually became plain that they were outdistancing us.

"The only way we could keep up with them is if we had some Big People with us," Lezek said.

I said that yes, Anna's children could run as fast as a deer, but an ordinary human with weapons and a backpack could not.

"I hate to lose our only contact with the local inhabitants, but I'm afraid that the two of you are right," Sir Odon said. "We'll pitch camp here and rest for a day before we head back to continue mapping the river."

Chapter Seventeen

FROM THE DIARY OF JOSIP SOBIESKI

written February 4, 1249,
concerning June 12, 1248

A few days later, while we were sitting around a fire, Taurus said, "I've been thinking about those deer people, and you know, I don't think that they were herding the deer after all."

"So?" Sir Odon said. "Just what do you think they were doing?"

"I think that they were *following* the deer. I mean, think about it. They weren't ahead of the animals, they were behind them at all times. When the animals moved, they moved, and they didn't dare stop, for fear of being left behind. When the deer stopped for a while, they could stop, too, and try to talk to us. You could see that they *were* curious about us, and they *were* friendly enough. But when the deer started to move again, they packed up everything in a hurry and left. I think they did that because they *had* to do that. They eat the deer, they wear the deer, and they ride behind the deer. I'd be willing to bet that they protect the deer as well. Without the deer, they would be absolutely nothing! So they *must* follow them wherever they go."

Sir Odon thought awhile and said, "You know, that's almost crazy enough to be the truth! To think that a whole tribe of people are in effect enslaved to a herd of deer! Amazing!"

"But are the people really the slaves?" Father John said. "It is the deer that are slaughtered and eaten. It is the deer that pull the sleighs. And I'll tell you, I examined some of those sleigh draft animals, and they were castrated males. Do masters permit their slaves to castrate them?"

"But it is the deer who decide where both the herd and the tribe are going," Sir Odon said.

Zbigniew said, "Maybe the people don't *care* where they're going, as long as the deer are there. Perhaps the deer know best where the better grazing is to be found. I mean, who would know better than a deer where the best food for a deer is?"

"I suppose so," Sir Odon said. "But it is still one of the strangest relationships that I have ever witnessed."

"I can tell you have never met Komander Sliwa," Lezek said. "He has six wives and everybody in the family is happy. Now, *there* is a strange relationship!"

A few days later we found the iron deposit. At first all we saw were several small mines that must have been used sporadically by native blacksmiths. They were little more than holes in the ground, actually, and scattered over several square miles.

But then, when Father John noticed that the ore from all of the mines was identical, he suggested that the whole area must have a huge seam of iron ore under it. We dug a half-dozen small pits, and found iron in every one of them!

We spent a further three weeks at the site, digging dozens of holes to define just how big the thing was, and digging a deep hole in the center of it, like a well, to find out how thick the ore seam was. Any way we figured it, there was more iron available than the army could use in three hundred years!

We surveyed the area, and sketched in some grandiose plans for equipment to mine and clean the ore, and then started to work our way back, making preliminary drawings for a series of canals and locks to get the ore down the river to the Baltic.

We were all vastly excited about the possibilities ahead of us, because according to the army policy statement concerning explorers, we would all be getting a percentage of the profits of the mine. Not a huge percentage, but as Kiejstut put it, "A small part of infinity is still very large!"

Our plans called for specially built steamships, designed to hold bulk cargoes of coke or iron ore, to run between the Vistula and the Torne, with steel-making plants at the mouths of both rivers. Coke from Poland would be shipped to the plant on the Torne, and then the ships would be filled with iron ore to be shipped back to Poland. It would be a most efficient operation!

We then discovered there were four seasons up there in the north. They were June, July, August, and winter.

By the time we made it back to our base camp, three months had gone by. The short northern summer was over, and the rivers were all frozen over. We suddenly realized that our carefully drawn plans for two gross miles of canals and locks were all a waste of time! If they were built, they would be useless for most of the year.

So we started all over, and this time we designed a railroad. Fortunately, we could use the same surveys, and do the design work at our base camp, which was wonderful, since we again had some variety in our meals. For the last six weeks, while on the trail, we had been eating nothing but fresh venison, and even that delight became very tiresome after a while.

Our radio messages concerning our find were well-received on the ship, and as they were getting back to Poland every month, we heard that Lord Conrad was pleased with us. It seems that the seam of magnetite at Three Walls was almost depleted, and another source of high-grade iron ore was urgently needed. We were now certain that our discovery would not be ignored.

On less important topics, our garden had been surprisingly productive, considering that it had only about five weeks of growing season. When we got back, we found a half acre of plants that had matured, but were mostly frost-killed and rotted. The potatoes, beets, and other root crops could be salvaged, but little else was saved.

Nonetheless, the long days of sunlight did allow for a decent enough harvest, except for the fact that a farmer would have to do all of his work, from plowing to harvest, in only five weeks, and it didn't seem likely that a man could make a living that way. Maybe gardening would be a hobby for some of the workers at the steel plant we would build here.

We made a few quick excursions back up the river, to check on a few alternate railroad routes and to bring back more samples of the ore for the metallurgists, but for the most part, the balance of our year on the Torne was spent at our base camp.

Once, coming back from the ore site, we crossed the tracks of the deer people, but we didn't meet any of them. We found out later, over the radio, that they had been contacted by two of the other explorer lances, southwest of there, toward Sweden. Hopefully, the others would learn more about those strange people than we had.

Before the Baltic froze over, a few people from the ship dropped by, to pick up our ore samples, along with our maps and drawings, and drop off some fresh fruits and vegetables, but army policy was that an explorer lance should spend at least a year at a site, so we did.

Once it became really cold, having the cave was a godsend. It was pleasantly warm in there compared to what it was outside.

A cave stays the same temperature all year around. This temperature is the average of all the outside temperatures in the area over the past several years. At least, that's what our data showed once we'd collected it over a year.

In fact, recording the temperature, along with the weather and the time the sun rose and set, was about all we did for the last six months in camp. Cooking, eating, and sleeping were the only other things we had to do besides writing up what had happened the summer before.

I expanded my notes to cover my entire life up to then. That is to say, this is when I wrote most of the journal you now hold, although now that I've gotten this far, I think I might continue with it.

At the Winter Solstice, the opposite of the Midnight Sun happened. One day the sun never does come up. But you cannot celebrate something that doesn't happen, so we didn't.

We tried trapping fur-bearing animals, using traps we made according to one of the manuals we had with us. Either there weren't any animals to be trapped or we didn't know what we were doing, or both, but the project was not successful.

We did find a large bear, or rather, he found us. Apparently, the cave had been his winter home, and he vigorously objected to our possession of it. This was only fair, since we objected to his repossession of the premises with even greater vigor. The bear made it all the way through the doorway before dying with over a dozen bullets in him. Bear meat was a refreshing change from venison, and we made his pelt into a rug.

Kiejstut and I managed to catch Sir Odon with the old outhouse trick, but it just isn't as much fun when the shit is frozen solid.

Lezek and Kiejstut wrote quite a few songs that winter, and some of them have gotten popular around the Explorer's School. When next you hear "Under the Midnight Sun," or "The Baltic Challenger," or even "Ten Thousand to One, Against Us," also known as "The Mosquito Song," think of them, up there in the cold.

Mostly, we told a lot of long, tall stories, played a lot of games, and read every army manual we had with us at least twice. We loudly bemoaned the fact that we had neither beer nor fair ladies with us. We sang and played our horns, violins, guitars, drums, and recorders, and with so much time to practice, we became better with them. We lived, but I think that if we had not been such good friends in the first place, we might have killed each other just to have something interesting to do.

In fact, there was a killing in the lance to the southeast of us. Apparently, the man just went crazy from sitting around with nothing to do. He killed one of his teammates and injured two others before he was shot dead. Madness.

Sitting unloved and sober in the cold and dark, my lance made a few resolutions. We swore that on our next mission, we would bring a year's supply of strong drink with us, even if it had to be that powerful white lightning stuff that Lord Conrad liked. Also, our next mission would either have to be someplace where they had women, or we would smuggle in our own. And mainly, wherever it was, it had darned well better be warm!

written January 12, 1250,
concerning June 1249

Again I find time weighing heavily on me, as I sit alone in my cabin, steaming across the Atlantic Ocean, and far away from my one true love. I might as well bring this journal up to date.

Finally, the birds of the Arctic began to return, the ice on the Baltic started to break, and the long winter ended. We were told to leave everything behind, except for our journals, our weapons, and our personal equipment. All the rest would be of use to those who would follow us. We asked if that included the chest of money we had brought but hadn't found a use for, and they said yes, leave that, too.

We sealed up and buried the cave entrance as we had done once before, but only after Sir Odon counted the money twice and made us all sign a paper saying that we had left the money and everything else behind pursuant to orders. I'd never seen him quite so nervous before, but then I'd never seen anyone ordered to abandon a quarter of a million pence before, either.

Well, a quarter million pence less all of our back pay, up to the first of next month. We didn't want to be penniless on the trip back to the Explorer's School.

We were personally welcomed on board the *Baltic Challenger* by Baron Siemomysl and Baron Tadaos with a party, mostly because we had found the most valuable thing of any of the explorer lances. You see, our superiors would get a cut of the profits on the mine, just as we would.

We all smiled and shook hands, and they all smiled and shook hands, and everybody said uninteresting things, and nobody said anything original, since everything important had already been said months ago, over the radio. They fed us well, with fantastically delicious fresh egg omelets, crispy salads, and fresh green garden vegetables. And we drank, and drank well.

It was a wonderful thing that they had beer on the ship, and we had been too long sober. We were all astounded at the *amount* we could drink, several gallons per man, without even falling over. I think that our bodies were telling us that we needed it.

At Gdansk we got our new orders. We were to forward our journals and equipment to the Explorer's School. I sent them my journals, but shipped my big war chest home, since in his letters, my brother had asked about all the new weapons and equipment, and I wanted to show him.

We were further ordered to take three months off, with pay. This gave Fritz, Kiejstut, and Taurus time enough to visit home, something they had not been able to do in many years, since before the Mongol invasion.

Kiejstut stayed right on the ship, since it would be making one more round to pick up the last of the explorer lances, while putting off over a dozen mercantile support groups at the permanent stations that had been selected, and in doing so would be steaming right past Lithuania.

When I asked why our lance hadn't been sent to Lithuania, since we already had someone who spoke the language, the barons told me that at the time, they hadn't known exactly where Lithuania was, and anyway, they hadn't thought of it.

Then they asked me why I hadn't suggested it, and I had to say that I hadn't thought of it, either. When we got Kiejstut into the conversation, he said he had traveled to Poland by land. He had never thought of going home by water until now.

Fritz considered taking the ship around the Baltic to get to Szczecin, and going home from there, but a study of the new maps convinced him it would be just as fast to go home by way of Okoitz, where he could get a little sexual release first.

He said, "That way I will be less likely to rape and pillage and rape again, all my bloody way across the Holy Roman Empire!"

The seven of us took a leisurely riverboat trip in pleasant early summer weather up the Vistula, to Sionsk, where Father John left us. He had to report to the Archbishop at Gniezno, before visiting his family at Poznan.

Lezek's family and Zbigniew's foster family lived on army ranches near Sieciechow, and Fritz, Taurus, and I were persuaded to visit with them for a day or two before continuing on home.

Sir Odon declined the offer, so we left him aboard to continue his way south. It was his loss, for their families gave us a fine welcome, and we enjoyed our stay there immensely.

The workers at both of the ranches, one for aurochs and the other for young Big People, were members of the army just as we were. But it seemed to them that we were the ones out doing all the exciting things while they were stuck living humdrum, ordinary lives. It seemed to me that I had just spent the winter in a cave bereft of beer and female company, while they had spent the time pleasantly with their families.

As Lezek put it, "The grass is always greener over somebody else's septic tank."

I was particularly taken with Zbigniew's foster sister, Maria. Because of her, I delayed my departure from the ranch for almost a week, and the others stayed around as well. I was about to propose matrimony, until my friends convinced me that I was thinking with my gonads rather than with my head. They said I had been too long without a woman, and that before I did anything irreversible, I should go spend a week or two with the girls from the cloth factory at Okoitz. Then I should come back and talk seriously with Maria's father.

New Big People were always coming of age, that is, "remembering" everything their mothers had known at the time of their voluntary conception. When this process was completed, the adult Big People, who automatically became members of the army, went out to their assigned military duty stations. It was customary to send them in the company of a little person, preferably one of knight's rank or higher.

We were asked by the assignment clerk if we would care to help out and deliver some of them to Three Walls, which was near the Warrior's School, our next duty assignment. Taurus said he wished he could oblige them but he wanted to go back to his homeland, in the Ukraine, where he had an uncle and some cousins he had not seen in many years, before returning to the Explorer's School. The clerk said that the trip would cause no difficulty, since we had ten weeks to make the delivery. He said that it was always good for the Big People to see some of the outside world before going to work.

Essentially, we were each being offered the services of one of Anna's fabulously valuable children for the rest of our vacations, and yes, of course we'd be happy to help them out!

Starting at dawn the next day, Taurus headed southeast for the Ukraine, while Fritz and I galloped south along the Vistula, stopped for a quick lunch in Sandomierz, and then had supper in Cracow on the same day, before we got to Okoitz before dark! This was less than half the time it would have taken had we gone by riverboat, although they ran around the clock. Neither the Big People nor we humans had ever made that trip by land before, but our mounts knew the way.

It was the first time I had ever been privileged to ride one of those lovely creatures, and being on Margarete was a joy never to be forgotten. She gave me such a tremendous feeling of speed and power! What's more, she remembered me from when I was a little boy at Okoitz who knew her ancestor Anna! She *really did* have all of Anna's memories.

I had never had a horse before, much less one of the Big People. I was unsure of how to take proper care of her, and Fritz was almost as ignorant as I was, since as a farmer his father had kept only oxen. Rather than risk causing the ladies any discomfort, we paid the stable keeper at the inn double the usual rates, and told him they must get the very best of everything. The next morning Margarete said that she was satisfied, so I considered the money well spent.

Fritz and I spent only a single night carousing in the Pink Dragon Inn at Okoitz, and then he went on his way, to his home near Worms, in the Holy Roman Empire. He was excited at the prospect of going home a true, belted knight, with eight pounds of gold on his uniform, a gold-hilted sword, a modern pistol, and a pouch full of silver at his belt, riding on one of Anna's famous children!

"My parents will burst with pride, and my old friends will turn purple with envy!"

I visited my parents the next morning, and it was the same old story. Everyone was glad to see me again except for my father, who *still* would not talk to me.

I went back to my room in the inn. I sat alone and thought about my problem with my father. I thought for a long while. I'd already tried using every intermediary possible. The priest. My mother. My sisters and brother. Even the in-laws. I was just going to have to settle the problem myself, somehow.

It took me a while to get up my courage, but a few days later I confronted my father. I actually stood in his path and wouldn't let him past without talking to me. I asked him just what he expected of me, and he said nothing. I begged to know just what great crime I had committed, that he should treat me this way for so many years, and he wouldn't talk!

I had to hold him by both arms to keep him in front of me, but still he would not say a single word to me. Finally, he tried to break away. I spun him around to face me again, and when he still wouldn't say a word, I hit him.

Just once, but in the mouth and as hard as I could.

He just stood there, bleeding and looking at me, and still he would not speak to me! Even looking into his eyes, I could not fathom what he was thinking.

I left Okoitz the next morning with the intention of reporting in early to the Explorer's School. There simply wasn't anything else I wanted to do.

I never saw Lezek's foster sister again, but sometimes I think that I should have.

Chapter Eighteen

FROM THE DIARY OF CONRAD STARGARD

June 2, 1249

Once again I sat in my office, planning the next expedition of the Explorer's Corps.

The Baltic had been mapped and a number of commercial possibilities examined. The fishing grounds were rich, much better than they had been in the twentieth century. Plans for six motorized fishing boats and a fish-processing plant built into a *Challenger*-sized hull were under way.

There were good trading possibilities in the fur trade, in amber, and in timber. The army's commercial products, from window glass to padlocks, had all been very well received.

But most important was the discovery of the vast iron ore deposit in what would someday be northern Sweden, in my old time line. I thought (and hoped) that this was the deposit that made Swedish steel so famous! Coming as it did, just when our seam of magnetite at Three Walls was running out, it reaffirmed my conviction that God was truly on my side! Plans to exploit the wonderful discovery were going ahead at full speed.

Exploration continued as well, with two ships and six dozen explorer lances currently out on the shores of the Kattegat, the Skagerrak, and the North Sea, from the English Channel to the Orkney Islands.

Now it was time to take a big bite.

We needed rubber, or at least some sort of durable, flexible, insulating material, and our chemical industry wasn't anywhere near advanced enough to produce decent plastics.

The only place I knew of where rubber trees could be found was in South America, or Brazyl, as I had named it on my maps.

What we needed was in the Amazon Rain Forest, a place I had heard a lot of mixed messages about. On one hand, there were dozens of horror stories about schools of man-eating piranhas, evil natives with blowguns, and vast clouds of carnivorous insects, not to mention leeches a half a yard long that sucked only warm blood. The place apparently abounded with poisonous darts, poisonous trees, poisonous fishes, poisonous frogs, and poisonous everything else.

On the other hand, I had seen travelogues that made it all look very attractive, with a balmy climate, friendly natives, and good swimming, since the alligators and piranhas were overrated bogeymen.

The truth, as always, was probably somewhere in the middle, but I doubt if it was anything our men couldn't handle. So far, the Explorer's Corps had done an admirable job, with only two fatalities, and those were caused by insanity, probably brought on by a case of cabin fever. Other companies had lost more men than that while engaged in farming!

The Amazon River should be easy enough to find, since it's right on the equator. Just head south until the North Star touches the horizon, and then turn right, and straight on till morning. There's no way they could miss it.

Once on the river, every third lance would be equipped with a riverboat, since land transportation in those swamps would be difficult.

Coming up with a riverboat that could be knocked down and packed in containers for shipment wasn't a problem. I'd put engineering on it a month ago, and a prototype would be ready within the week.

Besides finding rubber, and convincing the natives to collect it for us in return for steel knives, salt, and whatever else they wanted, our explorers would try to get to the headwaters of the Amazon. There, in the Andes Mountains, is a civilized area, inhabited by the Incas. These Indians have lots of gold and silver, but no iron or steel. Such a country could make a wonderful trading partner!

As I was pondering these pleasant thoughts, a very attractive and very naked young lady walked into my office, and my first thought was, *Oh my God! Not again!*

In the thirteenth century, in northern Europe, a naked lady had much in common with a woman of the twentieth century wearing a bikini bathing suit. On the one hand, it was neither immoral nor illegal, but on the other hand, it was not exactly always appropriate!

But she just stood there, with huge blue eyes and blond hair, wearing nothing but a slightly vacant smile. Not even pubic hair. I realized that I knew her, or rather that I had met her.

In partial payment for stranding me in the thirteenth century, my time-traveling cousin Tom had given me a vacation once in his apartment, which was located in what he called a "temporal bubble." It seemed to be able to exist in any time, and in any place, or even *without* a time or a place.

This girl had been the cook, the maid, and the whatever-else-you-needed there. She was not human, but was rather a bioengineered creation with a lot in common with the Big People, like my first mount, Anna.

"Well, hello there, Maude," I said in English, which had been the only language she had been able to speak. "What can I do for you?"

She just looked at me, confused, and then said, "I'm sorry, sir, but I don't understand you," in Polish.

"You speak Polish now, but not English?" I said in Polish.

"Yes, sir."

"So they reprogrammed you for a new language?"

"Yes, sir."

"If they did that, my cousin Tom must intend for you to stay here."

"Yes, sir."

Except for the fact that she could speak and looked human instead of like a horse, she was just like Anna. They both had absolutely literal minds. If you didn't ask exactly the right question, you wouldn't get the right answer.

That, and they were both so totally *nice* that they would never let you know you had hurt their feelings, so you had to work hard at not hurting them in the first place.

"If my cousin gave you a message for me, please tell it to me."

"Yes, sir. Tom said that you needed a bodyguard. He said that you had already ruined me as a servant. He said that you might as well have me stand guard over you."

She said that in her pleasant voice, with the same, unvarying plastic smile on her face, like a characterless automaton. Yet I knew that deep inside she was no such thing, any more than Anna was.

"He said that I had 'ruined' you? Was it because you slipped me that *Handbook of Chemistry and Physics*?"

"Yes, sir. Yes."

She had to answer both questions, but she wouldn't expand on her answers unless you asked her to. Sometimes, you got used to it after a while.

"Do you feel that I have ruined you?"

"No, sir."

"That's good, because I want to be your friend. I want you to like it here. You're not sorry that you came, are you?"

"No, sir."

"Good, because this can be a very nice place. Now then. My cousin sent you here to be a bodyguard. Do you know anything about that job? I mean, do you know how to fight?"

"Yes, sir. Yes."

"With what sort of weapons? Or do you fight empty-handed?"

"I fight with any weapons, sir. Yes."

"Hmm. I know that you are a lot stronger than you look. Let's go through a few judo throws, slowly, without hurting each other. You can do that, can't you?"

"Yes, sir."

I got up from behind my desk and walked around it toward

her. Small and slender, she couldn't have weighed ninety pounds, while I am large. Slowly, with exaggerated motions, I pretended to swing a fist at her. And just as slowly, and a good deal more gracefully, she put me into a hip throw, had me completely airborne, and just as gently set me down on my back on the floor. At one point, there, she was supporting my entire weight with one hand around my belt.

"Yes. That was very good, Maude. You certainly know that part of your job. Can you handle a sword?"

"Yes, sir."

"A knife? Our pistols, and other firearms?"

"Yes, sir. Yes."

"Very good. Later on we'll go down to the armory and you can pick out whatever you want," I said. "Now then, up until now, you worked for Tom. He wanted you to be a perfect personal servant, and that's how you act. Now you work for me. I don't want you to act like a servant. Around here, even the servants don't act like servants. I want you to act like a human being. I want you to *be* a human being, for all practical purposes. Do you understand that?"

"No, sir."

"Well, first off, one 'sir' per conversation is sufficient, or better yet, call me 'your grace,' since that's my proper title. But only once per conversation. Clear?"

"Yes, your grace."

"Good. From now on I want you to answer not only with what I specifically ask for, but also with any further information that you think I might need, or want to know."

"Yes . . . But how do I know what you already know? How do I know what you want to know?"

"You have to guess. Watch the other people around here, and listen to them. Try to imitate their word patterns. If and when you talk too much, or too little, I'll let you know. Just remember that I like you a lot, and just because I correct you, it doesn't mean that I don't like you."

"Yes," she said, with the same vacant smile.

On the one hand, it is difficult to become angry with something that looks like a pretty, naked blond girl who is being absolutely agreeable. But on the other hand, her literal mindset was driving me right up the wall! Deep down inside, she really did have feelings, and I wanted her to develop that side of herself. I didn't dare scream at her for fear of crushing her. All I could do was keep on prattling at her as though she was an idiot, which she certainly wasn't.

"Good. Next, I want to talk about facial expressions. You have been smiling all of the time, because that is what you were taught to do. Real people use their facial expressions to convey their emotions. When they're happy, they smile, when they're sad, they frown, or they cry. When they're angry, well, they look like they're angry. Understand?"

"Yes, but most of the time I don't feel anything."

"I think you have more feelings than you realize. If you let them out more often, I think they will grow, in time. In fact, you might want to practice your facial expressions in front of a mirror, until you get them right. Sometimes it can work backward. Smiling can make you happy, just as being happy can make you smile."

"Yes, I will do that when I can."

"That was very good! One last item, before I take you out and introduce you around. Clothing. Tom didn't see any need for your sort of person to wear clothing, but now you have to do that. People here wear clothing, most of the time when they're not alone. We'll have to get you fixed up with a suitable wardrobe."

For the first time, I saw her frown.

"But I don't *like* clothes. They're scratchy and uncomfortable. Do I *have* to wear them?"

"Your language and facial expressions are showing a lot of improvement. But as to clothing, yes, it will be necessary. It gets cold around here, after all."

"I am comfortable at any temperature between minus ten and plus fifty degrees Celsius. I am not comfortable in clothing."

"That's quite a range. Incidentally, remind me later to give you a set of conversion tables between the metric system that you are used to and the army system we use around here. But on clothing, well, there will be some times when clothing will be necessary. You can't go to church naked, for example. We'll find you some things that aren't uncomfortable. Something loose fitting and made of soft linen or silk, perhaps. On the other hand, behind closed doors, well, around here you can dispense with clothing if you have to."

"Yes."

"Good. Now, is there anything else we need to talk about right now?"

"Yes. Reproduction. Do you want me to start producing children?"

"Uh, no. Not for a while, at least."

"But you are producing neohorses at a maximum rate."

"True, but that's not quite the same thing. They look like horses and you look exactly like a human being."

"But I'm stronger than humans are. I'm faster. I'm more honest. I have a perfect memory. There are many things that my daughters could do for you better than ordinary people could. Why should appearance be so important?"

I told myself to stand and take it. I'd asked her to act like a human, after all, and she was trying her best to do it. Also, her questions were good, and I didn't have any good answers for them.

"Maude, I haven't thought this thing through. Give me some time. For now, do not reproduce. Let's leave it at that for a while."

"Yes."

"Sometimes, you can just nod your head for 'yes.'"

I pressed the buzzer that called my secretary, Zenya, into my office. When she came in, she tried hard not to stare at or to even notice the naked girl in the office until I introduced them.

"Maude, this is Zenya. She is a good friend of mine, and you can trust her. Pay close attention to what she tells you."

Maude nodded yes.

"Zenya, this is Maude. She will be my bodyguard from now on. Put her on the payroll at four pence a day, and with a drawing account for as much as she needs. Then I want you to see about getting her some clothes, enough so that she is ready for any occasion, including church. She is not used to wearing clothing, so I want you to make sure that they are as comfortable as possible. You will have to show her *how* to wear them, as well. Fix her up with a room in my household's chambers, and get her settled in. Make sure that she has everything she needs. Then, when you've done that, take her down to the armory, and let her have anything she wants."

"Yes, sir," Zenya said. "Will there be anything else?"

"Yes. Over the next few weeks, I want you to spend a lot of time with Maude. She's not used to our ways yet. Try to be her big sister. Help her out whenever she needs it. And one other thing. Find out how she got into my office, past the guards at the gate, past all the people in the outer office, and past your desk. Or, try to find out, anyway."

The girls left together, talking quietly.

And I sat down to have another think session. I knew that Tom's professional Peeping Toms—the people he calls the Historical Corps—have everything in the world, throughout all of history, completely bugged. They say that they are writing the definitive history of mankind, but I have some doubts about them. Be that as it may, I knew Tom would be told everything I said out loud concerning him.

I looked up at the ceiling. "Hey, Tom! Thanks for the present!"

Actually, I really was very grateful to Tom for sending me Maude. I had no doubts that if anything could save me from the next bad guy, lunatic, or hired assassin, Maude would do it. Having her around would make everyone in my household safer, especially the children.

Not only was Maude absolutely deadly, but her appearance would cause any intruder to greatly underestimate her, to his certain sorrow.

Back in Tom's apartment, she'd had the habit of standing absolutely still when she wasn't needed for anything. It would have been easy to mistake her for a statue. Maybe I should have a few lifelike statues of her made, and put them around where an intruder would see them. Then the third one he saw wouldn't even be noticed, until she removed his testicles, teeth, and eyeballs.

Having Maude around would be very worthwhile.

But I also knew that having a few million Maudes around would not be good for my army, for my country, or for my race. What I didn't know was *why* it would be so bad for us, why having a third intelligent species around would be so disastrous. There had to be a good rationalization for my gut-level feeling.

I was still pondering it when I got the report that we were being invaded again.

Chapter Nineteen

FROM THE JOURNAL OF JOSIP SOBIESKI

January 13, 1250,
concerning June 2, 1249

I was just outside of Okoitz when I heard the alarm bell ringing, the big one that was rung at noon on the first Saturday of the month so people would know what it sounded like. I had never heard it rung in earnest before.

My duty station was at the Explorer's School, and it was my job to get there as quickly as possible. I urged Margarete forward, and we flew south along the trail. When we were almost there, I suddenly realized I was making a mistake.

I had sent all of my equipment, including my armor and most of my weapons, to my parents' home back in Okoitz. I had intended to show my brother the improvements made since he had helped fight the Mongols. Because of my difficulties with my father, I totally forgot about it. I had hardly spoken to my brother at all.

There was no point in showing up during an emergency without my arms and armor. I would be as useless as an empty pistol. I told Margarete to turn around, and we galloped back to Okoitz.

When I got to my parents' rooms, my mother was there arming herself, since she was a platoon leader in the Lady's Militia. She told me that she had put my war chest in my brother's room.

I went there, stripped off my class A uniform, and zipped on the summer-weight gambezon. I put on the leg armor, zipping shut the internal air compartments. The system was such that fresh air was pumped over my body whenever I moved. Without it, wearing armor in the summer was like walking around in an oven.

I got into the rest of my armor. Since I was now at least temporarily a horseman, I clipped my decorative saber as well as my shoulder sword, pistol, and bayonet to my weapons belt, and buckled it on. I decided against the big war helm since you need better visibility when mounted. My open-faced casque made more sense.

Hurriedly, I put my money and three days' worth of dried rations in my pouch, and I threw everything else back into the war chest. I filled my canteen, picked up my rifle, and went back to the stable to get Margarete.

As I mounted her I saw Lord Conrad mounting his white Big Person, Silver. I couldn't help admiring his golden armor, and he noticed me looking at it.

"Yes, it's gaudy, but it's important that messengers can find me quickly on the battlefield. But why do you have that Big Person, Josip?" he asked.

I explained that I was on leave, and that the clerk at the Big People's Ranch had asked me to deliver Margarete to her duty station at Three Walls.

"Well, Sir Josip, all leaves are canceled. Just now, you'll both be of more use to the army on the battle line than at the Explorer's School. You might as well ride out with me."

I was flattered that he knew not only my name and rank, but my duty assignment as well.

A small blond woman of incredible beauty ran up and placed

herself at Lord Conrad's left, almost as though guarding him, except that she was smiling. Save for a weapons belt, she was naked. Totally naked. She was most obviously an adult, but she didn't have hair on either her groin or her armpits! I'd never seen such a thing!

"Maude, you'll get hurt down there! Climb up and ride with Sir Josip, here." She climbed up, not behind me, but right up into my lap! She was still smiling, as, indeed, was I.

Lord Conrad turned to me, smiled, and said, "I owe you a few for finding that iron ore deposit. You might as well carry this banner, since my usual herald is on leave. Once we get going, just ride by my left side. *Komander Wladyclaw, is everyone ready? Then FORWARD! FOR GOD AND POLAND!*"

Suddenly, no shit, there I was, armed and armored, riding out to battle on a Big Person at the side of Lord Conrad himself! I had the Battle Flag of Poland in my hand, and an unbelievably beautiful woman riding naked on my lap, smiling up at me!

Behind us, a full company of warriors followed, all mounted on Anna's children, the first such company I had ever seen. After we left the gates of Okoitz, a platoon of men rode past us, to take up the point and vanguard positions.

Their saddles had the high and flaring saddle bow of the traditional knight's warkak, but the cantle was low, for ease of mounting. Their war plans apparently did not include jousting with the lance, although they each carried one. It went from a socket at their right heel to a clip on the cantle. Since they were all on Big People, they did not use reins, bridles, or spurs.

I noticed that their armor was different from mine, and more slender, I suppose because a horseman does not need as much cooling ventilation as a footman does. I found out later that their armor weighed twice what mine did, and was capable of stopping a Mongol spear. They could afford the extra weight because they didn't have to carry it. The Big Person did.

Their close-fitting armet-style helmets fastened through a swivel to the body plates, like my war helm. They narrowed at the neck, where a hinge allowed some up-and-down motion. Rather than a single eyeslit, the visor was more open, but covered with a heavy mesh work that wouldn't quite let an arrow in.

Their weapons were different, too. The lances were much longer than usual, and the handguards were shaped like an elongated ball, rather than the usual cone. Their sabers were longer and heavier than most I'd seen, and there was a ring for the thumb, on the side, near the hilt. Altogether, they were more businesslike than the gold-hilted dress saber I wore.

Besides a rifle in a saddle holster, they each carried two pistols in belt holsters, the six-shooters I had heard about but never before seen, and they each carried another gun—no, *two* other guns—holstered ahead of the saddle. They were bigger than a pistol, yet shorter than a rifle. They had a big ammunition clip, similar to those used on the old swivel guns, but it fit into the *bottom* of the gun, rather than the expected top.

I guessed that they might hold three dozen rounds each. Two dozen more clips were sheathed about their mounts' necks and shoulders, armoring them. More ammunition was stored behind the riders, protecting their mounts' rumps. This company was prepared to put an incredible amount of lead into the air.

Fighting the Mongols, Lord Conrad discovered he had not prepared enough ammunition for the huge numbers of enemies he found arrayed against us. Apparently, he had made sure that next time things would be different. Somewhere, I read that generals are always ready to fight the last war again, and properly this time.

The Big People wore other armor, as well, protecting everything from the belly up, except where the saddles and ammunition clips were.

Of course, as I was noticing these men, they were looking at me, or more likely, at the naked woman in my arms. A few of them smiled and gave me the "crossed thumbs" signal, for luck, but none of them could say anything, not when I was riding next to Lord Conrad.

All of this was interesting, even glorious, but I was bothered by one or two items. To wit, I had no idea where we were going or why we were going there.

I could not ask Lord Conrad about it, because we were going at a full gallop, at the astounding speed that only a Big Person can run at, and also because he was so far above me that I dared not speak until spoken to.

There was the lady in my arms, however, and she wasn't wearing any insignia of rank, or much of anything else. What does one say to a naked lady? I didn't know. It wasn't covered in the army's course on proper social behavior.

I decided that it might be best to ignore, as best I could, her outfit, or rather her lack of one. So I said hello, and that my name was Josip.

She said, "Yes, sir."

She was smiling. She was always smiling.

I said that considering the circumstances, she shouldn't be so formal, and that I understood her name was Maude.

"Yes."

I didn't know if that was an improvement, but I kept on smiling. I asked her if she knew what was happening.

She said, "Yes."

I said, you do?

She said, "Yes."

I said, could you tell me what is happening?

She said, "Yes."

I said, can you say anything besides "yes"?

She said, "Yes."

I gritted my teeth, and thought about it for a while. Something like this had happened to me a long time ago, when I'd tried to question Anna, the first Big Person. I said, please tell me what is happening; specifically, what is the cause of the alarm in the first place, and what does Lord Conrad plan to do in response to whatever it is that is happening?

And she said, "I thought you'd never ask! One of the airplanes that the Eagles fly was on its usual dawn patrol. It was this morning. It flies along the border between Poland and the Holy Roman Empire. It goes from Szczecin to Eagles Nest. The pilot noticed some unusual activity. He went down to investigate. He saw an army. It had two thousand horsemen. It had four thousand foot soldiers. It was proceeding from the direction of the March of Brandenburg. It was heading toward the frontier castle town of Lubusz."

I asked if that was one of Lord Conrad's "snowflake" forts.

"The building program is proceeding north on the Odra. It hasn't gotten that far yet. Lubusz is a traditional stone-and-wood fortification. It's manned by the traditional nobility. Lord Conrad thinks that this attack was intended as a preemptive strike by the Margrave of Brandenburg. He wants to gain the territory before we can properly fortify it. The enemy has already burned several peasant villages in their path. That was why the pilot noticed them in the first place. Lord Conrad has called up the thirty-six companies nearest to the invasion point. Those farthest away are being taken forward by the twenty-two riverboats available for service on the Odra. The first units should have already arrived at Lubusz. The balance will be there by tomorrow night. This company should arrive on scene by midnight. Noncombatants are being evacuated—"

I interrupted her, saying thank you, and that she was very informative. There was an amazing amount of stuff in this pretty little bottle, once you got the stopper out of it!

I asked her if she was new to Okoitz.

She said, "Yes." She was still smiling.

Not this again, I thought. But last time, when I said please, she answered in full. More than full. So I said, please tell me everything about your life before you got to Okoitz.

"You can't mean everything. I will tell you that I worked for Tom. I took care of his apartment. I kept it clean. I ordered supplies. I cooked for him and his guests. I did everything else that I was told. I served Lord Conrad for two weeks when he was there. I liked him. Lord Conrad wanted a certain book that Tom had. Tom didn't want to give it to him. I put the book into Lord Conrad's suitcase. Tom was not happy with me. He had me retrained as a bodyguard. He sent me to Lord Conrad. I got there today."

This Tom must have been a remarkable man, a duke, at least, to have so many beautiful servants that he could give them away when they annoyed him!

I said that she seemed to be a very talented lady, and asked her to please tell me how the women dressed in Lord Tom's domains. Of course, what I was after was some hint as to why she seemed to think that riding off to war, naked and in the arms of a complete stranger, was an ordinary thing to do.

What I got was a quarter hour's worth of long descriptions told in short sentences, concerning a series of the most outlandish costumes I have ever heard of! It was only with great difficulty that I was finally able to interrupt her. I asked her to please tell me what *she* wore back there.

"Nothing."

I asked why she wore nothing when all the other ladies wore such diverse clothing. Please.

"Because I am not a lady. I am a wench."

So the nobility wore clothing, but they forbade it to the commoners? And I had thought that *our* nobility had too many privileges!

I said that now that she was with us, she could dress as she pleased.

"No. I cannot. Lord Conrad says that I must wear clothes to church, and also to other places."

I said that I should hope so! Of course she had to wear clothes to church!

"Why is that? What is church?"

I was totally flabbergasted. She didn't know what a church was? She had never even heard of religion? I had to ask her three or four times in different ways to make sure I understood her properly.

I mean, religion has always been so big a part of my life that I rarely even think about it. I am not even sure if I've mentioned it in my journals, any more than I have mentioned the fact that I was breathing. But this beautiful woman had never even heard of God! She didn't know who Jesus was! I was shocked, and there was nothing for it but to spend the rest of the day and much of the evening talking about religion.

At first Maude was as surprised as I was. In all her life, she had never wondered at how the world got here, how we humans came to be, and what it was all for. It had never even occurred to her that these things *should* be wondered at. But once I explained the basics to her, she was absolutely fascinated!

After a few hours, we stopped at a clear stream to let the Big People drink and eat, and to have a quick bite ourselves. I was glad that I'd brought some field rations with me, because no one even suggested that anyone should cook some food. I found out that the riders with us were all members of the old nobility, who would rather eat dried meat than demean themselves by cooking it.

I asked Maude if she was hungry, offering what I had; some dried fruit, dried meat, and hard biscuits.

"You eat this?" she said.

I said yes, when necessary, when there wasn't time to cook something better. "Then I must eat it also."

And eat it she did, chewing tough beef jerky as though it was a delicate pastry and she was famished. She quickly finished most of my three days' supply, slowing only when she noticed that I wasn't keeping up with her. Soon, between us, we emptied the pouch of everything but the money I'd left at the bottom. I'd had to explain what that was, because I feared that she might try to eat it, too. This was a very strange lady! Still, a man can put up with a lot if the girl is pretty enough.

She then drank my canteen dry, and when I refilled it from the stream, she was surprised that water was available there. When I asked, she said that she had never seen a stream before. I could now sympathize with Lord Conrad when I'd told him that I'd never seen a river.

Since I didn't know what to make of all of this, I said nothing, and once we were under way again, I renewed our discussion of religion.

I think that I quite outdid myself in my eloquence, for nothing so encourages a young man than to have an eager, beautiful young woman breathlessly listening to his every word. I did good work that day in the cause of Christ, for by day's end Maude was well on her way to becoming a good Christian.

And I did good work in my own cause as well, for by nightfall I was sure that she was as in love with me as I was with her.

By the time we got to Lubusz, at midnight, talking so long in the wind of our travel had made my voice quite hoarse. We had made only two quick stops during the day, and seven hours in the saddle is a lot. My body ached. Having even a small lady on my lap as well as a large flag in my hand, well, they did not help.

Worse still, my armor had been designed for an infantryman, and not for riding on someone who looked like a horse. My buttocks were covered with chain mail inside a canvas covering. This was not uncomfortable to occasionally sit down on, but after a long day in the saddle, I think that the individual rings had worked their way right into my privy members! Also, the thigh plates and knee caps were not made with a horse in mind, and had abraded vast areas of the only skin my mother had given me.

I was sore of body, but I really didn't mind, for I was in love.

I pitched a small dome tent next to Lord Conrad's great one, at his bidding, and went gratefully to my bed. The wiser heads, the captains and the lords, would be up for most of the night, conferring about the military situation, but young fellows like me had nothing to do but obey orders when the time came.

Maude stood behind Lord Conrad, to guard him, but from what little I heard through the walls of the tents, I think that perhaps her nakedness bothered some of the local officials. Lord Conrad bid her go to sleep. Having nowhere else to go, she came into my tent, and since it was too small for her to even stand up in, she lay down at my side.

I had stripped off my armor and gambezon, and when she laid a hand on my back, she said that my muscles were sore and tight. I had to admit that this was true, and she said that she had the cure for it.

I'd had my back rubbed before, but it was nothing like this! She started at my toes and fingertips, and worked her way upward and inward, carefully loosening every muscle, every tendon, every joint. Softly, she massaged back to life every square bit of skin on my entire body. She eliminated pains I had not even known I had, and replaced them with the most sensual of all glowing pleasures. I gloried in her golden touch.

I told her that I no longer had to wonder at what Heaven would be like, for now I knew!

I offered to return the favor on her body, but she said no. She had worked to relax me, and would not see her work wasted. I thought of suggesting sex, and thought that if I asked politely, she would oblige. But then I thought better of it. Best to put that off, for the time, for this was the woman I would marry.

Chapter Twenty

FROM THE JOURNAL OF JOSIP SOBIESKI

January 14, 1250,
concerning June 3, 1249

The bugles got us up at dawn. Maude and I went to mass, and I said the Army Oath with the other troops. Maude stood with us, listening but of course not joining in. We ate a quick breakfast, with little Maude again eating three times as much as I did, and I was barely in my armor when Lord Conrad came by.

"There isn't time to teach you how to operate a submachine gun, but you might as well take these," he said, handing me a pair of the six-shot pistols and holsters that his new company wore. "They use the same ammunition as that single shot of yours, and their action is simple enough. Just point it and pull the trigger. To load, they break open like your old gun. As for you, young lady, some of the natives have complained about your choice of costume, so tie this around your waist."

He handed Maude a strip of cloth that I recognized as part of the tablecloth in his tent. With poor grace, she took off her weapons belt and wrapped herself from waist to knees.

"This morning, we are going to conduct a raid on the Brandenburg vanguard. This company is a prototype for what the entire army will be like in ten years, and I need to know just how effective it is in actual combat. Josip, stay to my left no matter what happens. Your main job is to hold the Battle Flag high so that anyone who needs me can find me. After you've done that, try to stop anyone who is trying to kill me, or you, or Maude. Maude, your job is to stick close to us and stop anyone from the other army from hurting us. Got that, you two? Your function is to be defensive only! No stupid heroics allowed, and never leave my side!"

"Yes, sir, your grace."

"Good. Mount up."

While I saddled Margarete, Maude put her weapons belt back on. She carried a pistol like those I now wore, a long, thin sword with the handguard removed, a small dagger and two small throwing knives, all without hilts, and a small, one-handed shield of the sort called a buckler. I asked her why she didn't like handguards or hilts.

"They waste weight and space," she said.

I asked if she wasn't afraid of getting her hand cut.

"No."

I gritted my teeth, said please, and asked why she would not get her hand cut by her opponent's blade.

"Because I will not put my hand where my enemy puts his weapon."

I asked if a similar theory was working with regard to her lack of any sort of armor.

"Yes."

I said nothing, since there wasn't anything I could do to change the matter, even if I managed to win the argument, which wasn't likely. With Maude again on my lap, we were at Lord Conrad's side long before the rest of the company was ready. We could have taken longer with breakfast.

We rode out, as before, with Lord Conrad and his humble flag bearer in the lead. During the night, thousands of army troops had come up and made camp surrounding the old castle town of Lubusz. They cheered us on, but we rode out without them. Apparently, Lord Conrad's idea of a fair fight, or at least an amusing one, was to attack with odds of six thousand to three hundred—twenty to one—against us.

As before, a platoon soon passed us to take up the point. A bit later one of our aircraft, a graceful machine with two engines, flew overhead and dropped a short spear with a long red ribbon attached. One of our troops broke ranks, retrieved it, and brought it to Lord Conrad. He unscrewed the head, removed a message, and read it. He nodded, put the paper in his pocket, and discarded the spear. We rode on.

In perhaps a quarter hour we heard gunfire up ahead of us, gunfire like I had never heard before. The submachine guns fired at an incredibly fast rate, each one of them spewing out hundreds of bullets a minute!

We got to a rise where we could see what was going on up ahead, and Lord Conrad motioned for me to stop there with him. Then, somehow, Maude was no longer on my lap. She was standing on Silver's rump, behind Lord Conrad, and I had not seen her traverse the space between the two points!

Lord Conrad turned and looked up at her, apparently as surprised by her action as I was.

"Are you going to be all right up there?" he asked.

"Yes, your grace."

He was about to object further, but then he just shook his head, lifted his binoculars, and looked back at the battle.

I tried to put her strange actions out of my mind. My instincts told me to protect her, to keep her from all danger, and yet Maude seemed completely relaxed and totally confident. There wasn't anything I could do to change anything, so I didn't try.

I looked at the battle going on up ahead. Or perhaps I should call it a slaughter. The enemy cavalry had been advancing up the road in a column two men wide, and our men had come at them, also two men wide.

Our opponents had apparently dropped their lances to charge, but hadn't gotten very far, since our men pulled out their submachine guns and began spraying bullets at the Germans. I say spraying because I don't believe they could possibly have been aiming and shooting properly, not at a full gallop, with a submachine gun in each hand. I noticed that the Big People had the sense to drop their heads down low while this procedure was going on.

The pair of warriors at the head of our column were perforce doing more shooting than the rest, and when their guns were emptied, they dropped off to the side of the road to let those behind them pass while they reloaded. Those men who passed them soon dropped out in turn, with the result that we quickly had a column of two charging at a gallop between rows of men who were reloading.

When the balance of the first platoon, some forty-three men or so, had passed, the first pair took a position at the end of our column. It was a sort of continuously recycling action.

When the two columns met, the front ranks of the enemy were dead, many times over, and our troops continued onward, on both sides of them, pushing the zone of slaughter ever backward, almost as fast as the incredibly swift Big People could run. Any fallen enemy who showed signs of life was soon shot again by the troops racing past him.

The other platoons were catching up to the first, and they joined in on the recirculating battle.

Lord Conrad motioned for us to reenter our column, near the end, and we went forward to get a closer view of what was happening. For the longest while it was just a matter of riding with the flag in my left hand and a pistol in my right, beside a long line of dead men and horses, none of them ours.

I often glanced over at Maude, anxious for her safety, but she was standing on the rump of a galloping Big Person, looking as calm as if she were standing in line at the mess hall.

The great majority of the fallen were wearing plate armor, of the sort the army sold to anyone who could afford it. They had worn it in the same fashion as our traditional Polish nobility did, brightly polished and on the outside.

Everything in the center of the road was perforated and bloody. Everything toward the sides was trampled into blood pudding.

Even the weapons and armor were so badly mangled that few of them would make good trophies to hang on a wall.

Eventually, we ran out of dead men and dead horses. Now it was just dead men. We had come up on their infantry, pikers, most of them—just as I had once been—with the second most popular weapon being a huge, two-handed broadsword. They were still all on the road, still mostly in ranks of four.

They hadn't tried to run away, but I think it was not due to any great courage on their part. I think what was happening to them was all too strange and had happened all too quickly for any of them to react to it. Indeed, most of the swords I saw were still in their sheaths.

The shooting was going on ahead of us throughout all of this, and troops who were reloading and waiting for their turn again lined the side of the road. When we were about twenty men from the front of the line, the shooting slowed, then almost stopped.

Soon we were passing the baggage train, horse-drawn wagons, hundreds of them, with men, women, and even some children in the drivers' seats, or on top of the baggage. They were all holding their hands up high above their heads, wide-eyed and frightened, but still alive. I was glad to see that our men had the decency and good sense to spare the noncombatants.

But riding past the prisoners without shooting meant that none of our men were stopping to reload, which had the unexpected effect of leaving behind live enemies—the only prisoners we had—completely unguarded!

I was about to mention this to Lord Conrad when he noticed the problem himself.

"Damn!" he shouted. "Nothing ever works out right the first time! Halt!" He stopped about fifty men to guard the baggage train, and had them shouting to those who passed by that living enemies had to be guarded. He sent the rest on to continue the destruction.

Getting this sorted out put us at the back of the line again, and by the time we got to the front, some two dozen of our men were surrounding a very ornate carriage. We had captured the Margrave of Brandenburg, himself!

Again Lord Conrad took charge, while most of our people, some one hundred men or so, went on to murder the enemy's rear guard. The remaining two hundred were doing guard duty back up the road.

The margrave was a great, obese man who was dressed in a heavy blue and burgundy velvet doublet that I thought must be very warm for the weather, and indeed he was sweating profusely. Between his massive gold necklace and the gold on his belt and weapons, he might have been wearing as much wealth as the average soldier in our army did, or at least one who had fought against the Mongols.

He'd had three ladies with him in his oversized carriage. They were all attractive young women, if overdressed, but none of them gave Maude the slightest competition.

Maude, incidentally, was still standing on Silver's rump, still smiling, and still wearing nothing but a part of a tablecloth about her hips. She had ridden there, standing up, throughout the entire fight!

As chance would have it, none of the troops guarding the margrave at the moment spoke any German, and neither did Lord Conrad. A call for someone bilingual in German went out, but the problem was soon solved by one of the men riding in a slightly less ornate carriage, just behind the first one.

This rather pompous person introduced himself thusly:

"I am the King of Heralds at Brandenburg, and I offer my considerable services in translating for you."

"Thank you. Your 'considerable services' are needed. I am Duke Conrad of Mazovia, Sandomierz, and Little Poland, Hetman of the Christian Army. I take it that this man is the Margrave of Brandenburg, and that these other men are notables on his staff?" Lord Conrad said, without bothering to get down from Silver, and with Maude's bare breasts bobbing above his head.

"Quite so, your grace. May we offer you our parole and our promise of our good conduct, until such time as we can pay our ransoms?"

"You may offer, but I will not accept. You men are all under arrest. The charges are rape, murder, arson, assault, battery, breaking and entering, robbery, disorderly conduct, and such other crimes as I may later think up. Komander Wladyclaw! Strip-search these men, and once they're naked, tie their hands behind their backs and march them, under strict guard, back to Lubusz for trial."

While the herald was busily translating to the increasingly horrified margrave, Komander Wladyclaw said, "Yes, sir. What about these ladies, here?"

"Put them with the other noncombatants. Tell all those people that we are going to let them live, providing they obey orders, and that we will release them after they have done their Christian duty to their own dead. Then put that whole crowd to work, cleaning up this mess. Have them strip and bury the dead men and horses along the side of the road."

"Do you want the heads up on pikes, sir?"

"What I want really doesn't matter here, I'm afraid. This army was Christian, and the Church would have a fit if we decapitated them all. But see to it that every grave has a big cross over it. That should have a sufficient psychological effect. Oh, and send a rider back to Lubusz with the news, and have them send up the infantry as soon as possible to help out here. Send other riders with spare Big People to the villages that were burned by the Germans. Try to bring some witnesses to Lubusz."

"Yes, sir. What would you think of putting the dead warhorses' heads up on pikes?"

"An excellent suggestion, Komander. Act on it."

"Thank you, sir. What if any of the Germans are still alive?"

"Give them medical attention, by all means. What we want here is as many people as possible telling how just one of our companies ripped up an entire invading army," Lord Conrad said.

By this time the herald and the margrave had finished being astounded at Lord Conrad's pronouncement, and the troops were carrying out their orders over loud protests in German.

The herald said, "But Lord Conrad, this is madness! How can you accuse us of such crimes?"

"While you were invading my country, your troops sacked and burned at least eleven villages. That's enough arson to get you all hanged. I don't have proof of the murders, rapes, and the rest of it just yet, but I'm sure that we'll have it by tomorrow."

"But that was a simple act of war! Who cares about the damned peasants?"

"I do."

"But it was the soldiers who killed those peasants, not us!"

"You ordered them to come here, so the responsibility is yours. If it makes you feel any better, we've already killed all of your soldiers."

"But surely, Lord Conrad, when you consider the size of the ransom that the margrave could pay, well, he's one of the richest men in all of Christendom! Surely that can convince you of the folly of your path!"

"I just had six thousand men butchered. Do you think that I did it for money? No, I don't want the margrave's money. I have plenty of my own. Actually, it's possible that *I'm* the richest man in Christendom."

"But the emperor, Frederick the Great, will never stand for this!"

"All Frederick can do is send in another army just like this one. If he does, it will meet the same fate. I don't think he is as much of a fool as the margrave is. Was."

"But you can't go killing a margrave! It's unheard of!"

"I can kill him, and I will. What's more, I want as many people as possible to hear about it. Your class of 'noblemen' seems to think that war is just an amusing game, a pleasant way to spend a summer. Well, it is not, not anymore. I need to communicate to people like you, in a meaningful way, the idea that murdering a lot of peaceful, innocent people wholesale, in war, is just as evil as killing them one at a time, in peacetime."

"But it's always been done that way."

"You just don't listen very good. *It's not done that way anymore.* But enough of this. It doesn't matter if you understand or not, because you are not the recipient of my message. You are part of the message itself. Guards, march these men away."

"But you can't do this to *me*! I'm a herald!"

"Bet?"

I watched seven naked old men walk barefoot back along the length of their slaughtered army, thinking—I'm sure—that this couldn't possibly be happening to high and wonderful noblemen like *them*.

Already, some of the people from the baggage train were stripping the dead, putting valuables, weapons, and clothing in separate piles. The dead were being laid out neatly by the side of the road. Chaplains from both armies were going down the rows, giving extreme unction. Behind them, men were digging graves.

Komander Wladyclaw came over and reported in to Lord Conrad.

"Your orders are being carried out, sir. I notice that some of the prisoners are stealing money and jewels from their own dead, sir."

"Let them. When the job is all done, probably sometime tomorrow, I want you to strip-search all of the noncombatants. Then I want you to give each of them five days' food from the captured supply wagons, and march them to the border, naked. The idea is, I want them to have some very vivid memories of what happened here. I want them to tell everybody who sees them that attacking Poland and the rest of the Christian Federation is a bad idea. Stripping them naked will force them to explain themselves, as well as let us recover our booty."

Chapter Twenty-One

FROM THE JOURNAL OF JOSIP SOBIESKI

written January 15, 1250,
concerning June 3, 1249

That evening, when the last of the petty details had been handled, I was still in Lord Conrad's tent, because no one had thought to dismiss me. He was sitting on a camp chair, slumped over and looking very tired.

I asked him if he knew that Maude could give a most refreshing back rub.

"That is an excellent idea, Josip. A truly wonderful idea. Yes. Maude, would you please oblige me?"

He was soon stretched out on his back on the carpet, enjoying Maude's calm ministrations. Maude had removed her skirt as soon as the last visitor had left, and I wondered at this strange preoccupation of hers. Still, it improved the view.

"Sir Josip, tell me, what are your thoughts on this day's events? Was I too brutal?"

Lord Conrad wanted my thoughts? I said that I was mostly impressed with the new armaments, especially those submachine guns. I had heard that in ten years' time every man in the army would be paired with a Big Person, and when that happened, we would be truly invincible. No one would dare to bother us.

"It's actually more like five years from now, not ten," he said. When he saw my surprised expression, he continued, "Just now, there are almost five thousand Big People. Most of them are involved with civilian occupations. More than four thousand of them are used to carry the mails, throughout Poland, Hungary, Bulgaria, and the Ruthenias. We have a school with a post office in almost every village in the Federation, and almost every one of them is visited by a Big Person five times a week. King Henryk has four dozen Big People for his entourage, so Prince Daniel, King Bella, and Tzar Ivan all have to have the same, or they pout.

"Very few Big People are involved with the military. Too few, as it turns out, but I never thought that the margrave would pull a stunt like this. There are about two thousand new Big People coming on line in the next few months, and they will all go to the Wolves, or similar groups.

"In a few years we'll be invincible, all right. That's what an army is really for, Josip. To be so big and so strong that it never has to hurt anyone. What happened today was an aberration. One noble fool, who didn't believe what people had told him about us, and was too proud to visit us peacefully, decided to attack us without warning. You see, I've often invited the margrave to visit us, to see what we've got, and he wouldn't do it. But I asked you about the brutality."

I said that once the attack had started, I didn't see how he could possibly have called it off. And if we killed all of them, well, wasn't it their idea to kill all of us? Wasn't that why the Germans crossed our borders in the first place?

"True. The attack went better than I expected. But I was referring to what I did later, to the margrave himself and his staff."

I said that I was a commoner. My knighthood notwithstanding, I was still just a baker's son. It always troubled me that the rich and the powerful people in this world could do unpleasant things to the likes of me and not be held responsible for it. They were not punished for the crimes they committed, if they were committed on some peasant. I said that I was glad at what he did to those fat old men! And that I'd be even gladder when I saw them all hung up by their necks on the scaffold.

I was just as glad when I found that our troops hadn't hurt those people on the baggage train. And I said I was gladder yet that he was going to let the noncombatants all go free, the next day. I said I would have done just the same things he had, if I had been in charge, and if I'd been smart enough to think fast on my feet, the way he always does.

"Thank you. You've relieved my mind, a bit. So tell me, what will you be doing next, Josip?"

I was surprised, and said that it was up to him, or maybe some assignment clerk somewhere. I guessed that I'd spend some time at the Explorer's School, and then go out with my lance to some strange new place or other.

"Where would you like to go?" He closed his eyes and smiled as Maude worked her magic on his body.

I said that I didn't really know, but that when we were spending last winter near the Arctic Circle, my lance made itself—well, I couldn't call it a vow, but a promise. We wanted our next job to be somewhere where it was *warm*! And after that, we wanted it to be a place where a man could find a drink and a willing young lady on occasion!

Lord Conrad laughed and rolled over so Maude could do his back. "Josip, you are truly the salt of the earth. But yes, there is just such an assignment in the offing. I don't know if you'll like the native brew, but I don't object to your bringing in your own supply, within reason, of course. I guarantee that the climate will be warm, maybe too warm, and while I can't make any promises about the quality of the ladies you'll find there, I will warrant that they do exist in quantity. And, as a bonus, none of them wear any more clothes than our lovely Maude, here."

I said, "Then in the name of Sir Odon's lance, sir, we hereby volunteer for duty."

"You'll get the assignment, especially since you all are very experienced with riverboats. I'm going to send Captain Odon up the biggest river in the world. Along with Knight Banner Josip, and certain others. But you'll hear more about it once all the plans are solidified. For now, well, I noticed that you were taking a certain interest in Maude, here."

Maude continued at her work as though nothing had been said about her.

I said that it was more than just that. I said that I loved her. Which, of course, is a hell of a thing to say right in front of a woman, when you haven't ever said it to her in private up till then. But it just sort of blurted itself out! And Maude still showed no reaction!

"I thought so. You have all the symptoms. First off, I want to say that whatever the two of you want to do, it's fine by me. But. And it's a very big *but*. I want you both to go as slowly as possible on this. There is a lot that you both don't know about each other, and if you get your emotions too involved before your heads are properly in gear, you will cause each other a lot of agony. I'm going to get some of those things out in the open right now, hopefully, to save you both a lot of future confusion and pain."

He sat up on the carpet and gestured for me to sit in the chair. Taking the only chair while he was on the floor seemed improper, but not as improper as disobeying a direct order. Maude kneeled down to form a circle with us, and waited silently.

"Maude, as you have no doubt noticed by now, this culture is far more complicated than the one that you are used to. I heard the two of you talking about religion yesterday, and that's good, but religion is actually one of the simpler things that you will be learning about. Where you were before, all you had to do was to obey one man, and everything would be all right. Here, you have to run your own life, and while that can be very rewarding, it can also be very complicated, confusing, and even frightening.

"There, much of the time, you were treated as though you were a simple machine. Here, we have many convoluted interrelationships with each other. Some of them are awkward. Some of them are very warm, very close, and very wonderful.

"Josip here is saying that he wishes to explore having such a relationship with you. He thinks perhaps that he would like to bond with you. That's something that I think you might not know anything about, but it could involve his living with you for the rest of his life, if you were willing. Sharing his whole life with you. It's very important, so take your time with it."

Maude nodded.

He turned to me.

"Your turn. The big shock for you, Josip, is that Maude here is not human. Her species is a bioengineered creation, much like Anna and her children. She looks like a human and talks like a human, but her mental processes are a lot like Anna's. Honest, noble, and trustworthy to the extreme in many ways, but astoundingly strange to us in others.

"Accordingly, she is stronger and faster than any mere human like you can ever hope to be. Will that hurt your masculine pride? Think about it.

"Then there is the fact that she is essentially immortal. She is so different from us that there aren't any diseases that can bother her. Her wounds heal quickly, and she can even regrow a severed limb, in time.

"Oh, if someone could tie her down and spend enough time on her with an axe, she'd die, but it would take a lot to kill her.

"Aside from something like that, she'll likely live forever. If you're looking for someone to grow old with, this is not the girl for you. If what you want is someone who will stay young and sexy, hang in there, but think it out first.

"Another thing is that this pretty girl cannot give you children. She has children just like Anna does, four at a time, and identical twins of their mother. They'll all be girls. In four years they'll be adults and remember everything she knows.

"They won't remember much about their childhood, and whether you give them loving care or ignore them completely won't make any difference. But they won't be *your* children, not biologically. Worse, I worry that they might seem to you to be less like daughters, and more like your wife's twin sisters, which could cause you a whole bale of emotional troubles.

"Add all that to the fact that you are dealing with someone who still has no idea of what human love is all about.

"She does know about sex. I don't actually know, since my sexual contact with Maude has been limited to scratching her behind the ear, but I suspect that she knows more about erotic enjoyment than both of us put together. Just remember that sex with her is *only* for enjoyment.

"So. It's getting late, and I hope that I've scared the both of you to the point that you will take things very, very slowly. Good night. Go away, both of you, and try to get at least some sleep tonight, Josip. Maude doesn't need any. Ever."

Outside, I disrobed completely and crawled into the small tent with Maude. Lord Conrad's extensive advice had left my head spinning, but I thought that if we would have to spend a lot of time getting to know one another, and if this nudity thing was so important to her, well, then I should go as far as I could to meet her halfway.

Without saying a word, she started rubbing me down, since this day had been, if anything, more taxing than the day before.

I asked Maude what she thought about what Lord Conrad had said to us.

"I don't know. On one small point, Lord Conrad was incorrect. My daughters will not look exactly like me. There are always small variations in the color of the eyes, the hair, and the skin, and in the shape of facial features. As to the rest, I have insufficient information to know what to think. What do you think?"

That was the first time that I had ever heard her ask me about anything personal. I considered it a good omen.

I said that the fact that she was not human didn't bother me in the least. Lord Conrad's first mount, Anna, was a good friend of mine when I was a child. She had always seemed perfectly human to me, for all that she looked like a horse. If anything, I had always thought of her as being a better person than most of the normal human people I have known.

As to children, I said I'd had so many strange difficulties with my father that I didn't think I really wanted to start a family, or to have any children of my own, anyway.

If I ever felt different, or if she ever wanted human kids, I supposed that we could always adopt children, or, with her permission, as an army knight, I could always get a second wife.

As to the fact that she was stronger and faster than I was, I said I couldn't see that it would bother me. After all, it's not as though I'd gotten any weaker. I was stronger than most men, and if I had any immodest pride, it's of the way I could usually think fast and talk myself out of trouble, without needing physical strength.

As to growing old, I said I thought it was going to be a problem for her to decide on, not me. Old married men that I knew had told me that their wives had changed so slowly over the years that they had never noticed it happening. If they didn't see somebody changing, why should I worry about not seeing somebody not changing? Then I asked her if I was making any sense.

"I understand much of what you say, but I don't know enough to understand it all."

I asked her to tell me this much, please. Did she like being around me? Was there anywhere else that she would want to be?

"Yes. No. You want me to say more. It is very pleasant to be around you, Josip. I feel very secure, being with you. I know that you will always know what to do. You are very polite. Your face and body are very well constructed."

I said, thank you. I guessed that that would have to do for the time being. I told her I loved her, and that I thought she was very beautiful.

"What is love? What is beauty?"

I said, oh my. I said that I would take a stab at beauty...

Which got us into another long, one-sided conversation. Nice, though.

One decision we did come up with was that since sex now existed only for enjoyment, we might as well enjoy ourselves. And yes, she was a garden of wondrous delights who far surpassed all others!

Chapter Twenty-Two

FROM THE JOURNAL OF JOSIP SOBIESKI

written January 16, 1250,
concerning June 4, 1249

The next day, I watched a crowd of some three thousand teamsters, cooks, prostitutes, leather workers, soldier's wives, armorers, noblemen's girlfriends, servants, blacksmiths, washerwomen, gamblers, craftsmen of all kinds, merchants of all types, and children of all of the above. All of the extra people these conventional armies felt obligated to bring along with them to war.

All of them but the smallest children had been stripped naked, each of them was clutching a week's supply of food, and every one of them was loudly bemoaning his or her lot in life, mostly in German, but also in something that was close to Polish.

Had they been defeated by almost anyone else but Lord Conrad, all of them would likely be dead, but none of them seemed to have considered that. Escorted by a company of our infantry, they walked slowly back to the Holy Roman Empire.

Some twenty-six of them who spoke passable Polish had come to us and asked permission to settle here, rather than to go back to the empire. Most of them were allowed to do so. After the others left, they were given back their clothing, all of their property, and even some of the army's money to help get them started.

Eighty-six of the children were found to have no living relatives and were being sent to Okoitz for eventual adoption. A list of them was given to a responsible-looking German merchant, in case any of the children's relatives turned up later.

Some two hundred fifty-one German soldiers were still alive, at last count, and were being given the best possible medical care.

When I asked about all this generosity, after the cold brutality of battle, Lord Conrad told me that to be successful in war and politics, you must be either very, very cruel, or very, very generous. He said that attempting any middle path was always disastrous. I've thought long on this piece of wisdom.

Someone had tried to skin some of the dead warhorses, but gave up on it since the hides were too badly damaged. Anyway, the army warehouses still held half the leather we got from the hides we took off those Mongol ponies, those many years ago.

By late afternoon we were back in Lubusz, attending an outdoor trial. It was attended by a few thousand people, mostly civilians who were curious but who didn't want to get involved.

Lord Conrad acted as both judge and prosecuting attorney, which wasn't proper in any legal system I'd ever heard of, but there weren't any suitable volunteers for either of the positions, since no one but his grace would dare to kill the margrave and offend the emperor. Nor was there a defense attorney, since no one wanted to offend Lord Conrad, either.

His grace simply announced that he was going to try the offenders for a long list of crimes, which he read. He then called up nine witnesses to the atrocities that the German soldiers had committed and publicly questioned them, one at a time. When they were finished, the list of crimes had grown to nineteen capital offenses.

He found all the defendants guilty of all crimes, and condemned them all to death. He also fined the margrave an amount equal to the value of all of his possessions, which he now claimed for the Christian Army.

He had all the defendants hung by the neck until they were dead, and then left them hanging up there, naked and unburied.

It wasn't really a trial at all. It was simply a statement that certain kinds of behavior would no longer be tolerated.

During the trial, Lord Conrad's regular herald, a man who spoke eleven languages, returned from leave and took over his regular duties. I was offered the option of returning to the Explorer's School, but since my leave still had months to run, they couldn't be expecting me, and there wouldn't be much for me to do there. I had no desire to go home and see my father again, and anyway, Maude would be staying with Lord Conrad, who would be needing a bodyguard more than ever, after this day's work became known.

I stayed with Lord Conrad and was made a messenger, an interesting job, since it let me meet all sorts of people and still spend my nights with Maude. It also had me in attendance when King Henryk arrived on the night of the trial.

The king burst into Lord Conrad's presence before the herald had half enough time to announce him. His majesty briskly strode in and stepped right up on top of Lord Conrad's table so he could point his finger and glare down at his grace.

"Damn you, Conrad, this time you've gone too damn far! Our agreement was that you should take care of the military and technical side of things, and that I should have complete charge of all things judicial and political. Trying and hanging the Margrave of Brandenburg was obviously both judicial and political, as well as being boneheadedly stupid! You have managed to turn a minor border incident into what will likely soon become a full-fledged war with the entire Holy Roman Empire! What possible excuse can you have for this fit of madness? Did you receive a head wound in the opening stages of the battle? Or has your swinish swiving of every underaged slut in sight finally rotted out your brains? Well? Speak up, or has the same foul disease that has turned your mind to sludge also corrupted your tongue?"

Lord Conrad looked up and was silent for a bit, and then said, mildly, "Good evening, your majesty. I trust that you had a pleasant trip here. Would you care for a glass of wine? The local mead has quite a lot to recommend it."

"Damn you, Conrad, I said answer me!"

"As you wish, Henryk. I received no wounds in battle, and I am suffering from no disease that I am aware of, but thank you for inquiring after my condition. With regards to health, though, may I express concern for yours? The camp table that you are standing on folds up nicely, but it isn't all that sturdy. You would ease my anxieties considerably if you stepped down from it."

"Step down? I'm half minded to step down! Right down from my throne! But I'll see you banished first, dammit! I tell you, Conrad, one of us has to go, and I'm not minded that it should be me!"

This last pronouncement was accompanied by a particularly violent gesture, and the table took the opportunity to collapse. It seemed a natural occurrence to me, but later that night Maude said she'd seen Lord Conrad kick out a leg support. To his credit, the king rode it down standing up, but the accident seemed to have a certain calming effect on him.

"Maude, would you get us another table, please, and a chair for his majesty?" Lord Conrad said. "Sir Josip, clear the wreckage."

The camp furniture was collapsible, but still quite substantially made, and I had to bend my knees to lift the broken tabletop without straining my back. My love was back in moments with a new, larger table and chair before I was through. She had a chair in one hand and was supporting a long table—level with the floor—with the other hand gripping only one short edge!

His majesty noticed this.

Sir Conrad said, "You see, your majesty, things are not always precisely as they appear. Now please sit down and relax. Have some of this mead. Now, personally, I don't consider an invasion by nine thousand people to be a 'minor border incident.' It was an attempt to invade us, and to permanently conquer territory. I did not conduct a formal trial for the margrave. I merely publicly explained why I was going to kill him. The emperor is not stupid enough to attack us. I am not going to resign and neither are you. You are doing too good a job, and anyway, you *like* being a king. Was there anything else that seemed to trouble your majesty?"

"Killing the margrave was a major diplomatic blunder. He is very influential in the empire."

"*Was* very influential, perhaps. Now, well, in the first place, he's dead, and in the second, he has been shown to be a damned fool. I expect that whatever political faction he controlled is already rapidly dispersing."

"Perhaps so, Conrad, but I wish you wouldn't do things like this."

"I was only doing my job. I am responsible for the safety of the realm. When we were attacked, I had to respond as quickly as possible, since they were killing some of our people every minute. I admit that the battle was more destructive than it should have been. I had originally intended only to attack their van, to slow them down, but we were trying out some new weapons and tactics, and they proved to be remarkably effective. A single company of our troops took out their entire army without stopping. Except for the civilians in the baggage train, of course."

The king looked astounded. "All that was done by a single company?"

"Yes, your majesty, less than three hundred men. So you see why we have nothing to fear from the empire. That company was a newly formed unit. The Wolves. It's composed entirely of scions of the old nobility. It is about the only strictly military organization in our army, since those guys would never stoop to doing the kind of manual labor that everybody else in the army does."

"I see. My vassals will be proud to learn of their sons' accomplishments. But tell me, what is the story about this strong, if somewhat underdressed, young lady here."

"Your majesty, let me introduce Maude. She's my new bodyguard."

Maude did an amazingly graceful curtsy, such as I had never seen done by a woman before, even by one wearing a great flowing gown. It made me want to see her dance.

Lord Conrad said, "Maude is not the underaged swinish slut that you almost called her. But she is not an ordinary human being, either. In fact, she has a lot in common with Anna's children, that you and your men have been riding for years. She was sent to me by my cousin when he heard about that attempted assassination."

"I hope that she's as good at guarding you as she is at carrying around furniture. You're going to need her services, especially after this last foolish stunt of yours. If the Germans can't get rid of you by ordinary military means, you know they will try all of the other possibilities. Do you have a food taster? You should, you know."

"When I'm in the field, I eat from the same pots that my men do, and I never stand first in line. At home, what meals I don't eat in the cafeterias are cooked for me by the ladies of my own household, and they're always tasting things while they're cooking. So far, there hasn't been a problem, Henryk."

"I shall pray to God that it stays that way. For your part, you might want to put on a few good food inspectors. The people who hate us aren't above poisoning a few thousand people if it means killing you with them. The Big People have a remarkable sense of smell, you know. It might be worthwhile having one of them sniff over all the foodstuffs coming in, as well as all that is set on your table. It's what I do."

"An excellent suggestion, Henryk. I'll act on it. Better still, Maude, what is your sense of smell like? Is it as good as that of the Big People?"

"Yes, your grace."

"Can you tell if food has been poisoned?"

"Yes. All ordinary poisons. The only really dangerous poisons commonly known in Europe come from certain mushrooms."

"Interesting. Thank you. From now on, part of your job will be to smell my food, any food that is put on the table, for that matter, before I eat it. And when we get back, tell the accountants to raise your pay to eight pence a day."

"Yes."

"Conrad, are we going to be seeing thousands of these attractive creatures growing up around your estates?" Henryk asked.

"I really don't know. I haven't thought it out yet, but I think perhaps not. It doesn't feel right, somehow, but I'm not quite sure why."

"Let me know when you decide. Remember that my father was killed by one of his own guards. I think that I'd rather like to have a few like her guarding my back, if she's as honest as a Big Person and as trustworthy."

"I'm sure she is, Henryk, but still, I hesitate. I think perhaps that her sort are actually better people than we humans are. What is our moral position if we are giving orders to our moral superiors?"

"What, indeed?"

"The problem isn't as obvious with the Big People, because they look like horses, and you constantly have to remind yourself that they're not animals. Maude looks like a woman, and I can't help thinking about her as though she was a human woman. For example, I knew intellectually that she was far tougher than I was, and thus was actually much safer, but I was nonetheless as nervous as a mouse during the battle, thinking about her being in danger, right behind me.

"Should there be more like her? If there were, should we be giving them orders? *Would* we be giving them orders? Or might they decide that we humans are so degenerate that they should take charge for our own good?"

"I see what is bothering you, and I'm glad that I don't have to make the decision. Ponder long before you do anything, Conrad.

Concerning more pressing matters, what am I to do when the emperor complains about this last little affair of yours?"

"Simple. You tell him that it was unfortunate that one of his subordinates was so foolish as to attack one of your subordinates, but since you are in a forgiving mood, you won't be demanding further reparations. You may also tell him that the score on the battlefield was six thousand for you and zero for him. And tell him that he can come and have another romp with us, whenever he's inclined. He won't take you up on it."

"At this point, I suppose that it is the only tactic that could work. You know, when I heard that the margrave was still hanging naked outside the town, I sent men to have him cut down. They returned to say that the corpse had already done that for itself. It seems that he was so fat that his body actually pulled loose from his head, like a pinch of bread dough being pulled off. I'm having coffins made for those seven men. Would you have their clothes sent to my camp? I want to send their bodies back to their families in the best shape possible."

"I'll see to it, Henryk."

"Thank you. Now, the last order of business is this counter-invasion that you have planned. Do you really think this is wise?"

"I think that it is necessary. When a puppy makes a mess on the floor, you have to rub his nose in it so he knows what he did wrong, and then you have to swat him, to punish him, or he'll do it again. Without the swat, he might even get to liking shit on his nose! Anyway, the margrave's lands have been in Slavic hands since time immemorial. The people on the land are not exactly Polish, but they are closer to us than to anyone else around. They have been under the German's thumb for about a hundred years now. They deserve their freedom."

"Conrad, when you start using words like 'freedom,' there is no reasoning with you. Any further conversation on the subject would simply be a waste of the breath God gave us. Do what you will, and I'll try to sweep up your mess, politically."

"You know that you enjoy it. What say that you and your people come with me and my forces as we take possession of our new province? That way, you could see to it that everything was done to your satisfaction."

"Yes, that would be for the best, Conrad. Let us know when you'll be leaving."

"With pleasure. Good night, your majesty."

Later that night, sitting around a small fire, I got out my recorder and played a few simple tunes for Maude. She was very surprised. She said that she had never seen people make music before. She had often heard music, but it had always been made by a machine. I was mystified, and wondered what sort of machine could play a recorder. I could imagine a machine beating a drum, but not, say, a violin, or a trumpet. But I let it pass and played some more for my love.

She said she liked it, and soon was standing and swaying, naked as always, in time with the music. After a while, seeing that I was watching her with pleasure, she slowly began to dance, with a beautiful, flowing sort of motion I had never seen a person use before. Some of the knights from the Wolves camp nearby were as fascinated as I was and came over to watch. Most people play some sort of musical instrument, and a few of the watchers brought drums, strings, and woodwinds to contribute what they could. Still others used whatever was available to tap and keep the strong beat.

Someone started playing a violin to a slightly faster beat, and I turned and recognized him to be Komander Wladyclaw. The drums picked it up, and the rest of us quickly joined in.

Maude's dancing sped up as well, and she began to add graceful skips and spins to her dance. Seeing that her poise and prowess were up to something fast, the violinist made the song beat faster yet, and what had begun as a simple shepherd's tune was becoming something that might be heard from a Gypsy camp!

Again Maude's dance stayed with the increased tempo, whirling around the campfire, adding leaps and flying spins that seemed too fast to be real! She would leap into the air, and seem almost to hover there for a time while spinning. She was at once as free as a forest butterfly, as pure as a child, and as erotic as is possible for a woman to be.

More of our troops were coming to the fire to see what was happening, and staying once they did. There must have been six dozen of them by then.

The komander took the beat faster yet, and still Maude kept up with it, leaping higher than any of her audience would have thought possible, with her feet higher than a tall man's head, and her head far above that. Yet she gave no sign that this was some athletic thing she was doing, but rather an artistic one, for it was not the feat itself, but the beauty of the thing that was important.

Komander Wladyclaw glanced at me, asking if we dared to take it faster, and I gave him a quick shake of my head. No one could possibly dance like this for long, and I was beginning to worry about my darling love. We did a few bars to bring things to an ending, and Maude went into an elaborate spin and bow.

The crowd exploded with applause, a wild shout that was heard for miles and went on forever while Maude scampered back to my side. I was surprised to see that she wasn't even breathing heavily.

The komander stood and formally bowed to Maude, something I'd never seen a nobleman do for a girl around a campfire before. The feeling was unanimous, for every single man there, your narrator included, well over a gross of us, stood and bowed to her as well.

Maude at first nodded acceptance of this praise, but then, deciding that something more was required, she stood and made an elaborate curtsy and bow back.

The komander asked, "My gracious lady, could we beg you for a repeat performance?"

Maude looked up at me, and I said that she had not danced for a long while, but that perhaps we could hope for another show tomorrow.

The truth was, her dance was erotic, and I was so aroused that my strongest—only—desire was to get Maude alone in the tent with me.

If the other knights were disappointed, they were also understanding.

Much later, Maude said, "They trained me to be an entertainer, but Tom was never interested in watching me. Did my dance please you?"

My first thought was that this Tom must be an incredible ass, but I didn't say it.

I told her that it was the most unbelievably beautiful thing I had ever seen, that she was now the darling of the Wolves, and probably the rest of the army as well. If she ever wanted to cease being a bodyguard, there was a career waiting for her in dancing.

"I could quit being a bodyguard?"

I said that of course she could. There was no slavery in Poland. This was the land of the free. She was a free person, and she could do whatever she wanted to do.

She took a while to consider this, and then said, "No. I will continue as I am."

I said that this was good and held her close to me. Watching all of the other men looking at her with admiration and even open lust in their eyes, I realized that she could easily have almost any man she wanted. It chilled me to think how easily I could lose her.

Chapter Twenty-Three

FROM THE JOURNAL OF JOSIP SOBIESKI

written January 17, 1250,
concerning June 5, 1249

In the morning, after mass and the recitation of our Army Oath, Maude and I breakfasted, and I armed myself. Since I felt there was no possibility of any fighting taking place, I left off my leg armor. The combination of wearing infantry armor and riding in a saddle for two days had left parts of my posterior blistered where it wasn't bleeding.

Lord Conrad noticed my less-than-complete uniform and asked me why I was breaking general combat orders during what was still, officially, an alert. When I explained, he ordered that I see the battalion's armorers and get fitted for a set of the new cavalry armor.

I found the armorers with nothing much to do that day, except to sort out battered, bloody enemy armor and decide what should be scrapped, what repaired, and what saved as souvenirs. Given the chance to do honest work, they all jumped at it, and soon I had a dozen of them working in my cause.

They never let me leave their camp for more than a few minutes, as they took a set of standard heavy stampings from their storage boxes and cut, filed, and fitted them to my body.

Three seamstresses were soon at work, taking the partially finished sections of a summer gambezon from storage. They were cut oversized, with only half the seams sewn. Soon they were trimming and sewing them into a new garment for me, to suit the armor. Small pieces of chain mail were sewn on, covering the armpits, the insides of the elbows, and the backs of the knees, where the armor plates could not protect me.

I was surprised that I had no protection for my lower buttocks and my privy members below the belt, but I was told that when mounted, the saddle would keep those parts protected.

I said that my Big Person had not come with a saddle with that high of a cantle. Their response was to issue me a chit that got me a new, Wolves-style saddle, with built-in holsters for two submachine guns and a rifle.

Nonetheless, I resolved that someday soon I would get myself an armored skirt to wear in case I had to fight on foot. If I had to, I'd pay for it myself!

Most helmets have one piece that protects the top, back, and sides of the head, and a separate visor to protect the face. My new helm was just the opposite. The front, top, and sides were of a piece, and the back hinged up to let you in.

By late afternoon, an astoundingly short period of time, I was gloriously arrayed in the latest style of personal protection. They even found time to polish the plates, giving them the mirror finish so prized by the old nobility.

I lacked only the panache of gray plumes worn by the Wolves to look like one of their number, and I found myself wondering where I might possibly buy some plumes of some other color. Perhaps red.

I strutted proudly back to our tent, thinking that Maude might be impressed, but I was disappointed. She thought of wearing anything but one's own skin as being silly, smelly, and scratchy. Ah, well. You can't please everybody. I wasn't bothered. In all events, *I* thought that I looked beautiful.

One night I asked Maude how, just before the battle, she had managed to get from my lap to Silver's rump without my seeing her get there.

"I jumped."

I asked why I hadn't seen her move.

"I jumped quickly, when you blinked. It's how you move in combat. You wait until people blink, or look in another direction, then you move quickly."

I said that I was amazed.

"Would you like me to demonstrate it for you?"

I said that she could do it later. For now, it wasn't worth getting out of bed for.

Looking at Maude, admiring the lovely curve of her hip, and flank, and breast, I mumbled something to myself about the Lilies of the Field. She heard me, and asked what I was talking about.

I said, " 'And why take ye thought for raiment? Consider the lilies of the field, how they grow; they toil not, neither do they spin: And yet I say to you, That even Solomon in all his glory was not arrayed like one of these.' " I told her that it was from Jesus Christ's Sermon on the Mount.

I'm not a Bible scholar, but that one has always stuck in my head. And how could any young man resist the chance to impress his love?

"Yes. That is exactly right. Christ would always know what is best. We should not care about our raiment," she said, and continued in her nudity.

Maude had a perfect memory, and after that she would quote those verses of Matthew whenever anyone objected to her lack of coverings. When I said that she had to look at these words in context, she wouldn't consider it. Christ had spoken, He could not possibly be mistaken, and that was that.

I began to understand the saying about how a little knowledge was a dangerous thing, and why the Church does not encourage laymen to read the Bible.

When I asked her to please not argue with the bishop about religion, she asked what a bishop was, and we were promptly into another long, one-sided conversation.

FROM THE DIARY OF CONRAD STARGARD

June 5, 1249

I spent the day preparing to invade a major part of the Holy Roman Empire. Ordering up six more battalions of infantry was the easy part. Harder was the fact that our infantry could not move efficiently without a railroad going where they wanted to go. You see, our equipment and tactics had all been designed with *defending* the country in mind. Until recently, very little work or thought had gone into offense.

Units like the Wolves could go anywhere fast, as much as four gross miles a day, but we only had a single company of them.

A platoon of men could pull their war cart six dozen miles a day when they were rolling on steel rails. With some men pulling and some men sleeping, they could go around the clock. Averaged out, they were much faster than the enemy's conventional cavalry.

Put the same platoon on a good conventional road, and the best they could do was about two dozen miles, since it took all of them, pulling hard, to move the heavy thing on a dirt surface. There was no possibility of rolling around the clock.

The existing roads from Lubusz to Brandenburg were not very good, and in some sections it was doubtful if a single platoon could make a war cart move at all!

We had to get our infantry into Brandenburg, and once there, we needed to give them some mobility.

Then, we not only had to take and to occupy Brandenburg—an area of about six thousand square miles—we had to bring it into our system, and fast!

If the conversion went quickly and smoothly, the bulk of the Slavic-speaking population would be eagerly on our side, and the former conquerors would be dispirited.

If we let the German-speaking minority have time to organize itself, we could see factional fighting and guerrilla warfare for many years.

Worse yet, in my old time line, Brandenburg had joined with Prussia to form the state that was the political basis of modern Germany and the cultural basis of the Nazi party. These were the people with the strutting jackboots, and the firm belief that all other peoples were subhuman, *untermensch*. I wanted to make sure that the thing didn't happen in this time line.

Making Brandenburg a part of Poland meant bringing in our schools, with their general stores and their post offices. It meant bringing in our farming methods, our seeds, and our farm machinery. It meant bringing in our uniform measurement system, our monetary system, and our judicial system.

All of which involved a lot of travel and transport.

There was nothing for it but to build railroads. Lots of railroads. Quickly.

What I was planning was to be one of the fastest construction projects in army history. Everything else in the entire nation would be made subordinate to this single project. Every bit of materials and manpower, anything that could be of use, would be rushed to Lubusz. No matter what project had to be put on hold, no matter where else the materials were needed, no matter what the men would rather be doing, the new rail line to Brandenburg came first.

Our existing rail lines were placed defensively, on the east bank of the Odra. A pontoon bridge would be thrown across the river at Lubusz, which would stay in business until a real, masonry bridge could be finished, or until the thaw next spring took it out.

Surveyors were to be out in droves, preparing the way for hundreds of crews of construction workers. A forest of trees would be felled to clear the right-of-way, and were to be just as quickly ripsawed into railroad ties, bridge trusses, and siding platforms. Demolition teams would be blowing out tree stumps wholesale with gunpowder, followed by thousands of men who would be out with picks, shovels, and wheelbarrows, leveling the roadbed.

Every horse and wagon we had taken from the invaders would be in use, as well as every additional bit of equipment we could get our hands on.

While all this intensive work was going on, the Eagles would keep their planes high above us, searching for any hostile move, and the Wolves would be patrolling our borders, sniffing out any enemy action.

We figured to lay three miles of track in the first week, and ten more miles of it on the day after. Once we got rolling, we hoped to be in Brandenburg in ten days, and two months later we would have a perimeter defensive road around the entire province.

Experienced Polish farmers who wanted more land would be recruited to move into every town and large village in Brandenburg, mostly on land once owned by the soldiers who had just tried to invade us. We would equip them with the best seeds, the newest machinery, and the new fertilizers. Once the locals saw the kind of crops they brought in, they'd be lining up to get with our system.

A construction platoon would get to town, and in two days a schoolhouse would be completed. It would have a windmill that pumped water from a new tube well up to a cistern on the roof, indoor plumbing with hot water, and a septic system. This technology was far ahead of what the people in Brandenburg had ever seen, and it should impress them considerably.

Each of our schools had a general store that sold a wide variety of our products, at better prices than could be found locally, and a catalogue sales arrangement that could get you just about anything at half the price people were used to. Of course, everything was bought and sold with our own uniform currency, and in terms of our uniform measurement system.

Each school had a post office, something nobody in Germany ever saw before.

These commercial operations supported the school system, so much so that we sometimes had to work not to make a profit!

Since this would be army territory, taxes would be completely eliminated, except for those levied by the local government. The Christian Army supported itself by its own efforts, the schools were self-supporting, and the Church took care of itself.

Once we were completely set up, the only people the locals would have to deal with would be someone speaking something close to their own native language, and not in the foreign German tongue.

That was the program, anyway. We were pretty confident it would work. Especially since King Henryk had agreed to handle the political problems for us.

Six companies of infantry had left for Brandenburg the morning after the battle. They were marching with two weeks' worth of dried food on their backs, without their pikes or war carts, but they had been equipped with the new rifles, even if they weren't perfectly trained with them.

The king and I would head out in the morning with the Wolves. We figured to get to Brandenburg before noon.

Chapter Twenty-Four

FROM THE JOURNAL OF JOSIP SOBIESKI

written January 18, 1250,
concerning September 18, 1249

I arrived at the Explorer's School at the last possible minute before my leave was up, an hour later than the rest of them.

Sir Odon checked me in and said, "Someday, Josip, you are going to be late, and then I will have to be very rude to you."

I said in that event, he could wait to hear my news until after all of the rest of the men in our lance had told me the stories of what had happened to them during their vacations. I called him "Captain Odon," which certainly got his attention, and I swore not to talk until last. All of my friends were dying of curiosity, but I just grinned at them and said that they had to buy all of the beer, as well, in payment for my news.

Since it was almost quitting time, we walked to the local Pink Dragon Inn, where I again insisted on not breaking my vow of silence until I heard their news.

A bare-breasted waitress brought us a round of beers, was paid, and then was ignored. We all felt wonderful, being back with our friends.

Kiejstut eagerly started our informal debriefing. He had been grandly welcomed into his home village, and treated as a returning hero by all of his old friends and relatives. He had been feasted and feted for almost every day of the first two weeks, until he had to beg people to let him get some rest. Everyone had to hear about every event in his long and illustrious army career.

His entire village had been converted to Christianity during the eight years he was away, and they cheered when they heard that he, too, was a convert.

He had given the bride away at his niece's wedding, and had been the godfather at no less than five christenings.

All the girls he had known before were married, with too many children, but there was a whole new crop of fine young maidens, eager to welcome home the conquering hero!

"It was like having two months in Okoitz, but all the girls were even prettier and spoke Lithuanian!"

He ended by saying that when he came back, it was in the company of eleven good Lithuanian boys who had come to the Warrior's School to join the Christian Army.

We all cheered at this new addition to our ranks, for the army was growing again. The massive construction projects of the last eight years had resulted in more than enough apartments, factories, and farms to provide homes and work for all of us. More growth meant, among other things, more promotions.

Taurus had a less happy story to tell, since a few months before he returned to the family farm near Kiev, his uncle had died. Two of his cousins still lived and were struggling to feed themselves and their families. They were working with worn-out tools and poor-quality seeds, and in an area that had still not fully recovered from the Mongol onslaught.

By their standards, Taurus was fabulously wealthy, and in truth, he was able to help them a lot. He bought seeds and fertilizers for them, and then he and Nadja, the Big Person, had helped them get all of their land plowed and planted. He bought them a new, modern steel plow, and a pair of good oxen to pull it with, along with dozens of new farm tools from the store at the new school in the next village.

He bought household goods that they badly needed—dishes, pots, and pans—and gave them to his only relatives. He bought their wives bolts of cloth to make clothing, bedding, and curtains with, and gave everyone, even the children, a new pair of boots. After that, he spent the rest of his vacation time helping them build a new barn, with materials that he paid for.

"But you know, somehow, everything I did, it just wasn't enough. I wish that I had never brought my full dress uniform along with all the gold on it. I told them that I couldn't possibly sell my decorations, but they thought I was holding out on them. They never believed that the Big Person I had ridden in on wasn't my property, that Nadja wasn't even a horse, but a person who could not be bought or sold. One night, one of their wives even suggested that I sell some of my weapons and give the money to them, since I was so rich!

"I tell you that I was glad to leave those people. I've never seen people that greedy, or that ungrateful, before. I don't think I will ever go back there again."

Sir Odon said that everyone at home was glad to see him, but then he saw his relatives every few months, normally, since they lived nearby, in Wroclaw. Mostly, he spent the time helping out in his father's carpentry shop until the invasion happened. Then he had been called up to operate a steamboat on the Odra.

Father John had a similar story. After reporting to his bishop, he went to Cracow, and spent the time at his father's new butcher shop until the invasion. Then he was sent to a snowflake fort on the Vistula. The priest there had gone with the men to Brandenburg, and he was to see to the women and children left behind.

After Taurus, Fritz, and I left them, Lezek and Zbigniew enjoyed themselves at home until they were called up, to work on an oil tanker on the Vistula. They were not overly pleased.

Fritz's story was almost identical to Kiejstut's, even though he came from Germany instead of Lithuania. He was treated like a hero by all and sundry, the local boy who went away and made good. On top of that, the local nobility treated him like an equal, inviting him to supper and taking him along on a stag hunt. The son of a baron had begun politely calling on Fritz's little sister, to her great delight.

A total of fourteen healthy German farm boys, three of them his cousins, came back with Fritz to join the Christian Army.

"Still and all, I'm glad that I was out of touch when Brandenburg invaded us. I would have followed orders, you understand,

and fought them if it came to that, but, you know, I'm glad that it *didn't* come to that."

Since they had all now faithfully told their stories, they turned and looked expectantly at me.

Just to have some more fun with them, I said that these were all wonderful stories, and that they had warmed my heart, but that it was getting late and we had a busy day ahead of us tomorrow.

I got up from the table and made it halfway to the door before I was tackled and brought to the ground. They picked me up, carried me back to the table, and sat me back down. Then they took away my beer, as punishment, they said, for my attempted desertion.

So I told them the whole story, taking my time, starting with the night Fritz and I spent at the Pink Dragon. I spent some time describing each of the girls in detail.

Sir Odon said, "Hurry it up, or I will be forced to hurt you."

I passed lightly over my problems with my father, and soon had myself riding out to war at Lord Conrad's side, sitting astride one of Anna's children with the Battle Flag of Poland in my hand, and the most beautiful woman in the world sitting naked on my lap.

My friends gave me a loud *whoop*! Fritz gave me back my beer. Even Father John was laughing. At their urging, I continued with the story. I told them of the battle, of the execution of the margrave, and of King Henryk's amazing chastisement of Lord Conrad. I got to the point where we were about to invade Brandenburg when I finished my beer.

I'd had my fun with my friends, but enough was enough, and it was time that I bought a round of beer, which I ordered.

"But what happened then?" Zbigniew said. "Tell us about the counterinvasion!"

I had to tell them that from then on in, the story became less interesting, even boring, except for my relationship with Maude, of course. Everything was so well planned, and everyone in our army performed so well, that everything went smoothly.

Before the enemy had time to think, we had more than seventy thousand troops in Brandenburg. That was ten times the fighting

men they'd had even before the invasion! The few German soldiers who were left were so shocked that they just stood around
like sheep and did what they were told. Before my vacation was
over, the bulk of the building program was completed, there were
railroads everywhere, and schools were in every village!

Already, most of our troops had gone home, but the Germans
knew we could be back there in a hurry if they ever got rude
with us.

Even Lord Conrad was back at Okoitz, and so was my new
love. I knew, because I rode all the way back at his side, with
Maude again on my lap!

Sir Odon said, "A marvelous story, Josip! But tell me, what was
all that about calling me a captain?"

With great casualness, I said that I must have forgotten that
part, but Lord Conrad had seen fit to tell me about our next mission. It seemed that they needed some explorers with experience
in riverboats to explore the biggest river system in the world.

I enjoyed their rapt attention. On a small stage not three yards
away, a scantily clad dancer undulated suggestively, but all eyes
at our table were on me. After two months of being little more
than a wall decoration in Lord Conrad's tent, it felt very good
to be important!

I told about how we would be bringing in six collapsible
steamboats and assembling them on-site. Many details were
still not settled, but his grace had promised me that the climate
would be warm, all year around, that there was plenty of wine
and beer, or something like it, available locally, but that we were
also welcome to bring in our own supply, within reason. Further,
we were assured that there were many young ladies available,
and all of them naked, since the local customs forbade them to
wear clothing.

My friends were all looking at me with expressions that mixed
delight with incredulity, so I continued.

I said that Lord Conrad was vastly pleased with us for finding the iron mine on our last mission, and that he considered
himself to be in our debt.

Promotions had been promised to us all, and incidentally, I had taken the liberty to volunteer our lance for the above mission. And whose turn was it to buy the next round of beer?

"I will buy the next round, in honor of your very creative fantasy," Sir Odon said. "But what you are saying cannot possibly be true. Even if you are not lying, you must be exaggerating shamelessly, but it is such a pleasant lie that I think we would all like to wallow in it for the rest of the night, at least."

I said he could believe whatever he chose, it made no difference, since we would probably be briefed on it in the morning.

Father John wanted to know about the people to be found on this river, and I said that they were primitive along the river, but there was a rich civilization at its headwaters, in the mountains. And none of them had ever heard of Christ.

You could see the good father's eyes glow.

As the evening went on, my friends decided that they almost believed me about the mission, but on calm reflection they insisted that for the most beautiful woman in the world to be in love with a person abjectly lacking in *any* social skills, and with such a deplorable level of personal hygiene, was simply absurd.

They said that I had obviously fallen off Margarete and landed on my head, since I was patently delusional. I sat there and acted smug.

The high point of the evening came when Maude walked into the inn, wearing her usual outfit and easily outshining all of the waitresses and dancers there. She sat down next to me, put her arm around my waist and her head against my shoulder.

She said, "I missed you. Let's go to bed."

Fritz muttered, as if to himself, "She doesn't like clothes because nothing looks good on her. Unbelievably good, for a fact."

My other friends couldn't speak, since all of their mouths were locked open.

I told Maude that I would like that, but first she must meet my friends. I introduced them to her, but she had already heard much about each of them, and they were still too stunned by her beauty to say very much, so I was soon able to break away from them and take Maude back to my room in the barracks.

Having her there was perhaps discouraged by certain army

regulations, but they were not well-enforced regulations if you didn't bother anybody.

I asked her how she had gotten to the school from Okoitz. "I ran."

A distance of eighteen miles, and she ran the whole way. It made sense, somehow.

Chapter Twenty-Five

FROM THE JOURNAL OF JOSIP SOBIESKI

written March 6, 1251,
concerning January 19, 1250

I find myself laid up in the base hospital with an unimportant infection in a small scratch on my foot, and again, with nothing better to do, I have resolved to bring my personal history up to date.

I stood at the rail of the *Atlantic Challenger*, hoping for a sight of one of the flying fishes that Lord Conrad had written about. After weeks at sea, my love for it was still growing. Its awesome size, its constantly changing colors, its infinite peace. Together they made it for me one of the greatest works of God.

We had been at sea for four weeks, and out of radio contact for the last fifteen days. The new radios were an improvement, but were far from perfect. I could no longer send messages to my love.

I missed Maude, more than everything else.

Through the months of preparation for this voyage, she and I had been together every possible moment. I spent my weekends at Okoitz with her, and she arranged to have every Wednesday and Thursday off to spend at the school. In this manner, we had six nights a week together.

Transportation was provided by the Big People, who seemed to take a special pleasure in watching our love affair. Once Maude got Lord Conrad to teach her a few words in English, we often rode Silver back and forth, since that lady ordinarily didn't get enough exercise.

There was no longer even the slightest doubt in either of us that ours was a love that would last forever. She promised that she would wait for me to return, and that when I did, we would be married.

At Okoitz, where she was still guarding Lord Conrad, she spent her time in constant reading, to learn everything she could about this strange new world she had been sent into. She took formal religious instruction, and was baptized a Christian, which removed any possible impediment to our marriage.

She even submitted to wearing clothing in public, to forestall any criticism. It was very light clothing, loose, and made of the softest Bulgarian cotton, but it was clothing for all of that.

I was sorely tempted to transfer to some other branch of the army so I would not have to leave her. Maude thought seriously of leaving Lord Conrad's employment and stowing away on the ship, but in the end calmer, more practical thoughts had prevailed.

I wanted to set up a proper household for her, and I thought it likely that if this voyage proved to be as successful as the last, my promotion to captain was assured. Thirty-two pence a day, plus her salary, if she wanted to remain working, plus whatever royalties I got for my share of the mine, when added to my savings would let us live a very comfortable life.

Standing with me on the docks, just before I left, she had a confession to make. Unbeknownst to everyone, Maude had had four children.

It seems that children of her species are born very small, no bigger than mice, which explained why no one had noticed her pregnancy. They require no more care than a safe place to live and a supply of food, any food that a human could eat.

She was paying the widow of a yeoman farmer, who lived in

the woods not far from Okoitz, to care for them and keep them hidden.

This was the first truly independent action I had ever seen her make, and naturally I was curious about it. She said she felt a responsibility to Lord Conrad, and that by herself, she could not give him the security he deserved and still have any life of her own. Her four daughters, in time, could see to it that he was guarded around the clock, and still have plenty of free time for themselves.

Also, with the four of them on duty, Maude would feel free to go anywhere with me.

When I asked if this had been done with Lord Conrad's permission, she said no. But he never had anything to say about whether any human woman should have children or not, and she was as free as they were, wasn't she?

I had to agree with her, but secretly I was glad I hadn't been asked about it before the deed was done.

When I returned, in a year or so, it would be not only to a wife, but to a family, of sorts, as well.

As I pondered all of this, Knight Banner Taurus came over from the fishing net crane. He didn't have to do the sampling personally. Like me, he now had a forty-two-man platoon working under him, most of them belted knights. I think he was doing it himself simply because he was bored with our shipboard inactivity.

"Another empty net. These equatorial oceans are not as rich as our northern seas."

I said that our sampling was still far too small for us to draw any solid conclusions.

"True, and anyway, I was getting sick of the cook's abortive attempts at trying to make five new kinds of fish a day edible. I wonder if we'll ever find out if it's a matter of bad fish or bad cooking. Can you believe that lately I have been developing a craving for some fresh venison, you know, from those northern deer?"

I said I could not believe it, but that I had heard there was some trade starting in what they were calling reindeer meat, preserved by the new canning process.

"Reindeer. That must be because they put reins on the animal when they use it to pull their sleds. Reasonable. Say, how well do you know Baron Tadaos? This is the third time he has captained the ship we were on, and I still don't know anything about him."

I said that the first time was at the Battle for the Vistula, when we were just out of grunt school. The last thing we'd wanted was an interview with a baron! On the Baltic, we only saw him a few times, and the one time we'd met socially, everybody was too polite to actually talk. And on this trip, he had thus far stayed on the bridge, where our presence wasn't welcome. So I was as ignorant as Taurus was. I asked why he wanted to know about the man.

"I don't know. Maybe it's just my imagination, but some tension is building, something seems strange. Have you heard that the North Star is almost under the horizon? We'll be turning west in a few hours."

I said we were almost on the equator, and that I had expected it would be hotter. A summer afternoon in Poland would often get as warm as it was on the ship.

"I think the water cools us. Before long, we will arrive at the land of Brazyl, if all goes well and Lord Conrad is right. Still, I have a very bad feeling that something is going to go very wrong."

I said that his grace was rarely mistaken. We might be on the river within the week. I reminded him that no Christian in all of recorded history had ever traveled this far before! A certain amount of anxiety was only normal. I told Taurus that maybe it was just the anticipation that was upsetting him.

I was wrong.

Captain Odon was red in the face and gesticulating vigorously at the ship's captain, Baron Tadaos, who was groping for a weapon, and had not drawn one only because he couldn't seem to decide between his sword, his pistol, or the huge Mongol bow hanging on the wall. The baron's face was white, and I was unsure which color was the worse danger signal.

Both of their jaws were moving up and down, their lips were

moving, and their faces were going through the most remarkable contortions, but they were up on the bridge, and what with the noise and the wind of our travel, those of us below on the main deck could not hear a word of what was being shouted.

Suddenly, Captain Odon raised both fists into the air, turned around, and stormed down the staircase toward the two dozen or so officers who were watching them. The baron hesitated for a moment or two, then charged after the explorer.

"It seems that our sublime leaders have concluded their learned consultations," Zbigniew said. "Perhaps at last we shall be enlightened as to their cause for concern."

I said that his florid language suggested he had been reading too many diplomatic papers in the *News Magazine*, and stressed the prudence of being prepared to disarm them both, if necessary.

"Stop running away, you insubordinate bastard! I gave you an order!" the baron said, grabbing our captain's arm.

"Insubordinate, hell! I am your co-komander on this mission! And I tell you that you are a bloody madman! We are in the middle of the ocean! We have not sighted land for weeks! An idiot child could tell that we are not on a fornicating river! Use your eyes, you senile old fool!" Captain Odon said, shaking loose his arm.

"And I tell you that I have my written orders, you mutinous bastard! Fuel consumption has been much higher than expected, and if we have headwinds, in addition to the contrary currents that you know damn well we can expect, this ship will have a hard time getting back to Gdansk!" the baron said.

"You still have more than half of your fuel left, and if there is any question of it running out, when we find land, we can cut you enough cordwood to get you to China! But right now we are on the ocean! We are not on a river! And trying to assemble the riverboats down in those waves is suicide for any man who goes down there, and murder for you to order them to do it!"

"Lord Conrad's notes clearly say that the Amazon River is so wide that in some places you cannot see the banks from the middle! And you tasted the last bucket of water we brought up from the side! There wasn't one bit of salt in it! It was river water! We are on a river, you bloody idiot!"

"I don't give a damn if it tastes like pure white lightning! The Baltic Sea is damn low on salt, and nobody saw you putting a riverboat on it! Those waves down there are two yards high, and any attempt to assemble a riverboat over the side will result in disaster! And even *if* we were on a river, it makes no sense to take a fragile, short-ranged riverboat who knows how damned far to land when you still have miles of water below your ship's keel! If this is a river, it is too big for the boats we brought, and the only thing to do is take the ship up it until it gets shallow enough and narrow enough to justify putting a small riverboat on it!" Captain Odon shouted.

"This ship is needed elsewhere, and we have a schedule to keep! Now get your cowardly ass in gear and do your job!"

"That's an illegal order and you damn well know it! Schedules? Now the filthy truth finally comes out! You are willing to kill a whole company of men just so you can make your paperwork look neat! My men are not going to get butchered just to satisfy your stupid brand of pigheadedness!"

"Captain, if you won't follow orders, then your men will! Get on with your job, because if you don't, this ship is turning back!" the baron said.

"You will do no such thing. You will not kill my men, and you will not abort this mission. It is too important to Lord Conrad for us to turn back now, when there isn't any good reason for it. The reason why you will not do anything stupid is that I have three times as many men as you do, and my men are much better armed! Now just continue steaming in the direction that we're going, and we'll find land eventually!"

And with that Captain Odon turned around and marched back to his cabin. The baron stood there, breathing hard, and then suddenly realized that there were two dozen men staring at him. He opened his mouth to shout something, and then thought better of it. He turned and strutted briskly back to his own cabin.

"With any luck, they'll both get drunk alone in their cabins, and the rest of us can do something sensible and save the mission," First Officer Seweryn Goszczynski said.

"That is a noble thought," Zbigniew said. "Does anybody have any idea what set them off?"

"It was a matter of the baron making a poorly thought-out suggestion—certainly, it wasn't an order at first—and your captain rather abruptly calling it stupid. You must understand that the baron has been around boats and ships for forty years now, and he was not pleased that a man less than half his age was made co-komander on this mission," a ship's radio operator said.

I said that the whole idea of having co-komanders was stupid, but since we were stuck with it, we junior officers ought to come up with a plan as to what to do if our superiors got into this same argument again, especially if they started giving the men strange and contradictory orders.

The first officer said, "If that happens, we must be prepared to disobey all illegal orders, which would mean turning this ship back for home, aborting the mission, and enduring our own courts-martial. Those of us that weren't hung would have our careers irretrievably damaged. If we didn't disobey them, and anybody got killed, as your captain is convinced would happen, we'd be up on charges anyway, for conveying an illegal order. We are all in an absolutely no-win situation, and that is probably what will save us. Both of our superiors have been acting like bloody idiots, but neither one of them is a *stupid* bloody idiot. They know what would happen as well as we do, and they both know that their best chance of getting out of this unscathed is to pretend that it didn't happen. I doubt if either of them will stick his head out of his cabin until we are ready to part company. For the time being, we will follow my standing orders and continue to sail west, until such time as we can find a sane place in which to assemble your riverboats."

"An excellent suggestion, sir, and one that the Explorer's Corps will endorse. We will also station as high-ranking a man as possible near our captain's door, to waylay him if he comes out to do something stupid. I suggest that your people perform the same service for the baron," Zbigniew said.

"You may count on it, sir. I further suggest that if our superiors wisely decide to pretend that all of this never happened, we would all be well-advised to contract a case of mass amnesia."

I said that he could count on *that*.

Chapter Twenty-Six

FROM THE JOURNAL OF JOSIP SOBIESKI

written March 7, 1251,
concerning January 21, 1250

Things went pretty much as First Officer Goszczynski said they would. Our superiors both declared themselves to be sick, and had their meals sent to their rooms. Slowly, the tension on board relaxed.

It was two days before we sighted land to starboard, and another day more until we had land to port. A further half day took us upriver to a point where we were no longer bothered by big ocean waves.

A council of officers decided we were at a position that both of our superiors could live with, had they been sufficiently well to attend the meeting. We were on the equator, and we were definitely on an absolutely huge river. The current was strong, the water was fresh, and we had banks on both side of us.

We dropped anchor, broke out the the premade floats that would be the bottoms of the riverboats, and started lowering them down to the water level. We soon had assembly crews working under the wings on both sides of the ship.

The floats were the same size as our standard containers so they could fit into the ship's storage conveyors. Each float had a removable top, and most of them already contained the cargo that the riverboats would be carrying. They bolted together easily.

The steam engines were another matter, since they were heavy, and had to be mounted mostly behind and on top of the floats. Assembling them was not as simple as the designers had hoped, what with the motion of the boats, the ship, and the water. We encountered several bothersome manufacturing defects, and as always, we were up against the innate perversity of inanimate objects.

Persevering, it was almost sunset when we had one boat assembled, another close to done, and a third boat started. An amazing thing was sighted then.

A lookout up in the crow's nest was the first to spot it, but I was taking a break on the rear deck at the time, so I saw the whole terrible affair.

There was a white line to the east, on the ocean horizon, going from shore to shore. I soon noticed that it was getting bigger, and thicker, somehow, but I had no idea what it was. Neither did any of the ship's officers to whom I shouted.

Still, when strange things happen, it is best to act cautiously and get the men out of danger, even if it might slow down the job at hand.

I ran to the port side of the ship, under the wing, and shouted at the men working down there to get back up into the ship, and to do it quickly. Then I ran to the starboard side and repeated my message.

When I got back to the rear railing, the strange phenomenon had grown to the point where it was obviously coming at us, and at a pretty fair speed. I ran around in a triangle again and told everybody to hurry up, no shit, this was serious. Some fool made a joke about how a dragon was coming, and if I hadn't been worrying about saving his life, I would have shot him!

Some of the men that I'd trained myself, the men from my own platoon, scrambled up the netting we had hung over both sides, and those men lived. The ones who were waiting for the lift to come back down to get them got into trouble.

It was moving so fast that by the time the men below saw the huge wave, it was almost too late to do anything about it.

It was just one, single huge wave, with no big waves in front of it, or behind, either. But it was more than ten yards high, and it stretched from bank to rocky bank across the river!

It hit the stern of the ship, and she bucked up so fast that I was knocked down flat to the deck, on my stomach. I went down so hard that the wind was knocked out of me and I could neither move nor breathe.

Then a vast sheet of greenish-white water came down on top of me, flattening me even more. The fact that I couldn't breathe became unimportant, since I was underwater, anyway. Worse, I saw that I was about to be washed off the deck and into the river. To this day, I don't know how I managed to grab one of the stanchions that supported the railing.

I think it must have been the work of my guardian angel.

At that, I was hard-pressed to hold on, at first because of the thousands of tons of water streaming by me, and then because the ship was still vigorously bouncing up and down. Even so, I was one of the first men on my feet. I staggered forward to try to assess the damage and see where I could be of help.

There were dozens and dozens of men lying about, many of them badly injured, from skinned knees to broken legs, and even one broken neck. Blood ran from the wet deck, out the scuppers and into the water. It hurt to pass by my friends without helping, but in spite of their obvious wounds, if those men were still alive, they were likely to stay alive a few more minutes.

That might not be true of the men down on the water. When I got under the wing of the bridge, I leaned over the railing and looked down. Of the two boats that had been in the water on that side, the completed one was gone without a trace. Only the half-finished boat, where they hadn't started mounting the engine, was still afloat, and it was severely damaged.

Men were down in the water, and the current was sweeping them away! Ignoring the broken and bleeding men around me, I threw every life ring I could find overboard, and helped a few uninjured men get three of the ship's barges into the water.

We cut two of the barges free, and hoped that the men overboard would be able to help each other into them. We kept the third boat tethered, and a seaman slid down to it to see what he could do down there to help.

I ran to the port side of the ship, only to find Lezek doing the same job there that I had just done on the starboard. Here, too, the nearly finished boat was simply gone.

Kiejstut came up from below and shouted that the boilers were out, flooded with water. We could not get the engines going to pick up our lost men. Together, we made it to the ship's steam launches, only to find them both smashed.

He looked at me desperately.

"The anchor," he said.

Without another word, we both ran to the bow.

I would have expected that the wave that did so much damage would have pulled loose our anchor, or broken the cable, but no, it was still holding us in one place while the fast current was taking our men farther away every minute.

The release mechanism was jammed, but a few vigorous swings with an axe freed it up, permanently. As the cable was whirling away, Kiejstut took a life ring with a long rope tied to it, passed the rope around the fast-moving cable, and made a slipknot at the end of it. Just before the last of the cable was gone, he had the end of it tied to a float.

I complimented his good thinking.

"I thought we might need the anchor again, and now we should be able to find it," he said. "Anyway, it looked expensive, and the baron might have made us pay for it!"

I looked about. With the ship now drifting with the river, it was at least getting no farther away from the men in the water. There didn't seem to be anything more that we could do for those men, so we went aft to help with the wounded.

Our captain and the baron both had miraculous recoveries when the disaster occurred, as was only to be expected, and after a few moments of confusion, the two of them cooperated remarkably well in getting things back together.

Within the hour we had a current list of the dead, the wounded, and the missing. There were over ten dozen men somewhere in the dark, fast-moving water. Zbigniew, Taurus, and Fritz were among them.

The mechanics were six long army hours getting the engine room pumped out, the boilers repaired and refired, and the ship under way. By then it was dawn, and we went in search of our missing men.

Out of the ship's crew of ninety-one, six men were dead, eighteen were too seriously injured to work, and fourteen were still missing.

Of the two hundred sixty-two explorers, nine were dead, thirty-three were severely injured, and eighty-five were still missing. Most of the men doing the riverboat assembly work were explorers.

During the night, twenty-six men had managed to swim back to the ship and were taken aboard. That wouldn't have happened if Kiejstut and I hadn't let loose the anchor. The baron noticed this, too, and made a note of it in our records. He also noted that if a storm had come up during the night, without engines or anchor, the ship could possibly have gone down to the bottom. He told us this verbally, and quite forcefully, but did not put it down in our records. A decent man, the baron.

One of the men who swam back that night was Fritz.

Overnight, the steam launches had been repaired, and with them a half mile to either side of us, we spent days sweeping back and forth across the river, and eventually out into the ocean. Lezek and I had set seven barges adrift, and in the end we recovered only four of them, with twenty-nine men aboard. Another eleven people were found alive in the warm river water.

Zbigniew and Taurus were still among the missing.

After a week of searching the river, the sea, and the surrounding shores for our missing comrades, we regretfully called off the search. The barges each contained a small emergency kit, but with even a few men on board, by this time the supplies would be long exhausted.

We had recovered a total of twenty-two floating corpses. The last dead man we pulled aboard was Taurus.

➤ ➤ ➤

Baron Tadaos called an officers' meeting, to sum up what had happened.

This was the first maritime disaster suffered by the Christian Army, and we were all painfully aware of our ignorance and our inexperience. Careful notes were written up by everyone on board, to be delivered to the Maritime Design Board at Gdansk. Hopefully, some of our stupider mistakes would not be repeated the next time disaster struck. We all knew that someday, somewhere, it would happen again.

The baron thought that the disaster might have been caused by a tidal bore. The Baltic Sea doesn't have tides, any more than the Mediterranean Sea does, so we Poles were fairly ignorant of such things. Baron Tadaos had heard of only one other river in the world that had such a wave, the Severn River, in England, although he had never been there. It was said that they were caused by the mouth of a river having a funnel shape, and a big, incoming tide getting somehow focused, and made larger, as it rushed up the river.

I understood very little of it. I had heard Lord Conrad's lecture on the causes of tides, but I had never actually seen one, until that disastrous time on the Amazon River.

I didn't want to see any more of them.

Fritz had an interesting report. He said, "I think that I now know why our fuel consumption has been so high. I was in the water when the big wave lifted the ship up, and I got a good look at our bottom. We have an underwater forest growing down there! Some of the weeds looked to be two yards long!"

"There has been some growth below the waterline before, in the northern seas, but nothing that bad," the baron said. "It must be all this warm water we've been steaming through. Does anybody have any ideas on how to get rid of it without a dry dock? No? Then we'll just have to live with it for now."

Only one of the ship's crew was still missing, mostly because the crew wore bright red work clothing and so were easier to find in the water. The dark green explorer uniforms did us a great disservice that week.

Zbigniew had not been found.

As the meeting was about to break up, Captain Odon announced that he was having a barrel of whiskey broken out and set up in the mess. He said it was time to mourn our dead.

In a few minutes I found myself at a table with what was left of our old lance. Captain Odon. Fritz. Lezek. Kiejstut. Me. The captain poured us each a big glass from the pitcher, and we held up our glasses, as if in a toast. Only nobody could think of anything appropriate to say, and we just drank in silence.

"I never expected Taurus to die an old man in bed," Kiejstut said. "He was just too crazy, underneath, for that. But I always imagined him going out swinging his axe at his enemies, the way he did during that fight against the Mongols, on the bank of the river. He must have killed dozens of them, running and screaming like a madman."

"I think that he truly was a madman then, so soon after his family had all been killed," Fritz said. "He even took a swipe at me before Sir Odon took his axe away from him."

I reminded them that a few of his people were still alive, although after his last leave, he hadn't liked them very much.

"I suppose they'll think better of him now," Lezek said. "By their standards, Taurus died rich, what with his gold, his savings, and his shares in the iron mine. They'll inherit all that, won't they?"

"I suppose so, unless he left a will, and I never heard of one," Captain Odon said. "I think that after this, I will go and have one written up for myself. The rest of you might want to do the same. The ship's purser knows something about the law."

"Inside, somehow, I was beginning to think that we were all immortal," Kiejstut said. "We were always so lucky. I mean, we all lived through the Battle for the Vistula. Only about one man in three did that, out of the more than nine thousand men who fought in it, and every one of us came through it alive and healthy. What were the odds against that happening?"

"Who knows?" the captain said. "Who knows what the odds are of Zbigniew still being alive? Or if he is, will we ever see him again? We all knew that we were engaged in a dangerous occupation, but whoever thought we would lose men this way? Those were two of the finest fighting men I've ever had the privilege of knowing. Who would have expected them dying, not in combat, but in what was, in the end, just an accident brought on by our own ignorance? Well, we still have our duties to the younger men. I'll talk to Taurus's platoon, and Zbigniew's as well. Gentlemen, men have died in every one of your platoons. You should go and comfort the living. Maybe later tonight we'll meet back here."

We left to talk to our knights and squires, but much later we were all sitting around the same table again, quietly drinking.

In the morning we said a special Mass for the Dead, recited our Army Oath, and then we went back to our duties.

We steamed back up the mighty river, and by luck one of the lookouts spotted the life ring that Kiejstut had attached to the anchor cable. An hour's hard labor got us back our anchor.

We anchored upstream of a wooded, uninhabited island, on the theory that if another tidal bore happened, the island would break its force. We started assembling riverboats again, while others went to the island and began chopping firewood, which was needed both to ensure that the ship got home and as fuel for our four remaining riverboats.

The disaster had cost us, in dead, missing, and seriously injured, almost two complete platoons of explorers, including two platoon leaders. Since we were also missing two boats, well, with some reshuffling of personnel, it worked out.

The baron was shorthanded by twenty-one men, and asked if we could help out, but Captain Odon said there were still thirty-four men on the sick list, and many of them would be capable of doing at least some work within a few days.

I could see that the baron wanted to say that taking care of the injured took up a lot of badly needed manpower, but I think he was still a little afraid of our captain, and kept silent.

A tall, straight tree on the west end of the island had been stripped of its branches. The base had been girdled so they couldn't grow back, and a big flag was nailed at the top, as a marker. It was agreed that the ship and the riverboats would meet back at this place in exactly three hundred sixty-five days.

It was decided that the captain would go with Father John and a platoon of men, and try to get to the headwaters of the Amazon, where there was supposed to be a gold-rich civilization.

I was to take my boat and search out the north side of the river, and Lezek was to take the south. Kiejstut and Fritz were to accompany the captain farther west and would be assigned to search and map some tributary.

We were to be friendly to the natives, to show them our products and see what they might have that would be of interest to us, but mostly we were to search for a rubber tree. This was described as having a white, sticky sap that, when dried, was stretchy, like raw pigskin.

Those men who had been logging on the island were apprehensive about finding a single kind of tree in that strange forest.

"God was feeling very creative when He made this place!" Fritz said. His hands were covered by a rash that he picked up on the island. "We must have cut down three or four hundred trees on that island, and I don't think that any two of them were of the same species. I tell you that every single tree, every single plant, was different from every other plant around it! These are not like the forests back home, where there might be only five kinds of trees and six kinds of bushes in ten miles of forest. We might have to search for years, and cut into thousands of trees before we find this rubber tree. And when we do, there won't be very many of them."

There was no way to answer that, so no one did.

Besides the rubber trees, we were each to try to set up five or six trading stations along the banks of the river. The natives would want our knives, we were told, if nothing else, and we would always be needing firewood for our steamboats.

We all began to realize that this would not be an easy mission to accomplish.

Chapter Twenty-Seven

FROM THE JOURNAL OF JOSIP SOBIESKI

written March 8, 1251,
concerning February 6, 1250

The river we were on was called the Amazon, which meant, in Ancient Greek, "without a breast." It was named after a tribe of vaguely Greek warrior women. The story was that they were archers, and to keep their right breasts from interfering with their shooting, they cut them off. Or some said that they burned them off.

It was a gruesome story, that young women would so mutilate themselves, and a stupid one besides. My mother and sisters are all good archers, and the women in my family have always been very well-endowed. None of them have ever noticed any difficulties with their breasts interfering with their shooting, and getting a nipple twanged by a bowstring would certainly be a noticeable event!

So why the biggest river in the world should be named after something that probably never happened, or shouldn't have happened if it did, was one of life's little mysteries, until the afternoon came for me to go out alone and try to meet some natives.

We soon found that it was hotter on the river than it had been at sea, but it wasn't impossibly hot. The only problem was that it was hot all the time, without a break, which sometimes made it hard to fall asleep. The air had so much water in it that if anything got wet, it never seemed to get dry again, and we all had to learn to survive while being damp.

We soon discovered that on this river, humans did not always hold their normal, exalted position at the top of the food chain. A vast horde of disrespectful creatures were always out to displace us!

There were some huge reptiles, five and six yards long, some of them, which seemed to be half mouth, that the men promptly dubbed "dragons." There were snakes that got even longer, but we saw no large land mammals at all, or at least none bigger than a man.

There was a leech that was half the length of a man's arm, and after I burned one off the leg of a screaming squire, we *both* had nightmares about it for a week.

There were insects about in annoyingly prodigious numbers. Some of them were beautiful, some were horrible, some were huge, and some were all three. But when it came to being bitten, it actually wasn't nearly as bad as it was in the summer north of the Arctic Circle.

I was sitting beneath a tree having lunch with Sir Tomaz, my senior lance leader, when a leaf, which had fallen from the tree onto his cheese, got up on six legs and calmly walked away!

He said, "You know, Sir Josip, we're not in Poland anymore."

There was always something new crawling out of a crack in the boards, or out from under a rotting log. Some of them were beautiful, but the manual said that the creatures with the brightest colors were usually those that didn't have to hide. Likely, there was something about them that was deadly. Especially the snakes.

My riverboat, which I promptly named the *Magnificent Maude*, was small by the standards of those on the Vistula. It held a platoon of men in about the same comfort as the old *Muddling Through* had held an entire company. Thirty yards long and eight wide, it was only a single story tall, except where the bridge was built above the engine room. Cargo was kept below the main floor, and most of the boat was one huge screened-in room, to let the breezes in and keep the bugs out. There were lightweight wooden blinds that could be rolled down in inclement weather, but it wasn't armed or armored, in the traditional sense. The only weapons we had were our usual personal rifles, swords, and sidearms.

By our standards, this was an obviously nonthreatening vehicle. However, standards vary, and soon it was very obvious that it scared the natives silly.

The first eleven times we approached a native village, the people started screaming and shouting as soon as we came into view. Sometimes they shot arrows, or threw spears at us, or used a thing that was like a big peashooter (the child's toy, not the steam-powered weapon) that they used to shoot a sort of needle.

They must put some sort of poison on those needles, or at least they did on the one that hit Sir Tomaz on the inside of the elbow. When he screamed with pain, I told him to act like a man, that it was only a tiny needle.

He insisted that it was poisoned, so we stripped off his armor, and I treated the small wound just like it was a snakebite, lancing it open and sucking the blood and poisons out. It was fortunate that I listened to him, because even with such treatment, his arm swelled up to be as big as his leg, and the area around the pinprick turned black. I think that without such treatment, he might have died.

But whether the villagers were aggressive or not, by the time we got there, the village would be completely empty. When we sat back and waited for them to return, they didn't. When we followed them into those incredibly tangled forests, either they shot at us some more, or we got completely lost, or, most often, both.

In the last two villages our program had been to take a few small things, foodstuffs, mostly, and leave in payment a small knife, and one of those machete swords that Lord Conrad was convinced would be so much in demand, hoping they would get the idea that we wanted to trade.

Maybe when we returned, in a few weeks, we would be more socially acceptable.

I resolved to try the twelfth village alone. We made a visual reconnaissance from over a mile away, and then I left the *Maude* out of sight around the bend so as not to frighten the villagers. I took a folding canvas boat in alone, but since the real Maude wouldn't want to marry an absolute fool, or a dead one, I wore my infantry armor, with the metal plates inside of clean, white coveralls. My cavalry armor had been left back in Poland.

I had a bag of steel tools, glass bead necklaces, salt tablets, dried fruit, and my recorder. I also carried a small camp chair, reasoning that a man looks less threatening sitting down than standing up.

When I came within sight of the village, I sat down and studied the place. It was subtly different from the other villages we had visited. The buildings were arranged differently, and the thatched roofs on the huts were much steeper.

The people were the big change, however. At the other villages, the people were a medium brown in color, like Gypsies, only a little darker. They all had dark eyes and straight black hair. The men did not grow beards, and neither sex had much in the way of body hair.

They tended to be short and thin-boned, and as in every place else in the world that I had ever heard of, the women were shorter than the men. As Lord Conrad had promised, no one wore clothing, although they did wear decorations, and some of those covered a lot.

The men looked to be fairly fit, and the young girls were often very attractive, but almost without exception, as soon as the women had children, they all became extremely fat. I found myself wishing that some of them would wear clothes.

These new people were much different. The men, or perhaps I should just say the "males," were short and brown, and they tended to be chubby. They seemed to be mainly involved with gardening when they weren't taking care of the children.

The women were larger than the males, or at least taller and better muscled. They carried bows and spears the way the males did in the other villages. While the males all had black hair, the women wore theirs bright red. It did not look to be a natural color, and I suspected it was a dye. Their nipples and private areas were also colored bright red.

And the women were white. Not flesh-colored, the way I am, but *white*. The color of a new sheet of paper. Not even Lord Conrad had ever talked about such a thing.

But one can sit and be amazed for only so long. It was time to attract some attention. I displayed my trade goods on the ground a few yards in front of me.

I got out my recorder, flipped up my visor, and started to play a simple shepherd's tune. Something I hoped would be interesting, calming, and proof that I wasn't out to hurt anyone.

I did not get the desired reaction.

Some children noticed me first. They ran home screaming, not to get Daddy, but for Mommy to come. Or at least, it was Mommy who came. Six mommies. They reminded me of, well, I never learned if there was a polite name for them, but the kind of women who don't like men but want to be just like them. It occurred to me that these might be the warrior women that the river was named after. I wondered if "without a breast" might be another way of saying "not very feminine."

I continued playing the same tune, to give them time to get used to it, and I continued smiling resolutely.

They stopped a few dozen yards from me and discussed me among themselves. Then one of them calmly notched an arrow and shot me.

Now, my suit was proof against Mongol arrows with steel heads. This woman's weapon might have had a quarter of the pull of a good Mongol recurved bow, and the arrow point was only flame-hardened wood, from the look of it. I didn't even stop playing, and the arrow bounced off my breastplate. I smiled.

Within seconds they launched an additional two spears, eight arrows, and two of those peashooter needles. Most of them hit me, but only the needles stood a chance of doing any harm. They might possibly get through because they were narrower than the rings in the chain mail that covered the cracks in my armor. I took my chances and continued playing "The Lonely Shepherdess."

An arrow and both needles stuck in my coveralls, and playing with one hand, still smiling, I plucked them out.

One of the women, the best looking of the bunch, if you like that sort, screamed and ran at me with a long, thin club held over her head. I stopped playing and stood up. She hit me on the head as hard as she could, but I was wearing one of the old-style, ring-around-the-collar war helmets, and while it was extremely loud, I barely felt her blow.

I was getting very irritated at these people's behavior, but orders are orders, and we were told to make nice to the natives. I gesticulated to the trade goods that she had trampled in getting to me. I stooped over, picked up a necklace, and offered it to her. I was doing a serious job of turning the other cheek, and that's right where she hit me next.

She spat on me! She knocked my hand and gift away, and spat right in my face! I was furious. I have never struck a woman in my life, and I don't ever intend to, but I *do* punish naughty children when it is obviously for their own good!

I grabbed her by the arm, sat down, and turned her over my knee! I pinned her left arm behind her back, immobilized her legs with my right leg, and swatted her bare buttocks as hard as I could with my open hand until my right arm got tired.

During this time, there were a lot of rude sounds being made, and her friends tried to do various sorts of damage to my person. I simply ignored them, and the ladies didn't quite manage to knock me over. I then decided that this particular attempt at international trade was a wasted effort. I stood up, dumping the increasingly loud lady on the ground, picked up my recorder, and walked back to my canvas boat.

A half dozen or so more weapons hit me in the back as I made my exit, but I didn't care. One arrow put a hole in my boat, but I ignored it, keeping with the image. As a consequence, I almost sank in my armor before I got back to the *Maude*.

Mostly, I was thinking about how wonderful it was that I had brought an entire barrel of Lord Conrad's Seven-Year-Old Aged Whiskey along for my own personal use. Well, I had let the platoon buy shares on it once we'd gotten here, but there was still plenty to be had for me!

As soon as I got back to the *Maude,* I drew myself a pitcher of whiskey, and sat down alone to drink it.

Somehow, when you are *really* mad, you just can't get drunk, no matter how much you drink. It just burns out of you before it can do you any good.

The last few weeks had cost me two of my best friends, and now I was separated from not only the woman that I loved, but from the rest of the old lance as well. Oh, my platoon was made up of some very fine men, but it just wasn't the same!

And after enduring two weeks of having people I was trying to help turn and run away from me, a most annoying perverted woman had spat in my face!

It was late, and except for a pair of sentries, both of whom were up on the bridge, everyone else was asleep. We were at anchor, a hundred yards from the shore. It was dark, except for a single, small kerosene anchor light. I was in my "cabin," a small screened-in porch at the front of the boat. My white armored coveralls were hanging in one assembled piece on the other side of the room, in the vague hope that they would dry out from the soaking they had gotten that afternoon. I was sitting naked in my chair, trying to cool off enough to sleep. Only I couldn't sleep. I couldn't even get drunk.

I heard a sound in the water that wasn't quite right. I was sure it wasn't one of those huge green lizards that lived in the river, that the men persisted in calling dragons. I didn't think that it was one of the big, savage-looking otters, either.

I slowly drew my sword from its place near my bed and waited. In a few minutes my patience was rewarded. I saw the outline of a hand come up onto the foredeck, followed smoothly by the rest of a solidly built female form. I swore under my breath and slowly laid my sword down on the deck. No son of my mother could deliberately kill a woman, not even when she was attacking me in the dark with some sort of knife in her hand.

I was sure now that she was the same one I had spanked.

She stealthily pushed through the screen door into my room, but she must not have seen me sitting in the dark, since she began to stalk my white coveralls. When she had her back to me, I ripped the sheet off my bed and threw it over her in one smooth motion. I thought this would confuse her, since the native bedding didn't run to bedsheets. If she didn't know what a sheet was, she probably wouldn't know what to do about one. I followed the sheet by a half a second, and the sheet, the woman, and I rolled around the floor, grappling, groping, and making rude noises.

When the sentries got there, I was on her back, with her legs gripped between mine, and her arms and torso wrapped in my arms.

"Excuse me, sir, but was this a situation with which you wanted help?" Tomaz said.

I said that of course I wanted help! I was subduing an intruder! How could he possibly imagine that I wouldn't want help?

"Well, sir, when you see a naked man and a naked woman rolling around on the floor with a bedsheet, I have learned that it is only prudent to ask, before joining in."

Still struggling with the violent woman, I told him that I was not inviting him to join in on an orgy. I wanted him to get some rope and some more help, and to get her immobilized.

In the end, it took five of us to get her properly trussed up. I explained to them that she had entered without permission, at night, and with a weapon in her hand. This was not ordinarily considered to be a friendly act, and therefore we would keep her tied up until further notice. I told the second lance that they would have the rewarding task of teaching her to speak Pidgin, and to have the job done within the week.

They carried her away, and eventually I got to sleep.

Chapter Twenty-Eight

FROM THE JOURNAL OF JOSIP SOBIESKI

written March 9, 1251,
concerning February 26, 1250

Over the next few days, four other men tried their luck at getting friendly with the natives, each with as little success as I'd had. They'd all used different approaches, but because of the universal aggressiveness of the natives, I'd insisted that they wear armor, and nobody objected.

To make matters worse, Fritz was doing just fine on the south side of the river. On the radio, he said that the natives were fascinated with steel tools and were making good progress at learning Pidgin. Neither Captain Odon nor Kiejstut could offer us any useful advice, either.

It was our captive who eventually solved the problem.

The first morning after her capture, someone found a set of manacles and leg irons in our supplies. They were apparently put there in anticipation of one of our people going crazy, as had happened once near the Arctic Circle, but they worked just fine on a supposedly sane native woman who merely wanted to kill me. They were safer, since she couldn't chew herself loose, and more humane, with no chance of cutting off her blood supply.

We soon discovered that her skin coloration was as artificial as that of her hair. She was actually covered from head to foot with white paint, which was now wearing off. Under it, her skin was the same color as all the rest of the native people, but considerably lighter. We speculated that the white paint stopped her from getting a suntan.

The first day, she resisted all attempts at teaching her Pidgin, until they decided they had to use the same methods one uses to train a dog. By giving her small bits of food, or even better, salt, along with lavish praise, whenever she did anything right, and a scolding when she did things wrong, they eventually got through to her. I would have forbidden the use of any actual abuse, of course, but no one ever suggested that they use it.

The second lance kept at least two men on her at all times, from dawn until quite late, and in a week they had her in a meaningful conversation.

She refused to tell us her name, since if we knew it, she said, we could work magic and witchcraft against her. We still needed to call her something, so after trying out the "Captive Princess," a particularly unsuitable name, we simply settled on calling her Jane.

She said that at first she and her people thought I was a ghost! It seems that the local ghosts are all big, bulky things that are pure white in color. She now agreed I was not a ghost, but she felt that it was a perfectly reasonable mistake.

When I pointed out that she, too, was colored white, Jane said that her people did that to scare their enemies, and anyway, she could not be confused with a ghost because her nipples were painted red. Everyone knew that ghosts did not paint their nipples red, so she was safe from any mistake.

I said this was obviously true, since Christian ghosts did not paint their nipples red, either. In fact, I had never heard of a ghost painting anything any color at all. It was all I could think of to say about a subject so weird.

She was gratified to hear this.

I told her that our ghosts were not white, and that our coveralls were white because that was the natural color of cotton. I asked, if we painted them a different color, would she still think we looked like ghosts?

She said, of course not. If we were not white, we could not be ghosts.

We lacked a supply of clothing dye on board, but with her help, we found a tree with a dark brown sap that did a decent job of coloring our armored coveralls to a dark tan. We steamed back to the first village we had stopped at, and people came out to see what we had to offer.

Their reaction to our tools was remarkable. It took me a while to realize that, except for the bones and teeth of certain fish and animals, these people had nothing they could cut with. They not only lacked flint for toolmaking, they lacked any sort of stone at all. These were not a Stone Age people. They hadn't gotten that far along!

I'd put a good edge on one of the machetes, and let the natives see me slicing up some shrubbery.

Bear in mind that these people had spent their lives living in the most tangled forest imaginable. Every day of their lives had been spent crawling under plants, stepping over them, walking around them, and getting swatted in the face by them. And up until the moment they had a good knife, there hadn't been anything they could do about it.

One fellow in particular was fascinated, staring and grinning as I easily chopped the branches from a strange-looking bush. I grinned back at him and handed him the machete

He took it and gave the bush a tentative chop. Leaves and branches fell to the ground. He screamed in triumph! He took off at a dead run, laughing and shouting, slashing away at the underbrush. We heard him making all manner of noises out in the forest for well over an hour before he finally came back, dripping with sweat and tree sap.

The look on his face was like that of a young man who had finally attained sexual relief!

We explorers attained sexual relief of a more substantial sort from the young ladies of the village.

It all started with the elders inviting us over for a drink, and I think there must have been something in that brew that encouraged sexual license. Soon, I was handed a very attractive young woman who turned out to be the chief's favorite new wife. I was required to have sex with her *as a proof of my friendship with the chief*!

The young women of the tribe were all very appreciative of the small gifts my men gave to them, and the elders of the tribe were seen to be actively encouraging their daughters to please us.

I would be most embarrassed if my mother ever heard about the mass sexual orgy that ensued. While I had made no promises to Maude concerning my own chastity, it had been my firm intention to stay sexually true to her. This proved to be impossible in the induced madness that enveloped us.

Perhaps I am merely making excuses for my own conduct, but in later conversations with my men, I learned that the most subdued of them copulated with at least seven of the natives, and I have mental images of literally dozens of different young ladies under me. We could not possibly have been that virile without some sort of external stimulation!

That drink would make a very profitable product if sold in Europe, but I don't think the Church would approve of its sale!

All this fornication was accompanied by equally heavy drinking by everyone in the village. I thought that my own people drank too much, but we were but children compared to these native villagers. They continued on with the party long after we were comatose. At least, when I awoke in the night to relieve myself, the dancing and drinking were still going strong, with not an explorer in sight near the campfire.

It was the following afternoon before most of us departed that village.

We left a lance of men behind, confident that they would get along well with the natives.

That evening, we thanked Jane, the warrior woman, for her help. We gave her a knife, a machete, and an axe, along with some necklaces she liked, a sharpening stone, and a bag of salt tablets that all of the natives craved. We then offered to take her back to her home village.

Jane refused to go. It seems that by spanking her for spitting on me, I had permanently dishonored her somehow in the eyes of her tribe. She said that when she swam out to our boat and tried to kill me, she had done it because she had already been drummed out of her tribe. She had come expecting us to kill her.

It was rather like what they say a Musselman does when he can no longer stand the pain of being alive. He puts on his best clothes, prepares his best weapons, mounts his best horse, and charges into his enemies, trying to kill as many of them as possible before they kill him. The custom is called "Running Amok."

Further conversation with our former captive convinced us that if we simply ejected her from the boat, without friends to guard her back, she would soon die in the forest. She had been useful to us thus far, and while we all found her masculine mannerisms in combination with her feminine body to be offensive, after consultation with my knights, I decided to let her stay aboard.

Over the next few weeks, we established three more trading stations and survived three more orgies, which the locals insisted on. When we tried to back out, they became extremely insulted, and it was only with great difficulty that we repaired the breach.

A number of changes came over Jane. As her body paint began to wear away, she looked like she was dying of some horrible skin disease. She made no attempt at replacing it, and in a few weeks the color was gone. The dye in her hair was growing out more slowly, but whatever dye she had used to stain her nipples and privy members seemed to be permanent. When someone questioned her about it, the painful process she described seemed to be something like tattooing.

When I asked her about her body paint, she said that she no longer had the right to wear her tribe's colors.

One of my men noticed her smearing herself with a clear tree sap and asked her about it. She said that it kept the insects from biting.

Now, this was a wonderful thing to hear, since we were constantly plagued by the little bastards. As things were, you had your choice of wearing a complete set of clothes, and suffocating, or you could strip down and be eaten by the mosquitoes. Naturally, he tried the stuff out.

It turned out that it did not exactly repel the bugs, but rather, it made your skin so sticky that they stuck to you but could not bite through the glue, so you did not get bitten. You had to learn to ignore the insects buzzing on your skin, and if you were going to wear the stuff at all, you had to go completely naked. It had the habit of gluing your clothes to your body.

At first we thought we had a salable product here, but on later thought, we decided that its limitations were too great for it to have a market in Europe. In time, however, we all got to using the stuff regularly, washing it off and replacing it twice daily.

But a bigger change in Jane was in her bearing, or maybe it was in her self-image. Perhaps it had something to do with being around heterosexual people, and noticing the way my men and I reacted to pretty native girls. Tomaz noticed it first.

He said, "Is it just me needing a woman, sir, or is Jane starting to act feminine?"

I said that maybe she was starting to pick up on our customs. I suggested that if he was thinking of getting physical with her, it was up to them, but I followed the lead of Lord Conrad and recommended he take it slow. If anything ever developed between the two, I never heard of it.

It had been raining nonstop for weeks, and joking reports from the lookouts contained sightings of Noah's Ark. I let it go and even laughed about it. Anything that raised the men's spirits was good.

At about this time, the radio died for good. The wet, the funguses, and the insects did electronic components no good at all. With the old style spark-gap transmitters and coherer-type receivers, you could putter with the things and completely rebuild them when you had to, and in time it would work again, after a fashion. With these modern things, well, once a tube burned out, it was useless, and no amount of fiddling, hard work, or prayer did you any good at all. We were out of tubes, and everything else was rusting vigorously.

Other things on board were wearing out and rotting much faster than usual. I was finding mushrooms growing in my locker, and any food that was not sealed in a glass jar or one of the new metal cans was rotten. It was good that we had mostly stopped wearing clothes, because our supply of uniforms wouldn't have lasted out the season, let alone a whole year.

The wood that our boat was made out of was starting to rot,

as well. It was brand-new, first-quality oak, most of it, and it was rotting! Before long I had three men navigating the boat, and eleven more working to keep it repaired!

With the four trading posts we had set up—with a lance of men at each—I had only two lances left on board. The plan was to go another gross miles upstream, map the river, and set up a fifth post if we found a suitable site. Then we would go back and visit the other posts. I hoped that at least one of them still had a working radio.

We rounded a bend in the huge river and found ourselves steaming across a huge lake. At least two other boats should have been ahead of us, but when we had a radio, neither of them had mentioned the lake to us. Still, they could not possibly have missed it.

Besides being very large, the lake had other peculiarities as well. There were trees growing right out of the water, and in some areas they grew so thick they blocked out the sun. The trees back home would drown if their roots were flooded, but there were thousands of kinds of strange trees in this forest, and most of them seemed to be healthy.

Jane could offer no advice, since her home was a gross miles away. Being a primitive, she was much like a peasant in never before having been far away from home. The lake was as new to her as it was to us.

We steamed on, keeping the north bank in sight in accordance with my instructions. We were surprised to find that some of the huge trees in their watery meadows had people living in them. I would have investigated further, but other problems surfaced.

Two men acquired painful infections in their privy members, with a white pus dripping out. I had never seen the like of it, and there was no mention of it in the medical manual. The salves we had were ineffective, and there was nothing for it but to wait and see if it went away.

The next day, eight of the sixteen people we had on board came down with a severe fever. Often delirious, they could do little but lie in their beds and either shiver or sweat profusely.

Again, none of our medications did these men any good, and their temperatures grew alarmingly high.

The day after, four more people were down with the fever. There were no longer enough of us to manage the boat, take care of the sick, and map the shoreline. When I felt myself getting light-headed, I had the boat tied up to one of the trees in the middle of the lake. There was nothing left that we could do but go to bed and see whether or not we would survive.

The fever came and went for many days. Most of the time, you were flat on your back, unable to move. Occasionally, you felt almost normal, for a while, and then you could get up and help out with those who were more badly off.

Only Jane stayed healthy, and I think that without her we all would have died.

I don't know how long we stayed tied to that tree. I lost all sense of time, and often there was no one awake enough to keep the logbook up to date. Jane by this time was speaking a mixture of Polish and Pidgin, but no one had even begun to teach her to read or write. As it was, she did yeoman service keeping us in water and food.

Chapter Twenty-Nine

FROM THE JOURNAL OF JOSIP SOBIESKI

written March 10, 1251,
concerning Date Unknown, 1250

After I don't know how many weeks or months, I awoke feeling almost healthy and certainly hungry. I called out, but no one answered. The room was dark, more so than the lowered blinds could account for. The bed wasn't level. As I looked around in the gloom, it seemed the floor had an undulating quality about it, and that the walls were no longer straight.

Sure that I was still delirious, I closed my eyes again and slept.

When I awoke once more, the room was somewhat lighter, but all else was the same. The floor really was bumpy and bent, the screened walls were far from straight, and the ceiling sagged. There were strange forest sounds about me, and I was sure the boat was no longer afloat.

I went to remove the sheet that covered me, and for the first time noticed my hand. It looked ancient and wrinkled, and my fingernails were incredibly long, longer than they had ever been, longer even than those that some European highborn ladies cultivate to prove they never have to work.

I fumbled for my bayonet, on the nightstand, to trim my nails with. When I pulled it from the sheath, it was rusty. I dropped it, and it knocked a deep dent in the floor.

Had months gone by? Years?

I touched my face, my beard, and found it to be very long, longer than my fingers. Before I fell sick, I had been cleanshaven.

I called out again, and again, no one answered.

Was I truly alone? Could all the others be dead? Surely they would never abandon me!

With great effort, I sat up in the bed and twisted so my feet were on the floor. I marveled at how thin my thighs had become. I felt my chest, and could feel every rib under my fingers.

I stood, shaking, and slowly made my way to the kitchen, expecting to see the remains of bodies scattered around. It was not as bad as I feared. Most of the beds in the common room were gone. There were four beds left, and they showed signs of use.

The kitchen was untidy, the breakfast dishes unwashed, but the scraps on them were no more than a few hours old. There was cold food left in a pot. I found a spoon, sat down, and ate. I drank a canteen filled with water, and then stumbled to the door to relieve myself in the latrine at the stern.

The forest came right up to the doorway. There was no sign

of the lake that we steamed in on. The *Magnificent Maude* was sitting on the forest floor, her formerly straight lines all bent and slumped, and she was in the process of rotting away. Ants swarmed over the hull.

I fought my way through the thick bushes to the latrine, only to find vegetation growing up through the toilet seat. I ripped the leaves away and sat down.

None of this made any sense at all.

My ears hummed with bird sounds, insect sounds, and what might be the distant scream of a monkey. Then, in the far background, I heard what had to be the regular thumping of an axe. It was a man, swinging an axe. Some of my crew were still alive, they were out there somewhere, doing something important.

Exhausted, but greatly relieved, I went slowly back to my bed and fell asleep.

I awoke to find Tomaz standing above me. He was dirty, bearded, and except for a silver cross hanging around his neck, he was completely naked. He had lost a third of his body weight since I had seen him last, but despite everything, I could see that he was healthy, or at least getting that way.

"Are you feeling better, sir?"

I said that I thought so, and asked how long I had been away.

"We are not sure, sir. For a while there, there was no one mobile and sane enough to keep up the log. Several months, at least."

I asked how many of us were still alive.

He sat down on the edge of my bed.

"There are five of us left, sir. You, me, Jane, Gregor, and Antoni. The other eleven are dead. They weren't even buried properly. The two priests were the first to die, so none of them were given extreme unction. Jane was alone through the worst of it, and there wasn't anything she could do but throw the bodies overboard. That was before the water went away."

Seeing the quizzical expression on my face, he continued.

"We weren't sailing across a lake, sir. We were going over a flooded forest. In a few months, once the rains stopped, the water all drained away and the forest became dry land again. It was just as well, because by then the boat was sinking, just rotting away. Something in this land doesn't like our northern lumber. Even the handles on our knives and axes have had to be replaced. Some of the local timber is pretty good, though. Jane has been a big help, there, since the trees around here are a lot like those around her home."

I asked about the chopping I'd heard earlier.

"There is a fair-sized river about a mile from here. Jane is showing us how to make a dugout *canoe*, a boat of the sort her people use. You probably heard us working on that. We have been trying to spend half our time on it. The rest is needed to find food. Most of our stores rotted, of course. All the dried peas and beans, all the grains. Only the canned and bottled things are left, and not much of them. When she was taking care of us all alone, Jane didn't have much time to go hunting, and in her tribe, it's the men who do the gathering. Luckily, she knew enough about what to look for to show us what to do."

I said that he made it sound like she was in charge.

"I suppose she is, sir, in a way. She knows this country, and we don't. She hasn't been giving orders, exactly, but when she makes a suggestion, we usually follow it."

I said that despite all that, she was still an outsider, and we were regular army. I supposed that I would have to do something about our command structure.

"Sir, you are not going to do anything about anything, not for a week at least. That's how long it took each of the rest of us to get to the point of doing useful work. That's all you have to do for now. Get well. Once you are up on your feet, I will relinquish my command to you, but not until then."

I asked him if he had taken command.

"To the extent that five naked, starving people constitute a command, yes. I had to. I am senior lance leader, after all, and the only knight you have left. Until recently, you have been out of your head, when you weren't comatose. Just relax, sir. In a week, you'll likely be up and around."

➤   ➤   ➤

Five days later I was able to hobble all the way down to the site where they were building the new boat. Jane had selected a huge tree as being suitable, and it had been chopped down. Although her methods called for burning it down, the men did it their way, but on later reflection they weren't sure which would have been faster. Certainly, burning would have been less work. The bark was removed, and with fire and axe they made the outside look like a double-ended boat.

Fires were started on the top of the log, while the outside of the boat was kept wet. By judicious burning and scraping, the thing was being hollowed out. Jane estimated that in two weeks they would be ready to leave.

It seemed to me they had built on a grander scale than necessary to carry five people. They said they planned to take all of the remaining trade goods with them, to trade with the other tribes along the way. Also, there had been six of us when they started the boat. Yashoo had died a week before I regained consciousness.

Moving the completed boat on rollers proved to be impossible without a block and tackle, and those aboard the *Maude* had all either rotted or been eaten by the ants. Again, the native way worked. We dug trenches under the boat and slid logs under it, which supported the thing as we dug a pit under the whole boat. Then we extended the pit into a canal all the way to the river. Water filled the canal, we dug out the supporting logs, and floated the boat out.

I found it remarkable that the native people had worked out whole technologies to get around their lack of a good cutting edge.

As we were loading the canoe with everything we would be taking with us, we came across the only item made of northern wood that had not rotted to uselessness. The whiskey barrel. It was completely sound, as were its contents. This was a pleasant surprise, for Lord Conrad had mentioned that a small amount of whiskey would purify water without the need to boil it. We toasted the old *Maude*, as well as our lost comrades, and then rolled the half-empty barrel down to the canoe.

We pushed off at dawn.

The dragons had always avoided us when we traveled in the *Maude*. I suppose that we frightened them. But they had seen a lot of native canoes, and they weren't afraid of smaller boats. We had to shoot dozens of them when they came too close, but dragons have a slow learning curve, and we had to thin them out everywhere we went. Their tails were good eating.

We made good progress downstream for the first few days, but there hadn't been any rain for some time, and the level of the water was dropping alarmingly. What had been a deep river became a sluggish creek. We often had to get out of the canoe and pull it through the shallow, muddy water. This was required more and more often as the long days wore on.

Eventually, we were reduced to unloading the boat in order to drag it farther. It soon became obvious that we would either have to stop our journey, until such time as the water level rose, or to abandon most of our weapons and supplies and try to make it back on foot with only what we could carry on our none too strong backs.

In this jungle, without our supplies, I did not think we could have survived a week.

On the other hand, finding enough food was no longer a problem. What little water was left in the river bottom was filled with fishes. Our food stocks were never very good, and while the fish were available, we set out to smoke as many of them as possible, for future use.

The water eventually got so low and the fish got so thick that you could just wade into the mud and grab them with your hands. We were doing that when Antoni started shaking uncontrollably and screaming. He had a fish in both of his hands and he couldn't let go of it! Gregor went to help him, and then suddenly Gregor couldn't let go of Antoni!

I'd seen something like that once when a man touched the wires on a big electrical generator. I knew that this couldn't be the same thing, but I didn't know what else to do. You can stop anything electrical by opening the circuit, so I got out my machete, which we all carried now in lieu of a sword, and chopped the fish in two.

Both men immediately fell into the muddy water. When I got to Antoni, I found that he wasn't breathing and didn't have a heartbeat. I dragged him to shore and administered CPR, while Tomaz went after Gregor.

Gregor's life signs were missing as well, and we worked on both men for almost half an hour. Eventually, Tomaz was successful with Gregor, and he lived. I failed to bring Antoni around.

There wasn't a mark on either of the men, and from Gregor's description of what happened to him, it didn't seem to be a poison. It looked like death by electrocution, but how could a fish electrocute anybody?

We buried Antoni in the sand by the dying river.

That evening, we were sitting around the campfire, depressed by the loss of yet another of our number. Conversation had waned, and I was starting to think about going to sleep, when two tiny men walked up to our fire, as bold as you please! They sat down and shared out between them a fish that we had baked but nobody had wanted to eat. Then they ate it, smiling and nodding at us!

We were stunned. These people looked like something out of a children's fairy tale! They were perfectly formed, well-proportioned, and even quite handsome, but neither of them came as high as my waist! I doubted if either of them could have weighed forty pounds. Yet these were adult men, well-muscled, and with underarm and genital hair.

When they had finished their meal, with gestures we offered to cook some more for them, but they declined. Nor were they interested in any smoked fish. They did accept some water from us, lightly laced as it was with whiskey, and appeared to enjoy it considerably.

I took out a small belt knife and began to whittle on a piece of wood. This got their attention! I gave the knife to one of them, and he was delighted with it. I think he was more amazed with the knife than we were with him. Tomaz gave a similar knife to the second little man, then got out a machete and showed them how to chop up a nearby bush.

We now had them sufficiently interested that I didn't think

they would run away on us. It was time to teach them how to speak Pidgin!

The first lessons hadn't gone very far when the bushes around us parted and a dozen or so additional people came out and sat around our campfire. They weren't all little men. Some of them were little women.

These new people were greeted by the two we had already made friends with, and it was obvious to us that they had stayed in the bushes to see what sort of reception we would give their friends.

Since the newcomers were well-armed with spears, bows, and peashooters, they had been prepared to come to the rescue, if we turned out to be the bad guys.

We were trying hard to be the good guys, and we were soon passing out smoked fish and very watered whiskey, and putting more fish on the fire to cook. I went to the canoe and came back with knives enough for everybody in the party, and things soon got very pleasant.

We were going to have to spend some time in this area, at least until the dry spell ended, and we were glad that we could now spend it with friends, albeit small ones.

Chapter Thirty

FROM THE JOURNAL OF JOSIP SOBIESKI

written March 11, 1251,
concerning Date Unknown, 1250

Just before we went to sleep, our guests went back into the forest. Even with a fire, and with a sentry awake, they did not feel comfortable out in the open. They couldn't have gone far, though, because they were back again at first light.

They waited respectfully as the three of us recited our morning oath. Later, once they learned Pidgin, they had us translate it for them, and many of them started reciting it with us, as did, eventually, Jane.

They called themselves the Yaminana, and they said that the land for miles around owned them. They really thought that way. They did not own the land. It owned them. Another curiosity was that they did not consider themselves to be "real." We, the big people, were the real people. They were just the Yaminana. To their minds, they were something between the animals and the real people, but not members of either group.

The women were mostly gatherers, collecting more than half the food the tribe ate. They took care of the children and did the cooking. As with the other tribes we had seen, these roles were maintained with great strictness. A woman of the Yaminana would no more go hunting than a European would fornicate with his mother!

The men were primarily hunters, waiting silently for hours until a bird, a snake, or a monkey came within the relatively short range of their weapons before shooting. They liked fish, but disliked being on the ground in the open, which fishing generally required. Thus, they were pleased when we brought in all the fish that everybody could carry, before we made the trip to their village.

They were experts with poisons and with traps. The only big predator, aside from the dragons and some of the snakes, was a big spotted cat. It was quite capable of killing a full-sized human, but the Yaminana did not fear it. Rather, it feared them, their poisoned arrows, and their traps. Usually, the big cat avoided the little people.

I know that we could never have survived had we stumbled unsuspectingly onto their village. They had to point out to us each of the deadly tricks that awaited the unwary. The worst, or at least the most common, were pointed sticks steeped in poison, which were stuck in the dirt along the trail. Step on one, and you were laid up for a month, if you were lucky. If not, you were dead.

Their village was largely built up in the trees. Indeed, it might have been them that I had spotted, months ago, just before the fevers hit my platoon. It made sense, given the small size of the people and the fact that the forest around here regularly flooded.

Their community was made up of perhaps four hundred people. Well over half of their population consisted of children, and we saw only a few really old people among them.

They were much lighter-skinned than the natives we had seen earlier, perhaps because of their habit of staying in the dense forest, out of the sun. Their hair was not as black as the others', either, but often shaded into a dark brown. They were tiny, with the adults averaging about a yard tall, yet their proportions were approximately those of normal people, except for the eyes, which were about the same size as my own. Placed in a tiny head, they seemed huge. All told, they were as attractive a people as I have ever seen.

They went about completely naked, avoiding all jewelry, decorations, clothing, and body paint, save for the ubiquitous insect sap.

If they needed something with them, such as their weapons, they carried them in their hands and never slung them over a shoulder, even while climbing trees. They didn't wear belts, baldrics, or anything like a backpack or pouch. We wondered if the reason was that, being small, if danger threatened, they wanted to be able to drop everything, to run, and to hide.

My men and I had long been reduced to wearing loincloths, a piece of old bedsheet going from the back of the belt to the front. The native chief objected to them, on the grounds of sanitation! He felt it was unhealthy to thus hold the body's natural dirt against it. We demurred, but a few days later our loincloths disappeared in the night.

The other tribes that we had met had insisted we indulge in an orgy with them. The attitude seemed to be that if we were not going to be their enemies, we must be their best friends.

No middle ground was possible. The little people had the same attitude, only more so.

When we were introduced to their elders, everyone was all smiles and nods since we couldn't speak with them yet. I gave the chief a knife, an axe, and a machete. He gave me his favorite new wife!

Not just to use, but to keep. Forever. This bothered me, for while I was sure that my love, Maude, would forgive my sexual indiscretions—once I told her of the peculiar circumstances—how could I possibly explain bringing home another woman?

I couldn't pronounce her name, since it contained two clicks and a whistle that were used in the local tongue as well as the usual vowels and consonants. I never learned to manage these strange sounds. The locals actually laughed at me every time I tried to pronounce them. But her name ended with "Booboo," and she didn't seem to mind me calling her that.

My problems were increased by the fact that I was attracted to her. She was a pretty little thing. She was perfectly, deliciously formed, and had all of her dimensions been doubled, I would have recommended her to any good friend.

But despite her full, pointed breasts, her slender waist, and her flaring hips, I could not quite convince myself that anyone that tiny could be an adult. And even if she was old enough, there was the physical problem of our relative sizes.

How could I possibly copulate with someone so tiny without doing her serious damage?

The chief made it very clear that this was the way things were done, and if I were to be so crass as to insult both him and his former wife, then we had best get out of his territory now, before he was forced to kill us.

Leaving then would have involved abandoning our supplies, and after seeing the defenses around the village, I shuddered at the prospect of trying to make our way overland, past other, doubtless equally well-protected villages.

With this incentive, I went through a native wedding ceremony, with Tomaz and Gregor at my side. My objections to marriage had made the elders suspicious, and they now felt that we should all become their relatives. Gregor was of the opinion that the natives simply had a surplus of young women to feed.

With the Yaminana, marriage had a lot to do with mutual care, making sure the other was well-fed, taking care of children, and love, in the true sense of the word. It had very little to do with sex. Anytime anyone wanted to have sex with another person, they simply asked, and the favor was generally granted on the spot. Except for reasons like illness, the fact that you were a man who had already done it once today, or that you had prior commitments, to fail to have sex with a person of the opposite sex who asked you politely was a serious, even deadly insult. With this situation, the best tactic was to ask any lady who caught your eye early in the day, so you could turn down the dogs later without fear of repercussions.

Heterosexual sex was enjoyed out in the open, and at all times of the day or night. Homosexuality and lesbianism were unknown. Strangely, the Yaminana had no clear idea of there being a connection between sex and children. They said that a woman had to have sex at least once in order to "open the path" for children, but after that, sex was just for fun, and children happened when they wanted to.

Sex proved to be quite possible with our new wives, and all the rest of the women in the tribe, for that matter, despite their small proportions. I always insisted that my partners be on top, however, for fear of hurting them.

Jane confused the Yaminana, so they ignored her. They did not like the idea of a woman hunting, although they grudgingly admired her abilities with a bow. To my knowledge, she neither asked nor was asked to have sex during her entire stay there.

They were vastly impressed with our guns. When a big, long-nosed sort of wild pig, with three toes, came into the village, I got the chief's permission to shoot it. One shot put it down, and I was later told that it would have taken the Yaminana hours to kill so big a beast, with the likely injury of several villagers.

The chief immediately insisted that I give him a gun, but fortunately he was too small to shoot one. At his first attempt with one, it knocked him flat on his back and badly bruised his arm. I was happy when he gave up on the idea. As mercurial as these people were, I didn't really want to see them with modern weapons.

Jane had long considered firearms to be instruments of the devil and refused to touch them.

The Yaminana didn't make pottery, and were noticeably more primitive than the other tribes we'd met. They seemed to be less intelligent, and even childlike in most things. They were charming, though, and brought out our paternal feelings. Their children were particularly endearing, and even Jane couldn't help but feel maternal around them, although she was ashamed to admit it.

Still, we wondered if the small size of their heads and brains had something to do with their lack of intellectual depth.

In the course of time, everyone in the tribe was speaking a version of Pidgin, and eventually they seemed to like it so much that they were abandoning their old language. They were a simple people, and they liked a simple language.

For the next six months we and our adopted tribe ate well. Generally, they would find the game, and we would kill it. They did most of the gathering and the hunting and snaring of small game, but our addition of wild pigs, dragons, and big snakes, one of which was fully nine yards long, more than paid our way.

We helped out in another way when the Yaminana were attacked by a neighboring tribe of full-sized people. This was after we had stayed with them for over three months, and we Europeans had regained much of our original strength. Some thirty warriors attacked us, but they didn't have army training, and they didn't have guns.

We killed eleven of them, nine by gunshot and two in hand-to-hand fighting without serious injury to ourselves. The Yaminana accounted for three more, with a loss of seven of their own number, all of them adult men. The women neither hunted nor fought, which was probably why they outnumbered the men.

After the battle we were horrified to watch our little friends gleefully butcher their fallen foes, and then cook them up for dinner!

The chief told me they had to eat their enemies, because the big people who had attacked in the first place wanted to capture some of the Yaminana in order to eat them.

When a Yaminana was eaten by an outsider, his soul was lost to the tribe. Eating their enemies was the only way to return the souls of their lost tribesmen to their families. And anyway, he told us, they were delicious!

Fortunately, he was not greatly offended when we refused to participate in the feast. It was enough that we had provided the main course.

After I had seen my little wife daintily nibbling off the last shreds of flesh clinging to a human femur, it was weeks before I could kiss her again.

I was also shocked when I saw Jane happily eating her share of the cannibal feast! She said that to her people, human flesh was just another kind of meat. On questioning her later, I found out why she had not eaten our own dead on the *Maude*; since those men had died of a sickness, the meat was tainted. As to Antoni, she had simply assumed we preferred fish, as she did.

The next day, with great ceremony, the Yaminana ate the bodies of their own tribesmen who had fallen in battle.

All of this cannibalism troubled me. I had not been able to make any progress at converting the Yaminana to Christianity and had even given up trying, until I could bring a priest back to do the job properly. Seeing these tiny people eating human flesh told me just how remiss I had been in doing my Christian duty toward them. I renewed my efforts to bring them to Christ, but again it was to no avail. I gave up and worked instead on my equipment. The stock of my rifle had rotted so badly that I was obliged to carve myself a new one, out of a native wood that Jane recommended.

The most important event during our stay with the Yaminana, from the army's viewpoint, happened during our first month with them.

Several of their very tiny children were playing a game with a ball, when it rolled into a stream. I waded in to get it for them and was surprised to find the ball shedded water like wax, but it was soft, like flesh. I gave the ball back to the children and went to talk about it with some of the adults.

I was told that the toy was made from the sap of a certain tree, which they were very happy to take me to. At last I had found the almost mythical rubber tree! In fact, there were quite a few of them out there.

I got Tomaz and Gregor and showed them my find. After that, we worked out an efficient way to bleed the trees without killing them, and collected as much of the sap as we could. Over the months, we turned some of it into balls, in the native fashion, and stored the rest in empty glass food jars. We also collected samples of the tree's bark and its leaves, to aid others in finding them.

After more than six months of only occasional rain, the great downpours returned in earnest, and the river began to fill. Our canoe had not rotted as our riverboat had, and we soon had all in order for our departure.

We tried to persuade our wives to stay behind, for we weren't at all sure what we would do with them back in Poland, or whether they would like it there. But our tiny ladies were adamant about going with us. We had told too many stories about what it was like in Europe, I suppose. Also, the elders insisted that we take them with us, and their continued goodwill would be important when we returned to establish a trading post here, to bring in the rubber.

We shoved off in much better physical shape than we had arrived in, and with our company now increased to seven. The trip back was long and arduous, but relatively uneventful. At least nobody died.

When we at last put in at the fourth trading post we had established, we found it deserted, as was the native village it had been built next to. A day's searching through the ruins of both gained us no enlightenment. There was no evidence of violence. The post and the village had not been burned, but simply abandoned. Near what must have been the church, we found more than two dozen graves, with wooden crosses over them, but no indications as to who was buried there. Profoundly disturbed, we went on east, to the next post.

The story was the same at the third post and at the second. My men were gone, the villagers were gone, and there was nothing to show why this had happened. It was not as though some other tribes had supplanted the ones we had befriended. The countryside seemed to be devoid of all human life.

At the first post, I found Sir Caspar, the lance leader I had left there a year before. The village behind him looked to have about a third of its former inhabitants left.

He was nearly as naked as we were, sporting little but some pants with the legs cut off, and a pair of native sandals, yet he saluted me in proper army fashion, and it seemed only proper to salute back, even though I stood before him naked and barefoot. In military fashion, I asked him to report.

"It was sickness, more than anything else, sir," he said. "I lost one man to a dragon, and three more to fevers. The people in the village were sick, too, but of some other disease, like the worst cold you ever saw. Nothing we tried did any good, and the native doctors couldn't do any better, on their people or on mine. I got word from the other posts that they were in trouble, but we didn't have any help to send to them. I was bedridden and my men were either dead or shaking with fevers. I haven't heard from the other posts in six months."

I asked him about any other riverboats, and he said they hadn't seen one since I left him there, a year ago.

We went into his native-style hut, and Gregor brought some whiskey up from the canoe. While the women went out in search of supper, I filled Sir Caspar and his men in on all that had happened to us since I had last seen him.

"My God. Then we six are all that are left of a platoon of forty-three men? What a disaster!" he said. "And why haven't the other three platoons come looking for us? Could they be in worse shape than we are?"

I said that I didn't know, but I intended to leave in the morning for the rendezvous point, at the island with the flag. I asked him if he wanted to join us.

"No, sir, I don't see how I can. Father David has been making progress here in converting those villagers who survived the plague. He wouldn't even consider leaving without orders from his superiors in Poland. Ronald and I couldn't possibly abandon him."

I saw his point, and promised to return, no matter what I found out. Before leaving, I asked if they had any clothes to spare. Sir Caspar offered me the shorts he was wearing. That was all he had. Even their bedding was gone. I, of course, declined his offer.

Later that night we took advantage of Father David's presence to go to confession.

In the morning, after we recited our Army Oath, we sang a proper mass, with Communion, for the first time in entirely too long. Then we left, heading east.

Chapter Thirty-One

FROM THE JOURNAL OF JOSIP SOBIESKI

written March 12, 1251,
concerning February 10, 1251

As we came in sight of the island, I could barely believe my eyes! The entire island had been logged over, and a dozen new buildings, all made of concrete—army fashion—were either completed or under construction! At least a full company of men were busily working. Above it all was a huge, multi-element yagi radio antenna.

As we tied our canoe up to one of the docks, a sentry looked at us with his mouth open, then ran to get his superior. He was wearing a clean, summer-weight class B uniform, and for the first time in half a year I was seriously conscious of my own nakedness.

I suddenly realized I was coming back a dismal failure. I had been sent out with a steam-powered riverboat, tons of supplies, and a platoon of forty-two healthy, well-educated young men. Now the boat was a rotten mound in the jungle, the supplies were gone, with almost nothing to show for them, and all the men were dead except for the two naked survivors next to me, plus three more, left behind at a trading post—out in the bush—with nothing to trade.

I had lost an incredible thirty-seven out of forty-two of the army's finest young men. If ever a platoon leader deserved to be shot, it was me.

I wasn't sure what their feelings would be about the four women with me. Jane, at least, had certainly earned the right to be one of us, and the others were our wives. I didn't know what army policy was toward non-Christian, native wives. But there was nothing to do but to brazen it out.

As we were unloading the canoe onto the dock, a group of clean, groomed, and uniformed men came out to us, and I was suddenly glad we had left the whiskey barrel back at the trading post. With it, I could see them adding drunkenness to the list of charges against me. Leading the group was Baron Siemomysl himself, the commander of the entire Explorer's Corps.

He was smiling!

He completely ignored military formality and said, "Sir Josip! My God, but it's good to see you alive! We were all worried about you! Welcome to Brazylport! Come, introduce me to your party."

I introduced the men and women of my group to my baron, and told him a bit about each of them. He seemed delighted with them, but he winced when he noticed the hand-carved stock on my rifle.

"Excellent! I see that you have brought back samples of rubber, besides. But for now, unless you have something urgent to tell me, rooms are being made ready for you, and I'm sure you would like a chance to freshen up."

Which was as polite a way as he could manage of saying that I probably didn't want to report in officially while I was buck naked.

The baron personally led us back to the married housing area, and gestured to the tree stumps and the soil denuded of vegetation.

"We had to clear the entire area in order to clean out all of the nastier plants and animals. We'll be replanting it soon, with safe, useful local plants. Perhaps some of your ladies can advise us on that."

When we got to the married housing area, some troops were just carrying a new set of furniture into a new building. Four women in Explorer uniforms greeted our ladies and whisked them away. I was glad to see that someone had talked Lord Conrad out of his silly "men only" policy for the corps.

The baron left, saying, "Come and see me as soon as you are ready."

We men were shown the way to the showers. An hour later, scrubbed, shaved, and with my hair properly cut, I walked to the commander's office in a new class A uniform, with my tattered logbooks and journals under my arm.

The baron returned my salute and politely asked me to sit down.

"Well, now. The short of it is that as soon as we realized the mistake we'd made, we got another expedition together as quickly as possible. Launching the first expedition without any experienced men was an unavoidable necessity, but sending your company out with riverboats that rotted apart in a few months, with radios that ceased to function in weeks, and with food supplies that went bad even quicker, was downright criminal. The army owes you and your men a serious apology, son.

"We've been here for four months now, and with the buildings mostly up, we've started doing what we came here to do. Namely, to get your people the kind of equipment you need, and to test it on-site. Our first ferrocrete riverboat will be coming down the ways in a few weeks, and then we can start exploring properly! We started testing special paints and preservatives the day we got here, and work is already being done on a radio that works in this humidity. But enough of that. Pour yourself a drink and tell me what has happened to you this past year."

I told him the whole story, and filled my glass several times in the telling. The short twilight of the tropics had started before I was through.

"That was quite a story, Captain Sobieski. Yes, you've been promoted, and your men have just been promoted along with you. We'll come up with something for your native warrior woman, as well. You all deserve it, and there is a lot of work around here that needs doing. We'll be working together for a long time to come. The rubber you brought in wasn't the first, but a third source of supply will be very valuable, and your discovery will certainly be exploited. Those Yaminana people of yours sound fascinating, and I look forward to talking to your pretty little Booboo as soon as possible."

I thanked the baron, but said that I was looking forward to a trip home to Poland before long. I had a young lady there who was waiting to be my bride.

"That brings me to a very painful topic, Captain. I got a message from Lord Conrad three days ago, and, well, you can't go home. None of us can. It was only a few weeks ago that enough men like you made it back to impress on us the magnitude of the disease problem. It now appears that at least half, and possibly as many as three-quarters, of your old company have died of disease. Furthermore, they died of diseases unknown in Europe.

"In order to replace you, if you went home, we would have to bring in at least two and perhaps as many as four other men, and then watch as one, or two, or three of them died of disease in the first year. And that's not the worst of it.

"If you went back home, you could be a carrier of any or all of the deadly diseases that have afflicted your company. You could start a plague that could wipe out half the population of Christendom! And the problem gets still worse.

"We have already started plagues among the native peoples of this continent! Diseases that don't seriously bother us are deadly to them. Out of ignorance, we may have committed one of the worst crimes in history! Whole villages have already been obliterated. In the end, by simply coming here, we may have caused more deaths than the Mongols did with all their armies, swords, and arrows! So you see, we can't possibly let any of our people go home until this problem is solved.

"Furthermore, we have another company of volunteers forming up in Poland, medical people who are going to come out here to try to find a cure for the plagues we've started. They are coming here *knowing* that most of them will be dead within the year. The survivors of that company won't be going home, either."

I sat back, stunned. It was too much, too big. This day I had been raised to the heights on seeing the new base, when I had feared to find nothing but an empty island. Then I was cast down at the thought of my own dismal failure, then lifted back up at the baron's pleasant welcome, and then cast down again by this horrible news.

I sat there, numb, unable to absorb it all.

After a while the baron said, "Is there anything else you want to know?"

I nodded yes, and asked about the others in my company, Captain Odon and the other platoon leaders.

"Captain Fritz came in a few weeks ago. He's on recuperative leave, but you'll find him around here somewhere. Sir Taurus, of course, was killed before you set out on your mission. Sir Kiejstut is dead. He died six months ago of some disease he picked up. They say that his ending was quick. Sir Lezek was reported to have been alive as of a few months ago, several hundred miles upriver. Of the others, we have no definite news."

So. I still had Fritz and probably Lezek. Maybe Captain Odon, maybe Father John. Maybe even Zbigniew, although that seemed remote. I was twenty-six years of age, and I felt old. Very, very old.

As I left, the baron's secretary passed me a note, saying that my men and the ladies were waiting for me at the mess hall, after which they would be at the inn. I had news for them, but I went to the radio room first.

I composed a message for my mother, and a much longer one for Maude, trying to tell her that I was well, but that I couldn't come home to her. I wrote and rewrote that message, but it never said exactly what I felt. No matter how I worded it, it still wasn't right. Finally, I just gave my first draft to the operator and asked him to get it out when he could.

I was told that the airwaves had been fairly clean for the last few days, and my messages would probably go through sometime tonight to the relay station in Portugal, and from there to Poland.

It was late when I got to the almost empty mess hall, but the cook scrounged me up some food. I barely noticed the entree, but the bread and the beer were so wonderful they almost cheered me up.

I found my party at the inn. I was surprised that the army would build an inn at so remote a site, but Lord Conrad was always concerned about the happiness of his men. It was just like every other Pink Dragon Inn, except the carved sign over the door showed one of the local dragons, painted pink, instead of the classical one.

I found my people scrubbed clean, pleasantly drunk, and comparatively well-dressed. The men at least were in proper uniform, and the ladies had been prevailed upon to wear short cotton skirts, at least.

When I asked, I found that they had heard of the orders forbidding return to Europe, so I wasn't forced to break that news to them. I told the men that the Christian Army was pleased with us, and congratulated them on their promotions, calling them Sir Gregor and Knight Banner Tomaz. After we drank to that, I explained that they could now refer to me as Captain Sobieski, if they did so respectfully, and with suitable bowing and groveling. They laughed, and we drank to that as well.

I told them that Jane was accepted as an army civilian scout, with the status of an army knight. The pay consisted of room, board, and equipment, plus eight pence a day, retroactive for a year. She didn't understand what most of this meant and was soon talking intensely with Knight Banner Tomaz.

Our wives had no clear idea why we were so happy about our promotions. Our increased pay had no meaning for them, since they didn't know what money was. Our increased status also meant little to them, because in the society they grew up in, small differences in status had little meaning. You were either the chief or you weren't. But at the inn, they were delighted with the music, the dancing, and the ambience of the place, and they were happy because everybody else was happy.

Looking at them, I was reminded that they were really very limited creatures, and a life with Booboo would be much different from the one I had long dreamed of with Maude. It seemed rude to even think it, but we three were permanently bonded with creatures that were, at best, pretty, amusing little puppy dogs. And at worst? I couldn't even imagine, but I was sure that it could become very bad indeed.

I knew that life must go on, but I wasn't at all sure that I wanted to go on with it.

Before my thoughts got too morose, Captain Fritz came in, bringing with him the eight men of his platoon who had survived the year. After introductions were made, our ladies were all surrounded by eager admirers. Fritz and I found ourselves at one end of the table, deep in conversation, discussing our year apart. It was almost like being home. Slowly, my mood revived.

I told my story to Fritz, and he nodded and shook his head in all the right places. He understood what I was saying because his life's experiences were so very like my own. As a good friend will, he let me tell the whole story almost without interruptions, before he started in on his own.

Fritz had found the natives on the south bank friendly from the start. They had immediately seen the value of our products, and were familiar with the concept of trade. If they believed in ghosts, they never talked about it. He thought that the huge width of the river must separate two very different nations.

The people he found did some hunting and gathering, but they were primarily agriculturalists. The dozens of plants they cultivated were completely unknown in Europe, and he saw rich possibilities in trade with them.

There was a kind of pea in which the pods grew at first aboveground, but then went underground as they matured, actually planting themselves! Dug up, roasted, and heavily salted, Fritz said they were wonderful with beer.

They had dozens of fruits he had never seen before, and most of them were delicious. One of them, which looked like a big hand grenade growing in a display of swords, was particularly good.

"On the other hand, nobody ever insisted that we participate in a mass orgy. I think I'll always envy you that one!"

Apparently, the native girls were not extremely interested in Fritz and his men. They were generally available, but only after you negotiated the size of the gift that was to be given to them in advance.

"The price was mud cheap, but it still smacked too much of prostitution for me to greatly enjoy it. I scratched the itch once a week or so, but it was mere gratification, and not love."

The only trouble that he encountered in the first few weeks happened when one of his men was urinating over the side of their riverboat.

"Sir Ian started screaming, and clutched his privy member. He bounced around for a bit, and then fell over onto his back, shouting the most blasphemous of oaths! I was the closest thing to a surgeon we had on board, so I had a half-dozen men hold him down while I examined him. I couldn't see a thing out of the ordinary, so I had him released.

"None of our medications had any beneficial effect, and we didn't yet have a native who could speak Pidgin well enough to question what passes for a doctor among them. Ian remained in great pain for three days, during which time he never urinated, and I began to fear that his bladder would burst. After consulting with the others, it seemed that the only thing to do was to cut the member open, to see what was causing the problem.

"We couldn't even get poor Ian drunk, since that would only have generated more urine. With six men holding the screaming knight down, I took a sharp, clean scalpel and sliced along the last half of the length of his penis. Pints of blood and a gallon of urine squirted out, but can you guess what else was in there?"

I shook my head, and Fritz continued.

"There was a tiny *fish*, stuck in the urine vessel! It had three little barbs, like a catfish, that had stuck into Ian's flesh, and that was what was blocking his pipe!

"All that we can imagine is that as he was relieving himself, the fish must have swum upstream, right up his urine and into his privy member! There seems to be no other way it could have happened. As you can imagine, we all used a bucket after that.

"Well, I sewed the man up, and he managed to live. That is, he lived until he came down with a fever, three months later."

The rest of his sad story was a matter of surviving a fever much as I had and then building a boat and getting back to the rendezvous. Lacking native advice, since those natives who had not died of their own plague had run away, it took him much longer than it did us to build a suitable boat.

"I managed to get more of my men back than you did, but I must admire the ladies you brought to replace some of those you lost. I've often had fantasies of having a girl so small that I could carry her along in my pouch, and your new wife comes close to that. If there are more like her where she comes from, I'm minded to go along with you when you return. But for tonight, what is the story on the warrior woman you brought back? I mean, is she really the sort who prefers other women?"

I said I honestly didn't know about the lady's sexual preferences. Her tribe was heterosexual, of course, with women marrying men, but from there on, the usual roles were reversed. She had fit into my team as one of the troops. None of us males had seen fit to make any advances toward her, as far as I knew, and she had made none toward us. I said that if Fritz wanted to try, he was free to do so, but I advised that he move with great caution, and that at no time should he dare to offend the woman. She could be quite deadly if she wanted to.

Fritz went over and talked to Jane, and in time their conversation became more and more animated, with both of them smiling hugely. Eventually, they walked out of the inn arm in arm. I wished them both well.

After a bit I noticed that my wife was either asleep from too much excitement or had passed out from too much to drink, and that in any event it was getting late. I bid the others good-bye, picked her up in my arms, and carried my little bride home.

Someone had mentioned that in the course of giving her a medical examination today, they had weighed her in at thirty-four and a half pounds. Cuddled up in my arms, she reminded me of a sleeping kitten. She was very pretty, very precious, but somehow something less than a real human being. I began to believe that her tribe's evaluation of themselves, that they were above the animals but below the true men, was essentially true.

By no stretch of the imagination could I imagine her becoming my true life partner. The pretty lady I had married in a pagan ceremony was in truth but a house pet.

Chapter Thirty-Two

FROM THE DIARY OF CONRAD STARGARD

February 26, 1251

I sat at my desk with my head in my arms. Father Ignacy was in Rome. He was a cardinal bishop now, and he was voting on who would be the next pope. Many said he himself would win the office. I suppose I was happy for him, but the truth was that I needed my confessor, more than at any time before in my life. I had sinned. Oh God, how I had sinned!

I had sent a company of my best men out on an ill-thought-out mission, and because of me, most of them were dead. Far worse still, I had been responsible for introducing all of the diseases of Europe into the New World, and native Americans were dying by the whole villageful!

Killing in time of war has never bothered me, but this horrible thing I had done was something far worse than that! It is one thing to kill fighting men who invade your country, and quite another to go to someone else's land and sicken every man, woman, and child there with deadly diseases!

It was undoubtedly still going on. The damage was still being done. People were still dying. We had no way to stop those diseases from spreading throughout half the world.

Maude came into my office and stood in front of my desk. She wasn't smiling.

"Josip sent me a message. He says he cannot come home. He says that if he did, he might spread diseases here in Europe."

"Yes, Maude. That, too, is another of my sins."

"You must not sit there and cry. You must talk to your cousin Tom. Tom knows about diseases. Tom knows all about living systems. If you ask him, he will help you. He will help Josip. You must talk to Tom."

"Tom has helped me out several times before, but I have never asked for help before," I said.

"You must talk to Tom. He will help you."

"You are right, of course. People are dying as we speak. This is no time for stupid pride." I looked up at the ceiling and said, *"Tom! Help me, Tom! I need your help!* If this disease problem isn't solved quickly, I am going to have to stop the entire exploration program! You will never see a worldwide culture! I won't be the cause of making things worse than they already are! I won't be responsible for bringing plagues and the Black Death all across the globe! If I have to, I'll build a ten-story concrete wall all around Europe, I swear I will!"

A door that hadn't been there before opened up in the wall behind me, and my cousin Tom, dressed in T-shirt, shorts, and tennis shoes, walked into the room. He had a handwritten Polish manuscript in one hand and three test tubes in the other.

"All right! All right! You don't have to start making threats!" He surprised me by speaking in Polish. I'd never heard him do that before. Thinking about it, I *had* called to him in Polish.

He set the manuscript on my desk, turned to me, and held up one of the test tubes.

"Okay. This is part one. What it does is mark every cell

in the body as being human. It must be given at least twelve hours before the next part is administered. That's six of your hours. We call it the butter, because that's what it looks like and tastes like. You can take it as often as you like, and for your regular troops, we recommend a pat of it every morning. That way, the treatment can be started immediately in the event of illness. Also, it doesn't spoil, and it's cheaper than real butter. You can make it even with your primitive technology. You just mix a sample of it with any fresh mammalian milk, and let it set for a day. That's also how you make the other two parts of this system.

"This second part is called the cheese, for obvious reasons. The dosage is nine grams per hundred kilograms of body weight, plus or minus twenty percent. It's a deadly poison, and will kill anything alive except for human cells that have been protected by part one, the butter. The person treated is poisonous to all other life-forms for the next six of your hours. Keep the patient away from plants and pets during that time period. That includes neohorses, wenches, and all the other bioengineered critters.

"The third part, the oil, replaces all of the body's symbionts that were killed off by part two. You drink a few grams of it the day after you take the cheese and rub about twice that amount on the skin.

"Now, nothing is perfect. When you use this system, all of your stomach flora are killed and you are in for a serious case of the runs. There are a few rare types of brain tumors that this system can't cure. The worst problem is that in the case of very large tumors, the tumor is killed, but sometimes having a big, dead mass in your body overloads the body's cleanup system, and that can kill the patient. The best way to be sure this doesn't happen is to go through the treatment every half year. That way, really big tumors don't have time to grow. Also, life spans and general health are increased with regular use.

"In the case of communicable diseases, the system will cure the patient, but then sometimes the patient will contract the same disease again. In that case, just repeat the cure. Eventually, given enough time, the body will develop a natural immunity to that particular disease.

"Any other questions you might have are answered in the manual I brought. You ought to read it thoroughly before you try using this stuff."

"Tom, thank you. This stuff sounds like magic!"

"By your standards, I suppose it is. One man's magic is another man's technology. This project consumed over nine million high-quality man-hours, which is good, since they needed something interesting to do. Anything else you need, ask for it. Within reason, of course, and as long as you don't ask me to violate causality. Well, hang in there."

"Thanks again, Tom."

He left my office by the same doorway that he came through, after which the door disappeared. Maude never left the room, and Tom never acknowledged her existence, which was typical of him.

I glanced at the other, normal door into my office and saw Baron Piotr and my secretary looking in with their mouths open.

"Your grace, you have some *very* strange relatives!" Piotr said.

"How long have you two been standing there?" I asked.

"Ever since we heard you shouting at the ceiling," Zenya said. "You called for help."

"Huh. I suppose I did. Well, don't talk about all this, all right? But for now, we've got work to do. Piotr, get this manuscript down to the print shop. I want six thousand copies run off by yesterday. This takes precedence over *everything*, including sleep. Got it? Then move!

"Zenya, get a radiogram off to the *Atlantic Challenger* and tell them to stay in port until they get a special shipment. If they've already left, tell them to turn around! I'll be down in the kitchen whipping up a few hundred gallons of these medicines. Move, girl!"

Chapter Thirty-Three

FROM THE JOURNAL OF JOSIP SOBIESKI

written March 1, 1255,
concerning March 1251 to April 1254

I have a few days of idle time before the next semester starts, so I might as well bring my autobiography up to date.

As I was lying in the hospital at Brazylport in 1251, the surgeons were saying they would probably have to amputate my infected left foot, when the *Atlantic Challenger* steamed in with a company of volunteers, two dozen milk cows, and the Cure. I was eating breakfast when a new doctor, fresh off the boat, came to see me.

"Don't worry about a thing," he said. "This won't be nearly as bad as what you've heard about."

I said I hadn't heard anything at all about the new medicine, but his last statement had indeed started me worrying.

"Really, there's nothing much to it. I went through it myself a week ago, when we crossed the sector line." When he saw the quizzical expression on my face, he continued. "They have divided the world up into thirty-three sectors, to contain communicable diseases. Every passenger and crew member on every ship that passes between two sectors has to take the Cure, all at the same time, to stop the spread of diseases between areas. Then they fumigate the whole ship, just to be on the safe side. It's a bother, but considering the number of deaths that were caused on both sides when your crew came to Brazyl, you have to admit that it will be worth it."

I agreed with him, and told him I was ready to start.

"You already have. The butter on the toast you just ate was the first part of it. I'll be back this evening to administer the second part, a piece of cheese. Good day."

I grumbled a bit about being medicated without my permission. Certainly, *I* had never done such a thing back when I was a corpsman. Still, I observed no noticeable change in myself, except for the way my foot was continuing to painfully rot away.

That evening, the doctor had me stripped naked and propped upright on a toilet by a beefy male nurse who had also taken some of the magical butter in the morning. Five other seriously ill patients were already sitting on the other toilets in the latrine. Armed guards at the doors kept any unauthorized personnel strictly out, since we were shortly to become very poisonous individuals.

The doctor then placed a carefully weighed slice of cheese on each of our tongues with a pair of tongs. It looked and tasted very ordinary, but he was treating it like the host, so I took it seriously as well.

In about a quarter hour I started itching. We were told that this was caused by the death of all the tiny animals that had previously taken up residence on our skins, and that shortly it would no longer concern us.

This turned out to be perfectly true, since I was soon vomiting and shitting great spews of unmentionable fluids from both ends of my person with such rapidity that I was usually unable to decide which end I should point at the toilet, and with such force that such of it as was reasonably aimed generally overshot the toilet and splattered on the wall behind. I managed all this while hopping around on my right foot, the left one being still blackened, rotten, and painful.

True to the doctor's promise, I hardly noticed any itching during this phase of my cure.

The worst of it was over by midnight. Sitting weakly on the toilet, I noticed a mosquito that landed on my hand, but I was too exhausted to shoo him away. It started to sting me, then stopped and fell over. Dead.

After a bit, my fellow patients and I were taken to the showers and washed, while another crew hosed down the latrine to ready it for the next batch of victims.

My left foot, which was, after all, the object of this exercise, looked worse than ever when they finally took me back to my room.

I felt much better in the morning, and even better yet after an attractive female nurse gave me the last part of the Cure, which included an all-over body massage with a special oil. I was walking again in three days, and my foot was completely healed in another week.

Amazing stuff, the Cure.

I was promptly put on the planning committee that was working on a program to stamp out the plagues we had started among the Brazylians. The areas we had stopped at were fairly well-mapped, and we knew the dates when each place was visited. We had to make some very uneducated guesses as to how fast the diseases would spread among the native populations. We then drew circles on the map with their centers at the points of contact and their radiuses proportional to the time the diseases had had to spread. These overlapping circles covered a depressingly large area.

We then set up two teams of workers. The A team was to contain the diseases, and stop them from spreading across the continent. They would surround the contaminated areas by making contact with all the native tribes on the periphery, convincing them of the seriousness of the threat, and giving the entire tribe the Cure. We would then give the Cure to the native doctors, teaching them how to use it and how to make more. The lack of milk animals among the natives was not a serious problem, since our tests had proven that mother's milk worked as well as any animal milk, and there was always a lactating woman about.

Once the contaminated areas were completely surrounded, the A team would start moving inward until they met up with members of the B team.

The B team would start at the points of contact and work outward, following the diseases through the jungle until the newly introduced diseases were wiped out. Actually, we would be eradicating most of the local diseases as well, so we would be partially compensating the natives for the damage we had caused them.

Time was of the absolute essence, since the longer it took to do the job, the farther the diseases would spread and the more people would die. Large numbers of people would be needed if we were to accomplish our objectives quickly, if at all. Army personnel would be coming as fast as we could transport them to Brazyl. Every ship that could possibly be spared from other tasks was called upon, but they could not begin to bring over enough people to do the job.

A major point of our plan was to enlist as many natives into the program as possible. Without their help, the job could take decades, and the death toll could be in the millions.

It took us three years to finish. For most of it, I ran the B team, while Fritz handled the A team. We each delegated most of the administrative duties and spent most of our time in the jungle, keeping in touch daily with the new radios.

Before we were through, over a quarter of the continent had been explored. Thirteen gross tribes were contacted, with people speaking over seven gross different languages, most of which we still haven't had time to properly record. Pidgin is rapidly becoming the universal second language in the entire continent.

At the end of the first year, one of our native teams found Zbigniew! He had lost a foot to some sort of jungle rot, but had found himself a place in a tribe living near the ocean shore as a shaman, storyteller, and toolmaker. He had a wife and a son when he was found, and he brought them both back with him to Brazylport. We put Captain Zbigniew on administrative work until the emergency was over, and now he serves with me on the faculty of the Explorer's School. He and his family have the house next to mine on faculty row.

Lezek was picked up from the trading station he was running despite impossible problems, and put to work as Fritz's deputy in his own area. Komander Lezek is currently on his way with a company of Explorers to see what India has to offer.

Halfway through the second year of the campaign, Captain

Odon and Father John came into one of our advanced posts in native canoes. They had found their native, gold-rich civilization, high in the western mountains. They found five separate nations up there, and none of them called themselves the Incas, but they had still made a major discovery.

Baron Odon is back in his beloved mountains again, as Ambassador to Hy Brazyl, and with him is Father John, now Archbishop of Hy Brazyl.

Komander Fritz ended up marrying Jane, and a few months later, with Jane's permission, he married a pretty little Yaminana girl as well. They are both with him and his new, half-native, both-sexes company, exploring yet another tributary of the Amazon, the greatest river system in the world.

The Yaminana are now carefully protected from their bigger neighbors, and, without losses due to either diseases or to warfare, their numbers are increasing rapidly. This despite the fact that many Yaminana maidens have elected to marry Europeans. It seems that we have a reputation among them for being very good husbands.

To date, there have been more than six dozen of these Yaminana-European marriages, and curiously, they have not resulted in a single child. We are all mystified as to the reason for this. Since the little people's full-sized neighbors were only interested in eating them, there had been no earlier marriages with other full-sized people, as far as anyone knew.

Also, while every other native tribe caught deadly diseases even from apparently healthy Europeans, the Yaminana had remained disease free around us, even before the Cure was introduced. Some of us have begun wondering if they really are a separate species, as their own folklore insists.

On the other hand, the Cure works on them, and it is only supposed to work on humans.

Another of life's mysteries.

Once the foreign diseases had been wiped out in Brazyl, the army establishment at Brazylport was reduced to a group sufficient to maintain communications and support for trade, the missionaries, and exploration. Anna's children, the Big People, have been introduced in large numbers to assist the army's humans. Where the natives have requested it, we have started building and staffing our combination schools, stores, post offices, and churches.

Most important, from my viewpoint, those of us who wanted to go home were finally permitted to do so. In the company of Baron Siemomysl, Captain Zbigniew, over a gross of other army personnel, and all of their families, we boarded a new *Express*-class ship for home. These were half again as fast and had three times the capacity of the *Challenger*-class ships that had once so impressed me. They operated only between large, well-established, deepwater ports.

I, of course, brought Booboo with me. As I had discovered years before, her lack of intellectual capability made her something of a house pet, but the truth is that it can be very *nice*, having a good house pet. She was cuddly, pretty, and always anxious to please. With patient training, she had learned to keep our apartment or cabin neat and clean, and in time I learned to love her for what she was.

Maude was waiting for me on the crowded dock as our ship, the *Brazylport Express*, pulled into Gdansk. Lord Conrad was with her, as were Maude's four children, Molly, Megan, Mary, and Melinda.

Lord Conrad was very polite to me, but soon begged off to speak with Baron Siemomysl. Maude greeted me warmly, and introduced me to her daughters, whose greeting kisses were almost improperly sexual. I introduced them to Booboo, and I could see in an instant that she and Maude would like each other. They hit it off perfectly, and each seemed to intuitively understand the other. I was much relieved. If they had hated each other, I don't know what I would have done.

The custom was now that each family in the army should have at least one Big Person attached to it. Margarete had asked to be in our family, and Maude accepted her in my name.

It was late in the day and arrangements had been made at a new hotel on the Vistula Lagoon, run by a company with a snowflake fort a few miles south. When I mounted Margarete, Maude climbed up on my lap, just like old times. Booboo joined

Molly, to get better acquainted. As we went slowly to the hotel, I mentioned the passion her daughters had put into their kisses.

"I know. They all love you as much as I do. They awoke loving you. I did not know that this would happen. In Tom's world, we did not have feelings. Here, I learned about my emotions. Now my daughters have my love along with my memories."

I was surprised about all this, and asked what we should do.

"You must love them as you love me. Then you must find them good men of their own."

I said that with thought, I could probably find four good men in the army.

"Four men to start. In time, we will need sixteen more."

Startled, I asked her to explain.

"It takes four like me to guard one man properly. If Lord Conrad had four guards, King Henryk would want two of them to guard himself. If King Henryk had such guards, Prince Daniel of the Ruthenias would want some, too. So would King Bela of Hungary. So would Tzar Ivan of Bulgaria. Then each leader would have only one guard. One guard is not enough. Also, I would have to guard Lord Conrad. There would be no one else. I could not spend all of my time with you. Thus, I had four children for Lord Conrad. I had four more for King Henryk. Also for King Bela, and for Prince Daniel, and for Tzar Ivan. It takes four years for my children to awaken. Before that time is up, the Federation of Christendom will expand. More kings will need to be guarded. So I have made more children now."

So I was now the head of a household with two wives, a Big Person, and twenty children! I certainly hoped that the Explorer's School was providing me with a big house! I said as much to Maude.

"There will never be more than twenty of my daughters there. They will awaken and leave as fast as I have young ones. We will soon have two more Big People. There will be as many Big People as there are adults in the household. The house provided to you is very large. Your household also will need at least three servants. There will be much work to do."

I had been thinking of a long, quiet time alone with Maude and Booboo. Apparently such was not to be!

The hotel was a remarkable building, done in a style I had never seen before. It was a squarish, boxy structure, with no thought at all taken for defense, having neither battlements, nor machicolations, nor even thick masonry walls. Except for the large windows, it was completely covered with large, porcelain plates, each a yard square. These plates were embossed with bright, polychromed designs and heraldic symbols.

I asked if people actually lived in that thing.

"It is the new style," Maude said. "It is very comfortable. The outer plates cover thick mats made of glass fibers. It is very warm in the winter. It is cool in the summer. Your new house is made the same way."

I said I was sure that Baron Piotr would love it, and hoped that our home would have fewer colors.

"I told them to use red and white. You will like it," Maude said.

I grunted. I didn't want to appear an old stick-in-the-mud, but I've always felt more comfortable in a building that looked defensible. Well-a-day. I was soon to be a properly married man, and my days of relative freedom would be gone forever.

I was married sooner than I thought, for the great hall of the hotel was all set up for my wedding. Everybody seemed to know about it except me! My family was there, Zbigniew was set to be my best man, and he had three wedding rings ready, for Maude, Booboo, and me. Lord Conrad acted as father of the bride for Maude, and Baron Siemomysl did the same for Booboo.

I had no objections to these proceedings, but I felt they should have given me some warning. I mean, it was only by good luck I was still in a State of Grace, so I could take Communion at the mass that followed.

No sooner was my short double marriage ceremony completed, with Maude as my first wife and Booboo as my second, than the whole thing was repeated for Captain Zbigniew, since he had not yet had proper Christian wedding ceremonies with either of his wives. This time, *I* was *his* best man.

After mass, there was a feast with all of the usual fooling around that is traditional at such events, and then the two trios of young newlyweds were whisked off to our respective rooms.

My whole family was there, including my in-laws and my father. Everything was so rushed that I didn't get a chance to talk with any of them, but in the reception line my father shook my hand!

That night in bed I made love with Maude first, and then Booboo. While I was patting myself on the back and telling myself that at thirty I still wasn't over the hill, that I could still make love with two women in less than an hour, Megan came into the room and said that she wanted to love me. Maude and Booboo took this as a perfectly reasonable request and made room for her in the oversized bed. And what's a man to do?

Maude had said that her daughters would look different from her, but except for hair color, I could hardly tell them apart. Had one of them come to me first, on the dock that afternoon, rather than staying a bit behind their mother, I could easily have embraced her rather than Maude. They had all looked at me wistfully as we were introduced, and the way they kissed, well, it wasn't what the usual girl will do with a stepfather.

So I made love with the girl. As she was leaving, Molly came in, to be followed in turn by Mary and then Melinda. It was long after midnight before I could get to sleep.

I think that the Cure must do other wonderful things for a man besides wiping out his germs.

The next morning, my father came up to my table in the hotel's restaurant and said, "Son, I have given this matter much thought, and I forgive you."

I looked at him calmly and said, "Father, I, too, have given this matter much thought. For fifteen years you have done everything in your power to make my life as unpleasant as possible. When I was a young boy of fifteen, I loved you and I needed you. Your senseless rejection of me hurt me very badly, when I had done nothing to harm you or yours, except to try to live my own life. I still don't understand why you were so angry with me, but I do know this:

"Now I am a man, and I say that any man who would so hurt

someone who loved him, and who continued hurting that person for so many years for no other reason than stupid pride, I say that such a man is an unspeakable asshole, and one with whom I will not associate.

"Father, I do *not* forgive you!"

And with that, I collected up my wives and daughters, we mounted our Big People, and we rode home.

I never spoke to my father again.